JIM TH

James Meyers Thompson was born in Anadarko, Oklahoma, in 1906. In all, Jim Thompson wrote twenty-nine novels and two screenplays (for the Stanley Kubrick films *The Killing* and *Paths of Glory*). Films based on his novels include: *Coup de Torchon (Pop. 1280), Serie Noire (A Hell of a Woman), The Getaway, The Killer Inside Me, The Grifters,* and *After Dark, My Sweet.*

JIM THOMPSON

THE GETAWAY

THE KILLER INSIDE ME

THE GRIFTERS

POP. 1280

PICADOR

This collection first published 1983 by Zomba Books, London

This edition published 1995 by Picador
an imprint of Macmillan Publishers Ltd
25 Eccleston Place, London SW1W 9NF
and Basingstoke

Associated companies throughout the world

ISBN 0 330 34288 6

5 7 9 8 6 4

A CIP catalogue record for this book is available from the British Library.

Typeset by Intype, London
Printed and bound in Great Britain by
Mackays of Chatham PLC, Chatham, Kent

CONTENTS

JIM THOMPSON

The way his name was printed on the covers—sleazy, dynamic and brash—made you feel like pieces of your teeth would break off if you growled it out too loudly. To my chagrin, I could not growl with what I felt was the appropriate level of laconic ferocity; but I did read Jim Thompson's books. It was twenty-odd years ago and you could pick up the paperbacks secondhand from a stall on Ashton market with "8p"—or if in good condition, "10p"—scrawled across the covers in thick felt-tip marker pen. At the time I didn't have much of a literary vocabulary with which to say why I prized Thompson's novels—they seemed, after all, a long way from "O"-level *Macbeth*—but I pressed them upon friends with all the evangelistic fervour of adolescence. They were usually returned with a wrinkling of brows and a greenish tinge around the gills, but then my peers didn't like Johnny Cash and The Tennessee Three either, so what the hell did they know? Thompson's final elevation into the pantheon came when my mother found me reading *The Killer Inside Me*—I vaguely remember the crude cover photo of a busty woman being strangled, or maybe knifed, by a man whose face was all in shadow; except for his smile—whereupon she informed me, solemnly, that whilst Westerns were fine, I "shouldn't be reading that kind of filth".

As I now re-read these superb novels I find that the gap between Thompson's extraordinary protagonists and the Thane of Cawdor is not that great after all. I have read dozens of officially great novels that have left barely a trace on my imagination (which is entirely my responsibility and not their authors') but Jim Thompson left images in my mind that have never been erased. Some of those images—and others with a power peculiar to yourself—you will find in this collection. No human brain can retain—or even discover—all the infinite and ever-changing details of even a single work of art; but a few bars of music whistled or hummed, a fragment of verse remembered, an image painted from the colourless pigment of words, the way an actor lights his cigarette and squints in the smoke: these small things are the true stuff of immortality, and of human connection across infinite time and space. Jim Thompson connects us—chillingly, yet almost cheerfully—with a darker side of human nature than any contemporary novelist I can think of. But then, thankfully for us, Thompson did not have to write with the suffocating presence of review pages and bestseller lists breathing over his shoulder.

In *The Getaway*, Jim gives us Doc and Carol McCoy, the most clinically accurate portraits of the psychopathic personality that I had ever read—until I reacquainted myself with Deputy Sheriff Lou Ford of *The Killer Inside Me* and Lilly Dillon, the protagonist's mother, in *The Grifters*. The McCoys are natural born killers who do not waste time worrying about their haircuts and tattoos; they are far too busy charming those who will become their victims should the latter take a single—often innocently unaware—step that might jeopardize their goal. This couple do not kill for pleasure or out of psychic depravity—and certainly not for a notoriety they seek to avoid at all costs—but with the uninvolved and unhesitating efficiency of garage mechanics changing a tyre. They are terrifying. As Doc and Carol find themselves pitching their reptilian self-interest—an interest, a *commitment*, so profound and so unquestioned as to approach the force of a biological imperative—against each other, Jim Thompson unfolds one of the most perverse love affairs in fiction; for Doc and Carol love each other deeply, right until the horrifyingly poetic, and beautifully ironic, end that awaits them.

On a stylistic level Thompson throws out vivid one-line character sketches like a man shelling peas: "He came up the street at the slow but sullenly steady pace of one who is performing an unavoidable and unfairly imposed task." Doc McCoy promptly gives this character—a Negro busboy—a five-dollar tip. And here is Doc's adversary, Rudy (who always wakes up feeling like "a snake with its head caught beneath a forked stick"): "Early in his infancy, the night and the sleep that was normal to it had become indelibly associated with terror; with being stumbled over, smothered under a drunken mountain of flesh. With being yanked up by the hair, held helpless by one meaty hand while the other beat him into insensibility." Rudy "Piehead" Torrento is not a psychopath but he *is* paranoid and, despite having suffered permanent and severe deformity of the skull at birth, he is also "very vain". With characteristic irony it is Rudy's paranoia that "forced him to survive long after the withered inner man had cried out for the peace of death".

It's hard to decide if the clinical cool of Thompson's gaze makes the vast cruelties inflicted on his characters seem more tolerable or more awful. The dying shrieks of a gut-shot man sound "strangely like laughter". Hiding for hours inside an excavated manure heap in the desert, the characters find that the heat brings hordes of flies and "swarms of corpse-colored grub worms, which dropped down on their heads and backs and crawled up under them from the floor". And as the McCoys calmly contemplate their astonishingly poetic doom, a great bell in the palace tower tolls the hour of twelve and "the band in the ballroom struck up the strains of 'Home Sweet Home' ".

Needless to say, all the most dazzlingly grim moments in *The Getaway* were excluded from the (nevertheless excellent) movie—even though it was directed by Sam Peckinpah himself, not a man famed for the weakness of his stomach.

I confess myself amazed at the multiple levels of sub-text and symbolism that Thompson infiltrates into these tales of crime and suspense, not because they are found in an unexpected quarter—the despised ghetto of genre fiction—but because such sophisticated poeticism is extraordinarily difficult to achieve. Personally I find such sophistication lacking in great swaths of contemporary Literary fiction. On the rare occasions that the average modern Literary writer stumbles onto a powerful image or image system he or she cannot resist wrapping it around themselves and parading up and down the page as if it were a designer dress. Thompson has the true poet's discipline—and the faith in the reader's imagination—of letting his images *appear* to perform a purely narrative function whilst leaving their symbolic meaning to either work on the subconscious or be unearthed by contemplation; or both.

Do not imagine, either, that Thompson's corpse-colored grubs and pie-headed paranoids crop up by chance. He is not a primitive, stumbling upon jewels whose value he is unaware of. Jim knows his Freud all right—he even quotes Kraeplin—and it is a particular satisfaction to me to return to novels which I read as a teenager for their visceral power and find—now that I'm a psychiatrist—that they effortlessly sustain a more informed study. Should anyone doubt this, consider the fact that Thompson wrote two movies for one of the more formally abstract of all film geniuses, Stanley Kubrick.

To continue with the Freudian theme, both *The Killer Inside Me* and *The Grifters* are full-blooded—and impishly aware—Oedipal sagas. Deputy Lou Ford—who self-consciously bores the pants off everyone in town so that they will never suspect the extreme depravity he nurses in his heart—is driven by a classical transference (projected onto certain unfortunate females) of the hatred he felt for the woman who raised him. But in a neat psychoanalytic twist this woman is not his real mother; she died giving birth to him. Thus Lou's misogynistic/matricidal killing spree begins at the moment of his birth.

Roy Dillon, in *The Grifters*, abandons his mother, Lilly (who is only thirteen years older than him), and takes as a lover another woman of similar age and appearance: a deadly Oedipal triangle from which only one character survives. Here, again, we are treated to a *tour de force* of vivid characterization. Roy's relationship to Lilly comes alive in a single sentence: "She had given him nothing when he needed it, when he was too small to get for himself, and he wasn't letting her into the game at this late date." When Roy leaves home at seventeen, he refuses Lilly's offer of money because she needs it for herself: after all, she always has. At this: "She flinched, as though he had struck her, and her face worked sickishly, and the trim size-nine suit seemed suddenly to hang on her: a cruel moral to a life that had gotten her everything and given her nothing. And for a moment, he almost relented. He almost pitied her."

I think that to find a moral like that in the hang of a *trim* size-nine suit is pretty goddamn cool; and, despite those "almosts", there is a strange tenderness that runs through *The Grifters*. The tenderness is also found in Thompson's treatment of the deformed killer Rudy in *The Getaway* and in other unexpected places, such as when Lilly is being tortured by Bobo Justus: "It was a timeless world, an endless hell . . . [A world] at once to be endured and unendurable. And the one possible relief was within her own small body. Scalding urine spurted from her loins. It seemed to pour from her in a flood. And Bobo stood up, releasing her, and she got up and went into the bathroom."

Parents come in for a hard time in these novels; or, rather, they tend to raise their children on the principle of "spare the rod and spoil the sociopath". Given that American culture is currently totally obsessed—to the verge of paralysis—with Oprah Winfrian psychobabble, it's fascinating to see Thompson handle similar themes forty years before they became fashionable. He does so with a bracing directness and a complete absence of the bleating victim-neuroticism that we must tolerate today. Thompson's abused children do not grow up into litigation-crazed twelve-step anonymiacs, but into violent criminals entirely aware of and at peace with their own corruption. Almost to a man and woman, the very concept of conscience is alien to them. The only self-betrayal is in not pursuing one's basest impulses to the end of the line. Thus when Nick Corey, the sheriff anti-hero of the rip-snorting black comedy *Pop. 1280*, is asked by an attorney, "Do you really think you can go on taking graft and robbing the county, and doing nothing to earn your money?", he amiably replies: "Why, I don't see how I can do much else if I want to stay in office."

And so page after page one comes across writing which is simply beautiful in its throwaway clarity and phrasing. Roy Dillon's thoughts, as he watches a bunch of failed grifters hunched in fear on a deserted railroad platform, could stand as an epitaph for all of Thompson's characters: "This, or something worse than this, was the fate of the unrooted. Men to whom roots were a hazard rather than an asset . . . One sour deal, and they were on the skids." And the only character who does have deep roots—Lou Ford in *Killer*—is indeed destroyed by them at the very moment he tries to break free.

Another description that might apply to them all—and perhaps to Thompson himself—is Roy's "People were his business, knowing them was. And the only way of knowing was to listen to them." This is also the secret of Doc McCoy's success, and of Lou Ford's. They listen whilst everyone else blabbers on with their own agenda, never suspecting that they are about to be taken down. People were certainly Thompson's business too, and as these novels demonstrate he knew them and presented them in a uniquely self-effacing way. In an age when so many Literary authors feel compelled to parade their own personalities across every paragraph, Thompson wisely gives the stage to his characters and keeps himself buried out of sight. No need here to speculate as to whether or not Jim himself was ever a master bank robber, a sheriff, a con man or a serial killer, or whether his father and mother indulged sado-masochistic practices in front of his juvenile eyes. Rather, Jim is a proponent of a more old-fashioned authorial technique; he uses his imagination to make things up. Re-reading these stories I can't help wondering if the novel of the imagination—rather than of thinly transposed personal experience—is on the decline.

I think not; for the work of the imaginative novelist hangs entirely on the complementary imaginative powers of his readers. That is where his faith resides: not in his publishers or his critics, good or bad, but in his readers. They are the ones who will turn his bare skeleton of words into living flesh, tormented minds, broken hearts and burning sunsets. In this sense Thompson is a great writer, a generous writer: the patron poet of the psychopath inside us all. This collected Picador edition is a cause for celebration and gratitude that a writer of this calibre—or rather his ghost—is at last receiving the recognition that he did not get in his lifetime. But if Thompson did not knowingly get that recognition from the review pages, then he got it from those who devoured his stories for what they are, lurid covers and all. Jim Thompson left his imprint on dozens of the writers—and film-makers—who followed him; and it is with a great sense of honour—and, I hope, of a great debt to some infinitesimal degree being repaid—that I write this introduction and invite you to enter his world. I doubt that your imagination will ever be quite the same again.

Tim Willocks
July 1995

THE GETAWAY

ONE

Carter "Doc" McCoy had left a morning call for six o'clock, and he was reaching for the telephone the moment the night clerk rang. He had always awakened easily and pleasantly; a man with not a regret for the past, and completely confident and self-assured as he faced each new day. Twelve years of prison routine had merely molded his natural tendencies into habit.

"Why, I slept fine, Charlie," he said, in his amiably sincere voice. "Don't suppose I should ask you the same question, eh? Ha-ha! Got my breakfast on the way, have you? Fine, attaboy. You're a gentleman and a scholar, Charlie."

Doc McCoy hung up the receiver, yawned and stretched agreeably, and sat up in the big, old-fashioned bed. Tipping the shade of the side-street window a little, he glanced at the all-night lunch-room a block away. A Negro busboy was just emerging from the place, a tray covered with a white cloth balanced on one hand. He came up the street at the slow but sullenly steady pace of one who is performing an unavoidable and unfairly imposed task.

Doc grinned sympathetically. It was the boy's own fault, of course. He should have known better than to boast to Charlie about the handsome tip "Mr. Kramer" had given him—known that Charlie would relieve him of delivering the tray from then on. Still—Doc went into the bathroom and began to wash—fair was fair; and a boy in a job like that probably needed every nickel he could get.

"You know how it is, Charlie," he explained ingratiatingly when the clerk arrived with his breakfast. "Now, with people like you and me, a few bucks either way doesn't make any difference, but—mind giving him this five-spot for me? Tell him I'll drop around and thank him personally when I get back in town."

The clerk beamed. Him and Mr. Kramer! People like *them*! He'd have given the five to that dish jockey even if Mr. Kramer hadn't fixed it so that he just about had to.

His face fell suddenly as the full import of Doc's words registered on him. "W-when you get back? You mean you're leavin'?"

"Just for two-three days, Charlie. A little business matter that can't wait. You bet I'm coming back, and I'm going to tack this time-out onto the end of my vacation."

"Well—" the clerk was almost weak with relief. "We—I—I guess you know we're sure glad to have you, Mr. Kramer. But believe me, I sure wouldn't be spending no vacation in this place if I was fixed like—if I was you. I'd be cuttin' it up out in Las Vegas, or . . ."

"No, no, I don't think you would, Charlie. You're too sensible. You'd get fed up mighty fast, just like I did. So you'd pick out a nice town where you could just laze around and take things easy, and meet some *real* people for a change." He nodded earnestly, then pressed a bill into the clerk's hand. "You'll look after everything for me while I'm gone, Charlie? I don't think I'll be taking anything more than a briefcase."

"You bet! But, gosh, Mr. Kramer, you don't need to give me twenty dollars just for . . ."

"But you need it to keep up with those beautiful babes you've got on the string." Doc urged him genially toward the door. "Thought I wasn't wise to you, hah? Didn't figure I'd know you were the town lady-killer—ha-ha! Well, take it easy, Charlie."

Charlie was eager to learn the basis for Mr. Kramer's flattering conclusions. But he found that somehow he had gotten out in the hall, and Mr. Kramer's door had closed in his face. Dreamily beaming, he went back downstairs to the desk.

Several signals were flashing on the tiny switchboard. Charlie answered them deliberately, stonily unapologetic in the face of inquiries as to whether he'd dropped dead or been on a vacation. Everyone ought to know by this time that he was the only night employee of the Beacon City Hotel. He had the whole shooting match to take care of from nine peeycm until nine ayem, so he had plenty to do besides just stick around the desk. And any time anyone got griped too much about it, they could go to another hotel—the nearest of which was twenty miles away.

Charlie had told a number of gripers where they could head in. Mr. Farley, the owner, had told him to. The way Farley—the stingy old jerk!—figured it, hardly anyone stayed at the Beacon City Hotel unless they had to, and he couldn't sell any more rooms with two night employees than he could with one.

Charlie yawned sleepily, and glanced at the oak-cased wall clock. Going behind the key rack, he doused his face at a dingy lavatory and dried on one of the cleaner sections of a soiled roller towel. Lady-killer, he thought, studying his pimpled reflection in the mirror. Oh, you beautiful babes!

Offhand, he could remember seeing only two or three girls in Beacon City who might even remotely qualify as truly beautiful babes; and none of these, as the saying is, had been able to see him at all. But—well, maybe he just hadn't been lookin' sharp enough. He hadn't gone about things right. Because that Mr. Kramer was one might-ee shrewd *hombre*, and if he had a fella sized up in a certain way . . .!

Leaving the desk, Charlie took up a position before the lobby window; hands folded behind him, rocking back and forth on the balls of his feet. The glass was so dusty and fly-specked as to serve inadequately as a mirror, and in it he was only mildly unappetizing.

Rose Hip, the Chinese laundryman's lovely daughter, tripped by on her way to business college. Charlie winked at her, and she stuck out her tongue at him. Charlie smirked knowingly.

There just wasn't much of anything stirring after that. As Charlie put it, you could have fired a machine gun down Main Street without hitting a soul. It was due to the recent changeover to daylight saving time, Charlie thought; folks hadn't got used to it yet. Maybe the clock said it was getting kind of late—seventeen minutes of eight—but it still wasn't seven to the people.

Charlie started to turn away from the window; then, hesitantly, hearing a familiar creak of cartwheels, he faced it again. The woman was old "Crazy" Cvec, the town scavenger. Her wobbly cart was piled high with cardboard cartons, rags and bottles. She was dressed in a ragged Mother Hubbard, an ancient picture hat, and toeless tennis shoes. A frayed cigar butt protruded from the corner of her sunken-in mouth.

When Charlie winked at her, her gums parted in an insane cackle and the butt dropped down the front of her gown. This sent her into paroxysms of crazy cackling, which she concluded by gripping the handle of the cart and kicking friskily backward with both feet. Charlie giggled lewdly. Lifting a foot, he shook his leg in the manner of a man who has got a bee up his trousers. Then . . .

"Well, I'll be damned," said a jeering voice. "Yes, sir, I will be damned."

It was Mack Wingate, bank guard and long-time resident of the hotel. Mack Wingate, dressed in his crisp gray-blue uniform and cap; his plump face twisted in a look of acid astonishment.

"So that's your girl friend," he said. "You and Crazy Cvec. Well, I guess you're gettin' the best of the bargain at that."

"Now, l-listen you!" The clerk was scarlet-faced, tremulously furious. "You better not—go and fill your inkwells! Clean out the spittoons!"

"'Spect you're feeling pretty proud, hey, Charlie? Me, now, I like 'em kind of ma-chure myself, and you sure got to admit old Crazy's matured. Hard to tell which stinks the ripest, her or the . . ."

"Yah!" said Charlie desperately. "I guess you know, don't you? You know all about her, don't you, Mack?"

"Now, don't you worry, boy. I know a real love match when I see it, and I ain't gonna come between you."

"Dang you, Mack! You—" he searched wildly for some effective threat. "You—I'm warning you for the last time, Mack! No more cooking in your room. You do it just once more, and . . ."

Wingate belched, emanating an odor of day-old rolls and coffee. "But you're goin' to let me bake your weddin' cake, ain't you, Charlie? Or was you figurin' on Crazy pickin' one up from the garbage?"

Charlie made a strangled sound. His shoulders slumped helplessly. He just wasn't any match for the bank guard. No one in town was. Anything you said to him, why, he just ignored it, and kept coming at you harder than ever. And he never got off of you until he got someone better to ride—which would be a darned long time in this case.

The guard gripped one of his inert hands, and shook it warmly. "Want to be the first to congratulate you, Charlie. You're really gettin' something when you get Crazy. Wouldn't say what it was exactly, but . . ."

"G-get out of here," Charlie whispered. "Y-you tell anyone about this, an' I'll . . ."

"Sure, now. Sure, you're kind of up in the air," said Mack Wingate with hideous sympathy. "It ain't every day in the week that a man gets hisself engaged. So don't you worry about sendin' out no announcements. I'll see to it that everyone . . ."

Charlie turned abruptly and went behind the desk. Mack laughed, snorted wonderingly and stared across the street.

On the opposite side, he stood poised for a moment, hand on the butt of his gun, and looked deliberately from left to right. Some two blocks away a car was slowly rounding the corner. No one was immediately nearby, except a storekeeper sweeping off his walk and a farmer driving a spring-seat wagon—and both were well known to him. Mack turned and unlocked the bank door.

Reaching quickly inside, he shut off the automatic alarm. He stepped up to and across the threshold; and, then—as it appeared to Charlie at least—Mack tripped over his own feet and went sprawling into the darkened interior.

The clerk hugged himself delightedly. He wanted to see the expression on Mack's face when he stuck his head out the door for a quick look around before locking it again. After a stupid tumble like that, he'd be a cinch to look out, Charlie figured. He'd be scared to death that someone'd seen him and would say something about it—a bank guard that couldn't do any better than that!—and you could just bet that someone was going to, if Mack said anything about something else.

Unfortunately, Charlie couldn't go on watching the door. Because just then, Mr. Kramer's light flashed on the switchboard. And he was *one* person Charlie never kept waiting.

And "Mr. Kramer," that prince of men, would be the first to say so.

TWO

It was doubtful whether Rudy Torrento had ever enjoyed a good night's sleep in his life. He was afraid of the dark. Early in his infancy, the night and the sleep that was normal to it had become indelibly associated with terror; with being stumbled over, smothered under a drunken mountain of flesh. With being yanked up by the hair, held helpless by one meaty hand while the other beat him into insensibility.

He was afraid to sleep, and equally fearful of awaking; from the dawn of his memory, the days had also been identified with terror. In the latter case, however, his fear was of a different kind. A cornered rat might feel as Rudy Torrento felt on coming into full consciousness. Or a snake with its head caught beneath a forked stick. It was an insanely aggressive, outrageously furious fear; a self-frightening, self-poisoning emotion, gnawing acidly at the man whose existence depended upon it.

He was paranoid; incredibly sharp of instinct; filled with animal cunning. He was also very vain. On the one hand, then, he was confident that Doc McCoy intended to kill him, as soon as he had served Doc's purposes, and on the other, he could not admit it. Doc was too smart to tangle with Rudy Torrento; he'd known that no one pulled a cross on Rudy.

When the first gray streaks of daylight seeped through the boarded-up windows of the old farmhouse, Rudy sat up groaning, eyes still closed, and began a frantic pummeling and massaging of his ribs. They had all been broken and rebroken before he was old enough to run. By now, they had long since grown together in a twisted mass of cartilage, bone and scar tissue, which ached horribly when he became chilled or when he lay long in one position.

Having pounded and rubbed them into a degree of comfort, he fumbled among his blankets until he found whiskey, cigarettes and matches. He took a long drink of the liquor, lighted and inhaled deeply on a cigarette, and suddenly—with planned suddenness—opened his eyes.

The punk, Jackson, was staring at him. Being a little slow on the trigger, compared with Rudy at least, he continued to stare for a moment longer.

Torrento beamed at him with sinister joviality. "Got a mug like a piece of pie, ain't I, kid? A chunk with the big end down."

"Huh—what?" The kid suddenly came alive. "Uh—ain't that funny? Guess I must've been sittin' here asleep with my eyes wide open."

Rudy's lips parted in a wolfish, humorless grin. He said yes, sir, it was funny as all hell. But not nearly so funny, of course, as the way he himself looked. "My maw's doctor did that for me, Jackie boy. The one that took care of her when I was born. I had a pretty big noggin on me, y'see, so just to make things nice and easy for her he kinda sloped it off to a point. That's how I got the handle—'Piehead' Torrento. Didn't know I had a real first name for a long time. Maybe you'd like to call me Piehead too, huh, Jackie boy?"

The kid jerked his head nervously. Even in the two-bit underworld of window smashers and jackrollers which had been his recruited ground, Rudy's sensitivity about his appearance was a legend. You didn't call him Piehead any more than you'd've called Benny Siegel "Buggsy." The mere mention of pie in his presence was apt to inspire him to murderous fury.

"You need some coffee, Rudy," the kid said mannishly. "Some good hot coffee and a couple of them snazzy sandwiches I bought last night."

"I asked you a question!"

"That's right, that's right, all right," the kid murmured vaguely, and he poured a steaming cup of coffee from the vacuum bottle; diffidently extended it, with a sandwich, toward the gangster.

For a moment Rudy remained motionless, staring at him out of fixed, too-bright eyes. Then, abruptly, he burst into laughter, for he had remembered something very funny. The kind of thing that would amuse him when nothing else would.

"You got a lot of guts, Jackson," he said, snorting and choking over the words. "A real gutsy ginzo, that's you."

"Well," the punk said modestly, "I wouldn't want to say so myself, but most anyone that knows me will tell you that when it comes to a showdown, why, uh . . ."

"Uh-huh. Well, we'll see, Jackson. We'll see what you got inside of you." Again Rudy was convulsed. And then, with one of his mercurial changes of mood, he was overwhelmed with pity for the kid.

"Eat up, Jackie," he said. "Catch onto some of that coffee and chow yourself."

They ate. Over second cups of coffee, Rudy passed cigarettes and held a light for the boy. Jackson felt encouraged to ask questions, and for once the gangster did not reply with insults or order him to shut up.

"Well, Doc didn't just *happen* to pick this Beacon City job," he said. "Doc never just happens to do anything. He has this plan, see, so he goes looking for exactly the right place to fit into it. Probably scouted around for two-three months, traveled over half a dozen counties, before he settled on Beacon City. First, he looks for a bank that ain't a member of the Federal Reserve System. Then—huh?" Rudy frowned at the interruption. "Well, why the hell do you think, anyway?"

"Oh. Oh, I see," the kid said quickly. "The Feds don't come in on the case, right, Rudy?"

"Right. The talk is that they're fixin' to cut themselves in on any bank robbery, but they ain't got around to it yet. Well, so anyway he checks that angle, and then he checks on interest rates. If a bank's paying little or nothing on savings, y'see, it means they got a lot more dough than they can loan out. So that tips Doc off on the most likely prospects, and all he has to do then is check their statements of condition—you've seen them printed in the newspapers, haven't you? How much dough they've got on hand and so on?"

"I've seen 'em, but they never made any sense to me. I mean, well, it always looks to me like they got just enough to pay their bills with. They ain't got any more at the end of the year than they had in the beginning."

Rudy chuckled. "I'm with you, Jackie. But they mean plenty to Doc. He can read them things like they were funny books."

"Plenty foxy, huh? A real brain." The kid shook his head admiringly, not noticing Rudy's sudden scowl. "But how come we're goin' so far out of our way to skim out, Rudy? Why go all the way up and across the country when we're only a few hundred miles from the border here?"

"You don't like it?" said Rudy. "You stupid sap, they'd be expecting us to travel in a beeline."

"Sure, sure," Jackson mumbled hastily. "What about that place we're holing up in? They really can't extradite us from there? Not no way?"

"You got nothing to worry about," Rudy told him. And again, for the moment, he was pitying. "There's this one old geezer, El Rey—that means The King, y'know, in Mex—well, him and his family, his sons and grandsons and nephews and so on, they run the place. The state or province or what the hell ever it's called. They really run it, know what I mean? They're the cops and the judges and the prosecutors and everything else. So long as you pay off and don't make no trouble with the locals, you're settin' pretty."

The kid whistled appreciatively. "But, look. What's to keep 'em from grabbing a guy's loot, and knocking him off? I mean—uh—well, I guess that wouldn't be so smart, would it? The word would get around, and they wouldn't get no more customers."

"Just about one like you, and they wouldn't want any more," Rudy grunted. "You'd spread them idiot germs around, an' the whole population would turn stupid."

"I'm sorry—I didn't mean nothin'."

"And you don't. A big fat zero, that's you," Rudy said. And that was the end of his pity.

They had shaved late the night before, and they managed a wash by tipping the water jug over one another's hands. They combed their hair, brushed their clothes thoroughly with a whisk broom, and then, completely dressed, checked each other's appearance.

They wore dark suits, white shirts, and hats of a semi-Homburg type. Except for their shoulder-holstered guns and their briefcases, they took nothing with them when they went out the back door to their car. The briefcases were large—much larger than they looked—and bore a bold-lettered OFFICE OF STATE above an equally bold-stamped BANK EXAMINER. The car, with its immensely souped-up motor, appeared to be just another black, low-priced sedan.

Jackson climbed in with the briefcases, swung open the door on the driver's side and started the motor. Rudy peered around the corner of the abandoned house. A truck had just passed on the way into Beacon City. There was nothing else in sight. Rudy leaped into the car, gunned the motor and sent it rocketing down the weed-bordered lane to the highway.

He whipped it into the highway, wheels skidding. He relaxed, slowing its speed, taking a long, deep breath. Maybe it wouldn't have mattered if someone had seen them coming out of the lane. They could have turned into it accidentally, or maybe to fix a tire on the buggy. Still, that was maybe, and maybes were bad stuff. A very small one, one that hadn't seemed big enough to kick out of the way, had tumbled Rudy the Piehead into Alcatraz for a ten-year fall.

He kept one eye on his wristwatch as he drove. They entered town on schedule to the minute, and Rudy spoke to the kid in a tight, quiet voice. "Now, this is going to be all right," he said. "Doc knows his job, I know mine. You're green, but it don't make any difference. All you got to do is just what you're told—just follow my lead—and we'll roll through it like smoke through a chimney."

"I—I'm not afraid, Rudy."

"Be afraid. What the hell? Just keep the cork on it."

At the corner two blocks above the bank, Rudy slowed the car into a crawl, swinging a little wide so that he could see down the main street. They were on schedule, but Mack Wingate, the bank guard, wasn't. Automatically, Rudy killed the motor, then began to fumble futilely with the starter. The kid turned to him, white-faced.

"R-Rudy—w-what's the . . ."

"Easy. Easy, Jackie boy," Rudy said, the words quiet, his nerves screaming murder. "Guard's a little late, see, but it don't mean a thing. If he doesn't show fast, we'll circle again and . . ."

The guard came out of the hotel, then started briskly across the street. Rudy stalled a few seconds longer, and then smoothly started the motor and rounded the corner. In little more than a minute after the guard had entered the bank, Rudy was parking in front of it.

He and Jackson got out of the car on opposite sides, the boy lingering a step or so behind him. Crossing the walk, their briefcases turned to display the official stamp on them, Rudy gave a curtly pleasant nod to the storekeeper and received a vacant stare in return. Leaning on his broom, the man continued to stare as Rudy rapped on the bank door.

The kid was panting heavily, crowding on Rudy's heels. The gangster called, "Hey, Wingate! Hurry it up," and then turned a flat, steady gaze on the storekeeper. "Yes?" he said. "Something wrong, mister?"

"Just about to ask you the same," the man said pertly. "Bank ain't in no trouble, is she?"

Very slowly, his eyes hardening, Rudy looked him over from head to foot. "The bank's not in any trouble," he said. "You trying to make some for it?"

"Me?" The man's head waggled in anxious protest. "I was just makin' talk, you know. Just joking."

"There's a law against that kind of joke," Rudy told him. "Maybe you'd better get a new one, huh?"

The storekeeper nodded feebly. He turned and tottered into his establishment, and Rudy and the kid entered the bank.

Rudy snatched up the key from the floor, and relocked the door. The kid let out a croak of amazement, one finger pointing shakily to the guard's sprawled body. "Lookit! It l-looks like he'd had a p-pencil pushed through his head."

"What are you, the coroner?" Rudy blazed. "Get his cap on! Peel out of your jacket, and put on his!"

"That fellow outside, Rudy. D-do you suppose he'll . . ."

Torrento gave him a stinging backhanded slap. Then, as the kid reeled, he caught his lapels and yanked him up to within an inch of his face. "There's just two people you got to worry about, know what I mean? Just you and me. And you keep on playin' the jerk, there'll only be one of us." Rudy gave him a hard bearing-down shake. "You got that? Think you can remember it?"

The glaze drained out of Jackson's eyes. He nodded; spoke quite calmly. "I'm all right now, Rudy. You'll see."

He put on the guard's jacket and cap, pulling the bill low over his forehead. Then, since Rudy was afraid that the dead man might panic the other employees into hysteria, they pitched his body into the railed-off desk area and pulled a rug over it.

Back in the lobby proper again, Rudy put the kid through a final rehearsal. He wasn't supposed to peek out the door, of course. Make like he was, by rattling the shade a little, but not really do it. And when he opened the door, he wasn't to show nothing of himself but his jacket sleeve and maybe the bill of his cap.

"You don't need to sell 'em, see? They don't know anything's wrong, or if they do there's nothing we can do about it. Now—" Rudy tapped on the glass top of one of the high, marble-pedestaled customer's desks. "Now, here's the code again. Here's how you'll know it's one of the wage slaves and not some Johnny-ahead-of-time wanting change for a quarter. There'll be a *knock-knock-knock*, like that, see? Then a *knock* and another *knock*. Three and two."

"I get it," Jackson nodded. "I remember, Rudy."

"Some code, huh? Must have took Doc two or three minutes to figure out with a pair of binoculars. But just the three employees will use the code; they'll show between now and eight-thirty. The big cheese gets here about a quarter of, and he don't knock. Just rattles the door latch and says, 'Wingate, Wingate!' "

Rudy glanced at the clock, gestured. They took up positions on opposite sides of the door, Rudy drew his gun, and there was a *knock-knock-knock*, and a *knock—knock*.

The kid hesitated, freezing for a split second. Then as Rudy nodded to him, gravely encouraging, his nerve returned and he opened the door.

THREE

Four months before, when it was certain that Doc was getting a pardon on his second and last jolt, his wife, Carol, had quarreled violently with him while visiting the prison. She announced that she was suing him for divorce, and had actually started proceedings against him; leaving them in abeyance, ostensibly, until she could acquire the money to carry them through. Soon afterward, with the announced intention of changing her name and making a new start in life, she boarded a train for New York—coach-class, unreserved seat—and that seemed to be that.

Except that she did not go to New York, did not and had never meant to get a divorce, and had in fact never for a moment entertained the slightest desire for any life other than the one she had.

Back in the beginning, perhaps, she had had some conscience-impelled notion of reforming Doc. But she could not think of that now without a downward quirk of her small mouth, a wince born more of bewilderment than embarrassment at the preposterousness of her one-time viewpoint.

Reform? Change? Why, and to what? The terms were meaningless. Doc had opened a door for her, and she had entered into, adopted and been adopted by, a new world. And it was difficult to believe now that any other had ever existed. Doc's amoral outlook had become hers. In a sense, she had become more like Doc than Doc himself. More engagingly persuasive when she chose to be. Harder when hardness seemed necessary.

Doc had teased her about this a time or two until he saw that it annoyed her. "A little more of *that*," he would say, "and we'll send you back to the bookstacks." And while Carol wasn't angered by his funning—it was almost impossible to be angry with Doc—neither did she appreciate it. It gave her a vague feeling of indecency, of being unfairly exposed. She had felt much the same way when her parents persisted in exhibiting one of her baby pictures; a trite display of infant nudity sprawled on a woolly white rug.

It was her picture, all right, and yet it really wasn't her. So why not forget it? Forget also that more than two decades after the picture was taken, she was just about as dishwater-dull, dumb and generally undesirable as a young woman could be.

She had been working as a librarian then; living with her stodgy, middle-aged parents and daily settling deeper into the pattern of spinsterhood. She had no life but the lifeless one of her job and home. She was fine-featured, her small body beautifully full. But people saw only the dowdy "sensible" clothes and the primness of her manner, and thought of her as plain and even homely.

Then Doc had come along—still on parole, he was already doing research on another job—and he had instantly seen the woman that she really was; and with his easy smile, his amiable persuasiveness, his inoffensive persistence, he had pulled that woman right out of her shell. Oh, it hadn't been a matter of minutes, of course. Or even days. She had been pretty skittish, as a matter of fact. Snubbing and glaring at him; putting him in what she thought of as "his place." But somehow you just couldn't do things like that with Doc. Somehow they seemed to hurt you worse than they did him. So she had relented—just a little—and the next minute, seemingly, she was through that marvelous door. And kicking it firmly shut behind her.

Her parents had washed their hands of her. *Some parents!* she thought contemptuously. She had lost her friends, her position in the community. *Some friends, some position!* She had acquired a police record.

> Carol (Ainslee) McCoy. No alias. Photo and f-prints reclaimed by court order. Three arrests; no trials or convictions. Susp. of complicity in murder, armed robbery, bank robbery, in consort with husb. "Doc"

(Carter) McCoy. May work as steno; general office. May appear attractive or unattractive, very friendly or unfriendly. Five feet, two in.; 110 lbs.; gray to green eyes; brown, black, red or light blonde hair. Age 30–35. Approach with caution.

Carol smiled to herself, winked at her reflection in the car's rearview mirror. *Some record!* It had more holes in it than their little fat heads.

Since her ostensible departure for New York, she had been working as a restaurant night cashier in a city some five hundred miles away. Under a different name, of course, and looking not at all like she looked now. Yesterday morning she had quit the job (to join her Army-sergeant husband in Georgia), slept all day, taken delivery on a new car and started driving toward Beacon City.

At eight o'clock in the morning she was within sixty miles of the town. After breakfasting on the rolls and coffee she had brought with her, and a quick wash in a filling station, she felt quite rested and high-spirited despite the long hours at the wheel.

Her rollneck cashmere sweater snugly emphasized her narrowness of waist, the flaring fullness below it and the rich contours above. A long-billed airman's cap was cocked pertly on her head, and her hair—tawny brown now—flounced out from beneath it in a jaunty ponytail. Her bobby-socked ankles tapered up into a pair of slacks which were really much less than skintight, although they did seem pretty well filled to capacity in at least one area.

She looked heartbreakingly young and gay. She looked—well, what was wrong with the word—sexy? Tingling pleasantly, Carol decided there was nothing at all wrong with it.

She had not seen Doc since their phony quarrel at the prison. Their only contact had been through brief, cautious and emotionally unsatisfying long-distance phone calls. That was the way it had to be, and Carol, like Doc—being so much a part of Doc—did not quarrel with what had to be. Still, that did not keep her from being almost deliriously happy that the long months of their separation were over.

Doc would be very pleased with her, she knew. With the way she looked; with everything she had done.

The car was a flashy yellow convertible. Stacked along with the baggage on the rear seat and floor were golf clubs, fishing rods, tennis rackets and other vacation impedimenta. The bags were bright with the stickers of assorted hotels and tourist courts. One of them contained a cap similar to her own, sunglasses and a gaudy sports jacket. That was all it held since it was meant to accommodate the loot from the bank.

They would be very conspicuous as they traveled, and the conspicuousness would give them safety. The more obvious and out in the open a thing was, Doc had taught her, the less likely it was to attract attention.

She began to drive slower, to glance more and more frequently at the dashboard clock and the speedometer's mileage indicator. At nine she saw a puff of black smoke spout up in the distance; then a billowing oily cloud of it. Carol nodded approvingly.

Doc was right on schedule, as always. The smoke signaled the successful accomplishment of the second half of his part in the robbery. Which meant, since one part was dependent upon the other, that he had also pulled off the first one.

She took another look at the clock, drove still more slowly. At the crest of a hill she stopped the car and began raising the canvas top. A truck and two cars went past, the driver of one slowing as though to offer help. Carol waved him on in a way that let him know that she meant it, then slid back behind the wheel.

She lighted a cigarette, flipped it away after a puff or two, and stared narrowly through the windshield. Nine-fifteen—no, it was almost nine-twenty. And she hadn't got the signal yet, the winking left headlight. True, one of those distant oncoming cars had suddenly disappeared from the highway—there went another one right now—but that didn't mean anything. There were many turnoffs; up through tree-lined farm lanes, or cutting between one farm and another.

In any event, Doc never made any last-minute changes in plans. If changes seemed indicated, he simply dropped the job, either permanently or until a later date. So, since he had said there would be a signal . . .

Carol started the car. She took a gun out of the glove compartment, shoved it into the waistband of her slacks and pulled her sweater over it. Then she drove on—*fast*!

*

Doc McCoy's breakfast had cooled before he could get rid of Charlie, the night clerk. But he ate it with an enjoyment which may or may not have been as real as was apparent. It was hard to tell with Doc: to know whether he actually did like something or someone as well as he seemed to. Nor is it likely that Doc himself knew. Agreeability was his stock in trade. He had soaked up so much of it that everything he touched seemed roseately transformed.

Doc's beaming good nature and the compelling personality that was its outgrowth were largely owing to his father, the widowed sheriff of a small down-south county. To compensate for the loss of his wife, the elder McCoy kept his house filled with company. Liking his job—and knowing that he would never get another half as good—he made sure of keeping it. He had never been known to say no, even to a mob's request for a prisoner. He was ready at all times to fiddle for a wedding or weep at a wake. No poker session, cockfight or stag party was considered complete without his presence; yet he was a steadfast church communicant and the ever-present guest at the most genteel social gatherings. Inevitably, he came to be the best-liked man in the county, the one man whom everyone honestly regarded as a friend. He also was the grossest incompetent and the most costly ornament in the county's body politic. But the only person who had ever faulted him—an opposition candidate—had barely escaped a wrathful lynching party.

Doc, then, was born popular; into a world where he was instantly liked and constantly reassured of his welcome. Everyone smiled, everyone was friendly, everyone was anxious to please him. Without being spoiled—his father's strictly male household took care of that—he acquired an unshakable belief in his own merit; a conviction that he not only would be but should be liked wherever he went. And holding such a conviction, he inevitably acquired the pleasant traits and personality to justify it.

Rudy Torrento planned to kill Doc, but he was resentfully drawn to him.

Doc intended to kill Rudy, but he by no means disliked Torrento. He only liked him less than he did certain other people.

His breakfast finished, Doc stacked the dishes neatly on the tray and set it outside his door. The maid was vacuuming the hall and Doc told her of his impending departure ("for a few days") and that she need not bother with his room until he had left. He inquired into the health of her rheumatic husband, complimented her on her new shoes, gave her a five-dollar tip, and smilingly closed the door.

He bathed, shaved and began to dress.

He was five feet, ten and one-half inches tall, and he weighed roughly one hundred and seventy pounds. His face was a little long, his mouth wide and a trifle thin-lipped, his eyes gray and wideset. His graying, sand-colored hair was very thin on top. In one of his sloping, unostentatiously powerful shoulders were two bullet scars. Aside from that, there was nothing to distinguish him from any number of forty-year-old men.

The stock and barrel of a rifle were slung by loops inside his topcoat. Doc took them out, hung the coat back in the closet, and began to assemble them. The stock was from an ordinary twenty-two rifle. The barrel, as well as the rest of the gun proper, had either been made or made over by Doc. Its most distinctive feature was a welded-on cylinder, fitted at one end with a plunger. It looked like, and was, a small air pump.

Doc slid a twenty-two slug into the breech, closed and locked it and rocked the slug into place. He began to pump, pumping harder as the resistance inside the air chamber grew. When he could no longer depress the plunger, he gave it several quick turns, sealing the end of the cylinder.

He smoked a cigarette and scanned the morning newspaper which Charlie had brought with his breakfast, pausing now and then to pick idly at an incipient hangnail. He reweighed his decision to dispose of Rudy, and could see no reason to change it. No reason, at least, of sufficient importance.

When they reached the West Coast, they would need to hole up temporarily; to reconsider, switch cars and break trail generally, before jumping into Mexico. It was wise to do that at any rate, even though it might not be absolutely necessary. And Rudy had lined up a place where they could take temporary sanctuary. It was a small tourist court, owned by some distant relatives of his. They were naturalized citizens, an almost painfully honest, elderly couple. But they had an unreasoning fear of the police, brought with them from the old country, and they were even more terrified of Rudy. So, reluctantly, they had submitted to his demands, on this occasion and several others.

Doc was confident that he could handle them quite well without

Rudy. He was confident that they would be even more rather than less cooperative if they knew that he had disposed of their fearsome kinsman.

Glancing at his watch, Doc lighted another cigarette and picked up the rifle. Standing back in the concealing shadows of the room, he took aim through the window, one eye squinted against the smoke from the dangling cigarette. The bank guard was due any minute now. He . . .

There was a knock on the door. Doc hesitated for a split second, then crossed the room in two long strides and opened the door a few inches. The maid thrust a handful of towels at him.

"Sorry to bother you, Mr. Kramer. Thought you might be needin' these."

"Why, that's very thoughtful of you," Doc said. "Just a moment and I'll . . ."

"Now, that's all right, Mr. Kramer. You given me too much already."

"But I insist," Doc said pleasantly. "You wait right here, Rosie."

Leaving the door ajar, he wheeled back across the room and raised the rifle, sighting it as he moved. Mack Wingate was just stepping across the bank's threshold, had almost disappeared into its dark interior. Doc triggered the gun and there was a sharp, sighing sound, like the sudden emission of breath.

He didn't wait to see the guard fall; when Doc shot at something he hit it. With a more powerful rifle his aim would have been just as accurate at five hundred yards as it had been at fifty.

He gave the maid a dollar bill, again thanking her for her courtesy. Closing and relocking the door, he got the clerk on the phone.

"Charlie, does that train into the city leave at nine-twenty or nine-thirty? Fine, that's what I thought. No, no cab, thanks. I can use a little walk."

He hung up the phone, reloaded the rifle, and again pumped up the pressure. He unfastened the stock, locked it up in his briefcase, and put the rest back in the loops of the topcoat.

He lifted the coat out, draped it loosely over one arm. He walked back and forth with it for a moment, then nodded with satisfaction and hung it back in the closet. Rudy wouldn't expect him to have the rifle. It should come as a complete surprise to him. But just in case it didn't . . .

I'll think of something, Doc assured himself. And went to work on a more immediate problem.

His luggage contained an unusual number of toiletries: bath salts, hair tonics and the like. More accurately, it contained the *containers* of these items, which were filled not with what their labels indicated but such oddly assorted things as naphtha, crude oil, a gauze-wrapped quarter-stick of dynamite, and the movements from two watches.

They formed the ingredients of two incendiary smoke bombs. Doc began to assemble them, first spreading the newspaper out on the bed to protect its coverings. A few fine beads of sweat formed on his forehead. The movements of his fingers were sure, but extremely delicate.

The dynamite itself—which he sliced into two pieces—he regarded as safe, and a mere quarter-stick of it as virtually harmless (to one familiar with its action) even if exploded. No, dynamite was all right. Dinah was easygoing, tolerating almost anything short of outrage. The danger lay in that cute little black cap she wore when being readied for action. They—the percussion caps—were about the size of an after-dinner mint, and their behavior was anything but good. And tiny as they were, one of them was more than enough to remove a man's hand.

Doc was glad when his job was finished, glad that he would never again have to take on a similar job. The bombs could have been purchased ready-made, of course, but Doc distrusted the purveyors of such items. They might talk; besides, they lacked the incentive to turn out top-grade merchandise, anything less than which was apt to prove fatal to the purchaser.

Doc put the bombs in his wastebasket and crumpled the soiled newspaper over them. He scrubbed his hands in the bathroom and turned down the turned-up cuffs of his shirt. For no conscious reason, he sighed.

He'd been on tougher jobs than this one, but never one where so much depended on its success. Everything he had was on the line here; everything that he and Carol had. He was pushing forty-one. She was almost fourteen years younger. So, one more fall, one more prison stretch and—and that would be that.

The thoughts stirred muddily in the bottom of his mind. Unrecognized and unadmitted; manifested only in an unconscious sigh.

He had not taken another look at the bank, since seeing that Rudy and the kid had gotten in all right. He'd had work to do, and there'd been no point in looking. If there was trouble, he'd be able to hear it.

Now, however, he looked again, and was just in time to see the bank president enter its door. The door closed abruptly, almost catching the heel of his shoe. Doc winced and shook his head, unconsciously as he had sighed.

It was ten minutes of nine. Doc adjusted his tie and put on his suit jacket. Now it was five minutes of. He picked up the wastebasket and stepped out into the hall.

He went down the faded red carpet to the end of the hall, then turned right into a short side corridor. A metal trash can stood between the back stairs and the side-street window. Doc poked the papers into the can, idly glancing up and down the street.

His luck was far better than he could have hoped for.

A flatbed farm truck was parked rear end first at the curb. Next to it was a sedan, its windows rolled up tightly. But next to them, parked to windward of them, was another truck—loaded almost to the level of the hotel's second-floor windows.

And what it was loaded with was baled hay!

Doc gave the street another quick up and down glance. Then he tossed the bombs, lofting one between the truck's cab and bed, the other onto the load of hay.

He picked up the wastebasket and returned to his room. It was two minutes of nine now—two minutes before the bombs were set to explode—and three or four people were gathered in front of the bank, waiting for it to open.

Doc completed his arrangements for leaving, slowly counting off the seconds.

FOUR

The time lock on the bank's vault was set for eight-fifty. Slightly more than ten minutes later, Rudy and Jackson had cleared it of cash—dollar bills and coins excepted—and several thick packages of negotiable securities.

The banker lay sprawled on the floor, half-dead from Rudy's pistol-whipping. Stumbling over his unconscious body, Rudy gave him a savage kick in the face, turned half-crazed eyes upon the kid. The fear had filled him now, the furious outraged fear of a cornered rat. It would simmer down in time, solidify into the murderous trigger-quick wiliness which had guided him in and out of so many tight places. Which forced him to survive long after the withered inner man had cried out for the peace of death. Now, however, there was nothing but the raging fear, and he had to strike out at something. At anything.

"You hear anything out there?" He jerked his head toward the street. "Well, did you?"

"Hear anything? W-what . . ."

"The bombs, you long-eared jerk! Any commotion."

"Huh-uh. But I don't guess we could, could we, Rudy? I mean, there in the vault we—N-no! D-don't!"

The kid strangled on a scream. He tried to claw the gun from his belt. Then he toppled forward, clutching at his half-disemboweled abdomen; at the guts which Torrento had mockingly credited him with having.

Rudy giggled. He made a sound that was strangely akin to a sob. Then he wiped his knife on a blotter, returned it to his pocket and picked up the two briefcases.

He carried them to the bank door, set them down again. He turned and looked meditatively at the bank's three employees. They were scattered about the lobby floor, their mouths sealed with tape, their wrists and ankles bound with more tape. They looked at him, their eyes rolling to show the whites, and Rudy hesitantly fingered his knife.

They'd have him tabbed for the robbery, for killing the kid. And if things broke wrong, Doc would doubtless manage to tag him with the guard's death. Trust Doc to keep himself in the clear, him and his smart little sneak of a wife! But anyway, these yokels could finger him—pick his wedge-shaped map out of a million mug shots. So as long as he couldn't be fried or have his neck popped but once anyhow, why not . . .

He took the knife out again. He went from employee to employee, slashing the bonds of their ankles, kicking and cursing and yanking them to their feet.

Shoving them ahead of him, he herded them back inside the vault. He swung the door shut on them, gave the knob a few spins.

There'd been no point in killing them. He'd been seen coming into the joint, and he was a cinch to be seen leaving. There was a hell of a racket outside and it was growing by the second, and even in here you could get a whiff of smoke. But still, someone, a lot of someones, would see him leave. The best he could hope for was that none of 'em would try to do anything about it.

None of 'em did. Doc had figured right. They had too much else to be interested in to pay any attention to him. And after all, what was so funny about a guy coming out of a bank during banking hours?

The side street was jammed with people, surging back toward the walks occasionally when the wind-driven smoke threatened to envelop them. Sparks showered upward from the burning hay. A gas tank exploded, sending a speckled fountain of fire into the air. The crowd roared, jamming back into the intersection, and the people in the intersection tried to push forward. Several man in red helmets were scurrying about, shouting and gesturing futilely. Other red-helmeted men were lunging up the street, dragging a two-wheel hose cart behind them. The bell in the courthouse cupola tolled steadily.

Rudy loaded the briefcases into the car. He made a U-turn, honking for a couple of yokels to get out of the way, and headed out of town.

A block away, Doc stepped down from the walk to the street and climbed in with him. They rode on, Rudy grinning meanly to himself as he noted the careless caution with which Doc handled his coat. McCoy asked him how they had made out.

"Two hundred in bonds. Maybe a hundred and forty in cash."

"A hundred and forty?" Doc's eyes flicked at him. "I see. Must've been a lot of ones and silver."

"So maybe there's more, dammit! You think I figured it up on an addin' machine?"

"Now, Rudy," Doc said soothingly, "no offense. How did it go with the youngster?"

"What d'you mean, how'd it go? How'd you plan it to go?"

"Of course. Too bad," Doc said vaguely. "I always feel bad when something like that is necessary."

Rudy snorted. He jammed a cigarette into his mouth, put his left hand in his jacket pocket, ostensibly seeking a match. It came out with a heavy automatic which he leveled across his lap.

"Get rid of the rifle, Doc. Toss it out in the ditch."

"Might as well." Doc didn't appear to notice the automatic. "Doesn't look like we're going to need it."

He lifted the rifle, muzzle first, and dropped it out of the window. Rudy let out another snort.

"Doesn't look like we're gonna need it!" he mocked. "Well, you ain't going to need that rod in your jacket either, Doc, so—*don't move for it*! Just take the jacket off and toss it in the back seat."

"Listen, Rudy . . ."

"Do it!"

Doc did it. Rudy made him lean forward, then backward, swiftly scanning his trousers. He nodded, gave Doc permission to light a cigarette. Doc turned a little in the seat, eyes sorrowful beneath the brim of his hat.

"This doesn't make sense, Rudy. Not if it's what I think it is."

"That's what it is. Exactly what you'd figured for me."

"You're wrong, Rudy. I shouldn't have to tell you that. How would I get by at Golie's without you? They're your relatives, and if Carol and I pulled in there by ourselves . . ."

"They'd probably give you a gold watch," Rudy said sourly. "Don't kid me, Doc. You think I'm stupid or something?"

"In this case, yes. Perhaps we might get along as well without you, but . . ."

"As well? You'd be a hell of a lot better off, and you know it!"

"I don't agree with you, but let it go. You'll need us, Rudy. Carol and me."

"Huh-uh. Just a different car, and some other duds. Yeah, and your share of the take. That's all."

Doc hesitated, looked through the windshield. He glanced at the speedometer. "Too fast, Rudy. We're liable to pick up a cop."

"You mean we're ahead of schedule," Rudy grinned. "That's what you mean, ain't it?"

"Give Carol the signal, at least. She'll think there's trouble if you don't. Might even lam out on us."

"Not on you." Rudy's laugh was enviously angry. "She'll know you was going to bump me, and . . ."

"No, Rudy. How . . ."

". . . and she'll figure you got caught in a snarl, so she'll move right on in and try to get you out of it."

Doc didn't argue the point. In fact, he ceased to argue at all. He simply shrugged, turned around in the seat and was silent.

Coming so quickly, his apparent resignation bothered Rudy. Not because he was afraid Doc had a fast one up his sleeve. Obviously he couldn't have. The feeling came from something else—the irksome, deeply rooted need to justify himself.

"Look, Doc," he blurted irritably. "I wasn't burned over what you was going to do to me. You'd've been a sap to do anything else, and I'd be a sap to do anything else. So what's there to cry about?"

"I didn't realize I was crying."

"And you got no right to," Rudy said doggedly. "Look. A hundred and forty in cash. Maybe a hundred and twenty-five out of the bonds. Call it a quarter of a million all together. That ain't no dough in a three-way split—not when it's the last you're going to get and you got to hole up with The King all your life. He doesn't put out anything without cash on the line, and plenty of it."

"Exactly." Doc smiled witheringly. "So it would be an excellent idea not to simply live up your cash, wouldn't it? To use it in such a way that you'd be sure of a generous income as long as you lived."

"How you mean?" Rudy waited. "Like startin' a tamale parlor, huh?" he jeered. "Or maybe a gambling casino?" He waited again. "You're goin' to run competition with The King?"

Doc laughed softly. The laugh of an adult at a small child's antics. "Really, Rudy. In your case, I'd suggest a circus. You could be your own clown."

Rudy scowled and licked his lips uncertainly. He started to speak, stopped himself. He cleared his throat and made another attempt.

"Uh, what'd you have in mind, Doc? Dope, maybe? Smuggling? I figured them things was sewed up, but—ah, to hell with you, Doc! I'm holding aces and you're trying to buy out with hot air."

"Fine, so why don't we let it go at that?" Doc said easily.

Rudy's foot eased up on the gas. Two emotions warred within him: ingrained suspicion and inherent terror of being in want. Doc was conning him—or was he? Would a smoothie like Doc go out on a limb unless he saw a better one to grab? And—and what did a guy do when he ran out of dough, and he couldn't take it away from someone else?

"You ain't got a thing, Doc," he mumbled. "You got something, what you got to lose by telling me about it?"

"Very little—but what would you have to gain? Take such a simple matter as Mexico's foreign policy, its relations, I should say, on a global basis, as compared to those of its Latin-American neighbors. The situation isn't going to change any. Or if it does, it will be to a still more favorable position. It's tied directly to the monetary market—the foreign exchange rate, to use the more popular term—and with inflationary tendencies being what they are, and with gold staked at thirty-five dollars an ounce, the potential for the right kind of operator is . . ."

Doc let his voice trail away. "Never mind, Rudy," he said pleasantly. "It seems simple enough to me, but I didn't really expect you to understand. It's something that's confused a great many highly intelligent people, men who were very successful in their own particular professions."

"Like double-talk maybe?" Rudy scoffed. But he said it rather feebly. There were certain words, phrases, that rang a bell in his mind. Foreign exchange—inflationary tendencies—monetary market. The terms were identified with news stories which he invariably skipped over, but he guessed they probably meant heavy sugar to a lot of people.

"Like double-talk," Doc was saying. "Yes, that's exactly the way it would sound to you. And I can't say that I blame you a bit. It would probably sound the same way to me if I hadn't spent most of my last four-year stretch reading up on it."

"Well . . ."

"No, it's no use, Rudy," Doc said firmly. "I wish I could. It's a good deal—and a perfectly legitimate one—and you'd have been just the right man to hold down one end of it. But I can't make it any clearer than I have, so there's nothing more to be said."

Rudy was not a fast thinker—if the weird processes of his mind could be called thinking. But when he made a decision, he made it fast. Abruptly he dropped the gun into his pocket and said, "All right, Doc. I'm not buying just yet, but I'll take an option."

Doc nodded. He didn't trust himself to speak.

"I'm keeping your gun," Rudy went on. "I'm taking any iron that Carol has when she shows. We stop at night, you two get tied up. We stop for grub or something during the day, one of you stays with me. Either one of you tries anything, that'll be it. Know what I mean? Okay?"

"I know exactly what you mean," Doc purred, "and naturally it's okay."

They crossed a bridge over a small creek. Immediately on the other side, Rudy turned the car straight down the road's embankment, then down the bank of the creek. The wheels bounced high in the air; the steering wheel jerked and spun in his hands. Rudy fought it around to his left, heading the car up the rocky bed of the stream with its shallow trickles of water. A couple of hundred yards farther on, beneath a cloaking arbor of trees, he brought it to a stop.

Doc took a handkerchief from his pocket, mopped at his forehead. He said mildly that he was afraid his neck was broken.

Rudy laughed. Doc got out of the car and removed his hat, continuing the mopping process as Rudy climbed out.

"You kill me, y'know, Doc?" Rudy was still snorting over the joke. "You really slay me sometimes. I . . ."

"So what's wrong with that?" Doc said. And as Rudy burst into renewed laughter, he took a gun from his hat and fired.

"Got him right through the heart," Doc told Carol. "One of those very rare instances where a man actually died laughing."

"Just so he died." Carol grimaced. "That's one character I could never feel easy around. I always had a feeling that he was just about ready to jump at me from the one side I wasn't watching."

"Alas, poor Rudy," Doc murmured. "But how have you been, my dear—to move from the ridiculous to the sublime?"

"We-el—" Carol slanted a sultry glance at him. "I think I'll be a lot better tomorrow. You know. After I get a good night's sleep."

"Tut, tut," said Doc. "I see you're still a very wicked young woman."

They had driven through Beacon City, commenting wonderingly on the smoke, looking curiously at the milling throngs; and now they were far down the highway on the other side of town. Doc was driving, since Carol had driven all night. She sat sidewise in the seat, facing him, her legs curled under her.

Their eyes kept meeting. They kept smiling at each other. Doc patted one of her small round flanks, and she held his hand for a moment, gripping it almost fiercely.

"What are you worried about, Doc?"

"Worried?"

"I can always tell. Is it Golie's? You think that if Rudy isn't with us . . ."

Doc shook his head. "No trouble there. I wouldn't say I was worried about anything. Just puzzled in a troubled sort of way about our friend Beynon."

"Oh," said Carol. "Oh, yeah."

Beynon was an attorney, the chairman of the pardon and parole board. Doc's pardon had been bought from him, and there was still fifteen thousand dollars due on the purchase price. He owned a tiny ranch up in the far corner of the state. A bachelor, he lived on it when he was not occupied with some legal case or his official duties. They were going there now.

"Doc—" Carol was staring through the windshield. "Let's make a switch. Head right into Mexico from here."

"We couldn't do it, baby. It's too obvious. We're too close."

"But you haven't been connected with the job. With any kind of break at all, it'll be days before you are."

"That doesn't help much. Not when the job's this big and this close to the border. They'll have road blocks up fifty miles this side of El Paso. Everyone'll get a shakedown. Anyone trying to cross over had better be strictly clean and able to prove it, or he's in the soup."

"Well—but the other way, Doc. Beynon is miles off of our route, and if you think he may be up to something, why—why . . ."

"Skip him?" Doc gave her a thoughtful look. "Is that what you were going to suggest, Carol?"

"Why not? What could he do about it?"

Doc smiled wryly, almost irritated with her. Leave Beynon holding the sack for his fifteen thousand? A man with his connections who knew as much about them as he did? It was too preposterous to discuss. They were due at his ranch just as quickly as they could get there from Beacon City, and they had damned well better not dally along the way.

"What could he do?" Carol repeated stubbornly. "Why pay him off, if he's going to make trouble anyway?"

"I don't know that he is. If he's planning to, however, and if I can't talk him out of it—" Doc left the sentence unfinished, his shrewd eyes thoughtful behind the obscuring sunglasses.

Beynon hadn't run according to form. What he had done was completely out of character, and having acted in such a way, he must have a motive which did not appear on the surface.

Doc stroked his jaw, shook his head absently.

"How did he add up to you, Carol?" he asked. "I mean aside from the fact that he's an ambitious man with plenty of uses for money. Did he do or say anything that would indicate why he would go for a deal like this one?"

Carol didn't answer him. Doc was about to repeat the question when he saw that she was asleep.

FIVE

Doc went to New York the spring that he graduated from high school, a few weeks after his father's death. He was too young to hold political office, and there were no worthwhile jobs in the town. On the other hand, he was convinced, as were his countless friends, that he would be virtually able to pick and choose from the many opportunities available in a large city.

Things didn't work out that way. He had no difficulty in getting jobs, even in those times of economic depression. But he held none of them more than a few weeks. He was a disrupting influence, throwing any establishment he went into out of kilter. Other employees tended to gather around him, leaving their work undone. Minor supervisors coddled and favored him, to the detriment of morale. As an upper-echelon executive, he would have been invaluable to any company. But he qualified neither in years nor experience for anything but the lowliest jobs. And in that capacity he was simply a nuisance.

Working briefly and rarely, he lived largely on credit and small loans. He worried about these obligations (you did not let down your friends, his father had taught him), and he readily acquiesced when a bar owner-creditor offered to wipe the slate clean, and even gift him with a small bonus, in return for a "little favor."

The favor was done; the barkeep collected on his burglary insurance. A few days later he introduced Doc to the proprietor of a floating crap game—a man who needed big money in a hurry and could not depend on gambling to get it. Doc was glad to cooperate with him. He stuck up the game, with some subtle assistance from the proprietor, and they split the proceeds.

Later on, the gambler having introduced him to some "right" boys, Doc stuck up one of his games again, without prearrangement and without splitting. Nor did this in any way violate his father's code about friendship. On the contrary, the elder McCoy had believed that a man's best friend is himself, that a non-friend was anyone who ceased to be useful, and that it was more or less a moral obligation to cash in any persons in this category, whenever it could be done safely and with no chance of a kick-back.

Doc was made for crime, the truly big operations which he rapidly moved into. No one could get on the inside of a job as easily as he, no one could plan so shrewdly, no one was so imperturbable and cool-headed.

He liked his work. Beginning a stiff prison sentence at age twenty-five he still remained loyally committed to it. His take for the last five years had been more than a hundred thousand a year. For that kind of money, a man could afford to sit it out for a while. He could use his enforced leisure to relax, make new contacts, improve his criminal knowledge and plan new jobs.

Doc's ensuing eight years behind bars were entirely comfortable and often highly enjoyable. After all, a prison cannot function without the cooperation of its inmates; it cannot do so satisfactorily at least, or for very long. So a man who can lead his fellow prisoners, who can deliver their cooperation or withhold it, can get almost anything he asks for. And about the only deprivation Doc suffered was the loss of his income.

Given the same circumstances, he could have taken his second and last prison sentence as lightly as he had the first. But the circumstances differed crucially. He was married—and to a woman almost fourteen years his junior. And he was thirty-six years old.

Doc didn't fret about the situation. He never missed a meal, nor a night's sleep, nor spent a moment in futile regret. He had just one problem—to get out before getting out became pointless. Very well then, if that was what had to be done, he would do it.

He had left sixty thousand dollars on the outside with Carol. With that, and a topflight criminal lawyer, he managed to get his twenty-year sentence reduced to ten. It was a long step on the road to freedom; barring upsets, he would qualify for parole in approximately seven years. But that wasn't good enough for Doc. The seven years might as well be seventy as he saw it. And he wanted no more paroles. Trying to operate while on parole was what had put him where he was.

There were four members of the pardon and parole board, in addition to its chairman, Beynon. Exercising his unusual privileges, Doc approached them one by one. The middle-aged woman member fell for him; he was able to buy her with conversation. The three men members were open to a cash proposition.

Unfortunately Doc had run very, very low on money. He didn't have nearly the amount needed for the three-man buy. And his lawyer, who was usually open to a "good" proposition himself, refused to play banker. "Not that I don't trust you, Doc," he explained. "I know I'd get mine right off the top of your first job. The point is there wouldn't be any job, because there ain't going to be any pardon. You'd've talked this over with me in the first place, I'd've told you you were wasting your time."

"But I'd have four members. A majority of the board."

"Majority, schmority! Three of 'em are crooks, and the gal's a well-meaning imbecile. Beynon would veto them. If they tried to crowd him, he'd start swinging. Kick up such a stink that you'd probably have to do the rest of your time in the hole."

"Turn it around then. If they can't push him, can he push them?"

"He *could*. He could make 'em do a skirt dance on the capitol steps if he took a notion. But lay off, Doc. He didn't get that way by going for the fast dollar."

"Good for him. The better the reputation, the less the risk."

"Yeah?" The lawyer smiled bitterly. "Like to meet a guy that almost got disbarred for offering Beynon a cigar? Well, shake hands."

Doc wasn't convinced. He'd dealt with Honest Johns before, and they'd never turned out as pure as they were supposed to be. So he arranged to see Beynon alone—and that was about all he did. Just saw him. And excused himself as quickly as he could. He was too shrewd—too able an interpreter of a man's expression, the tone of his voice, his overall attitude—to do anything else. Beynon obviously wanted him to make the bribe attempt. It was also obvious that he had some very unpleasant plans for Doc as soon as it was made.

"So I'll have to think of something else," Doc told Carol on her next visit. "I don't know what it will be, but Beynon's definitely out."

"Maybe not. We can't be sure unless we try."

"I'm sure. Beynon won't take."

"You mean he never has," Carol persisted. "He won't take from you or the lawyer. Ordinarily he wouldn't take from me. But suppose I'd broken up with you, Doc—that it looked like I had. Then he'd have a double out for himself in case anyone got nasty. If I were through with you, then naturally I wouldn't be giving him a bribe. And when a man's wife quits him, it's supposed to be punishment. Don't you see, Doc? I wouldn't have any reason to bribe him, and he *would* have a reason for giving you a break."

It sounded pretty flimsy to Doc. But Carol wanted to try; and it was pressing four years since he had entered the penitentiary. So he told her to go ahead.

Two months passed before he saw her again. No one could have been more surprised than he when she reported success. Beynon would sell him a pardon. The price five thousand cash, fifteen thousand within ninety days.

News of the robbery had been on the air since ten-thirty that morning. Carol and Doc listened to it, the radio turned to a whisper, as they ate lunch at a roadside drive-in.

Rudy had been identified from rogues' gallery photographs. Except for Jackson, whom he had killed, there was no mention of a confederate. Rudy had robbed the bank. Rudy had driven boldly out of town with "more than three hundred thousand dollars in swag." The authorities were "puzzled" as to how he had gained entry into the bank to kill the guard. But no one raised the question as to whether he *had* shot Wingate.

That would happen in about two days, Doc mused, as he turned the car back into the highway. The trajectory of the bullet, and the bullet itself, would instigate inquiries about "an unnamed businessman who had been vacationing in Beacon City." And in two or three more days the businessman would be named, along with his "business." But by that time it wouldn't matter.

The news broadcast ended, gave way to a disc jockey. Carol started to doze again, and Doc leaned over to switch off the radio. Then, abruptly, he turned it up. And he and Carol listened silently, tensely, to a late news bulletin.

It was over in a moment. Carol turned the switch, turned slowly, wide-eyed, toward Doc.

"Doc . . .?"

Doc hesitated, then shook his head firmly. "Huh-uh. After all, it happened almost sixty miles away from Beacon City. It couldn't have anything to do with . . ."

"Why couldn't it? Who else would do a thing like that?"

"Anyone could have. Some drunk that lost his head. Some gun-happy teenager."

"You don't really believe that, Doc. I know you don't," Carol said. "You didn't kill him. Rudy's still alive."

Aimed straight at the heart, Doc's bullet felled Rudy Torrento like a streak of lightning. He stopped breathing, all conscious movement. His eyes glazed, his wedge-shaped face became a foolish, frozen mask, and he crumpled silently backward, an idiot doll cast aside by its master.

The back of his head struck against a rock in the bed of the stream. The impact deepened and extended his deathlike state. So, far from giving him a second bullet, Doc McCoy hardly gave him a second glance.

And less than thirty minutes after Doc's departure, Rudy came to life again.

His head ached horribly, and his first move was to roll on his stomach and batter the offending rock with his fists. Then memory returned and terror surged through him, and he hurled himself to his feet, clawing. Clawing off his coat and holster. Ripping open his shirt and undershirt. Ripping aside their bloody mess, and seeing and feeling—seeing-feeling—the scarlet frightfulness of his flesh.

He snarled, whimpered, whined. All silently, his vocal cords constricted. He threw back his head and let out a long, silent howl; the shivering, heart-breaking cry of a dying animal. That was taken care of then; the last ceremony which instinct demanded. Now he could begin the actual business of dying. He breathed more and more rapidly. Feverish, poison-filled air rushed into his lungs, his heart raced and stuttered, and his body began to jerk and stiffen.

I knew it, he thought dully, almost with his last thoughts. Back there years ago, back when I was just a kid, back as far as I can remember, I knew it'd be like this. Everything gettin' colder and colder, and the darkness getting deeper and deeper, an'—I knew. I KNEW!

Knew. The word drummed through his mind, sending a signal back through the years, through thousands of miles, through the grim gray walls and chilled-steel cages of a maximum security prison. And back through time and distance came a voice which told Rudy the Piehead, one of the nation's top ten public enemies, that he was a foolish little child who knew nothing whatsoever.

Rudy blinked, and a little color came back into his fish-gray face. "Max—?" he whispered hopefully. "You—you here, Max?"

"*But of course I am. Where else would I be, when my leetle poy Rudy is in trouble? Now, do vot I tell you, instanter!*"

Rudy did so. He was quite alone, needless to say; alone with the whispering, half-dry stream and the deep shadows of the arching trees, and the salt-sweet smell of his own blood. But in his mind he was not alone. With him was the one person he had ever loved, or been loved by. Little Max. Herr Doktor Max. Max Vonderscheid, M.D., Ph.D., Psych.D.—abortionist, physician to criminals; a man who had never been able to say no to a need, regardless of laws and professional ethics.

He and Rudy had been cellmates for three years. Those years, in a so-called tough jug, had given the Piehead the only true happiness he had ever known. One does not forget such things, or such a man. Each of his actions, his words, becomes a thing to treasure.

Rudy stretched out flat on the ground, closed his eyes, relaxed as completely as he could, and held his breath for a moment. Then he began to count slowly, "One-two-three—" exhaling and inhaling in time with the count. When he had counted to ten three times, his breathing was near normal and his heart had ceased its wild palpitating. He kept his eyes shut, waiting, and the voice spoke to him again.

He had done well—oh, but werry goot! He had remembered that shock was the big killer; shock first, infection second. If one gave way to shock, even a very minor wound could prove fatal.

"But, Max—" Rudy knew a momentary return of panic. "It ain't minor! He wasn't ten feet away, and he shot me straight through the . . ."

Rudy sat up. A hoarse laugh welled in his throat. Shot through the ticker? Why, hell if that had happened he wouldn't be alive! He examined his torso again, wondering just what had happened and how.

The riddle remained one to an extent; rather, it had a bit of miracle mixed up in it. The metal-sheathed tip of the holster had obviously deflected the bullet ever so slightly, while it had been further deflected by the iron-hard botch of broken bones and cartilage that formed his rib cage. But still he was very lucky to be alive. And the wound was still nothing to laugh off.

Extending from a point immediately over his heart, the flesh had been furrowed bone-deep across his chest and halfway around the left side of his body. Probably because of the way he had fallen—his chest arching against his clothes and holster strap—he had bled relatively little, much less at any rate than he normally would have. But movement had opened the wound wide now, and he was losing blood at a dangerous rate.

He made a bandage with his undershirt, binding it tight with his belt and holster strap. That helped, but not much; nor did it help much more when he added his socks and handkerchief to the bandage. He had one thing left—two things rather—readily available for putting over the wound. The two thick sheafs of bills he had sequestered from the bank loot. But if he used them, got them bloody—and they probably wouldn't do a damned bit of good anyway . . .

Huh-uh. He had to keep that dough. As long as he had dough and a gun and a car—but above all, the dough—well, he had a chance. To live. To catch up with Doc and Carol. Beyond that—catching up with and killing them—he couldn't think at the moment. It seemed both a means and an end to him. In their deaths, somehow, he would find life for himself.

He climbed weakly into the car and gunned the motor, sending the vehicle roaring up and out of the creek bed and onto the road in a skidding series of jumps and jounces. It was the way it had to be. He lacked the strength for reconnoitering, the strength and the time. All he could do was come up fast, and hope for the best.

His luck held; no one was passing on the road. Luck continued with him as he skirted Beacon City's outer streets and took to the highway again on the other side. Then swiftly, with his blood, it began to flow away.

He fumbled in the glove compartment of the car, took out a half-filled pint of whiskey. He took a cautious drink, then feeling warmed and stronger, a bigger one. He capped the bottle with one hand, dug cigarettes from his pocket. He found one that was still usable and lit up, drawing the smoke deep into his lungs. Suddenly, for no reason—except that he was drunk—he guffawed.

Laughing, he took another drink, another long puff on the cigarette. Abruptly the bottle fell from his hand, and the car swerved crazily toward the ditch.

The cigarette saved him. As he fought to avoid the ditch, he jammed the burning butt between his palm and the steering wheel, and the pain screamed his mind awake, gave it the complete alertness that it needed. But it began to fade almost as soon as it came. He was conscious; then surely, swiftly, he was losing consciousness again.

"*Foolish Rudy. So little blood he has, and he mixed that with alcohol!*"

Rudy brought the car to a weaving stop. Awkwardly, gasping with weakness, he raised and turned himself in the seat, reached down onto the rear floor. His fingers found what they were seeking. Closing them with shaky tightness, he flopped down into the seat again.

The two sandwiches were dry and stale. The coffee in the vacuum bottle was cold and tasted sour. But Rudy consumed all of it, and all of the food.

Had to eat when you were losing blood. Had to pack the chow down to come off a jag. Had to—had to . . .

Had to get to a doctor.

He was driving again. He could not remember starting up, but the wind was whipping into his face and the highway was leaping madly beneath the car.

"D-doctor," he mumbled drowsily. "Got tuh hurry'n see a—see Doc an' . . ."

Awareness flooded over him again. He cursed savagely, bitterly, his dark face contorting into a baffled scowl.

How could he go to a doctor? There'd be other people around; patients, a nurse, maybe the guy's wife. And even if he could take care of them and get treated, then what? So, sure, he'd bump off the sawbones as soon as the job was done, but that wouldn't help. Doctors were busy guys. People were always calling on them, dropping in on them, and . . .

"Not necessarily, my poy! Not with a certain kind of doctor. Oh, perhaps he would haf calls. But they would be relatively few, and the callers being under no such dire necessity as would prevail in . . ."

Rudy brushed the sweat from his eyes. He began to slacken his speed, to study the occasional R.F.D. mailboxes at the side of the highway.

Country doctor? Was that it huh-uh. Country docs didn't live in the country. Right in town, same's any other kind. And if one of 'em was killed or missing, the heat'd be on fast. Faster than fast this close to that bank job. Wouldn't take no Eddie Hoover to figure out that—that . . .

The highway began to blur; everything began to blur, to sink into a kind of gray fuzziness. He crouched forward over the wheel, brushing constantly at his eyes. Just before he lost consciousness completely, he turned into a side road.

He could remember doing nothing after that, yet he did a great deal. As much as he would have if he had been fully aware of his reactions. The frightful present no longer existed; he was reborn, free of all fear and the hideous savagery which festered in it. For Little

Max was with him. Max Vonderscheid of the leonine head and the dwarfed hunchbacked body. And he was laughing in a way he had never laughed before, or since.

"Aw, haw, haw! Now you're kidding me again, you little old Dutch bugger, you!"

"But vot iss so funny, my poor paranoid friend? You should read Jonathan Svift. It vill gif you a better perspective.

"Vy not? Der schooling has many parallels. Even it might be said that he must know much more of medicine and anatomy than your proud M.D. The basic difference? Only that der patients are usually more deserfing and inwariably less demanding."

Rudy came back into consciousness as quickly as he had gone out of it.

He was awake—and considerably refreshed—the moment the other car turned into the side road.

He had crouched down on the floorboards before passing out, lying on the seat from the waist up. Thus he could not be seen, unless someone peered directly into the car. And now he remained hidden, making no move except to firm the grip on the gun he had kept in his hand.

No move was necessary. He had already done everything that could be done in just such an emergency. Both windows on the left side were rolled down. The right wheels were parked on the edge of the roadside ditch. The rearview mirror was twisted to an angle which permitted him to see without raising his head.

It was a black-and-white patrol car. There were two men in it, one young, one middle-aged; apparently a rookie and a regular. They got out on opposite sides of the vehicle and started forward that way. Hands on gun butts, but they kept well apart from one another. Moving up on the suspect objective from different directions.

This, of course, was and is the proper procedure, never to be deviated from under any circumstances. Due to the way the car was parked, however, it would have been bothersome if not impossible to carry it through. And since the vehicle was obviously empty, it seemed unnecessary.

So after a moment's pause, one of them shrugged and the other laughed, and they came on together. Almost shoulder to shoulder. Just that once they violated regulations.

And a split second after Rudy reared up over the seat, both of them were dead.

He took their guns and ammunition. He whipped his car round in a U-turn, running partly over the older man's body, and took to the highway again.

He knew what he had to do now, and the knowledge gave him strength. It also amused him, and he laughed as he had when Max Vonderscheid gave him the tip which he was now about to use.

Now, wasn't that somethin' though? Who'd ever think of a dodge like that?

Getting yourself fixed up by a vet, a horse doctor!

SIX

Doc McCoy's greatest vice and major virtue was his sureness. He had been right so often and so long that he could not conceive the possibility of being anything else. Genially, he might charge himself with error, good-naturedly accept the blame for another's mistake. But that was just Doc—part of his masquerade. In his heart he was never wrong—never, that is, about anything that really mattered. And to have a doubt raised as to whether he had actually killed Rudy—a thing at once simple yet vital—made him as near to angry as he ever came.

"I'll tell you, Carol," he said, a trace of fiddle-string tightness in his voice. "I don't know who shot those two cops. I don't care. All I know is that it was not done by Rudy Torrento."

"Well—if you say so, Doc. But . . ."

"Look at it this way. I wasn't a great deal farther from Rudy than I am from you. Suppose I decided to plug you right now. Do you think I'd kill you or not?"

Carol laughed uneasily. He was smiling at her; joking, of course. No one knew better than she how much Doc thought of her, the lengths he was willing to go to for her sake. But if she *hadn't* known—if she *hadn't* been sure that Doc wanted and needed her just as much after the bank robbery as before . . .

The thought nettled her. She spoke in a tone, a manner, that was almost an identical match for his. "Suppose I decided to plug you right now," she said, smiling, playful—steady-eyed. "Do you think I'd kill you or not?"

"I'm sorry," Doc said warmly. "To answer your question—I wouldn't blame you if you did exactly like that."

"I don't like being shut up, Doc. I don't intend to be."

"And you're quite right, my dear."

"So don't talk to me that way again. Never, ever, understand? I know you didn't mean it like it sounded, but . . ."

Doc turned the car off onto a country road. Stopping just over the crest of a little hill, he turned silently and took his wife into his arms. He kissed her, drew her more and more tightly to him. He kissed her again, his sure hands pressing and caressing her small hard-soft body.

And afterward, as they drove on, they were again one with each other; each an extension of the other.

Their brief flare-up was forgotten. There was no more mention of Rudy. Carol was glad to be convinced, to be sure that Rudy was dead.

Mostly they were silent, happy and content merely to be together. But as the sun sank lower in the sky, there was more talk of Beynon. The man—his motives, rather—still bothered Doc. It was difficult to believe that the parole chief meant to grab all the bank loot, instead of the relatively small share he had agreed to accept. To think that such a man would commit murder—as he would have to—for any amount of money was nothing short of ridiculous. On the other hand, was it any more ridiculous than his ostensible sellout—at the risk of his career and reputation—for a mere pittance?

Carol was of little help with the riddle. She seemed indifferent to its answer; a little bored, dully withdrawn. Then, a few miles from Beynon's place she brightened, turned almost gaily to her husband. "I've got an idea, Doc. Let me take Beynon his fifteen grand."

"You?" Doc gave her a quick glance. "Without me, you mean?"

"Yes. You take the money satchel, and . . ."

"And just where would I take it to? Where would I wait? At the side of the road, or at one of these little inland villages—some wide place in the road where every stranger gets the big-eye and maybe an interview by the town clown?"

"We can work it out. Please, Doc. What do you say?"

"That I can't believe you're serious," said Doc evenly. "I appreciate your concern for me, of course, but—" he shook his head. "It just wouldn't do, lamb. As I mentioned before. If Beynon is planning something, we've got to know about it now. We've got to get it settled now."

"I could settle it."

"But he wouldn't bring things to a showdown if you were by yourself. In any event, the kind of settlement—if one is necessary—is something I'd want to decide on myself."

Carol started to say something else, then shrugged and lapsed into silence. Doc lighted a cigarette and extended the package, and she shook her head wordlessly.

They skirted a small village, its church spires poking up through a grove of trees. Doc slowed the car to make a quick study of the road map, then resumed his former speed. A few miles farther on, he turned into a narrow dirt road which stretched ribbonlike up through the hills.

It was less than an hour before sunset now, and a chill south-westerly wind was stirring. Back in the hills, Doc got an occasional glimpse of a ranch house or an outbuilding. He didn't like that. In this isolated area their car could be seen for a very long way, and one as conspicuous as theirs was certain to be remembered.

The trail met with another. At the rutted intersection, two mail-boxes stood catercornered to each other. On one of them, crudely printed in black paint, was the name Beynon. Doc stopped the car and looked carefully around the lonely, rolling terrain.

Apparently the intersection was not visible from either of the two houses which must be nearby. He considered this fact, murmuring absently that Beynon's place should be just over the next hill to their right.

Carol responded with a murmur of agreement. Doc scratched his cheek thoughtfully, then reached into the back of the car and lifted the money satchel into the front seat.

He opened it, sorted out fifteen thousand dollars and put it in the inside pocket of his coat. Then, as long as it was something that needed to be done anyway, he gave Carol a few hundred dollars in small bills, stuffed his wallet with a few hundred more, and assembled a third sheaf totaling perhaps a thousand. This was scat money—dough to be kept readily available. Doc fastened it together with two of the bank's paper money bands, laid it in right at the top of the suitcase and closed and locked it again.

Then he got out, unlocked the trunk and put the suitcase inside. He did not lower the trunk lid immediately; instead, catching Carol's eye in the rearview mirror, he gave her a grin and a wink.

"That idea of yours," he smiled. "If you don't mind a variation of it, along with a little cramping . . ."

Carol's face lit up. She hopped out of the car and came around to the rear; pulling the gun from her belt, she checked its chamber with two crisp metallic clicks before shoving it back into place. The action sent a frown flickering through Doc's eyes. He laid a hand on her arm as she started to climb into the trunk.

She was to take it very easy, he cautioned. To do nothing without his lead. Beynon was not a killer. He was a very prominent man. And they—she and Doc—had a long way to travel.

Carol nodded that she understood. She climbed into the trunk, and Doc lowered the lid, leaving the lock off the latch.

As he had supposed, Beynon's place was only a few hundred yards away, just over the crest of the nearest hill. The house was one of those old-fashioned ranch dwellings, two-storied and painted white, with a long veranda or "gallery" extending across the front.

Down the slope to the rear of the house was a large red barn, cow partitioned down one side to provide a garage for Beynon's car. Adjoining it was a plank corral, which opened at the far end into a lushly grassed pasture. Grazing in it were a couple of riding horses and a few head of white-faced cattle. Beynon kept no employees; the ranch, if it could be called that, was merely a hobby with him. When business affairs took him away, a neighbor looked after his small amount of livestock.

Doc parked the car in the yard beneath a gnarled cottonwood tree. He got out, casually brushing at his clothes, and looked around. It was very quiet. The big old house, with its shadow-black windows, seemed never to have been occupied. Beynon's car—a three-year-old model—was in the garage, but there was no sign of him.

Doc strolled across the yard, whistling tunelessly, softly. He stepped up on the porch. The front door was open. Through the screen he called, "Beynon," and stood waiting, listening. There was no answer—no sound. But that in itself, the no-sound, the complete silence, was an answer.

Doc opened the screen. He slammed it again—from the outside. Then he stepped down from the porch and strode silently around the house to the back door. It also stood open, and the screen was unlatched. He peered in, eyes squinting against the shadows. With a soft sigh, he walked in.

Beynon sat at the long kitchen table, his head pillowed in his arms. On the checkered oilcloth in front of him was a tipped-over glass, and a half-empty quart bottle of whiskey.

Drunk, Doc thought, with less tolerance than was customary to him. The great man had troubles, so he got drunk.

Picking up a glass from the sink, he walked around the table and sat down opposite the parole chief. He poured himself a drink, took a sip of it, and lighted a cigarette. Deliberately he spewed smoke at the man across from him—it was probably the least startling way of any to wake him up. Beynon's head, with its wild mass of black hair, jerked irritably; then, abruptly, he sat up.

Except for a very faint thickness of speech, he seemed quite sober. Either he had spilled much more of that whiskey than he had drunk, or he had slept it off. His burning, black eyes were clear. They were as contemptuous, as knowing of Doc as they had been back at the prison.

Doc smiled, made a small gesture with his glass. "I hope you don't mind? It's been a rather trying day."

"Where's your wife?" Beynon said.

"We're traveling in different cars. She'll be along in an hour or so."

"How nice of her," Beynon said in his rich, musical voice. "How very, very nice of her to come to see me." He poured himself a drink, threw it down at a gulp. "Or perhaps she isn't," he said. "Perhaps her comings and goings have ceased for all time."

Doc shrugged idly. "If you're inferring that I killed her . . ."

"Where's Rudy, McCoy? Where's your friend Torrento? He's in another car, too?"

"Yes. And neither he nor the car is moving in case you're interested. I thought you'd be primarily interested in knowing that I have the bank money in my car."

This was bait. Beynon didn't rise to it. Doc waved it at him again.

"You've received five thousand dollars from me, from my wife rather. I agreed to pay fifteen thousand more. Frankly—" Doc turned on his sincerest look, "frankly, I don't think that's enough, Mr. Beynon. We didn't get as much out of this job as we hoped to, but that's no fault of yours. And . . ."

"Three people have been killed, so far, McCoy. Whose fault would you say that was?"

"Oh, now—" Doc spread his hands. "You mustn't feel . . ."

"Car—your wife told me that no one would be killed. She swore to it."

"I'm sorry. I imagine she was simply trying to spare your feelings. But getting back to the subject . . ."

"It's still murder, McCoy. How many more will there be before all this is over? If it is ever all over. How many more lives will I have on my hands?"

Doc hesitated, started to attempt some soothing comment. Then he leaned forward a little, spoke with abrupt bluntness. Beynon, he said, had best stop fretting about others. He had, or would have, plenty to worry about on his own account. "It's just a matter of time until the Beacon City job is pinned on me. When it is, the man responsible for my pardon—you, in other words—will have some very tough questions to answer."

"And there's just one answer for them. That I'm a murderer and a thief." Beynon looked at him strangely; a dully wondering look. "So you did anticipate it. You knew exactly what it would cost me. My career, disgrace, disbarment. Maybe a long stretch in prison myself. You knew all that, and yet—yet . . ."

"Now, you're exaggerating the situation," Doc cut in smoothly. "You'll have an uncomfortable time of it, but it won't be nearly as bad as that. You've got a lot of friends, a simon-pure reputation. It's an accepted fact that you've never taken a dishonest dime in your life. Under the . . ."

"Never a dime, McCoy?" Beynon laughed thickly. "You wouldn't say I'd taken about thirty of them?"

"I was saying," Doc said, "that under the circumstances you should come through this fine. About the worst you can be charged with is gross bad judgment."

He paused, frowning slightly as Beynon laughed again. Faintly, almost lost in the night breeze, he heard a metallic squeak. The opening—or perhaps the closing—of the car's trunk.

"Bad judgment," he repeated, his eyes holding the parole chief's. "Now, that's not so terrible, is it? It shouldn't be so hard to face considering that instead of fifteen thousand more, you're getting—well—twenty seven and a half?"

"Twenty-seven and a half, eh?" Beynon nodded gravely. "Twenty-seven thousand, five hundred just for facing that. And how much do you think I should have, McCoy, for facing myself?"

"Nothing," Doc said. "Not a damn penny."

He was tired, weary of coddling Beynon. He saw no reason to. The man wasn't going to do anything rash; he wasn't going to do anything period. He simply wanted to whine—make a big display of the conscience which had been conveniently asleep at the time he had sold out his office.

"You're a crook," Doc went on. "A particularly rotten kind. Now, stop fighting the fact. Just accept it and make the most of it. Believe me, you won't find it so bad."

"I see." A skull's grin wreathed Beynon's haggard face. "You see us as two of a kind, is that it?"

"No," Doc said equably, "you're much worse than I am. You knew the kind of man I was—and I've never pretended to be any other kind. You knew, if you're not a complete idiot, that I play rough when I think it's necessary. You didn't have to give me a pardon; no one twisted your arm. You did it for money, and damned little of it at that. The kind of money that—yes?"

Beynon's grin widened. He said softly. "Now, aren't you mistaken about that, McCoy? Wasn't there another factor involved, and did I have a choice?"

"I don't know what it would be."

"No," Beynon nodded slowly. "No, you really don't, do you? I was certain that you did, that it was a put-up job. I was convinced of it, despite some very wishful thinking to the contrary. But now—a small drink, Mr. McCoy? Or, no, I think the circumstances call for a large one."

With grave courtesy, he slopped whiskey into Doc's glass. Then he filled his own, pursing his lips sympathetically as Doc brushed the drink aside. "I don't blame you a bit, sir. Oh, believe me, I understand your feelings. You might say they were identical with my own at one time."

"I'm in a hurry," Doc snapped. "What are you talking about?"

"You still don't see it? Well, perhaps it will help if I mention the word blackmail."

"Blackmail? What..."

"A highly original kind, Mr. McCoy. Almost an attractive kind. To elaborate, one is forced to go along with the wishes of the blackmailer, whether or no. But the mailed fist—or should I say the muddy fist?—also contains a prize; something delectable indeed. One is even allowed to sample it generously, by way of making sure that it is worth the cooperation which one is forced to extend..."

He let his voice trail away. He waited deliberately, prolonging the delicate torture, deepening the sickish heart-tightening suspense. Then, although nothing more needed to be said, he resumed talking. He spelled the thing out, speaking with a false sympathy that was worse than any hatred. Speaking with lewdly gleaming eyes, his wide mouth salaciously wet.

He's drunk, Doc thought. He's lying. He's sore, so he's striking back, digging at the one spot where it will hurt.

In the whispering twilight there was a minutely exploratory movement of the screen door. His attention riveted on Beynon, Doc didn't hear it.

"Take it a little at a time," Beynon was saying. "Approach the matter from all sides. One—" he held up a finger, waggled it in pseudo-courtroom fashion. "One, we have an extremely attractive woman, one who has thoroughly demonstrated her desirability. Two—" he put up a second finger, "we have the woman's husband, probably the most skilful bank robber in the country, who is serving a long prison sentence. Three—" another finger, "we have a powerful politician, a man who is in a position to free the robber husband. Why should he be freed? Well, naturally, to rob a bank, thus leaving the woman and the politician comfortably fixed for life, the ill winds peculiar to public office notwithstanding. Secondly—would you care to guess at the second—but by no means the lesser—motive, Mr. McCoy? Very well, then..."

His voice purred on, pushing and twisting the knife; moving Doc

McCoy off balance, hacking away at the one thing he had trusted and believed in.

"Consider, Mr. McCoy. Our robber is notoriously ingenious and deadly. He is also devoted to his wife. If he lost her to another man, he would quite likely kill both of them at the soonest opportunity—at the end of his prison sentence, that is. This didn't appeal to them at all, of course. Yet unless they gave each other up and resigned themselves to a life of modest or no comforts, there was only one alternative. To free the bank robber, let him make them wealthy, and then, having lured him to an isolated spot such as this . . ."

Beynon leaned forward, his voice dropping to a harsh conspiratorial whisper. "Then, Mr. McCoy, when he is off guard, when he is no longer sure of where he stands, whether he is captured or captor, when, being sure, he still would not dare to move; then, Mr. McCoy—*kill him!*"

Doc heard the screen at last. Heard it close—firmly, with no attempt at silence.

Out of the corner of his eye, he saw Carol move out of the shadows. And he saw the gun, held very steady, in her hand.

Was it pointed at him? If he moved, would it be pointed at him—blasting him into oblivion before his move could be completed?

It would, he was sure. Carol was practical. She could be as merciless as he. Undoubtedly she had heard much if not all that Beynon had said. If she thought that he, Doc, believed the man—and was he so hard to believe? mustn't there be a great deal of truth in what he said—if she thought that he believed Beynon, and was about to act accordingly . . .

He didn't know what to do. With extreme cleverness—or with drunken, conscience-stricken truthfulness—Beynon had so fixed things that any move or no move could be fatal.

"This—this is stupid," he said, his voice amused but deeply sincere; making the words at once a statement and a plea. "Did you really think I'd fall for a sucker pitch like that?"

"A trick question," Beynon pointed out promptly. "You don't know whether it is or isn't a sucker pitch. To be fair, neither do I. Obviously, I believed little Carol—*our* Carol, shall I say?—at one time. But with three men killed in spite of her promise that there would be none—well, was just that one promise of hers a lie or were all of them? Another thing . . ."

"That's enough," Doc broke in. "It was a good try, Beynon, but . . ."

"Another thing—" Beynon raised his voice. "She may have been entirely sincere and truthful with me. It may be that she just didn't know there would be three murders—in addition, of course, to your own. But seeing my dismay at the killings, and fearful that I might be a frail reed to tie to . . ."

It was wicked, cruel. And still he wasn't through. Beaming falsely, he drove home the final nail in Doc's cross of doubt.

"Carol, sweetheart—" Beynon pushed back his chair and stood up, extended one arm in an embracing gesture. "I hope you won't think ill of her, Mr. McCoy. After all, you were locked up for a long time—your first separation since your marriage, wasn't it?—and she's a healthy, vigorous young woman with perhaps more than her share of . . ."

Carol let out a low moan. She came at him with a rush, and jammed the gun into his stomach. And the room rocked with its stuttering explosions.

Beynon shrieked wildly; it sounded strangely like laughter. He doubled at the waist, in the attitude of a man slapping his knees; then collapsed, dead, riddled with bullets, before his body completed its somersault.

The gun dropped from Carol's fingers. She stood very straight, eyes squeezed shut, and wept helplessly.

"He-he was lying, Doc. The mean, h-hateful, dirty—! I wish I could kill him again . . .!"

"There, there now. Don't let it throw you." Doc held her in his arms, caressed her with hands that were still damp with sweat. "I'll get you a drink of booze here, and . . ."

"He *was* lying, Doc! Y-you believe me, don't you? There wasn't anything at all like—like he said."

"Of course there wasn't," Doc said warmly. "I never thought for a moment that there was."

"I-I was just friendly. J-just pretended to be. I couldn't help it. I had to be nice, make him want to know me, or he wouldn't have . . ."

It was a moment before Doc realized that she was talking about only the one facet of Beynon's story: her supposed or actual infidelity. That was all that bothered her, all that she was denying. Which must mean that there was nothing else to deny.

It was a comforting thought, and he hugged her to him fiercely with a kind of shamed ardor. Then he realized that if the undisputed part of the story was false, the other must be true. And he had to fight to keep from shoving her away.

"T-that's why I didn't want to come here, Doc. I-I was afraid he'd say something—m-make up a lot of lies, just to get even with me, and . . ."

Doc sat down on a chair and pulled her onto his lap. Smiling lovingly, he got her to take a drink, gently dried her tears with his handkerchief.

"Now, let's look at it this way," he said. "You wanted to get me out. The only way you could do it was to compromise him, so—wait, now! There had to be something between you. After all, if you didn't have a club to swing over his head, how . . ."

He broke off. The look in her eyes stopped him. He forced a laugh which sounded reasonably genuine, then stood up, lifting her in his arms.

"A very clever man," he smiled. "It's hard not to admire him. But I think we've let his gag bother us enough, so suppose we forget it?"

Carol brightened a little. "Then you do believe me, Doc?"

"Believe you?" Doc said warmly. "Now, why wouldn't I believe you, my dear?"

He carried her upstairs and laid her down on a bed. She clung to his hand when he started to straighten, made him sit down at her side while she told him how she had compromised Beynon. It sounded reasonable. Doc seemed satisfied. Urging Carol to try to rest, he went back downstairs and lugged Beynon's body down into the basement.

It was the work of a few minutes to bury the corpse in the coal bin. Afterward he stood at the corner sink, scrubbing his hands and arms with gritty mechanics' soap, drying them on a handful of waste cloth. Then, lost in thought, he remained where he was, a brooding shadow in the near blackness of the basement.

Carol. Why couldn't he accept her explanation? Beynon was a hard drinker at times. Carol had had to call at his apartment to talk to him. So, playing upon his weakness, she had got him so drunk that he passed out. And he was still dead to the world early the next morning when she slipped out of the place. That was all she had had to do, except, of course, to make sure that she was seen coming and going by the elevator operator and desk clerk. That was all—more than enough. For a man of Beynon's prominence—the head of the state's pardon and parole board—to have the wife of a notorious criminal in his apartment for an all-night stay . . .

Nothing else was necessary, so doubtless nothing else had taken place. As for the bribe money—well, as long as Beynon was stuck, there was no point in refusing a bit of salve.

It all fitted, Doc thought. Yet piece by piece, item by item, he could knock it apart. His mind moved around and around in a circle, disbelieving each time it was on the point of believing.

He was ready to admit that his shaky faith was a personal thing. As a professional criminal, he had schooled himself against placing complete trust in anyone. And as a criminal, he had learned to link infidelity with treachery. It revealed either a dangerous flaw in character, or an equally dangerous shift in loyalties. In any case, the woman was a bad risk in a game where no risk could be tolerated.

So . . .

Abruptly, Doc broke the agonizing circle of his thoughts. He stood off from himself, standing this fretful, teetering creature that he was now alongside the suave, sure and unshakable Doc McCoy; and the comparison made him squirm.

Now, no more of this, he lectured himself; he smiled softly. No more, either now or later.

Carol had mopped up the kitchen floor. Now she was at the oil stove, measuring coffee into an enamel pot. Doc walked over to her and put his arms around her. She turned hesitantly, a little fearfully, and looked up into his face.

Doc kissed her enthusiastically. He said mock-seriously, "Madam, were you aware that you had a damn fool for a husband?"

"Oh, Doc! Doc, honey!" She clung to him, burying her face against his chest. "It's my fault. I wanted to tell you the truth right back at the beginning, but . . ."

"But you were afraid I'd react exactly the way I did," Doc said. "That coffee smells good. How about some sandwiches to go with it?"

"All right. But shouldn't we be beating it out of here, Doc?"

"Well," Doc grinned wryly, "of course, I wouldn't recommend an indefinite stay. But there's no great rush that I can see." He sauntered over to the refrigerator, peered inside and lifted out a butt of baked ham. "Beynon wouldn't have known exactly when we'd show up. Therefore, he'd have made sure that no one else dropped in on him tonight."

"I guess I shouldn't have killed him, should I, Doc? It's going to make things tough for us."

Doc laid plates and silver on the table. He set out butter and bread. He said that Beynon's death was regrettable but unavoidable; when an accessory to a crime collapsed so completely, there was nothing to do but kill him. "I don't know just how tough it'll make things for us. Maybe not at all. But it certainly forces us to change our plans."

Carol nodded, and lifted the coffee from the stove. "Want to put the cream on for me, honey?" she said; then, "Just how will it change them?"

"Well, here's the way I add it up." Doc sat down at the table, and carved meat onto their plates. "Our car must have been spotted on the way up here. At least we have to assume that it was. Still playing it safe, we can't rule out the possibility that someone got a look at us. Maybe some kid stalking a rabbit near the road, or a nosy housewife with time on her hands and a pair of binoculars . . ."

"It could happen," Carol agreed. "We change out of these duds, then. Leave the car here and take Beynon's."

"Right. We try to make it appear that the three of us have gone off somewhere together, and that we'll be coming back. But—" Doc took a sip of his coffee. "Here's where the rub comes in. We don't know what Beynon's plans were, his appointments. For all we know he may have been due to see or call someone tomorrow morning, or someone may have been scheduled to see or call him here. Then there's the livestock—that's the real tip-off. When Beynon shows up missing, without having notified his part-time hired hand—" Doc shook his head. "We'll have to get off the road. We can't risk it a moment longer than we absolutely have to."

"No, we can't, can we?" Carol frowned. "We hole up with someone, then?"

"What gave you that idea? Who would we hole up with?"

"Well, I just thought that if—weren't you supposed to have a good friend out this way? Somewhere near Mexico, I mean? You know, that old woman—Ma Santis."

Doc said, regretfully, that he didn't have. Ma Santis was on the other side of Mexico, the Southern California side. At least, it had been rumored that she was there, although no one seemed to know where. "I don't know that she's even alive, but it's my guess that she probably isn't. When you get as well known as Ma Santis and her boys, people have you cropping up around the country for years after you're dead."

"Well. If there's no place for us to hole up . . ."

"I think we'd better be moving," Doc pushed back his plate and stood up. "We can talk about it while we're getting ready."

They cleared up the dishes and put them away. They changed into conservative clothes. As for talk—a discussion of their plans—there was very little. The decision was made for them. One saw it as readily as the other. They had to travel far faster than they had planned, and it was unsafe to use the highways. So there was only one thing they could do.

Aside from putting the kitchen to rights and smoothing out the upstairs bed, they did nothing to expunge the signs of their brief presence in the house. Doc did suggest that they wipe everything off to remove their fingerprints, but that was a joke and Carol grinned dutifully. Criminals are not nearly so cautious about fingerprints as is popularly supposed. Not, at least, the big-time operators who treat crime as a highly skilled profession. They know that an expert fingerprint man might work all day in his own home without picking up an identifiable set of his own prints. They also know that fingerprints are normally only corroborative evidence; that they will probably be tabbed for a certain crime, and the alarm set to ringing for them, long before they are tied to the job by fingerprints—if they ever are.

Doc filled Beynon's car with gasoline from a drum in the garage, also filling two five-gallon cans which he put in the rear of the car. He drove the car out into the yard, and Carol drove the convertible inside, and then they were on their way.

A couple of hours' driving got them off of the county roads and back onto the highway. They paused there briefly to consult their road maps, picking out the most practical route to Kansas City. The town was far to the north, farther rather than nearer their ultimate destination. But that, of course, was its advantage. It was the last place they would be expected to go. As a jumping-off place, it offered no clue as to what their destination might be.

Their plan was to abandon the car at Kansas City and take a train westward. It was not, they knew, an ideal one. You are confined on a train. You are part of a relatively small group, and thus more easily singled out. Still, there was only one alternative—to go by plane—and a train was by far the best bet.

The night was chill, and speeding north it grew colder. In the heaterless car Carol shivered and snuggled close to her husband. He patted her protectively, remarked that it was a shame they had had to give up the convertible. "It was a nice car. I imagine you put a lot of thought into picking it out, didn't you?"

"Oh, well—" Carol's small shoulder shrugged against his. "It was nice of you to say that, Doc," she added. "Even to think about me being disappointed or uncomfortable at a time like this."

Doc said it was nothing at all; it came perfectly natural to anyone as generally splendid as he. Carol reproved him with a delicate pinch.

They rode cozily shoulder to shoulder, and somehow, despite the dropping temperature, the car seemed to grow warmer. Carol was comfortably pert. Doc was Doc; tender, amusing, restful—exuding the contagious good humour of complete self-confidence.

So it had been on nights past. The good nights (the good seems always to be in the past) before Doc's prison stretch. Just what broke the spell Carol could not have said. But gradually she found herself withdrawing; moving over to her own side of the seat. Gradually she began to study Doc's words, the tone of his voice, the play of expression over his homely-handsome face.

Doc may or may not have noticed the change—may or may not have without knowing which was the case. Characteristically, and up to a point, he did not always allow himself to know what he thought or what he felt. He had come to a decision, decided on a certain course of conduct. If an obstacle could not be circumvented, ignore it. As long as it could be. Or until a better course suggested itself.

A couple of hours before dawn, he refueled the car from the two gas cans. Driving on again, he at last asked Carol if something was troubling her. "If I've done or said anything . . ."

"You haven't," she said. "I suppose that that's—well, never mind. Don't pay any attention to me, Doc."

"Now, of course, I'll pay attention to you," Doc said genially. "Now and at all other times. So let's get this thing straightened out, whatever it is."

"Well, it's really nothing, but—" she hesitated, laughed with nervous apology. "I guess it just occurred to me that if you—if you felt a certain way, I probably wouldn't know it."

"Yes?" His voice tilted upward. "I'm not sure I understand."

"I'm talking about Beynon!"

"Beynon?" He gave her a curious look. "But what's there to say about him? You explained everything. I believed you. It's all settled."

Silence closed over the car again. They raced through the headlight-tunneled night, and the black walls slapped shut behind them. Time and space were the immediate moment. Behind and beyond it there was only the darkness.

Doc shifted in the seat and got cigarettes out of his pocket. He lighted two of them and passed one to her. And after a time, after it was finished, she drew close to him again.

He drew her a trifle closer. He pulled the tail of his topcoat from beneath him and tucked it over her knees.

"Better?" he asked softly.

"Better," she nodded. Because it was. It was warmer. Friend or foe, there was at least someone with her, and anything was better than the utter loneliness.

"I understood what you were talking about," he went on quietly. "I simply didn't know how to reply to it. Or what to do about it."

"I know, Doc."

"It leaves me without a corner to go to. If I'm agreeable, it's pretense. If I'm not, that also is cause for alarm. You see, my dear? You just can't think that way. It's foolish and it's dangerous, and—you do see that don't you?"

"I see it," she nodded; and then desperately, with what was almost a cry, "Then it is all right, Doc? Honestly? You're not sore or suspicious about—anything? Everything's just like it always was?"

"I said so. I've done everything I could to show you."

"But you might do that anyway! You might act just as sweet as pie, and all the time you'd be planning t-to—to . . ."

"Carol," said Doc soothingly. "My poor darling little girl."

And she sobbed harshly, sighed, and fell asleep against his shoulder.

SEVEN

It was early afternoon when Doc let Carol out of Kansas City's Union Railroad Terminal. Being much the "cooler" of the two of them—much less likely to be identified—she kept the money satchel with her. While Doc drove away to dispose of the car, she entered the station and headed for the coach ticket windows. At one of them she bought a one-way ticket to Los Angeles. At another, far removed, she bought a second one. Then, hesitantly, with a look at the lobby clock, she again picked up the money bag and her overnight case.

It was almost an hour until train time—Doc had previously checked the schedule by telephone. He wouldn't be showing up until the next to last minute, so she had almost an hour to kill—and to remain in sole custody of approximately two hundred and fifty thousand very hot, very bloody dollars.

She had never faced such nerve-wracking responsibility before. It had had to be hers, but still, with part of her mind, she was resentful that it had been thrust upon her.

She looked around the vaulted lobby, then, lurching a little from the weight of the bag, she started for the women's rest room. After a dozen steps or so, she set the bag down, started to shift it to her other hand. And in a blur of movement—in her fear and nervousness it seemed a blur—she saw it snatched up from the floor.

It was a redcap, one of several who had so far proffered their services. But at the moment he had no identity for Carol. He was just a hand, an arm, a half-turned back—a something that was about to make off with the bag.

Taking in her expression, he said, "Hope I didn't startle you, ma'am. Just thought I'd . . ."

"*You give that here!*" With a wild grab, she recovered the satchel. "You hear me? You give . . ."

"Kind of looks like you already got it, ma'am." He grinned at her pleasantly. "Ain't that so? Now, how about letting me check it for you?"

"No!" She backed away from him. "I mean, I don't want it checked. I j-just . . ."

"Put it on the train for you, then. Mighty heavy bag for a little lady like you to carry."

"No! And you'd better get away from me, or I'll—I'll . . ."

"Well, yes, ma'am," he said coldly. "Yessiree, ma'am!"

Regaining some control of herself, she mumbled a grimacing word of apology. Very conscious that his eyes were following her, she hurried down the vaulted lobby. Her arm ached. She was panting, sweating with exertion. She had a feeling that everyone in the place was watching her, wondering about her.

At long last—after hours, miles, seemingly—she got out of the waiting room proper and into a wing of the building. She paused there gratefully, setting the bag against the wall and resting the toe of one shoe against it.

Her breath came back; she patted the sweat from her face, became cooler, calmer. In a half-resentful way she felt ashamed of herself. There had been no reason for her panic. The bag looked like any other bag. If the police had been alerted, there wasn't a chance in ten thousand they'd be able to spot her. All she had to do was follow Doc's instructions: stay in the crowd, keep the bag with her at all times, carry it onto the train herself. It was simple enough. It was what she knew she should do, without being told by Doc. But . . .

No buts. It was what she had to do. Checkroom attendants were always losing things. Handing them out to the wrong people, banging bags around until they flew open. There were similar risks in dealing with redcaps, baggage porters. Nothing ever happened, naturally, to a two-dollar suitcase with a few bucks' worth of clothes in it. But let the bag contain something hot—money or jewelry or narcotics, or part of a dismembered corpse—and sure as shootin' there was a foul-up.

It happened all the time. You needed only to read the newspapers to know that it did.

Doc had been fearful that the bag would be too heavy for her. She had lifted it, assured him that she could manage it. She had also assured him—and pretty shortly at that—that her nerves were equally up to the job. But that had been then, and somehow everything had changed since then. The sureness which she had felt with him had melted away; and suddenly, with a spur of panic, she knew why.

Not only had she never faced any such responsibility as this before, she had never faced any that remotely approached it. Nothing of do-or-die importance; nothing without Doc to guide her and work with her. She had thought that she had; Doc had tactfully let her think so. But invariably they had been a team. The one thing she had swung on her own was the Beynon deal; and that obviously, and regardless of the consequences, was something that would have been a lot better left unswung.

Actually, she hadn't been around very much. She was virtually untraveled. Until she met Doc, she'd never been out of her hometown. Since then, there'd been considerable travel by car, but she'd made only one train trip in her life.

She wasn't used to railroad stations. Even without the money bag she would have felt some unsureness.

Which I'd damn well better get over, she thought grimly. If Doc caught me acting like this, standing off in a corner by myself . . .!

He wouldn't like it. Far too much had already happened that he didn't like.

Resolutely, she picked up the bag and started back to the waiting room. The resolution lasted for a few steps, and then she began to slow, to hesitate. If only she could get rid of the thing for a few minutes. Long enough to make sure that she hadn't been spotted; to get a drink, to clean up a little. The drink, particularly, she needed. A good stiff jolt to pull her together again and . . .

She heard a dull clang of metal against metal; jumped a little, her eyes swerving toward it. But it was only someone slamming the door of a baggage locker. She started to move on toward the waiting room, and then her heart did a little skip-jump of relief, and she swung almost gaily toward the row of lockers on the other side of the wing.

She would be taking no chance in leaving the bag in a private locker. Doc couldn't object to it—in fact, he didn't even need to know about it. She could recover the bag before he showed up at the station.

She crossed the marble-paved foyer, set down the satchel and overnight case. She got a quarter out of her purse and stooped in front of an empty locker. Frowning, she sought in vain for the coin slot. Straightening again, she had started to read the metal instruction plate when a young man sauntered by. A young-oldish man with a small brown moustache and prematurely graying hair.

He was neatly dressed, engaging of manner. He would have been handsome except for the slight sharpness of his features.

"Kind of a Chinese puzzle, isn't it?" he said. "Well, here's how you work it."

Before Carol could object to the intrusion, he had taken the quarter from her hand, inserted it in the elusive slot and swung open the door. "Imagine you want to keep the dressing case with you, right?" he smiled. "Well, in we go with the big boy, then. Now—" he slammed and rattled the door, "we'll just test this to make sure that it's locked; maybe you'd better test it, too."

Carol tested it. He handed her a yellow-flanged locker key, courteously brushed aside her thanks, and sauntered off toward the waiting room.

In the station's bar-and-grill ladies' room, Carol touched up her makeup and allowed her suit to be brushed off by the attendant. Then, going out to the bar, she ordered and drank two double martinis. She wanted a third—not the drink itself so much as the excuse it would provide for remaining there. Just to stay there a little longer, where it was cool and shadowed and quiet, and feel the strength and the confidence spread through her. To feel *safe*.

But the hands of the clock pointed forbiddingly. It was barely ten minutes until the train time.

Draining the last drop from her glass, she hurried out of the bar. She located her locker, inserted the key and turned it. Or tried to. It wouldn't turn. It didn't fit.

Her stomach cramped convulsively and the two drinks rose up in her throat. Swallowing nauseously, she removed the key and examined it; read the number with bewildered disbelief.

That couldn't be right! She *knew* that the bag had gone into this locker, the one here on the end. But according to this key . . .

She located the other locker, the one numbered to correspond with the key. Hands shaking, she opened it, and of course, it was empty.

A voice boomed and echoed over the public address system: "Last call for the California umtumm—the California something-or-other, departing from Gate Three in exacklum fi'min-utts. Passengers will kine-ly take their seats on the California . . ."

Five minutes!

Feverishly she returned to the first locker, fought again to unlock it. Again, as on the first occasion, the effort was futile. The drinks struggled upward again. The heat, after the air-conditioned bar, beat and pounded through her brain.

She weaved a little. Foolishly, because there was nothing else to do, she started back toward the second locker, the one the key fitted. And then she stopped dead in her tracks. Up near the entrance, hat pulled low over his eyes, Doc was watching her. Watching and then coming toward her.

A few steps away, he faced up to the locker bank, fumbling in his pocket as though seeking a coin. His terse whisper whipped at her from the corner of his mouth. "Simmer down and talk fast. What happened?"

"I-I don't know, Doc! I put the bag in that locker back there, but I've got the key to . . ."

"To another locker, one that's empty, right? What did he look like?"

"He? What do you . . .?"

"Will you in the name of all hell hurry! Someone helped you. Put the bag in for you, then switched keys on you. It's one of the oldest con gags in the country."

"But—well, how was I to know?" she lashed out. "You leave me to do everything . . ."

"Easy, babe, easy. I'm not blaming you." His voice became a purring calm, the intense calm above a raging subterranean storm. "How long since you left the bag? When you first came in, maybe an hour?"

"No. Not more than thirty minutes. But . . ."

"Good. He'd expect you to leave it longer than that. If he operates on form, he'll try to hit several times before he pulls out." He stepped back from the lockers, jerked his head. "Move. Go ahead of me. If you spot him, give me the office."

"But, Doc. You shouldn't . . ."

"There's a lot of things that shouldn't have been done!" His tone was a whip again. "Now, *move*!"

She started off at a fast walk, then broke into a faster one as his long stride kept him almost on her heels. At what was almost a trot she reached the waiting room, swept it with an anxious glance. Prodded by an urgent cough from Doc, she made a hasty survey of the adjacent areas.

Then—and now she was really trotting—she headed for the train gates. The jarring of her high heels shot fire up her ankles. A button of her blouse became undone, and she ran clutching at the gap with one hand. Frantically, she raced down the corridor, a notorious criminal on the trail of a quarter of a million stolen and restolen dollars, and somewhere within her the child she had been, the child that she was in this baffling and fearful moment, wept with sullen self-pity. It—it wasn't fair! She was tired and sick, and she didn't want to play any more. She'd never wanted to play in the first place!

And it was all so useless. The man would be gone now, no matter what Doc said. He had the money, and he'd keep it. And they, they'd have nothing. The whole nation looking for them, and no means of escape. No money but the relatively little they were carrying.

She tripped and almost fell. She caught herself, half-turned in pain and anger on Doc. And then she saw him, the thief.

He was at a row of lockers near the train gates; no more than twenty feet away from the uniformed station attendant who stood at Gate Three—*their* gate—consulting his watch. Smiling engagingly, he was opening a locker for a well-dressed elderly woman, placing two expensive cowhide bags inside.

He slammed the door, tested it. He handed her a key and picked up the money satchel. Tipping his hat, he turned away. And suddenly he saw Carol.

His expression never changed. He took a step straight toward her, smiling, apparently on the point of calling a hello. And then, with a movement that was at once abrupt and casual, he disappeared behind the lockers.

"Doc—" Carol gestured feebly.

But Doc had already spotted the satchel, identified the thief for what he was. He strode past her, and after a moment's indecision she followed him.

By the time she had gotten behind the lockers, neither Doc nor the thief were in sight. They had disappeared as quickly and completely as though the floor had opened and swallowed them up. She turned, started to retrace her steps—and if she had, she would have seen the thief hasten through the train gate, with Doc following in brisk pursuit. Instead, however, she continued along the row of lockers, turned into the aisle formed by another row, and thence on to the end of that before coming out into the open again. By which time, of course, Doc and the thief were long gone from view.

She stood there in the corridor, looking this way and that, seeming to shrink, to grow smaller and smaller in its lofty vastness. She had never felt so bewildered, so lost, so alone. Doc—where had he gone? How could she find him? What would happen if she couldn't?

Reason told her that he must have followed the thief onto the train. But—and here reason questioned its own statement—would a smart thief choose the train as an escape route? And would Doc have followed without a word or sign to her?

He'd have been in a hurry, of course. He would doubtless assume that she was heeling him, even as he was heeling the thief. But—suppose she was wrong. Suppose the pursuit had led back up into the station.

She wouldn't know that he wasn't on the train until she had looked, and by that time . . .

She shivered at the thought. Herself on the train, and Doc here—the two of them separated in a hostile and watchful world. He wouldn't dare to make inquiries, to look for her; even to wait around the station for her return. For that matter, he could not be sure that she hadn't taken a powder on him. After last night, that drunken hateful talk of Beynon's . . .

Maybe Doc had run out on her! Maybe he'd recovered the money and abandoned her! He was sore, she thought; more accurately, suspicious. She needed him, but he did not need her. And when Doc no longer needed a person . . .

The trainman looked at her sharply. Then, with a final glance at his watch, he slipped it into his pocket and started through the gate.

"Mister!" Carol hurried toward him. "Did a couple of men go through here just now? A rather tall older man and a man with a . . ."

"A couple of men?" The trainman was irritably amused. "Lady, there's probably been a hundred. I can't . . ."

"But this was just in the last minute or so! The one in front would have had gray hair and a little mustache!"

"Were they catching the train for California?"

"I—I don't know. I mean, I think they were but . . ."

"Well, if they were, they went through here. If they weren't, they didn't." He fidgeted impatiently with the gate. "What about you? You taking the train?"

"I don't know!" Carol almost wailed. "I mean, I'm not sure whether I should or not. Can't you remember . . ."

"No I can't," he cut her off shortly. "Kind of seems like they did, but I wouldn't say for sure."

"But it's so important! If you'd just . . ."

"Lady—" his voice rose. "I told you I wasn't sure whether I saw 'em or not, and that's all I can tell you, and if you're taking the train you'll have to do it right now. It's already two minutes late pulling out."

"But . . ."

"Make up your mind, lady. What's it going to be?"

Carol looked at him helplessly. "I guess," she said. "I guess I really should—shouldn't . . ."

"Yes?" he snapped. "Well?"

Scowling, he waited a second or two more. Then, as she remained undecided, he slammed the gate and went down the ramp.

EIGHT

The barn was pleasantly cool—clean and sweet-smelling with the aroma of fresh straw and new hay. In one of the rear stalls a sway-backed horse nickered contentedly. From a partitioned-off kennel, also in the rear, came the happy yapping of a litter of puppies.

There were two box stalls at the front, small floored rooms open at the aisle end. Rudy Torrento was in one, propped up on a cot while the veterinarian worked over him. Opposite him, in the other, was the doctor's wife. The doc's name was Harold Clinton, so she, of course, was Mrs. Clinton. Fran, her husband called her, when he wasn't addressing her sweetishly as hon or pet or lambie. But Rudy didn't think of her by any of those handles.

He's seen this babe before—her many counterparts, that is. He knew her kin, distant and near. All her mamas, sisters, aunts, cousins and what have you. And he knew the name was Lowdown with a capital L. He wasn't at all surprised to find her in a setup like this. Not after encountering her as a warden's sister-in-law, the assistant treasurer of a country bank, and a supervisor of paroles. This babe got around. She was the original square-plug-in-a-round-hole kid. But she never changed any. She had that good old Lowdown blood in her, and the right guy could bring it out.

Seated on a high stool with her bare, milk-white legs crossed and her chin cupped demurely in the palm of her hand, she watched moist-lipped as her husband completed his work. She wore an expensive-looking plaid skirt, somewhat in need of cleaning and pressing, and a tight white sweater of what appeared to be cashmere. Her shoes were scuffed, their spike heels slightly run over. But her corn-colored hair was impeccably coiffured, and her nails glistened with bright red polish.

She'd do, Rudy decided; yes, sir, little Miss Lowdown would do just fine. But that red polish would have to go, even if her eensie-teensie pinkies went right along with it.

He caught her eye, and winked at her. She frowned primly, then lowered her lashes and smoothed the sweater a degree tighter. Rudy laughed out loud.

"Feeling better, eh?" The doctor straightened, beamed down at him professionally. "That's the glucose. Nothing like a good intravenous feeding of glucose to pull a man together fast."

"Ain't it the truth?" Rudy grinned. "Bet you didn't know that, did you, Mrs. Clinton?"

She murmured inaudibly, then tittered that she couldn't even spell glucose. Rudy told her that her husband was a plenty smart man. "Plenty," he repeated. "I've been tinkered over by high class M.D.s that didn't know half the medicine your old man does."

"Well, uh, thank you." Clinton's thin face flushed with pleasure. "I only wish that the people around here, uh, shared your high opinion."

"Yeah? You mean to say they don't?"

"Well . . ."

"They don't," his wife cut in curtly. "They think he's a dope."

Clinton blinked at her from behind his glasses. He was either unoffended, or resigned to such offenses; doubtless the last, Rudy decided. "Now, uh, Fran," he said mildly, "I don't believe I'd put it quite that way. It's just that they're rather set in their ways, and, uh, a young man like me—someone probably more interested in the theory of disease than actual practice—why . . ."

"So the sun don't rise and set here," Rudy said. "If the people aren't smart enough to appreciate you, why not go someplace where they are?"

"Where—where they are?" The doctor hesitated. "I'm afraid I don't know, uh, where—how . . ."

Rudy let it lay for the moment. He asked how his condition appeared to the doctor, and Clinton replied that it was excellent. "You have a wonderful constitution, Mr. Torrento. Might even say—ha-ha—that you had the constitution of a horse."

"Ha-ha," said Fran Clinton. "That's really good, Harold."

"It's a riot," Rudy said. "But what about the bandages, Clint—the wound? How often should I have it looked after?"

"Well, a couple of times a day perhaps. That's barring any unusual developments."

"How you mean, unusual?"

"Well, uh, fever. Any signs of gangrene or putrefaction. But I'm sure there won't be any. Just have it changed and rebandaged a couple of times a day for the next couple of days, and—and—" His voice died suddenly. He went on again, his eyes evading Rudy's. "On second thoughts, it might be wiser if you didn't have it tended at all. Might just irritate the wound, you know. Keep it from healing."

"It might," Rudy nodded. "I wouldn't know. You wouldn't maybe be kidding me would you, Clint, old boy?"

"K-kidding you? Why would I . . ."

"Because you want to get rid of me pronto, and you figure that if I need any taking care of, you'll be elected to do it."

Rudy pulled the heavy .38 from his belt, twirled it by the trigger guard and let the butt smack into his palm. Grinning savagely, he took aim at the doctor's stomach.

"Now, maybe, you'd better have a good big third thought," he said. "Just think real careful and give me the truth. Will I need more lookin' after, or won't I?"

"Y-you'll—y-y-y—" It was as far as the doctor could get.

"I'll need it, huh?" Rudy flipped the gun again and shoved it back into his belt. "Well, that's all I wanted to know. Just shoot square with me, and you got no more trouble than a flea in a dog pound. Now," he added casually, "I guess you want me to clear out of here."

Clinton nodded, weakly apologetic, as he sagged down onto a canvas camp stool. "Oh, well, you did promise, Mr. Torrento. You said that . . ."

"And I'll keep my promise," Rudy lied, "if that's the way you want it. I'll leave, and you'll call the cops, and . . ."

"N-no! No, we won't, Mr. Torrento! I . . ."

". . . and then maybe tonight, maybe five years from now, you'd have a visitor. It'd probably be me, because I got quite a rep for breaking out of tight spots. But if I didn't make it, some pal of mine would. Anyway, you'd have a visitor—like the guy that fingered Willie Sutton had one—and you know what he'd do to you, Clint, to you and the little lady here, before he did you a big favor and killed you?"

He told them, threatened them with what would happen; lips wolfishly drawn back from his teeth; eyes holding them with an unwinking reptilian gaze. He finished the discourse, and the sudden silence was like a scream.

A drop of sweat rolled shinily down the veterinarian's nose. His wife gulped and clapped a hand to her mouth, spoke through the lattice of her fingers.

"We—we won't call any cops," she said whitely. "He even looks like he's going to, and I'll murder him myself!"

"Well, now, maybe he'd feel that he had to," Rudy said. "I'm hot as a three-dollar pistol. I need medical attention. Say I've got a three to one chance of getting away, and you're giving me the best of it. Wouldn't you figure it that way, Clint?"

Clinton cleared his throat. He opened his mouth to speak, then closed it again. Rudy beamed at him falsely.

"Kind of one of those hell-if-you-do-or-don't propositions, ain't it, Clint? You holler copper and you and Frannie get your clocks fixed. You don't do it, and you're still in the soup. They got enough on me to fry me six times. That'd bring you and Fran in on accessory raps for forty or fifty years."

"A-accessories?" the doctor stammered. "But how would they know that . . ."

"I'll tell them," Rudy said cheerfully. "I'd name you as accessories."

"B-but—but, why? After we'd helped . . ."

"Because I'd figure you were boobs," Rudy said, "and boobs I got a very low boiling point for."

Clinton shook his head in bewilderment. Helplessly, hopefully, he looked at his wife. There was some indefinable change in her expression, something that carried a chill shock and yet seemed entirely natural to her. He had a feeling that he had never seen her before; that she was at once a stranger to him and an old friend of Torrento's.

"What," she said, "is the proposition—Rudy?"

"What do you think? That you and Clinty boy go along with me."

"And?"

"I fork up for a new car. I pay all expenses, and me, I wouldn't kick on a little expense like a mink jacket. You get anything you want, as soon as we're where we're safe to buy it. You cross the country first-class, and when we hit California there'll be a ten-grand bonus."

Her eyes gleamed softly. "That sounds good," she murmured. "That sounds real good, Rudy."

"Good, hell," Rudy said. "It's perfect. Big dough for you, a new car, and a swell trip. And not a chance in the world of getting caught. Clint bandages me up so that no one can see what I look like—I been in a bad accident, see? Then . . ."

"I won't do it." Clinton had found his voice at last. "We are not going with you, Mr. Torrento."

"You shut up!" His wife glared at him fiercely. "I guess I've got something to say about what we're going to do!"

"Now, take it easy," Rudy said. "What's wrong with the deal, Clint? I thought it added up good for you, but maybe I could sweeten it a little."

"What's wrong with it?" The doctor waved his hands wildly. "Why—why everything's wrong! I'm a respected citizen, a professional man. I can't just throw everything I am overboard, and go gallivanting across the country with a—uh—I couldn't do it for any amount of money!"

"Why couldn't you?" Rudy asked interestedly.

"Well—uh—because! I just got through telling you!"

"The respected citizen gimmick? But you ain't going to be one, remember? You won't be very long, anyway, unless you figure on being a dead one with a hide full of broken bones and a pound of raw hamburger for a face."

"He's already dead," his wife snapped contemptuously. Then, her manner changing, she slid off the stool, crossed the aisle and knelt at Clinton's side. "Now, Harold, hon," she coaxed, "why do you want to act like this? Don't you love me any more? Don't you want me to be happy? We could have such a wonderful life together, hon. Not having to worry and fret about money all the time, and people respecting and looking up to you, instead of laughing and joking like . . ."

"But, Fran!" The doctor squirmed. "I—you know I love you and want you to be happy, but . . ."

"That's been your whole trouble, hon. Money. You just didn't have the money to get started off right. Oh, I know how smart and wonderful my lambie is, even if I haven't always acted like it, and I could just absolutely cry sometimes when I think how different it could be for him. Just think of it, lambie! Starting out in a new place, with everything we need to make a good impression. Good clothes, and a swell car and a decent place to live. And a real office for you, hon. A nice big office, and a fine big laboratory where you could carry on your experiments . . ."

She held him close, and over his shoulder she winked at Rudy. Clinton twitched and sputtered, simultaneously attempting—it seemed—to return her embrace and disengage himself from it. His protests grew weaker and fewer. Finally, as a last resort, he professed a willingness to take on the enterprise, he *wanted* to do it. But the potential danger made it unthinkable.

"We might have an accident, and they'd find out who Mr. Torrento was. Or the police might just stop us on suspicion—you know, one of those routine investigations. A lot of criminals get caught that way and . . ."

"A lot of people get nibbled to death by wild ducks," Rudy yawned. "But I'll tell you what I'll do, Clint. We get a bad break like you mention, and you and Fran can be hostages. I'll back you up on it. You're helping me because I'd've killed you if you hadn't."

Clinton sighed, and gave up. All his life he had given up. He didn't know why it was like that; why a man who wanted nothing but to live honestly and industriously and usefully—who, briefly, asked only the privileges of giving and helping—had had to compromise and surrender at every turn. But that was the way it had been, and that apparently was the way it was to be.

"I suppose it doesn't seem to you that I'm giving up much, Mr. Torrento," he said dully. "But to me—" he paused, his eyes straying to the swaybacked mare, and his voice gathered new strength. "They're awfully smart, Mr. Torrento. You wouldn't believe how smart and, uh, nice they can be. Why, you take something like a pig or even a garter snake, and pet it and feed it and fix up whatever's wrong with it—just treat it like you'd want to be treated if you were what it is . . ."

"Oh, put it in a book." His wife jumped to her feet. "We've got things to do."

Rudy's car was driven into the weed-choked and rocky pasture, buried beneath a stack of moldering hay. (It is still there if anyone cares to look.) The doctor's business and professional affairs were wound up by two brief telephone calls, ending his lease and turning over his practice to another veterinarian. Neither the landlord nor the other vet was surprised by this action, or its nominal abruptness. Clinton had been barely eking out an existence. The rundown acres and the tumbledown house, rented furniture, had discouraged far more resourceful and tenacious tenants than he.

After taking Rudy's temperature again and urging him to rest, Clinton drove away in his ancient jalopy. He had more than three thousand dollars of Rudy's money in his wallet. His destination was a nearby city, where the cash purchase of a car would arouse no suspicion.

Fran Clinton waved him a loving goodbye from the doorway of the barn, then sauntered back, hips swinging, and resumed her stool opposite Rudy. "Well," she smirked, "how'd you like the way I handled stupid?"

"The doc, you mean?" Rudy crooked a finger at her. "Come here."

"What for?"

Rudy stared at her steadily, not answering. The knowing smile on her face wavered a little, but she slid off the stool and came across the aisle. She started to step up into the stall where Rudy lay. Without the slightest change of expression, he kicked her in the stomach;

watched unwinking, as she landed floundering and groaning in the straw of the aisle.

She staggered to her feet, gasping, eyes tear-washed with anger and pain. She asked furiously just what was the big idea anyway? Just who the hell did he think he was anyway? Then, weakly, as he continued to stare at her in silence, she began to weep.

"I d-didn't do anything. I-I tried to be n-nice, and do what you wanted me to, and y-you . . ."

She was overwhelmed with self-pity. Blindly, as though drawn by a magnet, she came close to Rudy again. And he hooked her, stumbling, into the stall with his foot, brought her down on her knees with a yank of a viselike hand. The hand went to the back of her head. Her mouth crushed cruelly against his. She gasped and struggled for a moment; then, with a greedy moan, she surrendered, squirming and pressing her softness against him.

Abruptly, Rudy pushed her away. "You get the idea?" he said. "When I tell you to do something, you do it. Fast! Think you can remember that?"

"Oh, yes," she said, eyes glowing softly. "Anything you say, Rudy. You just tell me and—and whatever it is—I'll . . ."

He told her what she was to do. Then, as she looked at him, face falling, he pointed up the command with a twist of her arm. "Now, hop to it," he said. "Get that red paint off your claws. It's making me sick."

NINE

Doc followed the thief through the gate to the train, then down the winding ramp to the loading platform. The man was nowhere in sight when he emerged from the tunnel. But Doc had not expected him to be. Stepping behind a nearby pillar, he waited watchfully. And after a minute or two the thief edged out from behind another pillar and started back up the platform.

Doc confronted him abruptly. "All right, mister," he said. "I'll just—" His hand grasped for the bag, almost gripped the handle. The thief twisted it, yanked, and trotted back down the platform. Doc strode after him.

He had made a mistake, he knew. Back there in the station he should have shouted at the thief, shouted that he *was* a thief. In which case the man would certainly have dropped the bag and fled. But he had been afraid to call out, had even believed that it wouldn't be necessary. Caught red-handed, the thief would—or should—hightail it.

Unfortunately, the man was as unobliging as he was discerning. He had stolen this tall gent's bag, or his wife's bag. The wife had been nervous as all hell about it, and now this guy, her husband, was making no outcry at all. That must be because he couldn't.

So the thief made off, taking the bag with him. More than a little hopeful that Doc would not risk pursuing him. As much exultant as dismayed when he saw that Doc was right after him. This must be something big that he had latched onto. And with Doc unable to squawk, he stood a good chance of getting away with it. Or at least a part of it. He could demand a split of whatever the bag contained.

The thief was very cocksure, it should be said; in his particular branch of crime, he had to be. Also—and it is hardly necessary to point this out—he had known no criminals of Doc McCoy's caliber.

Only two doors of the train were open, one in the Pullman section, the other to admit coach passengers. The thief approached the latter, squeezing himself in line behind an elderly couple. The conductor stopped them as they started to climb aboard.

"Tickets, tickets, please," he intoned impatiently. "See your ticket, lady, mister."

It developed that the tickets were at the bottom of the lady's handbag. While she fumbled for them anxiously, the thief eased around her and got a foot on the steps.

"Ticket? Ticket, mister?" the conductor called to him.

But the thief was already in the car.

The conductor glowered. The elderly woman produced one of the two necessary tickets, then, pawing for the other, she spilled a handful of small change onto the platform. Immediately she and her husband stopped to gather it up. The conductor implored them to please step aside, folks. "Tickets, tickets. Kindly show your tickets." But he himself was pushed aside as the other passengers pressed forward, began to clamber aboard by twos and threes. And what with one thing and another, he not only was unable to check their tickets but he ceased to give a damn whether he did.

With a heavenward gesture, he stalked away to converse with a sympathetically grinning brakeman.

Meanwhile, Doc was on the train, trailing the thief by less than a car length.

The man had turned right, heading toward the front of the train. He moved with relatively little haste as long as he was within Doc's view. But losing him momentarily in passing from one car to another, he began to run. His intent or, rather, hope was to get off the train and leave Doc on it. But that would take time, as his hurried attempt to open a connecting door proved. He would need at least a couple of minutes to jump off and lose himself and so he ran.

The passengers became fewer and fewer as he neared the front of the train. He raced through one car in which there were none at all; and then, coming to the door at its end, he stopped short. The car ahead was a dingy, straw-seated smoker. It was wholly empty, like the one he was in, and it adjoined the first of the express cars. In other words, he could go no farther. And he still lacked the time, or was afraid that he did, to make his escape.

His thief's mind weighed the situation, made an almost instantaneous decision. Darting through the drapes of the men's rest room, he yanked down the window shade, tossed the bag onto the leather couch and pressed the catches which held it shut. He was going to get *something* out of this frammis. Make sure, at least, that there was something to get. After all, the world was full of screwballs and it just might be that there was nothing in this keister but old matchbook covers or . . .

He gasped when he saw what was in it. Automatically, he grabbed a thick packet of bills and shoved them into his inside coat pocket. Then, hearing an approaching telltale sound, he slammed the bag shut, pushed it under the couch, and flattened himself against the wall by the doorway.

The train jerked and began to move. Doc's swift footsteps came closer. Then the drapes rustled, and in the mirror above the lavatory the thief saw his pursuer glance inside.

There was a muttered curse of disappointment. Then the drapes fell back into place, and the car door wheezed open and shut. The thief stayed where he was, motionless, hardly breathing. Some thirty seconds passed. The train slowly gathered speed. It still wasn't going too fast for a man to jump off, but . . .

There was a muted clang. The grating and scraping of metal against metal. Then silence save for the clicking of the wheels. Exultantly, the thief let out his breath.

He pulled the bag from beneath the couch and stepped out into the vestibule. The metal platform above the steps was swinging free, and the lower half of the exit door was partly open. The thief laughed out loud. What a break! Boy, what a break! Him speeding toward California with a satchelful of dough, and the guy back there at the station looking for him. And he couldn't raise a beef about his loss!

Grinning, he reclosed and locked the exit door. He entered the next car, the smoker, threw two seats together and tossed the bag onto the overhead rack. He sat down, placing his feet comfortably on the seat ahead of him.

And Doc moved away from the rear wall of the car, and sat down at his side. The thief gaped; his stiff lips framed a silent question. Doc jerked his head over his shoulder. "Back there," he said. "In the same place you were, approximately, when you hid in the rest room. I'll tell you something," he added. "Whenever you can see someone in a mirror, you can also be seen."

"B-but—" the thief shook his head helplessly. "But . . ."

"I wanted to get you out of the rest room, and it wouldn't have looked well to carry you—just in case someone was looking. And of course you'd head this way instead of going back the way you came." He smiled unpleasantly, prodding the thief's ribs with his gun. "That's the mark of a punk, you know. He loves a cinch. I'd jumped the train, supposedly, and it was traveling fast. But you were still too gutless to go back into the cars. You were afraid I might spot you from the platform and hop back on."

He was very annoyed with the thief. The man had given him an extremely bad time, and he was apt to receive an even worse one from Carol as an aftermath. He had seen her just before he sat down, motioned to her as she hesitantly entered the car behind. And while he couldn't tell much about her expression at that distance, he could see that she was angry. He had known that she must be before she showed up; as soon as, having cornered the thief, he had had time to think of anything else.

"Put the rod away, mister." The thief was smiling, getting back his nerve. "You aren't going to use it."

"That's another mark of a punk," Doc told him. "He doesn't know when to be frightened."

"You can't use it. You can't make any kind of rumble. If you could you'd've already done it." He winked at Doc companionably. "We're two of a kind, mister. You . . ."

"Now that," Doc said, "is carrying things too far." And he whipped the gun barrel upward.

It smashed against the point of the thief's chin. His eyes glazed, and his body went into a sacklike sag. Methodically, Doc locked an arm around his head, braced the other across his back and jerked.

It was over in a split second. If a man can die instantly, the thief did.

Doc tilted the seat back a little, adjusted the man's body to a slightly reclining position. He placed his feet on the seat ahead, and pulled his hat over his eyes.

Doc studied the corpse critically. He gave it a few minor touches—closing the staring eyes, putting one of the limp hands into a coat pocket—and was satisfied. To all appearances the man was asleep. Even Carol thought he was—or would have, if she had not known otherwise.

She sat down facing Doc, her anger somewhat weakened by the relief at being reunited with him. He hadn't had it very easy either, she guessed. And the terrifying mixup at the station was probably more her own fault than his. Still . . .

She couldn't quite locate the cause of her anger; explain, in absolute terms, why she had viewed him and almost everything he had done with distrust and distaste practically from the moment of their post-robbery meeting. It wasn't so much what he'd done, she supposed, as what he had not. Not so much what he was, as what he was not. And in her mind she wailed bridelike for what she had lost—or thought she had; for something that had never existed outside of her mind.

He doesn't treat me like he used to, she thought. He's not the same man any more.

"Carol—" Doc spoke to her a second time. "I said I was sorry, dear."

She looked at him coldly, shrugged. "All right. What's the pitch now?"

"That depends. Has the conductor collected your ticket—no? Well, that's good. But he did see you when you got on?"

Carol shook her head. "The train was already moving. If the porter hadn't hopped off and helped me—well, never mind. The less said about that the better."

"Perhaps. For the moment at least." Doc looked back through the door, saw the conductor trudging up the aisle of the next car. "Now give me one of the tickets—for my friend here—and just follow my lead."

The conductor was grumbling, complaining, almost before he reached them. What was the sense in their coming way up here? It was uncomfortable for them, and it made things hard on him. Doc murmured apologies. Their friend had wanted to visit the diner; having come this far in the wrong direction, he had decided to remain.

"My wife and I are getting off at the first stop," he added, profferring a bill along with the ticket. "We hadn't planned to . . ."

"You're getting off?" the conductor exploded. "This isn't some commuter's local, mister. You shouldn't have got on without a ticket; shouldn't've stayed on any way."

"And we hadn't planned to. But this gentleman wasn't feeling well and . . ."

"Then he shouldn't have got on either! Or he ought to've bought himself some Pullman space." He jabbed a train check into the window clip, yanked a coupon from the ticket book and tossed it down onto the seat. "You don't have enough money there, mister," he snapped at Doc. "The first scheduled stop for this train is ten o'clock tonight."

Carol's mouth tightened nervously. Ten o'clock—more than nine hours from now! They could never maintain the masquerade of the "sleeping" man that long. The conductor was already studying him narrow-eyed, turning a suspicious gaze toward Doc.

"What's the matter with him anyway?" he said. "He acts like he was drunk or doped or something. Here, you," he started to grab the corpse by the shoulder. "What . . ."

Doc caught his hand, grimly rose up from the seat. "I'll tell you what's the matter with him," he said. "He got a bad jostling when he boarded the train. Started up an old neck injury. You didn't notice because you were off chatting with a friend instead of minding your job. But I've got several witnesses to the fact that it happened, and if you're looking for trouble I'll be glad to supply it."

The conductor's mouth opened and reopened. He swallowed heavily. Doc softened his tone, warmed him with a look of man-to-man sympathy.

"Now, I know a man can't be everyplace at once," he said. "I don't always follow rules right to the letter, and I don't expect anyone else to. And as long as my friend isn't seriously injured, we're both inclined to forget the matter. On the other hand . . ."

He let the words hang in the air. The conductor glanced at his watch, took out a receipt book. "Suppose we pull a stop for you in about an hour? I could do it sooner, I guess, but we might get a flag there anyway, and . . ."

"An hour? That will be fine," Doc said.

"And, uh, everything'll be okay with your friend? I mean, you don't think he'll, uh . . ."

"File a complaint? Don't give it a thought," Doc said heartily. "I'll guarantee that he won't."

He sat down again as the conductor left, and tucked the railroad ticket into the breast pocket of the dead man's coat. Carol watched him, a little misty-eyed, feeling a sudden resurgence of the slavish devotion and adoration which had been about to be lost to the past.

Everything had been such a mess. Everything had seemed so different—she, Doc—everything. But now the mess was gone, the mistakes and misunderstandings brushed away—or aside. And Doc was exactly the same Doc she had dreamed of and longed for these last four years.

Relief engulfed her. Relief and gratitude at being snatched back from a last-straw, not-to-be-borne peril. She had been sinking, coming apart inside, and Doc had saved her and made her whole again. Impulsively she reached out and squeezed his hand.

"Doc," she said. "Do me a favor?"

"Practically anything," Doc said instantly into her mood.

"If I ever get nasty again, give me a good hard kick in the pants."

Doc said he would have to investigate the possibility of breakage first; he had a very delicate foot. Then he laughed and she laughed. And quivering with the movement of the train, the dead man seemed to laugh too.

When they got off the train, Doc waved a smiling good-bye toward the window, then advised the conductor that his friend was doing nicely. "I gave him some aspirin and he's going back to sleep for a while. That's all he needs, just rest and quiet."

The conductor said there was no reason at all why the gentleman shouldn't get it. "He can sleep till Doomsday as far as I'm concerned!"

Doc thanked him for his courtesy and gave him a warm handshake. As the train pulled out, the conductor examined the bill he had received during the handshaking process. And glowing pleasantly—telling himself you could always spot a gentleman—he started back down the line of cars. His happy musings were interrupted with nerve-shattering suddenness by a screamed demand to "Stick 'em up!"

The owner of the voice had been crouching between two seats. He was about seven, dressed in cowboy regalia, and equipped anachronistically with a toy machine gun.

"What are you doing here?" the conductor gasped, his hair slowly settling back to his scalp. "I've told you about fifteen times already to stay with your moth . . ."

"Bang, bang, bang!" The boy screamed. "You're an old stinky booger man, an' I'm gonna shoot you dead!"

He dropped into a crouch, triggered the gun. It chattered and barked realistically. Even more realistic was the water which jetted from its muzzle, and sprayed the conductor's starched white shirtfront. The conductor grabbed at him. The boy fled, screaming with laughter, shrieking insults and threats, spreading consternation through the next six cars until he reached the sanctuary of his mother. She responded to his pursuer's complaints with a kind of arch crossness.

"Oh, my goodness! Such a fuss over one little boy. Do you expect him to just sit still with his hands folded?"

She glanced around, smiling, at the other passengers, soliciting approval. None was forthcoming. The conductor said that he expected her to keep an eye on her son; to see that he cease his rambunctious ramblings forthwith.

"I mean that, lady. I'm insisting on it. I don't want to find that young man outside of this car again."

"But I just don't *understand*!" The woman frowned prettily. "What possible *difference* does it make if the poor child moves around a little? He's not hurting anything."

"But he might get hurt. In fact," the conductor added grimly, "he's very likely to. And you'd be the first to complain if he did."

He trudged away, reflecting that it was such brats and such mothers who provided unanswerable argument for the proponents of capital punishment. *Bang, bang, bang!* he brooded bitterly. *Ol' stinky booger man*. I'd like to booger-man him!

If he could have looked ahead a few hours—but he could not, fortunately. It would have been much to bear, in his mood, to see the boy acclaimed, however briefly, as brave, bold, brilliant and, in sum, a national hero.

Which is just what happened.

Doc McCoy had a fairly good map of the United States in his mind, surprisingly detailed, and as up-to-date as he could keep it. So, leaving the train, he inquired about a remembered landmark—although it was ten years since he had been in the area. And learning that it was still in existence, he and Carol taxied out to the place.

It was some five miles out on the highway, a family-style roadhouse set down amidst several acres of picnic grounds. They had lunch inside the establishment; then, taking several bottles of beer with them, they located a secluded picnic table and settled down for the brief wait until nightfall.

They could not get a car before then; at any rate, it would not be wise to attempt it. And the way they intended to get it made night travel advisable. A hot car was always cooler at night—providing, of course, that its loss was unreported. People weren't so alert. There was a sharp reduction in the risk of raising some yokel who knew the owner.

"And there's no big hurry," Doc pointed out. "I've got a hunch that our late traveling companion will go right on sleeping, undisturbed, until that ten o'clock stop. Even if they found out the nature of his slumber before then, it wouldn't matter much. The body has to be posted. That takes time, and it can't be done in just any hick village. Then there's the conductor's story of an old neck injury—along with the conductor's guilty conscience—to add confusion to the proceedings." He laughed softly. "If I know anything about human nature, he'll swear that our friend was alive and in good health at the time we left him."

Carol nodded, laughing with him. This was the old Doc talking, *her* Doc. She wanted more of his warming reassurance, and Doc did his best to supply it.

"Of course, we will be suspected of bringing about the gentleman's death," he went on. "Sometime tomorrow, say, when the conductor has come clean and it's definitely determined that the broken neck was inflicted rather than accidental. But who are we, anyway? What good is our description if they don't have a channel for it? Now, if there was anything to indicate we were bank robbers, we'd be tabbed in five minutes. Just as quickly as a batch of 'wanted' cards could be run through the sorter."

"It's not going to happen," Carol said firmly. "So let's not talk about it."

"Right," Doc said. "No point to it at all."

"But it's still smart to get off the highway. One more night is as much as we can risk."

"Well, that may be putting it a little strong. We won't be tagged with Beynon's car, and we helped our chances with that long jump north. Let's just say that the railroad still seems like our best bet."

Obviously, he continued, they couldn't go back to the line they'd been on. In fact, any of the due-west routes were a poor risk; unless—and the time element precluded this—they were able to take one across the northern rim of the United States.

"So I'd say we do this. Pull another swingback; get completely away from this east-west travel route. We can push hard tonight, make Tulsa or Oklahoma City by morning, and take a southern route train. We can miss Los Angeles that way. Come into California through the Carriso Gorge, and then straight on into San Diego. We can make it in forty-eight hours if everything goes all right."

"And it will, Doc." Carol squeezed his hand. "I know it!"

"Of course it will," Doc said.

Actually, he was more than a little uneasy about the situation. There was much that he disliked about it. But since it could not be changed, he put the best possible face on it, if he was secretly, perhaps subconsciously, annoyed at the necessity for doing so.

Much of their predicament was Carol's fault. She should have been absolutely frank with him about Beynon. Failing that—having made that one serious error—she should have kept the bag with her at the Kansas City station. That was little enough to expect of her, wasn't it? It was simply enough. But she had had to blunder again, again forcing him to plan extemporaneously, which was another way of saying dangerously. And now, instead of being properly apologetic, willing to look the facts in the face, she had to be cajoled and bolstered up.

If I'd known she was going to be like this, he thought—and left the thought at that. He took another drink of the beer, smiling at her, inwardly grinning the wry, pained grin of a man who has bumped his elbow.

"Doc." She was looking down at the table, idly scratching at the chipped paint with a fingernail. "Doc." She raised her eyes. "I've changed a lot, haven't I? You think I have."

"Oh, well," Doc began. "After all, it's been . . ."

"You seem the same way to me, Doc. Almost like a stranger at times. I mean—well, I don't mean it as though I was criticizing or blaming you or anything. I've seemed to have done something dopey every time I turned around, and you've been a damn sight nicer about it than you should have been. But . . ."

"Now, don't feel that way." Doc laid a hand over hers. "We've had some bad luck. We've never been involved in anything quite like this before."

"I don't think that's the trouble. Not the real trouble. We had our difficulties before, and they didn't seem to matter. We were so much closer, and—" she hesitated, thoughtfully. "I guess that's it, isn't it? We kind of are strangers. We aren't the same people we were four years ago."

"Essentially the same," Doc disagreed. "Let's say that perhaps we've forgotten what those people were like. In toto, I mean. We've forgotten their bad times, the occasions when they rubbed each other the wrong way, and remembered only the good."

"Well—maybe. Yes," she added. "I suppose this is it."

"I know it is. Just as soon as we've gotten a little reacquainted—have time for something besides running . . ."

"Doc." She looked down at the table again, a faint blush spreading over her cheeks. "I think we should, you know, get really acquainted again. I think we've just about got to. Very soon. C-can't we—isn't there some way we could manage to—be together?"

Doc murmured that he was sure they could. Beneath the table, he pressed her ankle with his, and the silken flesh quivered in response.

He began to feel a lot better about her, about everything. His inherent optimism reasserted itself, smothering his worried, re-creating him in the delightful and irresistible image that had burned so bright in Carol's memory.

"I know we can't lay over, stop anywhere," she said. "But, well, do you suppose we could travel together on the train? Take a state-room or a bedroom, and . . ."

Doc said he thought so; he was pretty sure of it (although he wasn't sure). "We'll count on it, anyway. *I'll* count on it, my dear."

And Carol blushed and squirmed deliciously.

In the deceptive half-light of dusk, Doc walked down the highway a couple of hundred yards and took cover behind a hedgerow. Carol, meanwhile, took up a position at the edge of the picnic grounds—protected by the thickening shadows of the driveway but within a quick step of the road.

Doc heard two cars stop for her, then speed on again almost before they had stopped. Soon there was a third car, and the opening and slamming of a door. And Doc came out of his place of concealment.

The car stopped for him jerkily; Carol was holding a gun in the driver's ribs. Doc climbed into the back seat and, putting a gun to the man's head, ordered him to relinquish the wheel. The man did so, fearfully, too frightened for speech, limbs stiff and numb as he slid over in the seat. With Carol driving, they moved on again.

Naturally, the car was from out-of-state; had it borne local license plates, Carol would never have gotten into it. The owner was a salesman, a man of about thirty-five with a plump well-fed face and a wide good-natured mouth. Doc spoke to him soothingly, putting him as much at ease as the circumstances would allow.

"We're sorry to do this," he apologized. "Believe me, we've never done anything like it before. But we ran out of money, and the wife can't take another night on the road, so—I hope you understand. You're a married man yourself, I take it."

The salesman wasn't. He'd tried the double harness once and it hadn't worked.

"Oh, that's too bad," Doc murmured. "Now, I wonder if you could drive us down into Oklahoma? I can get some money there, and . . ."

"S-sure, I could! Glad to!" The salesman was pitiful in his eagerness. "Naw, I really mean it. I was figuring on taking a fling at Tulsa myself, just for kicks, y'know. I'm not due back in Chicago for three days yet, but I already made all my calls and . . ."

Doc slugged him with the gun barrel. The man grunted, and slumped forward. Carol gave him a shove, pushed him down on the floor of the car.

"Side road, Doc?" She spoke over her shoulder.

Back on the train, the boy in the cowboy suit napped, dined and resumed his wanderings. After a longer absence than usual, he returned to his mother, shouting brassily that he had just killed a robber man. "I did so, too!" he screamed, as she laughed, indulgently. "I told him to stick 'em up an' he didn't so I poked him an' he fell over dead, an' the money he stole fell out of his pocket an' I got it! I got it right here!" He pulled a thick sheaf of bills from his blouse, waved them about excitedly. Across the aisle, a man reached out and took it from him; frowned, startled, as he read the imprint on the paper banding. The Bank of Beacon City! Why, that was the place that had been robbed yesterday morning! He jumped up and went in search of the conductor.

Doc frisked the salesman, taking his wallet and all other identification. Then, with the whispering of the car's radio fading behind him, he dragged the man down the ditch to the culvert and placed the gun muzzle inside his mouth. He triggered the gun twice. He shoved it back into his belt, began squeezing the now faceless body into the culvert.

"Doc!" Carol's voice came to him urgently. "*Doc!*"

"Be right with you," he called back easily. "Just as soon as I . . ."

The car's starter whirred. The motor coughed, caught and roared. Doc hastily clambered up the side of the ditch, yanked open the door and climbed in.

"What's the matter?" he demanded. "Can't I leave you for two minutes without . . ."

Then he broke off, listened incredulously to the newscaster's staccato voice:

". . . The man has been positively identified as Doc (Carter) McCoy, notorious bank robber and criminal mastermind. Police are certain that the woman with him is his wife, Carol. Their descriptions follow . . ."

TEN

Rudy Torrento and the Clintons started for California the morning after his arrival at their place. He was running a slight temperature, feeling worse than he had the day before. And Clinton suggested anxiously that they take it very easy for a day or so. But Rudy, fearful that Doc and Carol might get away from him, wouldn't hear of it. They were going to make California in three days, see? Three days and nights of steady driving. He himself would take a turn at the wheel if he had to, and if he *did* have to, they'd wish that he hadn't.

Then, late that evening, he heard the news about Doc and Carol; knew immediately that there was no longer any need for hurry. For certainly they would not be able to. The way things looked to him, he could probably roller-skate his way to California—and Golie's tourist court—and get there ahead of them.

So he informed the Clintons amiably that he had changed his mind. He'd decided to take Clinty-boy's advice after all, because what the hell was the use of having a doctor if you didn't listen to him? Anyway, they'd take it easy like Clint said, just take their time and get a little fun out of the trip; and they'd start in right now by turning in at a good motel.

They took connecting cabins, but only for the sake of appearances. They used only one of them, the three of them sleeping crosswise and partly disrobed in one bed, with Fran Clinton in the middle.

"Now we won't be getting lost from each other," Rudy explained, grinning. "Clint won't have to worry about me sneakin' off to the police, and reporting him for practicing medicine without a license."

Mrs. Clinton smirked lewdly. Rudy winked at her husband. "It's okay with you, ain't it, Clint? You've got no objections?"

"Why, no. No, of course not," Clinton said hastily. "It's, uh, very sensible." And he winced as his wife laughed openly.

He did not know how to object. In his inherent delicacy and decency, he could not admit that there was anything to object to. He heard them that night—and subsequent nights of their leisurely journey westward. But he kept his back turned and his eyes closed, feeling no shame or anger but only an increasing sickness of soul.

Just inside the border of California, they stopped for a picnic lunch at a roadside tourist park. Afterward, while Rudy dozed in the car and Fran Clinton thumbed through a movie magazine, her husband wandered off among the trees.

He did not return. When they found him, he was lying face down in a pool of blood, one of his small hands still gripping the razor blade with which he had cut his throat.

Rudy dropped down to the ground at his side. Clutching himself, he began to rock back and forth, groaning and gasping with what Mrs. Clinton mistook for a paroxysm of laughter. She could hardly be blamed for her error. She had never seen Rudy grief-stricken; the Piehead, overwhelmed by sorrow or laughter, appeared much the same.

So she began to laugh—with him, she thought. And Rudy came abruptly out of his fit and slugged her in the stomach. He beat her black and blue; everywhere but in her face. Except that he needed her, he would have beaten her to death. Then he made her carry the body into the bushes and cover it over with rocks.

She never again gave him reason to beat her. On the contrary, no one could have been more worshipful or watchful of his whims. Yet hardly a day passed after their arrival at Golie's that he did not pound and pummel her at least once. Because she annoyed him with her groveling. Because he was restless. Because he was very worried about Doc.

"Come on, boy," he would mumble fiercely, sitting hunched in front of the radio. "You can do it, Doc! You done it before, an' you can do it again!"

He seldom mentioned Carol in these injunctions; seldom thought of her. She would be with Doc, and as long as he was safe, so was she. Rudy couldn't see them as splitting up, getting fed up to the point of wanting to split. Like 'em or not, those two were really nuts about each other. And Rudy was sure that nothing short of prison or death could break them up. Just in case, though . . .

Rudy grinned evilly, considering the impossible possibility of a falling out between Carol and Doc. It couldn't happen, but if it did, it wouldn't change a thing.

Carol needed Doc; she'd never been on the run before, and she'd never make it without him. And because she wouldn't, Doc couldn't split with her or let her split with him. She'd be too apt to rattle the cup on him. Buy herself a deal at his expense.

They were tied together, bound together inextricably. And Rudy roared with crazy laughter when he thought what would happen if either attempted any untying. That would be something to see, one of them trying to get the jump on the other. Hell, it would be like trying to do something with your right hand without letting the left know about it.

They were still very hot news. Rudy himself was mentioned frequently but the focus was mainly on Carol and Doc.

They'd been seen in New York, Florida, and New Orleans. They'd boarded a train for Canada, a plane for South America, a ship for the Straits Settlements. It was mostly nut stuff, Rudy guessed, the kind of hooroosh that always sprang up around a big name or a big kill. But not all of it.

Doc had friends everywhere. The really slick rumor-planting—the stuff that got more than a second look from the cops—would be their work, done to repay an old favor or simply to give a hand to a brother in need. One of their stunts even had Rudy going for a while.

Two stiffs were found in a burned-down house in Washington D.C. They were charred beyond recognition, but of a size with Carol and Doc, and the woman's almost melted ring bore the inscription *D. to C.* As a clinching bit of evidence, the fire-blackened refrigerator was found to contain several packets of small bills, all banded with Bank of Beacon City tape.

The police were sure they had found the remains of Carol and

Doc. So, almost, was Rudy. Then some eager beaver of a lab hound had managed to raise a latent print on the man's corpse, establishing him indisputably as an underworld in-and-outer who had acquired a bad name for reliability. And with this much to go on, the police hunted out the printing shop where the bank bands had been obtained. Aside from admitting that they had been made from his stock and type, the owner denied all knowledge of them. He was of the opinion, however, that the bank had been turned out during a burglary of his shop—said burglary having been duly reported to the police several days before.

So the hoax was exposed, if not the hoaxers. No one seemed interested in learning their identity. No one seemed to care who the woman had been. Rudy wondered about her in his weirdly oblique way, and was sullenly envious of Doc. The in-and-outer had been a bum, a no-good with neither the physical attractiveness nor the cash to attract a lady friend. So, apparently, Doc's friends had arbitrarily provided him with one. Just any dame that met certain specifications. They weren't sore at her, as they were with the man. It was a hundred to one that they didn't even know her. They'd snatched her and bumped her simply to help Doc.

Rudy was forced to admit that he had no such good friends. Even little Max Vonderscheid would never kill anyone to help him. Not that he cared; if a double-crosser like Doc had friends, then he could do without 'em. But just the same . . .

"Come on, Doc," he pleaded. "Come to Rudy, Doc. What the hell's holding you up anyway?"

ELEVEN

Flight is many things. Something clean and swift, like a bird skimming across the sky. Or something filthy and crawling; a series of crablike movements through figurative and literal slime, a process of creeping ahead, jumping sideways, running backward.

It is sleeping in fields and river bottoms. It is bellying for miles along an irrigation ditch. It is back roads, spur railroad lines, the tailgate of a wildcat truck, a stolen car and a dead couple in lovers' lane. It is food pilfered from freight cars, garments taken from clotheslines; robbery and murder, sweat and blood. The complex made simple by the alchemy of necessity.

You cannot do what you must unaided. So throughout your struggling, your creeping and running, your thieving and killing, you are on the hunt for help. And if you live, you find it, sooner or later. Rudy Torrento found his sooner, in the Clintons. Doc found his later in a family of migratory farm workers; sharecroppers turned crop tramps.

There were nine of them, husband and wife and seven stair-step children—the youngest a toddling tot, the eldest a rawboned boy who was the scantling shadow of his father. They were camped alongside the muddy trickle of a creek. Two of the tires on their ancient truck were flat, and its battery stood on the ground. Their clothes were ragged but clean. When Doc emerged from the underbrush and approached them, trailed nervously by Carol, they drew together in a kind of phalanx; and the same look of wary phlegmatism was on every one of their suntanned faces.

Carol had no reason to be nervous. Doc knew people; and having been born among them, he knew this kind very well. Their existence was centered around existing. They had no hope of anything more, no comprehension that there might be anything more. In a sense they were an autonomous body, functioning within a society which was organized to grind them down. The law did not protect them; for them it was merely an instrument of harassment, a means of moving them on when it was against their interest to move, or detaining them where it was to their disadvantage to stay.

Doc knew them well. He knew how to talk to them.

Beyond a casual nod, he ignored the man's wife and brood. They had no authority, and to imply any to them would have been discourteous. Drawing the man aside, he spoke to him circuitously; casually hunkering down on his heels, talking with the man's own languid caution. Sometimes whole minutes passed in silence. And speaking, they seemed to discuss almost everything but the subject at hand.

Yet they understood each other, and they came to an agreement quite quickly. Doc gave the man some bills, not many and none of them large. For integrity cannot be bought, and they were simply men in need assisting one another. Then the man gave drawled instructions to his family.

"These here folks is friends," he said. "They'll be movin' on with us. We don't let on about it to no one, not any peep or whistle."

He sent the eldest boy and the second eldest into town for "new" secondhand tires, a battery and food. In the morning they headed westward, and lying prone in the rear of the truck, Doc and Carol heard the woman's cracked voice raised in a spiritual and they smelled the smoke from the man's nickel see-gar.

The seven children were squeezed into the truck bed with them, the bigger ones sitting with slumped shoulders to accommodate themselves to its low canvas cover. They were all around them, shielding them from view, hiding them as effectively as though they had been at the bottom of a well. But close as they were physically, they were still worlds apart.

Carol smiled at one of the girls, and received a flat stare in return. She started to pat the tot's head, and barely jerked her hand back in time to avoid being bitten. The eldest boy protectively took charge of the child. "Wouldn't do that no more, ma'am," he advised Carol with chill politeness. "He don't cotton none to strangers."

The truck's best speed was barely thirty miles an hour. Despite their early starts and late stops, they seldom made two hundred miles a day. Their food was monotonously unvaried, practically the same from one meal to the next. Salt pork and gravy, biscuits or mush, and chicory coffee for breakfast. For lunch, mush or biscuits and salt pork eaten cold while they rode. And for dinner, there was more biscuits, and pork and gravy, with perhaps some sweetnin' (sorghum) and a poke salad—greens boiled with pork into a greasy, tasteless mess.

Doc ate heartily of everything. Nauseated by the stuff, Carol ate no more than she had to to stay alive. She acquired a painful and embarrassing stomach complaint. Her small body ached constantly from the jouncing and bouncing of the truck. She became very bitter of Doc; the more so because she knew her predicament was her own fault, and because she dared not complain.

These people didn't like her. They tolerated her only because she was Doc's woman (his *woman*, for Pete's sake!). And without Doc, she would be lost.

Whether the family knew who they were—the most wanted criminals in the country—is a moot point. But reading no newspapers, having no radio, living in their own closemouthed world of existing to exist, it is unlikely that they did. And probably they would have turned their back on the opportunity to inform themselves.

These folks was feedin' them. These folks' business was their own business.

Ask no questions an' you'll hear no lies.

Curiosity killed the cat.

Leave well enough be, an' you'll be well enough.

The old truck limped westward, carrying Doc and Carol far beyond the danger zone of roadblocks and police checks, and into the whilom safety of California. And there, after another day or so of travel, they parted company with the family.

Doc didn't want them to know his and Carol's destination, to get any closer to it than they already were. That would be asking for trouble, and asked-for trouble was usually gotten. Moreover, the family did not wish to go any farther south—into an area that was traditionally hostile to vagrants or anyone who might possibly become vagrant. And they hoped to have other fish to fry, or rather, apples to pick in the Pacific Northwest.

So there were monosyllabic farewells, a final exchange of money; then the family moved on, and Carol and Doc remained behind . . . Quite inappropriately in the City of Angels.

Doc was dressed in blue overalls and a jumper, and a striped railroad worker's cap. He carried himself with a pronounced stoop; a pair of old-fashioned steel-rimmed glasses were perched on the end of his nose, and he peered over them nearsightedly as he paid for his ticket from a snap-toy money pouch. A metal lunch basket was tucked under one arm. Beneath his clothes—and Carol's—was an outsize money belt.

Carol came into the railroad station several minutes after him. She also was stooped, cronelike of figure. She wore a long, shapeless black dress, and under the shadow of her head shawl her face was wizened and sunblack.

They boarded the train separately, Carol taking a rear seat, Doc entering the men's lounge. Then, when their tickets had been collected and the train was well out of the yards, he came out and sat down at her side.

He opened the lunch bucket and took out a pint bottle of whiskey. He drank from it thirstily, wiped the neck with his sleeve, and extended it toward Carol.

She shook her head, her nose wrinkling distastefully. "Do you have to keep hitting that stuff?" she frowned.

"*Keep* hitting it?" He returned her frown. "That's the first drink I've had in days."

"Well, it's one too many at a time like this! If you ask me, I . . ."

"But I didn't." He took another long drink, then returned the bottle to the lunch bucket. "Look," he said reasonably. "What do you want to do anyway? Break up? Go it on your own? I'd like to know."

"As if you didn't already know! What the hell difference does it make what I want to do?"

"Well," said Doc. "Well, then."

Actually, he did not want to be separated from her. Even if it had been practical, he would not have wanted it. And despite anything she said or did, he knew that she felt the same way. They were still in love—as much as they had ever been. Strangely, nothing had changed that.

His eyes drifted shut. He wondered where the family of sharecroppers was by now, and subconsciously he wished that he was still with them. It hadn't been at all bad, that long creeping journey across half of the United States. Nothing to do but ride and ride, with every day exactly like the one before. No worries, no decisions to make. Above all the freedom, in fact the necessity, *not* to talk.

He had never before realized the blessedness of silence—the freedom to be silent, rather, if one chose. He had never realized, somehow, that such blessedness might be his privilege. He was Doc McCoy, and Doc McCoy was born to the obligation of being one hell of a guy. Persuasive, impelling of personality; insidiously likable and good-humored and imperturbable. One of the nicest guys you'd ever meet, that was Doc McCoy. They broke the pattern when they made him.

And, of course, Doc *did* like people and he liked to be liked. And he'd been well compensated for his efforts in that direction. Still—well, there you were. It had become an effort, something else that he hadn't realized.

Maybe he was just very tired, he thought wearily. And very worried. Because exactly what they were going to do after they got to Golie's, he didn't know.

"Doc," Carol said. "What's the next step, after we get to Golie's?"

Doc grimaced. She can read my mind, he thought. "I'm thinking about it," he said. "I haven't decided, yet."

"You don't know, do you? You haven't any plan."

"Now, that's putting it a little strong. I'll have to check around, and—" Her scornful smile stopped him. "All right," he said, "I don't know."

She waited, staring at him demandingly. He fumbled the lunch bucket open and took another drink. He gestured with it diffidently, then quickly recapped it and put it away.

"I—it would have been simple enough ordinarily," he explained. "I mean, if we could have made it before they had the alarm out for us. Coming back from Mexico, you're apt to get a pretty thorough going over. But going over, they hardly take a second look at you. You can just walk across the border, or drive across and . . ."

"All right! But that's what we *could* have done!"

"Well—maybe we still can. There doesn't seem to be much noise out here about us. Maybe . . ."

He broke off, unable to continue so palpable a lie. Perhaps there wasn't any general search for them on the West Coast, but the border patrol would certainly have been alerted.

"We'll see," he mumbled. "I'll have to look around. Maybe I can get a line on Ma Santis."

"Ma Santis!" Carol let out a disgusted snort. "Just like that you're going to get a line on Ma Santis, huh? You already told me you thought she was dead, and even if she wasn't I'd like to know how you're going to get a line on her or anyone else. You can't make any inquiries. You can't go wandering around and . . ."

"That's right. I can't," Doc said curtly; and he got up and entered the rest room.

Seated on the long leather couch, he lighted a cigarette, looked wearily out into the moonlit night. He had always thought this was the most beautiful stretch of country in the world, this area of orange and avocado groves, of rolling black-green hills, of tile-roofed houses—all alike yet all different—stretching endlessly along the endless expanse of curving, white-sand beach. He had thought about retiring here some day and, though the idea was preposterous, he still thought about it. He could see himself and Carol on the patio of one of those incredible gay houses. Barbecuing a steak perhaps, or sipping tall drinks while they stared out to sea. There would be a cool breeze blowing in, temperately cool and smelling of salt. And . . .

"Doc—" Carol murmured suddenly from the doorway.

He said, "Coming," and rejoined her in the seat. And she patted his hand and gave him a lingering smile.

"You know something, Doc?" she whispered. "This will be our first night together. Our first night together and alone."

"So it will!" Doc made his voice hearty. "It doesn't seem possible, does it?"

"And I'm not going to let anything spoil it either. Nothing! We'll just pretend like we don't have a worry in the world tonight. Just push everything out of our minds and have ourselves a nice long hot bath, and something to eat and—and . . ."

She squeezed his hand. Almost fiercely.

"Sandy-Egg-O!" bawled the conductor. "Next stop is San Diego!"

TWELVE

The cabdriver accepted Doc's tip with a grunt of surprise; he'd figured this pair for stiffs and maybe even no-pays. They were some kind of foreigners, he guessed, and they didn't know their way around yet. And he hastened to place himself at their disposal.

"Maybe you folks would like to go somewhere for a bite to eat?" he suggested. "After you, uh, get cleaned up a little I mean."

"Well—" Doc glanced at Carol. "I'm not sure just how long we'll . . ."

"Or I could bring you something if you don't want to go out.

Sandwiches, chicken an' French fries, maybe some Chinese or Mexican food. Anything you say, beer, booze, or baloney, and no service charge. Just my cab fare and waitin' time."

"Suppose you wait a moment," Doc said. "I'll have to see about a cabin."

Fat little Golie was nervous, but then Golie almost always was; he had things to make him that way. So Doc couldn't say just what it was that made him feel uneasy. He stalled over the selection of a cabin, finally choosing one at the far end of the court. But his effort to smell out the trouble he felt, to get at the source of his hunch, was unavailing.

Leaving the office, he gave the cabdriver his cabin number and a twenty; ordered two chicken dinners, cigarettes and a carton of coffee. The cabdriver saluted and sped away, and Doc and Carol went down the long single row of cabins to the last one.

He unlocked the door, switched on the light.

Carol yanked down the shade, pirouetted, and flopped down on the bed, kicking her legs high into the air. "Boy," she breathed. "Does this ever feel good!" Then, wiggling her finger at him, "Come here you! Right this minute!"

Doc took a step toward her, then stopped short, frowning. "Listen! Do you hear anything?"

"Oh, now, Doc. Of course, I hear something. After all, we're not the only people in the court."

Doc stared at her absently, his brow furrowed with thought. Carol jumped up and put her arms around him. Leaned into him, smiling up into his face. This was to be their night together, didn't he remember? Their first night in more than four years. So would he kindly stop acting foolish and jumpy, and . . .

"That's it!" Doc's eyes narrowed suddenly. "Golie's family! There was none of 'em around, didn't you notice? Not even that overstuffed wife of his, and she hasn't been twenty feet away from the place since she came here. We've got to get out of here, Carol! Now!"

"G-get out? But—but . . ."

"He's sent them away somewhere, don't you see? He must have! And there's only one reason why he would have."

"But—" Carol looked at him incredulously. "But why? What could . . ."

"I don't know! It doesn't matter! It may be too late already, but . . ."

It was too late. There was a crunch of gravel outside. Then a polite knock on the door, and a woman's soft voice.

"Mr. Kramer? Miz' Kramer?"

Doc stiffened, whipped a gun from beneath the bib of his overalls. He gripped Carol's arm, held it for a moment, then nodded to her.

"Yes?" Carol called. "Who is it, please?"

"The maid, ma'am. I brought you some towels."

Doc glanced into the bathroom, and slowly shook his head. He pointed at Carol's dress, mouthed a silent speech.

"Could you just leave them on the step, please? I'm undressed."

There was silence for a long moment, a whispering so faint that it might have been anything but a whisper. But that was the tip-off. There was someone with this maid, if it was a maid. Someone who was giving her instructions.

Doc looked around swiftly. He squeezed Carol's arm again and pointed toward the bathroom, and his lips formed the word "Window." Carol shook her head violently and tried to hang onto him; then winced and nodded whitely as he gave her arm another painful squeeze.

He raised the window silently. He heard the maid say, "I can't leave 'em outside, ma'am. Maybe your husband can come and get 'em."

"Just a moment, please," Carol called back. "He's in the bathroom right now."

Doc dropped through the window. He tiptoed along the rear of the house and around the side, and peered carefully around the corner.

Rudy! The gun in his hand jerked involuntarily. How in the hell!

He put it out of his mind; the wonderment, the sense of being unbearably put upon. Facts were facts, something to be accepted and dealt with, and the fact was that Rudy was here.

There was a woman with him—it was Fran Clinton—but she didn't appear to be armed. Gun in hand, Rudy stood to one side of her, his head turned away from Doc.

He didn't want to use the gun, of course. He could no more afford a racket than Doc and Carol could. His objective and Doc's would be exactly the same—to settle their score silently and unseen in the privacy of the cabin.

Doc hefted his gun, raised the barrel level with his shoulder. He edged silently around the corner of the building.

Rudy first—with one skull-crushing blow from the gun. Then, before the woman could move or yell, a hard left hook with his free hand.

Eyes fixed on them, Doc slowly raised and lowered his foot. It came down on an up-cornered brick, one of several that had once formed the border of a flower bed. And he fell headlong.

Falling, he triggered the gun; it was all he could do now.

Instantly Rudy whirled, gun blazing, whirling the woman in front of him. But his bullets passed above Doc, and Doc's drilled through the woman and into him.

And in seconds they lay dead on the ground, one of Rudy's hands still holding her arm behind her back.

From a couple of blocks away, the cabdriver heard the racket. But he did not place it as coming from Golie's, and certainly he did not connect it with his recent fares. Then he saw Doc and Carol running down the street toward him—*and, hey! look at the old gal run, would you?*—and puzzled he stopped the cab and got out.

"Somethin' wrong, folks? Somebody givin' you some trouble?"

"Yes," Doc told him. "I'll explain it while you're driving us into the city."

"Into Diego? But what about your grub? What . . ."

Doc jabbed a gun into his stomach, gave him a shove toward the cab. "Do you want to go on living? Do you? Then do what I tell you!"

The driver obeyed, but sullenly. With the dragging deliberation of the very stubborn. As they reached the highway and turned toward town, he gave Doc a self-righteous glare.

"This won't get you nothing," Mac," he said. "I don't know what you're after, but this won't get you a thing."

Doc looked at him, tight-lipped. In the back seat, Carol leaned forward anxiously. "Doc—I think he's right. There's probably an alert out for us already. Golie'll spill everything now. How far can we get in this circus wagon?"

Doc asked her curtly how far they would get without it. With an alert on the air, what chance did they have of grabbing another car? "The cops won't know what we're traveling in. Or whether we're traveling in anything. Maybe we can make it to the border before they find out."

"*To* the border! But what . . ."

"You'll never do it, Mac," the driver cut in doggedly. "The best thing you can do is give yourselves up. Now—*oof*!"

"Like it?" Doc gave him another prod with the gun. "Want some more?"

Teeth gritted, the man shook his head.

"All right, then," Doc said mildly. "Make a left here, and head straight up Mission Valley until I tell you to turn."

The cab swung left. They sped down the curving, cliff-shadowed road, and after a time Doc spoke over his shoulder to Carol. They couldn't get through the border gates, he said. That, obviously, would be impossible. But they might be able to slip across the line at some unguarded point.

"People do it all the time," he went on. "It's not the best bet in the world, and we'll still have problems if and when we get across, but . . ."

"You won't make it," the driver broke in, dogged again. "Not anywhere near the gates where you'll be tryin'. I know that border, mister, and I'm telling you . . ."

His sentence ended in a scream. The cab swerved, and he turned pain-crazed eyes on Doc. "You t-try that again!" he gasped. "You do that again and see what happens!"

Doc promised that he wouldn't do it again. "Next time I'll shoot you. Now go right at this next turn. We're hitting crosstown to the Tijuana highway."

The cab made the turn with an angry skidding of tires. They raced up the steep road into Mission Hills, then down the long arterial street which skirts San Diego's business district. The traffic began to thicken. There was the wail of a siren—fading eerily into the distance.

Above the windshield the blurred murmuring of the radio squawk box became a crisp voice:

"Cab Seventy-nine! Cab Seventy-nine! Come in, Seventy-nine . . ."

The driver was elaborately disinterested. Doc glanced at the identification plate on the instrument panel, and spoke to him sharply. "That's you. Answer it!"

"What d'you want me to say?"

"Tell her you've got a couple of people on a sightseeing tour. You'll be tied up for about an hour."

"Sightseeing tour?" The driver squirmed in the seat, leaned slightly over the wheel. "She won't never go for that, mister. She'll know I got a couple of crooks headin' for Tijuana."

"Wh-at?" Doc frowned. "How will she know?"

"She just will. She'll even know where we are right now. Just making the turnoff for National City."

Doc got it then. He linked the driver's seemingly senseless speech with the breathless silence of the squawk box. And savagely, his nerves worn raw, he smashed the gun barrel into the man's stubborn, doughish face.

He smashed it; he smashed it again. The driver groaned and flung himself against the door of the car. It shot open, and he went tumbling and bouncing into the street.

The door swung shut again. Doc fought the wheel of the cab, swinging it out of the path of an oncoming vehicle. There was a frozen silence from Carol; a wondering silence. Then, answering her unspoken question, the voice of the squawk-box:

"Seventy-nine? Seventy-nine—I read you, Seventy-nine . . ."

Doc found the switch and closed it.

He turned off the highway, sped along roughly parallel to it on a gravel country road.

He asked, "Is there a radio back there?" And Carol said there was none.

It didn't matter, of course. They both knew what would be happening by now.

The county road got them around National City. Then, implacably, it veered back toward the highway.

Doc tried to get away from it. Lights turned off, he weaved the cab through a network of outlying side streets. That got them only a little farther south, and in the end they were led back to the highway. Doc stopped just short of it, his mind racing desperately to the lazy throb of the cab's motor.

Take to the fields—run for it on foot? No, no, it was too late. As impractical and impossible as trying to hook another car.

Well, then, how about—how about moving in on one of these suburbanites? Holing up with them, holding the family hostage until there was a chance to make a break for it?

No again. Not with them penned in in so small an area. Holing up would simply eliminate the almost no-chance they had now.

Doc shrugged unconsciously. He watched the intermittent flash of lights in front of them, listened to the *swish-flick* of the cars speeding past the intersection. And finally, since there was nothing else to do, he drove back onto the highway again.

Other cars whipped past them, and laughter, snatches of happy conversation spilled out into the night. Pleasure seekers; people in a hurry to begin their evening of wining and dining across the border, and with nothing more to fear than a hangover in the morning.

People who had *earned* their good time.

Doc drove slowly. For once in his life, he had no plan. He saw no way out. They could not turn back. Neither could they cross the border, through the gates or any other way.

The police had only to wait for them. To close in the net until they were snared in it.

After a time he turned off the highway again, pursuing a winding trail until it came to a dead end by the ocean. He backed up, headed back in the direction from which he had come. And then he was again on the highway, moving south.

The other cars were not moving so quickly now. They shot past the cab, then a few hundred yards beyond they began to slow. And peering into the distance, Doc saw why.

So did Carol; and she spoke for the first time in minutes. Spoke with a tone that was at once angry, frightened, and a little gleeful. "Well, Doc. What do you figure on doing now?"

"Do?"

"The roadblock. What are you going to do?" Her voice broke crazily. "Just drive on into it? Just keep on going, and say yessir, I'm D-Doc McCoy, and th-this is my wife, Carol—and—a-and . . ."

"Shut up!" Doc cut in. "Look!"

"Don't you tell me t-to—look at what?"

"Just ahead of us there. That thing at the side of the road."

It seemed to be suspended some six feet above the roadside

embankment, an illuminated oblong blob topped by a larger and shadowy blob. Then, as the cab crept towards it, the outlines of the two blobs became clearer, revealed themselves as a woman's face beneath a man's hat.

She was holding a flashlight in her hand, shining the beam into her face. Swinging loosely from her other hand was a shotgun. A rawboned giant of a woman, she wore overalls and a sheepskin coat. She stared at them—at the cab rather; flicked the beam of the flashlight across it.

Then she made a brief swinging motion with it, the light disappeared, and so did she.

Doc let out a suppressed shout. He glanced over his shoulder quickly, waited for the two cars behind him to pass.

Carol shook him fiercely. "Doc, what's the matter with you? Who—what was that?" And Doc laughed a little wildly, babbled that he couldn't believe it himself. And then he slammed the cab into low gear, cut the wheels to the right, and went roaring up over the embankment and into the field.

It was wasteland, an expanse of eroded topsoilless rock. Ahead of them, the tall shadow of the woman beckoned, then moved away swiftly, guided them up over a rise in the land and down into a cuplike valley.

There was a house there, a dark, deserted-looking shack. Two great forms came bounding from behind it—mastiffs—and streaked toward the cab in deadly silence. But the woman spoke, gestured to them, and they came meekly to heel. Trotted along with her as she strode past the shack, and on into the darkness beyond it.

"Doc! Do you hear me? I want to know what this is all about!"

Doc didn't answer her. It was in his mind perhaps that he had already explained fully; and all his thoughts now were on the woman and the deliverance which she represented.

About a hundred yards beyond the house, she came to a stop; turned and faced them, beckoned them forward slowly until they were almost upon her. Then she stopped them with a pushing motion of her hand and yanked open the door of the cab. "Got anything in here that you want to save, Doc? Well, pile out then. We're gettin' rid of it for good."

They piled out. Just back of the point where the woman had been standing was a broad crater, the dull gleam of moonlight on dark water.

"Gravel pit," the woman explained succinctly. "Ain't got no bottom to it that I ever found. Now, we'll just give this buggy a good hard push . . ."

They pushed, straining, then trotting sluggishly as the cab gathered speed. Then, at a warning grunt from the woman, they came to a halt. And the cab shot over the brink of the pit, descended with a resounding splash and disappeared beneath the oily surface.

The woman turned and gripped Doc's hand. "Doc, you're a sight for sore eyes, and that's a fact. Couldn't hardly believe it was you when I got the word on the radio tonight."

"And you, needless to say, are also a sight for sore eyes," Doc murmured. "You were waiting for us down there on the highway?"

"Yep. Knew you was headin' this way. Just took a chance on you spotting me. Incidentally," her voice altered slightly, "not that I really give a whoop, but what happened between you and Rudy?"

"Well—" Doc hesitated. "You know Rudy. He never was quite right in the head and he'd gotten a lot worse. The more reasonable you tried to be with him, why . . ."

"Yeah, sure. Finally blew his top, huh? Well, I been expecting it for a long time." The woman shook her head wisely. "But to hell with the poor devil. Right now we got to hide you an'—and . . ."

She paused with rough delicacy, glancing at Carol.

Doc apologized hastily. "I'm sorry. Ma—Mrs. Santis—I'd like you to meet my wife, Carol."

It is scarcely to be wondered at that Carol's handshake had been a little limp. She had heard so much of this gaunt, craggy-faced woman for so long that she had almost come to regard her as a myth.

Ma Santis. Daughter of a criminal, wife of a criminal, mother of six criminal sons. Two of Ma's boys had died in gun battles with the police; two others—like their father—had died in the electric chair. Of the remaining two, one was in jail, and the other, Earl, was at liberty. The Santises were hill people, rebels and outlaws rather than criminals in the usual sense of the word. They never forgot a favor nor forgave an injury. They were that rare thing in the world of crime, people with a very real sense of honor. In another era, they might have been pirates or privateers or soldiers of fortune. It was their misfortune and perhaps the nation's as a whole that they had been born into a civilization which insisted upon conformity and pardoned no breakage of laws, regardless of one's needs or motives.

The Santises were unable to conform. They would have died, and did die, rather than attempt to. And now at age sixty-four, and after more than twenty years in prison, Ma was as completely unreconstructed as she had been at fourteen.

Her son Earl was living over in the black country, she explained. Doin' enough farming to look respectable, and livin' high on the hog from cached loot. "Been so long since me or him turned a trick that people plumb forgot all about us," Ma chuckled. "So I figures we'll probably get a good goin' over here at my place, but no more'n t'any other. You just hole up where I put you until Earl shows up, an'—by the by, you was headin' for El Rey's, Doc?"

"That's right."

"Well, don't you never doubt you'll make it," Ma said firmly. "Me'n Earl, we helped plenty of friends to get there—Pat Gangloni, Red Reading, Ike Moss an' his woman. 'Course, you're maybe a little hotter'n any of them, but—come here."

She turned and went back to the brink of the pit; squatted there, pointing with the beam of her flashlight. "You see that? Them two clumps of bushes? Now look right below them, there at them kind of shady places just under the water line."

"I see them," Doc nodded. "Caves?"

"You could call 'em that. Really ain't much more than holes. Just about big enough to crawl into and get out of sight, but that's all you need, ain't it?" Ma laughed jovially.

Doc hesitated, shooting a quick glance at Carol's taut face. "It—you think this is necessary, Ma? I mean . . ."

"Wouldn't have you do it if I didn't think so." There was a hint of tartness in her voice. "It ain't so bad, Doc. There's fresh air seeps in from somewhere, and it ain't really so cramped. Pat Gangloni took it, and you know Pat. Makes two fellas your size with half a man left over."

Doc forced himself to laugh at the joke. "We'll have to strip, I suppose?"

"I'd say so. Unless you want to keep on your unmentionables. They's blankets down there, an' it's kind of hot anyways."

"Fine," Doc said. "Well . . ."

He unbuttoned his jumper and dropped it to the ground. He sat down and began taking off his shoes and socks. Ma looked at Carol. She said, "Prob'ly need a rope," and disappeared into the darkness.

Carol remained standing, motionless, making no move to remove her clothes.

"Carol," Doc said. Then, "Carol!"

"No-no," Carol said shakily. "No, I can't! How do I know that— that . . ."

"You're with me. You're riding on my ticket. Now get out of those clothes!"

He stood up, stripped out of the jeans. He unbuckled the money belt and dropped it on top of the pile of clothing. He waited a moment, working up an encouraging smile, storing up warmth for his voice. Then, hand outstretched, he took a step toward Carol.

She backed desperately away from him. "N-no! *No!*" she gasped. "I know what you're planning! You'll get me down there and . . ."

"Stop it! What else can you do, anyway?"

"I know you! I'd never get back up again! She's your friend, not mine! She— y'you'd leave me down there under the ground and . . ."

"Well, here we are." Ma Santis was suddenly back with them. "Trouble?"

"I'm sorry," Doc said. "My wife's a little upset."

"Uh-huh," Ma drawled. "Thought she kind of sounded like she was. Me, I'm just a leetle upset myself. Figured I was goin' a long ways to do you two a favor, and now I ain't so sure. Like to get set straight before I go any farther."

Doc repeated that he was sorry. Ma shifted the shotgun under her arm, and behind her the two mastiffs suddenly came to attention. She waited, staring stonily at Carol. And as if from some great distance, Carol heard her own voice; felt her face stiffen in a conciliatory smile.

She was sorry. She hadn't meant what she said. She was grateful to Ma. She . . .

She broke off, stooping to pull the voluminous black dress over her head. Almost eagerly she unfastened the money belt, made a tentative gesture of offering it to the older woman. Ma motioned laconically with the gun. "Just drop it on the pile. An' don't worry about none of it showin' up missing."

"You help yourself to as much as you want," Doc said warmly. "I mean that, Ma. We . . ."

Ma nodded. She knew he meant it, but she wasn't needin' nothing. "Always thought you was a hell of a guy, Doc. Heard a thing or two to the contrary, but you was always square with me an' mine. Ain't a one of us that didn't think the world of you."

"And I've felt exactly the same way about all of you, Ma."

"But," she continued, "I ain't buyin' in on no one else's fight. I ain't putting myself any further in the middle than I am already. You two got a quarrel, which I hope you ain't, you settle it somewhere else. Elsewise, I'll do the settlin' and it won't be no fun for the party that starts the trouble."

She paused, looking from one to the other, waiting for their acknowledgements of her statement. Carol's was somewhat readier than Doc's.

"Well, that's fine," Ma said mildly. "Now there's some water in them holes; prob'ly a little stale but you can drink it if you're thirsty enough. No grub, o' course. You can do without for as long as you're down there. No smokin' and no matches; ain't enough air to allow it. Well, that about does it, I guess. Want me to help you down, Doc?"

Doc shook his head. "I can make it all right, thanks. Have you any idea how long it will be, Ma?"

"Well, I'd say tomorrow night. But you know how it is, Doc. Come see, come sah." She laughed throatily. "Oh, yeah, I knew I was forgettin' something. Sleepin' pills. Can't tell you where they are exactly, but just feel around an' you'll find 'em."

"Oh, fine. I was just going to ask about them. Now, if you'll just give me a little light for a moment, Ma . . ."

Ma squatted again, beamed the flashlight down the wall of the pit. Doc studied it, gave her shoulder a pat of thanks, and poised himself on the brink.

"Good night," he said, and shooting a smile at Carol, "and a very good night to you, my dear."

Then he jumped, stiff-legged.

There was an audible grunt as he struck the water.

He went under, and he came up. And then, getting a grip on the bushes, he pushed himself under again.

And stayed under.

"Now, there," Ma said quietly, "there is one hell of a guy. Just in case you didn't know it."

"I know it," Carol said.

She took the rope that Ma handed her, took a turn around her waist with it. Bellying down on the ground, she got her legs over the edge of the pit and squirmed slowly backward. She paused there, half-suspended in space, breathing very rapidly. Then she looked up and gave Ma the nod to lower her.

"Got somethin' on your mind?" Ma held her where she was for the moment. "Maybe you better unload it while you can."

"I—nothing, I guess. I was just going to ask about the sleeping pills. I mean, why you and Doc seem to take it for granted that we'll need them."

"Why?" Ma frowned incredulously. "Hey, you ain't been around much, have you, honey?"

"Well—I used to think so."

"Uh-huh," Ma said. "Mmm-hum. Well, I'll tell you somethin' about them pills. Don't you doubt that you'll need 'em. An' don't wait to take 'em until you do. You gulp you down some right to begin with, an' when them wears off . . ."

She tugged upward on the rope, then slacked off on it. Carol swung off at the brink, and moved slowly down toward the water.

"Yes?" she called, shivering as her feet touched the water. "When they begin to wear off?"

"Take some more," Ma said.

The hole lay on a slant and for its first two or three feet it was largely filled with water, making it all but impossible to breathe until one had navigated it.

Carol came through it at a frantic scramble; continued to scramble forward with eyes closed, breath held, until her head butted against the rock at the end of the hole. And then gratefully, gasping in the air, she let herself go prone.

Strangely, it was not absolutely dark. Wherever the faint seepage of air came from, there was an equally faint seepage of light, if only the relative light of the night outside, to relieve the blackness of this hidden cave.

It was like being in a coffin, she thought. A dimly lit, well-ventilated coffin. It wasn't uncomfortable; not yet at least. Merely confining. As long as one was content to remain in it, and did not try to get out . . .

Abruptly, she cut off the thought.

Fumbling in the dimness, running her hands up to the end of the hole, she encountered the oval canvas-covered surface of a water canteen. She shook it, felt the swish and swing of the liquid inside. She laid it down again and continued to fumble until she found a small tightly capped bottle. She got the cap off and sniffed the contents. Taking out one of the capsules, she pinched it and touched her tongue to it.

Mildly bitter; a faintly salty taste. She dropped it back into the bottle and screwed the lid back on.

She didn't need that stuff. She wasn't going to take anything that made her any more helpless than she was already. Ma had told her, in so many words, that she had nothing to fear. She and Doc were both under Ma's protection, until they struck out on their own again. But just the same, she wasn't knocking herself out with goof balls. Ma might be absolutely on the square. She might be. But Doc could outsmart someone like her, without even halfway trying. And if he decided to have things his own way, and if he thought it was safe—well, never mind. But no sleeping pills for her.

If they *were* sleeping pills.

Her mind moved around and around the subject, moving with a kind of fuzzy firmness. With no coherent thought process, she arrived at a conviction—a habit with the basically insecure; an insecurity whose seeds are invariably planted earlier, in under- or over-protectiveness, in a distrust of parental authority which becomes all authority. It can later, with maturity—a flexible concept—be laughed away, dispelled by determined clear thinking. Or it can be encouraged by self-abusive resentment and brooding self-pity. It can grow ever greater until the original authority becomes intolerable, and a change becomes imperative. Not to a radical one in thinking; that would be too troublesome, too painful. The change is simply to authority in another guise which, in time, and under any great stress, must be distrusted and resented even more than the first.

Thrashing it—and herself—Carol wondered why she feared Doc as she did—how she could fear him and be unable to trust him. And yet love him as she could never love another.

Even now, despite her fear and distrust, she would have given anything to have him with her.

He was always, or virtually always, so calm and self-assured. He always knew just what to do, and how to do it. He could be breaking apart inside and you'd never know it from the way he acted. He'd be just as pleasant and polite as if he didn't have a care in the world. You had to be careful with someone like that. You could never know what he was thinking. But . . .

She sighed uxoriously, squirming a little. Doc McCoy—one hell of a guy, Ma had called him. And that had seemed to say it all.

There just wasn't anyone else in the world like Doc, and there never would be.

She toyed with the bottle of pills. Then, turning on her side, she tapped on the wall with it. He couldn't be too far away from her, just a few feet through this coldly sweating rock. If she could make him hear her, and if he would reply to it—well, it would be nice. Each would be comforted, she persuaded herself, to know that the other was all right.

She tapped and listened. Tapped and listened. She frowned, with a kind of angry nervousness. Then, brightening, she turned and tapped on the opposite wall. Perhaps he was there, on that side. After all, he just about had to be, didn't he? He had to be on one side or the other.

She tapped and listened. Tapped and listened.

The silence between tappings pressed in around her. It became an aching thing, a void crying to be filled. It was unbearable, and since the unbearable cannot be borne, her imagination, that friendly enemy, stepped in.

Quite clearly, she heard Doc's answering taps. Well, not clearly perhaps—the imagination does have its limitations—but she did hear them.

She tapped and he—it—tapped. The signals went back and forth.

A great relief spread through her; and then, on its heels, overlaying it, an increasing restlessness and irritation.

What was the point in just tapping, in just making a meaningless noise? Now, if she could send him a message. Ask him, tell him to—to . . .

But maybe he'd already thought of that. And thought it was impossible. And maybe it was.

She pushed herself back against the wall, then measured the space to the opposite wall. There seemed to be enough room, for two people, that is. It could get to be a tight squeeze, of course, you couldn't continue it indefinitely. But just for a little while, an hour or so, it would be fine.

The overhead space? Well. She placed her palms against the roof of the hole, gave a start at its nearness to her. In the dimness it had seemed much farther away. She pushed on it, not realizing that she was pushing. And suddenly she pounded on it with her fists.

She stopped that very quickly, and lay very still for a few minutes until the wild pounding of her heart had stopped. Then, pushing herself with heels and elbows, she began to scoot toward the entrance.

Water touched her feet. She jerked them away from it. She let them slide into it again, and remain there for a moment. And then with resentful resignation she withdrew them. For obviously she couldn't leave this place, go back out into the pit. Someone might see her. For all she knew, the place might be swarming with cops by this time. At any rate, the water was very deep—bottomless, Ma had said—and she could swim very little. If she should be unable to find the hole Doc was in, or if she was unable to get into it or get back into this one . . .

Perhaps *they* had planned it that way. *They* hoped and expected that she would try to leave, knowing that she would drown if she did.

But, anyway, leaving was out of the question. She had to stay here until she was got out, as—her pendulum mind swinging back again—she assured herself she would be. Doc would get her out. After all, she was his wife and they'd been through a lot together, and she'd done a lot for him. And—and—if he'd really wanted to get rid of her, he'd had plenty of chances before this.

He'd get her out all right, as soon as it was safe.

Ma would make him.

It was just a little roomier, down here near the entrance to the hole. The roof was just a little higher. She measured the distance with her upstretched palms, thinking that there was almost room enough to sit up. And no sooner had the thought entered her mind than she knew she must sit up.

She had to. She could not remain prone, or lie half-propped up on her elbows another minute.

Tucking her chin against her chest, she raised herself experimentally. Six inches, a foot, a foot and a half, a—the stone pressed against her head. She shoved against it stubbornly, then with a suppressed "*Ouch!*" she dropped back to the floor.

She rested for a moment, then tried again. A kind of sideways try this time, with her knees pulled upward. That got her up a little farther, though not nearly far enough. But it did—or seemed to—show her how the trick could be done.

She was very lithe and limber, more so now than ever after the arduous thinning-down of their cross-country journey. So she sucked her stomach in, drew her knees flat against it, and pressed her chin down against them. And thus, in a kind of flat ball, she flung herself upward and forward.

Her head struck the roof with a stunning bump, then skidded along it gratingly, leaving a thin trail of hair and scalp. She would have stopped with the first painful impact, but the momentum of her body arced her onward. And then at last she was sitting up. Or rather, sitting, bent forward as she was, it would have been far from accurate to say that she was sitting *up*.

The roof pressed upon her neck and shoulders. Her head was forced downward. Her widespread legs were flattened against the floor, and, to support herself, she had her hands placed between them. She raised one of them to brush at her face, but the strain was so intolerable that she hastily put it back in use as a brace.

She rested, breathing heavily, finding it difficult to breathe at all in that constricting position; thinking, Well, at least I know I can do it now. I can sit up if I want to. Then, as the awkward pose became agonizing, she tried to lie down again. And was held almost motionless exactly as she was.

She couldn't accept the fact. It was too terrible. Now, surely, she thought, if I got into this, I can get out of it. If I can sit up, then I can s—I can lie down again.

"Of course I can," she spoke, grunted, aloud. "Why not, anyway?"

There was, of course, every reason why not. It was impossible to draw her legs up, as she had in the first instance. Almost impossible to move them at all. As for balling herself up—well, she already was; even more than she had been originally. But now there was no give in the ball. Her body was like an overburdened spring, so heavily laden that it can only go down farther and never up.

"No," she said quietly. "No."

Then, on an ascending note, "No, no, n-no!"

She waited, panting, the blood running to her head and her hair tumbled over her eyes. Her wrists throbbed, and her elbows ached with sugary pain. And suddenly they doubled under her and her torso lurched downward, and a tortured scream burbled from her lips.

Sobbing painfully, she braced herself again. Tears ran down her face, and she could not brush them away. And in her agony and growing hysteria, that seemed the most unbearable thing of all.

"C-can't—can't even raise a finger," she wept. "Can't even r-raise a . . ."

Then, so softly that she could hardly be heard, "Ma said tomorrow night. Tomorrow night, prob'ly."

The words trickled off into silence. Her panting grew more labored. She wheezed and coughed, groaned with the jerking of her body, and her tears ran harder.

"I—I can't—stand—it!" she gasped. "You hear me? *I can't stand it!* Can't stand it, can't stand it, *c-caa-an't stand eet, can't stand ee-yaahhhhhh* . . ."

She screamed and the pain of the exertion caused her to scream even louder, and that scream wrung still another from her throat. She writhed and screamed, gripped in a frenzy of pain and fury. Her head pounded against the roof and her heels dug and kicked into the floor, and her elbows churned and banged and scraped against the imprisoning sides of the hole.

Blood mingled with the tears on her face. It streamed down her back, over her arms and legs and thighs. From a hundred tiny cuts and scratches and bruises it came, coating her body; warm red blood—combining slippery with the dust of the cave.

She never knew when she broke free. Or how. Or that she had. She was still struggling, still screaming, when she got the cap off the pill bottle and upended it into her mouth . . .

Peevishly, she came up out of the pleasant blackness. Something was gripping her ankle, and she tried to jerk away from it. But the thing held tight. It yanked, skidding her down the hole, peeling more hide from her body. She cried out in protest, and the cry was choked off suddenly as water closed over her.

Choking and kicking, she slid out of the hole and into the pit. It was night again—or night still? And in the moonlight, she looked blurrily into the flattest eyes she had ever seen.

"I'm Earl," he grinned, showing twisted teeth. "Just hold tight now, and I'll getcha . . ."

"Leggo!" She flung herself frantically backward. "Just leave me alone! I don't want to go anywhere! P-please, please, don't make me! Just let me s-stay where . . ."

She made a grab for the bushes, tried to pull herself back into the hole. Treading water, Earl gave her a hard slap in the face.

"Son of a gun," he mumbled, getting a rope around her waist, signaling to Ma and Doc. "Wasn't forty-eight hours enough for yuh?"

THIRTEEN

Covered by odds and ends of sacking, Doc and Carol lay in the rear of Earl's old truck and were taken joltingly back through the hills to a country road, and thence on several miles to the so-called farm where Earl lived. It was a shabby, rundown place with a grassless junk-littered yard, a cow, a few chickens, a couple of acres of fruit trees and two or three more of truck crops. Inside the weatherbeaten house, however, with its bare warped floors and boarded up windows, there was an outsize color TV set, a huge deep freeze and a refrigerator, and an enormous wood-fuel range.

Earl was obviously proud of these possessions, and Doc complimented him on them. Laconically, trying to conceal his pleasure, Santis took a large beef roast from the oven and slapped it platterless on the table. As he whacked it into great bleeding chunks, Ma set out other "vittles"—cold boiled cabbage, bread, a pot of coffee, a gallon jug of bonded whiskey—and tin cups and plates. They all sat down then, and everyone but Carol began to eat hungrily. She sat dazed and listless, her stomach turning queasily, hardly able to tolerate the sight and the smell of the food.

Ma gave her an appraising look, and reached for the whiskey jug. She filled a tin cup—pronounced *tin*-cup—half full of the white liquid and thrust it across the table.

"Now, you drink that," she ordered. "Go on! Don't make me tell you twice."

Carol drank it. She swallowed hastily, trying to swallow back the sickness, and then a comforting fire spread through her stomach, and a little color came back into her face.

"Now, eat," Ma said. And Carol ate. And after the first few bites, the food tasted very good to her.

Both of her eyes were slightly blackened. Her mouth was puffy and bruised, and her face and hands were a mass of scratches and cuts. But no one commented on her appearance, or inquired into the why of it. Old hands in the sleazy bypaths of crime, they could pretty well guess what had happened to her.

She kept her eyes on the plate, taking no part in their conversation. As indifferent to it as though it had nothing to do with her.

Needless to say, she and Doc were still very hot. It would be impossible for them to sneak across the Mexican border, and make their way down into the interior by land. But Ma and Earl had lined up a good seaward contact—the captain of a small Portuguese fisherman who had handled similar ventures for them before.

"No one with the kind of heat you two got, o'course." Ma took a swig of whiskey, belched and wiped her mouth with the back of her hand. "He's stallin' now, trying to weasel out of the deal. But he'll come around in a day or so, soon's he sees it ain't getting him nowheres."

"You mean," Doc frowned warily, "you mean he knows who we are?"

Ma said sure, naturally the fellow knew. "Who else would be skippin' the country right now? But don't you worry none about it, Doc. He knows all about us Santises, and you got nothing to worry about."

"I see," Doc said. "Yes, I'm sure you're right."

Roy Santis would be getting out of prison in another year or so. That would make three of them on the loose, not to mention their manifold kinsfolk and friends. And no one who was even slightly familiar with the Santis reputation would do anything to offend them. Anyone who did, in hope of reward or in fear of punishment, would never live to brag about it.

The meal over, Earl filled a crockery jug with water and led Carol and Doc down through his gullied backyard to a haystack-size mound of manure. It was partly dug out, roofed over with boards which were in turn covered with manure. Facing away from the house, the entrance was covered with a piece of canvas which was smeared with cow dung, dried now but apparently applied when wet.

Diffidently Earl handed Doc the water jug. "Get you some grub too, if you want it, Doc. Just figured you'd want to do your eatin' at night when you could come outside."

"Of course," Doc said. "We won't want a thing now, Earl."

"Well—oh, yeah. No smokin'—guess you don't need me to tell you that. Don't believe I'd even light a match if I was you. Little smoke or fire shows a long ways off."

"I understand. There won't be any," Doc promised.

"Ever chaw? Got an extra plug with me you can have."

"Well, now, that might be all right," Doc said. "Thank you very much, Earl."

Earl went back to the house. Doc politely held the canvas door aside, and waited for Carol to precede him.

It was an hour or so before dawn. Without a word, Carol curled up on the floor and was almost immediately asleep again. Doc hunkered down against the wall and took a chew of tobacco. He had slept himself out during the past two days and nights. Now sleeping was something to be done when he could no longer stay awake; something to be conserved against the boredom of wakefulness. He chewed and spat, carefully covering up the spittle each time. Occasionally he looked at the dark shadow that was Carol, and his eyes became brooding and thoughtful.

With the first rays of sunlight, the manure pile began to gather heat. By ten o'clock, when Carol came suddenly awake, Doc had stripped himself naked except for his shoes and socks, and was sitting cross-legged on his pile of clothes.

He shook his head warningly as she broke into startled laughter, then grinned in good-natured self-deprecation. "Which would you say was the funniest?" he whispered. "Me or the symbolism of the situation?"

"I can't decide." She laughed softly. "Maybe I'd better get into the act myself."

She undressed, wiping away the sweat with her clothes, making a cushion of them as Doc had with his. And now that they were alone, Doc showed a great deal of concern about her many cuts and bruises. Carol made little of them; she deserved them, she said, for making a darned fool of herself. But she was pleased by his solicitude, and completely rested and relaxed, she felt very kindly toward him.

Head tilted to one side, she gave him an impish look. Then, leaning forward suddenly, she took his bristled face in her hands and . . .

A soggy mass struck her on the forehead, slid down across her face. She sat back abruptly, scrubbing and brushing at herself. "Gaah!" she spat disgustedly, nose wrinkled. "Ugh! Of all the filthy, messy . . ."

"Now, that was a shame," Doc said. "It's the heat, I suppose. It softens this stuff up and . . ."

"Please!" She grimaced. "Isn't it bad enough without you drawing me a picture?"

That was the end of any lovemaking. Doc withdrew behind the calm mask of his face, and Carol sank back into her former listlessness. As the long hours dragged by, she talked to herself silently; jeered at the vague *they* and *them* for the fools that they were.

A lot of fun, isn't it? Oh, sure! Just like the movies. Real dramatic and exciting. Two big, bad, brainy bank robbers, hiding naked in a pile of manure!

The heat brought hordes of flies. It brought out swarms of corpse-colored grub worms, which dropped down on their heads and backs or crawled up under them from the floor. And it brought a choking, eye-watering stench, which seemed to seep through every pore of their skins.

Once, in desperation, Carol started to swing back the canvas door.

But Doc pushed her away from it firmly. "You know better than that. Try a chew of tobacco."

"Tobacco? That'll kill the smell of this stuff?"

"No. But it'll take the taste of it out of your mouth."

She hesitated, then held out her hand. "Gimme. I can't be any sicker than I am already."

She took a small chew. It did make her sicker, but it was a different kind of sickness, and even that was a relief.

She and Doc sat chewing and spitting, not bothering to cover the spittle, not having to. The manure dripped and plopped down on it. And the flies swarmed, and the bugs crawled. And so the long day dragged on, and at last it was night.

Earl carried several pails of water down from the house, and they were able to douse away some of the filth. But the stench and the tobacco-tainted taste of it remained with them. It flavored the little food they were able to eat; in their imagination they could even taste it in the whiskey which Earl served them from a hip-pocket bottle.

There was no one at the house, so Earl had to get back to it quickly. Which meant that Carol and Doc could not linger in the open as they had hoped to. Reluctantly they went back beneath the canvas door flap and into the wretchedness of another night. Doc settled himself down to as much comfort as he could create. Carol moved restlessly from one spot to another on the filthy floor.

Why? she whispered fiercely. Why did they have to be *here?* First those terrible underwater holes that even a rat would have run from, and now this—this—place. It didn't make sense. After all, there'd been plenty of heat on them after they'd jumped the train, and they'd had to hide then. But never had they'd holed up in anything as bad as the Santises had provided.

"We were on the move then," Doc pointed out mildly. "We weren't pinned down in so small an area."

"I don't care! I say we could hide just as well in some place that we could at least *stand*—that was endurable, I mean."

Doc said that they seemed to have endured thus far. Then, patiently, he went on to explain that the best hiding place was always the one which seemed utterly impossible for human habitation. The water holes, for example; as she had said, even a rat would have shied from them. And now the manure pile. If it was nauseously repellent even at a distance, who would expect anyone to take refuge inside of it?

Carol listened dully. Then ceased to listen. Or to think. She'd better not complain any more, she guessed. Her position was uncertain enough as it was. Unlike Doc, however, she had not schooled herself to accepting what she could not change, so she simply deadened herself to it. Lapsing into a blind, blank lifelessness where time was at once endless and nonexistent.

They were in the manure pile for two more nights and days.

On the third night, Earl came down to them without his usual burden of provisions.

"Grab yourself a bite at the house," he explained. "Get cleaned up, too. Looks like you're on your way."

Earl lounged on the porch, his pack of vicious-looking curs romping around him. Seated around the kitchen table were Ma, the boat captain, Carol and Doc. Carol's hair was cut short to her head. Both she and Doc wore rolled-up stocking caps, jeans, and loosely fitting sweat shirts. To all appearances they were one with the captain's crew—his three kinsmen who stood behind his chair, beaming, frowning, smiling, as the case might be, in exaggerated imitation of his expression.

Right now they were all frowning.

"But twenty-five thousan'!" The captain rolled his eyes heavenward. "What is twenty-five thousan' for such a risk? A mere pittance!"

"Then it ain't really the risk you mind," Ma said drily, "long as you get paid enough for it. That's the way it sizes up, Pete?"

"Well . . ."

"Sure it is. So you got a bigger risk, and you're gettin' bigger money. Twice what you ever got before. An' that's more'n fair, and it's all you're gonna get."

The two money belts were on the table. Ma opened them, and counted out an equal amount from each.

Melodramatically, the captain continued his protests. "It will not do, señora! Me, I do not mind. We are old friends, an' with friends one is generous. But my crew—" he turned and shook his head at them. "You see? They will not do it! They insis' that . . ."

"Who you kiddin'?" Ma laughed. "Them ginks don't even know what we're talkin' about."

The captain scowled, then, his manner undergoing a complete change, he also laughed. "Well, one must always try, yes? Even with friends, it is no less than a duty. But now that we are agreed . . ."

He reached for the money. Ma dropped a hamlike hand over it.

"When you get back," she said. "When I get the word from these people that they got to where they were goin', safe an' sound an' with all their belongings."

"But—but," the captain sputtered, coloring. "You think I am stool pigeon? You do not trust me, yes?"

"Huh-uh. Didn't say nothin' like that."

"Then why? An' suppose there is trouble? What if I could not come back, eh?"

"Then you wouldn't get no money. An'," she gave him a steady look, "you wouldn't need none, Pete."

His eyes fell. He mumbled weakly that the matter was really nothing to dispute about; he was quite content to wait for his money. Ma nodded, wadded the bills into a roll and tucked it into the front of her dress.

Earl came in from the porch. Everyone shook hands, and Doc suggested lightly that Ma and Earl come along on the journey. They demurred, grinning at each other as though exchanging some secret joke. "Guess not, Doc. Me 'n' Earl kind of likes it here."

"Yeah," said Earl. "Yes, sir, we like it real well here."

"An' o' course, we couldn't leave now, nohow. Not with Roy still in the pen."

Doc said that he understood. There was an awkward moment of silence with no one seemingly able to speak or move. And then, prompted by something in Ma's attitude, Doc felt constrained to proffer payment for the help which she and Earl had rendered.

"I'd really feel much better about it," he said with wholly insincere sincerity. "I know you've said you don't need any money, but . . ."

"We-el, let's see now," Ma said. "What you think it's been worth to you, Doc?"

"Why—" he kept his smile warm, but there was a cold lump in his stomach. Several times already he had mentally totted up the money in the belts and divided it by two. "Why, I wouldn't put a figure on it, Ma. It's worth whatever you say it is, and whatever you say is a hundred percent okay with me."

"How'd five grand strike you?"

Five! He'd been expecting—well, he didn't know just what. But when people tapped you on a deal like this, it was usually for most of what you had. And there was nothing you could do but like it.

"It's not enough," he declared, generous in his relief. "I'd be getting a bargain at ten."

"Knew you'd take it that way." Ma wagged her head with satisfaction. "Told Earl you would, didn't I, son? But it ain't for us, Doc. What I had in mind was, if you're sure that five or ten won't pinch you . . ."

"Ten. And it doesn't matter if it does pinch!"

"Well, I'd like you to pass it on to Pat Gangloni. I told you he was down there, I guess. He wasn't carryin' very heavy when he skipped, an' I been pretty concerned about him."

"Good old Pat," Doc said. "I'll see that he gets it, Ma."

"I'd o' helped him myself. But he was in an' out awful fast, an' I didn't have nothin' I could get at in a hurry. So," she wrung his hand, "I'm right pleased you'll be looking out for him. Know you mean to or you wouldn't say so."

"It's as good as done," Doc promised. "After all, Pat's a mighty good friend of mine, too."

They rode in the captain's car with Doc in the front seat between him and one of his crew, and Carol in the rear between the remaining two crewmen. Fog was thickening over San Diego, slowly descending upon the bay. The car crept through it cautiously, coming into the quay from the north, then circling the city's civic center, and returning from the south.

The boat was a sturdy fifty-footer, tied up about halfway down the long wharf. There were other seagoing craft on either side of it, a shrimp fisherman and a pleasure launch, but both were silent and dark. The captain parked the car and put the keys in the glove compartment. (It would be picked up by one of his many kinsmen.) He opened the door, spoke quickly in Portuguese and English. "Now, we are in a hurry; so we must be to go out with the tide. But we are not running. We go slow fast, yes?"

His teeth gleamed in a nervous smile. He got out and the others followed him, and they moved with unhurried haste across the quay. The captain leaped aboard, held out his hands to Carol. Doc landed on the deck a second behind her, and calling low-voiced instructions over his shoulder, the captain showed them to his tiny cabin. It was to be theirs for the voyage. He himself would bunk with the crew.

He closed the door behind him; and there was a murmuring of voices, a blurred confusion of sounds. Then the roar—quickly muted—of the boat's twin diesels. And they moved out into the bay.

The captain came back, drew the shades over the portholes and turned on the light. "You will be very quiet, yes?" He smiled his white, nervous smile. "On the water, the sound she travels far."

He left again. Almost imperceptibly, the boat gathered speed. They slid deeper and deeper into the fog, and the gray mass of it closed in behind them.

Doc prowled about the cabin, automatically inspecting it as he did any place that was strange to him. He was looking for nothing in particular. Simply looking. Most top-drawer criminals have this habit. It had saved Doc's life several times, conversely bringing about the loss of another's life or other's lives on each occasion.

He checked the small shelf of books, and the first-aid cabinet. He looked under the bunk, smiling an apology at Carol who had lain down on it. He poked through the pigeonholes of the desk, located a key ring and unlocked and examined each of the drawers. Relocking them—and leaving their contents exactly as he had found them—he turned his attention to the heavy chest at the foot of the bunk.

It was padlocked at either end. Doc made a selection from the keys on the ring, found the appropriate ones on the first try and raised the heavy oak lid. There was a quantity of grayish blankets inside; also, bedded between them, several boxes of ammunition, two repeating rifles and two twelve-gauge double-barreled shotguns. Doc's eyes lit up. Then, almost absently, he loaded the shotguns, laid them at the top of the chest and lowered the lid. He put the locks back on their staples—not locked, although they appeared to be. That completed his inspection and its corollary activities, and he rehid the keys in their pigeonhole and fixed himself a drink.

Lying in the bunk, Carol watched her husband for a few moments, then turned on her side and closed her eyes. His behavior was merely another variation of a norm. If there was anything more than that behind it, he would tell her. When and if the telling became necessary.

She slept.

Almost immediately, it seemed, she came awake again.

Out there in the night, there was a peculiar echo to the boat's diesels. Or, no, it wasn't an echo, but the mounting purr of another engine. And against the blinded portholes, pushing stubbornly through the fog, was a fuzzy beam of light.

The cabin was dark. There was silence—tense, expectant—and then Doc's harsh whisper. Carol could see him now, feel him sitting at her side. And near the door she saw the white flash of the captain's teeth.

"You do what I tell you to, Pete. My wife and I will do the rest."

"No! Please, señor! I cannot—it is not necessary! Only a small launch, no more than three men, I know! All . . ."

"That makes it all the better."

"Please! I tell you we do not have to! I swear it, and I know thees Coast Guard. Am I a stranger to them? Have I not made this same run many times? We will chat for a few moments, perhaps, and . . ."

"And they'll hold you up in the meantime. Find out who you are, and where you're headed. Get all the dope they need to have us nailed by a cruiser."

"But—but—" there was a desperate sob in the darkness. "But later, señor? What of that? His position will have been known, and it will be known that I, my boat, was . . ."

"You can blame it on me. My wife and I slipped on board without your knowledge, and took charge of your guns and ammunition."

"Ha! They will believe such a story?"

"Why not? It's a pretty good one." Doc paused ominously. "In fact, I'd say it was a lot better than the other one."

"You say! It is easy for—what other one?"

"The one you'd have to tell Ma Santis. Not that it would do you any good, Pete. Nothing you could tell her would do any good."

"But . . ."

The captain sighed heavily. The purr of the motor launch swelled to a sluggish drone.

"I don't like it either, Pete," Doc said earnestly. "I hate killing, and I particularly hate this. But what else can I do?"

"What else?" It scarcely sounded like the captain's voice. "Yes, what else, señor? What could possible be dearer than one's own life?"

He turned and left. A moment later there was a cry of "Ahoy, there! Ahoy, *Elena Isabella*!" Then a gentle bump and the scraping of wood against wood.

Doc cocked the shotguns. He handed one of them to Carol, and silently opened the two portholes.

There were three men in the launch: a gunner, the steersman, and its captain, a young lieutenant. He stood with one foot braced on the side of his boat, cap pushed back on his head. The steersman slouched nearby, an elbow hooked over the windshield. Hands in his pockets, the gunner stood by his stern-mounted machine gun.

Doc studied him. He put a restraining hand on Carol's arm. Wait! Perhaps the three would draw closer together.

"What's the big hurry, Pete?" The lieutenant spoke in an amiable drawl; a friend addressing a friend. "Weren't trying to run away from me, were you?"

"R-run?" the captain laughed shakily. "Who runs? Who is in a hurry?"

"Didn't bait up tonight, did you? Why not?"

"Why? Because I did so this afternoon. Also I iced, fueled, provisioned, keesed my wife . . ."

"Okay, okay," the lieutenant chuckled. "Got any coffee in the galley? Jack, bring us our bucket back there."

The gunner came forward with a tin lunch pail. The lieutenant extended it upward, holding onto him for support.

"*Now!*" said Doc.

He got the two of them, almost cutting them in half at the waist with one double blast. They doubled over, toppled down into the dark water between the two boats. Carol's shot got the steersman in the face and chest. He was still alive when two of the fisherman's crew tossed him over the side, and blinded, faceless, he managed to struggle to the surface. Mercifully one of the men crushed his skull with an axe. Then they chopped a hole in the bottom of the launch, and leaped back aboard their own craft.

The diesels roared frantically. The boat lunged at the waves, lunged through them like a terrified thing. Running as though it could never run far enough, as though it would run forever. And then, as the hours passed, slowing. For what was done was done, and for now, at least, there was no need to run.

As for Carol and Doc . . .

They lay in one another's arms; replete, reunited at last. And Doc held her very close, stroked her head protectively. For she was his wife, much dearer to him than the average wife to the average husband. And if circumstances compelled him to think of her as an opponent—and he was not sure that they did, just yet—it was with no less love and a very great deal of regret.

She shivered against him, made muffled sounds against his chest. He emitted a few husbandly there-theres, murmured that everything was all right now. Then, realizing that she was laughing, he gave her a tender kiss. "Now, what's so funny, hmmm?"

"Y-you! I—I—don't be angry, Doc, but . . ."

"Of course I won't be. Now what did I do that amused you?"

"N-nothing! It was—well, just you!" She snickered delightedly. "You never really planned on staying in Mexico, did you? You never stopped hoping you could. Someday, somehow, you intended to do it. I could tell. I watched your expression when we were coming down on the train to San Diego, and—and . . ."

"And?"

"Well, you know. Now you can't. Not after that deal tonight."

"Correction," Doc said. "Now *we* can't."

FOURTEEN

The tiny area where El Rey is uncrowned king appears on no maps and, for very practical reasons, it has no official existence. This has led to the rumor that the place actually does not exist, that it is only an illusory haven conjured up in the minds of the wicked. And since no one with a good reputation for truth and veracity has ever returned from it . . .

Well, you see?

But it is there, all right.

Lying in a small coastal group of mountains, it suffers from sudden and drastic changes in climate. It is almost impossible to dress for it, the barely adequate clothes of one hour becoming a sweltering burden the next. And somehow, doubtless as an outgrowth of these climatic phenomena, one is always a little thirsty. Still, many tropical and semitropical climates have these same disadvantages, and worse. And there is this to be said for El Rey's kingdom: it it healthy. Disease is almost unknown. Even such man-created maladies as malnutrition and starvation are minus much of their normal potency, and a man may be almost consumed by them before he succumbs to them.

It is an excellent place in many ways. Healthy. Possessed of a climate to suit every taste. Protected by the largest per capita police force in the world. Yet there is constant grumbling among its expatriate guests. One of the commonest causes of complaint, strangely, is that all accommodations—everything one must buy—are strictly first class.

Not that they are exorbitantly priced, understand. On the contrary. A four-bathroom villa, which might cost several thousand a month in some French Riviera resort, will rent for no more than a few hundred. But you can get nothing for less than that. You must pay that few hundred. It is the same with food and drink, nothing but the very best; with clothes, cosmetics, tobacco, and a hundred other things. All quite reasonably priced for what they are, but still worrisomely expensive to people who have just so much money and can get no more.

El Rey manifests great concern over these complaints, but there is a sardonic twinkle in his ageless old eyes. Naturally, he provides only the best for his guests. Isn't it what they always wanted elsewhere? Didn't they insist on having it, regardless of cost? Well, then! He goes on to point out that less exquisite accommodations and material goods would encourage an undesirable type of immigrant; persons his present guests would not care to be identified with. For if they did, they obviously would not be what they were nor be where they were.

Watching their assets trickle, nay, pour away on every side, people scheme and struggle feverishly to economize. They cut down on food, they do without drink, they wear their clothes threadbare. And the result is that they are just as much out of pocket as if they had bought what they did without.

Which brings us to the subject of El Rey's bank, another cause for bitter complaint.

The bank makes no loans, of course. Who would it make them to? So the only available source of revenue is interest, paid by the depositor rather than to him. On balances of one hundred thousand dollars or more, the rate is six percent; but on lesser sums it rises simply, reaching a murderous twenty-five percent on amounts of fifty thousand and under. Briefly, it is almost imperative that a patron keep his account at or above the one hundred thousand figure. But he may not do this by a program of skimping and doing without. When one's monthly withdrawals fall under an arbitrary total—the approximate amount which it should cost him to live at the prevailing first-class scale—he becomes subject to certain "inactive account" charges. And these, added to his withdrawals, invariably equal that total.

This is just about as it has to be, of course. El Rey must maintain an elaborately stocked commissary; and he can only do so on a fixed-patronage basis. Such is the rule in almost every first-class resort. A certain tariff is collected from every guest, and whether he uses what he pays for is strictly up to him.

To strike another analogy: no one is compelled to deposit his money in El Rey's bank. But the resort management, specifically the police, will assume no responsibility if it is stolen—as it is very likely to be. There is good reason to believe that the police themselves do the stealing from nondepositors. But there is no way of proving it, and certainly nothing to be done about it.

So the complaints go on. El Rey is unfair. You can't win against him. ("You would argue fairness with me, señor. But why should you expect to win?") He listens courteously to all grievances, but you get no satisfaction from him. He tosses your words back at you, answers questions with questions, retorts with biting and ironic parables. Tell him that such and such a thing is bad, and suggest a goodly substitute, and he will quote you the ancient proverb about the king with two sons named Either and Neither. "An inquiry was made as to their character, señor. Were they good or bad boys, or which was the good and which the bad. And the king's reply? 'Either is neither and Neither is either.' "

People curse him. They call him the devil, and accuse him of thinking he is God. And El Rey will nod to either charge. "But is there a difference, señor? Where is the difference between punishment and reward when one gets only what he asks for?"

Most immigrants to the kingdom come in pairs, married couples or simply couples. For the journey is an arduous one, and it can seldom be made without the devoted assistance of another. In the beginning, each will handle his own money, carefully contributing an exact half of the common expenses. But this is awkward, it leads to arguments, and no matter how much the individual has he is never quite free of the specter of want. So very soon there is a casual discussion of the advantages of a joint account, and it is casually agreed that they should open one. And from then on—well, the outcome depends on which of the two is the shrewder, the more cold-blooded or requires the least sleep.

And whoever is the survivor, and thus has the account at his disposal, will not be alone long. He will be encouraged to seek out another partner, or one will seek him out. And when their association terminates, as it must, there will be still another.

The process goes on and on; inevitable, immutable. As simple as ABC.

Mention was made of El Rey's police; the protection they provide the populace. But this is a word of broad implications. If one is to protect, he may not annoy. He must remember that life belongs to the living. He will be wise to refrain from stepping over the line of his obvious duty to harry down a miscreant who may not exist.

Sluggings are unheard of in El Rey's dominion. No one is ever shot, stabbed, bludgeoned, strangled, or brought to death by the usual agencies of murder.

In fact, there are no murders. Officially, there are none. The very high death rate derives from the numerous suicides and the immigrant's proclivity for fatal accidents.

The fine swimming pools of the various villas are rarely used. The horses in the public stables grow fat for want of exercise, and the boats stand rotting in their docks. No one fishes, no one hunts, no one plays golf, tennis, or darts. Briefly, except for El Rey's annual grand ball, there is almost no social life. Anyone approaching another is suspect or suspicious.

Doc hardly knew what to do with himself. One day, a few months after his arrival, he took a walk up into the hills; and there, nestled in a pleasant valley and hidden from the city, he came upon a village. The one street was attractively cobblestoned; the buildings were freshly whitewashed. Drifting to him on the breeze came the smell of roasting peppery meat. The only people in sight were two men down near the end of the street, who were sweeping the cobblestones with long-handled brooms. Doc recognized them; he raised his hand in a half-salute. But not seeing him apparently, they finished their sweeping and disappeared inside a building.

"Yes, señor?" A blue-uniformed *carabinero* stepped out of a nearby doorway. "I may be of service?"

"Nothing," Doc smiled. "I thought for a moment that I recognized those two men."

"The streetsweepers? They are friends of yours?"

"Oh, no. Not at all. Hardly know them as a matter of fact."

"I see. Well, they are newly arrived, those two. They will live here now, in case you should wonder about their absence from their usual haunts."

Doc looked around; commented on the pleasing appearance of the place. The *carabinero* agreed that everything was indeed well kept. "It is required. Each resident contributes such labor as he is able to."

"Uh-huh," Doc nodded. "It's a cooperative, right? The labor is contributed in lieu of money."

"That is right, señor."

"Mmm-hmm." Doc took another appreciative look around. "Now, I was wondering. My wife and I have a very nice villa in the city, but . . ."

"No, señor. You would not be eligible for admittance here."

"Well, now, I don't know about that," Doc began. But the officer cut him off.

He *was* sure that Doc was not eligible. When he became so, he would be notified. "You may depend on it, señor. Meanwhile, perhaps you would like to walk around—see what your future home will be like."

Doc said that he would, and they started down the wide, sparkling street. Smoke rolled up from the chimneys of the houses, but no one stood in their doorways or looked out their windows, and hardly a sound came from any of them. The high dry air seemed unusually warm, and Doc paused and mopped his face. "Where's the *cantina*? I'll buy the drinks."

"There is none, señor. You can buy no drinks here."

"Well, some coffee then."

"That neither, señor. No drink or food of any kind."

"No?" Doc frowned. "You mean everything has to be brought out from the city? I don't think I'd like that."

The officer slowly shook his head. "You would not like it, señor. But, no, that is not what I mean. Nothing is brought from the city. Nothing but the people themselves."

The words seemed to hang suspended in the air, a brooding message painted upon the silence. The *carabinero* seemed to study them, to look through them and on into Doc's eyes. And he spoke gently as though in answer to a question.

"Yes, señor, that is the how of it. No doubt you have already noticed the absence of a cemetery."

"B-but—" Doc brushed a shaky hand across his mouth. "B-but . . ."

That smell that filled the air. The odor of peppery, roasting flesh. Peppers could be had anywhere, for the picking, the asking, but the meat . . .

'Quite fitting, eh, señor? And such an easy transition. One need only live literally as he has always done figuratively."

He smiled handsomely, and the gorge rose in Doc's throat; it was all he could do to keep from striking the man.

"Fitting?" he snarled. "It—it's disgusting, that's what it is! It's hateful, hideous, inhuman . . ."

"Inhuman? But what has that to do with it, señor?"

"Don't get sarcastic with me! I've taken care of better men than you without . . ."

"I am sure of it. That is why you are here, yes? But wait—" he pointed. "There is one who knows you, I believe."

The man had just emerged from one of the houses. He was well over six feet tall, some five or six inches perhaps. And his normal weight should have been—indeed it *had* been—no less than two hundred and fifty pounds. But what it was now could not possibly be more than a third of that.

His eyes were enormous in the unfleshed skull's head of his

face. His neck was no larger than Doc's wrist. It was incredible that he could be alive; but of course, the climate is very healthy in El Rey's kingdom and many people live to a hundred years and more.

He staggered toward Doc, mouthing silently in his weakness. In his helpless silence, the exaggerated slowness of his movements, he was like a man caught up in some terrifying nightmare.

"Pat—" Doc's voice was a sickened whisper. "Pat Gangloni." Automatically, he recoiled from the apparition, and then, bracing himself he stepped forward deliberately and took Gangloni into his arms. "It's all right, Pat. Take it easy, boy. You're okay now." He patted the skeleton's shoulders, and Gangloni wept silently.

The *carabinero* watched them, an unaccustomed sympathy in his eyes.

"A sad case," he murmured. "Oh, but very sad. He is unable to resign himself. Already he has been here far longer than many."

"Never mind that!" Doc turned on him angrily. "Can you get me a car—a cab? Something to get him out of here?"

"We-el, yes. It will take a little time, but I can do it."

"Well, do it then! Go on!"

"Your pardon, señor." The *carabinero* didn't move. "You would take him out of here, you said. Out of here to where?"

"Where? Why, to my home, naturally! Someplace where I can take care of him. Get him back on his feet."

"And then, señor?"

"Then?"

"You will continue to provide for him?"

"Why, uh—" Doc slowed down a little. "Well, yes, of course. I suppose so. I mean—uh . . ."

"You would be required to, señor. As long as you were able to provide for yourself. It would be so pointless otherwise. So cruel. Inhuman, as you said a moment ago."

Gangloni began to shudder violently. He could not talk, but he could hear; like the man in the nightmare, he knew what was going on. Doc made a feeble attempt to free himself, and the skeleton arms tightened around him.

"He is a good friend, eh? You owe him much." The *carabinero* was sympathy personified. "I can understand. In this one, I would say, there is an inner fineness. He is a man of beliefs, principles—distorted and twisted perhaps, but . . ."

Doc abruptly broke free of Gangloni. He backed away on the cobblestones; grimacing, mumbling apologetically.

"I-I'll have to come back later. I—you know. Make some arrangements first. T-talk with my wife. Sure it'll be all right, b-but—but you know. How women are, I mean. I—I—*Pat! Don't look at me like that! Don't . . .*"

He turned and began to run.

On the suddenly chill breeze the *carabinero*'s voice followed him. "*Hasta la vista, señor.* Until we meet again."

You tell yourself it is a bad dream. You tell yourself you have died—you, not the others—and have waked up in hell. But you know better. You know better. There is an end to dreams, and there is no end to this. And when people die they are dead—as who should know better than you?

El Rey does only what he has to. His criminal sanctuary is a big improvement over most. He does not kill you for your loot. He gives you value for money. He runs a first-class place, and he could not do so if you were allowed to be miserly. Nor can he permit you to linger on when your money is gone. There would be no room for newcomers if he did; and allowed to accumulate, you and your kind would soon take over. You would be in his place, and he would be in yours up on that cobblestoned street with its sparkling whitewashed buildings. And he knows this. He and his native subjects know it. It explains their delight in irony, in symbolism; in constantly holding a mirror up to you so that you must see yourself as you are, and as they see you.

No, it is impossible to deceive yourself. The kingdom is there, maps and officialdom to the contrary. It is there, call it what you like. All things considered, it is probably the very best place of its kind. And its bad features, such as they are, derive not from El Rey but his guests.

He will not cheat you. He will not kill you. He cannot and will not provide for you, but he will not put an end to your life, no matter how long you live. And in that strangely salubrious climate, you seem to live an eternity.

*

In El Rey's dominion there is one night of the year—the night of the annual grand ball—when there are no "suicides" or fatal "accidents." Everyone is politely but thoroughly searched before entering the *Palacio del Rey*, where the fete is held. Everyone is advised that any misfortune to a guest will be regarded with great displeasure. It has been many years since any such misfortune occurred, and the victim's plunge from a fourth-floor window actually was accidental. But everyone present was fined heavily, and the supposed instigator of the accident—the woman's husband—suffered total confiscation of his bank account. So today, not only does no one make an untoward move, but everyone shows the greatest concern for the welfare of everyone else. Raise your voice slightly, and you are immediately the target of a hundred anxious eyes. Reach suddenly for a handkerchief or cigarette, and a dozen people move toward you.

Very distinguished in white tie and tails, Doc McCoy stood on the promenade border of the great ballroom; beaming out over the swirling assemblage of dancers, bowing to this couple, smiling at that one, courteously inclining his head toward another. Perfectly groomed, his temples touched with gray, he was the very picture of a gentleman at ease, of well-bred charm. But he had seldom been less at ease, or more thoroughly miserable.

His physical discomfort—his numbed feet and aching back—was largely attributable to the wives of El Rey's two chief justices. Neither of the ladies was over five feet tall, yet their combined weight was considerably more than a quarter of a ton. And they were as near to being inexhaustible as anyone Doc had ever met. He had danced with them by turns, murmuring exquisite apologies as they walked giggling on his feet, whispering compliments as his back screamed at the constant bending. Oh, he had buttered up the ladies, but good; for they were known to be ogres in private, and virtually the masters of their henpecked husbands. Then, while he was silently congratulating himself, he had seen Carol dance by in the arms of the chief of police. And he knew that his agonized efforts had been wasted. The chief of police against the chief justices; if there was any advantage, it was on Carol's side. She might suffer for it, perhaps, if he became one of the dominion's suicides or accident victims. But that would do him no good whatsoever.

It was now more than an hour since he had seen either her or the chief of police, and his anxiety was growing. He would have to think very fast, or this might well be the last grand ball he would ever attend.

He made a final survey of the ballroom. Then turning, apparently unseeing as a fat feminine hand waved to him across the throng, he strolled down the palm-bordered promenade. And for some reason his mind went back to that long-ago day in Kansas; to the picnic grounds where he and Carol had gone after leaving the train.

"*. . . need to get acquainted again, Doc. We just about have to!*"

Doc smiled wryly to himself. Get acquainted? Oh no, they didn't need to. What had actually troubled them was that they knew each other too well. They lived by taking what they wanted. By getting rid of anyone who got in their way or ceased to be useful to them. It was a fixed pattern with them; it *was* them. And in the event of a showdown, they would show no more mercy toward each other than they had toward so many others . . .

Wrapped in thought, Doc sauntered down the promenade, absently glancing through the doorways of the innumerable parlors, drawing rooms and bars. From one of them, fat Ike Moss called a muffled greeting to him; gestured, his mouth stuffed to a long delicacy-laden table. But Doc smilingly shook his head, and passed on. Ike Moss, he thought distastefully. How gross, how completely lacking in a sense of propriety could the man be? Only last week his wife had drowned in her bath, yet here he was dressed to the nines, and gobbling down everything in sight.

Probably raided the icebox after he finished her off, Doc thought. And he chuckled silently at the picture that came into his mind.

He came to a small billiard room; started on past it. Then he paused abruptly, straightened his shoulders, and went through the doorway.

Dr. Max Vonderscheid was at the one pool table. His dwarfed hunchbacked body was dressed in rusty black, the tails of the ill-fitting suit almost touching the floor. And his gray leonine head rose only a few inches above the table. But still he appeared austerely handsome and dignified; and he sent the pool balls caroming about the green with almost magical accuracy.

He pocketed the last two with a difficult double-bank shot. Doc applauded lightly, and Vonderscheid set the cue on the floor butt down, and leaned on it looking at him. "Yes, Herr McCoy? I may be of service to you?"

His speech was almost unaccented; Doc had observed that it almost always was except when he was around El Rey. He and El Rey were seemingly on very good terms, the latter making extraordinary concessions to the doctor with regard to rent and other expenses. Still, Vonderscheid had to have some kind of income, and he couldn't have much of a practice here.

"Yes?" There was a peculiar gleam in the hunchback's eyes. "You cannot, perhaps, make up your mind?"

"Sorry," Doc said hastily. "I was so absorbed in watching your game that—but, yes, I believe you can be of help to me. I, uh—the truth is I'm very worried about my wife. I don't think she's at all well."

"I see. So?"

"Well—" Doc lowered his voice. "It's of a highly confidential nature, Doctor. I'd want to discuss it in absolute privacy."

Vonderscheid turned and glanced around the room, his gaze lingering for the merest moment on a palm-sheltered corner nook. Brows raised, he turned back to Doc again. "This would seem to be private enough," he said. "Yes, this should do perfectly. So what is it about your wife, and why do you bring the matter to me?"

Doc began a cautious explanation. He had not nearly finished when Vonderscheid interrupted with an impatient gesture. "If you please, Herr McCoy! So much talk for so commonplace a deed! You want me to examine your wife, yes? To suggest that she would do well to have one, with no mention that it is your suggestion. And then you wish me to tell her that she is in need of an operation. To convince her of it. And during the course of the operation, I am to . . ."

"No point in spelling it out," Doc said quickly. "After all, a great many people die in surgery. Now if you'd, uh, care to give me an estimate of your fee . . ."

"If I did it, there would be none. To remove either you or your wife from society would be both pleasure and privilege. Unfortunately I cannot do it. My name is Vonderscheid, not Katzenjammer. I am a doctor, not an assassin."

"Now just a moment," Doc frowned. "I'm afraid you misunderstood me, Doctor. You surely don't think that I . . ."

"If you please!" Vonderscheid cut him off with a bang of the cue. "Do not ask me what I think of you or your wife, of what you have done with your good bodies, your strong minds, your unlimited opportunities. If only half so much I had had, or poor Rudy Torrento . . ."

"So that's it," Doc said, angrily sardonic. "You and Rudy were friends, so naturally . . ."

He broke off. Vonderscheid had moved back a step, stood gripping the cue with both hands. He wagged it with an ominous movement, and Doc discovered he had nothing more to say.

"You are quite through, McCoy?" The doctor grinned at him furiously. "Then I will finish. Rudy was my friend, yes. He was insane; he had been brutalized almost from birth; he had been made into what he was and he could not have been anything else. He had never had a friend, so I became one to him. I did not regard him as a criminal. No more, merely because I have broken laws, do I consider myself one. So! So that is all, Herr McCoy, except for two things. Your wife approached me only a few minutes ago with a proposition similar to your own. In fact, she should still be here." He pointed to the cluster of potted palms. "So in case you should wish to condole with one another . . ."

He laughed wickedly, tossed his billiard cue onto the table and walked out.

Doc bit his lip. He remained where he was for a moment, and then, with a kind of dreary nonchalance, he walked around the table and skirted the palms.

Carol had a portable bar drawn up in front of her. Silently he sat down at her side, and silently she fixed him a drink, her eyes warmly sympathetic. "He was pretty rough on you, Doc. I'm sorry."

"Oh, well," Doc sighed. "I hope he wasn't equally nasty with you, my dear."

"I don't care about myself. I've been told off by experts. But someone like you, someone that everyone has always liked . . ."

She gave his hand a soothing pat, and Doc turned to her with thoughtful wonderment. "Do you know," he said, "I believe you really love me."

"Love you?" she frowned. "Why, of course I do. Don't you love me?"

"Yes," Doc nodded slowly. "Yes, Carol, strangely enough I love you very much. I always have and I always will, and I could never love anyone else."

"And I couldn't either. I—oh, Doc. *Doc!*"

"And it doesn't make any difference, does it, Carol? Or does it?"

"Does it?" She dabbed her eyes with her handkerchief. "T-tell me it does, Doc, and I'll tell you it does. And what the hell difference will it make?"

Doc nodded vaguely. He refilled their glasses. In the palace tower a great bell began to toll the hour of twelve. And in the ballroom the band struck up the strains of *Home Sweet Home*.

"Well," Carol said. "I guess it's just about over, Doc."

"Yes," Doc said. "Just about over, Carol."

"You!" she said, and her voice was suddenly angry, frightened, tortured. "I'll drink a toast to you, Doc darling!"

"Why, how kind of you," Doc said, and he touched his glass to hers. "What will it be?"

"To you! To you and our successful getaway!"

"And to you, my dear," Doc said. "And another such victory."

THE KILLER INSIDE ME

ONE

I'd finished my pie and was having a second cup of coffee when I saw him. The midnight freight had come in a few minutes before; and he was peering in one end of the restaurant window, the end nearest the depot, shading his eyes with his hand and blinking against the light. He saw me watching him, and his face faded back into the shadows. But I knew he was still there. I knew he was waiting. The bums always size me up for an easy mark.

I lit a cigar and slid off my stool. The waitress, a new girl from Dallas, watched as I buttoned my coat. "Why, you don't even carry a gun!" she said, as though she was giving me a piece of news.

"No," I smiled. "No gun, no blackjack, nothing like that. Why should I?"

"But you're a cop—a deputy sheriff, I mean. What if some crook should try to shoot you?"

"We don't have many crooks here in Central City, ma'am," I said. "Anyway, people are people, even when they're a little misguided. You don't hurt them, they won't hurt you. They'll listen to reason."

She shook her head, wide-eyed with awe, and I strolled up to the front. The proprietor shoved back my money and laid a couple of cigars on top of it. He thanked me again for taking his son in hand.

"He's a different boy now, Lou," he said, kind of running his words together like foreigners do. "Stays in nights; gets along fine in school. And always he talks about you—what a good man is Deputy Lou Ford."

"I didn't do anything," I said. "Just talked to him. Showed him a little interest. Anyone else could have done as much."

"Only you," he said. "Because you are good, you make others so." He was all ready to sign off with that, but I wasn't. I leaned an elbow on the counter, crossed one foot behind the other and took a long slow drag on my cigar. I liked the guy—as much as I like most people, anyway—but he was too good to let go. Polite, intelligent: guys like that are my meat.

"Well, I tell you," I drawled. "I tell you the way I look at it, a man doesn't get any more out of life than what he puts into it."

"Umm," he said, fidgeting. "I guess you're right, Lou."

"I was thinking the other day, Max; and all of a sudden I had the doggonedest thought. It came to me out of a clear sky—the boy is father to the man. Just like that. The boy is father to the man."

The smile on his face was getting strained. I could hear his shoes creak as he squirmed. If there's anything worse than a bore, it's a corny bore. But how can you brush off a nice friendly fellow who'd give you his shirt if you asked for it?

"I reckon I should have been a college professor or something like that," I said. "Even when I'm asleep I'm working out problems. Take that heat wave we had a few weeks ago; a lot of people think it's the heat that makes it so hot. But it's not like that, Max. It's not the heat, but the humidity. I'll bet you didn't know that, did you?"

He cleared his throat and muttered something about being wanted in the kitchen. I pretended like I didn't hear him.

"Another thing about the weather," I said. "Everyone talks about it, but no one does anything. But maybe it's better that way. Every cloud has its silver lining, at least that's the way I figure it. I mean, if we didn't have the rain we wouldn't have the rainbows, now would we?"

"Lou . . ."

"Well," I said, "I guess I'd better shove off. I've got quite a bit of getting around to do, and I don't want to rush. Haste makes waste, in my opinion. I like to look before I leap."

That was dragging 'em in by the feet, but I couldn't hold 'em back. Striking at people that way is almost as good as the other, the real way. The way I'd fought to forget—and had almost forgot—until I met her.

I was thinking about her as I stepped out into the cool West Texas night and saw the bum waiting for me.

TWO

Central City was founded in 1870, but it never became a city in size until about ten-twelve years ago. It was shipping point for a lot of cattle and a little cotton, and Chester Conway, who was born here, made it headquarters for the Conway Construction Company. But it still wasn't much more than a wide place in a Texas road. Then, the oil boom came, and almost overnight the population jumped to 48,000.

Well, the town had been laid out in a little valley amongst a lot of hills. There just wasn't any room for the newcomers, so they spread out every which way with their homes and businesses, and now they were scattered across a third of the county. It's not an unusual situation in the oil-boom country—you'll see a lot of cities like ours if you're ever out this way. They don't have any regular city police force, just a constable or two. The sheriff's office handles the policing for both city and county.

We do a pretty good job of it, to our own way of thinking at least. But now and then things get a little out of hand, and we put on a clean-up. It was during a clean-up three months ago that I ran into her.

"Name of Joyce Lakeland," old Bob Maples, the sheriff, told me. "Lives four-five miles out on Derrick Road, just past the old Branch farm house. Got her a nice little cottage up there behind a stand of blackjack trees."

"I think I know the place," I said. "Hustlin' lady, Bob?"

"We-el, I reckon so but she's bein' mighty decent about it. She ain't running it into the ground, and she ain't takin' on no roustabouts or sheepherders. If some of these preachers around town wasn't rompin' on me, I wouldn't bother her a-tall."

I wondered if he was getting some of it, and decided that he wasn't. He wasn't maybe any mental genius, but Bob Maples was straight. "So how shall I handle this Joyce Lakeland?" I said. "Tell her to lay off a while, or to move on?"

"We-el," he scratched his head, scowling—"I dunno, Lou. Just—well, just go out and size her up, and make your own decision. I know you'll be gentle, as gentle and pleasant as you can be. An'

I know you can be firm if you have to. So go on out, an' see how she looks to you. I'll back you up in whatever you want to do."

It was about ten o'clock in the morning when I got there. I pulled the car up into the yard, curving it around so I could swing out easy. The county license plates didn't show, but it wasn't deliberate. It was just the way it had to be.

I eased up on the porch, knocked on the door and stood back, taking off my Stetson.

I was feeling a little uncomfortable. I hardly knew what I was going to say to her. Because maybe we're kind of old-fashioned, but our standards of conduct aren't the same, say, as they are in the east or middle-west. Out here you say yes ma'am and no ma'am to anything with skirts on; anything white, that is. Out here, if you catch a man with his pants down, you apologize . . . even if you have to arrest him afterwards. Out here you're a man, a man and a gentleman, or you aren't anything. And God help you if you're not.

The door opened an inch or two. Then, it opened all the way and she stood looking at me.

"Yes?" she said coldly.

She was wearing sleeping shorts and a wool pullover; her brown hair was as tousled as a lamb's tail, and her unpainted face was drawn with sleep. But none of that mattered. It wouldn't have mattered if she'd crawled out of a hog-wallow wearing a gunny sack. She had that much.

She yawned openly and said "Yes?" again, but I still couldn't speak. I guess I was staring open-mouthed like a country boy. This was three months ago, remember, and I hadn't had the sickness in almost fifteen years. Not since I was fourteen.

She wasn't much over five feet and a hundred pounds, and she looked a little scrawny around the neck and ankles. But that was all right. It was perfectly all right. The good Lord had known just where to put that flesh where it would *really* do some good.

"Oh, my goodness!" She laughed suddenly. "Come on in. I don't make a practice of it this early in the morning, but . . ." She held the screen open and gestured. I went in and she closed it and locked the door again.

"I'm sorry, ma'am," I said, "but—"

"It's all right. But I'll have to have some coffee first. You go on back."

I went down the little hall to the bedroom, listening uneasily as I heard her drawing water for the coffee. I'd acted like a chump. It was going to be hard to be firm with her after a start like this, and something told me I should be. I didn't know why; I still don't. But I knew it right from the beginning. Here was a little lady who got what she wanted, and to hell with the price tag.

Well, hell, though; it was just a feeling. She'd acted all right, and she had a nice quiet little place here. I decided I'd let her ride, for the time being anyhow. Why not? And then I happened to glance into the dresser mirror and I knew why not. I knew I couldn't. The top dresser drawer was open a little, and the mirror was tilted slightly. And hustling ladies are one thing, and hustling ladies with guns are something else.

I took it out of the drawer, a .32 automatic, just as she came in with the coffee tray. Her eyes flashed and she slammed the tray down on a table. "What," she snapped, "are you doing with that?"

I opened my coat and showed her my badge. "Sheriff's office, ma'am. What are *you* doing with it?"

She didn't say anything. She just took her purse off the dresser, opened it and pulled out a permit. It had been issued in Fort Worth, but it was all legal enough. Those things are usually honored from one town to another.

"Satisfied, copper?" she said.

"I reckon it's all right, miss," I said. "And my name's Ford, not copper." I gave her a big smile, but I didn't get any back. My hunch about her had been dead right. A minute before she'd been all set to lay, and it probably wouldn't have made any difference if I hadn't had a dime. Now she was set for something else, and whether I was a cop or Christ didn't make any difference either.

I wondered how she'd lived so long.

"Jesus!" she jeered. "The nicest looking guy I ever saw and you turn out to be a lousy snooping copper. How much? I don't jazz cops."

I felt my face turning red. "Lady," I said, "that's not very polite. I just came out for a little talk."

"You dumb bastard," she yelled. "I asked you what you wanted."

"Since you put it that way," I said, "I'll tell you. I want you out of Central City by sundown. If I catch you here after that I'll run you in for prostitution."

I slammed on my hat and started for the door. She got in front of me, blocking my way.

"You lousy son-of-a-bitch. You—"

"Don't you call me that," I said. "Don't do it, ma'am."

"I did call you that! And I'll do it again! You're a son-of-a-bitch, bastard, pimp . . ."

I tried to push past her. I had to get out of there. I knew what was going to happen if I didn't get out, and I knew I couldn't let it happen. I might kill her. It might bring *the sickness* back. And even if I didn't and it didn't, I'd be washed up. She'd talk. She'd yell her head off. And people would start thinking, thinking and wondering about that time fifteen years ago.

She slapped me so hard that my ears rang, first on one side then the other. She swung and kept swinging. My hat flew off. I stooped to pick it up, and she slammed her knee under my chin.

I stumbled backward on my heels and sat down on the floor. I heard a mean laugh, then another laugh sort of apologetic. She said, "Gosh, sheriff, I didn't mean to—I—you made me so mad I—I—"

"Sure," I grinned. My vision was clearing and I found my voice again. "Sure, ma'am, I know how it was. Used to get that way myself. Give me a hand, will you?"

"You-you won't hurt me?"

"Me? Aw, now, ma'am."

"No," she said, and she sounded almost disappointed. "I know you won't. Anyone can see you're too easy-going." And she came over to me slowly and gave me her hands.

I pulled myself up. I held her wrists with one hand and swung. It almost stunned her; I didn't want her completely stunned. I wanted her so she would understand what was happening to her.

"No, baby"—my lips drew back from my teeth. "I'm not going to hurt you. I wouldn't think of hurting you. I'm just going to beat the ass plumb off of you."

I said it, and I meant it and I damned near did.

I jerked the jersey up over her face and tied the end in a knot. I threw her down on the bed, yanked off her sleeping shorts and tied her feet together with them.

I took off my belt and raised it over my head . . .

I don't know how long it was before I stopped, before I came to my senses. All I know is that my arm ached like hell and her rear end was one big bruise, and I was scared crazy—as scared as a man can get and go on living.

I freed her feet and hands, and pulled the jersey off her head. I soaked a towel in cold water and bathed her with it. I poured coffee between her lips. And all the time I was talking, begging her to forgive me, telling her how sorry I was.

I got down on my knees by the bed, and begged and apologized. At last her eyelids fluttered and opened.

"Don't," she whispered.

"I won't," I said. "Honest to God, ma'am I won't ever—"

"Don't talk." She brushed her lips against mine. "Don't say you're sorry."

She kissed me again. She began fumbling at my tie, my shirt; starting to undress me after I'd almost skinned her alive.

I went back the next day and the day after that. I kept going back. And it was like a wind had been turned on a dying fire. I began needling people in that dead-pan way—needling 'em as a substitute for something else. I began thinking about settling scores with Chester Conway, of the Conway Construction Company.

I won't say that I hadn't thought of it before. Maybe I'd stayed on in Central City all these years, just in the hopes of getting even. But except for her I don't think I'd ever have done anything. She'd made the old fire burn again. She even showed me how to square with Conway.

She didn't know she was doing it, but she gave me the answer. It was one day, one night rather, about six weeks after we'd met.

"Lou," she said, "I don't want to go on like this. Let's pull out of this crummy town together, just you and I."

"Why, you're crazy!" I said. I said it before I could stop myself. "You think I'd—I'd—"

"Go on, Lou. Let me hear you say it. Tell me"—she began to drawl—"what a fine ol' family you-all Fords is. Tell me, we-all Fords, ma'am, we wouldn't think of livin' with one of you mizzable ol' whores, ma'am. Us Fords just ain't built that way, ma'am."

That was part of it, a big part. But it wasn't the main thing. I knew she was making me worse; I knew that if I didn't stop soon I'd never be able to. I'd wind up in a cage or the electric chair.

"Say it, Lou. Say it and I'll say something."

"Don't threaten me, baby," I said. "I don't like threats."

"I'm not threatening you. I'm telling you. You think you're too good for me—I'll—I'll—"

"Go on. It's your turn to do the saying."

"I wouldn't want to, Lou, honey, but I'm not going to give you up. Never, never, never. If you're too good for me now, then I'll make it so you won't be."

I kissed her, a long hard kiss. Because baby didn't know it, but baby was dead, and in a way I couldn't have loved her more.

"Well, now, baby," I said, "you've got your bowels in an uproar and all over nothing. I was thinking about the money problem."

"I've got some money. I can get some more. A lot of it."

"Yeah?"

"I can, Lou. I know I can! He's crazy about me and he's dumb as hell. I'll bet if his old man thought I was going to marry him, he—"

"Who?" I said. "Who are you talking about, Joyce?"

"Elmer Conway. You know who he is, don't you? Old Chester—"

"Yeah," I said. "Yeah, I know the Conways right well. How do you figure on hookin' 'em?"

We talked it over, lying there on her bed together, and off in the night somewhere a voice seemed to whisper to forget it, *forget it, Lou, it's not too late if you stop now.* And I did try, God knows I tried. But right after that, right after the voice, her hand gripped one of mine and kneaded it into her breasts; and she moaned and shivered . . . and so I didn't forget.

"Well," I said, after a time, "I guess we can work it out. The way I see it is, if at first you don't succeed, try, try again."

"Mmm, darling?"

"In other words," I said, "where there's a will there's a way."

She squirmed a little, and then she snickered. "Oh, Lou, you corny so and so! You slay me!"

. . . The street was dark. I was standing a few doors above the cafe, and the bum was standing and looking at me. He was a young fellow, about my age, and he was wearing what must have been a pretty good suit of clothes at one time.

"Well, how about it, bud?" he was saying. "How about it, huh? I've been on a hell of a binge, and by God if I don't get some food pretty soon—"

"Something to warm you up, eh?" I said.

"Yeah, anything at all you can help me with, I'll . . ."

I took the cigar out of my mouth with one hand and made like I was reaching into my pocket with the other. Then, I grabbed his wrist and ground the cigar butt into his palm.

"Jesus, bud!"—He cursed and jerked away from me. "What the hell you tryin' to do?"

I laughed and let him see my badge. "Beat it," I said.

"Sure, bud, sure," he said, and he began backing away. He didn't sound particularly scared or angry; more interested than anything. "But you better watch that stuff, bud. You sure better watch it."

He turned and walked off toward the railroad tracks.

I watched him, feeling sort of sick and shaky; and then I got in my car and headed for the labor temple.

THREE

The Central City Labor Temple was on a side street a couple of blocks off of the courthouse square. It wasn't much of a building, an old two-storey brick with the downstairs rented out to a pool hall and the union offices and meeting hall on the second floor. I climbed the stairs, and went down the dark corridor to the end where a door opened into several of the best and largest offices in the place. The sign on the glass read:

CENTRAL CITY, TEXAS
Building Trades Council
Joseph Rothman, Pres.

and Rothman opened the door before I could turn the knob.

"Let's go back here in the rear," he said, shaking hands. "Sorry to ask you to come around so late, but with you being a public official and all I thought it might be best."

"Yeah," I nodded, wishing I could have ducked seeing him entirely. The law is pretty much on one side of the fence out here; and I already knew what he wanted to talk about.

He was a man of about forty, short and stocky, with sharp black eyes and a head that seemed too big for his body. He had a cigar in his mouth, but he laid it down after he sat down at his desk, and began rolling a cigarette. He lit it and blew smoke over the match, his eyes shying away from mine.

"Lou," the labor leader said, and hesitated. "I've got something to tell you—in the strictest confidence, you understand—but I'd like you to tell me something first. It's probably a pretty touchy subject with you, but . . . well, how did you feel about Mike Dean, Lou?"

"Feel? I'm not sure I know what you mean, Joe?" I said.

"He was your foster brother, right? Your father adopted him?"

"Yes. Dad was a doctor, you know—"

"And a very good one, I understand. Excuse me, Lou. Go on."

So that's the way it was going to be. Spar and counter-spar. Each of us feeling the other out, each of us telling things he knows damn well the other fellow has heard a thousand times. Rothman had something important to tell me, and it looked as though he was going to do it the hard—and careful—way. Well, I didn't mind; I'd play along with him.

"He and the Deans were old friends. When they got wiped out in that big flu epidemic, he adopted Mike. My mother was dead—had been dead since I was a baby. Dad figured Mike and me would be company for each other, and the housekeeper could take care of two of us as easily as one."

"Uh-huh. And how did that strike you, Lou? I mean, you're the only son and heir and your dad brings in another son. Didn't that rub you a little the wrong way?"

I laughed. "Hell, Joe, I was four years old at the time, and Mike was six. You're not much concerned with money at that age, and, anyway, Dad never had any. He was too soft-hearted to dun his patients."

"You liked Mike, then?" He sounded like he wasn't quite convinced.

"Like isn't the word for it," I said. "He was the finest, swellest guy that ever lived. I couldn't have loved a real brother more."

"Even after he did what he did?"

"And just what," I drawled, "would that be?"

Rothman raised his eyebrows. "I liked Mike myself, Lou, but facts are facts. The whole town knows that if he'd been a little older he'd have gone to the chair instead of reform school."

"No one *knows* anything. There was never any proof."

"The girl identified him."

"A girl less than three years old! She'd have identified anyone they showed her."

"And Mike admitted it. And they dug up some other cases."

"Mike was scared. He didn't know what he was saying."

Rothman shook his head. "Let it go, Lou. I'm not really interested in that as such; only in your feelings about Mike . . . Weren't you pretty embarrassed when he came back to Central City? Wouldn't it have been better if he'd stayed away?"

"No," I said. "Dad and I knew Mike hadn't done it. I mean"—I hesitated—"knowing Mike, we were sure he couldn't be guilty." *Because I was. Mike had taken the blame for me*. "I wanted Mike to come back. So did Dad." *He wanted him here to watch over me*. "My God, Joe, Dad pulled strings for months to get Mike his job as city building inspector. It wasn't easy to do, the way people felt about Mike, as popular and influential as Dad was."

"That all checks," Rothman nodded. "That's my understanding of things. But I have to be sure. You weren't sort of relieved when Mike got killed?"

"The shock killed Dad. He never recovered from it. As for me, well all I can say is that I wish it had been me instead of Mike."

Rothman grinned. "Okay, Lou. Now it's your turn . . . Mike was killed six years ago. He was walking a girder on the eighth floor of the New Texas Apartments, a Conway Construction job, when he apparently stepped on a loose rivet. He threw himself backward so he'd fall inside the building, onto the decking. But the floors hadn't been decked in properly; there were just a few planks scattered here and there. Mike fell all the way through to the basement."

I nodded. "So," I said. "What about it, Joe?"

"What about it!" Rothman's eyes flashed. "You ask me what about it when—"

"As President of the building unions, you know that the Ironworkers are under your jurisdiction, Joe. It's their obligation, and yours, to see that each floor is decked in as a building goes up."

"Now you're talking like a lawyer!" Rothman slapped his desk. "The Ironworkers are weak out here. Conway wouldn't put in the decking, and we couldn't make him."

"You could have struck the job."

"Oh, well," Rothman shrugged. "I guess I made a mistake, Lou. I understood you to say that you—"

"You heard me right," I said. "And let's not kid each other. Conway cut corners to make money. You let him—to make money. I'm not just saying you're at fault, but I don't reckon he was either. It was just one of those things."

"Well," Rothman hesitated, "that's a kind of funny attitude for you to take, Lou. It seems to me you're pretty impersonal about it. But since that's the way you feel, perhaps I'd better—"

"Perhaps *I'd* better," I said. "Let me do the talking and then you won't have to feel funny about it. There was a riveter up there with Mike at the time he took his dive. Working after hours. Working by himself. But it takes two men to rivet—one to run the gun and one on the bucking iron. You're going to tell me that he didn't have any rightful business there, but I think you're wrong. He didn't have to be riveting. He could have been gathering up tools or something like that."

"But you don't know the whole story, Lou! This man—"

"I know. The guy was an iron tramp, working on a permit. He blew into town without a dime. Three days after Mike's death he left in a new Chevvy which he paid cash on the line for. That looks bad, but it doesn't really need to mean anything. He might have won the dough in a crap game or—"

"But you still don't know it all, Lou! Conway—"

"Let's see if I don't," I said. "Conway's company was the architect on that job as well as the contractor. And he hadn't allowed enough space for the boilers. To get 'em in, he was going to have to make certain alterations which he knew damned well Mike would never allow. It was either that or lose several hundred thousand dollars."

"Go on, Lou."

"So he took the boss. He hated it like hell, but he went ahead and did it."

Rothman laughed shortly. "He did, huh? I pushed iron on that job, myself, and—and—"

"Well," I gave him a puzzled look. "He did, didn't he? No matter what happened to Mike, your locals couldn't close their eyes to a dangerous situation like that. You're responsible. You can be sued. You could be tried for criminal collusion. You—"

"Lou." Rothman cleared his throat. "You're a hundred per cent right, Lou. Naturally we wouldn't stick our necks out for any amount of money."

"Sure," I smiled stupidly. "You just haven't thought this deal through, Joe. You've been getting along pretty good with Conway, and now he's taken a notion to go non-union, and naturally you're kind of upset about it. I reckon if you thought there'd really been a murder you wouldn't have waited six years to speak up."

"Yeah, I mean certainly not. Certainly, I wouldn't." He began rolling another cigarette. "Uh, how did you find out all these things, Lou, if you don't mind telling me?"

"Well, you know how it is. Mike was a member of the family, and I get around a lot. Any talk that's going around, I'd naturally hear it."

"Mmmm. I didn't realize there'd been so much gossip. In fact, I didn't know there'd been any. And you never felt inclined to take any action?"

"Why should I?" I said. "It was just gossip. Conway's a big business man—just about the biggest contractor in West Texas. He wouldn't get mixed up in a murder any more'n you people would keep quiet about one."

Rothman gave me another sharp look, and then he looked down at his desk. "Lou," he said softly, "do you know how many days a year an ironworker works? Do you know what his life expectancy is? Did you ever see an old ironworker? Did you ever stop to figure that there's all kinds of ways of dying, but only one way of being dead?"

"Well, no I reckon not," I said. "I guess I don't know what you're driving at, Joe."

"Let it go. It's not really relevant."

"I suppose the boys don't have it too easy," I said. "But here's the way I look at it, Joe. There's no law says that they have to stick to one line of work. If they don't like it they can do something else."

"Yeah," he nodded, "that's right, isn't it? It's funny how it takes an outsider to see through these problems . . . If they don't like it let 'em do something else. That's good, that's very good."

"Aw," I said, "it wasn't anything much."

"I disagree. It's very enlightening. You really surprise me, Lou. I've been seeing you around town for years and frankly you hardly struck me as a deep thinker . . . Do you have any solution for our larger problems, the Negro situation for example?"

"Well, that's pretty simple," I said. "I'd just ship 'em all to Africa."

"Uh-huh. I see. I see," he said, and he stood up and held out his hand. "I'm sorry I troubled you for nothing, Lou, but I've certainly enjoyed our talk. I hope we can get together again sometime."

"That would be nice," I said.

"Meanwhile, of course, I haven't seen you. Understand?"

"Oh, sure," I said.

We talked for a minute or two more, and then we walked to the outside door together. He glanced at it sharply, looked at me. "Say," he said. "Didn't I close that damned thing?"

"I thought you did," I said.

"Well, no harm done, I guess," he said. "Could I make a suggestion to you, Lou, in your own interests?"

"Why, sure you can, Joe. Anything at all."

"Save that bullshit for the birds."

He nodded, grinning at me; and for a minute you could have heard a pin drop. But he wasn't going to say anything. He wasn't ever going to let on. So, finally, I began to grin, too.

"I don't know the way of it, Lou—I don't know a thing, understand? Not a thing. But watch yourself. It's a good act but it's easy to overdo."

"You kind of asked for it, Joe," I said.

"And now you know why. And I'm not very bright or I wouldn't be a labor skate."

"Yeah," I said. "I see what you mean."

We shook hands again and he winked and bobbed his head. And I went down the dark hall and down the stairs.

FOUR

After Dad died I'd thought about selling our house. I'd had several good offers for it, in fact, since it was right on the edge of the downtown business district; but somehow I couldn't let it go. The taxes were pretty high and there was ten times as much room as I needed, but I couldn't bring myself to sell. Something told me to hold on, to wait.

I drove down the alley to our garage. I drove in and shut off the lights. The garage had been a barn; it still was, for that matter; and I sat there in the doorway, sniffing the musty odors of old oats and hay and straw, dreaming back through the years. Mike and I had kept our ponies in those two front stalls, and back here in the box-stall we'd had an outlaws" cave. We'd hung swings and acting bars from these rafters; and we'd made a swimming pool out of the horse trough. And up overhead in the loft, where the rats now scampered and scurried, Mike had found me with the little gi—

A rat screamed suddenly on a high note.

I got out of the car and hurried out of the big sliding door of the barn, and into the backyard. I wondered if that was why I stayed here: To punish myself.

I went in the back door of the house and went through the house to the front, turning on all the lights, the downstairs lights I mean. Then I came back into the kitchen and made coffee and carried the pot up into Dad's old office. I sat in his big old leather chair, sipping coffee and smoking, and gradually the tension began to leave me.

It had always made me feel better to come here, back from the time I was knee-high to a grasshopper. It was like coming out of the darkness into sunlight, out of a storm into calm. Like being lost and found again.

I got up and walked along the bookcase, and endless files of psychiatric literature, the bulky volumes of morbid psychology . . . Krafft-Ebing, Jung, Freud, Bleuler, Adolf Meyer, Kretschmer, Kraeplin . . . All the answers were here, out in the open where you could look at them. And no one was terrified or horrified. I came out of the place I was hiding in—that I always had to hide in—and began to breathe.

I took down a bound volume of one of the German periodicals and read a while. I put it back and took down one in French. I skimmed through an article in Spanish and another in Italian. I couldn't speak any of those languages worth a doggone, but I could understand 'em all. I'd just picked 'em up with Dad's help, just like I'd picked up some higher mathematics and physical chemistry and half a dozen other subjects.

Dad had wanted me to be a doctor, but he was afraid to have me go away to school so he'd done what he could for me at home. It used to irritate him, knowing what I had in my head, to hear me talking and acting like any other rube around town. But in time, when he realized how bad I had *the sickness*, he even encouraged me to do it. That's what I was going to be: I was going to have to live and get along with rubes. I wasn't ever going to have anything but some safe, small job, and I'd have to act accordingly. If Dad could have swung anything else that paid a living, I wouldn't even have been as much as a deputy sheriff.

I fiddled around Dad's desk, working out a couple of problems in calculus just for the hell of it. Turning away from the desk, I looked at myself in the mirrored door of the laboratory.

I was still wearing my Stetson, shoved a little to the back of my head. I had on a kind of pinkish shirt and a black bow tie, and the pants of my blue serge suit were hitched up so as to catch on the tops of my Justin boots. Lean and wiry; a mouth that looked all set to drawl. A typical Western-country peace officer, that was me. Maybe friendlier looking than the average. Maybe a little cleaner cut. But on the whole typical.

That's what I was, and I couldn't change. Even if it was safe, I doubted if I could change. I'd pretended so long that I no longer had to.

"Lou . . ."

I jumped and whirled.

"Amy!" I gasped. "What in the— You shouldn't be here! Where—"

"Upstairs, waiting for you. Now, don't get excited, Lou. I slipped out after the folks went to sleep and you know them."

"But someone might—"

"No one did. I slipped down the alley. Aren't you glad?"

I wasn't, although I suppose I should have been. She didn't have the shape that Joyce did, but it was a big improvement over anything else around Central City. Except when she stuck her chin out and narrowed her eyes, like she was daring you to cross her, she was a mighty pretty girl.

"Well, sure," I said. "Sure, I'm glad. Let's go back up, huh?"

I followed her up the stairs and into my bedroom. She kicked off her shoes, tossed her coat on a chair with her other clothes, and flopped down backwards on the bed.

"My!" she said, after a moment; and her chin began to edge outward. "Such enthusiasm!"

"Oh," I said, giving my head a shake. "I'm sorry, Amy. I had something on my mind."

"S-something on your mind!" Her voice quavered. "I strip myself for him, I shed my decency and my clothes for him and h-he stands there with 'something' on his m-mind!"

"Aw, now, honey. It's just that I wasn't expecting you, and—"

"No! And why should you? The way you avoid me and make excuses for not seeing me. If I had any pride left I'd—I'd—"

She buried her head in the pillow and began to sob, giving me an A-1 view of what was probably the second prettiest rear end in West Texas. I was pretty sure she was faking; I'd picked up a lot of pointers on women from Joyce. But I didn't dare give her the smacking she deserved. Instead I threw off my own clothes and crawled into bed with her, pulling her around facing me.

"Now, cut it out, honey," I said. "You know I've just been busy as a chigger at a picnic."

"I don't know it! I don't know anything of the kind! You don't want to be with me, that's what!"

"Why, that's plumb crazy, honey. Why wouldn't I want to?"

"B-because. Oh, Lou, darling, I've been so miserable . . ."

"Well, now that's a right foolish way to act, Amy," I said.

She went on whimpering about how miserable she'd been, and I went on holding her, listening—you got to do plenty of listening around Amy—and wondering how it had all started.

To tell the truth, I guess it hadn't started anywhere. We'd just drifted together like straws in a puddle. Our families had grown up together, and we'd grown up together, right here in this same block. We'd walked back and forth to school together, and when we went to parties we were paired off together. We hadn't needed to do anything. It was all done for us.

I suppose half the town, including her own folks, knew we were knocking off a little. But no one said anything or thought anything about it. After all we were going to get married . . . even if we were kind of taking our time.

"Lou!" she nudged me. "You aren't listening to me!"

"Why, sure, I am, honey."

"Well, answer me then."

"Not now," I said. "I've got something else on my mind, now."

"But . . . Oh, *darling* . . ."

I figured she'd been grabbing and nagging about nothing, as usual, and she'd forget about whatever I was supposed to answer. But it didn't work out that way. As soon as it was over and I'd reached her cigarettes for her, taking one for myself, she gave me another one of her looks and another, "Well, Lou?"

"I hardly know what to say," I said, which was exactly the case.

"You want to marry me, don't you?"

"Mar—but, sure," I said.

"I think we've waited long enough, Lou. I can go on teaching school. We'll get by a lot better than most couples."

"But . . . but that's all we'd do, Amy. We'd never get anywhere!"

"What do you mean?"

"Well, I don't want to go on being a deputy sheriff all of my life. I want to—well—be somebody."

"Like what, for example?"

"Oh, I don't know. There's no use in talking about it."

"A doctor, perhaps? I think that would be awfully nice. Is that what you had in mind, Lou?"

"I know it's crazy, Amy. But—"

She laughed. She rolled her head on the pillow, laughing. "Oh, Lou! I never heard of such a thing! You're twenty-nine-years old, and y-you don't even speak good English, and—and—oh, ha, ha, ha . . ."

She laughed until she was gasping, and my cigarette burned down between my fingers and I never knew it until I smelled the scorching flesh.

"I'm s-sorry, darling. I didn't mean to hurt your feelings, but— Were you teasing me? Were you joking with your little Amy?"

"You know me," I said. "Lou the laughing boy."

She began to quiet down at the tone of my voice. She turned away from me and lay on her back, picking at the quilt with her fingers. I got up and found a cigar, and sat down on the bed again.

"You don't want to marry me, do you, Lou?"

"I don't think we should marry now, no."

"You don't want to marry me at all."

"I didn't say that."

She was silent for several minutes, but her face talked for her. I saw her eyes narrow and a mean little smile twist her lips, and I knew what she was thinking. I knew almost to a word what she was going to say.

"I'm afraid you'll have to marry me, Lou. You'll have to, do you understand?"

"No," I said. "I won't have to. You're not pregnant, Amy. You've never gone with anyone else, and you're not pregnant by me."

"I'm lying, I suppose?"

"Seems as though," I said. "I couldn't get you pregnant if I wanted to. I'm sterile."

"*You?*"

"Sterile isn't the same thing as impotent. I've had a vasectomy."

"Then why have we always been so—why do you use—?"

I shrugged. "It saved a lot of explanations. Anyway, you're not pregnant, to get back to the subject."

"I just don't understand," she said, frowning. She wasn't at all bothered by my catching her in a lie. "Your father did it? Why, Lou?"

"Oh, I was kind of run down and nervous, and he thought—"

"Why, you were not! You were never that way!"

"Well," I said, "he thought I was."

"He *thought*! He did a terrible thing like that—made you so we can never have children—just because he thought something! Why, it's terrible! It makes me sick! . . . When was it, Lou?"

"What's the difference?" I said. "I don't really remember. A long time ago."

I wished I'd kept my mouth shut about her not being pregnant. Now I couldn't back up on my story. She'd know I was lying and she'd be more suspicious than ever.

I grinned at her and walked my fingers up the curving plane of her belly. I squeezed one of her breasts, and then I moved my hand up until it was resting against her throat.

"What's the matter?" I said. "What have you got that pretty little face all puckered up for?"

She didn't say anything. She didn't smile back. She just lay there, staring, adding me up point by point, and she began to look more puzzled in one way and less in another. The answer was trying to crash through and it couldn't make it—quite. I was standing in the way. It couldn't get around the image she had of gentle, friendly easy-going Lou Ford.

"I think," she said slowly, "I'd better go home now."

"Maybe you'd better," I agreed. "It'll be dawn before long."

"Will I see you tomorrow? Today, I mean."

"Well, Saturday's a pretty busy day for me," I said. "I reckon we might go to church together Sunday or maybe have dinner together, but—"

"But you're busy Sunday night."

"I really am, honey. I promised to do a favor for a fellow, and I don't see how I can get out of it."

"I see. It never occurs to you to think about me when you're making all your plans, does it? Oh, no! I don't matter."

"I won't be tied up too long Sunday," I said. "Maybe until eleven o'clock or so. Why don't you come over and wait for me like you did tonight? I'd be tickled to death to have you."

Her eyes flickered, but she didn't break out with a lecture like she must have wanted to. She motioned for me to move so she could get up; and then she got up and began dressing.

"I'm awfully sorry, honey," I said.

"Are you?" She pulled her dress over her head, patted it down around her hips, and buttoned the collar. Standing first on one foot then the other, she put on her pumps. I got up and held her coat for her, smoothing it around her shoulders as I helped her into it.

She turned inside my arms and faced me. "All right, Lou," she said briskly. "We'll say no more tonight. But Sunday we'll have a good long talk. You're going to tell me why you've acted as you have these last few months, and no lying or evasions. Understand?"

"Ma'am, Miss Stanton," I said. "Yes, ma'am."

"All right," she nodded, "that's settled. Now you'd better put some clothes on or go back to bed before you catch cold."

FIVE

That day, Saturday, was a busy one. There were a lot of payday drunks in town, it being the middle of the month, and drunks out here mean fights. All of us deputies and the two constables and Sheriff Maples had our hands full keeping things under control.

I don't have much trouble with drunks. Dad taught me they were touchy as all-hell and twice as jumpy, and if you didn't ruffle 'em or alarm 'em they were the easiest people in the world to get along with. You should never bawl a drunk out, he said, because the guy had already bawled himself out to the breaking point. And you should never pull a gun or swing on a drunk because he was apt to feel that his life was in danger and act accordingly.

So I just moved around, friendly and gentle, taking the guys home wherever I could instead of to jail, and none of them got hurt and neither did I. But it all took time. From the time I went on at noon until eleven o'clock, I didn't so much as stop for a cup of coffee. Then around midnight, when I was already way over shift, I got one of the special jobs Sheriff Maples was always calling me in on.

A Mexican pipeliner had got all hayed up on marijuana and stabbed another Mexican to death. The boys had roughed him up pretty badly bringing him in and now, what with the hay and all, he was a regular wild man. They'd managed to get him off into one of the "quiet" cells, but the way he was cutting up he was going to take it apart or die in the attempt.

"Can't handle the crazy Mex the way we ought to," Sheriff Bob grumbled. "Not in a murder case. I miss my guess, we've already given some shyster defense lawyer enough to go yellin' third-degree."

"I'll see what I can do," I said.

I went down to the cell and I stayed there three hours, and I was busy every minute of it. I hardly had time to slam the door before the Mex dived at me. I caught his arms and held him back, letting him struggle and rave; and then I turned him loose and he dived again. I held him back again, turned him loose again. It went on and on.

I never slugged him or kicked him. I never let him struggle hard enough to hurt himself. I just wore him down, little by little, and when he quieted enough to hear me I began talking to him. Practically everyone in this area talks some Mex, but I do it better than most. I talked on and on, feeling him relax; and all the time I was wondering about myself.

This Mex, now, was about as defenseless as a man could be. He was hopped up and crazy. With the booting around he'd had, a little bit more would never have been noticed. I'd taken a lot bigger chance with what I'd done to that bum. The bum could have caused trouble. This Mex, alone in a cell with me, couldn't.

Yet I didn't so much as twist a finger. I'd never hurt a prisoner, someone that I could harm safely. I didn't have the slightest desire to. Maybe I had too much pride in my reputation for not using force. Or maybe I figured subconsciously that the prisoners and I were on the same side. But however it was, I'd never hurt 'em. I didn't want to, and pretty soon I wouldn't want to hurt anyone. I'd get rid of her, and it would all be over for all time.

After three hours, like I say, the Mex was willing to behave. So I got him his clothes back and a blanket for his bunk, and let him smoke a cigarette while I tucked him in. Sheriff Maples peeped in as I was leaving, and shook his head wonderingly.

"Don't see how you do it, Lou," he swore. "Dagnab it, if I see where you get the patience."

"You've just got to keep smiling," I said. "That's the answer."

"Yeah? Do tell," he drawled.

"That's right," I said. "The man with the grin is the man who will win."

He gave me a funny look; and I laughed and slapped him on the back. "Just kidding, Bob," I said.

What the hell? You can't break a habit overnight. And what was the harm in a little kidding?

The sheriff wished me a good Sunday, and I drove on home. I fixed myself a big platter of ham and eggs and French fries, and carried it into Dad's office. I ate at his desk, more at peace with myself than I'd been in a long time.

I'd made up my mind about one thing. Come hell or high water, I wasn't going to marry Amy Stanton. I'd been holding off on her account; I didn't feel I had the right to marry her. Now, though, I just wasn't going to do it. If I had to marry someone, it wouldn't be a bossy little gal with a tongue like barbed-wire and a mind about as narrow.

I carried my dishes into the kitchen, washed them up, and took a long hot bath. Then I turned in and slept like a log until ten in the morning.

While I was having breakfast, I heard gravel crunch in the driveway; and looking out I saw Chester Conway's Cadillac.

He came right in the house without knocking—people had got in the habit of that when Dad was practicing—and back into the kitchen.

"Keep your seat, boy, keep your seat," he said, though I hadn't made any move to get up. "Go right on with your breakfast."

"Thanks," I said.

He sat down, craning his neck so that he could look at the food on my plate. "Is that coffee fresh? I think I'll have some. Hop up and get me a cup, will you?"

"Yes, sir," I drawled. "Right away, Mr. Conway, sir."

That didn't faze him, of course; that was the kind of talk he felt he was entitled to. He took a noisy swill of coffee, then another. The third time he gulped the cup was emptied. He said he wouldn't take any more, without my offering him any, and lighted a cigar. He dropped the match on the floor, puffed, and dusted ashes into his cup.

West Texans as a whole are a pretty high-handed lot, but they don't walk on a man if he stands up; they're quick to respect the other fellow's rights. Chester Conway was an exception. Conway had been *the* big man in town before the oil boom. He'd always been able to deal with others on his own terms. He'd gone without opposition for so many years that, by this time, he hardly knew it when he saw it. I believe I could have cussed him out in church and he wouldn't have turned a hair. He'd have just figured his ears were playing tricks on him.

It had never been hard for me to believe he'd arranged Mike's murder. The fact that *he* did it would automatically make it all right.

"Well," he said, dusting ashes all over the table. "Got everything fixed for tonight, have you? No chance of any slip-ups? You'll wind this thing right on up so it'll stay wound?"

"I'm not doing anything," I said. "I've done all I'm going to."

"Don't think we'd better leave it that way, Lou. 'Member I told you I didn't like the idea? Well, I still don't. That damned crazy Elmer sees her again no telling what'll happen. You take the money yourself, boy. I've got it all ready, ten thousand in small bills, and—"

"No," I said.

"—pay her off. Then bust her around a little, and run her across the county line."

"Mr. Conway," I said.

"That's the way to do it," he chuckled, his big pale jowls jouncing. "Pay her, bust her and chase her . . . You say something?"

I went through it again, real slowly, dealing it out a word at a time. Miss Lakeland insisted on seeing Elmer one more time before she left. She insisted on his bringing the dough, and she didn't want any witnesses along. Those were her terms, and if Conway wanted her to leave quietly he'd have to meet 'em. We could have her pinched, of course, but she was bound to talk if we did and it wouldn't be pretty talk.

Conway nodded irritably. "Understand all that. Can't have a lot of dirty publicity. But I don't see—"

"I'll tell you what you don't see, Mr. Conway," I said. "You don't see that you've got a hell of a lot of gall."

"Huh?" His mouth dropped open. "Wha-at?"

"I'm sorry," I said. "Stop and think a minute. How would it look if it got around that an officer of the law had made a blackmail pay-off—that is, if she was willing to accept it from me? How do you think I feel being mixed up in a dirty affair of this kind? Now, Elmer got into this trouble and he came to me—"

"Only smart thing he ever did."

"—and I came to you. And you asked me to see what could be done about getting her out of town quietly. I did it. That's all I'm going to do. I don't see how you can ask me to do anything more."

"Well, uh"—he cleared his throat—"maybe not, boy. Reckon, you're right. But you will see that she leaves after she gets the money?"

"I'll see to that," I said. "If she's not gone within an hour, I'll move her along myself."

He got up, fidgeting around nervously, so I walked him to the door to get rid of him. I couldn't take him much longer. It would have been bad enough if I hadn't known what he'd done to Mike.

I kept my hands in my pockets, pretending like I didn't see him when he started to shake hands. He opened the screen, then hesitated a moment.

"Better not go off anywhere," he said. "I'm sending Elmer over as soon as I can locate him. Want you to give him a good talking-to; see that he's got everything down straight. Make him know what's what, understand?"

"Yes, sir," I said. "It's mighty nice of you to let me talk to him."

"That's all right. No trouble at all," he said; and the screen slammed behind him.

A couple hours later Elmer showed up.

He was big and flabby-looking like his old man, and he tried to be as overbearing but he didn't quite have the guts for it. Some of our Central City boys had flattened him a few times, and it had done him a world of good. His blotched face was glistening with sweat; his breath would have tested a hundred and eighty proof.

"Getting started pretty early in the day, aren't you?" I said.

"So what?"

"Not a thing," I said. "I've tried to do you a favor. If you ball it up, it's your headache."

He grunted and crossed his legs. "I dunno, Lou," he frowned. "Dunno about all this. What if the old man never cools off? What'll me and Joyce do when the ten thousand runs out?"

"Well, Elmer," I said. "I guess there's some misunderstanding. I understood that you were sure your father would come around in time. If that isn't the case, maybe I'd better tell Miss Lakeland and—"

"No, Lou! Don't do that! . . . Hell, he'll get over it. He always gets over the things I do. But—"

"Why don't you do this?" I said. "Don't let your ten thousand run out. Buy you some kind of business; you and Joyce can run it together.

When it's going good, get in touch with your dad. He'll see that you've made a darned smart move, and you won't have any trouble squaring things."

Elmer brightened a little—doggoned little. Working wasn't Elmer's idea of a good solution to any problem.

"Don't let me talk you into it," I said. "I think Miss Lakeland has been mighty badly misjudged—she convinced me and I'm not easy to convince. I've stuck my neck out a mile to give you and her a fresh start together, but if you don't want to go—"

"Why'd you do it, Lou? Why'd you do all this for me and her?"

"Maybe money," I said, smiling. "I don't make very much. Maybe I figured you'd do something for me in a money way."

His face turned a few shades redder. "Well . . . I could give you a little something out of the ten thousand, I guess."

"Oh, I wouldn't take any of that!" *You're damned right I wouldn't.* "I figured a man like you must have a little dough of his own. What do you do for your cigarettes and gas and whiskey? Does your dad buy 'em for you?"

"Like hell!" He sat up and jerked out a roll of bills. "I got plenty of money."

He started to peel off a few bills—they were all twenties, it looked like—and then he caught my eye. I gave him a grin. It told him, plain as day, that I expected him to act like a cheapskate.

"Aw, hell," he said, and he wadded the roll together and tossed the whole thing to me. "See you tonight," he said, hoisting himself up.

"At ten o'clock," I nodded.

There were twenty-five twenties in the roll. Five hundred dollars. Now that I had it, it was welcome; I could always use a little extra money. But I hadn't planned on touching Elmer. I'd only done it to shut him up about my motives in helping him.

I didn't feel much like cooking, so I ate dinner in town. Coming home again I listened to the radio a while, read the Sunday papers and went to sleep.

Yes, maybe I was taking things pretty calmly, but I'd gone through the deal so often in my mind that I'd gotten used to it. *Joyce and Elmer were going to die. Joyce had asked for it. The Conways had asked for it. I wasn't any more cold-blooded than the dame who'd have me in hell to get her own way. I wasn't any more cold-blooded than the guy who'd had Mike knocked from an eight-storey building.*

Elmer hadn't done it, of course; probably he didn't even know anything about it. But I had to get to the old man through him. It was the only way I could, and it was the way it should be. I'd be doing to him what he'd done to Dad.

... It was eight o'clock when I waked up—eight of the dark, moonless night I'd been waiting for. I gulped a cup of coffee, eased the car down the alley and headed for Derrick Road.

SIX

Here in the oil country you see quite a few places like the old Branch house. They were ranch houses or homesteads at one time; but wells were drilled around 'em, right up to their doorsteps sometimes, and everything nearby became a mess of oil and sulphur water and red sun-baked drilling mud. The grease-black grass dies. The creeks and springs disappear. And then the oil is gone and the houses stand black and abandoned, lost and lonely-looking behind the pest growths of sunflowers and sage and Johnson grass.

The Branch place stood back from Derrick Road a few hundred feet, at the end of a lane so overgrown with weeds that I almost missed it. I turned into the lane, killed the motor after a few yards and got out.

At first I couldn't see a thing; it was that dark. But gradually my eyes became used to it. I could see all I needed to see. I opened the trunk compartment and located a tire tool. Taking a rusty spike from my pocket, I drove it into the right rear tire. There was a *poof!* and a *whish-ss!*. The springs squeaked and whined as the car settled rapidly.

I got a jack under the axle, and raised it a foot or so. I rocked the car and slid it off the jack. I left it that way and headed up the lane.

It took maybe five minutes to reach the house and pull a plank from the porch. I leaned it against the gate post where I could find it in a hurry, and headed across the fields to Joyce's house.

"Lou!" She stood back from the door, startled. "I couldn't imagine who—where's your car? Is something wrong?"

"Nothing but a flat tire," I grinned. "I had to leave the car down the road a piece."

I sauntered into the living room, and she came around in front of me, gripping her arms around my back and pressing her face against my shirt. Her negligee fell open, accidentally on purpose I imagine. She moved her body against mine.

"Lou, honey . . ."

"Yeah?" I said.

"It's only about nine and Stupid won't be here for another hour, and I won't see you for two weeks. And . . . well, you know."

I knew. I knew how *that* would look in an autopsy.

"Well, I don't know, baby," I said. "I'm kind of pooped out, and you're all prettied up—"

"Oh, I am not!" She squeezed me. "I'm always prettied up to hear you tell it. Hurry, so I can have my bath."

Bath. That made it okay. "You twisted my arm, baby," I said, and I swept her up and carried her into the bedroom. And, no, it didn't bother me a bit.

Because right in the middle of it, right in the middle of the sweet talk and sighing, she suddenly went still and pushed my head back and looked me in the eye.

"You *will* join me in two weeks, Lou? Just as soon as you sell your house and wind up your affairs?"

"That's the understanding," I said.

"Don't keep me waiting. I want to be sweet to you, but if you won't let me I'll be the other way. I'll come back here and raise hell. I'll follow you around town and tell everyone how you—"

"—robbed you of your bloom and cast you aside?" I said.

"Crazy!" she giggled. "But just the same, Lou . . ."

"I know. I won't keep you waiting, baby."

I lay on the bed while she had her bath. She came back in from it, wiping herself with a big towel, and got some panties and a brassiere out of a suitcase. She stepped into the panties, humming, and brought the brassiere over to me. I helped her put it on, giving her a pinch or two, and she giggled and wiggled.

I'm going to miss you, baby, I thought. *You've got to go, but I'm sure going to miss you.*

"Lou . . . You suppose Elmer will make any trouble?"

"I already told you," I said. "What can he do? He can't squawk to his dad. I'll tell him I changed my mind, and we'll have to keep faith with the old man. And that'll be that."

She frowned. "It seems so—oh, so complicated! I mean it looks like we could have got the money without dragging Elmer into it."

"Well . . ." I glanced at the clock.

Nine-thirty-three. I didn't need to stall any longer. I sat up beside her, swinging my feet to the floor; casually drawing on my gloves.

"Well, I'll tell you, baby," I said. "It *is* kind of complicated, but it has to be that way. You've probably heard the gossip about Mike Dean, my foster brother? Well, Mike didn't do that. He took the blame for me. So if you should do your talking around town, it would be a lot worse than you realized. People would start thinking, and before it was all over . . ."

"But, Lou. I'm not going to say anything. You're going to join me and—"

"Better let me finish," I said. "I told you how Mike fell from that building? Only he didn't fall; he was murdered. Old man Conway arranged it and—"

"Lou"—she didn't get it at all. "I won't let you do anything to Elmer! You mustn't, honey. They'll catch you and you'll go to jail and—oh, honey, don't even think about it!"

"They won't catch me," I said. "They won't even suspect me. They'll think he was half-stiff, like he usually is, and you got to fighting and both got killed."

She still didn't get it. She laughed, frowning a little at the same time. "But, Lou—that doesn't make sense. How could I be dead when—"

"Easy," I said, and I gave her a slap. And still she didn't get it.

She put a hand to her face and rubbed it slowly. "Y-you'd better not do that, now, Lou. I've got to travel, and—"

"You're not going anywhere, baby," I said, and I hit her again.

And at last she got it.

She jumped up and I jumped with her. I whirled her around and gave her a quick one-two, and she shot backwards across the room and bounced and slumped against the wall. She staggered to her feet, weaving, mumbling, and half-fell toward me. I let her have it again.

I backed her against the wall, slugging, and it was like pounding a pumpkin. Hard, then everything giving way at once. She slumped down, her knees bent under her, her head hanging limp; and then, slowly, an inch at a time, she pushed herself up again.

She couldn't see; I don't know how she could. I don't know how she could stand or go on breathing. But she brought her head up, wobbling, and she raised her arms, raised them and spread them and held them out. And then she staggered toward me, just as a car pulled into the yard.

"Guhguh-guhby . . . kiss guhguh-guh—"

I brought an uppercut up from the floor. There was a sharp *craack!* and her whole body shot upward, and came down in a heap. And that time it stayed down.

I wiped my gloves on her body; it was her blood and it belonged there. I took the gun from the dresser, turned off the light and closed the door.

Elmer was coming up the steps, crossing the porch. I got to the front door and opened it.

"Hiya, Lou, ol' boy, ol' boy," he said. "Right on time, huh? Thass Elmer Conway, always right on time."

"Half-stiff," I said, "that's Elmer Conway. Have you got the money?"

He patted the thick brown folder under his arm. "What's it look like? Where's Joyce?"

"Back in the bedroom. Why don't you go on back? I'll bet she won't say no if you try to slip it to her."

"Aw," he blinked foolishly. "Aw, you shouldn't talk like that, Lou. You know we're gonna get married."

"Suit yourself," I shrugged. "I'd bet money though that she's all stretched out waiting for you."

I wanted to laugh out loud. I wanted to yell. I wanted to leap on him and tear him to pieces.

"Well, maybe . . ."

He turned suddenly and lumbered down the hall. I leaned against the wall, waiting, as he entered the bedroom and turned on the light.

I heard him say, "Hiya, Joyce, ol' kid, ol' ol' k-k-k . . ." I heard a heavy thump, and a gurgling, strangled sound. Then he said, he screamed, "Joyce . . . Joyce . . . *Lou!*"

I sauntered back. He was down on his knees and there was blood on his hands, and a big streak across his chin where he'd wiped it. He looked up at me, his mouth hanging open.

I laughed—I had to laugh or do something worse—and his eyes squeezed shut and he bawled. I yelled with laughter, bending over and slapping my legs. I doubled up, laughing and farting and laughing some more. Until there wasn't a laugh in me or anyone. I'd used up all the laughter in the world.

He got to his feet, smearing his face with his big flabby hands, staring at me stupidly.

"W-who did it, Lou?"

"It was suicide," I said. "A plain case of suicide."

"B-but that d-don't make—"

"It's the only thing that does make sense! It was the way it was, you hear me? Suicide, you hear me? Suicide suicide suicide! I didn't kill her. Don't you say I killed her. SHE KILLED HERSELF!"

I shot him, then, right in his gaping stupid mouth. I emptied the gun into him.

Stooping, I curved Joyce's hand around the gun butt, then dropped the gun at her side. I went out the door and across the fields again, and I didn't look back.

I found the plank and carried it down to my car. If the car had been seen, that plank was my alibi. I'd had to go up and find one to put under the jack.

I ran the jack up on the plank and put on the spare tire. I threw the tools into the car, started the motor and backed toward Derrick Road. Ordinarily, I'd no more back into a highway at night without my lights than I would without my pants. But this wasn't ordinarily. I just didn't think of it.

If Chester Conway's Cadillac had been traveling faster, I wouldn't be writing this.

He swarmed out of his car cursing, saw who I was, and cursed harder than ever. "Goddamit, Lou, you know better'n that? You trying to get killed, for Christ's sake? Huh? What the hell are you doing here, anyhow?"

"I had to pull in there with a flat tire," I said. "Sorry if I—"

"Well, come on. Let's get going. Can't stand here gabbing all night."

"Going?" I said. "It's still early."

"The hell it is! It's a quarter past eleven, and that damned Elmer ain't home yet. Promised to come right back, and he ain't done it. Probably up there working himself into another scrape."

"Maybe we'd better give him a little more time," I said. I had to wait a while. I couldn't go back in that house now. "Why don't you go on home, Mr. Conway, and I'll—"

"I'm going now!" He turned away from the car. "And you follow me!"

The door of the Cadillac slammed. He backed up and pulled around me, yelling again for me to come on. I yelled back that I would and he drove off. Fast.

I got a cigar lit. I started the motor and killed it. I started it and killed it again. Finally, it stayed running, it just wouldn't die, so I drove off.

I drove up the lane at Joyce's house and parked at the end of it. There wasn't room in the yard with Elmer's and the old man's cars there. I shut off the motor and got out. I climbed the steps and crossed the porch.

The door was open and he was in the living room, talking on the telephone. And his face was like a knife had come down it, slicing away all the flabbiness.

He didn't seem very excited. He didn't seem very sad. He was just business-like, and somehow that made it worse.

"Sure, it's too bad," he said. "Don't tell me that again. I know all about how bad it is. He's dead and that's that, and what I'm interested in is her . . . Well, do it then! Get on out here. We ain't going to let her die, get me? Not this way. I'm going to see that she burns."

SEVEN

It was almost three o'clock in the morning when I got through talking—answering questions, mostly—to Sheriff Maples and the county attorney, Howard Hendricks; and I guess you know I wasn't feeling so good. I was kind of sick to my stomach, and I felt, well, pretty damned sore, angry. Things shouldn't have turned out this way. It was just plumb unreasonable. It wasn't right.

I'd done everything I could to get rid of a couple of undesirable citizens in a neat no-kickbacks way. And here one of 'em was still alive; and purple hell was popping about the other one.

Leaving the courthouse, I drove to the Greek's place and got a cup of coffee that I didn't want. His boy had taken a part-time job in a filling station, and the old man wasn't sure whether it was a good thing or not. I promised to drop by and look in on the lad.

I didn't want to go home and answer a lot more questions from Amy. I hoped that if I stalled long enough, she'd give up and leave.

Johnnie Pappas, the Greek's boy, was working at Slim Murphy's place. He was around at the side of the station when I drove in, doing something to the motor of his hot rod. I got out of my car and he came toward me slowly, sort of watchfully, wiping his hands on a chunk of waste.

"Just heard about your new job, Johnnie," I said. "Congratulations."

"Yeah." He was tall, good-looking; not at all like his father. "Dad sent you out here?"

"He told me you'd gone to work here," I said. "Anything wrong with that?"

"Well . . . You're up pretty late."

"Well," I laughed, "so are you. Now how about filling 'er up with gas and checking the oil?"

He got busy, and by the time he was through he'd pretty much lost his suspicions. "I'm sorry if I acted funny, Lou. Dad's been kind of nagging me—he just can't understand that a guy my age needs a little real dough of his own—and I thought he was having you check up on me."

"You know me better than that, Johnnie."

"Sure, I do," he smiled, warmly. "I've got plenty of nagging from people, but no one but you ever really tried to help me. You're the only real friend I've ever had in this lousy town. Why do you do it, Lou? What's the percentage in bothering with a guy that everyone else is down on?"

"Oh, I don't know," I said. And I didn't. I didn't even know how I could stand here talking to him with the terrible load I had on my mind. "Maybe it's because I was a kid myself not so many years ago. Fathers are funny. The best ones get in your hair most."

"Yeah. Well . . ."

"What hours do you work, Johnnie?"

"Just midnight to seven. Saturdays and Sundays. Just enough to keep me in pocket money. Dad thinks I'll be too tired to go to school on Mondays, but I won't, Lou. I'll make it fine."

"Sure, you will," I said. "There's just one thing, Johnnie. Slim Murphy hasn't got a very good reputation. We've never proved that he was mixed up in any of these car-stripping jobs, but . . ."

"I know." He kicked the gravel of the driveway, uncomfortably. "I won't get into any trouble, Lou."

"Good enough," I said. "That's a promise, and I know you don't break your promises."

I paid him with a twenty dollar bill, got my change and headed toward home. Wondering about myself. Shaking my head, as I drove. I hadn't put on an act. I *was* concerned and worried about the kid. Me, worried about *his* troubles.

The house was all dark when I got home, but it would be, whether Amy was there or not. So I didn't get my hopes too high. I figured that my standing her up would probably make her all the more determined to stay; that she was a cinch to crop up at the one time I didn't want any part of her. That's the way I figured it, and that's the way it was.

She was up in my bedroom in bed. And she'd filled two ash trays with the cigarettes she'd smoked. And mad! I've never seen one little old girl so mad in my life.

I sat down on the edge of the bed and pulled off my boots; and for about the next twenty minutes I didn't say a word. I didn't get a chance. Finally, she began to slow up a little, and I tried to apologize.

"I'm sure sorry, honey, but I couldn't help it. I've had a lot of trouble tonight."

"I'll bet!"

"You want to hear about it or not? If you don't, just say so."

"Oh, go on! I've heard so many of your lies and excuses I may as well hear a few more."

I told her what had happened—that is, what was *supposed* to have happened—and she could hardly hold herself in until I'd finished. The last word was hardly out of my mouth before she'd cut loose on me again.

"How could you be so stupid, Lou? How *could* you do it? Getting yourself mixed up with some wretched prostitute and that awful Elmer Conway! Now, there'll be a big scandal and you'll probably lose your job, and —"

"Why?" I mumbled. "I didn't do anything."

"I want to know why you did it!"

"Well, it was kind of a favor, see? Chester Conway wanted me to see what I could do about getting Elmer out of this scrape, so—"

"Why did he have to come to you? Why do you always have to be doing favors for other people? You never do any for me!"

I didn't say anything for a minute. But I thought, *That's what you think, honey. I'm doing you a favor by not beating your head off.*

"Answer me, Lou Ford!"

"All right," I said. "I shouldn't have done it."

"You shouldn't have allowed that woman to stay in this county in the first place!"

"No," I nodded. "I shouldn't have."

"Well?"

"I'm not perfect," I snapped. "I make plenty of mistakes. How many times do you want me to say it?"

"Well! All I've got to say is . . ."

All she had to say would take her the rest of her life to finish; and I wasn't even halfway in the mood for it. I reached out and grabbed her by the crotch.

"Lou! You stop that!"

"Why?" I said.

"Y-you stop it!" She shivered. "You s-stop or . . . Oh *Lou*!"

I lay down beside her with my clothes on. I had to do it, because there was just one way of shutting Amy up.

So I laid down and she swarmed up against me. And there wasn't a thing wrong with Amy when she was like that; you couldn't have asked much more from a woman. But there was plenty wrong with me. Joyce Lakeland was wrong with me.

"Lou . . ." Amy slowed down a little. "What's the matter, dear?"

"All this trouble," I said. "I guess it's thrown me for a loop."

"You poor darling. Just forget everything but me, and I'll pet you and whisper to you, mmm? I'll . . ." She kissed me and whispered what she would do. And she did it. And, hell, she might as well have done it to a fence post.

Baby Joyce had taken care of me, but good.

Amy pulled her hand away, and began brushing it against her hip. Then she snatched up a handful of sheet, and wiped—scrubbed—her hip with it.

"You son-of-a-bitch," she said. "You dirty, filthy bastard."

"Wha-at?" I said. It was like getting a punch in the guts. Amy didn't go in for cussing. At least, I'd never heard her do much.

"You're dirty. I can tell. I can smell it on you. Smell her. You can't wash it off. It'll never come off. You—"

"Jesus Christ!" I grabbed her by the shoulders. "What are you saying, Amy?"

"You screwed her. You've been doing it all along. You've been putting her dirty insides inside of me, smearing me with her. And I'm going to make you pay for it. If it's the l-last thing I ever d-do, I'll—"

She jerked away from me, sobbing, and jumped out of bed. As I got up, she backed around a chair, putting it between me and her.

"K-keep away from me! Don't you dare touch me!"

"Why, sure, honey," I said. "Whatever you say."

She didn't see the meaning yet of what she'd said. All she could think of was herself, the insult to herself. But I knew that, given enough time—and not much at that—she'd put all the parts of the picture together. She wouldn't have any real proof, of course. All she had to go on was guesswork—intuition—and that operation I'd had; something, thank God, which seemed to have slipped her mind for the moment. Anyway, she'd talk. And the fact that there wasn't any proof for what she said wouldn't help me much.

You don't need proof, know what I mean? Not from what I've seen of the law in operation. All you need is a tip that a guy is guilty. From then on, unless he's a big shot, it's just a matter of making him admit it.

"Amy," I said, "Amy, honey. Look at me."

"I d-don't want to look at you."

"Look at me . . . This is Lou, honey, Lou Ford, remember? The guy you've known all your life. I ask you, now, would I do what you said I did?"

She hesitated, biting her lips. "You did do it." Her voice was just a shade uncertain. "I know you did."

"You don't know anything," I said. "Just because I'm tired and upset, you jump to a crazy conclusion. Why, why would I fool around with some chippy when I had you? What could a dame like that give me that would make me run the risk of losing a girl like you? Huh? Now, that doesn't make sense, does it, honey."

"Well . . ." That had got to her. It had hit her right in the pride, where she was tenderest. But it wasn't quite enough to jar her loose from her hunch.

She picked up her panties and began putting them on, still standing behind the chair. "There's no use arguing about it, Lou," she said, wearily. "I suppose I can thank my lucky stars that I haven't caught some terrible disease."

"But dammit . . .!" I moved around the chair, suddenly, and got her in my arms. "Dammit, stop talking that way about the girl I'm going to marry! I don't mind for myself, but you can't say it about her, get me? You can't say that the girl I'm going to marry would sleep with a guy who plays around with whores!"

"Let me go, Lou! Let . . ." She stopped struggling, abruptly.

"What did you—?"

"You heard me," I said.

"B-but just two days ago—"

"So what?" I said. "No man likes to be yanked into marriage. He wants to do his own proposing, which is just what I'm doing right now. Hell, we've already put it off too long, in my opinion. This crazy business tonight proves it. If we were married we wouldn't have all these quarrels and misunderstandings like we've been having."

"Since that woman came to town, you mean."

"All right," I said. "I've done all I could. If you're willing to believe that about me, I wouldn't want—"

"Wait, Lou!" She hung on to me. "After all, you can't blame me if—" And she let it go at that. She had to give up for her own sake. "I'm sorry, Lou. Of course, I was wrong."

"You certainly were."

"When shall we do it, Lou? Get married, I mean."

"The sooner the better," I lied. I didn't have the slightest intention of marrying her. But I needed time to do some planning, and I had to keep her quiet. "Let's get together in a few days when we're both more ourselves, and talk about it."

"Huh-uh." She shook her head. "Now that you've—we've come

to the decision, let's go through with it. Let's talk about it right now."

"But it's getting daylight, honey," I said. "If you're still here even a little while from now, people will see you when you leave."

"I don't care if they do, darling. I don't care a teensy-weensie little bit." She snuggled against me, burrowing her head against my chest. And without seeing her face, I knew she was grinning. She had me on the run, and she was getting a hell of a kick out of it.

"Well, I'm pretty tired," I said. "I think I ought to sleep a little while before—"

"I'll make you some coffee, darling. That'll wake you up."

"But, honey—"

The phone rang. She let go of me, not very hurriedly, and I stepped over to the writing desk and picked up the extension.

"Lou?" It was Sheriff Bob Maples.

"Yeah, Bob," I said. "What's on your mind?"

He told me, and I said, Okay, and hung up the phone again. Amy looked at me, and changed her mind about popping off.

"Your job, Lou? You've got some work to do?"

"Yeah," I nodded. "Sheriff Bob's driving by to pick me up in a few moments."

"You poor dear! And you so tired! I'll get dressed and get right out."

I helped her dress, and walked to the back door with her. She gave me a couple of big kisses and I promised to call her as soon as I got a chance. She left then, a couple of minutes before Sheriff Maples drove up.

EIGHT

The county attorney, Howard Hendricks, was with him sitting in the back seat of the car. I gave him a cold-eyed look and a nod, as I got in the front, and he gave me back the look without a nod. I'd never had much use for him. He was one of those professional patriots, always talking about what a great hero he'd been in the war.

Sheriff Bob put the car in gear, clearing his throat uncomfortably. "Sure hated to bother you, Lou," he said. "Hope I didn't interrupt anything."

"Nothing that can't wait," I said. "She—I'd already kept her waiting five-six hours."

"You had a date for last night?" asked Hendricks.

"That's right"—I didn't turn around in the seat.

"For what time?"

"For a little after ten. The time I figured I'd have the Conway business finished."

The county attorney grunted. He sounded more than a mite disappointed. "Who was the girl?"

"None of your—"

"Wait a minute, Lou!" Bob eased his foot off the gas, and turned onto Derrick Road. "Howard, you're getting way out of line. You're kind of a newcomer out this way—been here eight years now, ain't you?—but you still ought to know better'n to ask a man a question like that."

"What the hell?" said Hendricks. "It's my job. It's an important question. If Ford had himself a date last night, it—well"—he hesitated—"it shows that he planned on being there instead of—well, uh—some place else. You see what I mean, Ford?"

I saw, all right, but I wasn't going to tell him so. I was just old dumb Lou from Kalamzoo. I wouldn't be thinking about an alibi, because I hadn't done anything to need an alibi for.

"No," I drawled, "I reckon I don't know what you mean. To come right down to cases, and no offense meant, I figured you'd done all the jawing you had to do when I talked to you an hour or so ago."

"Well, you're dead wrong, brother!" He glared at me, redfaced, in the rearview mirror. "I've got quite a few more questions. And I'm still waiting for the answer to the last one I asked. Who was the—"

"Drop it, Howard!" Bob jerked his head curtly. "Don't ask Lou that again, or I'm personally going to lose my temper. I know the girl. I know her folks. She's one of the nicest little ladies in town, and I ain't got the slightest doubt Lou had a date with her."

Hendricks scowled, gave out with an irritated laugh. "I don't get it. She's not too nice to sl—well, skip it—but she's too nice to have her name mentioned in the strictest confidence. I'm damned if I can understand a deal like that. The more I'm around you people the less I can understand you."

I turned around, smiling, looking friendly and serious. For a while, anyway, it wasn't a good idea to have anyone sore at me. And a guy that's got something on his conscience can't afford to get riled.

"I guess we're a pretty stiff-necked lot out here, Howard," I said. "I suppose it comes from the fact that this country was never very thickly settled, and a man had to be doggoned careful of the way he acted or he'd be marked for life. I mean, there wasn't any crowd for him to sink into—he was always out where people could see him."

"So?"

"So if a man or woman does something, nothing bad you understand, but the kind of thing men and women have always been doing, you don't let on that you know anything about it. You don't, because sooner or later you're going to need the same kind of favor yourself. You see how it is? It's the only way we can go on being human, and still hold our heads up."

He nodded indifferently. "Very interesting. Well, here we are, Bob."

Sheriff Maples pulled off the pavement and parked on the shoulder of the road. We got out, and Hendricks nodded toward the weed-grown trail which led up to the old Branch house. He jerked his head at it, and then turned and looked at me.

"Do you see that track through there, Ford? Do you know what caused that?"

"Why, I reckon so," I said. "A flat tire."

"You admit that? You concede that a track of that kind would have to be there, *if* you had a flat tire?"

I pushed back my stetson, and scratched my head. I looked at Bob, frowning a little. "I don't guess I see what you boys are driving at," I said. "What's this all-about, Bob?"

Of course, I did see. I saw that I'd made one hell of a bone-head play. I'd guessed it as soon as I saw the track through the weeds, and I had an answer ready. But I couldn't come out with it too fast. It had to be done easy-like.

"This is Howard's show," said the sheriff. "Maybe you'd better answer him, Lou."

"Okay," I shrugged. "I've already said it once. A flat tire makes that kind of track."

"Do you know," said Hendricks slowly, "when that track was made?"

"I ain't got the slightest idea," I said. "All I know is that my car didn't make it."

"You're a damned li—*Huh?*" Hendricks' mouth dropped open foolishly. "B-but—"

"I didn't have a flat when I turned off the highway."

"Now, wait a minute! You—"

"Maybe you better wait a minute," Sheriff Bob interrupted. "I don't recollect Lou tellin' us his tire went flat here on Derrick Road. Don't recall his sayin' anything of the kind."

"If I did say it," I said, "I sure as heck didn't mean to. I knew I had a puncture, sure; I felt the car sway a little. But I turned off in the lane before the tire could really go down."

Bob nodded and glanced at Hendricks. The county attorney suddenly got busy lighting a cigarette. I don't know which was redder—his face or the sun pushing up over the hills.

I scratched my head again. "Well," I said, "I reckon it's none of my business. But I sure hope you fellows didn't chew up a good tire makin' that track."

Hendricks' mouth was working. Bob's old eyes sparkled. Off in the distance somewhere, maybe three-four miles away, there was a *such-whush* as a mudhog drilling pump began to growl. Suddenly, the sheriff whuffed and coughed and let out a wild whoop of laughter.

"Haw, haw, haw!" he boomed. "Doggone it, Howard, if this ain't the funniest—haw, haw, haw—"

And then, Hendricks started laughing, too. Restrained, uncomfortable, at first; then, plain unashamed laughter. I stood looking on, grinning puzzledly, like a guy who wanted to join in but didn't know the score.

I was glad now that I'd made that bonehead mistake. When a man's rope slides off you once, he's mighty cautious about making a second throw.

Hendricks slapped me on the back. "I'm a damned fool, Lou. I should have known better."

"Say," I said, letting it dawn on me at last. "You don't mean you thought I—"

"Of course, we didn't think so," said Bob, warmly. "Nothing of the kind."

"It was just something that had to be looked into," Hendricks explained. "We had to have an answer for it. Now, you didn't talk much to Conway last night, did you?"

"No," I said. "It didn't seem to me like a very good time to do much talking."

"Well, I talked to him, Bob, I did. Rather he talked to us. And he's really raring and tearing. This woman—what's her name, Lakeland?—is as good as dead. The doctors say she'll never regain consciousness, so Conway isn't going to be able to lay the blame for this mess on her. Naturally, then, he'll want to stick someone else with it; he'll be snatching at straws. That's why we have to head him off on anything that looks—uh—even mildly peculiar."

"But, shucks," I said, "anyone could see what happened. Elmer'd been drinking, and he tried to push her around, and—"

"Sure. But Conway don't want to admit that. And he won't admit it, if there's any way out."

We all rode in the front seat going back to town. I was in the middle, squeezed in between the sheriff and Hendricks; and all of a sudden a crazy notion came over me. Maybe I hadn't fooled 'em. Maybe they were putting on an act, just like I was. Maybe that was why they'd put me in the middle, so I couldn't jump out of the car.

It was a crazy idea, of course, and it was gone in a moment. But I started a little before I could catch myself.

"Feelin' twitchy?" said Bob.

"Just hunger pains," I grinned. "I haven't eaten since yesterday afternoon."

"Wouldn't mind a bite myself," Bob nodded. "How about you, Howard?"

"Might be a good idea. Mind stopping by the courthouse first?"

"Huh-uh," said Bob. "We go by there and we're apt not to get away. You can call from the restaurant—call my office, too, while you're at it."

Word of what had happened was already all over town, and there was a lot of whispering and gawking as we pulled up in front of the restaurant. I mean, there was a lot of whispering and gawking from the newcomers, the oil workers and so on. The old timers just nodded and went on about their business.

Hendricks stopped to use the telephone, and Bob and I sat down in a booth. We ordered ham and eggs all around, and pretty soon Hendricks came back.

"That Conway!" he snapped, sliding in across from us. "Now he wants to fly that woman into Fort Worth. Says she can't get the right kind of medical attention here."

"Yeah?" Bob looked down at the menu, casually. "What time is he takin' her?"

"I'm not at all sure that he is! I'm the man that has the sayso on handling this case. Why, she hasn't even been booked yet, let alone arraigned. We haven't had a chance."

"Can't see that it makes much difference," said Bob, "as long as she's going to die."

"That's not the point! The point is—"

"Yeah, sure," drawled Bob. "You like to take a little trip into Fort Worth, Lou? Maybe I'll go along myself."

"Why, I guess I could," I said.

"I reckon we'll do that, then. Okay, Howard? That'll take care of the technicalities for you."

The waitress set food in front of us, and Bob picked up his knife and fork. I felt his boot kick mine under the table. Hendricks knew how things stood, but he was too much of a phony to admit it. He had to go on playing the big hero—the county attorney that didn't take orders from anyone.

"Now, see here, Bob. Maybe I'm new here, as you see it; maybe I've got a lot to learn. But, by God, I know the law and—"

"So do I," the sheriff nodded. "The one that ain't on the books. Conway wasn't asking you if he could take her to Fort Worth. He was telling you. Did he mention what time?"

"Well"—Hendricks swallowed heavily—"ten this morning, he thought. He wanted to—he's chartering one of the airline's twin-motor jobs, and they've got to fit it up with oxygen and a—"

"Uh-huh. Well, that ought to be all right. Lou and me'll have time to scrub up a little and pack a bag. I'll drop you off at your place, Lou, as soon as we finish here."

"Fine," I said.

Hendricks didn't say anything.

After a minute or two, Bob glanced at him and raised his eyebrows.

"Something wrong with your eggs, son? Better eat 'em before they get cold."

Hendricks heaved a sigh, and began to eat.

NINE

Bob and I were at the airport quite a bit ahead of time, so we went ahead and got on the plane and made ourselves comfortable. Some workmen were pounding around in the baggage compartment, fixing things up according to the doctor's instructions, but tired as we were it would have taken more than that to keep us awake. Bob began to nod, first. Then I closed my eyes, figuring to just rest them a little. And I guess I must have gone right to sleep. I didn't even know when we took off.

One minute I was closing my eyes. The next, it seemed like, Bob was shaking me and pointing out the window.

"There she is, Lou. There's cow town."

I looked out and down. I felt kind of disappointed. I'd never been out of the county before, and now that I was sure Joyce wasn't going to live I could have enjoyed seeing the sights. As it was I hadn't seen anything. I'd wasted all my time sleeping.

"Where's Mr. Conway?" I asked.

"Back in the baggage compartment. I just went back for a look myself."

"She—she's still unconscious?"

"Uh-huh, and she ain't ever going to be any other way if you ask me." He shook his head solemnly. "Conway don't know when he's well off. If that no-account Elmer wasn't already dead, he'd be swingin' from a tree about now."

"Yeah," I said. "It's pretty bad all right."

"Don't know what would possess a man to do a thing like that. Dogged if I do! Don't see how he could be drunk enough or mean enough to do it."

"I guess it's my fault," I said. "I shouldn't have ever let her stay in town."

"We-el . . . I told you to use your own judgment, and she was a mighty cute little trick from all I hear. I'd probably have let her stay myself if I'd been in your place."

"I'm sure sorry, Bob," I said. "I sure wish I'd come to you instead of trying to handle this blackmail deal myself."

"Yeah," he nodded slowly, "but I reckon we've been over that ground enough. It's done now, and there's nothing we can do about it. Talking and fretting about might-have-beens won't get us anywhere."

"No," I said. "I guess there's no use crying over spilled milk."

The plane began to circle and lose altitude, and we fastened our seat belts. A couple of minutes later we were skimming along the landing field, and a police car and ambulance were keeping pace with us.

The plane stopped, and the pilot came out of his compartment and unlocked the door. Bob and I got out, and watched while the doctor supervised the unloading of the stretcher. The upper part of it was closed in kind of a little tent, and all I could see was the outline of her body under the sheet. Then I couldn't even see that; they were hustling her off toward the ambulance. And a heavy hand came down on my shoulder.

"Lou," said Chester Conway. "You come with me in the police car."

"Well," I said, glancing at Bob. "I kind of figured on—"

"You come with me," he repeated. "Sheriff, you ride in the ambulance. We'll see you at the hospital."

Bob pushed back his Stetson, and gave him a hard sharp look. Then his face sort of sagged and he turned and walked away, his scuffed boots dragging against the pavement.

I'd been pretty worried about how to act around Conway. Now, seeing the way he'd pushed old Bob Maples around, I was just plain sore. I jerked away from his hand and got into the police car. I kept my head turned as Conway climbed in and slammed the door.

The ambulance started up, and headed off the field. We followed it. Conway leaned forward and closed the glass partition between our seat and the driver's.

"Didn't like that, did you?" he grunted. "Well, there may be a lot of things you don't like before this is over. I've got the reputation of my dead boy at stake, understand? My own reputation. I'm looking out for that and nothing but that, and I ain't standing on etiquette. I'm not letting someone's tender feelings get in my way."

"I don't suppose you would," I said. "It'd be pretty hard to start in at your time of life."

I wished, immediately, that I hadn't said it; I was giving myself away, you see. But he didn't seem to have heard me. Like always, he wasn't hearing anything he didn't want to hear.

"They're operating on that woman as soon as she gets to the hospital," he went on. "If she pulls through the operation, she'll be able to talk by tonight. I want you there at that time—just as soon as she comes out of the anaesthetic."

"Well?" I said.

"Bob Maples is all right, but he's too old to be on his toes. He's liable to foul up the works right when you need him most. That's why I'm letting him go on now when it don't matter whether anyone's around or not."

"I don't know as I understand you," I said. "You mean—"

"I've got rooms reserved at a hotel. I'll drop you off there, and you stay there until I call you. Get some rest, understand? Get rested up good, so's you'll be on your toes and raring to go when the time comes."

"All right," I shrugged, "but I slept all the way up on the plane."

"Sleep some more, then. You may have to be up all night."

The hotel was on West Seventh Street, a few blocks from the hospital; and Conway had engaged a whole suite of rooms. The assistant manager of the place went up with me and the bellboy, and a couple of minutes after they left a waiter brought in a tray of whiskey and ice. And right behind him came another waiter with a flock of sandwiches and coffee.

I poured myself a nice drink, and took it over by the window. I sat down in a big easy chair, and propped my boots up on the radiator. I leaned back, grinning.

Conway was a big shot, all right. He could push you around and make you like it. He could have places like this, with people jumping sideways to wait on him. He could have everything but what he wanted—his son and a good name.

His son had beaten a whore to death, and she'd killed him; and he'd never be able to live it down. Not if he lived to be a hundred and I damned well hoped he would.

I ate part of a clubhouse sandwich, but it didn't seem to set so well. So I fixed another big drink and took it over to the window. I felt kind of restless and uneasy. I wished I could get out and wander around the town.

Forth Worth is the beginning of West Texas, and I wouldn't have felt conspicuous, dressed as I was, like I would have in Dallas or Houston. I could have had a fine time—seen something new for a change. And instead I had to stay here by myself, doing nothing, seeing nothing, thinking the same old thoughts.

It was like there was a plot against me almost. I'd done something wrong, way back when I was a kid, and I'd never been able to get away from it. I'd had my nose rubbed in it day after day until, like an overtrained dog, I'd started crapping out of pure fright. And, now, here I was—

I poured another drink . . .

—Here I was, now, but it wouldn't be like this much longer. Joyce was bound to die if she wasn't dead already. I'd got rid of her and I'd got rid of *it*—the sickness—when I did it. And just as soon as things quieted down, I'd quit my job and sell the house and Dad's practice and pull out.

Amy Stanton? Well—I shook my head—she wasn't going to stop me. She wasn't going to keep me chained there in Central City. I didn't know just how I'd break away from her, but I knew darned well that I would.

Some way. Somehow.

More or less to kill time, I took a long hot bath; and afterwards I tried the sandwiches and coffee again. I paced around the room, eating and drinking coffee, moving from window to window. I wished we weren't up so high so's I could see a little something.

I tried taking a nap, and that was no good. I got a shine cloth out of the bathroom and began rubbing at my boots. I'd got one brushed up real good and was starting on the toe of the second when Bob Maples came in.

He said hello, casually, and fixed himself a drink. He sat down, looking into the glass, twirling the ice around and around.

"I was sure sorry about what happened there at the airport, Bob," I said. "I reckon you know I wanted to stick with you."

"Yeah," he said shortly.

"I let Conway know I didn't like it," I said.

And he said, "Yeah," again. "Forget it. Just drop it, will you?"

"Well, sure," I nodded. "Whatever you say, Bob."

I watched him out of the corner of my eye, as I went ahead rubbing the boot. He acted mad and worried, almost disgusted you might say. But I was pretty sure it wasn't over anything I'd done. In fact, I couldn't see that Conway had done enough to upset him like this.

"Is your rheumatism bothering you again?" I said. "Why don't you face around on the straight chair where I can get at your shoulder muscles, and I'll—"

He raised his head and looked up at me. And his eyes were clear, but somehow there seemed to be tears behind them. Slowly, slowly, like he was talking to himself, he began to speak.

"I know what you are, don't I, Lou? Know you backwards and forwards. Known you since you was knee high to a grasshopper, and I never knowed a bad thing about you. Know just what you're goin' to say and do, no matter what you're up against. Like there at the airport—seeing Conway order me around. A lot of men in your place would have got a big bang out of that, but I knew you wouldn't. I knew you'd feel a lot more hurt about it than I did. That's the way you are, and you wouldn't know how to be any other way . . ."

"Bob," I said. "You got something on your mind, Bob?"

"It'll keep," he said. "I reckon it'll have to keep for a while. I just wanted you to know that I—I—"

"Yes, Bob?"

"It'll keep," he repeated. "Like I said, it'll have to keep." And he clinked the ice in his glass, staring down at it. "That Howard Hendricks," he went on. "Now, Howard ought to've known better'n to put you through that foolishness this morning. 'Course, he's got his job to do, same as I got mine, and a man can't let friendship stand in the way of duty. But—"

"Oh, hell, Bob," I said. "I didn't think anything of that."

"Well, I did. I got to thinking about it this afternoon after we left the airport. I thought about how you'd have acted if you'd have been in my place and me in yours. Oh, I reckon you'd have been pleasant and friendly, because that's the way you're built. But you wouldn't have left any doubt as to where you stood. You'd have said, 'Look, now, Bob Maples is a friend of mine, and I know he's straight as a string. So if there's something we want to know, let's just up and ask him. Let's don't play no little two-bit sheepherders' tricks on him like he was on one side of the fence and we was on the other . . . That's what you'd have done. But me— Well, I don't know, Lou. Maybe I'm behind the times. Maybe I'm getting too old for this job."

It looked to me like he might have something there. He was getting old and unsure of himself, and Conway had probably given him a hell of a riding that I didn't know about.

"You had some trouble at the hospital, Bob?" I said.

"Yeah," he hesitated. "I had some trouble." He got up and poured more whiskey into his glass. Then, he moved over to the window and stood rocking on his heels, his back turned to me. "She's dead, Lou. She never came out of the ether."

"Well," I said. "We all knew she didn't stand a chance. Everyone but Conway, and he was just too stubborn to see reason."

He didn't say anything. I walked over to the window by him and put my arm around his shoulders.

"Look, Bob," I said. "I don't know what Conway said to you, but don't let it get you down. Where the hell does he get off at, anyway? He wasn't even going to have us come along on this trip; we had to deal ourselves in. Then, when we got back here, he wants us to jump whenever he hollers frog, and he raises hell when things don't go to suit him."

He shrugged a little, or maybe he just took a deep breath. I let my arm slide from his shoulders, hesitated a moment, thinking he was about to say something, then went into the bathroom and closed the door. When a man's feeling low, sometimes the best thing to do is leave him alone.

I sat down on the edge of the tub, and lighted a cigar. I sat thinking—standing outside of myself—thinking about myself and Bob Maples. He'd always been pretty decent to me, and I liked him. But no more, I suppose, than I liked a lot of other people. When it came right down to cases, he was one of hundreds of people I knew and was friendly with. And yet here I was, fretting about his problems instead of my own.

Of course, that might be partly because I'd known my problems were pretty much settled. I'd known that Joyce couldn't live, that she wasn't going to talk. She might have regained consciousness for a while, but she sure as hell wouldn't have talked; not after what had happened to her face . . . But knowing that I was safe couldn't entirely explain my concern for him. Because I'd been damned badly rattled after the murder, I hadn't been able to reason clearly, to accept the fact that I *had* to be safe. Yet I'd tried to help the Greek's boy, Johnnie Pappas.

The door slammed open, and I looked up. Bob grinned at me broadly, his face flushed, whiskey slopping to the floor from his glass.

"Hey," he said, "you runnin' out on me, Lou? Come on in here an' keep me company."

"Sure, Bob," I said. "Sure, I will." And I went back into the living room with him. He flopped down into a chair, and he drained his drink at a gulp.

"Let's do something, Lou. Let's go out and paint old cow town red. Just me'n you, huh?"

"What about Conway?"

"T'hell with him. He's got some business here; stayin' over for a few days. We'll check our bags somewheres, so's we won't have to run into him again, and then we'll have a party."

He made a grab for the bottle, and got it on the second try. I took it away from him, and filled his glass myself.

"That sounds fine, Bob," I said. "I'd sure like to do that. But shouldn't we be getting back to Central City? I mean, with Conway feeling the way he does, it might not look good for us—"

"I said t'hell with him. Said it, an' that's what I meant."

"Well, sure. But—"

"Done enough for Conway. Done too much. Done more'n any white man should. Now, c'mon and slide into them boots an' let's go."

I said, sure, sure I would. I'd do just that. But I had a bad callus, and I'd have to trim it first. So maybe, as long as he'd have to wait, he'd better lie down and take a little nap.

He did it, after a little grumbling and protesting. I called the railroad station, and reserved a bedroom on the eight o'clock train to Central City. It would cost us a few dollars personally, since the county would only pay for first-class Pullman fare. But I figured we were going to need privacy.

I was right. I woke him up at six-thirty, to give him plenty of time to get ready, and he seemed worse off than before his nap. I couldn't get him to take a bath. He wouldn't drink any coffee or eat. Instead, he started hitting the whiskey again; and when we left the hotel he took a full bottle with him. By the time I got him on the train, I was as frazzled as a cow's hide under a branding iron. I wondered what in the name of God Conway had said to him.

I wondered, and, hell, I should have known. Because he'd as good as told me. It was as plain as the nose on my face, and I'd just been too close to it to see it.

Maybe, though, it was a good thing I didn't know. For there was nothing to be done about it, nothing I could do. And I'd have been sweating blood.

Well. That was about the size of my trip to the big town. My first trip outside the county. Straight to the hotel from the plane. Straight to the train from the hotel. Then, the long ride home at night—when there was nothing to see—closed in with a crying drunk.

Once, around midnight, a little while before he went to sleep, his mind must have wandered. For, all of a sudden, his fist wobbled out and poked me in the chest.

"Hey," I said. "Watch yourself, Bob."

"Wash—watch y'self," he mumbled. "Stop man with grin, smile worthwhile—s-stop all a' stuff spilt milk 'n' so on. Wha' you do that for, anyway."

"Aw," I said. "I was only kidding, Bob."

"T-tell you somethin'," he said. "T-tell you somethin' I bet you never thought of."

"Yeah?"

"It's—it's always lightest j-just before the dark."

Tired as I was, I laughed. "You got it wrong, Bob," I said. "You mean—"

"Huh-uh," he said. "You got it wrong."

TEN

We got into Central City around six in the morning, and Bob took a taxi straight home. He was sick; really sick, not just hung-over. He was too old a man to pack away the load he'd had.

I stopped by the office, but everything was pretty quiet, according to the night deputy, so I went on home, too. I had a lot more hours in than I'd been paid for. No one could have faulted me if I'd taken a week off. Which, naturally, I didn't intend to do.

I changed into some fresh clothes, and made some scrambled eggs and coffee. As I sat down to eat, the phone rang.

I supposed it was the office, or maybe Amy checking up on me; she'd have to call early or wait until four when her schoolday was over. I went to the phone, trying to think of some dodge to get out of seeing her, and when I heard Joe Rothman's voice it kind of threw me.

"Know who it is, Lou?" he said. "Remember our *late* talk."

"Sure," I said. "About the—uh—building situation."

"I'd ask you to drop around tonight, but I have to take a little jaunt to San Angelo. Would you mind if I stopped by your house a few minutes?"

"Well," I said. "I guess you could. Is it something important?"

"A small thing, but important, Lou. A matter of a few words of reassurance."

"Well, maybe I could—"

"I'm sure you could, but I think I'd better *see* you," he said; and he clicked up the receiver.

I hung up my phone, and went back to my breakfast. It was still early. The chances were that no one would see him. Anyway, he wasn't a criminal, opinion in some quarters to the contrary.

He came about five minutes later. I offered him some breakfast, not putting much warmth into the invitation since I didn't want him hanging around; and he said, no, thanks, but sat down at the table with me.

"Well, Lou," he said, starting to roll a cigarette. "I imagine you know what I want to hear."

"I think so," I nodded. "Consider it said."

"The very discreet newspaper stories are correct in their hints? He tried to dish it out and got it thrown back at him?"

"That's the way it looks. I can't think of any other explanation."

"I couldn't help wondering," he said, moistening the paper of his cigarette. "I couldn't help wondering how a woman with her face caved in and her neck broken could score six bullseyes on a man, even one as large as the late unlamented Elmer Conway."

He looked up slowly until his eyes met mine. I shrugged. "Probably she didn't fire all the shots at one time. She was shooting him while he was punching her. Hell, she'd hardly stand there and take it until he got through, and then start shooting."

"It doesn't seem that she would, does it?" he nodded. "Yet from the smattering of information I can gather, she must have done exactly that. She was still alive after he died; and almost any one—well, two—of the bullets she put into him was enough to lay him low. Ergo, she must have acquired the broken neck et cetera, before she did her shooting."

I shook my head. I had to get my eyes away from his.

"You said you wanted reassurance," I said. "You—you—"

"The genuine article, Lou; no substitutes accepted. And I'm still waiting to get it."

"I don't know where you get off at questioning me," I said. "The sheriff and the county attorney are satisfied. That's all I care about."

"That's the way you see it, eh?"

"That's the way I see it."

"Well, I'll tell you how I see it. I get off questioning you because I'm involved in the matter. Not directly, perhaps, but—"

"But not indirectly, either."

"Exactly. I knew you had it in for the Conways; in fact, I did everything I could to set you against the old man. Morally—perhaps even legally—I share the responsibility for any untoward action you might take. At any rate, we'll say, I and the unions I head could be placed in a very unfavorable light."

"You said it," I said. "It's your own statement."

"But don't ride that horse too hard, Lou. I don't hold still for murder. Incidentally, what's the score as of to date? One or two?"

"She's dead. She died yesterday afternoon."

"I won't buy it, Lou—if it was murder. Your doing. I can't say offhand what I will do, but I won't let you ride. I couldn't. You'd wind up getting me into something even worse."

"Oh, hell," I said. "What are we—"

"The girl's dead, and Elmer's dead. So regardless of how funny things look—and this deal should have put the courthouse crowd into hysterics—they can't prove anything. If they knew what I know, about your having a motive—"

"For killing her? Why would I want to do that?"

"Well"—he began to slow down a little—"leave her out of it. Say that she was just an instrument for getting back at Conway. A piece of stage setting."

"You know that doesn't make sense," I said. "About the other, this so-called motive—I'd had it for six years; I'd known about Mike's accident that long. Why would I wait six years, and then all of a sudden decide to pull this? Beat some poor whore to a pulp just to get at Chester Conway's son. Now, tell me if that sounds logical. Just tell me, Joe."

Rothman frowned thoughtfully, his fingers drumming upon the table. "No," he said, slowly. "It doesn't sound logical. That's the trouble. The man who walked away from that job—if he walked away—"

"You know he didn't, Joe."

"So you say."

"So I say," I said. "So everyone says. You'd say so yourself, if you didn't know how I felt about the Conways. Put that out of your mind once, and what do you have? Why, just a double murder—two people getting in a brawl and killing each other—under kind of puzzling circumstances."

He smiled wryly. "I'd call that the understatement of the century, Lou."

"I can't tell you what happened," I said, "because I wasn't there. But I know there are flukes in murder the same as there are in anything else. A man crawls a mile with his brains blown out. A woman calls the police after she's shot through the heart. A man is hanged and poisoned and chopped up and shot, and he goes right on living. Don't ask me why those things are. I don't know. But I do know they happen, and so do you."

Rothman looked at me steadily. Then, his head jerked a little, nodding.

"I guess so, Lou," he said. "I guess you're clean, at least. I've been sitting here watching you, putting together everything I know about you, and I couldn't make it tally with the picture I've got of *that* guy. Screwy as things are, that would be even screwier. You don't fit the part, to coin a phrase."

"What do I say to that?" I said.

"Not a thing, Lou. I should be thanking you for lifting a considerable load from my mind. However, if you don't mind my going into your debt a little further . . ."

"Yes?"

"What's the lowdown, just for my own information? I'll concede that you didn't have a killing hate for Conway, but you did hate him. What are you trying to pull off?"

I'd been expecting that question since the night I'd talked to him. I had the answer all ready.

"The money was supposed to be a payoff to get her out of town. Conway was paying her to go away and leave Elmer alone. Actually—"

"—Elmer was going to leave with her, right?" Rothman got up and put on his hat. "Well, I can't find it in my heart to chide you for the stunt, despite its unfortunate outcome. I almost wish I'd thought of it."

"Aw," I said, "it wasn't nothing much. Just a matter of a will finding a way."

"Ooof!" he said. "What are Conway's feelings, by the way?"

"Well, I don't think he feels real good," I said.

"Probably something he ate," he nodded. "Don't you imagine? But watch that stuff, Lou. Watch it. Save it for those birds."

He left.

I got the newspapers out of the yard—yesterday afternoon's and this morning's—poured more coffee, and sat back down at the table.

As usual, the papers had given me all the breaks. Instead of making me look like a boob or a busybody, which they could have done easily enough, they had me down as a kind of combination J. Edgar Hoover–Lombroso, "the shrewd sheriff's sleuth whose unselfish intervention in the affair came to naught, due only to the unpredictable quirks of all-too-human behavior."

I laughed, choking on the coffee I was starting to swallow. In spite of all I'd been through, I was beginning to feel nice and relaxed.

Joyce was dead. Not even Rothman suspected me. And when you passed clean with *that* guy, you didn't have anything to worry about. It was sort of an acid test, you might say.

I debated calling up the newspapers and complimenting them on their "accuracy". I often did that, spread a little sunshine, you know, and they ate it up. I could say something—I laughed—I could say something about truth being stranger than fiction. And maybe add something like—well—murder will out. Or . . . the best laid plans of mice and men.

I stopped laughing.

I was supposed to be over that stuff. Rothman had warned me about it, and it'd got Bob Maples' goat. But—

Well, why shouldn't I, if I wanted to? If it helped to take the tension out of me? It was in character. It fitted in with that dull good-natured guy who couldn't do anything bad if he tried. Rothman himself had remarked that no matter how screwy things looked, seeing me as a murderer was even screwier. And my talk was a big part of me—part of the guy that had thrown 'em all off the trail. If I suddenly stopped talking that way, what would people think?

Why, I just about had to keep on whether I wanted to or not. The choice was out of my hand. But, of course, I'd take it kind of easy. Not overdo it.

I reasoned it all out, and wound up still feeling good. But I decided not to call the newspapers, after all. The stories had been more than fair to me, but it hadn't cost 'em anything; they had to fill space some way. And I didn't care too much about a number of the details; what they said about Joyce, for example. She wasn't a "shabby sister of sin." She hadn't, for Christ's sake, "loved not wisely but too well." She was just a cute little ol' gal who'd latched onto the wrong guy, or the right guy in the wrong place; she hadn't wanted anything else, nothing else. And she'd got it. Nothing.

Amy Stanton called a little after eight o'clock, and I asked her to come over that night. The best way to stall, I figured, was not to stall; not to put any opposition to her. If I didn't hang back, she'd stop pushing me. And, after all, she couldn't get married on an hour's notice. There'd be all sorts of things to attend to, and discuss—God, how they'd have to be discussed! Even the size of the douche bag to take along on our honeymoon! And long before she was through, I'd be in shape to pull out of Central City.

After I'd finished talking to her, I went into Dad's laboratory, lighted the Bunsen burner and put an intravenous needle and an ordinary hypodermic on to boil. Then, I looked along the shelves until I found a carton each of male hormone, ACTH, B-complex and sterile water. Dad's stock of drugs was getting old, of course, but the pharmaceutical houses still kept sending us samples. The samples were what I used.

I mixed up an intravenous of the ACTH, B-complex and water and put it into my right arm. (Dad had a theory that shots should never be given on the same side as the heart.) I shot the hormone into my hip . . . and I was set for the night. Amy wouldn't be disappointed again. She wouldn't have anything to wonder about. Whether my trouble had been psychosomatic or real, the result of tension or too much Joyce, I wouldn't have it tonight. Little Amy would be tamed down for a week.

I went up to my bedroom and went to sleep. I woke up at noon, when the refinery whistles began to blow; then, dozed off again and slept until after two. Some times, most of the time, I should say, I can sleep eight-ten hours and still not feel rested. Well, I'm not tired, exactly, but I hate to get up. I just want to stay where I am, and not talk to anyone or see anyone.

Today, though, it was different; just the opposite. I could hardly wait to get cleaned up, and be out and doing something.

I showered and shaved, standing under the cold water a long time because that medicine was really working. I got into a clean tan shirt, and put on a new black bow tie, and took a freshly pressed blue suit out of the closet.

I fixed and ate a bite of lunch, and called Sheriff Maples' house.

His wife answered the phone. She said that Bob was feeling kind of poorly, and that the doctor thought he'd better stay in bed for a day or two. He was asleep, right then, and she kind of hated to wake him up. But if there was anything important . . .

"I just wondered how he was," I said. "Thought I might drop by for a few minutes."

"Well, that's mighty nice of you, Lou. I'll tell him you called when he wakes up. Maybe you can come by tomorrow if he's not up and around by then."

"Fine," I said.

I tried to read a while, but I couldn't concentrate. I wondered what to do with myself, now that I did have a day off. I couldn't shoot pool or bowl. It didn't look good for a cop to hang around pool halls and bowling alleys. It didn't look good for 'em to go into bars. It didn't look good for them to be seen in a show in the daytime.

I could drive around. Take a ride by myself. That was about all.

Gradually, the good feeling began to leave me.

I got the car out, and headed for the courthouse.

Hank Butterby, the office deputy, was reading the paper, his boots up on the desk, his jaws moving on a cud of tobacco. He asked me if it was hot enough for me, and why'n hell I didn't stay home when I had a chance. I said, well, you know how it is, Hank.

"Nice goin'," he said, nodding at the paper. "Right pretty little piece they got about you. I was just fixin' to clip it out and save it for you."

The stupid son-of-a-bitch was always doing that. Not just stories about me, but everything. He'd clip out cartoons and weather reports and crappy poems and health columns. Every goddam thing under the sun. He couldn't read a paper without a pair of scissors.

"I'll tell you what," I said, "I'll autograph it for you, and you keep it. Maybe it'll be valuable some day."

"Well"—he slanted his eyes at me, and looked quickly away again—"I wouldn't want to put you to no trouble, Lou."

"No trouble at all," I said. "Here let me have it." I scrawled my name along the margin, and handed it back to him. "Just don't let this get around," I said. "If I have to do the same thing for the other fellows, it'll run the value down."

He stared at the paper, glassy-eyed, like maybe it was going to bite him. "Uh"—there it went; he'd forgot and swallowed his spit—"you really think . . .?"

"Here's what you do," I said, getting my elbows down on the desk and whispering. "Go out to one of the refineries, and get 'em to steam you out a steel drum. Then—you know anyone that'll lend you a welding torch?"

"Yeah"—he was whispering too. "I think I can borry one."

"Well, cut the drum in two, cut it around twice, rather, so's you'll have kind of a lid. Then put that autographed clipping inside—the only one in existence, Hank!—and weld it back together again. Sixty or seventy years from now, you can take it to some museum and they'll pay you a fortune for it."

"Cripes!" he said. "You keepin' a drum like that, Lou? Want me to pick you up one?"

"Oh, I guess not," I said. "I probably won't live that long."

ELEVEN

I hesitated in the corridor in front of Howard Hendricks' office, and he glanced up from his desk and waved to me.

"Hello, there, Lou. Come on in and sit a minute."

I went in, nodding to his secretary, and pulled a chair up to the desk. "Just talked to Bob's wife a little while ago," I said. "He's not feeling so good."

"So I hear." He struck a match for my cigar. "Well, it doesn't matter much. I mean there's nothing more to be done on this Conway case. All we can do is sit tight; just be available in the event that Conway starts tossing his weight around. I imagine he'll become resigned to the situation before too long."

"It was too bad about the girl dying," I said.

"Oh, I don't know, Lou," he shrugged. "I can't see that she'd have been able to tell us anything we don't already know. Frankly, and just between the two of us, I'm rather relieved. Conway wouldn't have been satisfied unless she went to the chair with all the blame pinned on her. I'd have hated to be a party to it."

"Yeah," I said. "That wouldn't have been so good."

"Though of course I would have, Lou, if she'd lived. I mean, I'd have prosecuted her to the hilt."

He was leaning backwards to be friendly since our brush the day before. I was his old pal, and he was letting me know his innermost feelings.

"I wonder, Howard . . ."

"Yes, Lou?"

"Well, I guess I'd better not say it," I said. "Maybe you don't feel like I do about things."

"Oh, I'm sure I do. I've always felt we had a great deal in common. What is it you wanted to tell me?"

His eyes strayed a second from mine, and his mouth quirked a little. I knew his secretary had winked at him.

"Well, it's like this," I said. "Now, I've always felt we were one big happy family here. Us people that work for the county . . ."

"Uh-huh. One big happy family, eh?" His eyes strayed again. "Go on, Lou."

"We're kind of brothers under the skin . . ."

"Y-yes."

"We're all in the same boat, and we've got to put our shoulders to the wheel and pull together."

His throat seemed to swell all of a sudden, and he yanked a handkerchief from his pocket. Then he whirled around in his chair, his back to me, coughing and strangling and sputtering. I heard his secretary get up, and hurry out. Her high heels went tap-tapping down the corridor, moving faster and faster toward the women's john until she was almost running.

I hoped she pissed in her drawers.

I hoped that chunk of shrapnel under his ribs had punctured a lung. That chunk of shrapnel had cost the taxpayers a hell of a pile of dough. He'd got elected to office talking about that shrapnel. Not cleaning up the county and seeing that everyone got a fair shake. Just shrapnel.

He finally straightened up and turned around, and I told him he'd better take care of that cold. "I'll tell you what I always do," I said. "I take the water from a boiled onion, and squeeze a big lemon into it. Well, maybe a middling-size lemon and a small one if—"

"Lou!" he said sharply.

"Yeah?" I said.

"I appreciate your sentiments—your interest—but I'll have to ask you to come to the point. What did you wish to tell me, anyway?"

"Oh, it wasn't any—"

"Please, Lou!"

"Well, here's what I was wondering about," I said. And I told him. The same thing that Rothman had wondered about. I put it into my words, drawling it out, slow and awkward.

That would give him something to worry over. Something besides flat-tire tracks. And the beauty of it was he couldn't do much but worry.

"Jesus," he said, slowly. "It's right there, isn't it? Right out in the open, when you look at it right. It's one of those things that are so plain and simple you don't see 'em. No matter how you turn it around, he just about had to kill her after he was dead. After he couldn't do it!"

"Or vice versa," I said.

He wiped his forehead, excited but kind of sick-looking. Trying to trap old simple Lou with the tire tracks was one thing. That was about his speed. But this had him thrown for a loop.

"You know what this means, Lou?"

"Well, it doesn't necessarily mean that," I said, and I gave him an out. I rehashed the business about fluke deaths that I'd given to Rothman. "That's probably the way it was. Just one of those damned funny things that no one can explain."

"Yeah," he said. "Of course. That's bound to be it. You—uh—you haven't mentioned this to anyone, Lou?"

I shook my head. "Just popped into my mind a little while ago. 'Course, if Conway's still riled up when he gets back, I—"

"I don't believe I would, Lou. I really don't think that'd be wise, at all."

"You mean I should tell Bob, first? Oh, I intended to do that. I wouldn't go over Bob's head."

"No, Lou," he said, "that isn't what I mean. Bob isn't well. He's already taken an awful pounding from Conway. I don't think we should trouble him with anything else. Something which, as you point out, is doubtless of no consequence."

"Well," I said, "if it doesn't amount to anything, I don't see why—"

"Let's just keep it to ourselves, Lou, for the time being, at least. Just sit tight and see what happens. After all, what else can we do? What have we got to go on?"

"Nothing much," I said. "Probably nothing at all."

"Exactly! I couldn't have stated it better."

"I tell you what we might do," I said. "It wouldn't be too hard to round up all the men that visited her. Probably ain't more than thirty or forty of 'em, her being a kind of high-priced gal. Bob and us, our crowd, we could round 'em up, and you could . . ."

I wish you could have seen him sweat. Rounding up thirty or forty well-to-do citizens wouldn't be any skin off our ass, the sheriff's office. He'd be the one to study the evidence, and ask for indictments. By the time he was through, he'd be *through*. He couldn't be elected dog-catcher, if shrapnel was running out his eyeballs.

Well, though, I didn't really want him to do it any more than he wanted to. The case was closed, right on Elmer Conway's neck, and it was a darned good idea to leave it that way. So, that being the case, and seeing it was about supper time, I allowed him to convince me. I said I didn't have much sense about such things, and I was sure grateful for his setting me straight. And that's the way it ended. Almost.

I gave him my recipe for curing coughs before I left.

I sauntered down to my car, whistling; think of what a fine afternoon it had been, after all, and what a hell of a kick there'd be in talking about it.

Ten minutes later I was out on Derrick Road, making a U-turn back toward town.

I don't know why. Well, I do know. She was the only person I could have talked to, who'd have understood what I was talking about. But I knew she wasn't there. I knew she'd never be there again, there or anywhere. She was gone and I knew it. So . . . I don't know why.

I drove back toward town, back toward the rambling old two-storey house and the barn where the rats squealed. And once I said, "I'm sorry, baby," I said it out loud. "You'll never know how sorry I am." Then I said, "You understand, don't you? In a few months more I couldn't have stopped. I'd have lost all control and . . ."

A butterfly struck lightly against the windscreen, and fluttered away again. I went back to my whistling.

It had sure been a fine afternoon.

I was about out of groceries, so I stopped at a grocery and picked up a few, including a steak for my dinner. I went home and fixed myself a whopping big meal, and ate every bite of it. That B-complex was really doing its job. So was the other stuff. I began to actually look forward to seeing Amy. I began to want her bad.

I washed and wiped the dishes. I mopped the kitchen floor, dragging the job out as long as I could. I wrung the mop out and hung it up on the back porch, and came back and looked at the clock. The hands seemed to have been standing still. It would be at least a couple of hours yet before she'd dare to come over.

There wasn't any more work I could do, so I filled a big cup with coffee and took it up into Dad's office. I set it on his desk, lighted a cigar and started browsing along the rows of books.

Dad always said that he had enough trouble sorting the fiction out of so-called facts, without reading fiction. He always said that science was already too muddled without trying to make it jibe with religion. He said those things, but he also said that science in itself could be a religion, that a broad mind was always in danger of becoming narrow. So there was quite a bit of fiction on the shelves, and as much Biblical literature, probably, as a lot of ministers had.

I'd read some of the fiction. The other I'd left alone. I went to church and Sunday school, living as I had to live, but that was the end of it. Because kids are kids; and if that sounds pretty obvious, all I can say is that a lot of supposedly deep thinkers have never discovered the fact. A kid hears you cussing all the time, and he's going to cuss, too. He won't understand if you tell him it's wrong. He's loyal, and if you do it, it must be all right.

As I say, then, I'd never looked into any of the religious literature around the house. But I did tonight. I'd already read almost everything else. And I think it was in my mind that, since I was going to sell this place, I'd better be checking things over for value.

So I reached down a big leather-bound concordance to the Bible and blew the dust off of it. And I carried it over to the desk and opened it up; it kind of slid open by itself when I laid it down. And there was a picture in it, a little two-by-four snapshot, and I picked it up.

I turned it around one way, then another. I turned it sideways and upside down—what I thought was upside down. And I kind of grinned like a man will, when he's interested and puzzled.

It was a woman's face, not pretty exactly, but the kind that gets to you without your knowing why. But where the hell it was, what she was doing, I couldn't make out. Offhand, it looked like she was peering through the crotch of a tree, a white maple, say, with two limbs tapering up from the bole. She had her hands clasped around the limbs, and . . . But I knew that couldn't be right. Because the bole was divided at the base, and there were stumps of chopped off limbs almost tangent to the others.

I rubbed the picture against my shirt, and looked at it again. That face was familiar. It was coming back to me from some faraway place, like something coming out of hiding. But it was old, the picture I mean, and there were kind of crisscross blurs—of age, I supposed—scarring whatever she was looking through.

I took a magnifying glass and looked at it. I turned it upside down, as it was supposed to be turned. Then, I kind of dropped the glass and shoved it away from me; and I sat staring into space. At nothing and everything.

She was looking through a crotch, all right. But it was her own.

She was on her knees, peering between them. And those crisscross blurs on her thighs weren't the result of age. They were scars. The woman was Helene, who had been Dad's housekeeper so long ago.

Dad . . .

TWELVE

I was only like that for a few minutes, sitting there and staring, but a world of things, most of my kid life, came back to me in that time. *She* came back to me, the housekeeper, and she had been so much of that life.

"*Want to fight, Helene? Want to learn how to box . . .*"

And:

"*Oh, I'm tired. You just hit me . . .*"

And:

"*But you'll like it, darling. All the big boys do it . . .*"

I lived back through it all, and then I came to the end of it. That last terrible day, with me crouched at the foot of the stairs, sick with fear and shame, terrified, aching with the first and only whipping in my life; listening to the low angry voices, the angry and contemptuous voices in the library.

"I am not arguing with you, Helene. You're leaving here tonight. Consider yourself lucky that I don't prosecute you."

"Oh, ye-ss? I'd like to see you try it!"

"Why, Helene? How in the world could you do such a thing?"

"Jealous?"

"You—a mere child, and—"

"Yes! That's right! A mere child. Why not remember that? Listen to me, Daniel. I—"

"Don't say it, please. I'm at fault. If I hadn't—"

"Has it hurt you any? Have you harmed anyone? Haven't you, in fact—I should ask!—gradually lost all interest in it?"

"But a child! My child. My only son. If anything should happen—"

"Uh-huh. That's what bothers you, isn't it? Not him, but you. How it would reflect on you."

"Get out! A woman with no more sensibilities than—"

"I'm white trash, that's the term, isn't it? Riffraff. I ain't got that ol' quality. All right, and when I see some hypocritical son-of-a-bitch like you, I'm damned glad of it!"

"Get out or I'll kill you!"

"Tsk-tsk! But think of the disgrace, Doctor . . . Now I'm going to tell you something . . ."

"Get—"

"Something that you above all people should know. This didn't need to mean a thing. Absolutely nothing. But now it will. You've handled it in the worst possible way. You—"

"I . . . please, Helene."

"You'll never kill anyone. Not you. You're too damned smug and self-satisfied and sure of yourself. You like to hurt people, but—"

"No!"

"All right. I'm wrong. You're the great, good Dr. Ford, and I'm white trash, so that makes me wrong . . . I hope."

That was all.

I'd forgotten about it, and now I forgot it again. There are things that have to be forgotten if you want to go on living. And somehow

I did want to; I wanted to more than ever. If the Good Lord made a mistake in us people it was in making us want to live when we've got the least excuse for it.

I put the concordance back on the shelf. I took the picture into the laboratory and burned it, and washed the ashes down the sink. But it was a long time burning, it seemed like. And I couldn't help noticing something:

How much she looked like Joyce. How there was even a strong resemblance between her and Amy Stanton.

The phone rang. I wiped my hands against my pants, and answered it, looking at myself in the laboratory-door mirror—at the guy in the black bow tie and the pink-tan shirt, his trouser legs hooked over his boot tops.

"Lou Ford, speakin'," I said.

"Howard, Lou. Howard Hendricks. Look. I want you to come right down . . . down to the courthouse, yeah."

"Well, I don't know about that," I said. "I kind of—"

"She'll have to wait, Lou. This is important!" It had to be, the way he was sputtering. "Remember what we were talking about this afternoon? About the—you know—the possibility of an outside party being the murderer. Well, you, we were dead right. Our hunch was right!"

"Huh!" I said. "But it couldn't—I mean—"

"We've got him, Lou! We've got the son-of-a-bitch! We've got the bastard cold, and—"

"You mean he's admitted it? Hell, Howard, there's always some crank confessing to—"

"He's not admitting anything! He won't even talk! That's why we need you. We can't, uh, work on him, you know, but you can make him talk. You can soften him up if anyone can. I think you know him, incidentally."

"W-who—yeah?"

"The Greek's kid, Johnnie Pappas. You know him; he's been in plenty of trouble before. Now, get down here, Lou. I've already called Chester Conway and he's flying out from Fort Worth in the morning. I gave you full credit—told him how we'd worked on this idea together and we'd been sure all long that Elmer wasn't guilty, and . . . and he's pleased as punch, Lou. Boy, if we can just crack this, get a confession right—"

"I'll come down," I said. "I'll be right down, Howard."

I lowered the receiver hook for a moment, figuring out what had happened, what must have happened. Then, I called Amy.

Her folks were still up so she couldn't talk much; and that was a help. I made her understand that I really wanted to see her—and I did—and I shouldn't be gone too long.

I hung up and took out my wallet, and spread all the bills out on the desk.

I hadn't had any twenties of my own, just the twenty-five Elmer'd given me. And when I saw that five of them were gone, I went limp clear down to my toenails. Then I remembered that I'd used four in Fort Worth on my railroad ticket, and that I'd only broken one here in town where it would matter. Only the one . . . with Johnnie Pappas. So . . .

So I got out the car, and drove down to the courthouse.

Officer Deputy Hank Butterby gave me a hurt look, and another deputy that was there, Jeff Plummer, winked and said howdy to me. Then Howard bustled in and grabbed me by the elbow and hustled me into his office.

"What a break, huh, Lou?" He was almost slobbering with excitement. "Now, I'll tell you how to handle it. Here's what you'd better do. Sweet talk him, know what I mean, and get his guard down; then tighten up on him. Tell him if he'll cooperate we'll get him off with manslaughter—we can't do it, of course, but what you say won't be binding on me. Otherwise, tell him, it'll be the chair. He's eighteen years old, past eighteen, and—"

I stared at him. He misread my look.

"Oh, hell," he said, jabbing me in the ribs with his thumb. "Who am I to be telling you what to do? Don't I know how you handle these guys? Haven't I—"

"You haven't told me anything yet," I said. "I know Johnnie's kind of wild, but I can't see him as a murderer. What are you supposed to have on him?"

"Supposed, hell! We've got"—he hesitated—"well, here's the situation Lou. Elmer took ten thousand bucks out there to that chippy's house. He was supposed to have taken that much. But when we counted it up, five hundred dollars was missing . . ."

"Yeah?" I said. It was like I'd figured. That damned Elmer hadn't wanted to admit that he didn't have any dough of his own.

"Well, we thought, Bob and I did, that Elmer had probably pissed it off in a crap game or something like that. But the bills were all marked, see, and the old man had already tipped off the local banks. If she tried to hang around town after the payoff, he was going to crack down on her for blackmail . . . That Conway! They don't put many past him!"

"It looks like they've put a few past me," I said.

"Now, Lou"—he clapped me on the back. "There's no reason to feel that way at all. We trusted you implicitly. But it was Conway's show, and—well, you *were* there in the vicinity, Lou and—"

"Let it go," I said. "Johnnie spent some of the money?"

"A twenty. He broke it at a drugstore last night and it went to the bank this morning, and it was traced back to him a couple hours ago when we picked him up. Now—"

"How do you know Elmer didn't blow in the dough, and it's just now beginning to circulate?"

"None of it's shown up. Just this one twenty. So— Wait, Lou. Wait just a minute. Let me give you the whole picture, and we'll save time. I was entirely willing to concede that he'd come by the money innocently. He pays himself there at the filling station, and oddly enough that pay comes to exactly twenty dollars for the two nights. It looked all right, see what I mean? He could have taken the twenty in and paid himself with it. But he couldn't say he did—wouldn't say anything—because he damned well couldn't. There's damned few cars stopping at Murphy's between midnight and eight o'clock. He'd have to remember anyone that gave him a twenty. We could have checked the customer or customers, and he'd have been out of here—*if* he was innocent."

"Maybe it was in his cash drawer at the start of his shift?"

"Are you kidding? A twenty-dollar bill to make change with?" Hendricks shook his head. "We'd know he didn't have it, even without Slim Murphy's word. Now, wait! Hold up! We've checked on Murphy, and his alibi's airtight. The kid—huh-uh. From about nine Sunday night until eleven, his time can't be accounted for. We can't account for it, and he won't . . . Oh, it's a cinch, Lou, anyway you look at it. Take the murders themselves—that dame beaten to a pulp. That's something a crazy kid would lose his head and do. And the money; only five hundred taken out of ten grand. He's overwhelmed by so much dough, so he grabs up a fistful and leaves the rest. A kid stunt again."

"Yeah," I said. "Yeah, I guess you're right, Howard. You think he's got the rest cached somewhere?"

"Either that or he's got scared and thrown it away. He's a set-up, Lou. Man, I've never seen one so pretty. If he dropped dead right now I'd consider it a judgment from heaven, and I'm not a religious man either!"

Well, he'd said it all. He'd proved it in black and white.

"Well, you'd better get busy, now, Lou. We've got him on ice. Haven't booked him yet, and we're not going to until he comes through. I'm not letting some shyster tell him about his rights at this stage of the game."

I hesitated. Then I said, "No, I don't reckon that would be so smart. There's nothing to be gained by that . . . Does Bob know about this?"

"Why bother him? There's nothing he can do."

"Well, I just wondered if we should ask him—if it would be all right for me to—"

"Be all right?" He frowned. "Why wouldn't it be all right . . .? Oh I know how you feel, Lou. He's just a kid; you know him. But he's a murderer, Lou, and a damned cold-blooded one. Keep that in your mind. Think of how that poor damned woman must have felt while he was beating her face in. You saw her. You saw what her face looked like. Stew meat, hamburger—"

"Don't," I said. "For Christ's sake!"

"Sure, Lou, sure." He dropped an arm around my shoulders. "I'm sorry. I keep forgetting that you've never become hardened to this stuff. Well?"

"Well," I said. "I guess I'd better get it over with."

I walked downstairs to the basement, the jail. The turnkey let me through the gate and closed it again; and we went down past the bullpen and the regular cells to a heavy steel door. There was a small port or peephole in it, and I peered through it. But I couldn't see anything. You couldn't keep a light globe in the place, no matter what kind of guard you put over it; and the basement window, which was two-thirds below the surface of the ground, didn't let in much natural light.

"Want to borrow a flash, Lou?"

"I guess not," I said. "I can see all I need to."

He opened the door a few inches, and I slid inside, and he slammed it behind me. I stood with my back to it a moment, blinking, and there was a squeak and a scrape, and a shadow rose up and faltered toward me.

He fell into my arms, and I held him there, patting him on the back, comforting him.

"It's all right, Johnnie boy. Everything's going to be all right."

"J-jesus, Lou. Jesus Jesus Ca-christ. I knew—I kn'new you'd come, they'd send for you. But it was so long, so long and I began to think maybe—maybe—you'd—"

"You know me better'n that, Johnnie. You know how much I think of you."

"S-sure." He drew a long breath, and let it out slowly; like a man that's made land after a hard swim. "You got a cigarette, Lou? These dirty bastards took all my—"

"Now, now," I said. "They were just doing their duty, Johnnie. Have a cigar and I'll smoke one with you."

We sat down side-by-side on the bolted-down bunk, and I held a match for our cigars. I shook the match out, and he puffed and I puffed, and the glow came and went from our faces.

"This is going to burn the old man up." He laughed jerkily. "I guess— He'll have to know, won't he?"

"Yes," I said. "I'm afraid he'll have to know, Johnnie."

"How soon can I leave?"

"Very soon. It won't be long now," I said. "Where were you Sunday night?"

"To a picture show." He drew hard on his cigar, and I could see his jaw beginning to set. "What's the difference?"

"You know what I mean, Johnnie. Where'd you go after the show—between the time you left it and started to work?"

"Well"—*puff, puff*—"I don't see what that's got to do with this. I don't ask you"—*puff*—"where you—"

"You can," I said. "I intend to tell you. I guess maybe you don't know me as well as I thought you did, Johnnie. Haven't I always shot square with you?"

"Aw, hell, Lou," he said, shamed. "You know how I feel about you, but— All right, I'd probably tell you sooner or later anyway. It was"—*puff*—"here's the way it was, Lou. I told the old man I had this hot date Wednesday, see, but I was afraid of my tires, and I could pick up a couple of good ones cheap an' hand him back something each week until I got 'em paid for. And—"

"Let me sort that out," I said. "You needed tires for your hot-rod and you tried to borrow the money from your father?"

"Sure! Just like I said. And you know what he says, Lou? He tells me I don't need tires, that I gad around too much. He says I should bring this babe to the house and Mom'll make some ice cream, an' we'll all play cards or somethin'! For Christ's sake!" He shook his head bewilderedly. "How stupid can a person get?"

I laughed gently. "You got your two tires anyway, then?" I said. "You stripped a couple off a parked car?"

"Well—uh—to tell the truth, Lou, I took four. I wasn't meaning to but I knew where I could turn a couple real quick, an'—well—"

"Sure," I said. "This gal was kind of hard to get, and you wanted to be sure of getting over with her. A really hot babe, huh?"

"Mmmph-umph! Wow! You know what I mean, Lou. One of those gals that makes you want to take your shoes off and wade around in her."

I laughed again, and he laughed. Then it was somehow awfully silent, and he shifted uneasily.

"I know who owned the car, Lou. Soon as I get squared away a little I'll send him the money for those tires."

"That's all right," I said. "Don't worry about it."

"Are we—uh—can I—?"

"In just a little," I said. "You'll be leaving in a few minutes, Johnnie. Just a few formalities to take care of first."

"Boy, will I be glad to be out of here! Gosh, Lou, I don't know how people stand it! It'd drive me crazy."

"It'd drive anyone crazy," I said. "It does drive them crazy . . . Maybe you'd better lie down a while, Johnnie. Stretch out on the bunk, I've got a little more talking to do."

"But"—he turned slowly and tried to look at me, to see my face.

"You'd better do that," I said. "The air gets kind of bad with both of us sitting up."

"Oh," he said. "Yeah." And he lay down. He sighed deeply. "Say this feels pretty good. Ain't it funny, Lou, what a difference it makes? Having someone to talk to, I mean. Someone that likes you and understands you. If you've got that, you can put up with almost anything."

"Yes," I said. "It makes a lot of difference, and—that's that. You didn't tell 'em you got that twenty from me, Johnnie?"

"Hell, no! What do you think I am, anyway? Piss on those guys."

"Why not?" I said. "Why didn't you tell them?"

"Well, uh"—the hard boards of the bunk squeaked—"well, I figured—oh, you know, Lou. Elmer got around in some kind of funny places, an' I thought maybe—well, I know you don't make a hell of a lot of dough, and you're always tossing it around on other people—and if someone should slip you a little tip—"

"I see," I said. "I don't take bribes, Johnnie."

"Who said anything about bribes?" I could feel him shrug. "Who said anything? I just wasn't going to let 'em hit you cold with it until you figured out a—until you remembered where you found it."

I didn't say anything for a minute. I just sat there thinking about him, this kid that everyone said was no good, and a few other people I knew. Finally I said, "I wish you hadn't done it, Johnnie. It was the wrong thing to do."

"You mean they'll be sore?" He grunted. "To hell with them. They don't mean anything to me, but you're a square joe."

"Am I?" I said. "How do you know I am, Johnnie? How can a man ever really know anything? We're living in a funny world, kid, a peculiar civilization. The police are playing crooks in it, and the crooks are doing police duty. The politicians are preachers, and the preachers are politicians. The tax collectors collect for themselves. The Bad People want us to have more dough, and the Good People are fighting to keep it from us. It's not good for us, know what I mean? If we all had all we wanted to eat, we'd crap too much. We'd have inflation in the toilet paper industry. That's the way I understand it. That's about the size of some of the arguments I've heard."

He chuckled and dropped his cigar butt to the floor. "Gosh, Lou. I sure enjoy hearing you talk—I've never heard you talk that way before—but it's getting kind of late and—"

"Yeah, Johnnie," I said, "it's a screwed up, bitched up world, and I'm afraid it's going to stay that way. And I'll tell you why. Because no one, almost no one, sees anything wrong with it. They can't see that things are screwed up, so they're not worried about it. What they're worried about is guys like you.

"They're worried about guys liking a drink and taking it. Guys getting a piece of tail without paying a preacher for it. Guys who know what makes 'em feel good, and aren't going to be talked out of the motion . . . They don't like you guys, and they crack down on you. And the way it looks to me, they're going to be cracking down harder and harder as time goes on. You ask me why I stick around, knowing the score, and it's hard to explain. I guess I kind of got a foot on both fences, Johnnie. I planted 'em there early and now they've taken root, and I can't move either way and I can't jump. All I can do is wait until I split. Right down the middle. That's all I can do and . . . But, you, Johnnie. Well, maybe you did the right thing. Maybe it's best this way. Because it would get harder all the time, kid, and I know how hard it's been in the past."

"I . . . I don't—"

"I killed her, Johnnie. I killed both of them. And don't say I couldn't have, that I'm not that kind of a guy, because you don't know."

"I"—he started to rise up on his elbow, then lay back again. "I'll bet you had a good reason, Lou. I bet they had it coming."

"No one has it coming to them," I said. "But I had a reason, yes."

Dimly in the distance, like a ghost hooting, I heard the refinery whistles blowing for the swing shifts. And I could picture the workmen plodding in to their jobs, and the other shifts plodding out. Tossing their lunch buckets into their cars. Driving home and playing with their kids and drinking beer and watching their television sets and diddling their wives and . . . Just as if nothing was happening. Just as if a kid wasn't dying and a man, part of a man, dying with him.

"Lou . . ."

"Yes, Johnnie." It was a statement, not a question.

"Y-you m-mean I—I should take the rap for you? I—"

"No," I said. "Yes."

"I d-d-don't think—I can't, Lou! Oh Jesus, I can't! I c-couldn't go through—"

I eased him back on the bunk. I ruffled his hair, chucked him gently under the chin, tilting it back.

" 'There is a time of peace,' " I said, " 'and a time of war. A time to sow and a time to reap. A time to live and a time to die . . .' "

"L-lou . . ."

"This hurts me," I said, "worse than it does you."

And I knifed my hand across his windpipe. Then I reached down for his belt.

. . . I pounded on the door, and after a minute the turnkey came. He cracked the door open a little and I slid out, and he slammed it again.

"Give you any trouble, Lou?"

"No," I said, "he was real peaceful. I think we've broken the case."

"He's gonna talk, huh?"

"They've talked before," I shrugged.

I went back upstairs and told Howard Hendricks I'd had a long talk with Johnnie, and that I thought he'd come through all right. "Just leave him alone for an hour or so," I said. "I've done everything I can. If I haven't made him see the light, then he just ain't going to see it."

"Certainly, Lou, certainly. I know your reputation. You want me to call you after I see him?"

"I wish you would," I said. "I'm kind of curious to know if he talks."

THIRTEEN

I've loafed around the streets sometimes, leaned against a store front with my hat pushed back and one boot hooked back around the other—hell, you've probably seen me if you've ever been out this way—I've stood like that, looking nice and friendly and stupid, like I wouldn't piss if my pants were on fire. And all the time I'm laughing myself sick inside. Just watching the people.

You know what I mean—the couples, the men and wives you see walking along together. The tall fat women, and the short scrawny men. The teensy little women, and the big fat guys. The dames with lantern jaws, and the men with no chins. The bowlegged wonders, and the knock-kneed miracles. The . . . I've laughed—inside, that is—until my guts ached. It's almost as good as dropping in on a Chamber of Commerce luncheon where some guy gets up and clears his throat a few times and says, "Gentlemen, we can't expect to get any more out of life than what we put into it . . ." (Where's the percentage in that?) And I guess it—they—the people—those mis-matched people—aren't something to laugh about. They're really tragical.

They're not stupid, no more than average anyway. They've not tied up together just to give jokers like me a bang. The truth is, I reckon, that life has played a hell of a trick on 'em. There was a time, just for a few minutes, maybe, when all their differences seemed to vanish and they were just what each other wanted; when they looked at each other at exactly the right time in the right place and under the right circumstances. And everything was perfect. They had that time—those few minutes—and they never had any other. But while it lasted . . .

. . . Everything seemed the same as usual. The shades were drawn, and the bathroom door was open a little, just to let in a little light; and she was sprawled out on her stomach asleep. Everything was the same . . . but it wasn't. It was one of those times.

She woke up while I was undressing; some change dropped out of my pocket and rolled against the baseboard. She sat up, rubbing at her eyes, starting to say something sharp. But somehow she smiled, instead, and I smiled back at her. I scooped her up in my arms and sat down on the bed and held her. I kissed her, and her mouth opened a little, and her arms locked around my neck.

That's the way it started. That's the way it went.

Until, finally, we were stretched out close, side by side, her arm around my hips and mine around hers; limp, drained dry, almost breathless. And still we wanted each other—wanted something. It was like the beginning of the end.

She burrowed her head against my shoulder, and it was nice. I didn't feel like shoving her away. She whispered into my ear, kind of baby-talking.

"Mad at you. You hurt me."

"I did?" I said. "Gosh, I'm sorry, honey."

"Hurt real bad. 'Iss one. Punch elbow in it."

"Well, gosh—"

She kissed me, let her mouth slide off mine. "Not mad," she whispered.

She was silent then, waiting, it seemed, for me to say something. Do something. She pushed closer, squirming, still keeping her face hidden.

"Bet I know something . . ."

"Yeah, honey?"

"About that vas—that operation."

"What," I said, "do you think you know?"

"It was after that—after Mike—"

"What about Mike?"

"Darling"—she kissed my shoulder—"I don't care. I don't mind. But it was then, wasn't it? Your father got ex—worried and . . .?"

I let my breath out slowly. Almost any other night I could have enjoyed wringing her neck, but this was one time when I hadn't felt that way.

"It was about that time, as I recollect," I said. "But I don't know as that had anything to do with it."

"Honey . . ."

"Yeah?"

"Why do you suppose people . . .?"

"It beats me," I said. "I never have been able to figure it out."

"D-don't some women . . . I'll bet you would think it was awful if—"

"If what?"

She pushed against me, and it felt like she was on fire. She shivered and began to cry. "D-don't, Lou. Don't make me ask. J-just . . ."

So I didn't make her ask.

Later on, when she was still crying but in a different way, the phone rang. It was Howard Hendricks.

"Lou, kid you really did it! You really softened him up!"

"He signed a confession?" I said.

"Better than that, boy! He hanged himself! Did it with his belt! That proves he was guilty without us having to screw around before a judge and put the taxpayers to a lot of expense, and all that crap!

Goddammit, Lou, I wish I was there right now to shake your hand!"

He stopped yelling and tried to get the gloat out of his voice. "Now, Lou, I want you to promise me that you won't take this the wrong way. You mustn't get down about it. A person like that don't deserve to live. He's a lot better off dead than he is alive."

"Yeah," I said. "I guess you're right at that."

I got rid of him and hung up. And right away the phone rang again. This time it was Chester Conway calling from Fort Worth.

"Great work, Lou. Fine job. Fine! Guess you know what this means to me. Guess I made a mistake about—"

"Yes?" I said.

"Nothing. Don't matter now . . . See you, boy."

I hung up again, and the phone rang a third time. Bob Maples. His voice came over the wire thin and shaky.

"I know how much you thought of that boy, Lou. I know you'd just about as soon it'd happened to yourself."

As soon? "Yeah, Bob," I said. "I just about would have."

"You want to come over and set a spell, Lou? Play a game of checkers or somethin'? I ain't supposed to be up or I'd offer to come over there."

"I—I reckon not, Bob," I said. "But thanks, thanks a heap."

"That's all right, son. You change your mind, come on over. No matter what time it is."

Amy'd been taking in everything; impatient, curious. I hung up and slumped down on the bed, and she sat up beside me.

"For heaven's sake! What was that all about, Lou?"

I told her. Not the truth, of course, but what was supposed to be the truth. She clapped her hands together.

"Oh, darling! That's wonderful. My Lou solving the case! . . . Will you get a reward?"

"Why should I?" I said. "Think of all the fun I had."

"Oh, well . . ." She drew away a little, and I thought she was going to pop off; and I reckon she wanted to. But she wanted something else worse. "I'm sorry, Lou. You have every right to be angry with me."

She lay back down again, turning on her stomach, spreading her arms and legs. She stretched out, waiting, and whispered:

"Very, very angry . . ."

Sure, I know. Tell me something else. Tell a hophead he shouldn't take dope. Tell him it'll kill him, and see if he stops.

She got her money's worth.

It was going to cost her plenty, and I gave her value received. Honest Lou, that was me. Let Lou Titillate Your Tail.

FOURTEEN

I guess I must have got to sweating with all that exercise, and not having any clothes on I caught a hell of a cold. Oh, it wasn't too bad; not enough to really lay me low; but I wasn't fit to do any chasing around. I had to stay in bed for a week. And it was kind of a break for me, you might say.

I didn't have to talk to a lot of people, and have 'em asking damned fool questions and slapping me on the back. I didn't have to go to Johnnie Pappas' funeral. I didn't have to call on his folks, like I'd have felt I had to do ordinarily.

A couple of the boys from the office dropped by to say hello, and Bob Maples came in a time or two. He was still looking pretty peaked, seemed to have aged about ten years. We kept off the subject of Johnnie—just talked about things in general—and the visits went off pretty well. Only one thing came up that kind of worried me for a while. It was on the first—no, I guess the second time he came by.

"Lou," he said, "why in hell don't you get out of this town?"

"Get out?" I was startled. We'd just been sitting there quietly, smoking and passing a word now and then. And suddenly he comes out with this. "Why should I get out?"

"Why've you ever stayed here this long?" he said. "Why'd you ever want to wear a badge? Why didn't you be a doctor like your dad; try to make something of yourself?"

I shook my head, staring down at the bedclothes. "I don't know, Bob. Reckon I'm kind of lazy."

"You got awful funny ways of showin' it, Lou. You ain't never too lazy to take on some extra job. You put in more hours than any man I got. An' if I know anything about you, you don't like the work. You never have liked it."

He wasn't exactly right about that, but I knew what he meant. There was other work I'd have liked a lot better. "I don't know Bob," I said, "there's a couple of kinds of laziness. The don't-want-to-do-nothin' and the stick-in-the-rut brand. You take a job, figuring you'll just keep it a little while, and that while keeps stretchin' on and on and on. You need a little more money before you can make a jump. You can't quite make up your mind about what you want to jump to. And then maybe you make a stab at it, you send off a few letters, and the people want to know what experience you've had—what you've been doin'. And probably they don't even want to bother with you, and if they do you've got to start right at the bottom, because you don't know anything. So you stay where you are, you just about got to, and you work pretty hard because you know it. You ain't young any more and it's all you've got."

Bob nodded slowly. "Yeah . . . I kinda know how that is. But it didn't need to be that way with you, Lou! Your dad could've sent you off to school. You could've been a practicin' doctor by this time."

"Well," I hesitated, "there'd been that trouble with Mike, and Dad would've been all alone, and . . . well, I guess my mind just didn't run to medicine, Bob. It takes an awful lot of study, you know."

"There's other things you could do, and you lack a lot of bein' broke, son. You could get you a little fortune for this property."

"Yeah, but . . ." I broke off. "Well, to tell the truth, Bob, I have kind of thought about pulling up stakes, but—"

"Amy don't want to?"

"I haven't asked her. The subject never came up. But I don't reckon she would."

"Well," he said slowly, "that's sure too bad. I don't suppose you'd . . . No, you wouldn't do that. I don't expect no man in his right mind would give up Amy."

I nodded a little, like I was acknowledging a compliment; agreeing that I couldn't give her up. And even with the way I felt about her, the nod came easy. On the surface, Amy had everything plus. She was smart and she came from a good family—which was a mighty important consideration with our people. But that was only the beginning. When Amy went down the street with that round little behind twitching, with her chin tucked in and her breasts stuck out, every man under eighty kind of drooled. They'd get sort of red in the face and forget to breathe, and you could hear whispers, "*Man, if I could just have some of that.*"

Hating her didn't keep me from being proud of her.

"You trying to get rid of me, Bob?" I said.

"Kind of looks as though, don't it?" he grinned. "Guess I did too much thinkin' while I was laying around the house. Wondering about things that ain't none of my business. I got to thinkin' about how riled I get sometimes, having to give in to things I don't like, and hell, I ain't really fit to do much but what I am doin'; and I thought how much harder it must be on a man like you." He chuckled, wryly. "Fact is, I reckon, you started me thinking that way, Lou. You kind of brought it on yourself."

I looked blank, and then I grinned. "I don't mean anything by it. It's just a way of joking."

"Sure," he said, easily. "We all got our little pe-cul-ye-arities. I just thought maybe you was gettin' kind of saddle-galled, and—"

"Bob," I said, "what did Conway say to you there in Fort Worth?"

"Oh, hell"—he stood up, slapping his hat against his pants—"can't even recollect what it was now. Well, I guess I better be—"

"He said something. He said or did something that you didn't like a little bit."

"You reckon he did, huh?" His eyebrows went up. Then they came down and he chuckled, and put on his hat. "Forget it, Lou. It wasn't nothing important, and it don't matter no more, anyways."

He left; and, like I said, I was kind of worried for a while. But after I'd had time to think, it looked to me like I'd fretted about nothing. It looked like things were working out pretty good.

I was willing to leave Central City; I'd been thinking about leaving. But I thought too much of Amy to go against her wishes. I sure wouldn't do anything that Amy didn't like.

If something should happen to her, though—and something *was* going to happen—why, of course, I wouldn't want to hang around the old familiar scenes any more. It would be more than a soft-hearted guy like me could stand, and there wouldn't be any reason to. So I'd leave, and it'd all seem perfectly natural. No one would think anything of it.

Amy came to see me every day—in the morning for a few minutes on her way to school, and again at night. She always brought some cake or pie or something, stuff I reckon their dog wouldn't eat (and that hound wasn't high-toned—he'd snatch horseturds on the fly), and she hardly nagged about anything, that I remember. She didn't give me any trouble at all. She was all sort of blushy and shy and shamed like. And she had to take it kind of easy when she sat down.

Two or three nights she drew the bath tub full of warm water and sat in it and soaked; and I'd sit and watch her and think how much she looked like *her*. And afterwards she'd lie in my arms—just lie there because that was about all either of us was up to. And I could almost fool myself into thinking it was *her*.

But it wasn't *her*, and, for that matter, it wouldn't have made any difference if it had been. I'd just been right back where I started. I'd have had to do it all over again.

I'd have had to kill her the second time . . .

I was glad Amy didn't bring up the subject of marriage; she was afraid of starting a quarrel, I guess. I'd already been right in the middle of three deaths, and a fourth coming right on top of 'em might look kind of funny. It was too soon for it. Anyway, I hadn't figured out a good safe way of killing her.

You see why I had to kill her, I reckon. Or do you? It was like this:

There wasn't any evidence against me. And even if there was some, quite a bit, I'd be a mighty hard man to stick. I just wasn't that kind of guy, you see. No one would believe I was. Why, hell, they'd been seeing Lou Ford around for years and no one could tell them that good ol' Lou would—

But Lou could do it; Lou could convict himself. All he had to do was skip out on a girl who knew just about everything about him there was to know—who, even without that one wild night, could probably have pieced some plenty-ugly stuff together—and that would be the end of Lou. Everything would fall into place, right back to the time when Mike and I were kids.

As things stood now, she wouldn't let herself think things through. She wouldn't even let herself start to think. She'd cut up some pretty cute skylarks herself, and that had put a check on her thinking. And I was going to be her husband, so everything was all right. Everything had to be all right . . . But if I ran out on her—well, I knew Amy. That mental block she'd set up would disappear. She'd have the answer that quick—and she wouldn't keep it to herself. Because if she couldn't have me, no one else would.

Yeah, I guess I mentioned that. She and Joyce seemed pretty much alike.

Well, anyway . . .

Anyway, it had to be done, as soon as it safely could be done. And knowing that, that there was just no other way out, kind of made things easier. I stopped worrying, thinking about it, I should say. I tried to be extra pleasant to her. She was getting on my nerves, hanging around so much. But she wouldn't be hanging around long, so I thought I ought to be as nice as I could.

I'd taken sick on a Wednesday. By the next Wednesday I was up, so I took Amy to a prayer meeting. Being a school teacher, she kind of had to put in an appearance at those things, now and then, and I sort of enjoy 'em. I pick up lots of good lines at prayer meetings. I asked Amy, I whispered to her, how she'd like to have a little manna on her honey. And she turned red, and kicked me on the ankle. I whispered to her again, asked her if I could Mose-y into her Burning Bush. I told her I was going to take her to my bosom and cleave unto her, and anoint her with precious oils.

She got redder and redder and her eyes watered, but somehow it made her look cute. And it seemed like I'd never seen her with her chin stuck out and her eyes narrowed. Then, she doubled over, burying her face in her songbook; and she shivered and shook and choked, and the minister stood on tiptoe, frowning, trying to figure out where the racket was coming from.

It was one of the best prayer meetings I ever went to.

I stopped and bought some ice cream on the way home, and she was giggling and breaking into snickers all the way. While I made coffee, she dished up the cream; and I took part of a spoonful and chased her around and around the kitchen with it. I finally caught her and put it in her mouth, instead of down her neck like I'd threatened. A little speck of it got on her nose and I kissed it away.

Suddenly, she threw her arms around my neck and began to cry.

"Honey," I said, "don't do that, honey. I was just playing. I was just trying to give you a good time."

"Y-you—big—"

"I know," I said, "but don't say it. Let's don't have any more trouble between us."

"D-don't"—her arms tightened around me, and she looked up through the tears, smiling—"don't you understand? I'm j-just so happy, Lou. So h-happy I c-can't s-s-stand it!" And she burst into tears again.

We left the ice cream and coffee unfinished. I picked her up and carried her into Dad's office, and sat down in Dad's big old chair. We sat there in the dark, her on my lap—sat there until she had to go home. And it was all we wanted; it seemed to be enough. It was enough.

It was a good evening, even if we did have one small spat.

She asked me if I'd seen Chester Conway, and I said I hadn't. She said she thought it was darned funny that he didn't so much as come by and say hello, after what I'd done, and that if she were me she'd tell him so.

"I didn't do anything," I said. "Let's not talk about it."

"Well, I don't care darling! He thought you'd done quite a bit at the time—couldn't wait to call you up long distance! Now, he's been back in town for almost a week, and he's too busy to—I don't care for my own sake, Lou. It certainly means nothing to me. But—"

"That makes two of us, then."

"You're too easy-going, that's the trouble with you. You let people run over you. You're always—"

"I know," I said. "I think I know it all, Amy. I've got it memorized. The whole trouble is that I won't listen to you—and it seems to me like that's about all I ever get done. I've been listening to you almost since you learned how to talk, and I reckon I can do it a while longer. If it'll make you happy. But I don't think it'll change me much."

She sat up very stiff and straight. Then, she settled back again, still holding herself kind of rigid. She was silent for about the time it takes you to count to ten.

"Well, just the same, I—I—"

"Yeah?" I said.

"Oh, be quiet," she said. "Keep still. Don't say anything." And she laughed. And it was a good evening after all.

But it *was* kind of funny about Conway.

FIFTEEN

How long should I wait? That was the question. How long could I wait? How long was it safe?

Amy wasn't crowding me any. She was still pretty shy and skittish, trying to keep that barbed-wire tongue of hers in her mouth—though she wasn't always successful. I figured I could stall her off on marriage indefinitely, but Amy . . . well, it wasn't just Amy. There wasn't anything I could put my finger on, but I had the feeling that things were closing in on me. And I couldn't talk myself out of it.

Every day that passed, the feeling grew stronger.

Conway hadn't come to see me or spoken to me, but that didn't necessarily mean anything. It *didn't* mean anything that I could see. He was busy. He'd never given a whoop in hell for anyone but himself and Elmer. He was the kind of a guy that would drop you when he got a favor, then pick you up again when he needed another one.

He'd gone back to Fort Worth, and he hadn't returned. But that was all right, too. Conway Construction had big offices in Fort Worth. He'd always spent a lot of time there.

Bob Maples? Well, I couldn't see that he was much different than ever. I'd study him as the days drifted by, and I couldn't see anything to fret about. He looked pretty old and sick, but he *was* old and he had been sick. He didn't have too much to say to me, but what he did have was polite and friendly—he seemed hell-bent on being polite and friendly. And he'd never been what you'd call real talky. He'd always had spells when you could hardly get a word out of him.

Howard Hendricks? Well . . . Well, something was sure enough eating on Howard.

I'd run into Howard the first day I was up after my sick spell; he'd been coming up the steps of the courthouse, just as I was heading down them to lunch. He nodded, not quite looking at me, and mumbled out a "H'are you, Lou?" I stopped and said I was feeling a lot better—still pretty weak, but couldn't really complain any.

"You know how it is, Howard," I said. "It isn't the flu so much as the after-effects."

"So I've heard," he said.

"It's kind of like I always say about auty-mobiles. It's not the original cost so much as the upkeep. But I reckon—"

"Got to run," he mumbled. "See you."

But I wasn't letting him off that easy. I was really in the clear now, and I could afford to open up a little on him. "As I was sayin'," I said, "I reckon I can't tell you much about sickness, can I, Howard? Not with that shrapnel you got in you. I got an idea about that shrapnel, Howard—what you could do with it. You could get you some X-rays taken and print 'em on the back of your campaign cards. Then on the other side you could have a flag with your name spelled out in thermometers, and maybe an upside down—what do you call them hospital piss-pots? Oh, yeah—urinal for an exclamation mark. Where'd you say that shrapnel was anyway, Howard? Seems like I just can't keep track of it, no matter how hard I try. One time it's in—"

"My ass"—he was looking at me now, all right—"it's in my ass."

I'd been holding him by the lapel to keep him from running off. He took my hand by the wrist, still staring at me, and he pulled it away and let it drop. Then he turned and went up the steps, his shoulders sagging a little but his feet moving firm and steady. And we hadn't passed a word between us since then. He kept out of my way when he saw me coming, and I did him the same kind of favor.

So there was something wrong there; but what else could I expect? What was there to worry about? I'd given him the works, and it had probably dawned on him that I'd needled him plenty in the past. And that wasn't the only reason he had to act stiff and cold. Elections were coming up in the fall, and he'd be running as usual. Breaking the Conway case would be a big help to him, and he'd want to talk it up. But he'd feel awkward about doing it. He'd have to cut me out of the credit, and he figured I'd be sore. So he was jumping the gun on me.

There was nothing really out of the way, then. Nothing with him or Sheriff Bob or Chester Conway. There wasn't a thing . . . but the feeling kept growing. It got stronger and stronger.

I'd been keeping away from the Greek's. I'd even stayed off the street where his restaurant was. But one day I went there. Something just seemed to pull the wheels of my car in that direction, and I found myself stopping in front of it.

The windows were all soaped over. The doors were closed. But it seemed like I could hear people inside; I heard some banging and clattering.

I got out of my car and stood by the side of it a minute or two. Then I stepped up on the curb and crossed the walk.

There was a place on one of the double doors where the soap had been scraped away. I sheltered my eyes with my hand and peered through it; rather I started to peer through it. For the door opened suddenly, and the Greek stepped out.

"I am sorry, Officer Ford," he said. "I cannot serve you. We are not open for business."

I stammered that I didn't want anything. "Just thought I'd drop by to—to—"

"Yes?"

"I wanted to see you," I said. "I wanted to see you the night it happened, and it hasn't been off my mind since. But I couldn't bring myself to do it. I couldn't face you. I knew how you'd feel, how you'd be bound to feel, and there wasn't anything I could say. Nothing. Nothing I could say or do. Because if there'd been anything . . . well, it wouldn't have happened in the first place."

It was the truth, and God—God!—what a wonderful thing truth is. He looked at me in a way I didn't like to name; and then he looked kind of baffled; and then he suddenly caught his lip under his teeth and stared down at the sidewalk.

He was a swarthy middle-aged guy in a high-crowned black hat, and a shirt with black sateen protectors pulled over the sleeves; and he stared down at the sidewalk and looked back up again.

"I am glad you did come by, Lou," he said quietly. "It is fitting. I have felt, at times, that he regarded you as his one true friend."

"I aimed to be his friend," I said. "There weren't many things I wanted much more. Somehow, I slipped up; I couldn't help him right when he needed help worst. But I want you to know one thing, Max. I—I didn't hurt—"

He laid a hand on my arm. "You need not tell me that, Lou. I do not know why—what—but—"

"He felt lost," I said. "Like he was all alone in the world. Like he was out of step, and he could never get back in again."

"Yes," he said. "But . . . yes. There was always trouble, and he seemed always at fault."

I nodded, and he nodded. He shook his head, and I shook mine. We stood there, shaking our heads and nodding, neither of us really saying anything; and I wished I could leave. But I didn't quite know how to go about it. Finally, I said I was sorry he was closing the restaurant.

"If there's anything I can do . . ."

"I am not closing it," he said. "Why should I close it?"

"Well, I just thought that—"

"I am remodeling it. I am putting in leather booths and an inlaid floor and air-conditioning. Johnnie would have liked those things. Many times he suggested them, and I suggested he was hardly fitted to give me advice. But now we will have them. It will be as he wanted. It is—all that can be done."

I shook my head again. I shook it and nodded.

"I want to ask you a question, Lou. I want you to answer it, and I want the absolute truth."

"The truth?" I hesitated. "Why wouldn't I tell you the truth, Max?"

"Because you might feel that you couldn't. That it would be disloyal to your position and associates. Who else visited Johnnie's cell after you left?"

"Well, there was Howard—the county attorney—"

"I know of that; he made the discovery. And a deputy sheriff and the jailer were with him. Who else?"

My heart gave a little jump. Maybe . . . But, no, it was no good. I couldn't do that. I couldn't bring myself to try it.

"I don't have any idea, Max," I said. "I wasn't there. But I can tell you you're on the wrong track. I've known all those boys for years. They wouldn't do a thing like that any more than I would."

It was the truth again, and he had to see it. I was looking straight into his eyes.

"Well . . ." he sighed. "Well, we will talk again, Lou."

And I said, "You bet we will, Max," and I got away from him.

I drove out on Derrick Road, five-six miles out. I pulled the car off on the shoulder, up at the crest of a little hill; and I sat there looking down through the blackjacks but I didn't see a thing. I didn't see the blackjacks.

About five minutes after I'd stopped, well, maybe no more than three minutes, a car drew up behind mine. Joe Rothman got out of it, and plodded along the shoulder and looked in at me.

"Nice view here," he said. "Mind if I join you? Thanks, I knew you wouldn't." He said it like that, all run together, without waiting for me to reply. He opened the door and slid into the seat beside me.

"Come out this way often, Lou?"

"Whenever I feel like it," I said.

"Well, it's a nice view all right. Almost unique. I don't suppose you'll find more than forty or fifty thousand billboards like that one in the United States."

I grinned in spite of myself. The billboard had been put up by the Chamber of Commerce; and the words on it were:

You Are Now Nearing
CENTRAL CITY, TEX.
'Where the hand clasp's a little stronger.'
Pop. (1932) 4,800 Pop. (1952) 48,000
WATCH US GROW!!

"Yeah," I said, "that's quite a sign, all right."

"You were looking at it, then? I thought that must be the attraction. After all, what else is there to see aside from those blackjacks and a little white cottage? The murder cottage, I believe they call it."

"What do you want?" I said.

"How many times were you there, Lou? How many times did you lay her?"

"I was there quite a few times," I said. "I had reason to be. And I'm not so hard up for it that I have to lay whores."

"No?" He squinted at me thoughtfully. "No, I don't suppose you would be. Personally, I've always operated on the theory that even in the presence of abundance, it's well to keep an eye out for the future. You never can tell, Lou. You may wake up some morning and find they've passed a law against it. It'll be un-American."

"Maybe they'll put a rider on that law," I said.

"Prohibiting bullshit? I see you don't have a legal type of mind, Lou, or you wouldn't say that. There's a basic contradiction in it. Tail we can do without, as our penal institutions so righteously prove; tail of the orthodox type, that is. But what could you substitute for bullshit? Where would we be without it?"

"Well," I said. "I wouldn't be listening to you."

"But you're going to listen to me, Lou. You're going to sit right here and listen, and answer up promptly when the occasion demands. Get me? Get me, Lou?"

"I got you," I said. "I got you right from the beginning."

"I was afraid you hadn't. I wanted you to understand that I can stack it up over your head, and you'll sit there and like it."

He shook tobacco into a paper, twirled it, and ran it across his tongue. He stuck it in the corner of his mouth, and seemed to forget about it.

"You were talking with Max Pappas," he said. "From what I could judge it was a reasonably friendly conversation."

"It was," I said.

"He was resigned to the fact of Johnnie's suicide? He had accepted it as suicide?"

"I can't say that he was resigned to it," I said. "He was wondering whether someone—if someone was in the cell after I left, and . . ."

"And, Lou? And?"

"I told him, no, that it couldn't have been that way. None of the boys would be up to doing such a thing."

"Which settles that," Rothman nodded. "Or does it?"

"What are you driving at?" I snapped. "What—"

"Shut up!" His voice toughened, then went smooth again. "Did you notice the remodeling he's doing? Do you know how much all that will cost? Right around twelve thousand dollars. Where do you suppose he got that kind of money?"

"How the hell do I—"

"Lou."

"Well, maybe he had it saved."

"Max Pappas?"

"Or maybe he borrowed it."

"Without collateral?"

"Well . . . I don't know," I said.

"Let me make a suggestion. Someone gave it to him. A wealthy acquaintance, we'll say. Some man who felt he owed it to him."

I shrugged, and pushed my hat back; because my forehead was sweating. But I was feeling cold inside, so cold inside.

"Conway Construction is handling the job, Lou. Doesn't it strike you as rather odd that he'd do a job for a man whose son killed his son."

"There aren't many jobs that he don't handle," I said. "Anyway, it's the company, not him; he's not in there swinging a hammer himself. More'n likely he doesn't even know about it."

"Well . . ." Rothman hesitated. Then he went on, kind of dogged. "It's a turnkey job. Conway's jobbing all the materials, dealing with the supply houses, paying off the men. No one's seen a nickel coming from Pappas."

"So what?" I said. "Conway takes all the turnkey stuff he can get. He cuts a half a dozen profits instead of one."

"And you think Pappas would hold still for it? You don't see him as the kind of guy who'd insist on bargaining for every item, who'd haggle over everything right down to the last nail? I see him that way, Lou. It's the only way I can see him."

I nodded. "So do I. But he's not in a real good position to have his own way right now. He gets his job like Conway Construction wants to give it to him, or he just don't get it."

"Yeah . . ." He shifted his cigarette from one side of his mouth to the other. He pushed it across with his tongue, his eyes narrowed on my face. "But the money, Lou. That still doesn't explain about the money."

"He lived closer," I said. "He could have had it, a big enough part, anyway, so's they'd wait on the rest. It didn't need to be in a bank. He could have had it salted away around his house."

"Yeah," said Rothman, slowly. "Yeah, I suppose so . . ."

He turned back around in the seat, so that he was looking through the windshield instead of me—instead of *at* me. He flicked his cigarette away, fumbled for his tobacco and papers, and began rolling another one.

"Did you get out to the cemetery, Lou? Out to Johnnie's grave?"

"No," I said, "and I've sure got to do that, too. I'm ashamed I haven't done it before."

"Well—dammit, you mean that, don't you? You mean every word of it?"

"Who are you to ask that?" I snapped. "What did you ever do for him? I don't want any credit for it, but I'm the only man in Central City that ever tried to help that kid. I liked him. I understood him. I—"

"I know, I know," he shook his head, dully. "I was just going to say that Johnnie's buried in Sacred Ground . . . You know what that means, Lou?"

"I reckon. The church didn't call it suicide."

"And the answer, Lou? You do have an answer?"

"He was so awful young," I said, "and he hadn't ever had much but trouble. Maybe the church figured he'd been faulted enough, and tried to give him a break. Maybe they figured that it was sort of an accident; that he'd just been fooling around and went too far."

"Maybe," said Rothman. "Maybe, maybe, maybe. One more thing, Lou. The big thing . . . On the Sunday night that Elmer and the late occupant of yon cottage got it, one of my carpenters went to the last show at the Palace. He parked his car around in back at—now get this, Lou—at nine-thirty. When he came out, all four of his tires were gone . . ."

SIXTEEN

I waited and everything got pretty quiet. "Well," I said, finally, "that's sure too bad. All four tires, huh?"

"Too bad? You mean it's funny, don't you, Lou? Plumb funny?"

"Well, it is, kind of," I said. "It's funny I didn't hear anything about it at the office."

"It'd been still funnier if you had, Lou. Because he didn't report the theft. I'd hardly call it the greatest mystery of all time, but, for some reason, you fellas down at the office don't take much interest in us fellas down at the labor temple—unless you find us on a picket line."

"I can't hardly help—"

"Never mind, Lou; it's really not pertinent. The man didn't report the theft, but he did mention it to some of the boys when the carpenters and joiners held their regular Tuesday night meeting. And one of them, as it turned out, had bought two of the tires from Johnnie Pappas. They . . . Do you have a chill, Lou? Are you catching cold?"

I bit down on my cigar. I didn't say anything.

"These lads equipped themselves with a couple of piss-elm clubs, or reasonable facsimiles thereof, and went calling on Johnnie. He wasn't at home and he wasn't at Slim Murphy's filling station. In fact, he wasn't anywhere about that time; he was swinging by his belt from the window-bars of the courthouse cooler. But his hot rod was at the station, and the remaining two stolen tires were on it. They stripped them off—Murphy, of course, isn't confiding in the police either—and that ended the matter. But there's been talk about it, Lou. There's been talk even though—*apparently*—no one has attached any great significance to the event."

I cleared my throat. "I—why should they, Joe?" I said. "I guess I don't get you."

"For the birds, Lou, remember? The starving sparrows . . . Those tires were stolen after nine-thirty on the night of Elmer's and his lady friend's demise. Assuming that Johnnie didn't go to work on them the moment the owner parked—or even assuming that he did—we are driven to the inevitable conclusion that he was engaged in relatively innocent pursuits until well after ten o'clock. He could not, in other words, have had any part in the horrible happenings behind yonder blackjacks."

"I don't see why not," I said.

"You don't?" His eyes widened. "Well, of course, poor old Descartes, Aristotle, Diogenes, Euclid et al are dead, but I think you'll find quite a few people around who'll defend their theories. I'm very much afraid, Lou, that they won't go along with your proposition that a body can be in two places at the same time."

"Johnnie ran with a pretty wild crowd," I said. "I figure that one of his buddies stole those tires and gave 'em to him to peddle."

"I see. I see . . . Lou."

"Why not?" I said. "He was in a good position to get rid of them there at the station. Slim Murphy wouldn't have interfered . . . Why, hell, it's bound to have been that way, Joe. If he'd have had an alibi for the time of the murders, he'd have told me so, wouldn't he? He wouldn't have hanged himself."

"He liked you, Lou. He trusted you."

"For damned good reasons. He knew I was his friend."

Rothman swallowed, and a sort of laughing sound came out of

his throat, the kind of sound you make when you don't quite know whether to laugh or cry or get sore.

"Fine, Lou. Perfect. Every brick is laid straight, and the bricklayer is an honest upstanding mechanic. But still I can't help wondering about his handiwork and him. I can't help wondering why he feels the need to defend his structure of perhapses and maybes, his shelter wall of logical alternatives. I can't see why he didn't tell a certain labor skate to get the hell on about his business."

So . . . So there it was. I was. But where was he? He nodded as though I'd asked him the question. Nodded, and drew a little bit back in the seat.

"Humpty-Dumpty Ford," he said, "sitting right on top of the labor temple. And how or why he got there doesn't make much difference. You're going to have to move, Lou. Fast. Before someone . . . before you upset yourself."

"I was kind of figuring on leaving town," I said. "I haven't done anything, but—"

"Certainly you haven't. Otherwise, as a staunch Red Fascist Republican, I wouldn't feel free to yank you from the clutches of your detractors and persecutors—your would-be persecutors, I should say."

"You think that—you think maybe—"

He shrugged. "I think so, Lou. I think you just might have a little trouble in leaving. I think it so strongly that I'm getting in touch with a friend of mine, one of the best criminal lawyers in the country. You've probably heard of him—Billy Boy Walker? I did Billy Boy a favor one time, back East, and he has a long memory for favors, regardless of his other faults."

I'd heard of Billy Boy Walker. I reckon almost everyone has. He'd been governor of Alabama or Georgia or one of those states down south. He'd been a United States senator. He'd been a candidate for president on a Divide-the-Dough ticket. He'd started getting shot at quite a bit about that time, so he'd dropped out of politics and stuck to his criminal practice. And he was plenty good. All the high mucky-mucks cussed and made fun of him for the way he'd cut up in politics. But I noticed that when they or their kin got into trouble, they headed straight for Billy Boy Walker.

It sort of worried me that Rothman thought I needed that kind of help.

It worried me, and it made me wonder all over again why Rothman and his unions would go to all the trouble of getting me a lawyer. Just what did Rothman stand to lose if the Law started asking me questions? Then I realized that if my first conversation with Rothman should ever come out, any jury in the land would figure he'd sicked me on the late Elmer Conway. In other words, Rothman was saving two necks—his and mine—with one lawyer.

"Perhaps you won't need him," he went on. "But it's best to have him alerted. He's not a man who can make himself available on a moment's notice. How soon can you leave town?"

I hesitated. Amy. How was I going to do it? "I'll—I can't do it right away," I said. "I'll have to kind of drop a hint or two around that I've been thinking about leaving, then work up to it gradually. You know, it would look pretty funny—"

"Yeah," he frowned, "but if they know you're getting ready to jump they're apt to close in all the faster . . . Still, I can see your point."

"What can they do?" I said. "If they could close in, they'd be doing it already. Not that I've done—"

"Don't bother. Don't say it again. Just move—start moving as quickly as you can. It shouldn't take you more than a couple of weeks at the outside."

Two weeks. Two weeks more for Amy.

"All right, Joe," I said. "And thanks for—for—"

"For what?" He opened the door. "For you, I haven't done a thing."

"I'm not sure I can make it in two weeks. It may take a little—"

"It hadn't better," he said, "take much longer."

He got out and went back to his own car. I waited until he'd turned around and headed back toward Central City; and then I turned around and started back. I drove slowly, thinking about Amy.

Years ago there was a jeweler here in Central City who had a hell of a good business, and a beautiful wife and two fine kids. And one day, on a business trip over to one of the teachers' college towns he met up with a girl, a real honey, and before long he was sleeping with her. She knew he was married, and she was willing to leave it that way. So everything was perfect. He had her and he had his family and a swell business. But one morning they found him and the girl dead in a motel—he'd shot her and killed himself. And when one of our deputies went to tell his wife about it, he found her and the kids dead, too. This fellow had shot 'em all.

He'd had everything, and somehow nothing was better.

That sounds pretty mixed up, and probably it doesn't have a lot to do with me. I thought it did at first, but now that I look at it—well, I don't know. I just don't know.

I knew I had to kill Amy; I could put the reason into words. But every time I thought about it, I had to stop and think *why* again. I'd be doing something, reading a book or something, or maybe I'd be with her. And all of a sudden it would come over me that I was going to kill her, and the idea seemed so crazy that I'd almost laugh out loud. Then, I'd start thinking and I'd see it, see that it had to be done, and . . .

It was like being asleep when you were awake and awake when you were asleep. I'd pinch myself, figuratively speaking—I had to keep pinching myself. Then I'd wake up kind of in reverse; I'd go back into the nightmare I had to live in. And everything would be clear and reasonable.

But I still didn't know how to go about doing it. I couldn't figure out a way that would leave me in the clear or even reasonably in the clear. And I sure had to be on this one. I was Humpty-Dumpty, like Rothman had said, and I couldn't jiggle around very much.

I couldn't think of a way because it was a real toughie, and I had to keep remembering the *why* of it. But finally it came to me.

I found a way, because I had to. I couldn't stall any longer.

It happened three days after my talk with Rothman. It was a payday Saturday, and I should have been working, but somehow I hadn't been able to bring myself to do it. I'd stayed in the house all day with the shades drawn, pacing back and forth, wandering from room to room. And when night came I was still there. I was sitting in Dad's office, with nothing on but the little desk light; and I heard these footsteps moving lightly across the porch, and the sound of the screen door opening.

It was way too early for Amy; but I wasn't jittered any. I'd had people walk in before like this.

I stepped to the door of the office just as he came into the hall.

"I'm sorry, stranger," I said. "The doctor doesn't practice any more. The sign's just there for sentimental reasons."

"That's okay, bud"—he walked right toward me and I had to move back—"it's just a little burn."

"But I don't—"

"A cigar burn," he said. And he held his hand out, palm up.

And, at last, I recognized him.

He sat down in Dad's big leather chair, grinning at me. He brushed his hand across the arm, knocking off the coffee cup and saucer I'd left there.

"We got some talking to do, bud, and I'm thirsty. You got some whiskey around? An unopened bottle? I ain't no whiskey hog, understand, but some places I like to see a seal on a bottle."

"I've got a phone around," I said, "and the jail's about six blocks away. Now, drag your ass out of here before you find yourself in it."

"Huh-uh," he said. "You want to use that phone, go right ahead, bud."

I started to. I figured he'd be afraid to go through with it, and if he did, well, my word was still better than any bum's. No one had anything on me, and I was still Lou Ford. And he wouldn't get his mouth open before someone smacked a sap in it.

"Go ahead, bud, but it'll cost you. It'll sure cost you. And it won't be just the price of a burned hand."

I held onto the phone, but I didn't lift the receiver. "Go on," I said, "let's have it."

"I got interested in you, bud. I spent a year stretch on the Houston pea farm, and I seen a couple of guys like you there; and I figured it might pay to watch you a little. So I followed you that night. I heard some of the talk you had with that labor fellow . . ."

"And I reckon it meant a hell of a lot to you, didn't it?" I said.

"No, sir," he wagged his head, "hardly meant a thing to me. Fact is, it didn't mean much to me a couple nights later when you came up to that old farm house where I was shacked up, and then cut cross-prairie to that little white house. That didn't mean much neither, *then* . . . You say you had some whiskey, bud? An unopened bottle?"

I went into the laboratory, and got a pint of old prescription liquor from the stores cabinet. I brought it back with a glass; and he opened it and poured the glass half full.

"Have one on the house," he said, and handed it to me.

I drank it; I needed it. I passed the glass back to him, and he dropped it on the floor with the cup and saucer. He took a big swig from the bottle, and smacked his lips.

"No, sir," he went on, "it didn't mean a thing, and I couldn't stick around to figure it out. I hiked out of there, early Monday morning, and hit up the pipeline for a job. They put me with a jackhammer crew way the hell over on the Pecos, so far out I couldn't make town my first payday. Just three of us there by ourselves cut off from the whole danged world. But this payday it was different. We'd finished up on the Pecos, and I got to come in. I caught up on the news, bud, and those things you'd done and said meant plenty."

I nodded. I felt kind of glad. It was out of my hands, now, and the pieces were falling into place. I knew I had to do it, and how I was going to do it.

He took another swallow of whiskey and dug a cigarette from his shirt pocket. "I'm an understandin' man, bud, and the law ain't helped me none and I ain't helpin' it none. Unless I have to. What you figure it's worth to you to go on living?"

"I—" I shook my head. I had to go slow. I couldn't give in too easily. "I haven't got much money," I said. "Just what I make on my job."

"You got this place. Must be worth a pretty tidy sum, too."

"Yeah, but, hell," I said. "It's all I've got. If I'm not going to have a window left to throw it out of, there's not much percentage in keeping you quiet."

"You might change your mind about that, bud," he said. But he didn't sound too firm about it.

"Anyway," I said, "it's just not practical to sell it. People would wonder what I'd done with the money. I'd have to account for it to the government and pay a big chunk of taxes on it. For that matter—I reckon you're in a kind of a hurry—"

"You reckon right, bud."

"Well, it would take quite a while to get rid of a place like this. I'd want to sell it to a doctor, someone who'd pay for my Dad's practice and equipment. It'd be worth at least a third more that way, but the deal couldn't be swung in a hurry."

He studied me, suspiciously, trying to figure out how much if any I was stringing him. As a matter of fact, I wasn't lying more'n a little bit.

"I don't know," he said slowly. "I don't know much about them things. Maybe—you reckon you could swing a loan on it?"

"Well, I'd sure hate to do that—"

"That ain't what I asked you, bud."

"But, look," I said, making it good, "how would I pay it back out of my job? I just couldn't do it. I probably wouldn't get more than five thousand after they took out interest and brokerage fees. And I'd have to turn right around somewhere and swing another loan to pay off the first one, and—hell, that's no way to do business. Now, if you'll just give me four-five months to find someone who—"

"Huh-uh. How long it take you to swing this loan? A week?"

"Well . . ." I might have to give her a little longer than that. I wanted to give her longer. "I think that'd be a little bit quick. I'd say two weeks; but I'd sure hate—"

"Five thousand," he said, sloshing the whiskey in the bottle. "Five thousand in two weeks. Two weeks from tonight. All right, bud, we'll call that a deal. An' it'll be a deal, understand? I ain't no hog about money or nothin'. I get the five thousand and that's the last we'll see of each other."

I scowled and cussed, but I said, "Well, all right."

He tucked the whiskey into his hip pocket, and stood up. "Okay, bud. I'm goin' back out to the pipeline tonight. This ain't a very friendly place for easy-livin' men, so I'll stay out there another payday. But don't get no notions about runnin' out on me."

"How the hell could I?" I said. "You think I'm crazy?"

"You ask unpleasant questions, bud, and you may get unpleasant answers. Just be here with that five grand two weeks from tonight and there won't be no trouble."

I gave him a clincher; I still felt I might be giving in too easy. "Maybe you'd better not come here," I said. "Someone might see you and—"

"No one will. I'll watch myself like I did tonight. I ain't no more anxious for trouble than you are."

"Well," I said, "I just thought it might be better if we—"

"Now, bud"—he shook his head—"what happened the last time you was out wanderin' around old empty farm houses? It didn't turn out so good, did it?"

"All right," I said. "Suit yourself about it."

"That's just what I aim to do." He glanced toward the clock. "We got it all straight, then. Five thousand, two weeks from tonight, nine o'clock. That's it, and don't slip up on it."

"Don't worry. You'll get it," I said.

He stood at the front door a moment, sizing up the situation outside. Then he slipped out and off of the porch, and disappeared in the trees on the lawn.

I grinned, feeling a little sorry for him. It was funny the way these people kept asking for it. Just latching onto you, no matter how you tried to brush them off, and almost telling you how they wanted it done. Why'd they all have to come to me to get killed? Why couldn't they kill themselves?

I cleaned up the broken dishes in the office. I went upstairs and lay down and waited for Amy. I didn't have long to wait.

I didn't have long; and in a way she was the same as always, sort of snappy and trying not to be. But I could sense a difference, the stiffness that comes when you want to say or do something and don't know how to begin. Or maybe she could sense it in me; maybe we sensed it in each other.

I guess that's the way it was, because we both came out with it together. We spoke at the same time:

"Lou, why don't we . . ."
"Amy, why don't we . . ." } we said.

We laughed and said "bread and butter," and then she spoke again. "You do want to, don't you darling? Honest and truly?"

"Didn't I just start to ask you?" I said.

"How—when do you—"

"Well, I was thinking a couple of weeks would—"

"Darling!" She kissed me. "That was just what I was going to say!"

There was just a little more. That last piece of the picture needed one more little push.

"What are you thinking about, darling?"

"Well, I was thinking we've always had to do kinda like people expected us to. I mean—well, what were you thinking about?"

"You tell me first, Lou."

"No, you tell me, Amy."

"Well . . ."

"Well . . ."

"Why don't we elope," we said.

We laughed, and she threw her arms around me, snuggled up against me, sort of shivery but warm; so hard but so soft. And she whispered into my ear and I whispered into hers:

"*Bread and butter . . .*"

"*Bad luck, stay 'way from my darling.*"

SEVENTEEN

He showed up on, well, I guess it was the following Tuesday. The Tuesday after the Saturday the bum had shown up and Amy and I had decided to elope. He was a tall, stoop-shouldered guy with a face that seemed to be all bone and yellowish tightly drawn skin. He said his name was Dr. John Smith and that he was just passing through, he was just looking around in this section, and he'd heard—he'd thought, perhaps—that the house and the practice might be on the market.

It was around nine o'clock in the morning. By rights, I should have been headed for the courthouse. But I wasn't knocking myself out, these days, to get downtown; and Dad had always laid himself out for any doctors that came around.

"I've thought about selling it, off and on," I said, "but that's about as far as it's gone. I've never taken any steps in that direction. But come in anyway. Doctors are always welcome in this house."

I sat him down in the office and brought out a box of cigars, and got him some coffee. Then, I sat down with him and tried to visit. I can't say that I liked him much. He kept staring at me out of his big yellow eyes like I was really some sort of curiosity, something to look at instead of talk to. But—well, doctors get funny mannerisms. They live in an I'm-the-King world, where everyone else is wrong but them.

"You're a general practitioner, Doctor Smith?" I said. "I wouldn't want to discourage you, but I'm afraid the general practice field is pretty well the monopoly here of long-established doctors. Now—I haven't thought too much about disposing of this place, but I might consider it—now, I do think there's room for a good man in pediatrics or obstetrics . . ."

I let it hang there, and he blinked and came out of his trance.

"As a matter of fact, I am interested in those fields, Mr. Ford. I would—uh—hesitate to call myself a specialist, but—uh—"

"I think you might find an opening here, then," I said. "What's been your experience in treating nephritis, doctor. Would you say that inoculation with measles has sufficiently proven itself as a curative agent to warrant the inherent danger?"

"Well, uh—uh—" He crossed his legs. "Yes and no."

I nodded seriously. "You feel that there are two sides to the question?"

"Well—uh—yes."

"I see," I said. "I'd never thought about it quite that way, but I can see that you're right."

"That's your—uh—speciality, Mr. Ford? Children's diseases?"

"I haven't any speciality, doctor," I laughed. "I'm living proof of the adage about the shoemaker's son going barefooted. But I've always been interested in children, and I suppose the little I do know about medicine is confined to pediatrics."

"I see. Well, uh, as a matter of fact, most of my work has been in—uh—geriatrics."

"You should do well here, then," I said. "We have a high percentage of elderly people in the population. Geriatrics, eh?"

"Well, uh, as a matter of fact . . ."

"You know *Max Jacobsohn on Degenerative Diseases?* What do you think of his theorem as to the ratio between decelerated activity and progressive senility? I can understand the basic concept of course, but my math isn't good enough to allow me to appreciate his formulae. Perhaps you'll explain them to me?"

"Well, I—uh—it's pretty complicated . . ."

"I see. You feel, perhaps, that Jacobsohn's approach may be a trifle empirical? Well, I was inclined to that belief myself, for a time, but I'm afraid it may have been because my own approach was too subjective. For instance. Is the condition pathological? Is is psycho-pathological? Is it psycho-pathological-psychosomatic? Yes, yes, yes. It can be one or two or all three—*but* in varying degrees, doctor.

Like it or not, we must contemplate an *x* factor. Now, to strike an equation—and you'll pardon me for oversimplifying—let's say that our cosine is . . ."

I went on smiling and talking, wishing that Max Jacobsohn was here to see him. From what I'd heard of Dr. Jacobsohn, he'd probably grab this guy by the seat of his pants and boot him out into the street.

"As a matter of fact," he interrupted me, rubbing a big bony hand across his forehead, "I have a very bad headache. What do you do for headaches, Mr. Ford."

"I never have them," I said.

"Uh, oh? I thought perhaps that studying so much, sitting up late nights when you can't—uh—sleep . . ."

"I never have any trouble sleeping," I said.

"You don't worry a lot? I mean that in a town such as this where there is so much gossip—uh—malicious gossip, you don't feel that people are talking about you? It doesn't—uh—seem unbearable at times?"

"You mean," I said slowly, "do I feel persecuted? Well, as a matter of fact, I do, doctor. But I never worry about it. I can't say that it doesn't bother me, but—"

"Yes? Yes, Mr. Ford?"

"Well, whenever it gets too bad, I just step out and kill a few people. I frig them to death with a barbed-wire cob I have. After that I feel fine."

I'd been trying to place him, and finally it had come to me. It's been several years since I'd seen that big ugly mug in one of the out-of-town papers, and the picture hadn't been so good a resemblance. But I remembered it, now, and some of the story. I'd read about him. He'd taken his degree at the University of Edinburgh at a time when we were admitting their graduates to practice. He'd killed half a dozen people before he picked up a jerkwater Ph.D., and edged into psychiatry.

Out on the West Coast, he'd worked himself into some staff job with the police. And then a big murder case had cropped up, and he'd gotten hog-wild raw with the wrong suspects—people who had the money and influence to fight back. He hadn't lost his license, but he'd had to skip out fast. Now, well, I knew what he'd be doing now. What he'd have to be doing. Lunatics can't vote, so why should the legislature vote a lot of money for them?

"As a matter of fact—uh—" It was just beginning to soak in on him. "I think I'd better—"

"Stick around," I said. "I'll show you that corncob. Or maybe you can show me something from your collection—those Japanese sex goods you used to flash around. What'd you do with that rubber phallus you had? The one you squirted into that high school kid's face? Didn't you have time to pack it when you jumped the Coast?"

"I'm a-afraid you have me confused w-with—"

"As a matter of fact," I said, "I *do*. But you don't have me confused. You wouldn't know how to begin. You wouldn't know shit from wild honey, so go back and sign your report that way. Sign it shitbird. And you'd better add a footnote to the effect that the next son-of-a-bitch they send out here is going to get kicked so hard he'll be wearing his asshole for a collar."

He backed out into the hall and toward the front door, the bones in his face wobbling and twitching under the tight yellow skin. I followed him grinning.

He stuck a hand out sideways and lifted his hat from the halltree. He put it on backwards; and I laughed and took a quick step toward him. He almost fell out the door; and I picked up his briefcase and threw it into the yard.

"Take care of yourself, doc," I said. "Take good care of your keys. If you ever lose them, you won't be able to get out."

"You—you'll be . . ." The bones were jerking and jumping. He'd got down the steps, and his nerve was coming back. "If I ever get you up—"

"Me, doc? But I sleep swell. I don't have headaches. I'm not worried a bit. The only thing that bothers me is that corncob wearing out."

He snatched up the briefcase and went loping down the walk, his neck stuck out like a buzzard's. I slammed the door and made more coffee.

I cooked a big second breakfast, and ate it all.

You see, it didn't make a bit of difference. I hadn't lost a thing by telling him off. I'd thought they were closing in on me, and now I knew it. And they'd know that I knew it. But nothing was lost by that, and nothing else had changed.

They could still only guess, suspect. They had no more to go on than they'd ever had. They still wouldn't have anything two weeks—

well, ten days from now. They'd have more suspicions, they'd *feel* surer than ever. But they wouldn't have any proof.

They could only find the proof in me—in what I was—and I'd never show it to 'em.

I finished the pot of coffee, smoked a cigar, and washed and wiped the dishes. I tossed some bread scraps into the yard for the sparrows, and watered the sweet potato plant in the kitchen window.

Then, I got out the car and headed for town; and I was thinking how good it had been to talk—even if he had turned out to be a phony—for a while. To talk, really talk, for even a little while.

EIGHTEEN

I killed Amy Stanton on Saturday night on the fifth of April, 1952, at a few minutes before nine o'clock.

It had been a bright, crisp spring day, just warm enough so's you'd know that summer was coming, and the night was just tolerably cool. And she fixed her folks an early dinner, and got them off to a picture show about seven. Then, at eight-thirty, she came over to my place, and . . .

Well, I saw them going by my house—her folks, I mean—and I guess she must have been standing at their gate waving to 'em, because they were looking back and waving. Then, I guess, she went back into the house and started getting ready real fast; taking her hair down and bathing, and fixing her face and getting her bags packed. I guess she must have been busy as all-hell, jumping sideways to get ready, because she hadn't been able to do much while her folks were around. I guess she must have been chasing back and forth, turning on the electric iron, shutting off the bathwater, straightening the seams in her stockings, moving her mouth in and out to center the lipstick while she jerked the pins from her hair.

Why, hell, she had dozens of things to do, dozens of 'em, and if she'd just moved a little bit slower, ever so little—but Amy was one of those quick, sure girls. She was ready with time to spare, I guess, and then—I guess—she stood in front of the mirror, frowning and smiling, pouting and tossing her head, tucking her chin in and looking up under her brows; studying herself frontwards and sidewards, turning around and looking over her shoulder and brushing at her bottom, hitching her girdle up a little and down a little and then gripping it by both sides and sort of wriggling her hips in it. Then . . . then, I guess that must have been about all; she was all ready. So she came over where I was, and I . . .

I was ready too. I wasn't fully dressed, but I was ready for her.

I was standing in the kitchen waiting for her, and she was out of breath from hurrying so fast, I guess, and her bags were pretty heavy, I guess, and I guess . . .

I guess I'm not ready to tell about it yet. It's too soon, and it's not necessary yet. Because, hell, we had a whole two weeks before then, before Saturday, April 5th, 1952, at a few minutes before nine p.m.

We had two weeks and they were pretty good ones, because for the first time in I don't remember when my mind was really free. The end was coming up, it was rushing toward me, and everything would be over soon. I could think, well, go ahead and say something, do something, and it won't matter now. I can stall you *that* long; and I don't have to watch myself any more.

I was with her every night. I took her everywhere she wanted to go, and did everything she wanted to do. And it wasn't any trouble, because she didn't want to go much or do much. One evening we parked by the high school, and watched the baseball team work out. Another time we went down to the depot to see the Tulsa Flyer go through with the people looking out the dining car windows and the people staring back from the observation car.

That's about all we did, things like that, except maybe to drive down to the confectionery for some ice cream. Most of the time we just stayed at home, at my house. Both of us sitting in Dad's big old chair, or both of us stretched out upstairs, face to face, holding each other.

Just holding each other a lot of nights.

We'd lie there for hours, not speaking for an hour at a time sometimes; but the time didn't drag any. It seemed to rush by. I'd lie there listening to the ticking of the clock, listening to her heart beat with it, and I'd wonder why it had to tick so fast; I'd wonder *why*.

And it was hard to wake up and go to sleep, to go back into the nightmare where I could remember.

We had a few quarrels but no bad ones. I just wasn't going to have them; I let her have her own way and she tried to do the same with me.

One night she said she was going to the barbershop with me some time, and see that I got a decent haircut for a change. And I said—before I remembered—whenever she felt like doing that, I'd start wearing a braid. So we had a little spat, but nothing bad.

Then, one night she asked me how many cigars I smoked in a day, and I said I didn't keep track of 'em. She asked me why I didn't smoke cigarettes like "everyone else" did, and I said I didn't reckon that everyone else did smoke 'em. I said there was two members of my family that never smoked 'em. Dad and me. She said, well, of course, if you thought more of him than you do of me, there's nothing more to be said. And I said, Jesus Christ, how do you figure—what's that got to do with it?

But it was just a little spat. Nothing bad at all. I reckon she forgot about it right away like she did the first one.

I think she must have had a mighty good time those two weeks. Better'n any she'd ever had before.

So the two weeks passed, and the night of April fifth came; and she hustled her folks off to a show, and scampered around getting ready, and she got ready. And at eight-thirty she came over to my place and I was waiting for her. And I . . .

But I guess I'm getting ahead of myself again. There's some other things to tell first.

I went to work every working day of those two weeks; and believe me it wasn't easy. I didn't want to face anyone—I wanted to stay there in the house with the shades drawn, and not see anyone at all, and I knew I couldn't do that. I went to work, I forced myself to, just like always.

They suspected me; and I let 'em know that I knew. But there wasn't a thing on my conscience; I wasn't afraid of a thing. And I proved that there wasn't by going down. Because how could a man who'd done what they thought I had, go right on about his business and look people in the eye?

I was sore, sure. My feelings were hurt. But I wasn't afraid and I proved it.

Most of the time, at first, anyway, I wasn't given much to do. And believe me that was hard, standing around with my face hanging out and pretending like I didn't notice or give a damn. And when I did get a little job, serving a warrant or something like that, there was always a reason for another deputy to go along with me. He'd be embarrassed and puzzled, because, of course, they were keeping the secret at the top, between Hendricks and Conway and Bob Maples. He'd wonder what was up but he couldn't ask, because, in our own way, we're the politest people in the world; we'll joke and talk about everything except what's on our minds. But he'd wonder and he'd be embarrassed, and he'd try to brag me up—maybe talk me up about the Johnnie Pappas deal to make me feel better.

I was coming back from lunch one day when the hall floors had just been oiled. And they didn't make much noise when you stepped on them, and when you kind of had to pick your way along they didn't make any at all. Deputy Jeff Plummer and Sheriff Bob were talking, and they didn't hear me coming. So I stopped just short of the door and listened. I listened and I saw them: I knew them so well I could see 'em without looking.

Bob was at his desk, pretending to thumb through some papers; and his glasses were down on the end of his nose, and he was looking up over them now and then. And he didn't like what he had to say, but you'd never know it the way his eyes came up over those glasses and the way he talked. Jeff Plummer was hunkered down in one of the windows, studying his finger-nails, maybe, his jaws moving on a stick of gum. And he didn't like telling Bob off—and he didn't sound like he was; just easy-going and casual—but he was sure as hell doing it.

"No, sir, Bob," he drawled. "Been kind of studyin' things over, and I reckon I ain't going to do no spying no more. Ain't going to do it a-tall."

"You got your mind made up, huh? You're plumb set?"

"Well, now, it sure looks that way, don't it? Yes, sir, I reckon that's prob'ly the way it is. Can't rightly see it no other way."

"You see how it's possible to do a job if'n you don't follow orders? You reckon you can do that?"

"Now"—Jeff was looking—*looking*—real pleased, like he'd drawn aces to three kings—"now, I'm sure proud you mentioned that, Bob. I plain admire a man that comes square to a point."

There was a second's silence, then a *clink* as Jeff's badge hit the desk. He slid out of the window and sauntered toward the door, smiling but not with his eyes. And Bob cussed and jumped up.

"You ornery coyote! You tryin' to knock my eyes out with that thing? I ever catch you throwin' it around again, I'll whup you down to a nubbin."

Jeff scuffed his boots; he cleared his throat. He said it was a plumb purty day out, and a man'd have to be plain out of his mind to claim different.

"I reckon a man hadn't ought to ask you a question about all the hocus-pocus around here, now had he, Bob? It wouldn't be what you'd call proper?"

"Well, now, I don't know as I'd put it that way. Don't reckon I'd even prod him about why he was askin'. I'd just figure he was a man, and a man just does what he has to."

I slipped into the men's john and stayed there a while. And when I went into the office, Jeff Plummer was gone and Bob gave me a warrant to serve. By myself. He didn't exactly meet my eye, but he seemed pretty happy. He had his neck out a mile—he had everything to lose and nothing to gain—and he was happy.

And I didn't know whether I felt better or not.

Bob didn't have much longer to live, and the job was all he had. Jeff Plummer had a wife and four kids, and he was just about standing in the middle of his wardrobe whenever you saw him. People like that, well, they don't make up their mind about a man in a hurry. But once it's made up they hardly ever change it. They can't. They'd almost rather die than do it.

I went on about my business every day, and things were easier for me in a sense, because people acted easier around me, and twice as hard in another way. Because the folks that trust you, that just won't hear no bad about you nor even think it, those are the ones that are hard to fool. You can't put your heart in the job.

I'd think about my—those people, so many of them, and I'd wonder *why*. I'd have to go through it all again, step by step. And just about the time I'd get it settled, I'd start wondering all over again.

I guess I got kind of sore at myself. And at them. All those people. I'd think, why in the hell did they have to do it—I didn't ask 'em to stick their necks out; I'm not begging for friendship. But they *did* give me their friendship and they *did* stick their necks out. So along toward the last, I was sticking mine out.

I stopped by the Greek's place every day. I looked over the work and had him explain things to me, and I'd offer him a lift when he had to go some place. I'd say it was sure going to be one up-to-date restaurant and that Johnnie would sure like it—that he did like it. Because there hadn't ever been a better boy, and now he could look on, look down, and admire things the same as we could. I said I knew he could, that Johnnie was really happy now.

And the Greek didn't have much to say for a while—he was polite but he didn't say much. Then, pretty soon, he was taking me out in the kitchen for coffee; and he'd walk me clear out to my car when I had to leave. He'd hang around me, nodding and nodding while I talked about Johnnie. And once in a while he'd remember that maybe he ought to be ashamed, and I knew he wanted to apologize but was afraid of hurting my feelings.

Chester Conway had been staying in Fort Worth, but he came back in town one day for a few hours and I made it my business to hear about it. I was driving by his offices real slow, around two in the afternoon, when he came barging out looking for a taxi. And before he knew what was happening, I had him in charge. I hopped out, took this briefcase away from him, and hustled him into my car.

It was the last thing he'd've expected of me. He was too set back to talk, and he didn't have time to say anything. And after we were headed for the airport, he didn't get a chance. Because I was doing all the talking.

I said, "I've been hoping to run into you, Mr. Conway. I wanted to thank you for the hospitality you showed me in Fort Worth. It was sure thoughtful of you at a time like that, to think of me and Bob's comfort, and I guess I wasn't so thoughtful myself. I was kind of tired, just thinkin' of my own problems instead of yours, how you must feel, and I reckon I was pretty snappy with you there at the airport. But I didn't really mean anything by it, Mr. Conway, and I've been wanting to apologize. I wouldn't blame you a bit if you were put out with me, because I ain't ever had much sense and I guess I've made a hell of a mess of things.

"Now, I knew Elmer was kind of innocent and trusting and I

knew a woman like that just couldn't be much good. I shoulda done like you said and gone there with him—I don't rightly see how I could the way she was acting, but I shoulda done that anyway. And don't think I don't know it now, and if cussing me out will help any or if you want to get my job, and I know you can get it, I won't hold any grudge. No matter what you did it wouldn't be enough, it wouldn't bring Elmer back. An' . . . I never got to know him real well, but in a way kinda I felt like I did. I reckon it must've been because he looked so much like you. I'd see him from a distance sometimes and I'd think it was you. I guess maybe that's one reason I wanted to see you today. It was kinda like seein' Elmer again. I could sorta feel for a minute that he was still here an' nothing had ever happened. An' . . ."

We'd come to the airport.

He got out without speaking or looking at me, and strode off to the plane. Moving fast, never turning around or looking sideways; almost like he was running away from something.

He started up the ramp, but he wasn't moving so fast now. He was walking slower and slower, and halfway up he almost stopped. Then he went on, plodding, dragging his feet; and he reached the top. And he stood there for a second, blocking the door.

He turned around, gave the briefcase a little jerk, and ducked inside the plane.

He'd waved to me.

I drove back to town, and I guess I gave up about then. It was no use. I'd done everything I could. I'd dropped it in their plates, and rubbed their noses in it. And it was no use. They wouldn't see it.

No one would stop me.

So, on Saturday night, April 5th, 1952, at a few minutes before nine o'clock, I . . .

But I guess there's another thing or two to tell you first, and—but I *will* tell you about it. I want to tell you, and I will, exactly how it happened. I won't leave you to figure things out for yourself.

In lots of books I read, the writer seems to go haywire every time he reaches a high point. He'll start leaving out punctuation and running his words together and babble about stars flashing and sinking into a deep dreamless sea. And you can't figure out whether the hero's laying his girl or a cornerstone. I guess that kind of crap is supposed to be pretty deep stuff—a lot of the book reviewers eat it up, I notice. But the way I see it is, the writer is just too goddam lazy to do his job. And I'm not lazy, whatever else I am. I'll tell you everything.

But I want to get everything in the right order. I want you to understand how it was.

Late Saturday afternoon, I got Bob Maples alone for a minute and told him I wouldn't be able to work that night. I said that Amy and me had something mighty important to do, and maybe I wouldn't be getting in Monday or Tuesday either; and I gave him a wink.

"Well, now"—he hesitated, frowning. "Well, now, you don't think maybe that—" Then, he gripped my hand and wrung it. "That's real good news, Lou. Real good. I know you'll be happy together."

"I'll try not to lay off too long," I said. "I reckon things are, well, kind of up in the air and—"

"No, they ain't," he said, sticking his chin out. "Everything's all right, and it's going to stay that way. Now go on and buss Amy for me, and don't you worry about nothing."

It still wasn't real late in the day, so I drove out on Derrick Road and parked a while.

Then I went home, leaving the car parked out in front, and fixed dinner.

I stretched out on the bed for about an hour, letting my food settle. I drew water in the bath tub and got in.

I lay in the tub for almost an hour, soaking and smoking and thinking. Finally, I got out, looked at the clock and began laying out clothes.

I packed my gladstone, and cinched the straps on it. I put on clean underwear and socks and new-pressed pants, and my Sunday go-to-meetin' boots. I left off my shirt and tie.

I sat on the edge of the bed smoking until eight o'clock. Then, I went downstairs to the kitchen.

I turned the light on in the pantry, moving the door back and forth until I had it like I wanted it. Until there was just enough light in the kitchen. I looked around, making sure that all the blinds were drawn, and went into Dad's office.

I took down the concordance to the Bible and removed the four hundred dollars in marked money, Elmer's money. I dumped the drawers of Dad's desk on the floor. I turned off the light, pulled the door almost shut, and went back into the kitchen.

The evening newspaper was spread out on the table. I slid a butcher knife under it, and—and it was that time. I heard her coming.

She came up the back steps and across the porch, and banged and fumbled around for a minute getting the door open. She came in, out of breath kind of and out of temper, and pushed the door shut behind her. And she saw me standing there, not saying anything because I'd forgotten *why* and I was trying to remember. And, finally, I did remember.

So—or did I mention it already?—on Saturday night, the fifth of April 1952, at a few minutes before nine o'clock I killed Amy Stanton.

Or maybe you could call it suicide.

NINETEEN

She saw me and it startled her for a second. Then she dropped her two traveling cases on the floor and gave one of 'em a kick, and brushed a wisp of hair from her eyes.

"Well!" she snapped. "I don't suppose it would occur to you to give me a little help! Why didn't you leave the car in the garage, anyway?"

I shook my head. I didn't say anything.

"I'll swear, Lou Ford! Sometimes I think—and you're not even ready yet! You're always talking about how slow I am, and here you stand, on your own wedding night of all things, and you haven't—" She stopped suddenly, her mouth shut tight, her breasts rising and falling. And I heard the kitchen clock tick ten times before she spoke again. "I'm sorry, darling," she said softly. "I didn't mean—"

"Don't say anything more, Amy," I said. "Just don't say anything more."

She smiled and came toward me with her arms held out. "I won't, darling. I won't ever say anything like that again. But I do want to tell you how much—"

"Sure," I said. "You want to pour your heart out to me."

And I hit her in the guts as hard as I could.

My fist went back against her spine, and the flesh closed around it to the wrist. I jerked back on it, I had to jerk, and she flopped forward from the waist, like she was hinged.

Her hat fell off, and her head went clear down and touched the floor. And then she toppled over, completely over, like a kid turning a somersault. She lay on her back, eyes bulging, rolling her head from side to side.

She was wearing a white blouse and a light cream-colored suit; a new one, I reckon, because I didn't remember seeing it before. I got my hand in the front of the blouse, and ripped it down to the waist. I jerked the skirt up over her head, and she jerked and shook all over; and there was a funny sound like she was trying to laugh.

And then I saw the puddle spreading out under her.

I sat down and tried to read the paper. I tried to keep my eyes on it. But the light wasn't very good, not good enough to read by, and she kept moving around. It looked like she couldn't lie still.

Once I felt something touch my boot, and I looked down and it was her hand. It was moving back and forth across the toe of my boot. It moved up along the ankle and the leg, and somehow I was afraid to move away. And then her fingers were at the top, clutching down inside; and I almost couldn't move. I stood up and tried to jerk away, and the fingers held on.

I dragged her two-three feet before I could break away.

Her fingers kept on moving, sliding and crawling back and forth, and finally they got a hold of her purse and held on. They dragged it down inside of her skirt, and I couldn't see it or her hands any more.

Well, that was all right. It would look better to have her hanging onto her purse. And I grinned a little, thinking about it. It was so much like her, you know, to latch onto her purse. She'd always been so tight, and . . . and I guess she'd had to be.

There wasn't a better family in town than the Stantons. But both her folks had been ailing for years, and they didn't have much any more aside from their home. She'd had to be tight, like any damned fool ought to have known; because there wasn't any other way of being, and that's all any of us ever are: what we have to be. And I guessed it hadn't been very funny when I'd kidded her dead-pan, and acted surprised when she got mad.

I guess that stuff she'd brought to me when I was sick wasn't really crap. It was as good as she knew how to fix. I guess that dog of theirs didn't have to chase horses unless'n he wanted the exercise. I—

Why the hell didn't he come? Hell, she hadn't had a real breath now in almost thirty minutes, and it was hard as hell on her. I knew how hard it was and I held my own breath a while because we'd always done things together, and . . .

He came.

I'd locked the front screen, so that he couldn't just walk in, and I heard him tugging at it.

I gave her two hard kicks in the head and she rose off the floor, her skirt falling down off her face, and I knew there wouldn't be any doubt about her. She was dead on the night of— Then I went and opened the door and let him in.

I pushed the roll of marked twenties on him and said, "Stick this in your pocket. I've got the rest back in the kitchen," and I started back there.

I knew he would put the money in his pocket, and you do too if you can remember back when you were a kid. You'd walk up to a guy and say, "Here, hold this," and probably he'd pulled the same gag himself; he'd know you were handing him a horse turd or a prickly pear or a dead mouse. But if you pulled it fast enough, he'd do just what you told him.

I pulled it fast, and headed right back toward the kitchen. And he was right on my heels, because he didn't want me to get too far away from him.

There was just a little light, like I've said. I was between him and her. He was right behind me, watching me instead of anything else, and we went into the kitchen and I stepped aside quickly.

He almost stepped on her stomach. I guess his foot did touch it for a split second.

He pulled it back, staring down at her like his eyes were steel and she was a magnet. He tried to tug them away, and they'd just roll, going all-white in his head, and finally he got them away.

He looked at me and his lips shook as though he'd been playing a juice-harp, and he said:

"Yeeeeeeee!"

It was a hell of a funny sound, like a siren with a slippy chain that can't quite get started. "Yeeeeee!" he said. "Yeeeeee!" It sounded funny as hell, and he looked funny as hell.

Did you ever see one of those two-bit jazz singers? You know, trying to put something across with their bodies that they haven't got the voice to do? They lean back from the waist a little with their heads hanging forward and their hands held up about even with their ribs and swinging limp. And they sort of wobble and roll on their hips.

That's the way he looked, and he kept making that damned funny noise, his lips quivering ninety to the minute and his eyes rolling all-white.

I laughed and laughed, he looked and sounded so funny I couldn't help it. Then, I remember what he'd done and I stopped laughing, and got mad—sore all over.

"You son-of-a-bitch," I said. "I was going to marry that poor little girl. We were going to elope and she caught you going through the house and you tried to . . ."

I stopped, because he hadn't done it at all. But he *could* have done it. He could've done it just as easy as not. The son-of-a-bitch could have, but he was just like everyone else. He was too nicey-nice and pretendsy to do anything really hard. But he'd stand back and crack the whip over me, keep moving around me every way I turned so that I couldn't get away no matter what I did, and it was always now-don't-you-do-nothin' bud; but they kept cracking that old whip all the time they were sayin' it. And they—he'd done it all right; and I wasn't going to take the blame. I could be just as tricky and pretendsy as they were.

I could . . .

I went blind ma—angry seeing him so pretendsy shocked, "Yeeing!" and shivering and doing that screwy dance with his hands—hell, he hadn't had to watch *her* hands!—and white-rolling his eyes. What right did he have to act like that? I was the one that should have been acting that way, but, oh, no, I couldn't. That was their—his right to act that way, and I had to hold in and do all the dirty work.

I was as mad as all-hell.

I snatched the butcher-knife from under the newspaper, and made for him.

And my foot slipped where she'd been lying.

I went sprawling, almost knocking him over backwards if he hadn't moved, and the knife flew out of my hands.

I couldn't have moved a finger for a minute. I was laid out flat, helpless, without any weapon. And I could have maybe rolled a little and put my arms around her, and we'd have been together like we'd always been.

But do you think he'd do it? Do you think he'd pick up that knife and use it, just a little thing that wouldn't have been a bit of trouble? Oh, hell, no, oh, God, no, oh, Christ and Mary and all the Saints . . .?

No.

All he could do was beat it, just like they always did.

I grabbed up the knife and took off after the heartless son-of-a-bitch.

He was out to the street sidewalk by the time I got to the front door; the dirty bastard had sneaked a head start on me. When I got out to the walk, he was better'n a half-block away, heading toward the center of town. I took after him as fast as I could go.

That wasn't very fast on account of the boots. I've seen plenty of men out here that never walked fifty miles altogether in their lives. But he wasn't moving very fast either. He was sort of skipping, jerky, rather than running or walking. He was skipping and tossing his head, and his hair was flying. And he still had his elbows held in at his sides, and his hands doing that funny floppy dance, and he kept saying—it was louder now—that old siren was warming up—he kept saying, kind of screaming:

"Yeeeee! Yeeeeee! Yeeeeeeeee . . .!"

He was skipping and flopping his hands and tossing his head like one of those holy roller preachers at a brushwood's revival meeting. "Yeeeing!" and gone-to-Jesus and all you miserable sinners get right with Gawd like I went and done.

The dirty son-of-a-bitch! How low down can you get?

"MUR-DER!" I yelled. "Stop him, stop him! He killed Amy Stanton! MUR-DER . . .!"

I yelled at the top of my lungs and I kept yelling. And windows started banging up and doors slammed. And people ran down off their porches. And that snapped him out of that crap—some of it.

He skipped out into the middle of the street, and started moving faster. But I moved faster, too, because it was still dirt in this block, just one short of the business district, and boots are meant for dirt.

He saw that I was gaining a little on him, and he tried to come out of that floppy skippy stuff, but it didn't look like he could quite make it. Maybe he was using too much steam with that "Yeeeeing!"

"MURDER!" I yelled. "MUR-DER! Stop him! He killed Amy Stanton . . .!"

And everything was happening awful fast. It just sounds like it was a long time, because I'm not leaving out anything. I'm trying to tell you exactly how it was, so's you'll be sure to understand.

Looking up ahead, into the business district, it looked like a whole army of automobiles was bearing down on us. Then, suddenly, it was like a big plow had come down the street, pushing all those cars into the curb.

That's the way people are here in this section. That's the way they get. You don't see them rushing into the middle of a commotion to find out what's happening. There's men that are paid to do that and they do it prompt, without any fuss or feathers. And the folks know that no one's going to feel sorry for 'em if they get in the way of a gun or a bullet.

"Yeeeeee! Yeeeeee! Yeeeeeeeeeeeee!" he screamed, skipping and flopping.

"MUR-DER! He killed Amy Stanton . . ."

And up ahead a little old roaster swung crossways with the intersection and stopped, and Jeff Plummer climbed out.

He reached down on the floor and took out a Winchester. Taking his time, easy-like. He leaned back against the fender, one boot heel hooked through the wheel spokes, and brought the gun up to his shoulder.

"Halt!" he called.

He called out the one time and then he fired, because the bum had started to skip toward the side of the street; and a man sure ought to know better than that.

The bum stumbled and went down, grabbing at his knee. But he got up again and he was still jerking and flopping his hands, and it looked like he was reaching into his clothes. And a man *really* hadn't ought to do that. He hadn't even ought to look anything like that.

Jeff fired three times, shifting his aim easy-like with each shot, and the bum was dropping with the first one but all three got him. By the time he hit the dirt he didn't have much left in the way of a head.

I fell down on top of him and began beating him, and they had their hands full dragging me off. I babbled out the story—how I'd been upstairs getting ready and I'd heard some commotion but I hadn't thought much about it. And—

And I didn't have to tell it too good. They all seemed to understand how it was.

A doctor pushed through the crowd, Dr. Zweilman, and he gave me a shot in the arm; and then they took me home.

TWENTY

I woke up a little after nine the next morning.

My mouth was sticky and my throat dry from the morphine—I don't know why he hadn't used hyoscin like any damned fool should have—and all I could think of right then was how thirsty I was.

I stood in the bathroom, gulping down glass after glass of water, and pretty soon it began to bounce on me. (I'm telling you almost *anything* is better than morphine.) But after a while it stopped. I drank a couple glasses more, and they stayed down. And I scrubbed my face in hot and cold water, and combed my hair.

Then I went back and sat down on the bed, wondering who'd undressed me; and all at once it hit me. Not about her. I wouldn't think about that. But—well, this.

I shouldn't have been alone. Your friends don't leave you alone at a time like that. I'd lost the girl I was going to marry, and I'd been through a terrible experience. And they'd left me alone. There wasn't anyone around to comfort me, or wait on me or just sit and shake their heads and say it was God's will and she was happy, and I—a man that's been through something like that needs those things. He needs all the help and comfort he can get, and I've never held back when one of my friends was bereaved. Why, hell, I—a man isn't himself when one of these disasters strikes. He might do something to himself, and the least people can do is have a nurse around. And . . .

But there wasn't any nurse around. I got up and looked through the other bedrooms, just to make sure.

And I wasn't doing anything to myself. They'd never done anything for me, and I wasn't doing anything for them.

I went downstairs and . . . and the kitchen had been cleaned up. There was no one there but me. I started to make some coffee, and then I thought I heard someone out in front, someone cough. And I was so all-fired glad I felt the tears come to my eyes. I turned off the coffee and went to the front door and opened it.

Jeff Plummer was sitting on the steps.

He was sitting sideways, his back to a porch post. He slanted a glance at me, then let his eyes go straight again, without turning his head.

"Gosh, Jeff," I said. "How long you been out here? Why didn't you knock?"

"Been here quite a spell," he said. And he fingered a stick of gum from his shirt pocket and began to unwrap it. "Yes, sir, I been here quite a spell."

"Well, come on in! I was just—"

"Kinda like it where I am," he said. "Air smells real good. Been smellin' real good, anyways."

He put the gum in his mouth. He folded the wrapper into a neat little square and tucked it back into his pocket.

"Yes, sir," he said, "it's been smellin' real good, and that's a fact."

I felt like I was nailed there in the doorway. I had to stand there and wait, watch his jaws move on that gum, look at him not looking at me. Never looking at me.

"Has there . . . hasn't anyone been—?"

"Told 'em you wasn't up to it," he said. "Told 'em you was all broke up about Bob Maples."

"Well, I—*Bob*?"

"Shot hisself around midnight last night. Yes, sir, pore ol' Bob killed hisself, and I reckon he had to. I reckon I know just how he felt."

And he still didn't look at me.

I closed the door.

I leaned against it, my eyes aching, my head pounding; and I ticked them off with the pounding that reached from my head to my heart . . . Joyce, Elmer, Johnnie Pappas, Amy, the . . . Him, Bob Maples . . . But he hadn't known anything! He couldn't have known, had any real proof. He'd just jumped to conclusions like they were jumping. He couldn't wait for me to explain like, hell, I'd've been glad to do. Hadn't I always been glad to explain? But he couldn't wait; he'd made up his mind without any proof, like they'd made up theirs.

Just because I'd been around when a few people got killed, just because I happened to be around . . .

They couldn't know anything, because I was the only one who could tell 'em—show 'em—and I never had.

And I sure as hell wasn't going to.

Actually, well, logically, and you can't do away with logic, there *wasn't* anything. Existence and proof are inseparables. You have to have the second to have the first.

I held onto that thought, and I fixed myself a nice big breakfast. But I couldn't eat but a little bit. That darned morphine had taken all my appetite, just like it always does. About all I could get down was part of a piece of toast and two-three cups of coffee.

I went back upstairs and lighted a cigar, and stretched out on the bed. I—a man that'd been through what I had, belonged in bed.

About a quarter of eleven, I heard the front door open and close, but I stayed right where I was. I still stayed there, stretched out on the bed, smoking, when Howard Hendricks and Jeff Plummer came in.

Howard gave me a curt nod, and drew up a straight chair near the bed. Jeff sat down, sort of out of the way, in an easy chair. Howard could hardly hold himself in, but he was sure trying. He tried. He did the best he could to be stern and sorrowful, and to hold his voice steady.

"Lou," he said, "we—I'm not at all satisfied. Last night's events—these recent events—I don't like them a bit, Lou."

"Well," I said, "that's natural enough. Don't hardly see how you could like 'em. I know I sure don't."

"You know what I mean!"

"Why, sure, I do. I know just how—"

"Now, this alleged robber-rapist—this poor devil you'd have us believe was a robber and a rapist. We happen to know he was nothing of the kind! He was a pipeline worker. He had a pocket full of wages. And—and yes, we know he wasn't drunk because he'd just had a big steak dinner! He wouldn't have had the slightest reason to be in this house, so Miss Stanton couldn't have—"

"Are you saying he wasn't here, Howard?" I said. "That should be mighty easy to prove."

"Well—he wasn't prowling, that's a certainty! If—"

"Why is it?" I said. "If he wasn't prowling, what was he doing?"

His eyes began to glitter. "Never mind! Let that go for a minute! But I'll tell you this much. If you think you can get away with planting that money on him and making it look like—"

"What money?" I said. "I thought you said it was his wages?"

You see? The guy didn't have any sense. Otherwise, he'd have waited for me to mention that marked money.

"The money you stole from Elmer Conway! The money you took the night you killed him and that woman!"

"Now, wait a minute, wait a minute," I frowned. "Let's take one thing at a time. Let's take the woman. Why would I kill her?"

"Because—well—because you'd killed Elmer and you had to shut her up."

"But why would I kill Elmer? I'd known him all my life. If I'd wanted to do him any harm, I'd sure had plenty of chances."

"You know—" He stopped abruptly.

"Yeah?" I said, puzzled. "Why would I kill Elmer, Howard?"

And he couldn't say, of course. Chester Conway had given him his orders about that.

"You killed him all right," he said, his face reddening. "You killed her. You hanged Johnnie Pappas."

"You're sure not making much sense, Howard." I shook my head. "You plumb insisted on me talking to Johnnie because you knew how much I liked him and how much he liked me. Now you're saying I killed him."

"You had to kill him to protect yourself! You'd given him that marked twenty-dollar bill!"

"Now you really ain't making sense," I said. "Let's see; there was five hundred dollars missing, wasn't there? You claiming that I killed Elmer and that woman for five hundred dollars? Is that what you're saying, Howard?"

"I'm saying that—that—goddammit, Johnnie wasn't anywhere near the scene of the murders! He was stealing tires at the time they were committed!"

"Is that a fact?" I drawled. "Someone see him, Howard?"

"Yes! I mean, well—uh—"

See what I mean? Shrapnel.

"Let's say that Johnnie didn't do these killings," I said. "And you know it was mighty hard for me to believe that he had, Howard. I said so right along. I always did think he was just scared and kind of out of his mind when he hanged himself. I'd been his only friend, and now it sort of seemed like I didn't believe in him any more, an'—"

"His friend! Jesus!"

"So I reckon he didn't do it, after all. Poor little Amy was killed in pretty much the same way that other woman was. And this man—you say he had a big part of the missing money on him. Five hundred dollars would seem like a lot of money to a man like that, an' seeing that the two killings were so much alike . . ."

I let my voice trail off, smiling at him; and his mouth opened and went shut again.

Shrapnel. That's all he had.

"You've got it all figured out, haven't you?" he said, softly. "Four—five murders; six counting poor Bob Maples who staked everything he had on you, and you sit there explaining and smiling. You aren't bothered a bit. How can you do it, Ford? How can—"

I shrugged. "Somebody has to keep their heads, and it sure looks like you can't. You got some more questions, Howard?"

"Yes," he nodded, slowly. "I've got one. How did Miss Stanton get those bruises on her body? Old bruises, not made last night. The same kind of bruises we found on the body of the Lakeland woman. How did she get them, Ford?"

Shrap—

"Bruises?" I said. "Gosh, you got me there, Howard. How would I know?"

"H-how"—he sputtered—"how would you know?"

"Yeah?" I said, puzzled. "How?"

"Why, goddam you! You'd been screwing that gal for years! You—"

"Don't say that," I said.

"No," said Jeff Plummer, "don't say that."

"But"—Howard turned on him, then turned back to me. "All right, I won't say it! I don't need to say it. That girl had never gone with anyone but you, and only you could have done that to her! You'd been beating on her just like you'd beaten on that whore!"

I laughed, sort of sadly. "And Amy just took it huh, Howard? I bruised her up, and she went right ahead seeing me? She got all ready to marry me? That wouldn't make sense with any woman, and it makes no sense minus about Amy. You sure wouldn't say a thing like that if you'd known Amy Stanton."

He shook his head, staring, like I was some kind of curiosity. That old shrapnel wasn't doing a thing for him.

"Now, maybe Amy did pick up a bruise here and there," I went on. "She had all sorts of work to do, keepin' house and teaching school, and everything there was to be done. It'd been mighty strange if she didn't bang herself up a little, now and—"

"That's not what I mean. You know that's not what I mean."

"—but if you're thinking I did it, and that she put up with it, you're way off base. You sure didn't know Amy Stanton."

"Maybe," he said, "you didn't know her."

"Me? But you just got through sayin' we'd gone together for years—"

"I—" He hesitated, frowning. "I don't know. It isn't all clear to me, and I won't pretend that it is. But I don't think you knew her. Not as well as . . ."

"Yeah?" I said.

He reached into his inside coat pocket, and brought out a square blue envelope. He opened it and removed one of those double sheets of stationery. I could see it was written on both sides, four pages in all. And I recognized that small neat handwriting.

Howard looked up from the paper, and caught my eye.

"This was in her purse." *Her purse*. "She'd written it at home and was planning, apparently, to give it to you after you were out of

Central City. As a matter of fact"—he glanced down at the letter—"she intended to have you stop at a restaurant up the road, and have you read it while she was in the rest room. Now, it begins, 'Lou Darling . . .' "

"Let me have it," I said.

"I'll read—"

"It's his letter," said Jeff. "Let him have it."

"Very well." Howard shrugged; and he tossed me the letter. And I knew he'd planned on having me read it all along. He wanted me to read it while he sat back and watched.

I looked down at the thick double page, holding my eyes on it:

Lou, Darling:

Now you know why I had you stop here, and why I've excused myself from the table. It was to allow you to read this, the things I couldn't somehow otherwise say to you. Please, please read carefully, darling. I'll give you plenty of time. And if I sound confused and rambling, please don't be angry with me. It's only because I love you so much, and I'm a little frightened and worried.

Darling, I wish I could tell you how happy you've made me these last few weeks. I wish I could be sure that you'd been even a tiny fraction as happy. Just a teensy-weensie bit as much. Sometimes I get the crazy, wonderful notion that you have been, that you were even as happy as I was (though I don't see how you could be!) and at others I tell myself . . . Oh, I don't know, Lou!

I suppose the trouble is that it all seemed to come about so suddenly. We'd gone on for years, and you seemed to be growing more and more indifferent; you seemed to keep drawing away from me and taking pleasure in making me follow. (Seemed, Lou: I don't say you did do it.) I'm not trying to excuse myself, darling. I only want to explain, to make you understand that I'm not going to behave that way any more. I'm not going to be sharp and demanding and scolding and . . . I may not be able to change all at once (oh, but I will, darling; I'll watch myself; I'll do it just as fast as I can) but if you'll just love me, Lou, just act like you love me, I'm sure— Do you understand how I felt? Just a little? Do you see why I was that way, then, and why I won't be any more? Everyone knew I was yours. Almost everyone. I wanted it to be that way; to have anyone else was unthinkable. But I couldn't have had anyone else if I'd wished to. I was yours. I'd always be yours if you dropped me. And it seemed, Lou, that you were slipping further and further away, still owning me yet not letting yourself belong to me. You were (it seemed, darling, seemed) leaving me with nothing—and knowing that you were doing it, knowing I was helpless—and apparently enjoying it. You avoided me. You made me chase you. You made me question you and beg you, and—and then you'd act so innocent and puzzled and . . . Forgive me, darling. I don't want to criticize you ever, ever again. I only wanted you to understand, and I suppose only another woman could do that.

Lou, I want to ask you something, a few things, and I want to beg you please, please, please not to take it the wrong way. Are you—oh, don't be, darling—are you afraid of me? Do you feel that you have to be nice to me? There I won't say anything more, but you know what I mean, as well as I do at least. And you will know . . .

I hope and pray I am wrong, darling. I do so hope. But I'm afraid—are you in trouble? Is something weighing on your mind? I don't want to ask you more than that, but I do want you to believe that whatever it is, even if it's what I—whatever it is, Lou, I'm on your side. I love you (are you tired of my saying that?), and I know you. I know you'd never knowingly do anything wrong, you just couldn't, and I love you so much and . . . Let me help you, darling. Whatever it is, whatever help you need. Even if it should involve being separated for a while, a long while, let's—let me help you. Because I'll wait for you, however long—and it mightn't be long at all, it might be just a question of—well, it will be all right, Lou, because you wouldn't knowingly do anything. I know that and everyone else knows it, and it will be all right. We'll make it all right, you and I together. If you'll only tell me. If you'll just let me help you.

Now I asked you not to be afraid of me, but I know how you've felt, how you used to feel, and I know that asking you or telling you might not be enough. That's why I had you stop at this place, here at a bus stop. That's why I'm giving you so much time. To prove to you that you don't need to be afraid.

I hope that when I come back to the table, you'll still be there. But if you aren't, darling, if you feel that you can't . . . then just leave my bags inside the door. I have money with me and I can get a job in some other town, and—do that, Lou. If you feel that you must. I'll understand, and it'll be perfectly all right—honestly it will, Lou—and . . .

Oh, darling, darling, darling, I love you so much. I've always loved you and I always will, whatever happens. Always, darling. Always and always. Forever and forever.

Always and forever,
Amy

TWENTY-ONE

Well. WELL?

What are you going to do? What are you going to say?

What are you going to say when you're drowning in your own dung and they keep booting you back into it, when all the screams in hell wouldn't be as loud as you want to scream, when you're at the bottom of the pit and the whole world's at the top, when it has but one face, a face without eyes or ears, and yet it watches and listens . . .

What are you going to do and say? Why, pardner, that's simple. It's easy as nailing your balls to a stump and falling off backwards. Snow again, pardner, and drift me hard, because that's an easy one.

You're gonna say, they can't keep a good man down. You're gonna say, a winner never quits and a quitter never wins. You're gonna smile, boy, you're gonna show 'em the ol' fightin' smile. And then you're gonna get out there an' hit 'em hard and fast and low, an'—an' Fight!

Rah.

I folded the letter, and tossed it back to Howard.

"She was sure a talky little girl," I said. "Sweet but awful talky. Seems like if she couldn't say it to you, she'd write it down for you."

Howard swallowed. "That—that's all you have to say?"

I lit a cigar, pretending that I hadn't heard him. Jeff Plummer's chair creaked. "I sure liked Miss Amy," he said. "All four of my young 'uns went to school to her, an' she was just as nice as if they'd had one of these oilmen for a daddy."

"Yes, sir," I said. "I reckon she really had her heart in her work."

I puffed on my cigar, and Jeff's chair creaked again, louder than the first time, and the hate in Howard's eyes seemed to lash out against me. He gulped like a man choking down puke.

"You fellows getting restless?" I said. "I sure appreciate you dropping in at a time like this, but I wouldn't want to keep you from anything important."

"You—y-you!"

"You starting to stutter, Howard? You ought to practice talking with a pebble in your mouth. Or maybe a piece of shrapnel."

"You dirty son-of-a-bitch! You—"

"Don't call me that," I said.

"No," said Jeff, "don't call him that. Don't ever say anything about a man's mother."

"To hell with that crap! He—you"—he shook his fist at me—"you killed that little girl. She as good as says so!"

I laughed. "She wrote it down after I killed her, huh? That's quite a trick."

"You know what I mean. She knew you were going to kill her . . ."

"And she was going to marry me, anyway?"

"She knew you'd killed all those other people!"

"Yeah? Funny she didn't mention it."

"She did mention it! She—"

"Don't recall seeing anything like that. Don't see that she said anything much. Just a lot of woman-worry talk."

"You killed Joyce Lakeland and Elmer Conway and Johnnie Pappas and—"

"President McKinley?"

He sagged back in his chair, breathing hard. "You killed them, Ford. You killed them."

"Why don't you arrest me, then? What are you waiting on?"

"Don't worry," he nodded grimly. "Don't you worry. I'm not waiting much longer."

"And I'm not either," I said.

"What do you mean?"

"I mean you and your courthouse gang are doing spite work. You're pouring it on me because Conway says to, just why I can't figure out. You haven't got a shred of proof but you've tried to smear me—"

"Now, wait a minute! We haven't—"

"You've tried to; you had Jeff out here this morning chasing visitors away. You'd do it, but you can't because you haven't got a shred of proof and people know me too well. You know you can't get a conviction, so you try to ruin my reputation. And with Conway backing you up you may manage it in time. You'll manage it if you have the time, and I guess I can't stop you. But I'm not going to sit back and take it. I'm leaving town, Howard."

"Oh, no you're not. I'm warning you here and now, Ford, don't you even attempt to leave."

"Who's going to stop me?"

"I am."

"On what grounds?"

"Mur-suspicion of murder."

"But who suspects me, Howard, and why? The Stantons? I reckon not. Mike Pappas? Huh-uh. Chester Conway? Well, I've got kind of a funny feeling about Conway, Howard. I've got a feeling that he's going to stay in the background, he's not going to do or say a thing, no matter how bad you need him."

"I see," he said. "I see."

"You see that opening there behind you?" I said. "Well, that's a door, Howard, in case you were wonderin', and I can't think of a thing to keep you and Mister Plummer from walking through it."

"We're walking through it," said Jeff, "and so are you."

"Huh-uh," I said, "no I ain't. I sure ain't aimin' to do nothing like that, Mister Plummer. And that's a fact."

Howard kept his seat. His face looked like a blob of reddish dough, but he shook his head at Jeff and kept his seat. Howard was really trying hard.

"I—it's to your own interest as well as ours to get this settled, Ford. I'm asking you to place yourself—to remain available until—"

"You mean you want me to cooperate with you?" I said.

"Yes."

"That door," I said. "I wish you'd close it real careful. I'm suffering from shock, and I might have a relapse."

Howard's mouth twisted and opened, and snapped shut. He sighed and reached for his hat.

"I sure liked Bob Maples," said Jeff. "I sure liked that little Miss Amy."

"Sure enough?" I said. "Is that a fact?"

I laid my cigar down on an ashtray, leaned back on the pillow and closed my eyes. A chair creaked and squeaked real loud, and I heard Howard say, "Now Jeff"—and there was a sound like he'd sort of stumbled.

I opened my eyes again. Jeff Plummer was standing over me.

He was smiling down at me with his lips and there was a .45 in his hand, and the hammer was thumbed back.

"You right sure you ain't coming with us?" he said. "You don't reckon you could change your mind?"

The way he sounded I knew he hoped I wouldn't change it. He was just begging, waiting for me to say no. And I reckoned I wouldn't say all of even a short word like that before I was past saying anything.

I got up and began to dress.

TWENTY-TWO

If I'd known that Rothman's lawyer friend, Billy Boy Walker, was tied up in the East and was having trouble getting away, I might have felt different. I might have cracked up right off. But, on the other hand, I don't think I would have. I had a feeling that I was speeding fast down a one-way trail, that I was almost to the place I had to get to. I was almost there and moving fast, so why hop off and try to run ahead? It wouldn't have made a particle of sense and you know I don't do things that don't make sense. You know it or you will know it.

That first day and that night, I spent in one of the "quiet" cells, but the next morning they put me on ice, down in the cooler where I'd—where Johnnie Pappas had died. They—

How's that? Well, sure they can do it to you. They can do anything they're big enough to do and you're little enough to take. They don't book you. No one knows where you are, and you've got no one on the outside that can get you out. It's not legal, but I found out long ago that the place where the law is apt to be abused most is right around a courthouse.

Yeah, they can do it all right.

So I was saying, I spent the first day and night in one of the quiet cells, and most of the time I was trying to kid myself. I couldn't face up to the truth yet, so I tried to play like there was a way around it. You know. Those kid games?

You've done something pretty bad or you want something bad, and you think, well, if I can just do such and such I can fix it. If I can count down from a thousand backwards by three and a third or recite the Gettysburg address in pig-latin while I'm touching my little toes with my big ones, everything will be all right.

I'd play those games and their kin-kind, doing real impossible things in my imagination. I'd trot all the way from Central City to San Angelo without stopping. Or they'd grease the pipeline across the Pecos River, and I'd hop across it on one foot with my eyes blindfolded and an anvil around my neck. I'd really get to sweating and panting sometimes. My feet'd be all achy and blistered from pounding that San Angelo Highway, and that old anvil would keep swinging and dragging at me, trying to pull me off into the Pecos; and finally I'd win through, just plumb worn out. And—and I'd have to do something still harder.

Well, then they moved me down into the cooler where Johnnie Pappas had died, and pretty soon I saw why they hadn't put me there right away. They'd had a little work to do on it first. I don't know just how they'd rigged the stunt—only that that unused light-socket in the ceiling was part of it. But I was stretched out on the bunk, fixing to shinny up the water tower without using my hands, when all at once I heard Johnnie's voice:

"*Hello, you lovely people. I'm certainly having a fine time and I wish you were here. See you soon.*"

Yes, it was Johnnie, speaking in that sharp smart-alecky way he used a lot. I jumped up from the bunk and started turning around and looking up and down and sideways. And here his voice came again:

"*Hello, you lovely people. I'm certainly having a fine time and I wish you were here. See you soon.*"

He kept saying the same thing over and over, about fifteen seconds between times, and, hell, as soon as I had a couple minutes to think,

I knew what it was all about. It was one of those little four-bit voice recordings, like you've just about got time to sneeze on before it's used up. Johnnie'd sent it to his folks the time he visited the Dallas Fair. He'd mentioned it to me when he told me about the trip—and I'd remembered because I liked Johnnie and would remember. He'd mentioned it, apologizing for not sending me some word. But he'd lost all his dough in some kind of wheel game, and had to hitch-hike back to Central City.

"*Hello, you lovely people . . .*"

I wondered what kind of story they'd given the Greek, because I was pretty sure he wouldn't have let 'em have it if he'd known what it was going to be used for. He knew how I felt about Johnnie and how Johnnie'd felt about me.

They kept playing that record over and over, from maybe five in the morning until midnight; I don't know just what the hours were because they'd taken away my watch. It didn't even stop when they brought me food and water twice a day.

I'd lie and listen to it, or sit and listen. And every once in a while, when I could remember to do it, I'd jump up and pace around the cell. I'd pretend like it was bothering the hell out of me, which of course it didn't at all. Why would it? But I wanted 'em to think it did, so they wouldn't turn it off. And I guess I must have pretended pretty good, because they played it for three days and part of the fourth. Until it wore out, I reckon.

After that there wasn't much but silence, nothing but those faraway sounds like the factory whistles which weren't any real company for a man.

They'd taken away my cigars and matches, of course, and I fidgeted around quite a bit the first day, thinking I wanted a smoke. Yeah, *thinking*, because I didn't actually want one. I'd been smoking cigars for—well—around eleven years; ever since my eighteenth birthday when Dad had said I was getting to be a man, so he hoped I'd act like one and smoke cigars and not go around with a coffin-nail in my mouth. So I'd smoked cigars, from then on, never admitting to myself that I didn't really like them. But now I could admit it. I had to, and I did.

When life attains a crisis, man's focus narrows. *Nice lines, huh? I could talk that way all the time if I wanted to*. The world becomes a stage of immediate concern, swept free of illusion. *I used to talk that way all the time.*

No one had pushed me around or even tried to question me since the morning they'd locked me up. No one, at all. And I'd tried to tell myself that was a good sign. They didn't have any evidence; I'd got their goats, so they'd put me on ice, just like they'd done with plenty of other guys. And pretty soon they'd simmer down and let me go of their own accord, or Billy Boy Walker'd show up and they'd have to let me out . . . that's what I'd told myself and it made sense—all my reasoning does. But it was top-of-the-cliff sense, not the kind you make when you're down near the tag-end of the rope.

They hadn't tried to beat the truth out of me or talk it out of me for a couple of reasons. First of all, they were pretty sure it wouldn't do any good: you can't stamp on a man's corns when he's got his feet cut off. Second—the second reason was—they didn't think they had to.

They *had* evidence.

They'd had it right from the beginning.

Why hadn't they sprung it on me? Well, there were a couple of reasons behind that, too. For one thing, they weren't sure that it was evidence because they weren't sure about me. I'd thrown them off the track with Johnnie Pappas. For another thing, they *couldn't* use it—it wasn't in shape to be used.

But now they were sure of what I'd done, though they probably weren't too clear as to why I'd done it. And that evidence would be ready to be used before long. And I didn't reckon they'd let go of me until it was ready. Conway was determined to get me, and they'd gone too far to back down.

I thought back to the day Bob Maples and I had gone to Fort Worth, and how Conway hadn't invited us on the trip but had got busy ordering us around the minute we'd landed. You see? What could be clearer? He'd tipped his hand on me right there.

Then, Bob had come back to the hotel, and he was all upset about something Conway had said to him, ordered him to do. And he wouldn't tell me what it was. He just talked on and on about how long he'd known me and what a swell guy I was, and . . . Hell, don't you see? Don't you get it?

I'd let it go by me because I had to. I couldn't let myself face the facts. But I reckon you've known the truth all along.

Then, I'd brought Bob home on the train and he'd been babbling drunk, and he'd gotten sore about some of my kidding. So he'd snapped back at me, giving me a tip on where I stood at the same time. He'd said—what was it?—"*It's always lightest just before the dark* . . ."

He'd been sore and drunk so he'd come out with that. He was telling me in so many words that I might not be sitting nearly as pretty as I thought I was. And he was certainly right about that—but I think he'd got his words twisted a little. He was saying 'em to be sarcastic, but they happen to be the truth. At least it seemed so to me.

It *is* lightest just before dark. Whatever a man is up against, it makes him feel better to know that he *is* up against it. That's the way it seemed to me, anyhow, and I ought to know.

Once I'd admitted the truth about that piece of evidence, it was easy to admit other things. I could stop inventing reasons for what I'd done, stop believing in the reasons I'd invented, and see the truth. And it sure wasn't hard to see. When you're climbing up a cliff or just holding on for dear life, you keep your eyes closed. You know you'll get dizzy and fall if you don't. But after you fall down to the bottom, you open 'em again. And you can see just where you started from, and trace every foot of your trail up that cliff.

Mine had started back with the housekeeper; with Dad finding out about us. All kids pull some pretty sorry stunts, particularly if an older person edges 'em along, so it hadn't needed to mean a thing. But Dad had made it mean something. I'd been made to feel that I'd done something that couldn't ever be forgiven—that would always lie between him and me, the only kin I had. And there wasn't anything I could do or say that would change things. I had a burden of fear and shame put on me that I could never get shed of.

She was gone, and I couldn't strike back at her, yes, kill her, for what I'd been made to feel she'd done to me. But that was all right. She was the first woman I'd ever known; she *was* woman to me; and all womankind bore her face. So I could strike back at any of them, any female, the ones it would be safest to strike at, and it would be the same as striking at her. And I did that, I started striking out . . . and Mike Dean took the blame.

Dad tightened the reins on me after that. I could hardly be out of his sight an hour without his checking up on me. So years passed and I didn't strike out again, and I was able to distinguish between women and *the* woman. Dad slacked off on the reins a little; I seemed to be normal. But every now and then I'd catch myself in that dead-pan kidding, trying to ease the terrific pressure that was building up inside me. And even without that I knew—though I wouldn't recognize the fact—that I wasn't all right.

If I could have got away somewhere, where I wouldn't have been constantly reminded of what had happened and I'd had something I wanted to do—something to occupy my mind—it might have been different. But I couldn't get away, and there wasn't anything here I wanted to do. So nothing had changed; I was still looking for *her*. And any woman who'd done what she had would be *her*.

I'd kept pushing Amy away from me down through the years, not because I didn't love her but because I did. I was afraid of what might happen between us. I was afraid of what I'd do . . . what I finally did.

I could admit, now, that I'd never had any real cause to think that Amy would make trouble for me. She had too much pride; she'd have hurt herself too much; and, anyway, she loved me.

I'd never had any real cause, either, to be afraid that Joyce would make trouble. She was too smart to try to, from what I'd seen of her. But if she had been sore enough to try—if she'd been mad enough so's she just didn't give a damn—she wouldn't have got anywhere. After all, she was just a whore and I was old family, quality; and she wouldn't have opened her mouth more than twice before she was run out of town.

No I hadn't been afraid of her starting talk. I hadn't been afraid that if I kept on with her I'd lose control of myself. I'd never had any control even before I met her. No control—only luck. Because anyone who reminded me of the burden I carried, anyone who did what that first *her* had done, would get killed . . .

Anyone. Amy. Joyce. Any woman who, even for a moment, became *her*.

I'd kill them.

I'd keep trying until I did kill them.

Elmer Conway had had to suffer, too, on *her* account. Mike had taken the blame for me, and then he'd been killed. So, along with the burden, I had a terrible debt to him that I couldn't pay. I could never repay him for what he'd done for me. The only thing I could do was what I did . . . try to settle the score with Chester Conway.

That was my main reason for killing Elmer, but it wasn't the only one. The Conways were part of the circle, the town, that ringed me in; the smug ones, the hypocrites, the holier-than-thou guys—all the stinkers I had to face day in and day out. I had to grin and smile and be pleasant to them; and maybe there are people like that everywhere, but when you can't get away from them, when they keep pushing themselves at you, and you can't get away, never, never, get away . . .

Well.

The bum. The few others I'd struck out at. I don't know—I'm not really sure about them.

They were all people who didn't have to stay here. People who took what was handed them because they didn't have enough pride or guts to strike back. So maybe that was it. Maybe I think that the guy who won't fight when he can and should deserves the worst you can toss at him.

Maybe. I'm not sure of all the details. All I can do is give you the general picture; and not even the experts could do more than that.

I've read a lot of stuff by a guy—name of Kraepelin, I believe—and I can't remember all of it, of course, or even the gist of all of it. But I remember the high points of some, the most important stuff, and I think it goes something like this:

". . . difficult to study because so seldom detected. The condition usually begins around the period of puberty, and is often precipitated by a severe shock. The subject suffers from strong feelings of guilt . . . combined with a sense of frustration and persecution . . . which increase as he grows older; yet there are rarely if ever any surface signs of . . . disturbance. On the contrary, his behavior appears to be entirely logical. He reasons soundly, even shrewdly. He is completely aware of what he does and why he does it . . ."

That was written about a disease, or a condition, rather, called dementia praecox. Schizophrenia, paranoid type. Acute, recurrent, advanced.

Incurable.

It was written, you might say, about—
But I reckon you know, don't you?

TWENTY-THREE

I was in jail eight days, but no one questioned me and they didn't pull any more stunts like that voice recording. I kind of looked for them to do the last because they couldn't be positive about that piece of evidence they had—about my reaction to it, that is. They weren't certain that it would make me put the finger on myself. And even if they had been certain, I knew they'd a lot rather I cracked up and confessed of my own accord. If I did that they could probably send me to the chair. The other way—if they used their evidence—they couldn't.

But I reckon they weren't set up right at the jail for any more stunts or maybe they couldn't get ahold of the equipment they needed. At any rate, they didn't pull any more. And on the eighth day, around eleven o'clock at night, they transferred me to the insane asylum.

They put me in a pretty good room—better'n any I'd seen the time I'd had to take a poor guy there years before—and left me alone. But I took one look around and I knew I was being watched through those little slots high up on the walls. They wouldn't have left me in a room with cigarette tobacco and matches and a drinking glass and water pitcher unless someone was watching me.

I wondered how far they'd let me go if I started to cut my throat or wrap myself in a sheet and set fire to it, but I didn't wonder very long. It was late, and I was pretty well worn out after sleeping on that bunk in the cooler. I smoked a couple of hand-rolled cigarettes, putting the butts out real careful. Then with the lights still burning—there wasn't any switch for me to turn 'em off—I stretched out on the bed and went to sleep.

About seven in the morning, a husky-looking nurse came in with a couple of young guys in white jackets. And she took my temperature and pulse while they stood and waited. Then, she left and the two attendants took me down the hall to a shower room, and watched while I took a bath. They didn't act particularly tough or unpleasant, but they didn't say a word more than they needed to. I didn't say anything.

I finished my shower and put my short-tailed nightgown back on. We went back to my room, and one of 'em made up my bed while the other went after my breakfast. The scrambled eggs tasted pretty flat, and it didn't help my appetite any to have them cleaning up the room, emptying the enamel night-can and so on. But I ate almost everything and drank all of the weak luke-warm coffee. They were through cleaning by the time I'd finished. They left, locking me in again.

I smoked a hand-rolled cigarette, and it tasted good.

I wondered—no I didn't, either. I didn't need to wonder what it would be like to spend your whole life like this. Not a tenth as good as this probably, because I was something pretty special right now. Right now I was a hide-out; I'd been kidnapped, actually. And there was always a chance that there'd be a hell of a stink raised. But if that hadn't been the case, if I'd been committed—well, I'd still be something special, in a different way. I'd be worse off than anyone in the place.

Conway would see to that, even if doc Bony-face didn't have a special sort of interest in me.

I'd kind of figured that the doc might show up with his hard-rubber playthings, but I guess he had just enough sense to know that he was out of his class. Plenty of pretty smart psychiatrists have been fooled by guys like me, and you can't really fault 'em for it. There's just not much they can put their hands on, know what I mean?

We might have the disease, the condition; or we might just be cold-blooded and smart as hell; or we might be innocent of what we're supposed to have done. We might be any one of those three things, because the symptoms we show would fit any one of the three.

So Bony-face didn't give me any trouble. No one did. The nurse checked on me night and morning, and the two attendants carried on with pretty much the same routine. Bringing my meals, taking me to the shower, cleaning up the room. The second day, and every other day after that, they let me shave with a safety razor while they stood by and watched.

I thought about Rothman and Billy Boy Walker, just thought,

wondered, without worrying any. Because, hell, I didn't have anything to worry about, and they were probably doing enough worrying for all three of us. But—

But I'm getting ahead of myself.

They, Conway and the others, still weren't positive about that piece of evidence they had; and, like I say, they preferred to have me crack up and confess. So, on the evening of my second night in the asylum, there came the stunt.

I was lying on my side in bed, smoking a cigarette, when the lights dimmed way down, down to almost nothing. Then, there was a click and a flash up above me, and Amy Stanton stood looking at me from the far wall of the room.

Oh, sure, it was a picture; one that had been made into a glass slide. I didn't need to do any figuring at all to know that they were using a slide projector to throw her picture against the wall. She was coming down the walk of her house, smiling, but looking kind of fussed like I'd seen her so many times. I could almost hear her saying, "*Well, you finally got here, did you?*" And I knew it was just a picture, but it looked so real, it seemed so real, that I answered her back in my mind. "*Kinda looks that way, don't it?*"

I guess they'd got a whole album of her pictures. Which wouldn't have been any trouble, since the old folks, the Stantons, were awfully innocent and accommodating and not given to asking questions. Anyway, after that first picture, which was a pretty recent one, there was one taken when she was about fifteen years old. And they worked up through the years from that.

They . . . I saw her the day she graduated from high school; she was sixteen, that spring, wearing one of those white lacy dresses and flat-heeled slippers, and standing real stiff with her arms held close to her sides.

I saw her sitting on her front steps, laughing in spite of herself . . . *it always seemed hard for Amy to laugh* . . . because that old dog of theirs was trying to lick her on the ear.

I saw her all dressed up, and looking kind of scared, the time she started off for teachers' college. I saw her the day she finished her two-year course, standing very straight with her hand on the back of a chair and trying to look older than she was.

I saw her—and I'd taken a lot of those pictures myself; it seemed just like yesterday—I saw her working in the garden, in a pair of old jeans; walking home from church and kind of frowning up at the little hat she'd made for herself; coming out of the grocery store with both arms around a big sack; sitting in the porch swing with an apple in her hand and a book in her lap.

I saw her with her dress pulled way up high—she'd just slid off the fence where I'd taken a snap of her—and she was bent over, trying to cover herself, and yelling at me, "*Don't you dare, Lou! Don't you dare, now!*" . . . She'd sure been mad about me taking that picture, but she'd saved it.

I saw her . . .

I tried to remember how many pictures there were, to figure out how long they would last. They were sure in a hell of a hurry to get through with them, it looked like to me. They were just racing through 'em, it seemed like. I'd just be starting to enjoy a picture, remembering when it was taken and how old Amy was at the time, when they'd flash it off and put on another one.

It was a pretty sorry way to act, the way I saw it. You know, it was as though she wasn't worth looking at; like, maybe they'd seen someone that was better to look at. And I'm not prejudiced or anything, but you wouldn't find a girl as pretty and well-built as Amy Stanton in a month of Sundays.

Aside from being a slight on Amy, it was damned stupid to rush through those pictures like they were doing . . . like they seemed to be doing. After all, the whole object of the show was to make me crack up, and how could I do it if they didn't even let me get a good look at her?

I wasn't going to crack up, of course; I felt stronger and better inside every time I saw her. But they didn't know that, and it doesn't excuse them. They were lying down on the job. They had a doggone ticklish job to do, and they were too lazy and stupid to do it right.

Well . . .

They'd started showing the pictures about eight-thirty, and they should have lasted until one or two in the morning. But they had to be in a hell of a hurry, so it was only around eleven when they came to the last one.

It was a picture I'd taken less than three weeks before, and they *did* leave it on long enough—well, not long enough, but they let me get a good look at it. She and I had fixed up a little lunch that evening, and eaten it over in Sam Houston Park. And I'd taken this picture just as she was stepping back into the car. She was looking over her shoulder at me; wide-eyed, smiling but sort of impatient. Saying:

"*Can't you hurry a little, darling?*"

Hurry?

"*Well, I reckon so, honey, I'll sure try to.*"

"*When, Lou? How soon will I see you, darling?*"

"*Well, now, honey. I—I . . .*"

I was almost glad right then that the lights came back on. I never was real good at lying to Amy.

I got up and paced around the room. I went over by the wall where they'd flashed the pictures, and I rubbed my eyes with my fists and gave the wall a few pats and tugged my hair a little.

I put on a pretty good act, it seemed to me. Just good enough to let 'em think I was bothered, but not enough to mean anything at a sanity hearing.

The nurse and the two attendants didn't have any more to say than usual the next morning. It seemed to me, though, that they acted a little different, more watchful sort of. So I did a lot of frowning and staring down at the floor, and I only ate part of my breakfast.

I passed up most of my lunch and dinner, too, which wasn't much of a chore, hungry as I was. And I did everything else I could to put on just the right kind of act—not too strong, not too weak. But I was too anxious. I had to go and ask the nurse a question when she made the night check on me, and that spoiled everything.

"Will they be showing the pictures tonight?" I said, and I knew doggone well it was the wrong thing to do.

"What pictures? I don't know anything about pictures," she said.

"The pictures of my girl. You know. Will they show 'em, ma'am?"

She shook her head, a kind of mean glint in her eye. "You'll see. You'll find out, mister."

"Well, tell 'em not to do it so fast," I said. "When they do it so fast, I don't get to see her very good. I hardly get to look at her at all before she's gone."

She frowned. She shook her head, staring at me, like she hadn't heard me right. She edged away from the bed a little.

"You"— she swallowed— "you want to see those pictures?"

"Well—uh—I—"

"You *do* want to see them," she said slowly. "You want to see the pictures of the girl you—you—"

"Sure, I want to see 'em." I began to get sore. "Why shouldn't I want to see them? What's wrong with that? Why the hell wouldn't I want to see them?"

The attendants started to move toward me. I lowered my voice.

"I'm sorry," I said. "I don't want to cause any trouble. If you folks are too busy, maybe you could move the projector in here. I know how to run one, and I'd take good care of it."

That was a pretty bad night for me. There weren't any pictures, and I was so hungry I couldn't go to sleep for hours. I was sure glad when morning came.

So, that was the end of their stunt, and they didn't try any others. I reckon they figured it was a waste of time. They just kept me from then on; just held me without me saying any more than I had to and them doing the same.

That went on for six days, and I was beginning to get puzzled. Because that evidence of theirs should have been about ready to use, by now, if it was ever going to be ready.

The seventh day rolled around, and I was really getting baffled. And, then, right after lunch, Billy Boy Walker showed up.

TWENTY-FOUR

"Where is he?" he yelled. "What have you done with the poor man? Have you torn out his tongue? Have you roasted his poor broken body over slow fires? Where is he, I say?"

He was coming down the corridor, yelling at the top of his lungs; and I could hear several people scurrying along with him, trying to shush him up, but no one had ever had much luck at that and they didn't either. I'd never seen him in my life—just heard him a couple of times on the radio—but I knew it was him. I reckon I'd have known he'd come even if I hadn't heard him. You didn't have to see or hear Billy Boy Walker to know he was around. You could just kind of sense it.

They stopped in front of my door, and Billy Boy started beating on it like they didn't have a key and he was going to have to knock it down.

"Mr. Ford! My poor man!" he yelled; and, man, I'll bet they could hear him all the way into Central City. "Can you hear me? Have they punctured your eardrums? Are you too weak to cry out? Be brave, my poor fellow."

He kept it up, beating on the door and yelling, and it sounds like it must've been funny but somehow it wasn't. Even to me, knowing that they hadn't done a thing to me, really, it didn't sound funny. I could almost believe that they *had* put me through the works.

They managed to get the door unlocked, and he came bounding in. And he looked as funny—he should have looked as funny as he should have sounded—but I didn't feel the slightest call to laugh. He was short and fat and pot-bellied; and a couple of buttons were off his shirt and his belly-button was showing. He was wearing a baggy old black suit and red suspenders; and he had a big floppy black hat sitting kind of crooked on his head. Everything about him was sort of off-size and out-of-shape, as the saying is. But I couldn't see a thing to laugh about. Neither, apparently, could the nurse and the two attendants and old Doc Bony-face.

Billy Boy flung his arms around me and called me a "poor man" and patted me on the head. He had to reach up to do it; but he didn't seem to reach and it didn't seem funny.

He turned around, all at once, and grabbed the nurse by the arm. "Is this the woman, Mr. Ford? Did she beat you with chains? Fie! Fah! Abomination!" And he scrubbed his hand against his pants, glaring at her.

The attendants were helping me into my clothes, and they weren't losing any time about it. But you'd never have known it to hear Billy Boy. "Fiends!" he yelled. "Will your sadistic appetites never be satiated? Must you continue to stare and slaver over your handiwork? Will you not clothe this poor tortured flesh, this broken creature that was once a man built in God's own image?"

The nurse was spluttering and spluttering, her face a half-dozen different colors. The doc's bones were leaping like jumping-jacks. Billy Boy Walker snatched up the night-can, and shoved it under his nose. "You fed him from this, eh? I thought so! Bread and water, served in a slop jar! Shame, shame, fie! You did do it? Answer me, sirrah! You didn't do it? Fie, fah paah! Perjurer, suborner! Answer, yes or no!"

The doc shook his head, and then nodded. He shook and nodded it at the same time. Billy Boy dropped the can to the floor, and took me by the arm. "Never mind your gold watch, Mr. Ford. Never mind the money and jewelry they have stolen. You have your clothes. Trust me to recover the rest—and more! Much, much more, Mr. Ford."

He pushed me out the door ahead of him, and then he turned around real slow and pointed around the room. "You," he said softly, pointing them out one by one. "You and you and you are through. This is the end for you. The end."

He looked them all in the eye, and no one said a word and none of them moved. He took me by the arm again, and we went down the corridor, and each of the three gates were open for us before we got to 'em.

He squeezed in behind the wheel of the car he'd rented in Central City. He started it up with a roar and a jerk, and we went speeding out through the main gate to the highway where two signs, facing in opposite directions, read:

WARNING! WARNING!
Hitch-hikers May Be Escaped
LUNATICS!

He lifted himself in the seat, reached into his hip pocket, and pulled out a plug of tobacco. He offered it to me and I shook my head, and he took a big chew.

"Dirty habit," he said, in just a quiet conversational voice. "Got it young, though, and I reckon I'll keep it."

He spat out the window, wiped his chin with his hand, and wiped his hand on his pants. I found the makings I'd had at the asylum and started rolling a cigarette.

"About Joe Rothman," I said. "I didn't say anything about him, Mr. Walker."

"Why, I didn't think you had, Mr. Ford! It never occurred to me that you would," he said; and whether he meant it or not he sure sounded like it. "You know somethin', Mr. Ford? There wasn't a bit of sense in what I did back there."

"No," I said.

"No, sir, not a bit. I've been snorting and pawing up the earth around here for four days. Couldn't have fought harder getting Christ off the cross. And I reckon it was just habit like this chewing tobacco—I knew it but I kept right on chawing. I didn't get you free, Mr. Ford. I didn't have a thing to do with it. They *let* me have a writ. They *let* me know where you were. That's why you're here, Mr. Ford, instead of back there."

"I know," I said. "I figured it would be that way."

"You understand? They're not letting you go; they've gone too far to start backing water."

"I understand," I said.

"They've got something? Something you can't beat?"

"They've got it."

"Maybe you'd better tell me about it."

I hesitated, thinking, and finally I shook my head. "I don't think so, Mr. Walker. There's nothing you can do. Or I can do. You'd be wasting your time, and you might get Joe and yourself in a fix."

"Well, now, pshaw." He spat out the window again. "I reckon I might be a better judge of some things than you are, Mr. Ford. You—uh—aren't maybe a little distrustful, are you?"

"I think you know I'm not," I said. "I just don't want anyone else to get hurt."

"I see. Put it hypothetically, then. Just say that there are a certain set of circumstances which would have you licked—if they concerned you. Just make me up a situation that doesn't have anything to do with yours."

So I told him what they had and how they planned to use it, hypothetically. And I stumbled around a lot, because describing my situation, the evidence they had, in a hypothetical way was mighty hard to do. He got it, though, without me having to repeat a word.

"That's the whole thing?" he said. "They haven't got—they can't get, we'll say, anything in the way of actual testimony?"

"I'm pretty sure they can't," I said. "I may be wrong but I'm almost positive they couldn't get anything out of this—evidence."

"Well, then? As long as you're—"

"I know," I nodded. "They're not taking me by surprise, like they figured on. I—I mean this fellow I'm talking about—"

"Go right ahead, Mr. Ford. Just keep on using the first person. It's easier to talk that way."

"Well, I wouldn't cut loose in front of 'em. I don't think I would. But I'd do it sooner or later, with someone. It's best to have it happen now, and get it over with."

He turned his head a moment to glance at me, the big black hat flopping in the wind. "You said you didn't want anyone else to get hurt. You meant it?"

"I meant it. You can't hurt people that are already dead."

"Good enough," he said, and whether he knew what I really meant and was satisfied with it, I don't know. His ideas of right and wrong didn't jibe too close with the books.

"I sure hate to give up, though," he frowned. "Just never got in the habit of giving up, I reckon."

"You can't call it giving up," I said. "Do you see that car way back behind us? And the one up in front, the one that turned in ahead of us, a while back? Those are county cars, Mr. Walker. You're not giving up anything. It's been lost for a long time."

He glanced up into the rear-view mirror, then squinted ahead through the windshield. He spat and rubbed his hand against his pants, wiped it slowly against the soiled back cloth. "Still got quite a little ride ahead of us, Mr. Ford. About thirty miles isn't it?"

"About that. Maybe a little more."

"I wonder if you'd like to tell me about it. You don't need to, you understand, but it might be helpful. I might be able to help someone else."

"Do you think I could—that I'm able to tell you?"

"Why not?" he said. "I had a client years ago, Mr. Ford, a very able doctor. One of the most pleasant men you'd want to meet, and he had more money than he knew what to do with. But he'd performed about fifty abortions before they moved in on him, and so far as the authorities could find out every one of the abortion patients had died. He'd deliberately seen that they did die of peritonitis about a month after the operation. And he told me why—and he could've told anyone else why, when he finally faced up to the facts—he'd done it. He had a younger brother who was "unfinished," a prematurely born monstrosity, as the result of an attempted late-pregnancy abortion. He saw that terrible half-child die in agony for years. He never recovered from the experience—and neither did the women he aborted . . . Insane? Well, the only legal definition we have for insanity is the condition which necessitates the confinement of a person. So, since he hadn't been confined when he killed those women, I reckon he was sane. He made pretty good sense to me, anyhow."

He shifted the cud in his jaw, chewed a moment and went on. "I never had any legal schooling, Mr. Ford; picked up my law by reading in an attorney's office. All I ever had in the way of higher education was a couple years in agricultural college, and that was pretty much a plain waste of time. Crop rotation? Well, how're you going to do it when the banks only make crop loans on cotton? Soil conservation? How're you going to do terracing and draining and contour plowing when you're cropping on shares? Purebred stock? Sure. Maybe you can trade your razorbacks for Poland Chinas . . . I just learned two things there at that college, Mr. Ford, that was ever of any use to me. One was that I couldn't do any worse than the people that were in the saddle, so maybe I'd better try pulling 'em down and riding myself. The other was a definition I got out of the agronomy books, and I reckon it was even more important than the first. It did more to revise my thinking, if I'd really done any thinking up until that time. Before that I'd seen everything in black and white, good and bad. But after I was set straight I saw that the name you put to a thing depended on where you stood and where it stood. And . . . and here's the definition, right out of the agronomy books: 'A weed is a plant out of place.' Let me repeat that. 'A weed is a plant out of place.' I find a hollyhock in my cornfield, and it's a weed. I find it in my yard, and it's a flower.

"You're in my yard, Mr. Ford."

. . . So I told him how it had been while he nodded and spat and drove, a funny pot-bellied shrimp of a guy who really had just one thing, understanding, but so much of it that you never missed anything else. He understood me better'n I understood myself.

"Yes, yes," he'd say, "you had to like people. You had to keep telling yourself you liked them. You needed to offset the deep, subconscious feelings of guilt." Or, he'd say, he'd interrupt, "and, of course, you knew you'd never leave Central City. Overprotection had made you terrified of the outside world. More important, it was part of the burden you had to carry to stay here and suffer."

He sure understood.

I reckon Billy Boy Walker's been cussed more in high places than any man in the country. But I never met a man I liked more.

I guess the way you felt about him depended on where you stood.

He stopped the car in front of my house, and I'd told him all I had to tell. But he sat there for a few minutes, spitting and sort of studying.

"Would you care to have me come in for a while, Mr. Ford?"

"I don't think it'd be smart," I said. "I got an idea it's not going to be very long, now."

He pulled an old turnip of a watch from his pocket and glanced at it. "Got a couple hours until train time, but—well, maybe you're right. I'm sorry, Mr. Ford. I'd hoped, if I couldn't do any better, to be taking you away from here with me."

"I couldn't have gone, no matter how things were. It's like you say, I'm tied here. I'll never be free as long as I live . . ."

TWENTY-FIVE

You've got no time at all, but it seems like you've got forever. You've got nothing to do, but it seems like you've got everything.

You make coffee and smoke a few cigarettes; and the hands of the clock have gone crazy on you. They haven't moved hardly, they've hardly budged out of the place you last saw them, but they've measured off a half? two-thirds? of your life. You've got forever, but that's no time at all.

You've got forever; and somehow you can't do much with it. You've got forever; and it's a mile wide and an inch deep and full of alligators.

You go into the office and take a book or two from the shelves. You read a few lines, like your life depended on reading 'em right. But you know your life doesn't depend on anything that makes sense, and you wonder where in the hell you got the idea it did; and you begin to get sore.

You go into the laboratory and start pawing along the rows of bottles and boxes, knocking them on the floor, kicking them, stamping them. You find the bottle of one hundred percent pure nitric acid and you jerk out the rubber cork. You take it into the office and swing it along the rows of books. And the leather bindings begin to smoke and curl and wither—and it isn't good enough.

You go back into the laboratory. You come out with a gallon bottle of alcohol and the box of tall candles always kept there for emergencies. For *emergencies*.

You go upstairs, and then on up the little flight of stairs that leads to the attic. You come down from the attic and go through each of the bedrooms. You come back downstairs and go down into the basement. And when you return to the kitchen you are empty handed. All the candles are gone, all the alcohol.

You shake the coffee pot and set it back on the stove burner. You roll another cigarette. You take a carving knife from a drawer and slide it up the sleeve of your pinkish-tan shirt with the black bow tie.

You sit down at the table with your coffee and cigarette, and you ease your elbow up and down, seeing how far you can lower your arm without dropping the knife, letting it slide down from your sleeve a time or two.

You think, "*Well how can you? How can you hurt someone that's already dead?*"

You wonder if you've done things right, so's there'll be nothing left of something that shouldn't ever have been, and you know everything has been done right. You know, because you planned this moment before eternity way back yonder someplace.

You look up at the ceiling, listening, up through the ceiling and into the sky beyond. And there isn't the least bit of doubt in your mind. That'll be the plane, all right, coming in from the east, from Fort Worth. It'll be the plane she's on.

You look up at the ceiling, grinning, and you nod and say, "Long time no see. How you been doin' anyway, huh, baby? How are you, Joyce?"

TWENTY-SIX

Just for the hell of it, I took a peek out the back door, and then I went part way into the living room and stooped down so I could look out the window. It was like I'd thought, of course. They had the house covered from every angle. Men with Winchesters. Deputies, most of 'em, with a few of the "safety inspectors" on Conway's payroll.

It would have been fun to take a real good look, to step to the door and holler howdy to 'em. But it would have been fun for them, too, and I figured they were having far too much as it was. Anyway, some of those "inspectors" were apt to be a mite trigger happy, anxious to show their boss they were on their toes, and I had a little job to do yet.

I had to get everything wrapped up to take with me.

I took one last walk through the house, and I saw that everything—the alcohol and the candles and everything—was going fine. I came back downstairs, closing all the doors behind me—*all the doors behind me*—and sat back down at the kitchen table.

The coffee pot was empty. There was just one cigarette paper left and just enough tobacco to fill it, and, yeah—*yeah!*—I was down to my last match. Things were sure working out fine.

I puffed on the cigarette, watching the red-gray ashes move down toward my fingers; I watched, not needing to, knowing they'd get just so far and no further.

I heard a car pull into the driveway. I heard a couple of its doors slam. I heard them crossing the yard and coming up the steps and across the porch. I heard the front door open; and they came in. And the ashes had burned out, the cigarette had gone dead.

And I laid it in my saucer and looked up.

I looked out the kitchen window, first, at the two guys standing outside. Then I looked at them.

Conway and Hendricks, Hank Butterby and Jeff Plummer. Two or three fellows I didn't know.

They fell back, watching me, letting her move out ahead of them. I looked at her.

Joyce Lakeland.

Her neck was in a cast that came clear up to her chin like a collar, and she walked stiff-backed and jerky. Her face was a white mask of gauze and tape, and nothing much showed of it but her eyes and her lips. And she was trying to say something—her lips were moving—but she didn't really have a voice. She could hardly get out a whisper.

"*Lou . . . I didn't . . .* "

"Sure," I said. "I didn't figure you had, baby."

She kept coming toward me and I stood up, my right arm raised like I was brushing at my hair.

I could feel my face twisting, my lips pulling back from my teeth. I knew what I must look like, but she didn't seem to mind. She wasn't scared. What did she have to be scared of?

"*. . . this, Lou. Not like this . . .*"

"Sure, you can't," I said. "Don't hardly see how you could."

"*. . . not anyway without . . .*"

"Two hearts that beat as one," I said. "T-wo—ha, ha, ha—two—ha, ha, ha, ha, ha, ha, ha—two—J-Jesus Chri—ha, ha, ha, ha, ha, ha, ha—two Jesus . . ."

And I sprang at her, I made for her just like they'd thought I would. Almost. And it was like I'd signaled, the way the smoke suddenly poured up through the floor. And the room exploded with shots and yells, and I seemed to explode with it, yelling and laughing and . . . and . . . Because they hadn't got the point. She'd got that between the ribs and blade along with it. And they all lived happily ever after, I guess, and I guess—that's—all.

Yeah, I reckon that's all unless our kind gets another chance in the Next Place. Our kind. Us people.

All of us that started the game with a crooked cue, that wanted so much and got so little, that meant so good and did so bad. All us folks. Me and Joyce Lakeland, and Johnnie Pappas and Bob Maples and big ol' Elmer Conway and little ol' Amy Stanton. All of us.

All of us.

THE GRIFTERS

ONE

As Roy Dillon stumbled out of the shop his face was a sickish green, and each breath he drew was an incredible agony. A hard blow in the guts can do that to a man, and Dillon had gotten a hard one. Not with a fist, which would have been bad enough, but from the butt-end of a heavy club.

Somehow, he got back to his car and managed to slide into the seat. But that was all he could manage. He moaned as the change in posture cramped his stomach muscles; then, with a strangled gasp, he leaned out the window.

Several cars passed as he spewed vomit into the street, their occupants grinning, frowning sympathetically, or averting their eyes in disgust. But Roy Dillon was too sick to notice or to care if he had. When at last his stomach was empty, he felt better, though still not well enough to drive. By then, however, a prowl car had pulled up behind him—a sheriff's car, since he was in the county rather than the city of Los Angeles—and a brown-clad deputy was inviting him to step out to the walk.

Dillon shakily obeyed.

"One too many, mister?"

"What?"

"Never mind." The cop had already noticed the absence of liquor breath. "Let's see your driver's license."

Dillon showed it to him, also displaying, with seeming inadvertence, an assortment of credit cards. Suspicion washed off the cop's face, giving way to concern.

"You seem pretty sick, Mr. Dillon. Any idea what caused it?"

"My lunch, I guess. I know I should know better, but I had a chicken-salad sandwich—and it didn't taste quite right when I was eating it—but . . ." He let his voice trail away, smiling a shy, rueful smile.

"Mmm-hmm!" The cop nodded grimly. "That stuff will do it to you. Well"—a shrewd up-and-down look—"you all right now? Want us to take you to a doctor?"

"Oh, no. I'm fine."

"We got a first-aid man over at the substation. No trouble to run you over there."

Roy declined, pleasantly but firmly. Any prolonged contact with the cops would result in a record, and any kind of record was at best a nuisance. So far he had none; the scrapes which the grift had led him into had not led him to the cops. And he meant to keep it that way.

The deputy went back to the prowl car, and he and his partner drove off. Roy waved a smiling farewell to them and got back into his own car. Gingerly, wincing a little, he got a cigarette lit. Then, convinced that the last of the vomiting was over, he forced himself to lean back against the cushions.

He was in a suburb of Los Angeles, one of the many which resist incorporation despite their interdependence and the lack of visible boundaries. From here it was almost a thirty-mile drive back into the city, a very long thirty miles at this hour of the day. He needed to be in better shape than he was, to rest a while, before bucking the outbound tide of evening traffic. More important, he needed to reconstruct the details of his recent disaster, while they still remained fresh in his mind.

He closed his eyes for a moment. He opened them again, focussing them on the changing lights of the nearby traffic standard. And suddenly, without moving from the car—without physically moving from it—he was back inside the shop again. Sipping a limeade at the fountain, while he casually studied his surroundings.

It was little different from a thousand small shops in Los Angeles, establishments with an abbreviated soda fountain, a showcase or two of cigars, cigarettes, and candy, and overflowing racks of magazines, paperback books, and greeting cards. In the East, such shops were referred to as stationers' or candy stores. Here they were usually called confectionaries or simply fountains.

Dillon was the only customer in the place. The one other person present was the clerk, a large, lumpy-looking youth of perhaps nineteen or twenty. As Dillon finished his drink, he noted the boy's manner as he tapped ice down around the freezer containers, working with a paradoxical mixture of diligence and indifference. He knew exactly what needed to be done, his expression said, and to hell with doing a bit more than that. Nothing for show, nothing to impress anyone. The boss's son, Dillon decided, putting down his glass and sliding off the stool. He sauntered up toward the cash register, and the youth laid down the sawed-off ball bat with which he had been tamping. Then, wiping his hands on his apron, he also moved up to the register.

"Ten cents," he said.

"And a package of those mints, too."

"Twenty cents."

"Twenty cents, hmm?" Roy began to fumble through his pockets, while the clerk fidgeted impatiently. "Now, I know I've got some change here. Bound to have. I wonder where the devil . . ."

Exasperatedly, he shook his head and drew out his wallet. "I'm sorry. Mind cashing a twenty?"

The clerk almost snatched the bill from his hand. He slapped the bill down on the cash register ledge and counted out the change from the drawer. Dillon absently picked it up, continuing his fumbling search of his pockets.

"Now, doesn't that get you? I mean, you know darned well you've got something, but—" He broke off, eyes widening with a pleased smile. "There it is—two dimes! Just give me back my twenty, will you?"

The clerk grabbed the dimes from him, and tossed back the bill. Dillon turned casually toward the door, pausing, on the way out, for a disinterested glance at the magazine display.

Thus, for the tenth time that day, he had worked the *twenties*, one of the three standard gimmicks of the short con grift. The other two are the *smack* and the *tat*, usually good for bigger scores but not nearly so swift nor safe. Some marks fall for the twenties repeatedly, without ever tipping.

Dillon didn't see the clerk come around the counter. The guy was just there, all of a sudden, a pouty snarl on his face, swinging the sawed-off bat like a battering ram.

"Dirty crook," he whinnied angrily. "Dirty crooks keep cheatin' me and cheatin' me, an' Papa cusses me out for it!"

The butt of the bat landed in Dillon's stomach. Even the clerk was startled by its effect. "Now, you can't blame me, mister," he stammered. "You were askin' for it. I—I give you change for twenty dollars, an' then you have me give the twenty back an'—'an' "—his self-righteousness began to crumble. "N-now, you k-know you did, m-mister."

Roy could think of nothing but his agony. He turned swimming eyes on the clerk, eyes flooded with pain-filled puzzlement. The look completely demolished the youth.

"It w-was j-just a mistake, mister. Y-you made a m-mistake, an' I m-made a m-m-mistake an'—mister!" He backed away terrified. "D-don't look at me like that!"

"You killed me," Dillon gasped. "You killed me, you rotten bastard!"

"Nah! P-please don't say t-that, mister!"

"I'm dying," Dillon gasped. And, then, somehow, he had gotten out of the place.

And now, seated in his car and re-examining the incident, he could see no reason to fault himself, no flaw in his technique. It was just bad luck. He'd simply caught a goof, and goofs couldn't be figured.

He was right about that. And he'd been right about something else, although he didn't know it.

As he drove back to Los Angeles, constantly braking and speeding up in the thickening traffic, repeatedly stopping and starting—with every passing minute, he was dying.

Death might be forestalled if he took proper care of himself. Otherwise, he had no more than three days to live.

TWO

Roy Dillon's mother was from a family of backwoods white trash. She was thirteen when she married a thirty-year-old railroad worker, and not quite fourteen when she gave birth to Roy. A month or so after his birth, her husband suffered an accident which made her a widow. Thanks to the circumstances of its happening, it also made her well-off by the community's standards. A whole two hundred dollars a month to spend on herself. Which was right where she meant to spend it.

Her family, on whom she promptly dumped Roy, had other ideas. They kept the boy for three years, occasionally managing to wheedle a few dollars from their daughter. Then, one day, her father appeared in town, bearing Roy under one arm and swinging a horsewhip with the other. And he proceeded to demonstrate his lifelong theory that a gal never got too old to whip.

Since Lilly Dillon's character had been molded long before, it was little changed by the thrashing. But she did keep Roy, having no choice in the matter, and frightened by her father's grim promises to keep an eye on her, she moved out of his reach.

Settling down in Baltimore, she found lucrative and undemanding employment as a B-girl. Or, more accurately, it was undemanding as far as she was concerned. Lilly Dillon wasn't putting out for anyone; not, at least, for a few bucks or drinks. Her nominal heartlessness often disgruntled the customers, but it drew the favorable attention of her employers. After all, the world was full of bimbos, tramps who could be had for a grin or a gin. But a smart kid, a doll who not only had good looks and class, but was also *smart*—well, that kind of kid you could use.

They used her, in increasingly responsible capacities. As a managing hostess, as a recruiter for a chain of establishments, as a spotter of sticky-fingered and bungling employees; as courier, liaison officer, fingerwoman; as a collector and disburser. And so on up the ladder . . . or should one say down it? The money poured in, but little of the shower settled on her son.

She wanted to pack him off to boarding school, only drawing back, indignantly, when the charges were quoted to her. A couple thousand dollars a year, plus a lot of extras, and just for taking care of a kid! Just for keeping a kid out of trouble! Why, for that much money she could buy a nice mink jacket.

They must think she was a sucker, she decided. Nuisance that he was, she'd just look after Roy herself. And he'd darned well keep out of trouble or she'd skin him alive.

She was, of course, imbued with certain ineradicable instincts, eroded and atrophied though they were; so she had her rare moments of conscience. Also, certain things had to be done, for the sake of appearances: to stifle charges of neglect and the unpleasantness pursuant thereto. In either case, obviously, and as Roy instinctively knew, whatever she did was for herself, out of fear or as a salve for her conscience.

Generally, her attitude was that of a selfish older sister to an annoying little brother. They quarreled with each other. She delighted in gobbling down his share of some treat, while he danced about her in helpless rage.

"You're mean! Just a dirty old pig, that's all."

"Don't you call me names, you snot!"—striking at him. "I'll learn you!"

"Learn me, learn me! Don't even have enough sense to say teach!"

"I do, too! I did say teach!"

He was an excellent student in school, and exceptionally well-behaved. Learning came easily for him, and good behavior seemed simply a matter of common sense. Why risk trouble when it didn't make you anything? Why be profitlessly detained after school when you could be out hustling newspapers or running errands or caddying? Time was money, and money was what made the world go around.

As the smartest and best-behaved boy in his classes, he naturally drew the displeasure of the other kind. But no matter how cruelly or frequently he was attacked, Lilly offered only sardonic condolence.

"Only one arm?" she would say, if he exhibited a twisted and swollen arm.

Or if a tooth had been knocked out, "Only one tooth?"

And when he received an overall mauling, with dire threats of worse to come, "Well, what are you kicking about? They may kill you, but they can't eat you."

Oddly enough, he found a certain comfort in her backhanded remarks. On the surface they were worse than nothing, merely insult added to injury, but beneath them lay a chilling and callous logic. A fatalistic do-or-be-damned philosophy which could accommodate itself to anything but oblivion.

He had no liking for Lilly, but he came to admire her. She'd never given him anything but a hard time, which was about the extent of her generosity to anyone. But she'd done all right. She knew how to take care of herself.

She showed no soft spots until he was entering his teens, a handsome, wholesome-looking youth with coal-black hair and wide-set gray eyes. Then, to his secret amusement, he began to note a subtle change in her attitude, a softening of her voice when she spoke to him and a suppressed hunger in her eyes when she looked at him. And seeing her thus, knowing what was behind the change, he delighted in teasing her.

Was something wrong? Did she want him to clear out for a while and leave her alone?

"Oh, no, Roy. Really. I—I like being together with you."

"Now, Lilly. You're just being polite. I'll get out of your way right now."

"Please, h-honey . . ." Biting her lip at the unaccustomed endearment, a shamed flush spreading over her lovely features. "Please stay with me. After all, I'm—I'm y-your m-mother."

But she wasn't, remember? She'd always passed him off as her younger brother, and it was too late to change the story.

"I'll leave right now, Lilly. I know you want me to. You just don't want to hurt my feelings."

He had matured early, as was natural enough. By the time he was seventeen-going-on-eighteen, the spring that he graduated from high school, he was as mature as a man in his twenties.

On the night of his graduation, he told Lilly that he was pulling out. For good.

"Pulling out . . .?" She'd been expecting that, he guessed, but she wasn't resigned to it. "B-but—but you can't! You've got to go to college."

"Can't. No money."

She laughed shakily, and called him silly; avoiding his eyes, refusing to be rejected as she must have known she would be.

"Of course, you have money! I've got plenty, and anything I have is yours. You—"

" 'Anything I have is yours,' " said Roy, eyes narrowed appreciably. "That would make a good title for a song, Lilly."

"You can go to one of the really good schools, Roy. Harvard or Yale, or some place like that. Your grades are certainly good enough, and with my money—our money . . ."

"Now, Lilly. You know you need the money for yourself. You always have."

She flinched, as though he had struck her, and her face worked sickishly, and the trim size-nine suit seemed suddenly to hang on her: a cruel moral to a life that had gotten her everything and given her nothing. And for a moment, he almost relented. He almost pitied her.

And then she spoiled it all. She began to weep, to bawl like a child, which was a silly, stupid thing for Lilly Dillon to do; and to top off the ridiculous and embarrassing performance, she threw on the corn.

"D-don't be mean to me, Roy. Please, please don't. Y-you—you're b-breaking my heart . . ."

Roy laughed out loud. He couldn't restrain himself.

"Only one heart, Lilly?" he said.

THREE

Roy Dillon lived in a hotel called the Grosvenor-Carlton, a name which hinted at a grandeur that was wholly non-existent. It boasted one hundred rooms, one hundred baths, but it was purely a boast. Actually, there were only eighty rooms and thirty-five baths, and those included the hall baths and the two lobby restrooms which were not really baths at all.

It was a four-storey affair with a white sandstone façade, and a small, terrazzo-floored lobby. The clerks were elderly pensioners, who were delighted to work for a miniscule salary and a free room. The Negro bellboy, whose badge of office was a discarded conductor's cap, also doubled as a janitor, elevator operator, and all-round handyman. With such arrangements as these, the service left something to be desired. But, as the briskly jovial proprietor pointed out, anyone who was in a helluva hurry could hurry right on out to one of the Beverly Hills hotels, where he could doubtless get a nice little room for fifty bucks a day instead of the Grosvenor-Carlton's minimum of fifty a month.

Generally speaking, the Grosvenor-Carlton was little different than the numerous other "family" and "commercial' hotels which are strung out along West Seventh and Santa Monica and other arterial streets of West Los Angeles; establishments catering to retired couples, and working men and women who required a close-in address. Mostly, these latter, single people, were men—clerks, white collar workers and the like—for the proprietor was strongly prejudiced against unattached women.

"Put it this way, Mr. Dillon," he said, during the course of their initial meeting. "I rent to a woman, and she has to have a room with a bath. I insist on it, see, because otherwise she's got the hall bath tied up all the time, washing her goddamn hair and her clothes and every other damned thing she can think of. So the minimum for a room with a bath is seventeen a week—almost eighty bucks a month, just for a place to sleep and no cooking allowed. And just how many of these chicks make enough to pay eighty a month for a sleeping room and take all their meals in restaurants and buy clothes and a lot of frigging goo to smear on their faces that the good Lord gave 'em, and—and—you a God-fearing man, Mr. Dillon?"

Roy nodded encouragingly; not for the world would he have interrupted the proprietor. People were his business, knowing them was. And the only way of knowing was to listen to them.

"Well, so am I. I and my late wife, goddamn—God rest her, we entered the church at the same time. That was thirty-seven years ago, down in Wichita Falls, Texas, where I had my first hotel. And that's where I began to learn about chicks. They just don't make the money for hotel livin', see, and there's only one way they can get it. By selling their stuff, you know; tapping them cute little piggy banks they all got. At first, they just do it now and then, just enough to make ends meet. But pretty soon, they got the bank open twenty-four hours a day; why the hell not, is the way they see it. All they got to do is open up that cute little slot, and the money pours out; and it's no skin off their butts if they give a hotel a bad name.

"Oh, I tell you, Mr. Dillon. I've hotelled all over this wonderful land of ours, and I'm telling you that hookers and hotellin' just don't mix. It's against God's laws, and it's against man's laws. You'd think the police would be too busy catching *real* criminals, instead of snooping around for hookers, but that's the way the gravy stains, as the saying is, and I don't fight it. An ounce of prevention, that's my motto. If you keep out the chicks, you keep out the hookers, and you've got a nice clean respectable place like this one, without a lot of cops hanging around. Why, if a cop comes in here now, I know he's a new man, and I tell him he'd better come back after he checks with headquarters. And he never comes back, Mr. Dillon; he's damned well told that it ain't necessary, because this is a hotel, not a hook shop."

"I'm pleased to hear that, Mr. Simms," Roy said truthfully. "I've always been very careful where I lived."

"Right. A man's got to be," Simms said. "Now, let's see. You wanted a two-room suite, say, parlor, bedroom, and bath. Fact is, we don't have much demand for suites here. Got the suites split off into room with bath, and room without. But . . ."

He unlocked a door, and ushered his prospective tenant into a roomy bedroom, its high ceilings marking its pre-war vintage. The connecting door opened into another room, a duplicate of the first except that it had no bath. This was the former parlor, and Simms assured Roy that it could be converted back into one in short order.

"Sure, we can take out this bedroom furniture. Move back the parlor stuff in no time at all—desk, lounge, easy chairs, anything you want within reason. Some of the finest furnishings you ever saw."

Dillon said he would like to take a look at it, and Simms conducted him to the basement storeroom. It was by no means the finest he had ever seen, of course, but it was decent and comfortable; and he neither expected nor wanted anything truly fine. He had a certain image to maintain. A portrait of a young man who made rather a good living—just good, no better—and lived well within it.

He inquired the rental on the suite. Simms approached the issue circuitously, pointing out the twin necessities of maintaining a high-class clientele, for he would settle for nothing less, by God, and also making a profit, which was goddamn hard for a God-fearing man to do in those times.

"Why, some of these peasants we get in here, I mean that *try* to get in here, they'll fight you for a burned-out light globe. You just can't please 'em, know what I mean? It's like crackerjacks, you know, the more they get the more they want. But that's the way the cinnamon rolls, I guess, and like we used to say down in Wichita Falls, if you can't stand posts you better not dig holes. Uh, one hundred and twenty-five a month, Mr. Dillon?"

"That sounds reasonable," Roy smiled. "I'll take it."

"I'm sorry, Mr. Dillon. I'd like to shave it a little for you; I ain't saying I *wouldn't* shave it for the right kind of tenant. If you'd guarantee, now, to stay a minimum of three months, why—"

"Mr. Simms," said Roy.

"—why, I could make you a special rate. I'll lean over backward to—"

"Mr. Simms," Dillon said firmly. "I'll take the place on a year's lease. First and last months' rent in advance. And one hundred and twenty-five a month will be fine."

"It—it will?" The proprietor was incredulous. "You'll lease for a year at a hundred and twenty-five, and—and—"

"I will. I don't believe in moving around a lot. I make a profit in my business, and I expect others to make one in theirs."

Simms gurgled. He gasped. His paunch wriggled in his pants, and his entire face, including the area which extended back into his balding head, reddened with pleasure. He was a shrewd and practiced student of human nature, he declared. He knew peasants when he saw them, and he knew gentlemen; he'd immediately spotted Roy Dillon as one of the latter.

"And you're smart," he nodded wisely. "You know it just ain't good business to chisel where you live. What the hell? What's the percentage in chiselling a hotel for a few bucks—people you're going to see every day—if it's going to make 'em a little down on you?"

"You're absolutely right," Dillon said warmly.

Simms said he was damned tootin' he was right. Suppose, for example, that there was an inquiry about a guest of the peasant type. What could you honestly say about him anyway, beyond saying that he did live there and it was your Christian practice to say nothing about a man unless you could say something good? But if a *gentleman* was the subject of the inquiry, well, then, honesty compelled you to say so. He didn't simply *room* at the hotel, he *lived* there, a man of obvious character and substance who leased by the year and . . .

Dillon nodded and smiled, letting him ramble on. The Grosvenor-Carlton was the sixth hotel he'd visited since his arrival from Chicago. All had offered quarters which were equal to and as cheap or cheaper than those he had taken here. For there is a chronic glut of rooms in Los Angeles's smaller hotels. But he had found vaguely indefinable objections to all of them. They didn't *look* quite right. They didn't *feel* quite right. Only the Grosvenor-Carlton and Simms had had the right feel and look.

". . . one more thing," Simms was saying now. "This is your home, see? Renting like you do, it's just the same as if you were in an apartment or house. It's your castle, like the law says, and if you should want to have a guest, you know, a lady guest, why you got a perfect right to."

"Thank you for telling me," Roy nodded gravely. "I don't have anyone in mind at the moment, but I usually make friends wherever I go."

"O' course. A fine-looking young fellow like you is bound to have lady friends, and I bet they got class too. None of these roundheels that crumb a place up just by walking through the lobby."

"Never," Dillon assured him. "I'm very careful of the friends I make, Mr. Simms. Particularly the lady friends."

He was careful. During his four-year tenancy at the hotel he had had only one female visitor, a divorcee in her thirties, and everything about her—looks, dress, and manner—was abundantly satisfactory even to the discriminating Mr. Simms. The only fault he could find with her was that she did not come often enough. For Moira Langtry was also discriminating. Given her own way, something that Dillon frequently refrained from giving her as a matter of policy, she wouldn't have come within a mile of the Grosvenor-Carlton. After all, she had a very nice apartment of her own, a place with one bedroom, two baths and a wet bar. If he really wanted to see her—and she was beginning to doubt that he did—why couldn't he come out there?"

"Well, why can't you?" she said, as he sat up in bed phoning to her. "It's no further for you than it is for me."

"But you're so much younger, dear. A youthful female like you can afford to humor a doddering old man."

"Flattery will get you nowhere, mister"—she was pleased. "I'm five years older, and I feel every minute of it."

Dillon grinned. *Five* years older? Hell, she was ten if she was a day. "The fact is, I'm a little under the weather," he explained. "No, no, it's nothing contagious. I happened to trip over a chair the other night in the dark, and it gave me a nasty whack in the stomach."

"Well . . . I guess I could come . . ."

"That's my girl! I'd hold my breath if I wasn't panting."

"Mmm? Let's hear you."

"Pant, pant," he said.

"You poor thing," she said. "Moira'll hurry just as fast as she can."

Apparently, she had been dressed to go out when he called, for she arrived in less than an hour. Or, perhaps, it only seemed that way. He had got up to unlock the door preparatory to her arrival, and returning to the bed he had felt strangely tired and faint. So he had let his eyes drift shut, and when he opened them, a very little later seemingly, she was entering the room. Sweeping into it on her tiny, spike-heeled shoes; a billowing but compact bundle of woman with glossily black hair, and direct darkly-burning eyes.

She paused just inside the threshold for a moment, self-assured but suppliant. Posing like one of those arrogantly inviting mannequins. Then, she reached behind her, feeling for and finding the doorkey. And turning it with a soft click.

Roy forgot to wonder about her age.

She was old enough, was Moira Langtry.

She was young enough.

His silent approval spoke to her, and she gave a little twitch to her body, letting the ermine stole hang from one shoulder. Then, hips swaying delicately, she came slowly across the room; small chin outthrust; seemingly tugged forward by the bountiful imbalance within the small white blouse.

She stopped with her knees pressed against his bed, and looking upward he could see nothing but the tip of her nose above the contours of her breasts.

Raising a finger, he poked her in one then the other.

"You're hiding," he said. "Come out, come out, wherever you are."

She sank gracefully to her knees, let her dark eyes burn into his face.

"You stink," she said, tonelessly, the blouse shimmering with her words. "I hate you."

"The twins seem to be restless," he said. "Maybe we should put them to bed."

"You know what I'm going to do? I'm going to smother you."

He said, "Death, where is thy sting?" and then he was necessarily voiceless for a while. After an incredibly soft, sweet-smelling eternity, he was allowed to come up for air. And he spoke to her in a whisper.

"You smell good, Moira. Like a bitch in a hothouse."

"Darling. What a beautiful thing to say!"

"Maybe you don't smell good . . ."

"I do, too. You just said so."

"It could be your clothes."

"It's me! Want me to prove it to you?"

He did, and she did.

FOUR

When he first settled in Los Angeles, Roy Dillon's interest in women was prudently confined by necessity. He was twenty-one, an oldish twenty-one. His urge toward the opposite sex was as strong as any man's; flourishing even stronger, perhaps, because of the successes that lay behind him. But he was carrying light, as the saying is. He had looked around extensively and carefully before choosing Los Angeles as a permanent base of operations, and his capital was now reduced to less than a thousand dollars.

That was a lot of money, of course. Unlike the big-con operator, whose elaborate scene-setting may involve as much as a hundred thousand dollars, the short-con grifter can run on peanuts. But Roy Dillon, while remaining loyal to the short con, was abandoning the normal scheme of things.

At twenty-one, he was weary of the hit-and-get. He knew that the constant "getting"—jumping from one town to another before the heat got too hot—could absorb most of the hits, even of a thrifty man. So that he might work as hard and often as he safely could, and still wind up with the wolf nipping at the seat of his threadbare pants.

Roy had seen such men.

Once, on an excursion special out of Denver, he had run into a "mob" of them, poor devils so depleted in capital that they had had to pool their resources.

They were working in a monte swindle. The dealer was cast as the "wise guy," whom the others were determined to take. While he turned his head to argue with the two shills—holding the three cards open on his palm—the roper had drawn a small mark on the top card, winking extravagantly at Roy.

"Take him, pal!" His stage whisper was ridiculously loud. "Put down that big bill you got."

"The fifty or the hundred?" Roy whispered back.

"The hundred! Hurry!"

"Could I bet five hundred?"

"Well, uh, naw. You just better make it a hundred to start."

The dealer's conveniently outstretched hand was getting tired. The shills were running out of arguments to distract his attention. But Roy persisted with his cruel joke.

"How big is the marked card?"

"An ace, dammit! The other two are deuces! Now—"

"Does an ace beat deuces?"

"Does an—! Hell, yes, dammit! Now, bet!"

The other passengers in the bar car were catching on, beginning to grin. Roy laboriously took out his wallet, and took out a C-note. The dealer counted out a crumpled mass of ones and fives. Then, he shuffled, palming the marked ace for a marked deuce, and switching one of the deuces for an unmarked ace. One that was unmarked, that is, to the naked eye.

The showdown came. The three cards were slapped face down on the table. Roy studied them, squinting. "I can't see so good," he complained. "Let me borrow your glasses." And deftly, he appropriated the dealer's "readers."

Through the tinted glass, he promptly identified the ace, and pulled in the money.

The mob slunk out of the car, to the jeers of the other passengers. At the next town, a wide place in a muddy road, they jumped the train. Probably they had no funds to ride farther.

As the train pulled out, Roy saw them standing on the deserted platform, shoulders hunched against the cold, naked fear on their pale, gaunt faces. And in the warm comfort of the club car, he shivered for them.

He shivered for himself.

That was where the hit-and-get landed you, where it could land you. This, or something far worse than this, was the fate of the unrooted. Men to whom roots were a hazard rather than an asset. And the big-con boys were no more immune to it than their relatively petty brethren. In fact, their fate was often worse. Suicide. Dope addiction and the d.t.'s. The big house and the nut house.

Overhead and income were always in a neck-and-neck race. One sour deal, and they were on the skids.

And it wasn't going to happen to Roy Dillon.

For his first year in Los Angeles, he was strictly a square john. An independent salesman calling on small businessmen. Gliding back into the grift, he remained a salesman. And he was still one now. He had a credit rating and a bank account. He was acquainted with literally hundreds of people who would attest to the excellence of his character.

Sometimes they were required to do just that, when suspicion threatened to build into a police matter. But, naturally, he never called upon the same ones twice; and it didn't happen often anyway. Security gave him self-assurance. Security and self-assurance had bred a high degree of skill.

In accomplishing so much, he had had no time for women. Nothing but the casual come-and-go contacts which any young man might have. It was not until late in his third year that he had started looking around for a particular kind of woman. Someone who was not only highly desirable, but who would be willing to—even prefer to—to accept the only kind of arrangement which he was willing to offer.

He found her, Moira Langtry, that is, in church.

It was one of those screwball outfits which seem to flourish on the West Coast. The head clown was a yogi or a swami or something of the kind. While his audience listened as though hypnotized, he droned on and on of the Supreme Wisdom of the East, never once explaining why the world's highest incidence of disease, death, and illiteracy endured at the fount of said wisdom.

Roy was a little stunned to find such a one as Moira Langtry present. She just wasn't the type. He was aware of her puzzlement when she saw him, but he had his reasons for being here. It was an innocent way of passing the time. Cheaper than movies and twice as funny. Also, while he was doing very well as it was, he was not blind to the possibility of doing better. And a man just might see a way to do it at gatherings like these.

The audiences were axiomatically boobs. Mostly well-to-do boobs, middle-aged widows and spinsters: women suffering from a vague itch which might be scratched for a bundle. So . . . well, you never knew, did you?

You could keep your eyes open, without going out on a limb.

The clown finished his act. Baskets were passed for the "Adoration Offering." Moira tossed her program in one of them, and walked out. Grinning, Dillon followed her.

She was lingering in the lobby, making a business out of pulling on her gloves. As he approached, she looked up with cautious approval.

"Now, what," he said, "was a nice girl like you doing in a place like that?"

"Oh, you know." She laughed lightly. "I just dropped in for a glass of yogurt."

"Tsk, tsk. It's a good thing I didn't offer you a martini."

"It certainly is. I won't settle for less than a double Scotch."

They took it from there.

It took them rapidly to where they were now. Or reasonable facsimiles thereof.

Lately, today in particular, he sensed that she wanted it to take them somewhat further.

There was just one way of handling that, in his opinion. With the light touch. No one could simultaneously laugh and be serious.

He let his hand walk down her body and come to rest on her navel. "You know something?" he said. "If you put a raisin in that, you could pass as a cookie."

"Don't," she said, picking up his hand and dropping it to the bed.

"Or you could draw a ring around it, and pretend you're a doughnut."

"I'm beginning to feel like a doughnut," she said. "The part in the middle."

She sat up, swinging her legs off the bed, and got a cigarette from the reading stand. After it was lit, he took it for himself, and she got herself another.

"Roy," she said, "look at me."

"Oh, I am looking, dear. Believe me, I am."

"Now, please! Is—is this all we have, Roy? Is it all we're going to have? I'm not knocking it, understand, but shouldn't there be something more?"

"How could we top a thing like that? Tickle each other's feet?"

She looked at him silently, the burning eyes turning lackluster, staring at him from behind an invisible veil. Without turning her head, she extended a hand and slowly tamped out her cigarette.

"That was a funny," he said. "You were supposed to laugh."

"Oh, I am laughing, dear," she said. "Believe me, I am."

She reached down, picked up a stocking and began to draw it on. A little troubled, he pulled her around to face him.

"What are you driving at, Moira? Marriage?"

"I didn't say that."

"But that's what I asked."

She frowned, hesitating, then shook her head. "I don't think so. I'm a very practical little girl, and I don't believe in giving any more than I get. That might be pretty awkward for a matchbook salesman, or whatever you are."

He was stung, but he kept on playing. "Would you mind handing me my first aid kit? I think I've just been clawed."

"Don't worry. Kitty's had all her shots."

"The fact is, the matchbooks are just a sideline. My real business is running a whorehouse."

"Oh, fine. I was afraid it might be something shameful." Then, cutting him off firmly, pulling him back into line. "But you see what I'm driving at, Roy. We don't know a thing about each other. We're not friends. We're not even acquainted. It's just been early to bed and early to bed from the time we met."

"You said you weren't knocking it."

"I'm not. It's very necessary to me. But I don't feel that it should begin and end with that. It's like trying to live on mustard sandwiches."

"And you want pâté?"

"Steak. Something nourishing. Aah, hell, Roy"—she shook her head fretfully. "I don't know. Maybe it isn't on the menu. Maybe I'm in the wrong restaurant."

"Madame is too cruel! Pierre weel drown heemself in ze soup!"

"Pierre doesn't care," she said, "if madame lives or dies. He's made that pretty clear."

She started to rise, with a certain finality of movement. He caught her and pulled her back to the bed, pulled her body against his again. He felt her carefully. He smoothed her hair and kissed her lips.

"Mmm, yes," he said. "Yes, I'm sure of it. The sale is final, and no exchanges."

"Here we go again," she said. "Out into outer space, before we have our feet on the ground."

"I mean, I went to a great deal of trouble to find you. A very nice little partridge. Perhaps there are better birds in the bushes, but again there might not be. And—"

"—and a bird in bed is better than a bush. Or something. I'm afraid I'm crabbing your monologue, Roy."

"Wait!" He held onto her. "I'm trying to tell you something. That I like you and that I'm lazy. I don't want to look any further. So just show me the price tag, and if I can I'll buy."

"That's better. I have an idea it might be quite profitable for both of us."

"So where do we begin? A few evenings on the town? A fling at Las Vegas?"

"Mmm, no, I guess not. Besides, you couldn't afford it."

"Surprise," he said curtly. "I wouldn't even make you pay your own way."

"Now, Roy . . ." She rumpled his hair affectionately. "That isn't the kind of thing I have in mind, anyway. A lot of girls, glitter and glassware. If we're going some place, it ought to be at the other end of the street. You know. Relaxed and quiet, so that we can talk for a change."

"Well. La Jolla's nice this time of year."

"La Jolla's nice any time of year. But are you sure you can afford—"

"Keep it up," he warned her. "One more word of that song, and you'll have the reddest butt in La Jolla. People will think it's another sunset."

"Pooh! Who's afraid of you?"

"And get the hell out of here, will you? Go crawl back under your culvert! You've drained me dry and got me to splurge my life's savings, and now you want to talk me to death."

She laughed fondly, and got up. When she was dressed, she knelt again at his bedside for a goodbye kiss.

"Are you sure you're all right, Roy?" She smoothed the hair from his forehead. "You look rather pale."

"Oh, God," he groaned. "Will this woman never leave? She puts me through a double shift, and then she says I look pale!"

She left, smiling smugly. Very pleased with herself.

Roy arose wearily, his legs wobbling as he made the round trip to the bathroom. He dropped back down on the bed in a heap, a little worried about himself for the first time. What could be the cause of this, anyway, this strange overpowering fatigue? Not Moira, surely; he was used to her. Not the fact that he had eaten very little during the past three days. He often had spells when he didn't feel hungry, and this had been one of them. Whatever he ate bounced back, in a brownish-colored liquid. Which was strange, since he'd eaten nothing but ice cream and milk.

Frowning, he leaned forward and examined himself. There was a faint purplish-yellow bruise on his stomach. But it didn't hurt any more—unless he pushed on it very hard. He'd had no pain since the day he was slugged.

So . . .? He shrugged and lay back down. It was just one of those things, he guessed. He didn't feel sick. If a man was sick, he *felt* sick.

He piled the pillows on top of one another, and reclined in a half-sitting position. That seemed to be better, but tired as he was he was restless. With an effort, he reached his trousers from a nearby chair, and dug a quarter from the watch pocket.

Offhand, it looked like any other quarter, but it wasn't quite. The tail side was worn down, the head was not. Holding it back between the fleshy part of his first two fingers, hidden edgewise by them, he could identify the two sides.

He flipped it into the air, caught it and brought it down against his other hand with a *smack*. For this *was* the smack, one version of it. One of the three standard short-con gimmicks.

"Tails," he murmured, and there was tails.

He tossed the coin again, and called for heads. And heads came up.

He began closing his eyes on the calls, making sure that he wasn't unconsciously cheating. The coin went up and down, his palm deceptively smacking the back of his hand.

Heads . . . tails . . . heads, heads . . .

And then there was no smack.

His eyes closed, and stayed closed.

That was a little after noon. When he opened them again, twilight was shading the room and the phone was ringing. He looked around wildly, not recognizing where he was, not knowing where he was. Lost in a world that was as strange as it was frightening. Then, drifting back into consciousness, he picked up the phone.

"Yes," he said; and then, "What, what? How's that again?" For what the clerk was saying made no sense at all.

"A visitor, Mr. Dillon. A very attractive young lady. She says"—a tactful laugh—"she says she's your mother."

FIVE

At seventeen going on eighteen, Roy Dillon had left home. He took nothing with him but the clothes he wore—clothes he had bought and paid for himself. He took no money but the little in the pockets of his clothes, and that too he had earned.

He wanted nothing from Lilly. She had given him nothing when he needed it, when he was too small to get for himself, and he wasn't letting her into the game at this late date.

He had no contact with her during the first six months he was away. Then, at Christmas time, he sent her a card, and on Mother's Day he sent her another. Both were of the gooey sentimental type, dripping with sickly sweetness, but the latter was a real dilly. Hearts and flowers and fat little angels swarmed over it in an insanely hilarious montage. The engraved message was dedicated to Dear Old Mom, and it gushed tearfully of goodnight kisses and platters and pitchers of oven-fresh cookies and milk when a little boy came in from play.

You would have thought that Dear Old Mom (God bless her silvering hair) had been the proprietor of a combination dairy-bakery, serving no customer but her own little tyke (on his brand-new bike).

He was laughing so hard when he sent it that he almost botched up the address. But afterward, he had some sobering second thoughts. Perhaps the joke was on him, yes? Perhaps by gibing at her he was revealing a deep and lasting hurt, admitting that she was tougher than he. And that, naturally, wouldn't do. He'd taken everything she had to hand out, and it hadn't made a dent in him. He damned well mustn't ever let her think that it had.

So he kept in touch with her after that, at Christmas and on her birthday and so on. But he was very correct about it. He just didn't think enough of her, he told himself, to indulge in ridicule. It would take a lot better woman than Lilly Dillon to get to him.

The only way he showed his true feelings was in the presents they exchanged. For while Lilly could obviously afford far better gifts than he, he would not admit it. At least, he did not until the effort to keep up with or outdo her not only threatened his long-range objectives, but revealed itself for what it was. Another manifestation of hurt. She had hurt him—or so it looked—and childishly he was rejecting her attempts at atonement.

She might think that, anyway, and he couldn't let her. So he had written her casually that gift-giving had been over-commercialized, and that they should stick to token remembrances from then on. If she wanted to donate to charity in his name, fine. Boys' Town would be appropriate. He, of course, would make a donation in her name.

Say to some institution for Wayward Women . . .

Well, but that is getting ahead of the story, skipping over its principal element.

New York is a two-hour ride from Baltimore. At seventeen going on eighteen, Roy went there, the logical objective of a young man whose only assets were good looks and an inherent yen for the fast dollar.

Needing to earn—and to be paid—immediately, he took work selling on a flat commission. Door-to-door stuff. Magazines, photo coupons, cooking utensils, vacuum cleaners—anything that looked promising. All of it promised much and gave little.

Perhaps Miles of Michigan had made $1,380 his first month by showing Super Suitings to his friends, and perhaps O'Hara of Oklahoma earned ninety dollars a day by taking orders for the Oopsy-Doodle Baby Walker. But Roy doubted it like hell. By literally knocking himself out, he made as high as $125 in one week. But that was his very best week. The average was between seventy-five and eighty dollars, and he had to hump to get that.

Still it was better than working as a messenger, or taking some small clerical job which promised "Good Opportunity" and "Possibility To Advance" in lieu of an attractive wage. Promises were cheap. Suppose he went to one of those places and promised to be president some day; so how about a little advance?

The selling was no good, but he knew of nothing else. He was very irked with himself. Here he was nineteen going on twenty, and already a proven failure. What was wrong with him, anyway? What had Lilly had that he didn't have?

Then, he stumbled onto the twenties.

It was a fluke. The chump, the proprietor of a cigar store, had really pulled it on himself. Preoccupied, Roy had continued to fumble for a coin after receiving the change from the bill, and the fidgety storekeeper, delayed in waiting on other customers, had suddenly lost patience.

"For Pete's sake, mister!" he snapped. "It's only a nickel! Just pay me the next time you're in."

Then, he threw back the twenty, and Roy was a block away before he realized what had happened.

On the heels of the realization came another: an ambitious young man did not wait for such happy accidents. He created them. And he forthwith started to do so.

He was coldly told off at two places. At three others, it was pointed out—more or less politely—that he was not entitled to the return of his twenty. At the remaining three, he collected.

He was exuberant at his good luck. (And he had been exceptionally lucky.) He wondered if there were any gimmicks similar to the twenties, ways of picking up as much money in a few hours as a *fool* made in a week.

There were. He was introduced to them that night in a bar, whence he had gone to celebrate.

A customer sat down next to him, jostling his elbow. A little of his drink was spilled, and the man apologetically insisted on buying him a fresh one. Then he bought still another round. At this point, of course, Roy wanted to buy a round. But the man's attention had been diverted. He was peering down at the floor, then reaching down and picking up a dice cube which he laid on the bar.

"Did you drop this, pal? No? Well, look. I don't like to drink so fast, but if you want to roll me for a round—just to keep things even . . ."

They rolled. Roy won. Which naturally wouldn't do at all. They rolled again, for the price of four drinks, and this time the guy won. And, of course, that wouldn't do either. He just wouldn't allow it. Hell, they were just swapping drinks, friendly like, and he certainly wasn't going to walk out of here winner.

"We'll roll for eight drinks this time, well, call it five bucks even, and then . . ."

The *tat*, with its rapidly doubling bets, is murder on a fool. That is its vicious beauty. Unless he is carrying very heavy, the man *with-the-best-of-it* strips him on a relatively innocent number of winning rolls.

Roy's griftings were down the drain in twenty minutes.

In another ten, all of his honest money had followed it. The guy felt very bad about it; he said so himself. Roy must take back a couple bucks of his loss, and . . .

But the taste of the grift was strong in Roy's mouth, the taste and the smell. He said firmly that he would take back half of the money. The grifter—his name was Mintz—could keep the other half for his services as an instructor in swindling.

"You can begin the lessons right now," he said. "Start with that dice gimmick you just worked on me."

There were some indignant protests from Mintz, some stern language from Roy. But in the end they adjourned to one of the booths, and that night and for some nights afterward they played the roles of teacher and pupil. Mintz held back nothing. On the contrary, he talked almost to the point of becoming tiresome. For here was a blessed chance to drop pretense. He could show how smart he was, as his existence normally precluded doing, and do it in absolute safety.

Mintz did not like the twenties. It took a certain indefinable something which he did not have. And he never worked it without a partner, someone to distract the chump while the play was being made. As for working with a partner, he didn't like that either. It cut the *score* right down the middle. It put an apple on your head, and handed the other guy a shotgun. Because grifters, it seemed, suffered an irresistible urge to beat their colleagues. There was little glory in whipping a fool—hell, fools were made to be whipped. But to take a professional, even if it cost you in the long run, ah, that was something to polish your pride.

Mintz liked the smack. It was natural, you know. Everyone matched coins.

He particularly liked the tat, whose many virtues were almost beyond enumeration. Hook a group of guys on that tat, and you had it made for the week.

The tat must always be played on a very restricted surface, a bar or a booth table. Thus, you could not actually roll the die, although, of course, you appeared to. You shook your hand vigorously, holding the cube on a high point, never shaking it at all, and then you spun it out, letting it skid and topple but never turn. If the marks became suspicious, you shot out of a cup, or, more likely, a glass, since you were in a bar room. But again you did not really shake the die. You held it, as before, clicking it vigorously against the glass in a simulated rattle, and then you spun it out as before.

It took practice, sure. Everything did.

If things got too warm, the bartender would often give you a *take-out* for a good tip. Call you to the phone or say that the cops were coming or something like that. Bartenders were chronically fed up with drinkers. They'd as soon see them chumped as not, if it made them a buck, and unless the guys were their friends.

Mintz knew of many gimmicks other than the three standards. Some of them promised payoffs exceeding the normal short-con top of a thousand dollars. But these invariably required more than one man, as well as considerable time and preparation; were, in short, bordering big-con stuff. And they had one very serious disadvantage; if the fool tipped, you were caught. You hadn't made a mistake. You hadn't just been unlucky. You'd just had it.

There were two highly essential details of grifting which Mintz did not explain to his pupil. One of them defied explanation. It was an acquired trait, something each man had to do on his own and in his own way; i.e., retaining a high degree of anonymity while remaining in circulation. You couldn't disguise yourself, naturally. It was more a matter of *not* doing anything. Of avoiding any mannerism, any expression, any tone on pattern of speech, any posture or gesture or walk—anything at all that might be remembered.

Thus, the first unexplained essential.

Presumably, Mintz didn't explain the second one because he saw no need to. It was something that Roy must certainly know.

The lessons ended.

Roy industriously went to work on the grift. He acquired a handsome wardrobe. He moved to a good hotel. Indulging himself extravagantly, he still built up a roll of more than four thousand dollars.

Months passed. Then, one day, when he was eating in an Astoria-section lunchroom, a detective came in looking for him.

Conferring with the proprietor, he described Roy to a *t*. He had no photo of him, but he did have a police artist's reconstruction, and it was an excellent likeness.

Roy could see them looking down his way, as they talked, and he thought wildly of running. Of beating it back through the kitchen, and on out the back door. Probably the only thing that kept him from running was the weakness of his legs.

And then he looked at himself in the back-counter mirror, and he breathed a shuddery sigh of relief.

The day had turned warm after he left his hotel, and he'd checked his hat, coat and tie in a subway locker. Then, only an hour or so ago, he'd got a butch-style haircut.

So he was changed, considerably. Enough anyway to keep him from being collared. But he was shaken right down to his shoe soles. He sneaked back to his hotel room, wondering if he'd ever have the guts to work again. He stayed in the hotel until dark, and then he went looking for Mintz.

Mintz was gone from the small hotel where he had lived. He'd left months ago, leaving no forwarding address. Roy started hunting for him. By sheer luck, he found him in a bar six blocks away.

The grifter was horrified when Roy told him what had happened. "You mean you've been working here all this time? You've been working *steady*? My God! Do you know where I've been in the last six months? A dozen places! All the way to the coast and back!"

"But why? I mean, New York's a big city. Why—"

Mintz cut him off impatiently. New York *wasn't* a big city, he said. It just had a lot of people in it, and they were crammed into a relatively small area. And no, you didn't help your odds much by getting out of jampacked Manhattan and into the other boroughs. Not only did you keep bumping into the same people, people who worked in Manhattan and lived in Astoria, Jackson Heights, et cetera, but you were more conspicuous there. Easier to be spotted by the fools. "And, kid, a blind man could spot you. Look at that haircut! Look at that fancy wristwatch, and them three-tone sports shoes! Why don't you wear a black eye-patch, too, and a mouthful of gold teeth?"

Roy reddened. He asked troubledly if every city was like this. Did you have to keep jumping from place to place, using up your capital and having to move on just about the time you got to know your way around?

"What do you want?" Mintz shrugged. "Egg in your beer? You can usually play a fairly long stand in Los Angeles, because it ain't just one town. It's a country full of towns, dozens of 'em. And with traffic so bad and a lousy transportation system, the people don't mix around like they do in New York. *But*"—he wagged a finger severely—"but that still doesn't mean you can run wild, kid. You're a grifter, see? A thief. You've got no home and no friends, and no visible means of support. And you damned well better not ever forget it."

"I won't," Roy promised. "But, Mintz . . ."

"Yeah?"

Roy smiled and shook his head, keeping his thought to himself. *Suppose I did have a home, a regular place of residence? Suppose I had hundreds of friends and acquaintances? Suppose I had a job and—*

And there was a knock on the door, and he said, "Come in, Lilly," and his mother came in.

SIX

She didn't seem to have aged a year in the seven since he'd seen her. He was twenty-five, now, which meant that she was crowding thirty-nine. But she appeared to be in her very early thirties, say about thirty-one or -two. She looked like . . . like . . . Why, of course! Moira

Langtry! That was who she reminded him of. You couldn't say that they actually *looked* like each other; they were both brunettes and about the same size, but there was absolutely no facial resemblance. It was more a type similarity than a personal one. They were both members of the same flock; women who knew just what it took to preserve and enhance their natural attractiveness. Women who were either endowed with what it took, or spared no effort in getting it.

Lilly took a chair diffidently, unsure of her welcome, quickly explaining that she was in Los Angeles on business. "I'm handling playback money at the tracks, Roy. I'll be getting back to Baltimore as soon as the races are over."

Roy nodded equably. The explanation was reasonable. Playback—knocking the odds down on a horse by heavy pari-mutuel betting—was common in big-time bookmaking.

"I'm glad to see you, Lilly. I'd have been hurt if you hadn't dropped by."

"And I'm glad to see you, Roy. I—" She looked around the room, leaning forward a little to peer into the bathroom. Slowly, her diffidence gave way to a puzzled frown. "Roy," she said. "What's this all about? Why are you living in a place like this?"

"What's wrong with it?"

"Stop kidding me! It isn't you, that's what's wrong. Just look at it! Look at those corny clown pictures! That's a sample of my son's taste? Roy Dillon goes for corn?"

Roy would have laughed if he hadn't been so weak. The four pictures were his own additions to the decorations. Concealed in their box frames was his grifted dough. Fifty-two thousand dollars in cash.

He murmured that he had rented the place as he found it, the best that he could afford. After all, he was just a commission salesman and . . .

"And that's another thing," Lilly said. "Four years in a town like Los Angeles, and a peanut selling job is the best you can do! You expect me to believe that? It's a front, isn't it? This dump is a front. You're working an angle, and don't tell me you're not because I wrote the book!"

"Lilly . . ." His faint voice seemed to come from miles away. "Lilly, mind your own damned business . . ."

She said nothing for a moment, recovering from his rebuke,

reminding herself that he was more stranger than son. Then, half-pleading, "You don't have to do it, Roy. You've got so much on the ball—so much more than I ever had—and . . . You know what it does to a person, Roy. I—"

His eyes were closed. An apparent signal to shut up or get out. Forcing a smile, she said, okay, she wouldn't start scolding the minute she saw him.

"Why are you still in bed—s-son? Are you sick?"

"Nothing," he muttered. "Just . . ."

She came over to the side of the bed. Timidly, she put the palm of her hand to his forehead; let out a startled gasp. "Why, Roy, you're ice cold! What—" Light bloomed over his pillows as she switched on the table lamp. He heard another gasp. "Roy, what's the matter? You're as white as a sheet!"

"Nothin' . . ." His lips barely moved. "No s-sweat, Lilly."

Suddenly, he had become terribly frightened. He knew, without knowing why, that he was dying. And with the terrible fear of death was an unbearable sadness. Unbearable because there was no one who cared, no one to assuage it. No one, no one at all, to share it with him.

Only one death, Roy? Well, what are you kicking about?

But they can't eat you, can they? They can kill you, but they can't eat you.

"Don't!" he sobbed, his voice pushing up through an overpowering drowsiness. "D-don't laugh at me—I—"

"I won't! I'm not laughing, honey! I— Listen to me, Roy!" She squeezed his hand fiercely. "You don't seem to be sick. No fever or— Where do you hurt? Did someone hurt you?"

He didn't hurt. There had been no pain since the day of his slugging. But . . .

"Hit . . ." He mumbled. "Three days ago . . ."

"Three days ago? How? Where were you hit? What— Wait a minute, darling! Just wait until mother makes a phone call, and then—"

In what was record time for the Grosvenor-Carlton, she got an outside line. She spoke over the phone, her voice cracking like a whip.

". . . Lilly Dillon, doctor. I work for Justus Amusement Company out of Baltimore, and— *What*? Don't you brush me off, buster! Don't you tell me you never heard of me! If I have to have Bobo Justus call you—! Well, all right then. Let's see how fast you can get over here!"

She slammed down the receiver, and turned back to Roy.

The doctor came, out of breath and looking a little sullen; then, forgetting his wounded dignity, as his eyes drank in Lilly.

"So sorry if I was abrupt, Mrs. Dillon. Now, don't tell me this strapping young man can be your son!"

"Never mind that." Lilly chopped off his flattery. "Do something for him. I think he's in a pretty bad way."

"Well, now. Let's just see."

He moved past her, looked down at the pale figure on the bed. Abruptly, his light manner washed away, and his hand moved quickly; testing Roy's heart, probing for pulse and blood pressure.

"How long has he been like this, Mrs. Dillon?" —curtly, not turning to look at her.

"I don't know. He was in bed when I came in about an hour ago. We talked and he seemed to be all right, except that he kept getting weaker and—"

"I'll bet he did! Any history of ulcers?"

"No. I mean, I'm not sure. I haven't seen him in seven years, and—What's the matter with him, doctor?"

"Do you know whether he's been in any kind of accident during the last few days? Anything that might have injured him internally?"

"No . . ." She corrected herself again. "Well, yes, he was! He was trying to tell me about it. Three days ago, he was hit in the stomach—some bar-room drunk, I suppose . . ."

"Any vomiting afterward? Coffee-colored?" The doctor yanked down the sheet, nodding grimly at sight of the bruise. "Well?"

"I don't know . . ."

"What's his blood-type? Do you know that?"

"No. I—"

He dropped the sheet, and picked up the phone. As he summoned an ambulance, breaking the hotel's outside call record for the second time that day, he stared at Lilly with a kind of worried reproach.

He hung up the phone. "I wish you'd known his blood type," he said. "If I could have got some blood into him now, instead of having to wait until he's typed . . ."

"Is it . . . He'll be all right, won't he?"

"We'll do all we can. Oxygen will help some."

"But will he be all right?"

"His blood-pressure is under a hundred, Mrs. Dillon. He's had an internal hemorrhage."

"Stop it!" She wanted to scream at him. "I asked you a question! I asked you if—"

"I'm sorry," he said evenly. "The answer is, no. I don't think he can live until he gets to the hospital."

Lilly swayed. She got hold of herself; drawing herself straight, making her voice firm. And she spoke to the doctor very quietly.

"My son will be all right," she said. "If he isn't, I'll have you killed."

SEVEN

Carol Roberg arrived at the hospital at five in the afternoon, an hour before the beginning of her shift. The mere thought of being late to work terrified her, and, by coming so early, she could get a bargain-priced meal in the employees' cafeteria before going on duty. That was very important to Carol—a good meal at a low price. Even when she wasn't hungry, which was seldom, even in America where no one seemed ever to be hungry, she was always subtly worried about when she would eat again.

Her white nurse's uniform was so stiffly starched that it gave off little pops and crackles as she hurried down the marble corridor. Cut overlong, in the European fashion, it made her look like a child dressed in its mother's clothes; and the skirt and cuffs flared upward at the corners, seeming to set a pattern for her eyes, her mouth, her brows, and the tips of her short bobbed hair. All her features had an amusing turned-up look, and no amount of inner solemnity could conquer it. In fact, the more solemn she was, the more determinedly severe, the greater was the effect of suppressed laughter: a child playing at being a woman.

Entering the cafeteria, she moved straight to the long serving counter. Blushing self-consciously; careful to avoid looking at anyone who might be looking her way. Several times, here and elsewhere, she had been drawn into joining other diners. And the experience had been painfully awkward. The men, internes and technicians, made jokes which were beyond her limited idiom, so that she never knew quite what her response should be. As for the other nurses, they were nice enough; they wanted to be friendly. But there was a great gulf between them which only time could bridge. She did not talk or think or act as they did, and they seemed to take her ways as a criticism of theirs.

Carol took a tray and silverware from the serving counter, and studied the steamy expanse of food. Carefully, weighing each item against the other, she made her selections.

Potatoes and gravy were eight cents. Then the two-order would be fifteen, yes? A penny less.

"The two-order—?" The fat counter woman laughed. "Oh, you mean a double?"

"A double, yes. It is fifteen?"

The woman hesitated, looked around conspiratorially. "Tell you what, honey. We'll make it the same price as a single, hmm? I'll just go a little bit heavy with the spoon."

"You can do this?" Carol's turned-up eyes rounded with awe. "It would not cause trouble?"

"For me? Hah! I *own* this joint, honey."

Carol guessed that that made it all right. It would not be stealing. Her conscience comfortable, she also accepted the two extra sausages which the woman buried beneath her order of knockwurst and sauerkraut.

She was hesitating at the dessert section, about to decide that she could have a strudel in view of her other economies, when she heard the voices back down the line: the fat woman talking to another attendant.

"*. . . Kosher Kid can really put it away, can't she?*"

"*When she gets it for nothin', sure. That's how them kikes get ahead.*"

Carol froze for a moment. Then, stiffly, she moved on, paying her check and carrying her tray to a table in a distant corner of the room. She began to eat, methodically; forcing down the suddenly tasteless food until it once again became tasteful and desirable.

That was the way one had to do. To do the best one could, and accept things as they were. Usually, they did not seem so bad after a while; if they were not actually good, then they became so by virtue of the many things that were worse. Almost everything was relatively good. Eating was better than starving, living better than dying.

Even a simulated friendliness was better than none at all. People had to care—at least a little—to pretend. Her own kith and kin, immigrants like herself, had not always done that.

She had come to the United States under the auspices of relatives, an aunt and uncle who had fled Austria before the *anschluss*. Now well-to-do, they had taken her into their home and given her probationary status as a daughter. But with certain unstated stipulations: that she become one with them; that she live as they lived, without regard to how she had lived before. And Carol could not do that.

The ritual dining, the numerous sets of dishes, each to be used only for a certain kind of food, were almost offensive to her. So much waste in a world filled with want! Contrariwise, it seemed foolish to fast in the midst of abundance.

She was repelled by the bearded, pink-mouthed *Shiddem* for all his Judaic learning. To her he seemed a parasite, who should be forced to work as others did. She was shocked to find stupidity masquerading as pride—or what she thought of as stupidity: the imperviousness to a new language, and a new and possibly better way of life. All in all she was frightened by the conscientious apartness, sensing in it the seeds of tragedy.

Because they were good to her, or meant to be, she tried to be as they were. She was even willing to believe that they were right and that she was wrong. But mere trying, willingness, was not enough for them. They accused her of abandoning her faith, one that she could never remember knowing. Their tyranny, in its own way, seemed almost as bad as that she had fled from, and at last, she had had to flee from them.

Life outside the refugee world wasn't easy. The alternative to it often seemed to be a world with quite as many prejudices as the one she had left. But it was not always that way. There were some people who were completely indifferent to what she had been; that is, they were indifferent in a critical sense. They—the rare few: Mrs. Dillon was their best example—accepted her for what she was *now*. And—

She saw Mrs. Dillon approaching, moving past the other tables with her easy imperiousness. Hastily, Carol set down her teacup and came to her feet.

"Please sit down, Mrs. Dillon. I will get you some tea, yes? Some coffee? Something to eat—"

"Nothing," Lilly smiled, waving her back to her chair. "I won't be staying at the hospital this evening, and I wanted to talk to you before I left."

"There is something wrong? I—I have done—"

"No, you're doing fine. Everything's fine," Lilly assured her. "Get yourself some more tea, if you like. There's no hurry."

"I'd better not," Carol shook her head. "It is almost six, and the other nurse—"

"I'm paying the other nurse, too," Lilly said flatly. "She's working for me, not the hospital. If she doesn't want to work a little overtime for extra pay, she can quit."

Carol nodded and murmured meekly. This was a side of Mrs. Dillon she had never seen before. Lilly's smile returned.

"Now, just relax and rest easy, Carol. I like your work. I like you. I hope you like me, too—my son and I."

"Oh, I do, very much! You have been very nice to me."

"Why is it that you don't have a regular job? That you're just working extra?"

"Well . . ." Carol hesitated over her answer. "The hospital, almost every hospital, it graduates its own nurses, and I am not such a graduate. Then, the regular jobs, like in the doctors' offices, they usually want skills that I do not have. Often bookkeeping and shorthand, and—"

"I understand. How do you make out on this special duty work? All right?"

"Well, I do not always make so much," Carol said seriously. "It depends on how much work I can get, and that is not always a great deal. And, of course, there are the fees to the nurses' registry. But . . . well, it's enough, whatever. When I know more and when I better understand English—"

"Yeah, sure. How old are you, Carol?"

"Twenty-seven."

"Oh?" Lilly was surprised. "I wouldn't have thought you were that old."

"I feel much older, sometimes. Like I had lived forever. But, yes, I am twenty-seven."

"Well, no matter. Any boy friends? Going steady with anyone? No?" Lilly thought that was strange too. "Now, a girl like you must have had plenty of opportunities."

Carol shook her head, her upturned features humorously solemn. She lived in a furnished room, she pointed out, and she could not properly receive young men in it. Then, since it was necessary to work whenever she could, and since she worked irregular hours, it was not possible to plan ahead nor to be sure of keeping a social engagement if any were made.

"Also," she concluded, blushing, "also, the young men try to do certain things. They—often, I am greatly embarrassed."

Lilly nodded gently, feeling a strange tenderness toward the girl. Here was something, someone, absolutely real and the reality was all to the good. Perhaps, under different circumstances, she might have turned out as wholesome and honest—and *real*—as Carol was. But—she shook herself mentally—to hell with that noise.

She was what she was, and thus Roy had become what he was. And there was nothing to be done about her, assuming that she wanted anything done, but perhaps it wasn't too late to . . .

"You're probably wondering why I was so nosy. Inquisitive, I mean," Lilly said. "Well, it's like this. I don't want to jinx my son by saying that he's going to be all right, but—"

"Oh, I'm sure he will be, Mrs. Dillon! I—"

"Don't say it," Lilly said, sharply, knocking on the wooden top of the table. "It might bring bad luck. Let's just say that when and if he is able to leave the hospital, I'd like you to go on looking after him for a while. At my apartment, I mean. Do you think you'd like that?"

Carol nodded eagerly, her eyes shining. She'd already had more than two weeks of steady employment with Mrs. Dillon, more than she'd ever had before. What a wonderful thing it would be to go on working for her and her nice son, indefinitely.

"Well, that's fine, then," Lilly said. "It's all settled. Now, I've got to run along, but— Yes?"

"I was just wondering . . ." Carol hesitated. "I was wondering if—if Mr. Dillon would want me. He is always very kind, but . . ." She hesitated again, not knowing how to say what she meant without sounding impolite. Lilly said it for her.

"You mean Roy resents me. He's against anything I do simply because I do it."

"Oh, no. I did not mean that. Not exactly, anyway. I was just . . ."

"Well, it's close enough," Lilly smiled, trying to make her voice light. "But don't worry about it, dear. You're working for me, not him. Anything I do for him is for his own good, so it doesn't matter if he's a little resentful at first."

Carol nodded, a trifle dubiously. Lilly arose from her chair, and began drawing on her gloves.

"We'll just keep this to ourselves for the time being," she said. "It's just possible that Roy will suggest it himself."

"Whatever you say," Carol murmured.

They walked to the door of the cafeteria together. Then Lilly headed toward the lobby entrance, and Carol hurried away toward her patient's room.

The other nurse left as soon as they had checked the chart together. Roy gave Carol a weakly lazy grin, and told her that she looked very bad.

"You belong in bed, Miss Roberg," he said. "I'll give you part of mine."

"I do *not*!" Carol blushed furiously. "You will *not*!"

"Oh, but you do. I've seen girls with that look before. Bed is the only thing that will cure 'em."

Carol giggled unwillingly, feeling very wicked. Roy told her severely that she mustn't laugh about such things. "You'd better behave or I won't kiss you goodnight. Then, you'll be sorry!"

"I will *not*!" Carol blushed and wriggled and giggled. "Now, you *stop* it!"

Roy stopped the teasing after a minute or two. She was honestly embarrassed by it, he guessed, and he wasn't up to much fun-making himself.

Suspended from a metal stand on the left side of his bed was a jar of syrupy-looking blood. A tube extended from the upended top of it to a quill-like needle in his arm. On the right side of the bed, a similar device dripped saline water into the artery of his other arm. The blood and water had been fed into him thus since his arrival in the hospital. Lying constantly on his back with his arms held flat, he ached almost incessantly, his only relief coming when his body and arms became numb. Sometimes he found himself wondering if life was worth such a price. But the wondering was humorous, strictly on the wry side.

He'd had a long look at death, and he hadn't liked the look of it at all.

He was very, very glad to be alive.

Now that he was apparently out of danger, however, he did regret one thing—that it was Lilly who had saved his life. The one person to whom he wished to owe nothing, he now owed everything, a debt he could never repay.

He could fret and argue the matter in his mind. He could cite his own incredibly tough constitution, an irresistible will to live, as the true source of his survival. The doctors themselves had practically said as much, hadn't they? It was scientifically impossible, they'd said, for a man to live when his blood pressure and hemoglobin fell below a certain level. Yet his had been well below that level *when* he arrived at the hospital. Unassisted, he had been clinging to life on his own *before* anything had been done for him. So . . .

So nothing. He'd needed help fast, and Lilly had got it for him. Moira hadn't seen his need, he hadn't, no one had but Lilly. And just where, for that matter, had he got the mental and physical toughness to hold on until he had medical help? From strangers? Huh-uh.

Any way you looked at it, he owed his life to Lilly. And Lilly, unconsciously or deliberately, was making sure that he didn't forget it.

In a sweetly feline fashion, she'd put such a frost on Moira Langtry that Moira had stopped coming to the hospital after a couple of visits. She called every day, letting him know that she was concerned about him, but she didn't come back again. And Lilly often managed to be on hand at the time of her calls, practically restricting his end of the conversation to monosyllables.

Lilly obviously intended to break up his affair with Moira. Nor did her intentions end there. She'd selected a day nurse for him who was a real turtle, competent enough but homely as a mud fence. Then, by contrast, she'd picked a little doll for night duty, a kid that was bound to appeal to him even if Lilly hadn't given her a clear field with no competition.

Oh, he could see what was happening. Everywhere he looked, he could see the shadow of Lilly's fine hand. And just what could he do about it, anyway? Tell her to get the hell away and leave him alone? Could he say, "Okay, you saved my life; does that give you any claim on me?"

A doctor came in, not the one who had visited at the hotel—Lilly had dismissed him right at the beginning—but a merry-looking young man. Behind him came an orderly, wheeling a metal-topped cart. Roy looked at the implements on it, and let out a groan.

"Oh, no! Not that thing again!"

"You mean you don't like it?" The doctor laughed. "He's kidding us, isn't he, nurse? He loves to have his stomach pumped."

"Please." Carol frowned reprovingly. "It is not funny."

"Aah, you can't hurt this guy. Rally round now, and we'll get it over with."

The orderly held him on one side, one hand clamping over the intravenous needle. Carol held the needle into the other arm, her free hand poised over a bowl of tiny ice cubes. The doctor picked up a narrow rubber tube and pushed it up into his nose.

"Now, hold still, keedo. Hold still or you'll jerk those needles loose!"

Roy tried to hold still but he couldn't. As the tube went up into his nose and down into his throat, he jerked and struggled. Gagging, gasping for breath, he tried to break free of them. And the doctor cursed him merrily, and Carol pressed little ice lumps between his lips.

"Please to swallow, Mr. Dillon. Swallow the ice and the tube will go down with it."

Roy kept swallowing. At last the tube was down his throat and into his stomach. The doctor made some minor adjustments in it, moving it up and down slightly.

"How's that? Not hitting bottom, is it?"

Roy said he didn't think so. It seemed to be all right.

"Good." The doctor checked the glass receptacle to which the pump was attached. "I'll be back in thirty minutes, nurse. If he gives you any trouble, sock him in the stomach."

Carol nodded oddly. She looked after him, frowning, as he strode out of the room, then came over to the bed and patted away the sweat from Roy's face.

"I am sorry. I hope it does not bother you too much."

"It's all right." He felt a little abashed at the fuss he had made. "I'm just kind of conscious of it, you know."

"I know. The worst part is getting it down, but afterward it is not good. You cannot swallow well and your breathing is ever-so-slightly hampered, and never do you become accustomed to it. Always, there is the consciousness of something wrong."

"You sound like you'd been pumped yourself."

"I have been, many times."

"Internal bleeding?"

"No. I began to bleed after a time, but I was not bleeding to begin with."

"Yes?" he frowned. "I don't get you. Why were you being pumped out if—"

"I don't know." She smiled suddenly and shook her head. "It was a very long time ago. Anyway, it is not pleasant to talk about."

"But—"

"And I think you should not talk so much, either. You will just lie still, please, and do nothing to disturb your stomach contents."

"I don't see how there could be any contents."

"Well, anyway," she said firmly. And he let it go at that.

It was easy to drop the subject. Easy, in his insistent need to survive, to ignore all possible distractions. Years of practice had made it so easy that it was almost automatic.

He lay quietly, watching Carol as she moved about the room, seeing her youthful freshness as a refreshing relief from Moira. A very nice little kid, he thought, just about as nice as they came. So doubtless she must be left that way. On the other hand, wouldn't it be a little strange if a girl as attractive as she was had remained strictly on the nice side? Weren't the odds all against it? And if she did know the score . . .

Well, it was something to think about. Certainly, it would be a pleasant way of putting Lilly in her place.

The doctor returned. He checked the glass container of the pump, and chortled happily. "Nothing but bile. That's what he's full of, nurse, as if you didn't know."

He removed the stomach tube. Then, wonder of wonders, he ordered the intravenous needles removed from Roy's arms. "Why not? Why should we baby a goldbrick like you?"

"Oh, go to hell." Roy grinned at him, flexing his arms luxuriously. "Just let me stretch."

"Sassy, hmm. How about something to eat?"

"You mean that liquid chalk you call milk? Bring it on, brother."

"Nope. Tonight you get steak, mashed potatoes, the works. You can even have a couple of cigarettes."

"You're kidding."

The doctor shook his head, became serious. "You haven't bled any in three days. It's time your stomach resumed peristalsis, started toughening itself up, and it can't do it on liquids."

Roy was just a little uneasy. After all, it was *his* stomach. The doctor assured him that he had nothing to worry about.

"If your stomach won't take it, we'll just have to open you up and cut out a piece. No trouble at all."

He walked out, whistling.

Again, Carol looked after him, frowning. "That man! Ooh, I would like to shake him good!"

"You think it will be all right?" Roy asked. "To have solid food, I mean, I'm not particularly hungry, and—"

"Of course, it will be all right! Otherwise, you would not be allowed to have it."

She took one of his hands in hers, looked down at him so protectively that he wanted to smile. He restrained the impulse, clinging to her hand while he gently urged her into the chair at his side.

"You're a good little girl," he said softly. "I've never known anyone like you."

"T-thank you . . ." Her eyes fell, and her voice dropped to a whisper. "I have known no one like you either."

He lay studying her in the gathering twilight of the room, examining the small honest face with its tenderly upturning features; thinking how much she looked like some gravely innocent child. Then he turned on his side, and eased over near the edge of the bed.

"I'm going to miss you, Carol. Will I see you after I leave here?"

"I—I do not know." She was breathing heavily, still not looking at him. "I—I would like to, b-but I must work whenever I can, whenever I am c-called and—"

"Carol?"

"Y-yes."

"Come here."

He drew her forward by the hand, his free hand dropping around her shoulders. She looked up at last, eyes frightened, hanging back desperately. And then, suddenly, she was in his arms, her face pressed against his.

"Like me, Carol?"

"Oh, yes!" Her head jerked in assent. "So, so much! B-but—"

"Listen," he said. And then as she listened, waiting, he was silent. Putting on the brakes. Telling himself that this was as far as it should go.

But *was* it? He would need looking after for a while, wouldn't he? Lilly had hinted at something of the kind, suggesting that he stay in her apartment for a week or so. He'd been against it, of course, first because it was her suggestion, and secondly because it seemed pointless. With her away at the tracks so much, he'd still be on his own. But . . .

Carol shivered against him delicately. He started to shove her away; and, unwillingly, his arms tightened around her.

"I was just thinking," he said. "I'll still be a little rocky after I leave here. Maybe—"

"Yes?" She raised her head, smiled down at him excitedly. "You would want me to tend you for a while, yes? That is it?"

"You'd like that?"

"Yes! Oh, my, yes!"

"Well," he said, awkwardly. "We'll think about it. See what my mother has to say. I live in a hotel myself, so I'd have to stay at her place. And—"

"And it will be all right!" Her eyes were dancing. "I know."

"How do you mean?"

"I mean, it is what your mother wants! I—we were not going to say anything about it yet. She was not sure how you would feel, and—and—"

Her voice died away under his flat-eyed stare. Quick anxiety tugged at the tipped-up corners of her mouth.

"Please. T-there is something wrong?"

"Not a thing," he said. "No, sir, everything's just fine."

EIGHT

The fourth race was over. The trackside crowds surged back through the areaway which passed beneath the grandstand, and led into the vaulted arena of bars, lunch-rooms, and pari-mutuel windows. Some of them were hurrying, smiling broadly, or wearing smug, tight-lipped grins. They headed toward pay-off windows. Others, the majority, came more slowly, scanning their racing programs, tip sheets, and forms; their faces indifferent, desperate, angry, or sullen. These were the losers, and some of them went on through the exits to the parking lot, and some stopped at the bars, and most of them moved toward the bet windows.

It was still early in the day. There were still a lot of full pockets. The crowd would not shake out much before the end of the sixth race.

Lilly Dillon collected three bets at as many windows. Putting the money to one side in her purse—for it would have to be accounted for—she hurried toward the bet windows. Her betting money, the playback dough that came by wire each day, was already separated into sheafs of twenties, fifties and hundreds. She used the twenties as much as her limited time would allow, usually five and ten at a time. With the fifties she was more cautious; the hundreds were disposed of with downright stinginess.

Possibly, rather probably, much of her caution was wasted. The treasury agents had no interest in the betting; they were normally on the lookout only for wins, the cashing in of fistfuls of fifty and hundred-dollar tickets. And Lilly was not there to win, and seldom did. Her activities were largely precautionary, not usually concerned with favorites or semi-favorites. The odds on such horses pretty much took care of themselves. She dealt mainly in "likely" runners and long-shots, and they rarely wound up in the money. When they did, she collected on them only when it seemed absolutely safe. If it didn't, she simply let the winnings go, keeping the pari-mutuel tickets as a matter of record.

To an extent, she was a free agent. She had certain general instructions, but within them she was allowed and expected to use her own judgment. That didn't make things any easier for her, of course. On the contrary. It was a hard job, and she was well paid for it. And there were ways of adding to that pay.

Ways which Bobo Justus frowned upon, but which were very difficult to detect.

She strolled off toward one of the bars, her eyes shrewdly watchful behind the dark sunglasses. Several times she stopped quickly and picked up a discarded ticket, adding them to the ones in her purse. Losing tickets were usually thrown away. As long as they weren't torn or suspiciously trampled, she could count them as money spent.

A certain number of them, anyway. It wasn't something you could lean on too hard. She'd only gone overboard once at this meet, and that had been a mistake. Rather, she'd done it to cover a mistake.

It had happened almost three weeks ago, right after Roy had gone into the hospital. Perhaps that was how it had come about, she'd had her mind on him instead of her job. But, anyway, a real dog had come in at a hundred-and-forty for two. And she didn't have a dime down on him.

She'd been too frightened and worried to sleep that night. She'd been even more frightened the next day when the papers hinted at heavy off-track betting on the nag. As an expensive but necessary precaution, she'd sent five thousand dollars of her own money back to Baltimore—her pretended winnings on the horse. And apparently that had taken the heat off her, for she'd had no word from Bobo. But days passed before she was resting easy.

For a while, she was even carrying a gun when she went to the bathroom.

She stood at the bar, sipping a rum and cola, looking at the milling crowd with something approaching disgust. Where did they come from? she thought wearily. Why did they buck a stupid racket like this? Many of them were downright shabby. Some of them even had children with them.

Mothers with kids... Men in cheap sport-shirts and baggy slacks... Grandmothers with cigarettes dangling from their mouths.

Gaah! It was enough to turn a person's stomach.

She turned away from them, shifting wearily from foot to foot. She was wearing a sports outfit; a simple but expensive ensemble of fawn-colored slacks, blouse, and jacket, with flat-heeled buckskin Oxfords.

Everything was cool and lightweight, the most comfortable things she could put on. But nothing could compensate for her hours of standing.

As the fifth and sixth races dragged by, as she moved back and forth from the betting and pay-off windows, the struggle between her growing tiredness and the never-ending need to be alert almost reached a stalemate. It was hard to think of anything but sitting down, of resting for at least a few minutes. It was impossible to think about it. Need and necessity fought with one another, pulling her this way and that, tugging her forward and holding her back; adding unbearably to the burden she already carried.

There were seats in the grandstand, of course, but those were for yokels. By the time she got into the stands, she would be due at the windows. The effort of going back and forth would take more from her than it gave. As for the clubhouse, with its comfortable chairs and pleasant cocktail lounge, well, naturally, that was out. There was too much money floating around, too much heavy betting. The treasury boys loved the place.

She set down her cup of coffee—her third in the last hour—and trudged away toward the mutuel windows. The seventh race, the next to the last, was coming up. It always drew some of the day's heaviest play, and the yokels were rushing to buy tickets. As Lilly pushed her way through them, a sardonic thought suddenly struck her. And despite her weariness, she almost laughed out loud.

Now, isn't this something? she thought. *Twenty-five years getting out of the mob, and I'm right back in it. Hell, I've never even been away!*

She collected a couple of bets on the seventh, disposing of the money as she hurried toward the parking lot. There was nothing in the last race that couldn't be missed. By beating it out now, before the crowd swarmed down from the stands, she could avoid the last-minute traffic jam.

Her car was parked back near the gate, in a space as near to it as a big tip would buy. A convertible, it was a very good car but by no means the most expensive. Not even faintly flashy. Its one distinctive feature was something that couldn't be seen. A secret trunk compartment containing one hundred and thirty thousand dollars in cash.

As she approached the car now and saw the man standing beside it, Lilly wondered whether she'd ever live to spend the money.

NINE

Bobo Justus had wavy, iron-gray hair and a deeply-tanned, chiseled-looking face. He was a small man, short that is, but he had the head and torso of a six-footer. Knowing his sensitivity about his height, Lilly was grateful for her flat-heeled shoes. That was one thing in her favor at least. But she doubted that it would count for much, judging by his expression.

He addressed her tonelessly, his lips barely moving.

"You goddamned silly-looking pig! Driving a god-damned circus wagon! Why don't you paint a bull's-eye on it? Hang a couple of cowbells on the bumper?"

"Now, Bo. Convertibles are quite common in California."

"Convertibles are quite common in California," he mimicked her, weaving his shoulders prissily. "Are they as common as two-timing, double-crossing whores? Hah? Are they, you sneaky little slut?"

"Bo—" she looked around quickly. "Hadn't we better go some place private?"

He drew back a hand as though to slap her, then gave her a shove toward the car. "Get with it," he said. "The Beverly Hills. I get you alone, and I'm going to pop every pimple on your pretty pink butt!"

She started the car and drove out through the gate. As they joined the stream of town-bound traffic, he resumed his tight-lipped abuse.

Lilly listened attentively, trying to decide whether he was building up steam or letting it off. Probably the last, she guessed, since it had been almost three weeks since her blunder. Murderously angry, he probably would have taken action before this.

Most of the time she was silent, making no response except when it was asked for or seemed urgently indicated.

". . . told you to watch that fifth race, didn't I? And, by God, you really watched it, didn't you? I bet you stood there grinning clear to your ankles while the dog comes in at a hundred-and-forty per!"

"Bo, I—"

"How much did your pals cut you in for, huh? Or did they give you the same kind of screwing you gave me? What the hell are you, anyway—a stud-horse with tits?"

"I was down on the nag," Lilly said quietly. "You know I was, Bo. After all, you wouldn't have wanted me to bet it off the board."

"You were down on it, huh? Now, I'll ask you just one question. Do you want to stick to that story, or do you want to keep your teeth?"

"I want to keep my teeth."

"Now, I'll ask you one more question. Do you think I got no contacts out here? You think I couldn't get a report on the play on that horse?"

"No, I don't think that. I'm sure you could, Bo."

"That nag paid off at just the opening price. There wasn't hardly a flutter on the tote board from the time the odds were posted." He lit a cigarette, took a couple of quick angry puffs. "What kind of crap you handing me anyway, Lilly? There ain't enough action to tickle the tote, but you claim a five-grand win! Now, how about it, huh? You ready to fly straight or not?"

She drew in a deep breath. Hesitated. Nodded. There was only one thing to do now, to tell the truth and hope for the best.

She did so. Justus sat turned in the seat; studying, analyzing her expression throughout the recital. When she had finished, he faced back around again, sat in dead-pan silence for several minutes.

"So you were just stupid," he said. "Asleep at the switch. You think I'm going to buy that?"

Lilly nodded evenly. He'd already bought it, she said, three weeks ago; suspected the truth before he was told. "You know you did, Bo. If you hadn't, I'd be dead by now."

"Maybe you will be yet, sister! Maybe you'll wish you was dead."

"Maybe."

"I laid out better than a hundred yards for a screwing. Just about the highest-priced piece of tail in history. I figure on getting what I paid for."

"Then you'd better do some more figuring," Lilly said. "I'm not that kind of punching bag."

"Real sure about that, are you?"

"Positive. Give me a cigarette, please."

He took a cigarette from his package, and tossed it across the seat. She picked it up, and tossed it back to him.

"Light it please, Bo? I need both hands in this traffic."

She heard a sound, something between a laugh and a snort, anger and admiration. Then, he lit the cigarette and placed it between her lips.

As they rode on, she could sense the looks he slanted at her, almost see the workings of his mind. She was a problem to him. A very special and valued employee, one whom he actually liked, had yet erred badly. It was unintentional, her one serious mistake in more than twenty years of faithful service. So there was strong argument for forgiveness. On the other hand, he was showing unusual forbearance in allowing her to live, and more hardly seemed to be indicated.

Obviously, there was much to be said for both sides of the debate. Having forgiven so much, he could forgive completely. Or having forgiven so much, he need forgive no more.

They were almost at the hotel before he reached his decision.

"I got a lot of people working for me, Lilly. I can't have things like this happening."

"It never happened before, Bo." She fought to keep her voice level, free of any hint of begging. "It won't happen again."

"It happened once," he said. "With me, that's practically making a habit of it."

"All right," she said. "You're calling the shots."

"You got any kind of long coat in the car? Anything you can wear home over your clothes?"

"No." A dull ache came into her stomach.

He hesitated, then said it didn't matter. He'd lend her his raincoat. "Ought to be right in style out here. God-damnedest sloppiest-looking women I ever seen."

She stopped the car at the hotel entrance, and an attendant took charge of it. Bobo handed her out to the steps, then courteously gave her his arm as they entered the building. They crossed the lobby, Bobo holding himself very erect, and entered the elevator.

He had a suite on the fourth floor. Unlocking the door, he motioned for her to precede him. She did so, letting her body go limp, preparing herself for what she knew was coming. But you could never prepare for a thing like that—not fully. The sudden shove-blow sent her hurtling into the room, stumbling and tripping over her own feet. And finally landing in a skidding sprawl on the floor.

As she slowly picked herself up, he locked the door, drew the shades, and entered the bathroom, emerging immediately with a large towel. Crossing to the sideboard, he took a number of oranges from a bowl of fruit, dropped them into the towel and pulled up its ends to form a bag. He came toward her, swinging it loosely. Again, Lilly tried to brace herself with limpness.

She knew *the oranges*. She knew all such gimmicks, though never before had she been the victim of any. The oranges was an item from the dummy-chuckers" workbag, a frammis of the professional accident fakers.

Beaten with the fruit, a person sustained bruises far out of proportion to his actual injuries. He looked badly hurt when he was hardly hurt at all.

But he could be hurt. If he was hit hard enough and in certain areas of his body. Without feeling much pain at the time, he could have his internal organs smashed. Used in just the right way (or the wrong way), the oranges produced much the same effect as an enema or douche of plaster-of-Paris.

Bobo drew closer. He stopped in front of her. He moved to one side and a little behind her.

He gripped the towel with both hands. And swung.

And let the oranges spill harmlessly to the floor.

He gestured.

She bent to pick up the fruit. And then again she was sprawling. And his knees were in her back and his hand was against her head. And she was pinned, spreadeagled, against the carpet.

A couple passed in the hallway, laughing and talking. A couple from another planet. From the dining room—from another world—came the faint sound of music.

There was a click of a cigarette lighter, the smell of smoke. Then, the smell of burning flesh as he held the glowing coal against the back of her right hand. He held it with measured firmness, just enough to keep it burning without crushing it out.

His knees worked with expert cruelty.

The cigarette burned into her hand, and his knees probed the sensitive nerves of her spine.

It was a timeless world, an endless hell. There was no escape from it. There was no relief in it. She couldn't cry out. It was impossible even to squirm. The world was at once to be endured and unendurable. And the one possible relief was within her own small body.

Scalding urine spurted from her loins. It seemed to pour from her in a flood.

And Bobo stood up, releasing her, and she got up and went into the bathroom.

She held her hand under the ice-water tap, then patted it with a towel and examined it. The burn was ugly, but it didn't appear to be serious. None of the large veins were affected. She lowered her slacks and swabbed herself with a slightly moistened towel. That was about as much as could be done here. The raincoat would cover up her stained clothes.

She left the bathroom, crossed the lounge where Bobo was seated, and accepted the drink he gave her. He took out his wallet, and extended a thick sheaf of new bills.

"Your five grand, Lilly. I almost forgot."

"Thanks, Bo."

"How you making out these days, anyway? Stealing much from me?"

"Not much. My folks didn't raise any stupid kids," Lilly said. "I just clip a buck here and a buck there. It mounts up, but nobody gets hurt."

"That's right," Justus nodded approvingly. "Take a little, leave a little."

"I look on it this way," Lilly said, shrewdly enunciating his own philosophy. "A person that don't look out for himself is too dumb to look out for anyone else. He's a liability, right, Bo?"

"Absolutely! You're a thousand per cent right, Lil!"

"Or else he's working an angle. If he doesn't steal a little, he's stealing big."

"Right!"

"I like that suit, Bo. I don't know what there is about it, but somehow it makes you look so much taller."

"Yeah?" He beamed at her. "You really think so? You know a lot of people been telling me the same thing."

Their amiable talk continued as twilight slid into the room. And Lilly's hand ached, and the wet clothes burned and chafed her flesh.

She had to leave him feeling good about her. She had to make sure that the score between them was settled, and that he was actually letting her off so lightly.

They discussed several business matters she had handled for him in Detroit and the Twin Cities on her circuitous way to the coast. Bobo revealed that he was only in town for the day. Tomorrow he was heading back east via Vegas, Galveston, and Miami.

"Another drink, Lilly?"

"Well, just a short one. I've got to be running along pretty soon."

"What's the hurry? I thought maybe we could have dinner together."

"I'd like to, but . . ."

But it was best not to stay, best to quit while she was ahead. She'd been very, very lucky apparently, but luck could run out on you.

"I've got a son living here, Bo. A salesman. I don't get to see him very often, so . . ."

"Well, sure, sure," he nodded. "How's he making out?"

"He's in the hospital. Some kind of stomach trouble. I usually visit him every night."

"Sure, naturally," he frowned. "Gettin' everything he needs? Anything I can do?"

Lilly thanked him, shaking her head. "He's doing fine. I think he'll be getting out in a day or two."

"Well, you'd better run along," Bobo said. "A boy's sick, he wants his mother."

She got the raincoat out of the closet, and belted it around her. They said good night, and she left.

A little urine had trickled down her legs, making them itch and sting, and leaving an unpleasant sogginess in her shoes. Her underpants chafed and stung, and the seat of the slacks seemed to have soaked through. The ache in her right hand grew, spread slowly up into her wrist and arm.

She hoped she hadn't soiled Bobo's lounge. She'd been very lucky, considering the amount her blunder must have cost him, but a little thing like that might spoil it.

She picked up her car, and drove away from the hotel.

As she entered her apartment, she kicked out of her shoes, began flinging her clothes from her; leaving them in a trail behind her as she hurried toward the bathroom. She closed the door. Kneeling, she went down in front of the toilet as though it were an altar, and a great sob shook her body.

Weeping hysterically, laughing and crying, she began to vomit.

Lucky . . .

Got off easy . . .

Boy, am I lucky!

TEN

At a few minutes before noon, Moira Langtry came out of the arched door of the hospital and crossed the street to the parking lot. She'd risen unusually early that day in order to turn herself out with extra care, and the result was all that she could have hoped for. She was a brunette dream, a fragrant sultry-eyed vision of loveliness. The nurses had looked after her enviously as she tripped down the corridor. The doctors and interns had almost drooled, their eyes lingering on the delicate shivering of her breasts and the sensual swing of her rounded little hips.

Women almost always disliked Moira. She was glad that they did, taking it as a compliment and returning their dislike. Men, of course, were invariably drawn to her, a reaction which she expected and cultivated but was emotionally cold to. Very rarely did they appeal to her. Roy Dillon was one of the rare ones who did. In her own way, she had been faithful to him during the three years of their acquaintance.

Roy was fun. Roy stirred her. Man-wise, he was the luxury which she had clutched to herself no more than a half-dozen times in her life. Six men out of the hundreds who had had her body.

If she could put him to practical use, fine. She hoped and believed she could do just that. If not, she still wanted him, and she did not intend to have him taken from her. It wasn't, of course, that she absolutely couldn't do without him; women who got that way over a man were strictly for the movies. But she simply couldn't afford such a loss, its clear threat to her security.

When things reached the point where she couldn't hold a man, then she was finished. She might as well do a high brodie out of the nearest window.

So today she had risen early, knocking herself out to be a knockout. Thinking that by arriving at the hospital at an off-hour, she could see Roy alone for a change and tease his appetite for what he had been missing. It was highly necessary, she felt. Particularly with his mother working against her, and throwing that cute little nurse at him.

And today, after all the trouble she'd gone to, his damned snotty mother was there. It was almost as though Mrs. Dillon had read her mind, intuitively suspecting her visit to the hospital and busting her goddamned pants to be there at the same time.

Smoldering, Moira reached the parking lot. The pimply-faced attendant hastened to open the door of her car, and as she climbed into it, she rewarded him with a look at her legs.

She drove off the lot, breathing heavily, wishing that she could get Lilly Dillon alone in a good dark alley. The more she thought about her recent visit the angrier she became.

That's what you got for trying to be nice to people! You tried to be nice to 'em and they made you look like a fool!

"Please don't tell me that I can't really be Roy's mother, Mrs. Langtry. I'm rather tired of hearing it."

"Sorry! I didn't mean it, of course. You're about fifty, Mrs. Dillon?"

"Just about, dear. Just about your own age."

"I think I'd better leave!"

"I can give you a lift, if you like. It's only a Chrysler convertible, but it probably beats riding a bus."

"Thanks! I have my bicycle with me."

"Lilly. Mrs. Langtry drives a Cadillac."

"Not really! But don't you think they're rather common, Mrs. Langtry? I know they're a very good car, but it seems like every overdressed hustler you see these days is driving a Cadillac."

Moira's hands tightened on the wheel of the car.

She told herself that she could cheerfully kill Mrs. Dillon. She could strangle her with her bare hands.

At her apartment house, she turned the Cadillac over to the doorman, and went on through the lobby to the grill and cocktail lounge.

It was well into the noon-hour now. Many of the tables were occupied and waiters in smart white pea jackets were hurrying in and out of the kitchen with trays of delicately smelling food. One of them brought Moira an outsize menu. She studied it, hesitating over the filet mignon sandwich with stuffed mushrooms (6.75).

She was hungry. Breakfast had consisted of her usual unsweetened grapefruit and black coffee. But she needed a drink more than she needed food; two or three strong, reassuring drinks. And she could allow herself only so many calories a day.

Closing the menu, she handed it back to the waiter. "Just a drink now, Allen," she smiled. "I'll eat later on."

"Certainly, Mrs. Langtry. A martini, perhaps? Gibson?"

"Mmm, no. Something with a little more character, I believe. A sidecar, say, with bourbon instead of brandy. And, Allen, no Triple Sec, please."

"Emphatically!" The waiter wrote on his pad. "We always use Cointreau in a sidecar. Now, would you like the rim of the glass sugared or plain?"

"Plain. About an ounce and a half of bourbon to an ounce of Cointreau, and a twist of lime peel instead of lemon."

"Right away, Mrs. Langtry."

"And, Allen . . ."

"Yes, Mrs. Langtry?"

"I want that served in a champagne glass. A thoroughly chilled glass, please."

"Certainly."

Moira watched him as he hurried away, her carefully composed features concealing an incipient snicker. Now, wasn't that something, she thought. No wonder the world was going to hell when a grown man pranced around in a monkey suit, brown-nosing dames who made a big deal out of ordering a belt of booze! Where had it all started? she wondered. Where the beginning of this detour which had sidetracked civilization into mixing drinks with one hand and stirring up bombs with the other?

She thought about it, not thinking in those words, of course. Simply feeling that the times were out of joint with themselves, and that the most emphasis was put on the least-worthwhile pursuits.

What it all boiled down to really was everybody giving everybody else a hard time for no good reason whatever. And the hell of it was that there seemed to be no way of getting on the right track. You couldn't be yourself any more. If a woman ordered a straight double-shot with a beer chaser in a place like this, they'd probably throw her out. Ditto, if she asked for a hamburger with raw onions.

You just couldn't march to your own music. Nowadays, you couldn't even hear it . . . She could no longer hear it. It was lost, the music which each person had inside himself, and which put him in step with things as they should be. Lost along with the big, bluff man, the joking introspective man, who had taught her how to listen for it.

Cole Langley (Lindsey, Lonsdale). Cole "The Farmer" Langley.

Her drink came, and she took a quick sip of it. Then, with a touch of desperation, she half-emptied the glass. That helped. She could think of Cole without wanting to break up.

She and The Farmer had lived together for ten years, ten of the most wonderful years of her life. It had been a kind of camping-out living, the kind that most people would turn up their noses at, but it was that way by choice not necessity. With Cole, it seemed the only possible way to live.

They always traveled by chair-car in those days. They wore whatever they felt like wearing, usually overalls or khakis for him and gingham for her. When it was possible to obtain, Cole would have a two-quart jar of corn whiskey in a paper sack. Instead of eating in diners, they carried a huge lunch wrapped in newspapers. And every time the train stopped Cole would hop off and buy gobs of candy and cold drinks and cookies and everything else he could lay hands on.

They couldn't begin to eat so much themselves, naturally. Cole gloried in abundance, but he was a rather finicky eater and a very light drinker. The food and the booze were to pass around, and the way he did it no one ever refused. He knew just the right thing to say to each person—a line of scripture, a quote from Shakespeare, a homely joke. Before they'd been in the car an hour, everyone was eating and drinking and warming up to everyone else. And Cole would be beaming on them as though they were a bunch of kids and he was a doting father.

Women didn't hate her in those days.

Men didn't look at her the way they did now.

Friendliness, the ability to make friends, was The Farmer's stock in trade, of course. Something eventually to be cashed in on through small-town banks via a series of simple-seeming but bewildering maneuvers. But he insisted on regarding the payoffs as no more than a fair exchange. For mere money, a thing useless and meaningful in itself, he traded great hopes and a new perspective on life. And nothing was ever managed so that the frammis would show through for what it was. Always the people were left with hope and belief.

What more could they want, anyway? What could be more important in life than having something to hope for and something to believe in?

For more than a year, they lived on a rundown farm in Missouri, a rocky clay-soiled sixty acres with a completely unmodernized house and an outdoor privy. That was their best time together.

It was a two-hole privy, and sometimes they'd sit together in it for hours. Peering out at the occasional passers-by on the rutted red-clay road. Watching the birds hop about in the yard. Talking quietly or reading from the stack of old newspapers and magazines that cluttered one corner of the building.

"Now, look at this, Moira," he would say, pointing to an advertisement. "While the price of steak has gone up twenty-three cents in the pound in the last decade, the price of coal has only advanced one and one-half cents per pound. It looks like the coal dealers are giving us quite a break, doesn't it?"

"Well . . ." She didn't always know how to respond to him; whether he was just making an idle comment or telling her something.

"Or maybe they aren't, either," he'd say, "when you consider that meat is normally sold by the pound and coal by the ton."

Now and then, she'd come up with just the right answer, like the time he'd pointed out that "four out of five doctors" took aspirin, and what did she think about that, anyway?

"I'd say the fifth doctor was a lucky guy," she said. "He's the only one who doesn't have headaches." And Cole had been very pleased with her.

They got a lot of fun out of the advertisements. For years afterward, she would look at some nominally straightforward pronouncement and break into laughter.

Beware the wiry zone . . . Are germs lurking in your nooks and crannies? . . . You, too, can learn to dance!

Even now she laughed over them. But wryly, with sardonic bitterness. Not as she and Cole Langley had laughed.

One day, when he was trying to dig down to the bottom of the magazine pile, it toppled over, uncovering a small box-like structure with a hole cut in the top. A kid's toilet.

Moira had made some comment about its being cute. But Cole went on staring at it, the laughter dying in his eyes, his mouth loosening sickishly. Then he turned and whispered to her:

"I'll bet they killed the kid. I'll bet it's buried down there under us . . ."

She was stunned, speechless. She sat staring at him, unable to move or speak, and Cole seemed to take her silence for agreement. He went on talking, low-voiced, even more impellingly persuasive than he normally was. And after a time, there was no reality but the hideousness he created, and she found herself nodding to what he said.

No, no child should be allowed to live. Yes, all children should be killed at birth or as soon afterward as possible. It was the kindest thing to do. It was the only way to spare them the futile torment, the frustrating and senseless torture, the paradoxically evil mess which represented life on the planet Earth.

Subconsciously, she knew she was seeing him for the first time, and that the laughing, gregarious Cole was only a shadow fleeing its owner's convictions. Subconsciously, she wanted to scream that he was wrong, that there were no absolutes of any kind, and that the real man might well be fleeing the shadow.

But she lacked the vocabulary for such thoughts, the mentality to string them together. They wandered about in her subconscious, unguided and uncohered, while Cole, as always, was utterly convincing. So, in the end, she had been persuaded. She agreed with everything he said.

And suddenly he had started cursing her. So she was a faker, too! A stinking hypocrite! She could do nothing for herself and nothing for anyone else because she believed in nothing.

From that day on The Farmer was on the toboggan. They jumped from the sticks to St. Louis, and when he wasn't dead drunk he was shooting himself full of hop. They had a hefty hunk of loot—rather Moira had it. Secretly, in the way of many wives—although she was not legally his wife—she had been rat-holing money for years. But the substantial sum she had cached wouldn't last a month at the rate he was going, so, as she saw it, there was only one thing to do. She took up hustling.

There was no stigma attached to it in their professional circle. In fact, it was an accepted practice for a woman to prostitute herself when her man was low on his back. But whores *per se* were a dime a dozen and only girls with "class," the expensively turned-out dames, could pull down the big money. And Cole was infuriated by a classy Moira.

He grew fanatical in his charges that she was a hypocrite and "unbeliever," shouting down her pleas that she wished only to help him. Wildly, he declared that she was a whore at heart, that she had always been a whore, that she had been one when he met her.

That was not true. In her early working life, as a photographer's model and cocktail waitress, she had occasionally given herself to men and received gifts in return. But it wasn't the same as whoring. She had liked the men involved. What she gave them was given freely, without bargaining, as were their gifts to her.

So Cole's false charges, insensibly made though they were, began to hurt more and more. Perhaps he didn't know what he was saying, or perhaps he did. But even the innocent blow of a child can be painful, possibly more so than that of an adult since its victim cannot bring himself to strike back. His only recourse, when the pain becomes unbearable, is to put himself beyond the child's reach . . .

Moira's last memory of Cole "The Farmer" Langley was that of a wildly weeping man in overalls, shouting "Whore!" from the curb in front of their swank apartment house as a grinning cab-driver drove her away.

She wanted to leave the rat-holed money for him. Or half of it, at least. But she knew it was useless. It would either be stolen from him, or he would throw it away. He was beyond help—her help, in any event—and anything she might do would only prolong his agony.

What had happened to him, she didn't know. Deliberately, she had tried to avoid knowing. But she hoped that he was dead. It was the best she could hope for the man she had loved so much.

ELEVEN

Moira took a long sip of her third bourbon sidecar. Feeling just a little skittish (she had a horror of actual drunkenness), she grinned at the man who was approaching her table.

His name was Grable, Charles Grable, and he was the manager of the apartment house. Dressed in striped trousers and a black broadcloth morning coat, he had rather close-set eyes and a plump, peevish-looking face. His attempt to look stern, as he sat down, gave his small mouth a baby-like pout.

"Don't tell me, now," Moira said, solemnly. "You're Addison Simms of Seattle, and we had lunch together in the fall of 1902."

"What? What are you talking about?" Grable snapped. "Now, you listen to me, Moira! I—"

"How is your wiry zone?" Moira asked. "Are hidden germs lurking in your nooks and crannies?"

"Moira!" He leaned forward angrily, dropping his voice. "I'm telling you for the last time, Moira. I want your bill settled today! Every last penny of it, your rent and all the other charges you've run up! You either pay it, or I'm locking you out of your apartment!"

"Now, Charles. Don't I always pay my bills? Aren't they always settled . . . one way or another?"

Grable flushed, and looked over his shoulder. A half-pleading, half-whining note came into his voice.

"I can't do that any more, Moira. I simply can't! People staying over their leases, coming in ahead of their lease-dates—paying money that I don't show on the books! I—I—"

"I understand." Moira gave him a sad, sultry look. "You just don't like me any more."

"No, no, that's not it at all! I—"

"You don't either," she pouted. "If you did, you wouldn't act this way."

"I told you I couldn't help it! I—I—" He saw the lurking mockery in her eyes. "All right!" he snarled. "Laugh at me, but you're not making a thief out of me any longer. You're nothing but a cheap little—little—"

"Cheap, Charles? Now, I didn't think I was at all cheap."

"I'm through talking," he said firmly. "Either you settle up by five o'clock tonight or out you go, and I'll hold on to every thing you own!"

He stamped away with a kind of furtive indignation.

Moira shrugged indifferently, and picked up her drink. He's a secret sufferer, she told herself. *Stop getting up nights, men!*

She signaled for her check, penciled on a dollar tip for the waiter. As he nodded gracefully, pulling back her chair, she told him that he, too, could learn to dance.

"All you need is the magic-step," she said. "It's as simple as one-two-three."

He laughed politely. Cloud-nine kidding was old stuff in a place like this. "Like some coffee before you leave, Mrs. Langtry?"

"Thank you, no," Moira smiled. "The drinks were very good, Allen."

She left the lounge, and passed back through the lobby. Recovering her car, she headed toward the downtown business district.

All things considered, she had lived quite economically since her arrival in Los Angeles. Economically, that is, insofar as her own money was concerned. Of the boodle with which she had skipped St. Louis, she still had several thousand dollars, plus, of course, such readily negotiable items as her car, jewelry, and furs. But lately, she had had an increasingly strong hunch that her life here was drawing to a close, and that it was time to cash in wherever and whatever she could.

She hated to leave the city; particularly hated the idea that it would mean giving up Roy Dillon. But it didn't necessarily have to mean that, and if it did, well, it just couldn't be helped. Hunches were to be heeded. You did what you had to do.

Arriving downtown, she parked the car on a privately-operated lot. It was owned by a better-class jewelry store, one which she had patronized both as a buyer and seller, though largely the last. The doorman touched his cap and swung open the plate-glass doors for her, and one of the junior executives came forward, smiling.

"Mrs. Langtry, how nice to see you again! Now, how can we serve you today?"

Moira told him. He nodded gravely, and led her back to a small private office. Closing the door, he seated her at the desk and sat down opposite her.

Moira took a bracelet from her purse, and handed it to him. His eyes widened appreciatively.

"Beautiful," he murmured, reaching for a loupe. "A wonderful piece of workmanship. Now, let's just see . . ."

Moira watched him, as he snapped on a gooseneck lamp, and turned the bracelet in his clean, strong hands. He had waited on her several times before. He wasn't handsome; almost homely, in fact. But she liked him, and she knew that he was strongly attracted to her.

He let the loupe drop from his eye, shook his head with genuine regret.

"I can't understand a thing like this," he said. "It's something you almost never see."

"How . . . what do you mean?" Moira frowned.

"I mean this is some of the finest filigreed platinum I've ever seen. Practically a work of art. But the stones, no. They're not diamonds, Mrs. Langtry. Excellent imitations, but still imitations."

Moira couldn't believe him. Cole had paid four thousand dollars for the bracelet.

"But they must be diamonds! They cut glass!"

"Mrs. Langtry," he smiled wryly, "glass will cut glass. Practically anything will. Let me show you a positive test for diamonds."

He handed her the loupe, and took an eyedropper from his desk. Carefully, he dropped a minuscule amount of water on the stones.

"Do you see how the water splashes over them, slides off in a sheet? With real diamonds it won't do that. It clings to the surface in tiny droplets."

Moira nodded dully, and took the loupe from her eye.

"Do you happen to know where it was purchased, Mrs. Langtry?" I'm sure your money could be recovered."

She didn't know. Quite possibly Cole had bought it as a fake. "It isn't worth anything to you?"

"Why, of course it is," he said warmly. "I can offer you—well, five hundred dollars?"

"Very well, if you'll give me a check, please."

He excused himself, and left for several minutes. He returned with the check, placed it in an envelope for her and sat down again.

"Now," he said, "I hope you're not too badly disappointed with us. You'll give us an opportunity to serve you again, I hope."

Moira hesitated. She glanced at the small sign on his desk. *Mr. Carter.* The store was named Carter's. The owner's son, perhaps?

"I should have told you, Mrs. Langtry. With a valued customer, such as you, we'd be very happy to call at your home. It's not at all necessary for you to come to the store. If there's anything you think we might be interested in . . ."

"I have only one thing, Mr. Carter." Moira looked at him evenly. "*Are* you interested?"

"Well, I'd have to see it, of course. But—"

"You are seeing it, Mr. Carter. You're looking right at it."

He looked puzzled, then startled. Then, his face assumed something of the same expression it had worn when he was examining the bracelet.

"You know something, Mrs. Langtry? A bracelet like the one you sold us, we seldom run across anything like that. A fine setting and workmanship are usually indicative of precious stones. It always hurts me when I find they're not. I always hope"—he raised his eyes—"that I'm mistaken."

Moira smiled, liking him better than ever.

"At this point," she said, "I think I should say ouch."

"Say it for both of us, Mrs. Langtry," he laughed. "This is one of those times when I almost wish I wasn't married. Almost."

They walked to the entrance together, the lovely smartly-dressed woman and the homely, clean-looking young man. As they said goodbye, he held her hand for a moment.

"I hope everything straightens out for you, Mrs. Langtry. I do wish I could have helped."

"Just stay in there and pitch," Moira told him. "You're on the right team."

Very hungry by now, she had coffee and a small salad at a drugstore. Then, she returned to her apartment house.

The manager was on the lookout for her, and he was knocking at her door almost as soon as she had closed it. Curtly, he thrust an itemized bill at her. Moira examined it, her eyebrows raising now and then.

"A lot of money, Charles," she murmured. "You wouldn't have padded it a little, would you?"

"Don't you talk to me that way! You owe every doggone cent of it and you know it, and by golly you're going to pay it!"

"Maybe I could get the dough from your wife, do you suppose, Charlie? Maybe your kiddies would crack their piggy banks?"

"You leave them out of this! You go near my family, and I'll—I'll—" His voice broke into a pleading whine. "Y-you . . . you wouldn't do that would you, Moira?"

Moira gave him a disgusted look. "Oh, don't wet your pants, for God's sake! Mark the damned bill paid, and I'll get you the money."

She turned abruptly and entered her bedroom. Opening her purse, she took out a roll of bills and dropped it on the dressing table. Then, as she undressed swiftly, slipping into a sheer black negligee, her weary frown suddenly broke and she snickered.

Laughing silently, she spread herself out on the bed.

She often broke into such sudden fits of merriment. Faced with some unpleasant facet of the present, she would force her mind away from it, letting it wander vagrantly until it seized upon some ridiculous parallel of paradox. And then, for no apparent reason, she laughed.

Now, the laughter became briefly audible, and Grable called to her suspiciously from the vicinity of the doorway.

"What are you up to, Moira? What are you laughing about?"

"You wouldn't understand, Charlie; just a little item from the luncheon menu. Come on in."

He came in. He looked at her and gulped, then frantically pulled his gaze away.

"I want that m-money, Moira! I want it right now!"

"Well, there it is." The negligee fell open as she waved a bare foot at the dresser. "There's the money, and here's little Moira."

He strode toward the dressing table. Just before he reached it, his step faltered and he turned slowly around.

"Moira, I-I—" He stared at her, gulping again, licking back the sudden saliva from the corners of his babyish mouth. And this time he could not pull his eyes away.

Moira looked down at herself, following the course of his gaze.

"The automatic clutch, Charles," she murmured. "It comes with the de luxe upholstery and the high-speed wiry zone."

He made a little rush toward her. He stopped weakly, a hand held out in wretched appeal.

"P-please, Moira! Please, *please*, I've been good to you! I've let you stay h-here month after month, and . . . You will, won't you? Just—"

Moira said, nope, it couldn't be done. All passengers must pay as they entered, and no free passes or rebates. "That's a strict rule of the Intercourse Commerce Commission, Charles. All common carriers are governed by it."

"Please! You got to! *You j-just got to!*" Almost sobbing, he sagged down on his knees at the side of the bed. "Oh, God, God, God! D-don't make me—"

"Only one choice to a customer," Moira said firmly. "The lady or the loot. So what's it going to be?" And then, as he abruptly flung himself at her, "As if I didn't know . . ."

She lay looking up past his shoulder, trying to blot out his panting, thrusting presence. Forcing her mind away from him and to Roy Dillon.

Their last afternoon at the hotel. Why his sudden hemorrhage, anyway, a young guy with an apparently cast-iron stomach? What had happened to bring it on? Or was it really on the level? Could it be some angle his mother was working to break them up?

She looked like an angle-player! Plenty like one! You could see that she was sharp as a tack and twice as hard—anyone could see it that knew their way around. And she was loaded with dough, and . . .

Moira didn't want to think about her, the snotty little witch! Anything else, but not her! She'd like to *do* something about her, but—

She rolled her eyes at the ceiling. What a character this guy was! What a revolting character! He must be wearing forty dollars' worth of toilet water and hair gook, but it didn't really touch him. It was just sort of wrapped around him, like foil around a chunk of limburger, and when you got down under it—

Ooops! She tightened her lips quickly, her cheeks bulging with repressed merriment. She tried to jerk her mind away from its source, from that darned crazy menu. But it just wouldn't go away, and again she was shaking with laughter.

"Whassa matter?" gasped Grable. "How can you laugh at a—"

"Nothing. N-never mind, Charles. I j-just—ah, ha, ha, ha—I'm s-sorry, but—ahh, ha, ha, ha . . ."

Luncheon Special. Broiled hothouse tomato under generous slice of ripe cheese.

TWELVE

Lilly Dillon's apartment was on the top floor of a Sunset Strip building a few blocks east of the city limits of Beverly Hills. Rented furnished, it consisted of a bedroom, bath, powder room, kitchen, living room, and den. The den was on the rear or south side of the building, and a hospital bed had been put into it for Roy. He lay on it today, in pajamas and bathrobe, its head cranked up so that he could look out over unlimited miles of oil fields, ocean, and beach towns.

He felt lazy and comfortable. He felt restless and guilty. This was the beginning of his third week out of the hospital. He was fully recovered, and there was no valid excuse for his remaining here. And yet he lingered on. Lilly wanted him to. The doctors passively encouraged him to, seeing little to be gained by his protracted convalescence but a broad margin of safety in it.

The ruptured vessels of his stomach *could* open up again, under just the right circumstances. They *could* be re-ruptured. Thus, if he wished to remain completely inactive and beyond reach of the smallest risk, it was quite agreeable with the doctors.

Aside from Lilly and the matter of his health, Roy had another reason for staying on. A guilty reason, and one he tried not to admit to. She, Carol Roberg, was in the kitchen now, cleaning up their luncheon dishes and doubtless preparing a dessert for them. He didn't want any himself—he had gained almost seven pounds in the past two weeks—but he knew that she did. And not for the world would he have interfered.

Carol was very dainty about her eating, as she was about everything. But he had never seen anyone who could stow away so much food as quickly.

He wondered about that, her insatiable appetite, when he was not wondering about her in a different way. Most women he knew seemed hardly to eat anything. Moira for example. . . .

Moira. . . .

He squirmed uneasily as he recalled her visit this morning. He had told her yesterday in a subdued telephone conversation that Lilly was leaving the apartment early today, and suggested that she drop by. So she had come, pulling up startled when she saw Carol, then giving him a quick, questioning look.

Carol sat down in the living room with them. She apparently felt that it was only polite to do so, and she tried to make conversation about the weather and the usual routine topics. When, after what was probably the longest half-hour on record, she had finally excused herself and gone into the kitchen, Moira turned on him, tight-mouthed.

"I tried to send her out," Roy said helplessly. "I told her to take off for a few hours."

"*Tried* to? If it were me, you'd just said to beat it."

"I'm sorry," he said. "I wanted to be alone as much as you did."

He glanced quickly over his shoulder, then went down beside her chair and took her in his arms. She submitted to a kiss, but there was no response to it. He kissed her again, letting his hands rove over her body, probing the soft, sweet-scented curves. After weeks of enforced continence, and the constant temptation which Carol represented, he had never wanted Moira as much as he did at that moment. But abruptly she had pulled away from him.

"Just how much longer do you plan on staying here, Roy?" she asked. "When are you moving back to the hotel?"

"Well, I don't know exactly. Pretty soon, I imagine."

"You're not in much of a hurry, are you? You like it here?"

Roy said awkwardly that he had no complaints. He was being well taken care of—much better than he could be in a hotel—and Lilly was anxious to have him stay.

"Mmm, I'll bet she is, and I'll bet you're darned well taken care of, too!"

"What do you mean?"

"Are you kidding? I've seen the way you looked at that simpering little simp of a nurse! Either you're losing your grip, or you think she's too good to tumble. She is, but I'm not!"

"Oh, for God's sake . . ." He reddened. "Look, I'm sorry about today. If there was any way I could get rid of her without hurting her feelings . . ."

"Naturally, you couldn't do that. Oh, no!"

"Let's just say I wouldn't do it then," he said, tiring of apology.

"Well, forget it." She picked up her gloves, and stood up. "If it suits you, it suits me."

He followed her out into the hallway, trying to smooth over the rift without unbending too far. Liking her, desiring her more than he ever had, yet wary as always of any tightening of her hold upon him.

"I'll be out of here any day, now," he assured her. "I'm probably a hell of a lot more anxious than you are."

"Well . . ." She smiled tentatively, the dark eyes searching his face. "I'm not so sure of that."

"You'll see. Maybe we can go to La Jolla this weekend."

"Just maybe?"

"I'm practically sure of it," he said. "I'll give you a ring, hmm?"

So he had got things straightened out, for a time, at least, and after a fashion. But he had gotten nothing in return, nothing but the status quo, and unsatisfied desire squirmed in him relentlessly. Something was going to have to give, he told himself. With Moira's presence still lingering with him, with Carol so readily accessible . . .

Carol. He wondered just what he should do about her anyway. Or whether he should do anything about her. She looked completely virginal, and if she was, that was that. She'd remain that way, as far as he was concerned. But looks could be deceptive; and sometimes, when she consented to a kiss and she clung to him for a moment, well, he wasn't so sure about her status. Was, in fact, almost positive that he had judged it wrongly.

And in that case, of course . . .

She came in from the kitchen, bearing two cream-topped parfait glasses. He accepted one of them, and she sat down with the other. Smiling, he watched as she dipped into it, wanting to sweep her up in his arms and give her a hearty squeeze.

"Good?" he said.

"Wonderful!" she exclaimed enthusiastically. Then, looking up at him, pinking with self-consciousness. "All the time here, I am eating! You think I am such a pig, yes?"

Roy laughed. "If they made pigs like you, I'd start raising them. How about eating mine, too?"

"But it is yours. More I could not possibly eat!"

"Sure you can," he said, swinging his legs off the bed. "Will you come into the bedroom when you're through?"

"I will come now. You want your rubdown, yes?"

"No, no," he said quickly. "There's no hurry. Finish your ice cream first."

He crossed the deeply carpeted living room and entered the bedroom. Entering the bedroom, he hesitated for a long moment, almost deciding to stop now while he could. Then, swiftly, before he could change his mind, he flung off the robe and his pajama top and stretched out on the bed.

Carol came in a minute or two later. She started to get the alcohol bottle from the bathroom, and he held out his hand to her.

"Come here, Carol. I want to ask you something."

She nodded, and sat down on the edge of the bed. He drew her closer, bringing her face down to his; and, then, as their lips met, he began to draw her prone.

Nervously, her body suddenly stiffening, she tried to pull away. "Oh, no! Please, Roy. I—I—"

"It's all right. I want to ask you something, Carol. Will you tell me the truth?"

"Well"—she tried to muster a smile. "It is so important to you? Or perhaps you are teasing me again, yes?"

"It's very important to me," he said. "Are you a virgin, Carol?"

The smile washed abruptly from her face, and for a moment it was something completely blank. Then, a trace of color came back into it and her eyes fell, and almost imperceptibly she shook her head.

"No, I am not a virgin."

"You're not?" He was vaguely disappointed.

"I am not. Not by many times." Under its surface firmness, her voice shook slightly. "And now you will not like me any more."

"Not like you? Why, of course, I do. I like you more than ever!"

"B-but—" She smiled tremulously, began to glow with a kind of joyous incredulity. "You really mean it? You would not tease about so important a thing?"

"What's so important about it? Now, come on, honey!"

Laughing joyously, she allowed him to pull her down against him; hugged him with laughing wonderment. Oh, my, she said. She was so happy. And then, with no real resistance, bubbling with the happiness he had given her, "But—shouldn't we wait, Roy? You would not like me better?"

"I couldn't like you any better!" He tugged impatiently at her white uniform. "How do you get this damned thing—?"

"But there is something else you must know. You have a right to know. I—I cannot have children, Roy. Never."

That stopped him, made him hesitate, but only for a second. She had an awkward way of phrasing things, twisting them around hindside-to and putting the emphasis in the wrong places. So she couldn't have children and that was all to the good, but he would have taken care of that, anyway.

"Who cares?" he said, almost groaning in his hunger for her. "It's okay and it's okay if you're not a virgin. Now, can't you stop talking, for God's sake, and—"

"Yes! Oh, yes, Roy!" She clung to him in wondrous surrender, guiding his fumbling hands. "Also, I want to. And it is your right . . ."

The uniform fell away from her; the underthings. The innate modesty, the fears, the past. In the drape-drawn dimness of the room, she was reborn, and there was no past but only a future.

The purplish brand still lingered on her outflung left arm, but now it was merely a childhood scar; time dulled, shrunken by growth. It didn't matter. What is memorialized didn't matter—the sterilization, the loss of virginity—for he had said it didn't. So the thing itself was without meaning: the indelible imprint of the Dachau concentration camp.

THIRTEEN

She came out of the bathroom, modestly wearing her underthings now; still flushed and warm and glowing. Primly protective, she drew up the sheet and tucked it over his chest. "I must take care of you," she said. "Now, more than ever, you are most important to me."

Roy grinned at her lazily. She was sweet, a lot of woman, he thought. And about the most honest one he'd ever met. If she hadn't told him that she wasn't virginal . . .

"You are all right, Roy? You do not hurt any place?"

"I never felt better in my life," he laughed. "Not that I haven't been feeling okay."

"That is good. It would be terrible if I had given you hurt."

He repeated that he was feeling fine; she was just what he'd needed. She said seriously that she also had needed him, and he laughed again, winking at her.

"I believe you, honey. How long has it been, anyway, or shouldn't I ask?"

"How long?" She frowned a little, her head tilted in puzzlement. Then, "Oh," she said. "Well, it—it was—"

"Never mind," he said quickly. "Forget it."

"It was there." She extended the tattooed arm. "There also I was made sterile."

"There?" he frowned. "I don't . . . What's that, anyway?"

She explained absently, her smile fixing; the tilted-up eyes looking at him and through him toward something far beyond. Seemingly, she was speaking of the abstract, a dull and tenuous theorem scarcely worthy of recital. Seemingly, she was reading from a fairy tale, a thing so filled with terrors that they clung stagnating to one another; never advancing the plot or theme, physically motionless, merely horror piled upon horror until they sagged slowly downward, drawing the listener with them.

"Yes, yes, that is right." She smiled at him as though at a precocious child. "Yes, I was very young, seven or eight, I think. That was the reason, you see: to discover the earliest possible age at which a female might conceive. It can be very early in life, as young as five, I think.

But an average minimum age was being sought. With my mother and grandmother, it was the other way; I mean, how old could the female be. My grandmother died shortly after the beginning of the experiment, but my mother . . ."

Roy wanted to vomit. He wanted to shake her, to beat her. Standing apart from himself, as she was standing from herself, he was furious with her. Subjectively, his thoughts were not a too-distant parallel of the current popular philosophizing. The things you heard and read and saw everywhere. The pious mourning of sin; the joyous absolution of the sinners; the uncomfortable frowns and glances-askance at those who recalled their misdeeds. After all, the one-time friends, poor fellows, were now our friends and it was bad taste to show gas-stoves on television. After all, you couldn't condemn a people, could you? And what if they had done exactly that themselves? Should you make the same regrettable error? After all, they hated the reds as much as we did, they were as eager as we were to blow every stinking red in the world to hell and gone. And after all, those people, the allegedly sinned-against, had brought most of the trouble on themselves.

It was their own fault.

This was *her* own fault.

"Now, listen to me," he broke in on her angrily. "No, I don't want to hear any more, damnit! If you'd told me about it in the first place instead of just saying that—letting me think that—that—"

"I know," she said. "It was very bad of me. But I too was thinking something else."

"Well, now," he mumbled. "I don't want to put you in the wrong. I like you; I think the world of you, Carol. That's why I asked you what I did, told you it was important to me. I can see now how you might have taken it the wrong way, and I wish to God there was something I could do to square things up. But—"

But why did she keep looking at him that way, smiling that totally vacant smile; waiting for him to fill the vacuum with life? He had said he was sorry, apologized for something that was partially her own fault. But still she sat there waiting. Did she seriously expect him to give up his life, the only way of life acceptable to him, merely to correct a mistake? Well, she had no right to do so! Even if he could give what she had expected and apparently still desired, he would not do it.

She was a nice girl, and it wouldn't be fair to her.

"Now, I'll tell you what," he said, smiling ingratiatingly. "We can't change what's already happened, so why don't we just pretend it didn't happen? How will that be, hmm? Okay? We'll just forget this, and make a brand new start?"

She looked at him silently.

"Fine," Roy said briskly. "That's my sweet girl. Now, I'll skim on out of here, and let you finish dressing and—and, uh . . ."

He left, pulling on his robe as he went out of the room. Returning to the den, he flopped back down on the hospital bed, stared out unseeing at the panorama to the south; still seeing the girl in the bedroom. He'd put things very badly, he guessed. His usual glibness had failed him, just when he needed it most, and he'd sounded peevish and small-time.

What had happened to him? he wondered. What had gone wrong with his pitch?

It had been an honest mistake. She'd suffered no actual loss because of it. Why couldn't he make her understand that? Why, when he could so easily pull a real swindle without a kickback?

You can't cheat an honest man, he thought. And was unreasonably irritated by the thought.

He heard her approaching, the starchy rustle of her uniform. Working up a smile, he sat up and turned around.

She was wearing her coat, a quaintly old-world garment. She was carrying her small nurse's kit.

"I am leaving now," she said. "Is there anything you want before I go?"

"Leaving! But— Oh, now look," he said winningly. "You can't do that, you know. It's not professional. A nurse can't walk out on a patient."

"You do not need a nurse. We both know it. At any rate, I have ceased to be a nurse to you."

"But—but, damnit, Carol—"

She turned away from him, started for the door. He looked after her helplessly for a moment, then caught up with her and pulled her around facing him.

"Now, I'm not going to let you do this," he said. "There's no reason to. You need the job, and my mother and I both want you to have it. Why—"

"Let me go, please." She pulled away from him, again moving toward the door.

Hastily, he placed himself in front of her. "Don't," he begged. "If you're sore with me, okay; maybe you think you've got a right to be. But my mother's involved here. What will she think, I mean, what will I tell her when she comes home and finds you're—"

He broke off, reddening, realizing that he had sounded fearful of Lilly. A ghost of a smile touched Carol's lips.

"Your mother will be disappointed," she said, "but not surprised, I think. I have thought your mother did not understand you, but now I know that she does."

Roy looked away from her. He said curtly that that wasn't what he meant at all. "You've got some money coming to you, your wages. If you'll tell me how much . . ."

"Nothing. Your mother paid me last night."

"All right, then, but there's still today."

"For today, nothing. I gave nothing of value," she said.

Roy let out an angry snort. "Stop acting like a two-year-old kid, will you? You've got some money coming to you, and, by God, you're going to take it!" He snatched the wallet from his robe pocket, jerked out its contents and extended it toward her. "Now, how much? What do I owe you for today?"

She looked down at the money. Carefully, shuffling through it with a finger, she selected three bills and held them up.

"Three dollars, yes? I have heard that was the usual price."

"You seem to know," he snapped. "Aah, Carol, why—"

"Thank you. It is really too much."

She turned, crossed the carpet to the door and went out.

Roy raised his hands helplessly, and let them drop to his sides. That was that. You couldn't square a beef with a stupe.

He went into the kitchen, warmed up some coffee and drank it, standing up. Rinsing out his cup, he glanced at the clock above the stove.

Lilly would be home in a few hours. There was something he must do before she got here. It wouldn't make this Carol thing right with her, and it would mean tipping his hand, but it had to be done. For his own sake.

Dressing and going down to the street, he was just a little rocky.

But not because there was anything wrong with him, only from his long inactivity. By the time he had gotten a taxi and reached his hotel, he felt as strong as he ever had.

He was a little embarrassed by his reception at the hotel. Of course, he'd always worked to make himself likeable; that was an essential part of his front. But he was still warmed and vaguely discomfited at the way he was welcomed home (*home!*) by Simms and the owner's employees. He was glad that he didn't have to chump them; leave them up the creek, paddleless, where people who liked him were customarily left.

Flustered, he accepted their congratulations on his recovery, reassured them as to the present state of his health. He agreed with Simms that sickness came to all men, always inconveniently and unexpectedly, and that that was how the permanent waved.

At last, he escaped to his room.

He took three thousand dollars from one of the clown pictures. Then, having carefully replaced the picture on the wall, he left the hotel and went back to Lilly's apartment.

The place seemed strangely empty without Carol. Hungeringly empty as it always is when a familiar something or someone is no longer where it was. There is a haunting sense of wrongness, of things amiss. Here is a niche crying to be filled, and the one thing that will fill it will not.

Roaming restlessly from room to room, he kept listening for her, kept seeing her in his mind's eye. He could see her everywhere, the small stiffly-starched figure, the glossy tip-curling hair, the rose-and-white face, the small clean features, upturned in childlike innocence. He could hear her voice everywhere; and always he, *you*, was in what she said. . . . Did he want something? Was there something she could do for him? Was he all right? He must always tell her, please, if he wanted anything.

"You are all right, yes? It would be terrible if I had given you hurt."

He started to enter the bathroom, then came up short in the doorway. A towel was draped over the sink. Scrubbed, rinsed, and hung up to dry, but still faintly imbued with the yellowishness of washed-out blood.

Roy swallowed painfully. Then, he dropped it into the hamper and slammed down the lid.

The long hours dragged by, hours that had always seemed short until today.

A little after dusk, Lilly returned.

As usual, she left her troubles outside the door; came in with an expectant smile on her face.

"Why, you're all dressed! How nice," she said. "Where's my girl, Carol?"

"She's not here," Roy said. "She—"

"Oh? Well, I guess I am a little late, and of course you're all right." She sat down, made gestures of fanning herself. "Whew, that lousy traffic! I could make better time hopping on one foot."

Roy hesitated, wanting to tell her, glad of anything that would let him delay.

"How's your hand, the burn?"

"Okay," she waved it carelessly. "It looks like I'm branded for life, but at least it learned—taught—me something. Keep away from boobs with cigars."

"I think you should have it bandaged."

"No can do. Have to dip in and out of my purse too much. Anyway, it's coming along all right."

She dismissed the subject carelessly, pleased but somewhat embarrassed by his unusual concern. As the room grew silent, she took a cigarette from her purse; smiled gaily, as Roy hurried to light it.

"Hey, now, it looks like I really rate around here, doesn't it? A little more of this, and— What's that?"

She looked down at the money he had dropped into her lap. Frowning, she raised her eyes.

"Three thousand dollars," he said. "I hope it's enough to square us up, the hospital bills and all."

"Well, sure. But you can't— Oh," she said tiredly. "I guess you can, can't you? I hoped you were playing it straight, but I guess—"

"But you knew I wasn't," Roy nodded. "And now there's something else you've got to know. About Carol."

FOURTEEN

From Sunset Strip, a muted, gradually increasing clamor floated up to Lilly's apartment, the sounds of the dinner hour and the early beginnings of the nightclubs' day. Earlier, from about four until seven, there had been the racket of the business traffic: trucks, heavy and light pick-up, making their last deliveries of the day and turning tail toward the city; passenger cars, speeding and skidding and jockeying for position as they swarmed out from town to their own duchies of Brentwood, Bel Air, and Beverly Hills. The cars were of all kinds and sizes, from hot rods on up, but there was an awesome abundance—even a predominance, at times—of the upper bracket makes. Caught once in the Strip's traffic, Roy had examined its content and, except for two motorcycles and a Ford, he had seen nothing, for as far as he could see, but Cadillacs, Rolls-Royces, Lincolns, and Imperials.

Now, listening to the night's throbbing, Roy wished he was down there on the Strip, or practically any place but where he was. He had told Lilly about Carol as quickly as he could, anxious to get it over with. But brushed over, it had probably sounded worse than in detail. He had felt the need to go back through it again, to explain just how what had led into what. But that seemed only to worsen matters, making him appear to pose as an honest if earthy young man who had been put to shameful disadvantage by the wilful stupidity of a young woman.

There was just no good way of telling the story, he guessed. There simply wasn't, despite her definite non-prudishness and the fact she had never played the role of mother, as he saw it.

He gave a start as Lilly's purse slid to the floor with a thump. He bent forward to pick it up, then settled back uneasily as he saw what had fallen from the purse—a small, silencer-equipped gun.

Her hand closed around it. She straightened again, hefting it absently. Then, seeing his unease, her mouth twisted in a tight grin.

"Don't worry, Roy. It's a temptation, I'll admit, but it would cost me my permit."

"Well, I wouldn't want you to do that," Roy said. "Not after all the trouble I've already caused."

"Oh, now, you shouldn't feel that way," Lilly said. "You've paid your bill, haven't you?—tossed money at me like it was going out of style. You've explained and you've apologized; you didn't really do anything to explain or apologize for, did you? I was stupid. She was stupid—stupid enough to love and trust you, and to put the best possible interpretation on what you did and said. We were fools, in other words, and it's a grifter's job to take the fools."

"Have your own way about it," Roy snapped. "I've apologized, done everything I can. But if you want to get nasty—"

"But I always was nasty, wasn't I? Always giving you a hard time. There was just no good in me, never ever. And you damned well couldn't miss a chance to get back at me!"

"Wh-aat?" He looked at her sharply. "What the hell are you talking about?"

"The same thing you've spent your life brooding about and pitying yourself about, and needling me about. Because you had a hard time as a kid. Because I didn't measure up to your standards of motherhood."

Roy blurted out surlily that she hadn't measured up to anyone else's standards, either. Then, a little shamefaced, he tacked on a half-hearted retraction. "Now, I don't really mean that, Lilly; you just got me sore. Anyway, you've certainly done plenty out here, a lot more than I had any right to expect, and—"

"Never mind," she cut him off. "It wasn't enough. You've proved it wasn't. But there's a thing or two I'd like to get straight, Roy. To your way of thinking, I was a bad mother—no, I was, so let's face it. But I wonder if it occurred to you that I didn't look on myself that way at all."

"Well . . ." He hesitated. "Well, no, I don't suppose you did."

"It's all a matter of comparison, right? In the good neighborhoods you were raised in, and stacked up against the other mothers you saw there, I stank. But I didn't grow up in that kind of environment, Roy. Where I was raised, a kid was lucky if he got three months of school in his life. Lucky if he didn't die of rickets or hookworm or plain old starvation, or something worse. I can't remember a day, from the time I was old enough to remember anything, that I had enough to eat and didn't get a beating . . ."

Roy lit a cigarette, glancing at her over the match; more irritated than interested in what she was saying. What did it all amount to, anyway? Maybe she'd had a tough childhood—although he'd have to take her word for that. All he knew about was his own. But having had one, and knowing how it felt, why had she handed him the same kind of deal? She knew better. She hadn't been under the same ugly social pressures that had been brought to bear on her own parents. Why, hell, she was married and living away from home at about the age he'd finished grammar school!

Something about the last thought dug into him, cut through the layered rationalizations which warmed him in their rosy glow while holding her off in outer darkness. Irritably, he wondered just how soon he could decently break out of here. That was all he wanted. Not excuses, not explanations. Because of Carol, and because he did owe Lilly *something*, he himself had been cast in the role of apologizer and explainer. And, manfully, he had accepted it. But—

He became aware at last that the room was silent. Had been silent for some time. Lilly was leaning back in her chair, looking at him with a tiredly crooked smile.

"I seem to be keeping you up," she said. "Why don't you just run along and leave me to stew in my sins?"

"Now, Lilly—" He made a defensive gesture. "You've never heard me reproach you for anything."

"But you have plenty to reproach me for, haven't you? It was pretty lousy of me to be a child at the same time you were. To act like a child instead of a grown woman. Yes, sir. I was a real stinker not to grow up and act grown up as fast as you thought that I should."

Roy was stung. "What do you want me to do?" he demanded. "Put a halo on you? You're doing a pretty good job of that yourself."

"And making you look like a heel at the same time, hmm? But that's the way I am, you know: the way I've always been. Always picking on poor little Roy."

"Oh, for God's sake, Lilly—!"

"Now, I've got just one more thing to say. I don't suppose it will do any good, but I've got to say it, anyway. Get out of the grift, Roy. Get out right now and stay out."

"Why? Why don't you get out yourself?"

"Why?" Lilly stared at him. "Are you seriously asking me, *why?* Why, you brainless sap. I'd be dead if I even looked like I wanted out! It's been that way since I was eighteen years old. You don't get out of things like this—you're carried out!"

Roy wet his lips nervously. Maybe she wasn't exaggerating, although it was comforting to think that she must be. But he wasn't in her league, and he never would be.

"I'm strictly short-con, Lilly," he said. "Nothing but small-time stuff. I can walk away from it any time I want to."

"It won't always be small time. With you, it couldn't be. You're only twenty-five years old, and already you can lay out three grand without turning a hair. You're only twenty-five, and you've come up with a new angle on the grift—how to take fools for profit without changing hotels. So are you going to stop there?" Her head wagged in a firm negative. "Huh-uh. The grift's like everything else. You don't stand still. You either go up or down, usually down, but my Roy's going up."

Roy was guiltily flattered. He pointed out that however it was, it was still the con. It didn't have the dangers that the organized rackets had.

"It doesn't, huh?" Lilly asked. "Well, you could have fooled me. Now, I heard of a guy just about your age who got hit so hard in the guts that it almost killed him."

"Well, uh—"

"Sure, sure, that doesn't count. That's different. And here's something else that's different." She held up the burned hand. "Do you know how I really got that burn? Well, I'll tell you . . ."

She told him, and he listened sickishly; shamed and embarrassed. Unwilling to associate such things with his mother, and unable to connect them with himself. Insofar as he could, they tended to widen the rift that lay between him and Lilly.

She saw how he felt; saw that it was no use. A slow fury welled through her tired body.

"So that's that," she said, "and it doesn't have anything to do with you, does it? Just another chapter in the Perils of Lilly Dillon."

"And very interesting, too," he said, his voice light. "Maybe you should write a book, Lilly."

"Maybe you should write one," Lilly said. "Carol Roberg would make a good chapter."

Roy came stiffly to his feet. He nodded coldly, picked up his hat and started toward the door; then paused with a gesture of appeal. "Lilly," he said, "just what are you driving at, anyway? What more can I do about Carol than I've already done?"

"You're asking me," Lilly said bitterly. "You've actually got the guts to stand there and ask me what you should do!"

"But—you're suggesting that I should marry her? Ask her to marry me? Oh, now, come off it! What kind of break would that be for her?"

"Oh, God! God, God, God," Lilly moaned.

Coloring, Roy slammed on his hat. "I'm sorry I'm such a big disappointment to you. I'm going now."

Lilly looked at him, as he still hesitated, and remarked that she hadn't noticed. "That's the second time you've fooled me tonight," she said. "Now you see him and now you see him, and when he goes nobody knows."

He left abruptly.

Striding down the corridor, his steps slowed and he paused; teetered on the point of turning back. At about the same instant, Lilly jumped up from her chair, started toward the door, and herself paused in teetering indecision.

They were so much alike, so much a part of one another. They were that close—for a moment.

The moment passed; a moment before murder. Then, flouting instinct, each made his decision. Each, as he always had, went his own way.

FIFTEEN

Roy had his delayed dinner in a downtown restaurant. He ate hungrily, telling himself, and doubtless meaning it, that it was good to be eating in a restaurant. It was what he was used to. The subtle sameness of the food, whatever the restaurant, had a reassuring quality about it, not unlike a mother's milk to a child. In its familiar and dependable nurture, it bolstered one's believe-or-perish credo that the more things changed the more they remained the same.

Similarly, it was good to be back in his own hotel bed. For here also would be his own bed wherever it was; standardized, always ready and waiting for him, simultaneously providing the pleasurable prerequisites of permanence and impermanence. Perhaps, in his dreams, Carol briefly shared the bed with him, and he winced, almost crying out. But there were entirely amenable wraiths, also comfortably standardized, who came quickly to the rescue. They asked no more of him than he did of them, a sensual but immaculate penetration which achieved its end without mental or moral involvement. One bathed quickly or lingeringly, sans the danger of nearing the water.

So, all in all, Roy Dillon slept well that night.

Awakening early, he lay for a while in the presumable posture of all men awakening. Hands locked under his head, eyes gazing absently at the ceiling, letting his mind roam. Then, with a brisk abandonment of bed, he washed, dressed, and left the hotel.

He ate breakfast. He visited a barber shop, indulged himself in "the works" and went back to his two-room suite. After bathing, he put on completely fresh clothes, hat and shoes included, and again left the hotel.

He got his car from its parking lot, and turned it out into the traffic.

At first he felt a little awkward, nervous, after his prolonged absence from driving. But that passed quickly. In a few blocks he was himself again, moving the car along with automatic ease, driving with the same unthinking skill that a stenographer applies to a typewriter. He was part of this river of cars, aiding its sluggish tide and in turn aided by it. Without losing his identity, free to turn out of the tide when he chose, he still belonged to something.

Like many business establishments that had once been a traditional integrant of the downtown's whole, the jobbing house of Sarber & Webb was now set down in a quasi-residential district; commodiously released, for a restless hiatus, from the sprawling giant which would inevitably surround it again. The firm was housed in a roomy sandstone-and-brick building, a lofty one-storey high for perhaps three-fourths of its area. At the rear it jutted up to a storey-and-a-half, thus accommodating the company offices.

Roy put his car on the private lot at the side of the building. Whistling absently, his eyes approving as he surveyed the familiar scene around him, he took his briefcase from the car.

Someone else was looking them over too, he saw, but without his own casualness. A young man—well, perhaps he wasn't quite so young—in shirtsleeves but wearing a vest. A clerk in appearance, he stood well back on the wide sidewalk bordering the building, looking critically up and down and around, and occasionally jotting into a small notebook.

He turned and watched as Roy approached, his gaze uncompromising at first, incipiently disapproving. Then, as Roy came on, unflinching, and grinned and nodded, "Hi," the gaze registered a little warmth, and its proprietor nodded in return.

"Hi," he said, almost as though the word embarrassed him.

Roy passed on, grinning, mentally shaking his head.

A long, broad service counter stretched along the interior front of the building, breached at one end by a wicket. Behind it, racks of stock-shelves ranged rearward, bulging neatly with the thousand-odd items which were wholesaled by Sarber & Webb, and forming a half-dozen parallel aisles.

It was early, and he was the only salesman-customer in the place. Usually at this hour, most of the clerks were either having coffee across the street or propped up along the counter in clusters, smoking and talking until they could resign themselves to the day. But there was no such homey nonsense this morning.

Everyone was present, without a cigarette or coffee carton in sight. The aisles hummed with activity: the pulling of orders, inventorying, restocking, dusting, and rearranging. Everyone was busy, or—much harder—pretending to be busy.

Through the years, he had become friendly with all of them, and all came forward for a handshake and a word of congratulation on his recovery. But they wasted no time about it. Puzzled, Roy turned to the clerk who was opening a catalogue for him.

"What's hit this place?" he asked. "I haven't seen anyone as busy since the joint caught fire."

"Kaggs hit it, that's what!"

"Kaggs? Is that anything like the galloping crud?"

The clerk laughed grimly. "You can say that again! Brother." He brushed imaginary sweat from his brow. "If that son-of-a-bitch stays around much longer—"

Kaggs, he elaborated, was one of the home-office big shots, a seeming mixture of comptroller, trouble-shooter, and efficiency expert. "Came out here right after you went into the hospital—one of those college punks he looks like. And he ain't had a kind word for anyone. Ain't no one knows anything but him, and everyone's either a dope-off or a bum. Now, you know that's not so, Roy. You won't find a harder-workin', more efficient group of boys anywhere than we got right here!"

"That's right," Roy nodded agreeably, although it was very far from right. "Maybe he'll run me off, d'you suppose?"

"I was going to tell you. He *did* chop off several of the salesmen; just won't wholesale to 'em any more. And what kind of sense does that make? They're all selling on commission. If they don't sell, they don't make nothing, so—*psst*, here he comes!"

As Roy had suspected, Kaggs was the critical-looking young man he had seen outside the building. A split second after the clerk had spoken, he was upon them, shooting out his hand like a weapon.

"Kaggs. Home office," he said. "Glad to meet you."

"This is Mr. Dillon," the clerk said, nervously obsequious. "Roy's one of our best salesmen, Mr. Kaggs."

"He is the best," Kaggs didn't give the clerk a glance. "Which isn't saying much for this place. Want to talk to you, Dillon."

He turned, still clinging to Roy's hand as though to hustle him along. Roy remained where he was, pulling Kaggs back around with a jerk. He smiled pleasantly, as the home-office man blinked at him, startled.

"That was a pretty backhanded compliment, Mr. Kaggs," he said, "and I never let people get away with things like that. If I did, I wouldn't be a good salesman."

Kaggs considered the statement; nodded with curt judiciousness. "You're right, I apologize. Now, I'd still like to talk to you."

"Lead the way," Roy said, picking up his briefcase.

Kaggs led him back down the counter, abruptly swerving away from the wicket and moving toward the building entrance. "How about some coffee, okay? Sets a bad example; too much piddling around here already. But it's hard to talk with so many people trying to listen in."

"You don't seem to think much of them," Roy remarked.

Kaggs said crisply, as they started across the street, that he had no feelings at all about people in the abstract. "It depends on how they stack up. If they're on the ball, I've got plenty of consideration for 'em."

In the restaurant, he asked for milk as well as coffee, mixing the two together a little at a time as he sipped from his cup. "Ulcers," he explained. "Your trouble too, right?" Then, without waiting for an answer he went on:

"Had you spotted when you passed me this morning, Dillon. Nothing slobby or sloppy about you. Looked like you were going somewhere and you knew the way. Figured then that you must be Dillon; connected you with your sales right away. And when I said that it didn't say much for Sarber & Webb—your being the best man, I mean—I meant just that. You stack up as a top-flight man in my book, but you've had no incentive here. No one walking on your heels. Just a lot of half-asses, so the tendency's been not to stretch yourself. I'm bouncing the slobs, incidentally. Makes no difference to me if they are only on commission. If they're not making good money, they're not giving us good representation and we can't afford to have 'em around. What's your selling experience, anyway? Before you came here, I mean?"

"Selling's all I've done since I left high school," Roy said, not knowing what all this was leading up to but willing to go along for the ride. "You name it, I've sold it. All door-to-door stuff. Premiums, brushes, pots and pans, magazines."

"You're singing my song," Kaggs grinned crookedly. "I'm the guy who worked his way through college peddling subscriptions. You switched to business-house selling when you came with us; why?"

"It's easier to get into doors," Roy said, "and you can build up regular customers. The house-to-house stuff is mostly one-shot."

Kaggs nodded approvingly. "Ever supervise salesmen? You know; kind of head them up, keep 'em on their toes."

"I've run house-to-house crews," Roy shrugged. "Who hasn't?"

"I haven't. Don't have the talent for it, somehow."

"Or tact?" Roy smiled.

"Or tact. But never mind me; I do all right. The point is, Sarber & Webb need a sales manager. Should have had one right along. Someone who's proved he's a salesman and can handle other salesmen.

He'd have a lot of dead-wood to clear out, or put some sap back into 'em. Hire new men, and give 'em a good draw if they cut the stuff. What do you think?"

"I think it's a good idea," Roy said.

"Now, I don't know offhand what your best year's earnings have been. Around sixty-six hundred, I believe. But put it this way. We'll top your best year by fifteen hundred; make it eight thousand in round numbers. That's just a beginning, of course. Give you a year at eight, and if you're not worth a lot more than that by then I'll kick you the hell out. But I know you will be worth more. Knew you were my kind of man from the minute I saw you this morning. And now that we've got that settled, I'm going to borrow one of your cigarettes and have a real cup of coffee, and if my stomach doesn't like it I'll kick it the hell out, too."

Roy held out his cigarette package. In the rapid-fire delivery of Kaggs' talk, he had let its meaning slip away from him. And coming to him abruptly, hitting him like a blow, his hand gave a convulsive jerk.

Kaggs looked at him, blinking. "Something wrong? Incidentally, don't cigarettes and coffee bother you? Your ulcers, I mean."

Roy nodded, shook his head. "I, uh, it wasn't a bad ulcer. Just happened to be in a bad place. Struck a vein. I—look, Mr. Kaggs—"

"Perk, Roy. Perk for Percy, and smile when you say that. How old are you, Roy? Twenty-five or -six? Fine. No reason at all why you can't . . ."

Roy's mind raced desperately. *A sales manager!* Him, Roy Dillon, grifter de luxe, a sales manager! But he couldn't be, damnit! It would be too confining, too proscribed. He would lose the freedom of movement necessary to carrying on the grift. The job itself, the importance of it, would preclude any such activities. As a commission salesman, he might reasonably loiter in the places where the grift could be practiced. But as Sarber & Webb's sales manager—no! The slightest rumble would dump him cold.

He couldn't take the job. On the other hand, how could he turn it down, without arousing suspicion? How could you reasonably refuse a job that was right up your alley, one that was not only much better than the one you had but promised to become far, far better?

". . . glad to get this thing settled, Roy." Perk Kaggs was saying.

"Now, we've wasted enough time here, so if you're through with your coffee—"

"Mr. Kaggs—Perk," Roy said. "I can't take the job. I can't take it right away, I mean. This is the first day I've been up and around, and I just dropped by to say hello and—"

"Oh?" Kaggs looked at him judiciously. "Well, you do look a little pale. How soon will you be ready, a week?"

"Well, I—the doctor's checking me over in a week, but I'm not sure that—"

"Two weeks then. Or take a little longer if you have to. Be plenty of work, and you've got to be in shape for it."

"But you need a man right now! It wouldn't be fair to you to—"

"I take care of the being-fair-to-me department." Kaggs permitted himself an icy grin. "Things been going to hell this long. They can go a little longer."

"But—"

But there was nothing more to say. Perhaps he could think of an out for himself during the next week or so, but none occurred to him now.

They walked back across the street together, and then he went on by himself to his car. He got into it uncertainly, started the motor, then cut it off again.

What now? How could he pass the time that Kaggs had given him? Selling was out of the question, of course, since he was supposedly unready to work. But there was the other, his real occupation; the source of the wealth behind the four clown pictures.

He started the car again. Then, with a dismayed grunt, he again shut it off. Since work was out, so also was the grift. He wouldn't dare turn a trick. Not before the weekend, at least, when he would normally be idle and could unsuspiciously indulge in some on-the-towning.

The weekend. And this was only Wednesday.

He thought about Moira. With an unconscious frown, he dismissed her from his mind. Not today. It was too soon after Carol.

Starting his car for the third time, he drove around for a couple of hours, then had lunch at a drive-in and returned to the hotel. He spent a restless afternoon reading. He had dinner, and killed the evening at the movies.

Faced with more idleness the following day, he was again moved to call Moira. But somehow, without seeming to think about it, he rang Carol's number instead.

Coming to the phone drowsy-voiced, she said she could not see him. They had no reason to see each other.

"Oh, now, we might have," he said. "Why don't we get together and talk about it?"

She hesitated. "About what, exactly?"

"Well . . . you know. A lot of things. We'll have lunch, and—"

"No," she said firmly. "No, Roy. It is impossible, anyway. I am working regularly at the hospital now. Night duty. In the day, I must sleep."

"In the evening, then." Suddenly it had become very important that he see her. "Before you go to work. Or I can pick you up in the morning, after you finish. I . . ."

He rushed on. He had a new job, he explained. Or, well, he was *thinking* about taking a new job. He wanted her opinion on it, and—

"No," she said. "No, Roy."

And she hung up.

SIXTEEN

On the following day, he called Moira Langtry. But there again he was defeated. He was surprised as well as irritated, since, momentarily, she had seemed to welcome an early start on their La Jolla weekend, reversing herself in practically the same breath. It couldn't be done, she explained. At least, due to delicate womanly reasons, a periodic difficulty, it wouldn't be very practical. Tomorrow? Mmm, no she was afraid not. But the next day, Sunday, should be fine.

Roy suspected that she was simply a little miffed at him; that this was his punishment for his weeks of inattentiveness. Certainly, however, he was of no mind to plead with her, so he said casually that Sunday would be fine with him, too, and the arrangements were made on that basis.

He killed the rest of that day, or most of it, with a trip to the Santa Monica beaches. The next day being Saturday, he was free to hit the grift again. But after some mental shilly-shallying, he decided against it.

Let it go. He wasn't quite in the mood. He needed to snap out of himself a little more, to shake off certain disturbing memories which might add to the hazards of a profession which already had hazards enough.

He loafed through the day, he became broody; almost, he pitied himself. What a way to live, he thought resentfully. Always watching every word he said, carefully scrutinizing every word that was said to him. And never making a move that wasn't studiously examined in advance. Figuratively, he walked through life on a high wire, and he could turn his mind from it only at his own peril.

Of course, he was well-paid for his efforts. The loot had piled up fast, and it would go on piling up. But there was the trouble—it simply piled up! As useless to him as so many soap coupons.

Needless to say, this state of things would not go on forever; he would not forever live a second-class life in a second-class hotel. In another five years, his grifted loot would total enough for retirement, and he could drop caution with the grift which impelled it. But those five years were necessary to insure that retirement, filling it with all the things he had been forced to forgo. And just suppose he didn't live five years. Or even one year. Or even one day. Or—

The brooding exhausted itself. And him, as well. The interminable day passed, and he fell asleep. And then, wondrously, it was morning. Then, at last, he had something to do.

They were making the trip by train, the southbound one-o'clock, and Moira was meeting him at the station. Roy parked his car on the railroad lot—he would rent another for their holiday use—and took his bag out of the trunk.

It was only a quarter after twelve, far too early to expect Moira. Roy bought their tickets, gave the seat numbers and his bag to a well-tipped redcap, and entered the station bar.

He had a drink, stretching it out as he glanced occasionally at the clock. At twenty minutes to one, he got up from his stool and went back through the entrance.

This Sunday southbound was always crowded, carrying not only the civilian traffic but the swarms of Marines and sailors returning to their duty stations at Camp Pendleton and San Diego. Roy watched as they streamed through the numbered gates and down the long ramps which led to the trains. A little nervously, he again checked the time.

Ten minutes until one. That was enough time, of course, but not too much. The station was more than a block in depth, and the train ramp was practically a block long. If Moira didn't get here very quickly, she might as well stay home.

Five minutes until one.

Four minutes.

Sourly, Roy gave up and started back to the bar. She wouldn't do this deliberately, he was sure. Probably, she'd been caught in a traffic jam, one of the Gordian knots of snarled-up cars which afflicted the city's supposedly highspeed freeways. But, damnit, if she'd ever start any place a little early, instead of waiting until the last minute—!

He heard his name called.

He whirled and saw her coming through the entrance, trotting behind the redcap who carried her baggage. The man flashed a smile at Roy as he passed. "Do my best, boss. Just you stay behind me."

Roy grabbed Moira and hurried her along with him.

"Sorry," she panted. "Darned apartment house! Elevator stuck, an'—"

"Never mind. Save your breath," he said.

They raced the marble-floored length of the building, passed through the gate and on down into the seemingly endless stretch of ramp. At its far end a trainman stood, watch in hand. As they approached, he pocketed the watch, and started up the short side-ramp to the loading platform.

They followed him, passed him.

As the train pulled out, they caught the last car.

A train porter escorted them to their seats. Breathless, they slumped into them. And for the next thirty minutes, they hardly stirred.

At last, as they were pulling out of the town of Fullerton, Moira's head turned on the white-slipped seat back and she grinned at him.

"You're a good man, McGee."

"And you're a good woman, Mrs. Murphy," he said. "What's your secret?"

"Underwear in the chowder, natch. What's yours?"

Roy said his derived from inspirational reading. "I was reading a wonderful story just as you came in. Author named Bluegum LaBloat. Ever hear of him?"

"Mmm, it does sound slightly familiar."

"I think this is the best thing he's done," Roy said. "The setting is the men's washroom in a bus station, and the characters are a clean old man and a fat young boy who live in one of the coin toilets. They ask little of the world. Only the privacy incident to doing what comes naturally. But do they get it? Heck, no! Every time they begin to function—you should excuse the language—some diarrheal dope rushes up and drops a dime in the slot. And in his coarse surrender to need, their own desire is lost. In the end, fruition frustrated, they gather up the apple cores from the urinals and go off into the woods to bake a pie."

Moira gave him a severe look.

"I'm going to call the conductor," she declared.

"I couldn't buy your silence with a drink?"

"The silence I'll buy—a couple of hours of it, after that. You buy the drink, and be sure you rinse your mouth out with it."

Roy laughed. "I'll wait for you if you like."

"Go," Moira said firmly, closing her eyes and leaning back against the seat. "Go, boy, go!"

Roy patted her on the flank. Rising, he walked the two cars to the bar-lounge. He was feeling good again, back in form. The brooding introspectiveness of recent days had slipped from him, and he felt like swinging.

As he had expected, the lounge was crowded. Unless he could squeeze in with some group, which was what he intended to do, there was no place to sit.

He surveyed the scene approvingly, then turned to the attendant behind the small bar. "I'll have a bourbon and water," he said. "Bonded."

"Sorry, sir. Can't serve you unless you're seated."

"Let's see. How much is it, anyway?"

"Eighty-five cents, sir. But I can't—"

"Two dollars," Roy nodded laying two bills on the counter. "Exact change, right?"

He got his drink. Glass in hand, he started down the aisle, swaying occasionally with the movement of the train. Halfway down the car, he allowed himself to be swayed against a booth where four servicemen sat, jolting their drinks and slopping a little of his own on the table.

He apologized profusely. "You've got to let me buy you a round. No, I insist. Waiter!"

Vastly pleased, they urged him to sit down, squeezing over in the booth to make room. The drinks came, and disappeared. Over their protests, he bought another round.

"But it ain't fair, pal. We're buyin' the next time."

"No sweat," Roy said pleasantly. "I'm not sure I can drink another one, but . . ."

He broke off, glancing down at the floor. He frowned, squinted. Then, stooping, he reached slightly under the booth. And straightening again, he dropped a small dotted cube on the table.

"Did one of you fellows drop this?" he asked.

The tat rolled. The bets doubled and redoubled. With the deceptive swiftness of the train, the money streamed into Roy Dillon's pockets. When his four dupes thought about him later, it would be as a "helluva nice guy," so amiably troubled by his unwanted and unintended winnings as to make shameful any troubled thought of their own. When Roy thought about them later—but he would not. All his thinking was concentrated on *them*, the time of their fleecing; in keeping them constantly diverted and disarmed. And in the high intensity of that concentration, in fueling its white-hot flames, he had nothing of them left for afterthoughts. They enjoyed their drinks; his were tasteless. Occasionally, one of them went to the toilet; he could not. Now and then, they looked out the window, remarking on the beauty of the passing scenery—for it was beautiful with the snowy beaches, the green and gold of the groves, the blue-gray mountains and the white houses with red-tiled roofs: strikingly reminiscent of the South of France. But while Roy chimed in with appropriate comments, he did not look where they looked nor see what they saw.

At last, swarming up out of his concentration, he saw that the car had emptied and that the train was creeping through the industrial outskirts of San Diego, the terminus of the rail trip. Rising, wringing hands all around with the servicemen, he turned to leave the bar-lounge. And there was Moira smiling at him from its head.

"Thought I'd better come looking for you," she said. "Have fun?"

"Oh, you know. Just rolling for drinks," he shrugged. "Sorry I left you alone so long."

"Forget it," she smiled, taking his arm. "I didn't mind a bit."

SEVENTEEN

Roy rented a car at San Diego, and they drove out to their La Jolla hotel. It sat in a deep lawn, high on a bluff overlooking the Pacific. Moira was delighted with it. Breathing in the clean cool air, she insisted on a brief tour of the grounds before they went inside.

"Now, this is something like," she declared. "This is living!" And sliding a sultry glance at him. "I don't know how I'll show my appreciation."

"Oh, I'll think of something," Roy said. "Maybe you can rinse out my socks for me."

He registered for them, and they followed the bellboy upstairs. Their rooms were on opposite sides of a corridor, and Moira looked at him quizzically, demanding an explanation.

"Why the apartheid bit?" she said. "Not that I can't stand it, if you can."

"I thought it would be better that way, separate rooms under our own names. Just in case there's any trouble, you know."

"Why should there be any trouble?"

Roy said easily that there shouldn't be any; there was no reason why there should be. "But why take chances? After all, we're right across from each other. Now, if you'd like me to show you how convenient it is . . ."

He pulled her into his arms, and they stood locked together for a moment. But when he started to take it from there, she pulled away.

"Later, hmm?" She stooped before the mirror, idly prinking at her hair. "I hurried so fast this morning that I'm only half-thrown together."

"Later it is," Roy nodded agreeably. "Like something to eat now, or would you rather wait for dinner?"

"Oh, dinner by all means. I'll give you a ring."

He left her, still stooped before the mirror, and crossed to his own room. Unpacking his bag, he decided that she was curious rather than peeved about the separate rooms, and that, in any case, the arrangement was imperative. He was known as a single man. Departing from that singleness, he would have to use an assumed name. And where then was his protective front, so carefully and painfully built up through the years?

He was bound to the front, bound to and bound by it. If Moira was puzzled or peeved, then she could simply get over being puzzled or peeved. He wished he hadn't had to explain to her, since explanations were always bad. He also regretted that she had seen him operating in the club car. But the wish and the regret were small things, idly reflective rather than worrisome.

Anyone might do a little gambling for drinks. Anyone might be cautious about hotel registrations. Why should Moira regard the first as a professional activity, and the second as a cover for it—a front which must always accrue to him like a shadow?

Unpacked, Roy stretched out on the bed, surprisingly grateful for the chance to rest. He had not realized that he was so tired, that he could be so glad to lie down. Apparently, he reflected, he was still not fully recovered from the effects of his hemorrhage.

Lulled by the distant throb of the ocean, he fell into a comfortable doze, awakening just before dusk. He stretched lazily and sat up, unconsciously smiling with the pleasure of his comfort. Salt-scented air wafted in through the windows. Far off to the West, beneath a pastel sky, an orange-red sun sank slowly into the ocean. Many times he had seen the sun set off the Southern California coast, but each time was a new experience. Each sunset seemed more beautiful than the last.

Reluctantly, as the phone rang, he turned away from its splendor. Moira's voice came gaily over the wire.

"Boo, you ugly man! Are you buying me dinner or not?"

"Absolutely not," he said. "Give me one good reason why I should."

"Can't. Not over the phone."

"Write me a letter, then."

"Can't. No mail deliveries on Sunday."

"Excuses," he grumbled. "Always excuses! Well, okay, but it's strictly hamburgers."

They had cocktails on the hotel's patio bar. Then, driving farther on in to the city, they ate at a seafood restaurant jutting out over the ocean. Moira had declared an armistice with her diet, and she proved that she meant it.

The meal opened with a lobster cocktail, practically a meal in itself. Served with hot garlic-bread and a fresh green salad, the main course was a sizzling platter of assorted seafoods bordered by a rim of delicately-browned potatoes. Then came dessert—a fluffy cheese-cake—and pots of black, black coffee.

Moira sighed happily as she accepted a cigarette. "As I said earlier, this is living! I honestly don't think I can move!"

"Then, of course you don't feel like dancing."

"Silly," she said. "Whatever gave you an idea like that?"

She loved dancing, and she danced very well; as, for that matter, did he. More than once, he caught the eyes of other patrons on them; seeing them also, Moira pressed closer to him, bending her supple body to his.

After perhaps an hour of dancing, when the floor became oppressively crowded, they went for a moonlight drive up the coast, turning around and heading back at the city of Oceanside. The mounting waves of the night tide foamed with phosphorus. They came rolling in from the distant depths of the ocean, striking against the shore in a steady series of thunder-like roars. On the rocky outcrops of the shore, an occasional seal gleamed blackly.

It was almost eleven when Roy got them back to their hotel, and Moira was suppressing a yawn. She apologized, saying it was the weather, not the company. But when they stood again in front of their rooms, she held out her hand in good night.

"You don't mind, do you, Roy? It's been such a wonderful evening, I guess I just wore myself out."

"Of course you did," he said. "I'm pretty tired myself."

"You're sure now? You're sure you don't mind?"

"Beat it," he said, pushing her through the door. "It's okay."

But of course it wasn't okay, and he minded a great deal. He entered his own room, restraining an angry urge to slam the door. Stripping out of his clothes, he sat down on the edge of the bed; puffed surlily at a cigarette. A hell of a holiday, this was! It would serve her right if he walked out on her!

The phone tinkled faintly. It was Moira. She spoke with repressed laughter.

"Open your door."

"What?" He grinned expectantly. "What for?"

"Open it and find out, you fathead!"

He hung up and opened his door. There was a sibilant, "*Gangway!*" from the door opposite his. And he stood back. And Moira came skipping across the hall. Her black hair stood in a sedate pile on her head. She was completely naked. Gravely, a finger under her chin, she curtsied before him.

"I hope you don't mind, sir," she said. "I just washed my clothes, and I couldn't do a thing with them."

Then, gurgling, choking with laughter, she collapsed in his arms. "Oh, you!" she gasped. "If you could have seen your face when I told you good night! You looked s-so—so—*ah, ha, ha*—"

He picked her up and tossed her on the bed.

They had a hell of a time.

EIGHTEEN

But afterward, after she had gone back to her own room, depression came to him and what had seemed like such a hell of a time became distasteful, even a little disgusting. It was the depression of surfeit, the tail of self-indulgence's kite. You flew high, wide, and handsome, imposing on the breeze that might have wafted you along indefinitely; and then it was gone, and down, down, down, you went.

Tossing restlessly in the darkness, Roy told himself that the gloom was natural enough and a small enough price to pay for what he had received. But as to the last, at least, he was not convinced. There was too much of a sameness about the evening's delights. He had been the same route too many times. He'd been there before, so double-damned often, and however you traveled—backward, forward, or walking on your hands—you always got to the same place. You got nowhere, in other words, and each trip took a little more out of you.

Still, did he really want anything changed? Even now, in his misery, weren't his thoughts already reaching out and across the hall?

He flung his legs over the side of the bed, and sat up. Lighting a cigarette, pulling a robe around his shoulders, he sat looking out into the moonlit night. Thinking that perhaps it wasn't him or them—he or Moira—that had brought him to this gloomy despair. Perhaps it was a combination of things.

He didn't have his strength back yet. He'd used up a lot of energy in catching the train. And grifting after so long an idleness had been unusually straining on him. Then there'd been a lot of little things—Moira's curiosity about the separate rooms, for example. And that heavy dinner, at least twice as much as he needed or wanted. Then, after all that . . .

His mind went back to the dinner now, the enormous quantity and richness of it. And suddenly the cigarette tasted lousy to him, and a wave of nausea surged up through his stomach. He ran to the bathroom, a hand over his mouth, cheeks bulging. And he got there barely in time.

He rid himself of the food, every miserable mouthful of it. He rinsed out his mouth with warm water, then drank several glasses of cold. And immediately he began vomiting again.

Bending over the sink, he anxiously studied his stomach's washings, and to his relief he found them clear. There was no tell-tale trace of the brown that would signify internal bleeding.

Shivering a little, he tottered back to bed and pulled the covers over him. He felt a lot better now, lighter and cleaner. He closed his eyes, and was promptly asleep.

He slept soundlessly, dreamlessly; seeming to compress two hours of sleep in one. Awakening at about six-thirty, he knew he'd had his quota and that further sleep was out of the question.

He shaved, showered and dressed. That took no more than a half-hour, drag it out as he would. So there it was, only seven o'clock in the morning, and he as much at loose ends as if he was back in L.A.

Certainly, he couldn't call Moira at such an hour. Moira had indicated last night that she intended to sleep until noon, and that she would cheerfully murder anyone who awakened her before then. At any rate, he was in no hurry at all to see Moira. It was labor enough to pull himself together again, without the necessity of entertaining her.

Going down to the hotel coffee shop, he had some toast and coffee. But he only did it as a matter of discipline, of virtue. Regardless of nights-before, a man ate breakfast in the morning. He ate, hungry or not, or else he inevitably found himself in trouble.

Strolling down a white-graveled walk to the cliff above the ocean, he let his eyes rove aimlessly over the expanse of sea and sand: the icy-looking whitecaps, the blinking, faraway sails of boats, the sweeping, constantly searching gulls. Desolation. Eternal, infinite. Like Dostoyevski's conception of eternity, a fly circling about a privy, the few signs of life only emphasized the loneliness.

At this hour of the morning, a very little of it went a long way with Roy Dillon. Abruptly, he turned away from it and headed for the rented car.

The coffee and toast hadn't set at all well with him. He needed something to settle his stomach, and he could think of only one thing that would do it. A bottle of good beer, or, better still, ale. And he knew it was not to be found, so early in the day, in a community like La Jolla. The bars here, the cocktail lounges, rather, would not open until shortly before lunch. If there were morning drinkers in the town, and doubtless there were, they had their own private bars to drink from.

Turning the car toward San Diego, Roy drove out of the southerly outskirts of La Jolla and into the more humble districts beyond, slowing occasionally for a swift appraisal of the various drinking establishments. Many of them were open, but they were not the right kind. They would have only the West Coast beers, which, to Roy's way of thinking, were undrinkable. None of them, certainly, would have a good ale.

Nearing San Diego, he drove up Mission Valley for a mile or so; then, swinging up a long hill, he entered Mission Hills. There, after some thirty minutes of wandering about, he found what he was looking for. It wasn't a fancy place at all; not one of those glossy cocktail lounges where drinks were secondary to atmosphere. Just a good solid-looking bar, with an air that immediately inspired confidence.

The proprietor was counting cash into his register when Roy entered. A graying, wiry-looking man, with a tanned smile-wrinkled face, he nodded a greeting in the back-bar mirror. "Yes, sir, what'll it be?"

Roy put a name to it, and the proprietor said that certainly he had good ale: if ale wasn't good it was slop. "Give you imported or Ballantine's." Roy chose Ballantine's, and the proprietor was pleased at his gratified reaction.

"Good, huh? Y'know, I think I'll just have one myself."

Roy took an immediate liking to the guy, and the feeling was reciprocated. He liked the look of this place, its unassuming honesty and decency; the quiet pride of its owner in being its owner.

Within ten minutes they were on a first-name basis. Roy was explaining his presence in the town, using his holidaying as an excuse for off-hour drinking. Bert—the proprietor—revealed that he also shunned the pre-noon drink; but he was going on vacation tomorrow, so what was the harm, anyway?

Two men came in, downed a double-shot each, and hurried out again. Bert looked after them with a touch of sadness, and came back to Roy. That was no way to drink, he said. Occasionally, even the best of men needed a drink or two in the morning, but they shouldn't drink it that way.

As he left to wait on another customer, he brushed against a back-bar display stand of salted nuts, moving it slightly out of its original position. And staring absently in that direction, Roy saw something that made him frown. He stood up a little from his stool for another look, making sure of what he had seen. He sat down again, puzzled and troubled.

A punchboard! A punchboard in a place like this! Bert was no fool, either in the con or the everyday sense, but a punchboard was strictly a fool's item.

Back at the time when Roy was just starting out, there were still a few teams working the boards, one man planting them, the other knocking them over. But he hadn't seen any in years. Everyone had tipped long ago, and trying to plant a board now was the equivalent of asking for a busted jaw.

Of course, some small merchants and barkeeps still bought boards on their own, punching out the winning numbers at the start and thus giving the suckers no chance at all. But Bert wouldn't do that. Bert . . .

Roy laughed wryly to himself, took a foamy sip of the ale. What was this, anyway? Was he, Roy Dillon, actually concerned about the honesty or dishonesty of a barkeep or the possibility that he might be swindled?

Another customer had come in, a khaki-clad workman, and Bert was serving him a coke. Coming back down the bar with two fresh bottles of ale, he refilled their glasses. And Roy allowed himself to "notice" the board.

"Oh, that thing." The proprietor retrieved it from the back-bar and laid it in front of him. "Some fellow walked out and left it here three or four months ago. Didn't notice it until after he was gone. I was going to throw it away, but I get a customer now and then who wants to try his luck. So . . ." He paused tentatively. "Want to have a try? Chances run from a cent to a dollar."

"Well . . ." Roy looked down at the board.

Affixed to the top were five gold-colored imitation coins, representing cash prizes of five to one hundred dollars. Under each of them a number was printed. To win, one had only to punch out a corresponding number or numbers from the thousands on the board.

None of the winners had been punched out. Bert, obviously, was as honest as he looked.

"Well," said Roy, picking up the little metal key which dangled from the board, "what can I lose?"

He punched a few numbers, laying them out for Bert's inspection. On his sixth punch, he hit the five-dollar prize, and the proprietor smilingly laid the money on the counter. Roy let it lay, again poised the key over the board.

He couldn't tell Bert that this was a chump's gimmick. To do so would reveal knowledge that no honest man should have. Most certainly, and even though someone else was bound to do it, he couldn't take the man himself. The grift just wasn't for him today—or so he rationalized. There just wasn't enough at stake.

If he knocked off every prize on the board, the take would be under two hundred dollars. And naturally he'd never get away with knocking them all off. The pros of the racket had always gone for the big one and left the others alone. He, however, had already hit the five, so . . .

He punched out the ten-dollar number. Still smiling, pleased rather than disconcerted, Bert again laid money on the counter. Roy brought the key up for another punch.

This was the way to do it, he'd decided. The way to get the board out of circulation. One more prize—the twenty-five—and he'd point out that something must be screwy about the board. Bert would be obliged to get rid of it. And he, of course, would refuse to accept his winnings.

He punched out the third "lucky" number. Properly startled, he cleared his throat for the tip-off. But Bert, his smile slightly stiffened now, had turned to glance at the coke customer.

"Yes, sir?" he said. "Something else?"

"Yes, sir," the man said, his voice grimly light. "Yes, sir, there's something else, all right. You got a federal gambling-tax stamp?"

"*Huh!* What—"

"Don't have one, huh? Well, I'll tell you something else you don't have; won't have it long, anyway. Your liquor license."

"B-but—" Bert had paled under his tan. California liquor licenses are worth a small fortune. "B-but you can't do that! We were just—"

"Tell it to the state and Federal boys. I'm local." He flipped open a leather credential-case; nodded coldly at Roy. "You're pretty stupid, mister. No one but a stupe would knock a chump off for three balls in a row."

Roy looked at him evenly. "I don't know what you're talking about," he said. "And I don't like your language."

"On your feet! I'm arresting you for bunco!"

"You're making a mistake, officer. I'm a salesman, and I—"

"You giving me a hard time? Huh? *Hah?* Why, you grifting son-of-a-bitch—!"

He grabbed Roy by the lapels, yanked him furiously to his feet and slammed him up against the wall.

NINETEEN

First, there was the search; the turning out of pockets, the probing and slapping of garments, the hand brought up on either side of the testicles. Then came the questions, the demanded answers that were immediately labeled lies.

"Your right name, goddamn you! Never mind them phony credentials! All you hustlers got 'em!"

"That is my right name. I live in Los Angeles, and I've worked for the same company for four years—"

"Stop lying! Who's working the boards with you? How many other places you pulled this gimmick?"

"My health has been bad. I came down to La Jolla last night—a friend and I—on a holiday."

"All right, all right! Now, we're gonna start all over again and, by God, you better come clean!"

"Officer, there are at least a hundred businessmen here in town who can identify me. I've been selling to them for years, and—"

"Drop it! Drop that crap! Now, what's your right name!"

The same questions over and over. The same answers over and over. Now and then, the cop turned to the wall telephone to pass his information on for checking. But still, the information checking out, he would not give up. He knew what he knew. With his own eyes, he had seen the bunco worked, a punchboard swiftly knocked for three prizes. And Roy's perfect front notwithstanding, how could the clear evidence of grifting be ignored?

He was on the phone again now, his heavy face sullen as he got the answers to his questions. Roy sidled a glance at the bar owner, Bert. He looked at the punchboard on the counter fixedly, and again raised his eyes to Bert. Nodded to him ever so slightly. But he couldn't be sure that Bert got the message.

The cop slammed up the phone. He stared at Roy sourly, rubbed a meaty hand over his face. Hesitating, he tried to form the words which the situation called for, the apology which outraged instinct and flouted the evidence of his own eyes.

From up the bar, Roy heard a dull grinding sound, the garbage disposal.

He grinned quietly to himself. "Well, officer," he said. "Any more questions?"

"That's all." The cop jerked his head. "Looks like I maybe made a mistake."

"Yes? You slam me around and insult me, and treat me like a criminal. And then you say you maybe made a mistake. That's supposed to smooth everything over."

"Well—" mouth tight, choking over the words. "Sorry. 'Pologize. No offense."

Roy was content to settle for that. Savagely, the cop turned on Bert.

"All right, mister! I want the number of your liquor license! I'm turning you in for—for—*Where's that punchboard?*"

"What punchboard?"

"Damn you, don't you pull that crap on me! The board that was right there on the counter—the one that this guy was playing! Now, you either hand it over or I'll find it myself!"

Bert picked up a rag, and began mopping the counter. "I usually clean up this time of day," he said. "Clear up all the odds and ends of junk, and throw 'em down the garbage disposer. Now, I can't say that I remember any punchboard, but if there was one here . . ."

"You threw it away! Y-you think you can get away with that?"

"Can't I?" Bert said.

The cop stammered in furious incoherence. He said, "You'll see, by God, you'll see!" And turning savagely to Roy, "You too, mister! You ain't got me fooled a damned bit! I'm gonna be on the lookout for you, and the next time you hit this town—!"

He whirled and stalked out of the place. Grinning, Roy sat back down at his stool.

"Acts like he's sore about something," he said. "How about another ale?"

"No," Bert said.

"What? Now, look, Bert, I'm sorry if there was any trouble, but it was your punchboard. I didn't—"

"I know. It was my mistake. But I never make the same mistake twice. Now, I want you to leave and I don't want you to come back."

Another customer came in, and Bert began to wait on him. Roy arose and walked out.

The dazzling sunlight struck against his face, its strength doubled with the contrast of the cool and shadowed bar. The cold ale—how much had he drunk, anyway?—roiled in his stomach, then uneasily settled back. He wasn't drunk, by any means. He never got drunk. But it wasn't smart to start back to La Jolla without eating.

There was a small restaurant around the next corner, and he had a bowl of soup there and two cups of black coffee. Startled, he noticed the time as he left, five minutes after one, and he glanced around for a telephone. But the place apparently had none; no public phone, at any rate, so he went on out to his car.

It was probably best not to call Moira, he decided. The police would have called her, and he didn't want to make explanations over the phone.

He went back down the long hill to Mission Valley, then took the road left toward the coast. It was about twenty minutes' drive to La Jolla, twenty-five minutes at the outside. Then, he would be back at the hotel with Moira, lightly explaining the cop trouble as a—

A case of mistaken identity? No, no. Something more ordinary, something that might logically evolve from an innocent circumstance. This car, for example, was a rented car. The last driver might have been involved in a serious traffic violation; he had fled, say, from the scene of an accident. So when the police spotted the car this morning . . .

Well, sure, there were inconsistencies in the story: the police would have known it was a rented car by the license number. But that wasn't up to him to explain. He'd been the victim of a police booboo; who could figure out their mistakes?

A hell of a morning, he thought. It was Bert's punchboard. Why should he get tough with me? What the hell do I care what a barkeep thinks?

Near the intersection with Pacific Highway, the traffic about him thickened, and at the Highway itself it was stalled in a four-lane tangle which two cops where struggling to undo. That didn't jibe with the normal pattern of Monday in San Diego. Traffic wasn't this bad even during the shift-changes at the aircraft plants, and it was the wrong hour for that.

The cars crept forward slowly, Roy's car moving with them. Almost an hour later, near Mission Beach, he turned off the Highway and into a filling station. And here he learned the reason for the congestion.

The horses were running at Del Mar. It was the beginning of the local racing season.

In another thirty minutes, the traffic had thinned, and rejoining it, he reached La Jolla some twenty minutes later. So he was very late, and entering the hotel he called Moira's room from the lobby. There was no answer, but she had left a message for him with the clerk.

"Why, yes, Mr. Dillon. She said to tell you she'd gone to the races."

"The races?" Roy frowned. "You're sure?"

"Yes, sir. But she was only going to stay for part of the day's program. She'll be back early, she said."

"I see," Roy nodded. "By the way, was there a call from the police about me a couple of hours ago?"

The clerk admitted delicately that there had been, also revealing that there had been a similar call to Mrs. Langtry. "Naturally, we spoke of you in the highest terms, Mr. Dillon. It was, uh, nothing serious, I hope?"

"Nothing, thanks," Roy said, and he went on up to his room.

He stood for some time before the French windows, staring out at the sun-sparkled sea. Then, eyes hurting a little, he stretched out on the bed, letting his thoughts roam at will; piecing them together with hunch and instinct until they formed a pattern.

First there was her curiosity about the way he lived, the job he held. Why did he stay on, year after year, at a place like the Grosvenor-Carlton? Why did he cling, year after year, to a relatively small-time commission job? Then, there were her subtle complaints about their relationship: they didn't really *know* each other; they needed to "get acquainted." So he had arranged this excursion, a means of getting acquainted, and how did she use the time? Why, by putting him on his own, at every opportunity. And then sitting back to see what happened.

So now she knew; she must know. Her actions today proved that she did.

The police had called her about him, yet she had not been concerned. She had known that he would be all right, that just as his front had held up for years, it would continue to hold up in this trouble whatever that trouble was. So, having found out all that she needed to, she had gone off to the races.

The races. . . .

Abruptly, he sat up scowling, his mild annoyance with her turning to anger.

She had stalled on coming to La Jolla. After being so anxious for the trip, she had unreasonably found reason to postpone it—until this week.

Because this was the beginning of the Del Mar meet. And the tracks in the L.A. area were temporarily inactive.

Or . . . maybe not. He couldn't be absolutely sure that she was nosing into Lilly's business as she had nosed into his. It might be that she was simply sore at him for leaving her alone so long, and that she had gone to the races as a way of expressing her displeasure.

Moira returned to the hotel around four o'clock. Fretting humorously over the discomforts of her cab ride; pretending to pout at Roy for going off without her.

"I just thought I'd teach you a lesson, you big stinker! You're not mad, are you?"

"I'm not sure. I understand that the police called you about me."

"Oh, that," she shrugged. "What was the trouble, anyway?"

"You wouldn't have any idea?"

"Well . . ." She began to draw in a little bit. Coming over to the bed, she sat down gingerly at his side. "Roy, I've been wanting to talk to you for a long time. But before I could, I wanted to make sure that—"

"Let it ride a little," he said carelessly. "Did you see Lilly at the races?"

"Lilly? Oh, you mean your mother. Isn't she living in Los Angeles now?"

Roy said that she was. "But the L.A. meets closed last week. So she'd be down here at Del Mar, wouldn't she?"

"How do I know? What are you getting at, anyway?"

She started to get up. He held her, taking a grip on the front of her dress.

"Now, I'll ask you again. Did you see Lilly at the Del Mar track?"

"No! How could I? I sat in the clubhouse!"

Roy smiled thinly, pointing out her blunder. "And Lilly wouldn't be in the clubhouse, hmm? Now how did you know that?"

"Because I—I—" She colored guiltily. "All right, Roy, I saw her. I was snooping. But—it's not like you think! I was just curious about her, wondering why she'd come to Los Angeles. And she was always so nasty to me! I knew she was knocking me to you every chance she got. So I just thought who is she to be so high and mighty, and I talked with a friend of mine in Baltimore and—and—"

"I see. You must have some very knowledgeable friends."

"Roy," she begged. "Don't be angry with me. I wouldn't do anything to hurt her any more than I would you."

"You'd better never try," he said. "Lilly travels in some very fast company."

"I know," she nodded meekly. "I'm sorry, dear."

"Lilly didn't see you today?"

"Oh, no. I didn't hang around, Roy. Honest." She kissed him, smiling into his eyes. "Now, about us. . . ."

"Yes," he nodded. "We may as well go back to Los Angeles, hadn't we? You've found out what you wanted to know."

"Now, honey. Don't take it like that. I think I must have known for a long time. I was just waiting for the right opportunity to talk to you."

"And just what do you know about me, anyway?"

"I know you're a short-con operator. A very good one, apparently."

"You talk the lingo. What's your pitch?"

"The long end. The big-con."

He nodded; waited. She snuggled close to him, pressing his hand against her breast. "We'd make a hell of a team, Roy. We think alike; we get along well together. Why, darling, we could work for two months out of the year and live high for the other ten! I—"

"Wait," he said, gently pushing her away. "This isn't something to rush into, Moira. It's going to take a lot of talking about."

"Well? So let's talk."

"Not here. We didn't come here on business. We don't talk in here."

She searched his face, and her smile faded a little. "I see," she said. "You think it might be hard to give me a turndown here. It would be easier on the home grounds."

"You're smart," he said. "Maybe you're too smart, Moira. But I didn't say I was turning it down."

"Well . . ." She shrugged and stood up. "If that's the way you want it . . ."

"That's the way I want it," he said.

TWENTY

They caught the six o'clock train back to Los Angeles. It was crowded, as the train coming down had been, but the composition of the crowd was different. These passengers were largely business people, men who had put in a long day in San Diego and were now returning to their Los Angeles homes, or those who lived in San Diego and were due in Los Angeles early in the morning. Then, there were those few who had overstayed their weekends, and faced reproaches—or worse—when they arrived in the California metropolis.

The holiday spirit was definitely absent. A kind of moodiness pervaded the train, and some of it enveloped Moira and Roy.

They had a drink in the half-empty lounge. Then, discovering that the train carried no diner, they remained in the car for the rest of their ride. Seated in the cozy closeness of a booth, her thigh pressed warmly against his, Moira looked out at the aching loneliness of the sea, the naked and hungering hills, the houses closed firmly to all but themselves. The idea that she had propounded to him, something that was merely desired, became a tigerish must—a thing that had to be. It was either that or nothing, and so it had to be that.

She could not go on as she had the past few years, eking out her capital with her body, exchanging her body's use for the sustenance it needed. There were not enough years left, and the body inevitably used more than it received. Always, as the years grew fewer, the more rapidly the flesh depleted itself. So, an end to things as they had been. An end to the race with self. The mind grew youthful with use, increasing eagerly with the demands of its owner, anxious and able to provide for the body that gave it shelter, to imbue it with its own youth and vigor or a reasonable facsimile thereof. And thus the mind must be used from now on. The ever-lucrative schemes which the mind could concoct and put into practice. Her mind and Roy's, the two working together as one, and the money which he could and must supply.

Perhaps she had pushed her hand a little too hard; no man liked to be pushed. Perhaps her interest in Lilly Dillon had been a blunder; every man was sensitive about his mother. But no matter. What she suggested was right and reasonable. It would be good for both of them.

It was what had to be. And damn him, he'd better—!

He made some casual comment, nudging her for a response, and seething with her own thoughts she turned on him, her faced aged with hatred. Startled, he drew back, frowning.

"Hey, now! What's the matter?"

"Nothing. Just thinking about something." She smiled, dropping the mask so swiftly that he was not sure of what he had seen. "What was it you said?"

He shook his head; he couldn't remember what it was now. "But maybe I should know your name, lady. Your right one."

"How about Langley?"

"Langley . . ." He puzzled over it for a moment. Then, "*Langley!* You mean, The Farmer? You teamed with Farmer Langley?"

"That's me, pal."

"Well, now . . ." He hesitated. "What happened to him, anyway? I heard a lot of stories, but—"

"The same thing that happens to all of 'em, a lot of them I mean. He just blew up; booze, dope, the route."

"I see," he said. "I see."

"Now, don't you worry about him." She snuggled closer to him, misreading his attitude. "That's all over and done with. There's just us now, Moira Langtry and Roy Dillon."

"He's still alive, isn't he?"

"Possibly, I really don't know," she said.

And she might have said, *And I don't care*. For the knowledge had come to her suddenly, though unsurprisingly, that she didn't care, that she had never really cared about him. It was as though she had been hypnotized by him, overwhelmed by his personality as others had been; forced to go his way, to accept his as the right and only way. Yet always subconsciously resisting and resisting, slowly building up hatred for being forced into a life—and what kind of life was it, anyway, for an attractive young woman?—that was entirely foreign to the one she wanted.

It was nothing clear, defined. Nothing she was consciously aware of or could admit to. But still she knew, in her secret mind, knew and felt guilty about it. And so, when the blowup came, she had tried to take care of him. But even that had been a means of striking back at him, the final firm push over the brink, and subconsciously knowing this she had felt still more guilty and was haunted by him. Yet now, her feelings brought to the surface, she saw there was not and had never been anything to feel guilty about.

The Farmer had got what he deserved. Anyone who deprived her of something she wanted deserved what he got.

It was nine-fifteen when the train pulled into Los Angeles. She and Roy had a good dinner in the station restaurant. Then they ran through a light rain to his car, and drove out to her apartment.

She threw off her wraps briskly, turned to him holding out her arms. He held her for a moment, kissing her, but inwardly drawing back a little, subtly cautioned by something in her manner.

"Now," she said, drawing him down onto the lounge, "Now, we get down to business."

"Do we?" He laughed awkwardly. "Before we do that, maybe we'd better—"

"I can scrape up ten grand without much trouble. That would leave twenty or twenty-five for your end. There's a place in Oklahoma now, wide open if the ice is right. As good as Fort Worth was in the old days. We can move in there with a wire store, and—"

"Wait," said Roy. "Hold it, keed!"

"It would be perfect, Roy! Say, ten grand for the store, ten for the ice, and another ten for—"

"I said to hold it! Not so fast," he said, angering a little now. "I haven't said I was going to throw in with you."

"What?" She looked at him blankly, a slight glaze over her eyes. "What did you say?"

He repeated the statement, softening it with a laugh. "You're talking some tall figures. What makes you think I've got that kind of money?"

"Why, you must have! You're bound to!" She smiled at him firmly; a teacher reproving an errant child. "Now, you know you do, Roy."

"Do I?"

"Yes. I watched you work on the train, as slick an operator as I ever saw. You don't get that smooth overnight. It takes years, and you've been getting away with it for years. Living on a Square John income and taking the fools for—"

"And I've been doing some taking myself. Twice in less than two months. Enough to put me in the hospital here, and in San Diego today—"

"So what?" She brushed the interruption aside. "That doesn't change anything. All it proves is that it's time you moved up. Get up where there's big dough at stake and you don't have to stick your neck out every day."

"Maybe I like it where I am."

"Well, I don't like it! What are you trying to pull on me, anyway? What the hell are you trying to hand me?"

He stared at her, not knowing whether to laugh or be angry, his lips twitching uncertainly. He had never seen this woman before. He had never heard her before.

The rain whispered against the window. Distantly, there was a faint whirring of an elevator. And with it, with those sounds, the sound of her heavy breathing. Labored, furious.

"I'd better run along now," he said. "We'll talk about it some other time."

"We'll talk about it now, by God!"

"Then," he said quietly, "there's nothing to talk about, Moira. The answer is no."

He stood up. She jumped up with him.

"Why?" she demanded. "Just tell me why, damn you!"

Roy nodded, a glint coming into his eyes. He said that the best reason he could think of was that she scared the hell out of him. "I've seen people like you before, baby. Double-tough and sharp as a tack, and they get what they want or else. But they don't get by with it forever."

"Bull!"

"Huh-uh, history. Sooner or later the lightning hits 'em, honey. I don't want to be around when it hits you."

He started for the door. Wild-eyed, her face mottled with rage, she flung herself in front of him.

"It's your mother, isn't it? Sure, it is! One of those keep-it-in-the-family deals! That's why you act so funny around each other! That's why you were living at her apartment!"

"Wh-aat?" He came to a dead stop. "What are you saying?"

"Don't act so goddamned innocent! You and your own mother,

gah! I'm wise to you, I should have seen it before! Why, you rotten son-of-a-bitch! How is it, hmm? How do you like—"

"How do you like this?" Roy said.

He slapped her suddenly, catching her with a back-handed slap as she reeled. She leaped at him, hands clawed, and he grabbed her by the hair and flung her, and she came down sprawling on the floor.

A little wonderingly he looked at her, as she raised her smudged and reddened face. "You see?" he said. "You see why it wouldn't do, Moira?"

"You d-dirty bastard! *You're* going to see something!"

"I'm sorry, Moira," he said. "Good night and good luck!"

TWENTY-ONE

At the curb outside her apartment house, he lingered briefly before entering his car; relishing the rain against his face, liking the cool, clean feel of it. Here was normality, something elemental and honest. He was very glad he was out here in the rain instead of up there with her.

Back at his hotel, he lay awake for a time, thinking about Moira; wondering at how little sense of loss he felt at losing her.

Was tonight merely a finalizing of something that he had long intended to do? It seemed so; it had the feeling about it of the expected. It might even be that his strong attraction for Carol had been a reaction to Moira, an attempt to attach himself to another woman and thus be detached from her.

Carol. . . .

He fidgeted uncomfortably, then put her out of his mind. He'd have to do something about her, he decided. Some day soon, somehow, he'd have to smooth things over with her.

As for Moira . . .

He frowned, on the point of falling asleep, then relaxed with a shake of his head. No, no danger there. She'd gotten sore and blown her top, but she was probably regretting it already. At any rate, there was nothing she could do and she was too smart to try. Her own position was too tenuous. She was wide open for a smacking-down herself.

He fell into a deep sleep. Having slept so little the night before, he rested well. And it was after nine when he awakened.

He sprang out of bed, feeling good and full of energy, starting to plan the day's schedule as he reached for a robe. Then slowly, drearily, he sat back down. For here he was again as he had been last week. Here he was again, still, confronted by emptiness. Barred from his selling job, barred from any activity. Faced with a day, an endless series of days, with nothing to do.

Dully, he cursed Kaggs.

He cursed himself.

Again, hopefully hopeless, as he bathed and shaved, as he dressed and went out to breakfast, he sought some way out of the impasse. And his mind came up with the same two answers—answers which were wholly unacceptable.

One: He could take the sales manager's job—take it without further stalling around—and give up the grifting. Or, two: He could jump town and go to another city; begin all over again as he had begun when he first came to Los Angeles.

Breakfast over, he got into his car and began to drive, aimlessly, without destination; the most tiresome way of driving. When this became unbearable, as it very shortly did, he pulled in to the curb and parked.

Peevishly, his mind returned to the impossible problem.

Kaggs, he thought bitterly. That damned Perk (for Percival) Kaggs! *Why couldn't he have left me alone? Why did he have to be so damned sure that I—*

The futile thinking interrupted itself. His frown faded, and a slow smile played around his lips.

Kaggs was a man of snap judgment, a man who made up his mind in a hurry. So probably he would unmake it just as fast. He would take no nonsense from anyone. Given sufficient reason, and without apology, he would snatch back the sales manager's job as promptly as he had profferred it.

Roy called him from a nearby drugstore. He was still forbidden to work for a while (the doctor's orders), he said, but perhaps Kaggs would like to have lunch with him? Kaggs said that he seldom took time for lunch; he usually settled for a sandwich in his office.

"Maybe you should start going out," Roy told him.

"Oh? You mean on account of my ulcers? Well—"

"I mean on account of your disposition. It might help you to get along better with people."

He grinned coldly, listening to the startled silence that poured over the wire. Then, Kaggs said equably, "Well, maybe it would at that. Twelve o'clock suit you?"

"No, it doesn't. I'd rather eat at one."

Kaggs said, fine, that was better for him, too. "One o'clock then. The little place across the street."

Roy hung up the phone. He considered the advisability of showing up late for the appointment, and decided against it. That would be simply rudeness, crudeness. It would do nothing but arouse Kagg's suspicions.

Already, perhaps, he had pursued the line of brusqueness too far.

He arrived at the restaurant a little before one. They ate at a small table in the rear of the place, and somehow the meeting went pretty much as the first one had. Somehow, and much to Roy's annoyance, the feeling of empathy grew between them. Toward the end of the meal, Kaggs did a surprising thing—surprising, that is, for him. Reaching across the table, he gave Roy a shy slap on the shoulder.

"Feeling lousy, aren't you, boy? Like you could bite nails."

"What?" Roy looked at him startled. "What makes you think that?"

"You'd just have to; I know I would. A man can idle around so long, and then it begins to drive him nuts. Why don't you come back to the office with me for a while? Sort of look the set-up over."

"Well, I—you're busy, and—"

"So I'll put you to work, too." Kaggs stood up, smiling. "I'm kidding, of course. You can just look around; take a gander at the salesmen's file, if you like. Do what you want to, and pull out when you want to."

"Well . . ." Roy shrugged. "Why not?"

The question was rhetorical; he could think of no valid reason to decline. Similarly, finding himself in Kagg's office at Sarber & Webb, he was forced to accept the file which Kaggs showed in front of him. To show at least a semblance of interest in its various cards.

Resentfully, he saw himself a victim of Kaggs's highhandedness. Kaggs had taken charge of him again, as he had on that first day. But that wasn't really true. More accurately, he was his own victim, his own slave. He had made personality a profession, created a career out of steeling himself. And he could not stray far, or for long, from his self-made self.

He riffled through the cards, unseeing.

He began to see them, to read the meaning in them. They became people and money and life itself. And thoughtfully, one at a time, he took them out of the file and spread them out on the desk.

He picked up a pencil, reached for a lined pad of scratch paper . . .

As he worked, Kaggs gave him an occasional covert glance, and a smug smile tightened his thin lips. A couple of hours passed, and Kaggs arose and strolled over to his desk.

"How are you doing?"

"Sit down," Roy said, and as the other man obeyed, "I think this record system is all wrong, Perk. I don't want to tread on anyone's toes, whoever set it up, but—"

"Tread away. Nothing's sacred around here."

"Well, it's misleading, a waste of time. Take this man here. His gross sales for the week are six hundred and fifty dollars. His commission, over in this column, totals eighty-one dollars. What's his percentage of the week's sales?"

"I'd have to figure it up. Roughly, eight per cent."

"Not necessarily. Depending on what he sold, he might have some twenty-five per cent stuff in there. The point is, just what the hell was it that he sold? How much of it was practically loss-leader stuff, items that we have to sell in order to compete?"

Kaggs looked at him sharply; hesitated. "Well, of course, there's his sales slips; that's what his commissions were figured from."

"But where are the sales slips?"

"Accounting gets a copy, inventory gets a copy, and of course the customer gets one at the time of purchase."

"Why does inventory need a copy? The stuff is checked off at the time it leaves the shop, isn't it? Or at least it could be. You've got some duplicate effort if it isn't. Where you need a copy is here in the salesman's file."

"But—"

"Not in a file like this, of course. There isn't enough room. But it doesn't have to be like this. We don't have so many salesmen that we couldn't set up a separate file on each one, give each man a section in one of the filing cabinets."

Kaggs scratched his head. "Hmm," he said. "Well maybe."

"It ought to be done, Perk. It just about has to be if you're going to have a clear picture of what's going on. Tie the sale slips to the salesmen, and you know which men are selling and which are running a milk route. Order-takers. You know what items are moving and which need pushing, and which should be dropped entirely. Of course, you'll know all that eventually, anyway. But waiting can cost you a hell of a lot of money and—"

Roy broke off abruptly, suddenly abashed by his tone and his words. He shook his head, dismayed, like a man coming into wakefulness.

"Just listen to me," he said. "I come in here for the first time, and I start kicking your system to pieces."

"So kick it some more. Kick the crap out of it!" Kaggs beamed at him. "How are you feeling, anyway? Getting tired? Want to knock off for the day?"

"No, I'm okay. But—"

"Well, let's see then." Kaggs skidded his chair closer, and reached for a pencil. "What would you say to . . ."

An hour went by.

Two hours.

In the outer offices, one of the clerks turned a startled stare on her neighbor. "Did you hear that?" she whispered. "He was *laughing*! Old Picklepuss Kaggs laughed out loud!"

"I heard," said the other girl, grimly, "but I don't believe it. That guy never learned how to laugh!"

At five-thirty that evening, the telephone operator plugged in her night numbers and closed her board. The outer offices darkened and became silent, as the last of the office employees filed out. And at six, the downstairs workers departing to the muted clanging of the time-clock, the silence and the dimness became absolute.

At eight o'clock—

Perk Kaggs removed his glasses, and rubbed his eyes. He looked around, blinking absently, and a bewildered look spread over his face. With an amazed curse, he jumped to his feet.

"My God! Look at the time! Where the hell did the day go to?"

"What?" Roy frowned. "What's the matter, Perk?"

"Come on, you're getting out of here! Right this minute, damnit! My God—" Kaggs swore again. "I ask you to drop in for a few minutes and you put in a day's work!"

They had a late dinner together.

As they said good-night, Kaggs gave him a sharp searching glance. "Level with me, Roy," he said quietly. "You do want this job, don't you? You want to be a sales manager?"

"Well . . ." Roy hesitated for a flicker of a second.

There it was. Here was his chance to refuse. And he knew suddenly that he could refuse, without apology or explanation. He could say simply no, that he didn't want it, and that would be that. He could go back to his old life where he had left it. For something had happened between him and Kaggs, something that made them friends. And friends do not question each other's motives.

"Why, of course, I want it," he said firmly. "What gave you the idea that I didn't?"

"Nothing. I just thought that—nothing." Kaggs returned to his usual briskness. "To hell with it. To hell with you. Go home and get some sleep, and don't show up at the shop again until the doctor says you're ready!"

"You're the boss," Roy grinned. "'Night, Perk."

Driving back to the hotel, he started to rationalize his decision, to find some devious reason for doing what he had done. But that passed very quickly. Why shouldn't he take a job that he wanted to take? Why shouldn't a man want a friend, a real friend, when he has never before had one?

He put the car away and entered the hotel. The elderly night clerk hailed him.

"You had a phone call this morning, Mr. Dillon. Your mother."

"My mother?" Roy paused. "Why didn't you leave word for me where I work?"

"I was going to, sir, but she said not to bother. Didn't have time to wait, I guess."

Roy picked up a house phone, put in a call to Lilly's apartment. He hung up a moment or two later, puzzled, uneasy.

Lilly was gone. She had checked out of her apartment this morning, leaving no forwarding address.

He went upstairs. Frowning, he shucked out of his clothes and lay down on the bed. He tossed and turned for a while, worrying. Then, gradually, he relaxed and began to doze.

Lilly could take care of herself. There could be—must be—an innocent reason for her sudden move.

Del Mar . . . She might have moved there for the race meet. Or she might have found a more desirable apartment here in town that had to be taken immediately. Or perhaps Bobo Justus had suddenly recalled her to Baltimore.

He fell asleep.

After what seemed only an instant, he came awake.

Sunlight flooded the room. It was late in the morning. He was conscious that the phone had been ringing for a very long time. It was now silent, but its din was still in his ears. He started to reach for it, his senses dull, not fully free of the stupor of sleep, and there was a knock on the door, a steady knocking.

He crossed to it, opened it enough to look out. He blinked at the man there; then, the man identifying himself, stating his business with professional regret—apologizing for the errand that had brought him here—Roy let the door open wide.

And he stood shaking his head as the man came inside.

No, he shouted silently. It wasn't true! It was some stupid mistake! Lilly wouldn't be in Tucson! Why—why—

He said it aloud, glaring at his visitor. The latter pursed his lips thoughtfully.

"You didn't know she was in Arizona, Mr. Dillon? She didn't tell you she was going?"

"Of course, she didn't! Because she didn't go! I—I"—he hesitated, some of his caution asserting itself. "I mean, my mother and I weren't very close. We went our own ways. I hadn't seen her for almost eight years until she came here a few weeks ago, but—"

"I understand," the man nodded. "That jibes with our information, such as it is."

"Well, you're wrong, anyway," Roy said doggedly. "It's someone else. My mother wouldn't—"

"I'm afraid not, Mr. Dillon. It was her own gun, registered to her. The proprietor of the tourist court remembers that she was very distraught. Of course, it does seem a little odd that she'd use a gun with a silencer on it for . . . for something like that. But—"

"And she didn't! It doesn't make sense!"

"It never does, Mr. Dillon. It never makes sense when a person commits suicide . . ."

TWENTY-TWO

The man was slightly bald, heavy-set, with a plump, honest face. His name was Chadwick, and he was a Treasury Department agent. Obviously, he felt a little awkward about being here at such a time. But it was his job, distasteful though it might be, and he meant to do it. He did, however, lead into his business circuitously.

"You understand why I came rather than the local police, Mr. Dillon. It really isn't their affair, at least at this point. I'm afraid there may be some unpleasant publicity later on, when the circumstances of your mother's death are revealed. An attractive widow with so much money in her possession. But—"

"I see," said Roy. "The money."

"More than a hundred and thirty thousand dollars Mr. Dillon. Hidden in the trunk of her car. I'm very much afraid—" delicately; "I'm afraid she hadn't paid taxes on it. She'd been falsifying her returns for years."

Roy gave a wry look. "The body was discovered this morning; about eight o'clock, right? You seem to have been a very busy little man."

Chadwick agreed simply that he had been. "Our office here hasn't had time to make a thorough investigation, but the evidence is indisputable. Your mother couldn't have saved that much out of her reported income. She was a tax evader."

"How terrible! Too bad you can't put her in jail."

"Please!" Chadwick winced. "I know how you feel, but—"

"I'm sorry," Roy said quietly. "That wasn't very fair. Just what do you want me to do, Mr. Chadwick?"

"Well . . . I'm required to ask if you intend to lay claim to the money. If you care to say, that is. Possibly you'd rather consult a lawyer before you decide."

"No," Roy said. "I won't lay any claim to the money. I don't need it, and I don't want it."

"Thank you. Thank you, very much. Now, I wonder if you can give me any information as to the source of your mother's income. It seems obvious, you know, that there must have been tax evasions on the part of others, and—"

Roy shook his head. "I imagine you know as much about my mother's associates as I do, Mr. Chadwick. Probably," he added, with a tiredly crooked grin, "you know a hell of a lot more."

Chadwick nodded gravely, and stood up. Hesitating, hat in hand, he glanced around the room. And there was approval in his eyes, and a quiet concern.

Lilly's money had had to be impounded, he murmured; her car, everything she owned. But Roy mustn't think that the government was heartless in these matters. Any sum necessary for her burial would be released.

"You'll want to see to the arrangements personally, I imagine. But if there's anything I can do to help . . ." He took a business card from his wallet and laid it on the table. "If you can tell me when you might care to leave for Tucson, if you are going, that is, I'll notify the local authorities and—"

"I'd like to go now. Just as soon as I can get a plane."

"Let me help you," Chadwick said.

He picked up the phone, and called the airport. He spoke briskly, reciting a government code number. He glanced at Roy. "Get you out in an hour, Mr. Dillon. Or if that's too soon—"

"I'll make it. I'll be there," Roy said, and he began flinging on his clothes.

Chadwick accompanied him to his car, shook hands with him warmly as Roy opened the door.

"Good luck to you, Mr. Dillon. I wish we could have met under happier circumstances."

"You've been fine," Roy told him. "And I'm glad we met, regardless."

He had never seen the traffic worse than it was that day. It took all his concentration to get through it, and he was glad for the respite from thinking about Lilly. He got to the airport with ten minutes to spare. Picking up his ticket, he hurried toward the gate to his plane. And then, moved by a sudden hunch, he swerved into a telephone booth.

A minute or two later he emerged from it. Grim-faced, a cold rage in his heart, he went onto his plane.

It was a propellor job since his trip was a relatively short one, a mere five hundred and eighty miles. As it circled the field and winged south, a stewardess began serving the pre-luncheon drinks. Roy took a double bourbon. Sipping it, he settled back in his seat and gazed out the window. But the drink was tasteless and he gazed at nothing.

Lilly. Poor Lilly . . .

She hadn't killed herself. She'd been murdered.

For Moira Langtry was also gone from her apartment. Moira also had checked out yesterday morning, leaving no forwarding address.

There was one thing about playing the angles. If you played them long enough, you knew the other guy's as well as you knew your own. Most of the time it was like you were looking out the same window. Given a certain set of circumstances, you knew just about what he would do or what he had done.

So, without actually knowing what had happened, just how and why Lilly had been brought to her death, Roy knew enough. He could make a guess which came astonishingly close to the truth.

Moira had a contact in Baltimore. Moira knew that Lilly would be carrying heavy—that, like any successful operator, she would have accumulated a great deal of money which would never be very far from her. As to just how far, just where it might be hidden, Moira didn't know. She might look forever without finding it. Thus Lilly had had to be put on the run; for, running, she would take the loot with her, necessarily narrowing its possible whereabouts to her immediate vicinity.

How to make her run? No problem there. For a fearful shadow lies constantly over the residents of Uneasy Street. It casts itself through the ostensibly friendly handshake, or the gorgeously wrapped package. It beams out from the baby's carriage, the barber's chair, the beauty parlor. Every neighbor is suspect, every outsider, everyone period; even one's own husband or wife or sweetheart. There is no ease on Uneasy Street. The longer one's tenancy, the more untenable it becomes.

You didn't need to frighten Lilly. Only to frighten her a little more. And if you had a contact at her home base, someone to give her a "friendly warning" by telephone . . .

Roy finished his drink.

He ate the lunch which the stewardess served him.

She took the tray away and he smoked a cigarette, and the plane dropped lower over the desert and came into the Tucson glide pattern.

A police car was waiting for him at the airport. It carried him swiftly into the city, and a police captain took him into a private office and gave him such facts as he could.

". . . checked into the motor court around ten last night, Mr. Dillon. It's that big place with the two swimming pools; you passed it on the way into town. The night clerk says she seemed pretty jumpy, but I don't know that you can put much stock in that. People always remember that other people acted or looked or talked funny after something's happened to 'em. Anyway, your mother left a seven-thirty call, and when she didn't answer her phone one of the maids finally got around to looking in on her . . ."

Lilly was dead. She was lying in bed in her nightclothes. The gun was on the floor at the side of the bed. Judging by her appearance—*Roy winced*—she'd put the muzzle in her mouth and pulled the trigger.

There was no disarray in the room, no sign of a struggle, no suicide note. "That's about all we know, Mr. Dillon," the captain concluded, and he added with casual pointedness, "Unless you can tell us something."

Roy said that he couldn't and that was true. He could only say what he suspected, and such guilty suspicions would only damage him while proving nothing at all against Moira. It might make a little trouble for her, cause her to be picked up and questioned, but it would accomplish no more than that.

"I don't know what I could tell you," he said. "I've got an idea that she traveled with a pretty fast crowd, but I'm sure you're already aware of that."

"Yes."

"Do you think that it might not have been suicide? That someone killed her?"

"No," the captain frowned, hesitantly. "I can't say that I think that. Not exactly. There's nothing to indicate murder. It does seem strange that she'd come all the way from Los Angeles to kill herself and that she'd get into her nightclothes before doing it, but, well, suicides do strange things. I'd say that she was badly frightened, so afraid of being killed that she went out of her mind."

"That sounds reasonable," Roy nodded. "Do you think someone followed her to the motel? The person who'd frightened her, I mean."

"Possibly. But the place is on the highway, you know. People are coming in and out at all hours. If the guilty person was one of them, it would be practically impossible to tab him, and short of getting his confession to making a death threat, I don't know how we could stick him if he was tabbed."

Roy murmured agreement. There was only one thing more that he could say, one more little nudge toward Moira that he could safely give the captain.

"I'm sure you've already looked into it, captain, but what about fingerprints? Wouldn't they, uh—"

"Fingerprints," the officer smiled sadly. "Fingerprints are for detective stories, Mr. Dillon. If you dusted this office, you'd probably have a hard time finding a clear set of mine. You'd probably find hundreds of smudged prints, and unless you knew when they were made and just who you were looking for, I don't know what the devil you'd do with them. Aside from that, criminals at work have an unfortunate habit of wearing gloves, and many of the worst ones have no police record. Your mother, for example, had never been mugged or printed. I'm sorry—" he added quickly. "I didn't mean to refer to her as a criminal. But . . ."

"I understand," Roy said. "It's all right."

"Now, there are a few items of your mother's personal property which you'll want. Her wedding ring and so on. If you'll just sign this receipt . . ."

Roy signed, and was given a thin brown envelope. He pocketed it, the pitiful residue of Lilly's hard and harried years, and the captain escorted him back to the waiting police car.

The undertaking establishment was on a side street, a sedately imposing building of white stucco which blazed blindly in the afternoon sun. But inside it was almost sickeningly cool. Roy shivered slightly as he stepped into the too-fragrant interior; the manager of the place, apparently alerted to his coming, sprang forward sympathetically.

"So sorry, Mr. Dillon. So terribly sorry. No matter how we try to prepare for these tragic moments—"

"I'm all right." Roy removed his arm from the man's grasp. "I'd like to see my mother's—my mother, please."

"Shouldn't you sit down a moment first? Or perhaps you'd like a drink."

"No," Roy said firmly. "I wouldn't."

"It might be best, Mr. Dillon. It would give us a little time to, uh . . . Well, you understand, sir. Due to the unusual financial involvements, we have been unable to, uh, perform the cosmetic duties which we normally would. The loved one's remains—the poor dear face—"

Curtly, Roy cut him off. He understood, he said. Also, he said, enjoying the manager's wince of distaste, he knew what a bullet fired into a woman's mouth could do to her face.

"Now, I want to see her. Now!"

"As you wish, sir!" The man drew himself up. "Please to follow me!"

He led the way to a white-tiled room behind the chapel.

The cold here was icy. A series of drawers was set into one of the frostily gleaming walls. He gripped a drawer by its metal handle and gave it a tug, and it glided outward on its bearings. With an offended gesture, he stepped back and Roy advanced to the crypt and looked into it.

He looked and looked quickly away.

He started to turn away. And then, slowly, concealing his surprise, he forced his eyes back on the woman in the coffin.

They were about the same size, the same coloring; they had the same full but delicately-boned bodies. But the hands? *The hand!* Where was the evil burn that had been inflicted on it, where was the scar that such a burn must leave?

Well, doubtless it was on the hand of the woman who had killed this woman. The woman whom Moira Langtry had intended to kill, and who had killed Moira Langtry instead.

TWENTY-THREE

It was late evening when the dusty Cadillac reached downtown Los Angeles; pulled up a few doors short of the Grosvenor-Carlton. The driver leaned wearily over the wheel for a moment, limp with exhaustion, a little dizzy from sleeplessness. Then, resolutely, she raised her head, removed the tinted sunglasses, and studied herself in the mirror.

Her eyes were strained, bloodshot, but that didn't matter. They would probably be a hell of a lot worse, she suspected, before she was safely out of this mess. The glasses covered them, also helping to disguise her face. With the glasses on, and with the scarf drawn tightly around her head and under her chin, she could pass as Moira Langtry. She done it back at the Tucson motel, and she could do it again.

She made some minor adjustments on the scarf, pulling it a little lower on her forehead. Then, throwing off her weariness, subjecting it to her will, she got out of the car and entered the hotel.

The clerk greeted her with the anxious smile of the aged. He heard her request, a command, rather, and a touch of uncertainty tinged his smile.

"Well, uh, Mr. Dillon's out of town, Mrs. Langtry. Went to Tucson this morning, and—"

"I know that, but he's due back in just a few minutes. I'm supposed to meet him here. Now, if you'll kindly give me his key . . ."

"But—but—you wouldn't like to wait down here?"

"No, I would not!" Imperiously she held out her hand. "The key, please!"

Fumbling, he took the key from the rack and gave it to her. Looking after her, as she swung toward the elevator, he thought with non-bitterness that fear was the worst part of being old. The anxiety born of fear. A fella knew that he wasn't much good any more—oh, yes, he knew it. And he knew he didn't always talk too bright, and he couldn't really look nice no matter how hard he tried. So, knowing in his heart that it was impossible to please anyone, he struggled valiantly to please everyone. And thus he made mistakes, one after the other. Until, finally, he could no more bear himself than other people could bear him. And he died.

But maybe, he thought hopefully, this would be all right. After all, Mrs. Langtry and Mr. Dillon *were* good friends. And visitors did sometimes wait in a guest's room when the guest was out.

Meanwhile . . .

Entering Roy's room, the woman locked the door and sagged against it, briefly resting. Then, dropping the sunglasses and her modishly large handbag on the bed, she went resolutely to the four box-framed clown pictures. They had caught her attention the first time she had seen them—something that struck a jarring note; entirely incompatible with the known tastes of their owner. They couldn't have been there as decoration, so they must serve another purpose. And without seeing the symbolism in the four wisely grinning faces: Clotho, Lachesis, Atropos, and a fourth self-nominated Fate, Roy Dillon—she had guessed what the purpose was.

Now, prying loose the backs of the pictures, she saw that her guess was right.

The money tumbled out, sheaf after sheaf of currency. Stuffing it into her bag, she was struck with unwilling admiration for Roy; he must be good to have piled up this much. Then, stifling this emotion, telling herself that the theft would be good for him by pointing up the fruitlessness of crime, she finished her task.

Large as it was, the bag bulged with its burden of loot. She could barely close the clasp, and she wasn't at all sure that it would stay closed.

She hefted it, frowning. She put it under her arm, draping an end of the stole over it, checked her appearance in the mirror. It didn't look bad, she thought. Not *too* bad. If only the damned thing didn't fly open as she was passing through the lobby! She considered the advisability of leaving some of the money behind, and abruptly vetoed the idea.

Huh-uh! She needed the dough. Every damned penny of it and a lot more, besides.

She gave the mirror a final swift glance. Then, the purse clutched tightly under her arm, she crossed the door and unlocked it, pulled it open. And fell back with a startled gasp.

"Hello, Lilly," said Roy Dillon.

TWENTY-FOUR

The basic details of her story were just about what Roy expected them to be . . .

First there had been the warning call from Baltimore; then, responding to it, her frantic, unreasoning flight. She drove as hard as she could and as long as she could. When she could go no farther, she turned in at the Tucson tourist court.

The place had a garage, rather than individual car ports, and she hadn't liked that. But she was too tired to go farther; and since a garage attendant was on duty at all times, she could not reasonably object to the arrangement.

She put the loaded gun under her pillow. She undressed and went to bed. Yes, naturally she had locked her door, but that probably didn't mean much. Those places, motels and tourist courts, lost so many keys that they often had them made interchangeable, the same keys unlocking different doors. And that was doubtless the case here.

Anyway, she awakened hours later, with two hands clutching her throat. Hands that silenced any outcry she might make as they strangled her to death. She couldn't see who it was; she didn't care. She had been warned that she would be killed, and now she was being killed and that was enough to know.

She got the gun from under her pillow. Blindly, she had shoved it upward, into the face of her assailant. And pulled the trigger. And—and—

Lilly shuddered convulsively, her voice breaking. "God, Roy, you don't know what it was like! What it means to kill someone! All your life you hear about it and read about it, b-but—but when you do it yourself . . . "

Moira was in her nightclothes, an old trick of nocturnal prowlers. Caught in another's room, they lay it to accident, claiming that they left their own room on some innocent errand and somehow strayed into the wrong one.

There was a tagged key in Moira's pocket—the key to a nearby room. Also, it was the key to Lilly's predicament. It pointed to a plan, ready-made, and without thinking she knew what she must do.

She put Moira in her bed. She wiped her own fingerprints from the gun, and pressed Moira's prints upon it. She spent the night in Moira's room, and in the morning she checked out under Moira's name and with the dead woman's clothes.

Naturally, she couldn't take her own car. The car and the money hidden in it now belonged to Moira also. For Moira was now Lillian Dillon, and Lilly was Moira Langtry. And so it must always be.

"What a mess! And all for nothing, I guess. I was jake with Bobo all the time, but now that it's happened . . ." She paused, brightening a little. "Well, maybe it's a break for me, after all. I've been wanting out of the racket for years, and now I'm out. I can make a clean start, and—"

"You've already made a start," Roy said. "But it doesn't look very clean to me."

"I'm sorry," Lilly flushed guiltily. "I hated to take your money, but—"

"Don't be sorry," Roy said. "You're not taking it."

For a long moment, a silent second-long eternity, Lilly sat staring at her son. Looking into eyes that were her eyes, meeting a look as level as her own. So much alike, she thought, and the thought was also his. *Why can't I make him understand?* she thought. And he thought, *Why can't I make her understand?*

Shakily, a cold deadness growing in her heart, she arose and went into the bathroom. She bathed her face in the sink, patted it dry with a towel, and took a drink of water. Then, thoughtfully, she refilled the glass and carried it out to her son. "Why, thank you, Lilly," he said, touched by the small courtesy, disarmed by it. And Lilly told herself, *He's asking for it. I helped him when he was in a bind, and if he tries to hold out on me now, well he just hadn't better.*

"I have to have that dough, Roy," she said. "She had a bankbook in her purse, but that doesn't do me any good. I can't risk tapping it. All she had on her was a few hundred bucks, and what the hell am I going to do with that?"

Roy said she could do quite a bit with it. A few hundred would get her to San Francisco or some other not-too-distant city. It would give her a month to live quietly while she looked for a job.

"A job!" Lilly gasped. "I'm almost forty years old, and I've never held a legit job in my life!"

"You can do it," Roy said. "You're smart and attractive. There are any number of jobs you can hold. Just dump the Cad somewhere. Bury it. A Cad won't fit in with the way you'll be living, and—"

"Save it!" Lilly cut him off with an angry, knifing gesture. "You sit there telling me what to do—a guy so crooked that he has to eat soup with a corkscrew—!"

"I shouldn't have to tell you. You should be able to see it for yourself." Roy leaned forward, pleadingly. "A legit job and a quiet life are the only way for you, Lil. You start showing up at the tracks or the hot spots and Bobo's boys will be on you."

"I know that, damnit! I know I've got to lay low, and I will. But the other—"

"It's good advice, Lilly. I'm following it myself."

"Yeah, sure you are! I see you giving up the grift!"

"What's so strange about it? It's what you wanted. You kept pushing it at me."

"Okay," Lilly said. "So you're on the level. So you don't need the money, do you? You don't need or want it. So why the hell won't you give it to me?"

Roy sighed; tried to explain why: to explain acceptably the most difficult of propositions; i.e., that the painful thing you are doing for a person is really for his or her own good. And yet, talking to her, watching her distress, there was in his mind, unadmitted, an almost sadistic exulting. *Harking back to childhood, perhaps, rooted back there, back in the time when he had known need or desire, and been denied because the denial was good for him*. Now it was his turn. Now he could do the right thing—and yes, it was right—simply by doing nothing. *Now now now the pimp disciplining his whore listening to her pleas and striking yet another blow. Now now now he was the wise and strong husband taking his frivolous wife in hand. Now now now his subconscious was taking note of the bond between them, the lewd, forbidden and until now unadmitted bond. And so he must protect her. Keep her from the danger which the money would inevitably lead her to. Keep her available . . .*

"Now, look, Lilly," he said reasonably. "That money wouldn't last you forever; maybe seven or eight years. What would you do then?"

"Well . . . I'd think of something. Don't worry about that part."

Roy nodded evenly. "Yes," he said, "you'd think of something. Another racket. Another Bobo Justus to slap you around and burn holes in your hand. That's the way it would turn out, Lilly; that way or worse. If you can't change now, while you're still relatively young, how could you do it when you were crowding fifty?"

Fifty? There was an ancient sound about it and the odor of haggishness and the mouse-mouthed look of death . . .

And Carol? Ah, yes, Carol. A dear girl, a desirable girl. Perhaps, except for the until-now-unadmitted bond, THE girl. But as it was, only a ploy, a pawn in the game of life, death—and love—between Roy and Lillian Dillon. So—

"So that's how it is, Lil," Roy said. "Why I can't let you have the money. I mean, uh—"

His voice faltered weakly, his eyes straying away from hers.

After a moment, Lilly nodded. "I know what you mean," she said. "I think I know."

"Well—" he gestured, his hands suddenly awkward. "It's certainly simple enough."

"Yes," Lilly said. "It's simple enough. Very simple. And it's something else, too."

There was a peculiar glow in her eyes, a strange tightness to her face, a subdued huskiness to her voice. Watching him, studying him, she slowly crossed one leg over the other.

"We're criminals, Roy. Let's face it . . ."

"We don't have to be, Lil. I'm turning over a new leaf. So can you."

"But we've always had class. We've kept our private lives fairly straight. There's been certain things we wouldn't do . . ."

"I know! So there's no complications! I can—we can—"

The leg was swinging gently; hinting, speaking to him. Holding him hypnotized.

"Roy . . . what if I told you I wasn't really your mother? That we weren't related?"

"Huh!" He looked up startled. "Why, I—"

"You'd like that, wouldn't you? Of course you would. You don't need to tell me. Now, why would you like it Roy?"

He gulped painfully, attempted a laugh of assumed nonchalance. Everything was getting out of hand, out of his hands and into hers. The sudden awareness of his feelings, the sudden understanding of himself, all the terror and the joy and the desire held him thralled and wordless.

"Roy . . ." So softly that he could hardly hear it.

"Y-yes?" *He gulped again*. "Yes?"

"I want that money, Roy. I've got to have it. Now, what do I have to do to get it?"

Lilly, he said, or tried to say it, and perhaps he did say some of what he meant to. Lilly, you know you can't go on like you were; you know you'll be caught, killed. You know I'm only trying to help you. If you didn't mean so much to me, I'd let you have the damned money. But I've got to stop you, I—I—

"Maybe—" she was going to be fair about this. "You mean you really won't give it to me, Roy? You won't? Or will you? Can't I change your mind? What can I do to get it?"

And how could he tell her? How say the unsayable? And yet, as she arose, moved toward him with the tempting grace with which Moira had used to move—*Moira, another older woman, who had in essence been Lilly*—he tried to tell her. And jumbled as it was, it was enough for Lilly.

"Why don't you finish your water, dear?" she said. And gratefully, welcoming this brief respite, he raised the glass. And Lilly, her grip tight on the heavy purse, swung it with all her might.

It's my fault, she told herself; the way I raised him, his age, my age, wrestling and brawling him as though he were a kid brother; my fault, my creation. But what the hell can I do about that, now?

The purse crashed against the glass, shattering it. The purse flew open, and the money spewed out in a green torrent. A torrent splattered and splashed with red.

Lilly looked at it bewilderedly. She looked at the gushing wound in her son's throat. He rose up out of his chair, clutching at it, and an ugly shard of glass oozed out between his fingers. He said bubblingly. "Lil, I—w-whyy—" and then his knees crumpled under him, and he doubled over and pitched down upon the carpet of red-stained bills.

It was over that quickly. Over before she could explain or apologize—insofar as there was anything to explain or apologize for.

Matter-of-factly, she began to toe the unstained money to one side, gathering the bills into a pile. She tied them up in a towel from the bathroom, stowed it inside her clothes, and took a final look around the room.

All clear, it looked like. Her son had been killed by Moira, by someone who didn't exist. Sure, her own fingerprints were all over the room, but that wouldn't mean anything. After all, she'd been a visitor to Roy's room before his death, and, anyway, Lilly Dillon was officially dead.

And maybe I am, she thought. *Maybe I wish to God that I was!*

Bracing herself, she let her eyes stray down to her son. Abruptly a great sob tore through her body, and she wept uncontrollably.

That passed.

She laughed, gave the thing on the floor an almost jeering glance. "*Well, kid, it's only one throat, huh?*"

And then she went out of the room and the hotel, and out into the City of Angels.

POP. 1280

ONE

Well, sir, I should have been sitting pretty, just about as pretty as a man could sit. Here I was, the high sheriff of Potts County, and I was drawing almost two thousand dollars a year—not to mention what I could pick up on the side. On top of that, I had free living quarters on the second floor of the courthouse, just as nice a place as a man could ask for; and it even had a bathroom so that I didn't have to bathe in a washtub or tramp outside to a privy, like most folks in town did. I guess you could say that Kingdom Come was really here as far as I was concerned. I had it made, and it looked like I could go on having it made—being high sheriff of Potts County—as long as I minded my own business and didn't arrest no one unless I just couldn't get out of it and they didn't amount to nothin'.

And yet I was worried. I had so many troubles that I was worried plumb sick.

I'd sit down to a meal of maybe half a dozen pork chops and a few fried eggs and a pan of hot biscuits with grits and gravy, and I couldn't eat it. Not all of it. I'd start worrying about those problems of mine, and the next thing you knew I was getting up from the table with food still left on my plate.

It was the same way with sleeping. You might say I didn't really get no sleep at all. I'd climb in bed, thinking this was one night I was bound to sleep, but I wouldn't. It'd be maybe twenty or thirty minutes before I could doze off. And then, no more than eight or nine hours later, I'd wake up. Wide awake. And I couldn't go back to sleep, frazzled and wore out as I was.

Well, sir, I was layin' awake like that one night, tossing and turning and going plumb out of my mind, until finally I couldn't stand it no longer. So I says to myself, "Nick," I says, "Nick Corey, these problems of yours are driving you plumb out of your mind, so you better think of something fast. You better come to a decision, Nick Corey, or you're gonna wish you had."

So I thought and I thought, and then I thought some more. And finally I came to a decision.

I decided I didn't know what the heck to do.

TWO

I got out of bed that morning, and I shaved and took a bath, even if it was only Monday and I'd washed real good the Saturday before. Then, I put on my Sunday-go-to-meetin' clothes, my new sixty-dollar Stetson and my seventy-five-dollar Justin boots and my four-dollar Levis. I stood in front of the mirror, checking myself over real good; making sure that I didn't look like some old country boy. Because I was making a little trip to see a friend of mine. I was going to see Ken Lacey and get his advice about my problems. And I always try to look my best when I see Ken Lacey.

I had to pass Myra's bedroom on the way downstairs, and she had her door open to catch the breeze, and without realizing that I was doing it, I stopped and looked in. Then I went in and looked at her some more. And then I eased toward the bed on tippy-toe and stood looking down at her, kind of licking my lips and feeling itchy.

I'll tell you something about me. I'll tell you for true. That's *one* thing I never had no shortage of. I was hardly out of my shift—just a barefooted kid with my first pair of boughten britches—when the gals started flinging it at me. And the older I got, the more of 'em there were. I'd say to myself sometimes, "Nick," I'd say, "Nick Corey, you'd better do something about these gals. You better start carrying you a switch and whip 'em off of you, or they'll do you to death." But I never did do nothing like that, because I just never could bear to hurt a gal. A gal cries at me a little, and right away I'm giving in to her.

Well, though, to get back to the subject, I never had no shortage of women and they were all real generous with me. Which maybe don't seem to add up, the way I was staring at my wife, Myra. Licking my lips and feeling itchy all over. Because Myra was quite a bit older than I was and she looked every bit as mean as she was.

And believe me, she was one danged mean woman. But the way it is with me, I'm kind of single-minded, I get to thinking about something, and I can't think of anything else. And maybe I wasn't suffering any shortage, but you know how that is. I mean, it's kind of like eating popcorn. The more you have the more you want.

She didn't have a nightdress on, it being summer, and she'd kicked the sheet off. And she was kind of laying on her stomach, so that I couldn't see her face, which made her look a lot better.

So I stood there, staring and steaming and itching, and finally I couldn't stand it no longer and I started unbuttoning my shirt. "After all, Nick," I says to myself, "after all, Nick Corey, this here woman is your wife, and you got certain rights."

Well, I guess you know what happened. Or I guess you don't know either. Because you don't know Myra, which makes you about as lucky as a person can get. Anyways, she turned over on her back all of a sudden, and opened her eyes.

"And just what," she said, "do you think you're doing?"

I told her I was just getting ready to take a trip over to the county where Ken Lacey was sheriff. I'd probably be gone until late that night, I said, and we'd probably get real lonesome for each other, so maybe we ought to get together first.

"Huh!" she said, almost spitting the word at me. "Do you think I'd want you, even if I was of a mind to have relations with a man?"

"Well," I said. "I kind of thought maybe you might. I mean, I kind of hoped so. I mean, after all, why not?"

"Because I can hardly bear the sight of you, that's why! Because you're stupid!"

"Well," I said. "I ain't sure I can agree with you, Myra. I mean, I ain't saying you're wrong but I ain't saying you're right, either. Anyways, even if I am stupid, you can't hardly fault me for it. They's lots of stupid people in the world."

"You're not only stupid but you're spineless," she said. "You're about the poorest excuse for nothing I ever laid eyes on!"

"Well, looky," I said. "If you feel that way, why for did you marry me?"

"Listen to him! Listen to the beast!" she said. "As if he didn't know why! As if he didn't know that I had to marry him after he raped me!"

Well, that made me kind of sore, you know. She was always saying

I'd raped her, and it always made me kind of sore. I couldn't really argue about her saying I was stupid and spineless, because I probably ain't real smart—who wants a smart sheriff?—and I figure it's a lot nicer to turn your back on trouble than it is to look at it. I mean, what the heck, we all got trouble enough of our own without butting in on other people's.

But when she said I was a rapist, *that* was something else. I mean, there just wasn't a word of truth in it. Because it just didn't make sense.

Why for would a fella like me rape a woman, when he had so many generous gals chasing him?

"Well, I'll tell you about this rape business," I said, getting kind of red in the face as I rebuttoned my shirt. "I ain't saying you're a liar, because that wouldn't be polite. But I'll tell you this, ma'am. If I loved liars, I'd hug you to death."

Well, that really started her off. She started blubbering and bawling like a calf in a hail storm. And of course that woke up her half-witted brother, Lennie. So he came rushing in, blubbering and rolling his eyes and slobbering all over his chin.

"What you done to Myra?" he says, spraying spit for about twenty feet. "What you gone an' done to her, Nick?"

I didn't say anything, being busy dodging the spit. He went stumbling over to Myra, and she took him into her arms, glaring at me.

"You beast! Now look what you've done!"

I said, what the heck, I hadn't done nothing. Far as I could see, Lennie was pretty near always bawling and slobbering. "About the only time he ain't," I said, "is when he's sneaking around town, peeking in some woman's window."

"You—you bully!" she said. "Faulting poor Lennie for something he can't help! You know he's as innocent as a lamb!"

I said, "Yeah, well, maybe." Because there wasn't much else to say, and it was getting close to train time. I started toward the hall door, and she didn't like that, me walking out without so much as a beg-pardon, so she blazed away at me again.

"You better watch your step, Mr. Nick Corey! You know what will happen if you don't!"

I stopped and turned around. "What will happen?" I said.

"I'll tell the people in this county the truth about you! We'll see how long you'll be sheriff then! After I tell them you raped me!"

"I'll tell you right now what will happen," I said. "I'd be run out of my job before I could say scat."

"You certainly would! You'd better remember it, too!"

"I'll remember," I said, "an' here's something for you to remember. If I ain't sheriff, then I got nothing to lose, have I? It don't make a good gosh-damn about anything. And if I ain't the sheriff, you ain't the sheriff's wife. So where the heck will that leave you—you and your half-witted brother?"

Her eyes popped and she sucked in her breath with a gasp. It was the first time I'd spoken up to her for a long time, and it kind of took the starch out of her.

I gave her a meaningful nod, and went out the door. When I was about halfway down the stairs, she called to me.

She'd moved real fast, throwing on a robe and working up a smile. "Nick," she said, kind of cocking her head to one side, "why don't you come back for a few minutes, hmmm?"

"I guess not," I said. "I'm kind of out of the mood."

"We-el. Maybe, I could get you back in the mood. Hmmmm?"

I said I guessed not. Anyways, I had to catch a train, and I'd have to grab a bite to eat first.

"Nick," she said, sort of nervous-like. "You—you wouldn't do anything foolish, would you? Just because you're angry with me."

"No, I wouldn't," I told her. "No more'n you would, Myra."

"Well. Have a nice day, dear."

"The same to you, ma'am," I said. And then I went on downstairs, into the courthouse proper, and out the front door.

I almost took a header as I came out into the dusky haze of early morning. Because the danged place was being painted, and the painters had left their ladders and cans scattered all over everywhere. Out on the sidewalk, I looked back to see what kind of progress they'd been making. The way it looked to me, they hadn't made hardly any at all in the last two, three days—they were still working on the upper front floor—but that wasn't none of my butt-in.

I could have painted the whole building myself in three days. But I wasn't a county commissioner, and I didn't have a painting contractor for a brother-in-law.

Some colored folks had a cook-shack down near the railway station, and I stopped there and ate a plate of corn bread and fried catfish. I was too upset to eat a real meal; too worried about my worries. So I just ate the one plateful, and then I bought another order with a cup of chicory to take on the train with me.

The train came and I got on. I got a seat next to the window, and began to eat. Trying to tell myself that I'd really got Myra told off this morning and that she'd be a lot easier to get along with from now on.

But I knew I was kidding myself.

We'd had showdowns like the one this morning a lot of times. She'd threaten what she was going to do to me, and I'd point out that she had plenty to lose herself. And then things would be a little better for a while—but not really better. Nothing that really mattered was any better.

It wasn't, you see, because it wasn't a fair stand-off between me and her.

She had the edge, and when things came to a showdown, she knew I'd back away.

Sure, she couldn't lose me my job without being loser herself. She'd have to leave town, her and her low-down half-wit of a brother, and it'd probably be a danged long time before she had it as nice as she had it with me. Probably she'd never have it as nice.

But she *could* get by.

She'd have *something*.

But me . . .

All I'd ever done was sheriffin'. It was all I could do. Which was just another way of saying that all I could do was nothing. And if I wasn't sheriff, I wouldn't have nothing or be nothing.

It was a kind of hard fact to face—that I was just a nothing doing nothing. And that brought up something else for me to worry about. The worry that maybe I could lose my job without Myra saying or doing anything.

Because I'd begun to suspect lately that people weren't quite satisfied with me. That they expected me to do a little something instead of just grinning and joking and looking the other way. And me, I just didn't quite know what to do about it.

The train took a curve and began to follow the river a ways. By craning my neck, I could see the unpainted sheds of the town whorehouse and the two men—pimps—sprawled on the little wharf in front of the place. Those pimps had caused me a sight of trouble, a powerful sight of trouble. Only last week, they'd accidentally-on-purpose bumped me into the river, and a few days before they'd accidentally-on-purpose tripped me up in the mud. And the worst thing of all was the way they talked to me, calling me names and poking mean fun at me, and not showing me no respect at all like you'd naturally expect pimps to show a sheriff, even if he was shaking 'em down for a little money.

Something was going to have to be done about those pimps, I reckoned. Something plumb drastic.

I finished eating and went up to the men's lounge. I washed my hands and face at the sink, nodding to the fella that was sitting on the long leather bench.

He wore a classy black-and-white checked suit, high-button shoes with spats and a white derby hat. He gave me a long slow look, letting his eyes linger for a moment on my pistol belt and gun. He didn't smile or say anything.

I nodded at the paper he was reading. "What do you think about them Bullshevicks?" I said. "You reckon they'll ever overthrow the Czar?"

He grunted, still not saying anything. I sat down on the bench a few feet away from him.

The fact was, I wanted to relieve myself. But I wasn't sure that I ought to go on into the toilet. The door was unlocked, swinging back and forth with the motion of the train, and it looked like it must be empty. Still, though, here this fella was, and maybe that's what he was waiting for. So even if the place was empty, it wouldn't be polite to go in ahead of him.

I waited a little while. I waited, squirming and fidgeting, until finally I couldn't wait any longer.

"Excuse me," I said. "Were you waiting to go to the toilet?"

He looked startled. Then, he gave me a mean look, and spoke for the first time. "That's some of your business?"

"Of course not," I said. "I just wanted to go to the toilet, and I thought maybe you did, too. I mean, I thought maybe someone was already in there, and that's why you were waiting."

He glanced at the swinging door of the toilet; swinging wide now so that you could see the stool. He looked back at me, kind of bewildered and disgusted.

"For God's sake!" he said.

"Yes, sir?" I said. "I don't reckon there's anyone in there, do you?"

I didn't think he was going to answer me for a minute. But then he said, yeah, someone was in the toilet. "She just went in a little while ago. A naked woman on a spotted pony."

"Oh," I said. "But how come a woman's using the men's toilet?"

"On account of the pony," he said. "He had to take a leak, too."

"I can't see no one from here," I said. "It's funny I couldn't see 'em in a little place like that."

"You calling me a liar?" he said. "You saying a naked woman on a spotted pony ain't in there?"

I said, no, of course not. I wouldn't say nothing like that. "But I'm in kind of a hurry," I said. "Maybe I better go up to one of the other cars."

"Oh, no, you don't!" he said. "No one's calling me a liar and getting away with it!"

"I'm not," I said. "I didn't mean it that way at all. I just—"

"I'll show you! I'll show you I'm telling the truth! You're gonna sit right there until that woman and her pony comes out."

"But I gotta pee!" I said. "I mean, I really got to, sir."

"Well, you ain't leaving here," he said. "Not until you see I'm telling the truth."

Well, sir, I just didn't know what to do. I just didn't know. Maybe you would have, but I didn't.

All my life, I've been just as friendly and polite as a fella could be. I've always figured that if a fella was nice to everyone, why, they'd be nice to him. But it don't always work out that way. More often than not, it seems like, I wind up in a spot like I was in now. And I just don't know what to do.

Finally, when I was about to let go in my britches, the conductor came through taking up tickets, and I had a chance to get away. I tore out of there in such a hurry that it was maybe a minute before I could get the door open to the next car. And I heard a burst of laughter from the rest room behind me. They were laughing at me, I guess—the conductor and the man in the checked suit. But I'm kind of used to being laughed at, and anyway I didn't have time to think about it right then.

I dashed on up into the next car and relieved myself—and believe me it was a relief. I was coming back down the aisle, looking for a seat in that car so's I wouldn't run into the checked-suit fella again, when I saw Amy Mason.

I was pretty sure that she'd seen me, too, but she let on that she didn't. I hesitated by the seat next to her for a minute, then braced myself and sat down.

No one knows it in Pottsville, because we were careful to keep it a secret, but me and Amy was mighty thick at one time. Fact is, we'd've got married if her daddy hadn't had such strong objections to me. So we waited, just waiting for the old gentleman to die. And then just a week or so before he did, Myra hooked me.

I hadn't seen Amy since except to pass on the street. I wanted to tell her I was sorry, and try to explain things to her. But she never gave me the chance. Whenever she saw me, she'd toss her head and look away. Or if I tried to stop her, she'd cross to the other side of the street.

"Howdy, Amy," I said. "Nice morning."

Her mouth tightened a little, but she didn't speak.

"It's sure nice running into you like this," I said. "How far you ridin', if you don't mind my asking?"

She spoke that time. Just barely. "To Clarkton. I'll be getting ready to leave any moment now."

"I sure wish you was riding further," I said. "I been wanting to talk to you, Amy. I wanted to explain about things."

"Did you?" She slanted a glance at me. "The explanation seems obvious to me."

"Aw, naw, naw," I said. "You know I couldn't like no one better'n you, Amy. I never wanted to marry anyone in my life but you, and that's the God's truth. I swear it is. I'd swear it on a stack of Bibles, honey."

Her eyes were blinking rapidly, like she was blinking back the tears. I got hold of her hand and squeezed it, and I saw her lips tremble.

"Th-then, why, Nick? Why did—y-you—"

"That's what I been wanting to tell you. It's a pretty long story, and—looky, honey, why don't I get off at Clarkton with you, and we can get us a hotel room for a couple hours and—"

It was the wrong thing to say. Right at that time it was the wrong thing.

Amy turned white. She looked at me with ice in her eyes. "So that's what you think of me!" she said. "That's all you want—all you ever wanted! Not to marry me, oh, no, I'm not good enough to marry! Just to get me in bed, and—"

"Now, please, honey," I said. "I—"

"Don't you dare honey me, Nick Corey!"

"But I wasn't thinking about that—what you think I was thinking about," I said. "It was just that it'd take quite a while to explain about me and Myra, and I figured we'd need some place to—"

"Never mind. Just never mind," she said. "I'm no longer interested in your explanations."

"Please, Amy. Just let me—"

"But I'll tell you one thing, Mr. Nicholas Corey, and you'd better pass the word along to the proper quarters. If I catch your wife's brother peeking in *my* windows, there's going to be trouble. *Real* trouble. I won't put up with it like the other women in Pottsville do. So you tell her that, and a word to the wise is sufficient."

I told her I hoped she didn't ever do anything about Lennie. For her own sake, that is. "I got no more use for Lennie than you have, but Myra—"

"Humph!" She tossed her head and stood up as the train slowed down for Clarkton. "You think I'm afraid of that—that—her?"

"Well," I said, "it might be better if you was. You know how Myra is when she takes out after someone. By the time she gets through gossiping and telling lies, why—"

"Let me out, please."

She pushed past me and went on up the aisle, her head high, the ostrich plume on her hat dipping and swaying. As the train pulled out, I tried to wave to her where she stood on the platform. But she turned her head quickly, with another swoop of the ostrich plume, and started off up the street.

So that was that, and I told myself that maybe it was just as well. Because how could we ever mean anything to each other the way things stood?

There was Myra, of course, and there was going to be Myra, it looked like, until her or me died of old age. But Myra wasn't the only drawback.

Somehow, I'd gotten real friendly with a married woman, name of Rose Hauck. One of those involvements which I've always kind of drifted into before I knew what was happening. Rose didn't mean a thing to me, except that she was awful pretty and generous. But I meant plenty to her. I meant plenty-plenty, and she'd let me know it.

Just to show how smart Rose was, Myra considered her her very best friend. Yes, sir, Rose could put on that good an act. When we were alone, me and Rose that is, she'd cuss Myra until it actually made me blush. But when they were together, oh, brother! Rose would suck around her—honeyin' and dearie-in' her—until heck wouldn't have it. And Myra would get so pleased and flustered that she'd almost weep for joy.

The surest way of gettin' a rise out of Myra was to hint that Rose was something less than perfect. Even Lennie couldn't do it. He started to one time, just kind of hinted that anyone as pretty as Rose couldn't be as nice as she acted. And Myra slapped him clean across the room.

THREE

Maybe I didn't tell you, but this Ken Lacey I was going to visit was the sheriff a couple of counties down the river. Me and him met at a peace officers' convention one year, and we kind of cottoned to each other right away. He wasn't only real friendly, but he was plenty smart; I knew it the minute I started talking to him. So the first chance I got, I'd asked him advice about this problem I had.

"Um-hmmm!" he'd said, after I'd explained the situation and he'd thought it over for a while. "Now, this privy sits on public property, right? It's out in back of the courthouse?"

"That's right," I said. "That's exactly right, Ken."

"But it don't bother no one but you?"

"Right again," I said. "You see, the courtroom is on the downstairs rear, and it don't have no windows in back. The windows are up on the second floor where I live."

Ken asked me if I couldn't get the county commissioners to tear the privy down and I said no, I couldn't hardly do that. After all, a lot of people used it, and it might make 'em mad.

"And you can't get 'em to clean it out?" he asked. "Maybe sweeten it up a little with a few barrels of lime?"

"Why should they?" I said. "It don't bother no one but me. I'd probably call down trouble on myself if I ever complained about it."

"Uh-*hah*!" Ken nodded. "It'd seem right selfish of you."

"But I got to do something about it, Ken," I said. "It ain't just the hot-weather smell, which is plenty bad by itself, but that's only part of it. Y'see, there's these danged big holes in the roof that show everything that's going on inside. Say I've got some visitors in, and they think, Oh, my, you must have a wonderful view out that way. So they look out, and the only view they get is of some fella doing his business."

Ken said, "Uh-hah!" again, kind of coughing and stroking his mouth. Then, he went on to say that I really had a problem, a *real* problem. "I can see how it might even upset a high sheriff like you, Nick, with all the pre-occu-pations of your great office."

"You got to help me, Ken," I said. "I'm getting plumb frazzled out of my wits."

"And I'm *going* to help you," Ken nodded. "I ain't never let a brother officer down yet, and I ain't about to begin now."

So he told me what to do, and I did it. I sneaked out to the privy late that night, and I loosened a nail here and there, and I shifted the floor boards around a bit. The next morning, I was up early, all set to spring into action when the proper time came.

Well, sir, the fella that used the privy most was Mr. J. S. Dinwiddie, the bank president. He'd use it on the way home to lunch and on the way back from lunch, and on the way home at night and on the way in in the morning. Well, sometimes he'd pass it up, but never in the morning. By the time he'd got that far from his house his grits and gravy were working on him, and he just couldn't get to the privy fast enough.

He went rushing in that morning, the morning after I'd done my tampering—a big fat fella in a high white collar and a spanking new broadcloth suit. The floor boards went out from under him, and down into the pit. And he went down with them.

Smack down into thirty years' accumulation of night soil.

Naturally, I had him fished out almost as fast as he went in. So he wasn't really hurt none, just awful messed up. But I never saw one man so mad in all my borned days.

He hopped up and down and sideways, waving his fists and flinging his arms around, and yelling blue murder. I tried to toss some water over him to get the worst of the filth off. But the way he was hopping around and jumping every which way, I couldn't do much good. I'd throw the water at him in one place, and he'd be in another. And cuss! You never heard anything like it, and him a deacon in the church!

The county commissioners came running out, along with the other office holders, all of 'em pretty jittery to see the town's most important citizen like that. Mr. Dinwiddie recognized them somehow, although it's hard to see how he could with all that gunk in his eyes. And if he could have found a club, I swear he'd've clubbed 'em.

He cussed 'em up one side and down the other. He swore he'd file felony charges against them for criminal negligence. He yelled that he was going to file personal damage suits against them for wilfully perpetuating a public hazard.

About the only person he had a kind word for was me. He said that a man like me could run the county by himself, and that he was going to see that all the other officials were recalled, because they were just a needless expense and a menace to life and limb as well.

As things turned out, Mr. Dinwiddie never did get around to doing anything of the things he threatened to. But that sure settled the privy problem. It was gone and the pit was filled in within an hour; and if you ever feel like getting a punch in the nose, just tell the commissioners that there ought to be another courthouse privy.

Well, that's a sample of Ken Lacey's advice. Just one sample of how good it is . . .

Of course, some people might say it was no good at all, that it might have got Mr. Dinwiddie killed and me in a pack of trouble. They might say that the other advice Ken had given me was pure meanness, and meant to be hurtful rather than helpful.

But me, well, I'll always think good of people as long as I possibly can. Or at least I won't think bad about 'em until I absolutely have to. So I hadn't quite reached a decision about Ken as yet.

I figured I'd see how he acted today, what kind of advice he gave me before I made up my mind. If he stacked up even halfway good, I'd give him the benefit of the doubt. But if he didn't appear even that good . . .

Well, I'd know what to do about him.

I always know.

FOUR

I bought a bite of lunch from the train news butch, just a few sandwiches and some pie and potato chips and peanuts and cookies and sody-pop. About two o'clock that afternoon, we got into Ken Lacey's town, the county seat where he was high sheriff.

It was a real big place—probably four, five thousand people. The main street was paved, along with the square around the courthouse, and everywhere you looked there were wire-wheeled buggies and fancy fringe-topped carriages, and I even seen two, three auty-mobiles with eye-goggled dudes driving 'em and women in veils and linen dusters holding on for dear life. I mean, it was just like being in New York or one of them other big cities I've heard about. All that stuff to see, and the people so busy and used to excitement that they didn't pay it no mind at all.

Just for example, I passed this one vacant lot where there was the god-dangest dogfight going on that I ever did see. Kind of a battle royal between two hounds and a bulldog and a kind of spotty-assed mongrel.

Why, even if there hadn't been a fight, that mongrel would have been enough to make a fella stop and stare. Because I'm telling you, he was really something! He had this high ass in the back, all spotted and speckled like a cow had farted bran on him. But his front legs were so short that his nose almost rubbed on the ground. And one of his eyes was blue and the other'n was yaller. A real bright yaller like a woman's hair.

I stood there gawking, wishing that I had someone from Pottsville with me as a witness, because naturally no one'd ever believe, I'd really seen a dog like that. Then, I happened to look around, and hard as it was to tear myself away, I turned my back on that spectacle and went on toward the courthouse.

I just about had to, you know, unless I wanted people to think I was an old country boy. Because I was the only one that had stopped to look. There was so much going on in that city that no one would ever give a second glance to something like *that*!

Ken and a deputy named Buck, a fella I'd never met before, were sitting in the sheriff's office; slumped way down on their spines with their boots crossed out in front of 'em, and their Stetsons tilted over their eyes.

I coughed and scuffled my feet, and Ken looked up from under his hatbrim. Then he said, "Why, I'll be god-danged, if it ain't the high sheriff of Potts County!" And he rolled his chair over to me and held out his hand.

"Set down, set down, Nick," he said, and I sat down in one of the swivel chairs. "Buck, wake up and meet a friend of mine."

Buck was already awake, as it turned out, so he rolled over and shook hands like Ken had. Then, Ken kind of jerked his head at him, and Buck rolled over to the desk and got out a quart of white corn and a handful of stogies.

"This here Buck is the smartest deputy I got," Ken said, as we all had a drink and lit up. "Got a lot of initiative, Buck has. Don't have to tell him every god-danged thing he's supposed to do like you would some fellas."

Buck said all he'd ever done was to just try to do his duty, and Ken said, no, sir, he was smart.

"Like old Nick here. That's why he's sheriff of the forty-seventh largest county in the state."

"Yeah?" Buck said. "I didn't know they was but forty-seven counties in the state."

"Pre-zackly!" Ken said, sort of frowning at him. "How is things in Pottsville these days, Nick? Still booming?"

"Well, no," I said. "I wouldn't hardly say they was booming. Pottsville ain't exactly no real metropolis like you got here."

"Is that a fack?" Ken said. "Guess my recollection ain't as good as it used to be. Just how big is Pottsville, anyways?"

"Well, sir," I said, "there's a road sign just outside of town that says 'Pop. 1280,' so I guess that's about it. Twelve hundred and eighty souls."

"Twelve hundred and eighty souls, huh? Is them souls supposed to have people to go with 'em?"

"Well, yeah," I said, "that's what I meant. It was just another way of saying twelve hundred and eighty people."

We all had a couple more drinks, and Buck tossed his stogie in a gaboon and cut himself a chaw; and Ken said I wasn't pre-zackly correct in saying that twelve hundred and eighty souls was the same as twelve hundred and eighty people.

"Ain't that right, Buck?" Ken said, giving him a nod.

"Kee-rect!" Buck said. "You're a thousand per cent right, Ken!"

"Natcherly! So just tell old Nick why I am."

"Shorely," Buck said, turning toward me. "Y'see it's this way, Nick. That twelve hundred and eighty would be countin' niggers—them Yankee lawmakers force us to count 'em—and niggers ain't got no souls. Right, Ken?"

"Kee-rect!" Ken said.

"Well, now, I don't know about that," I said. "I wouldn't come out flat and say you fellas was wrong, but I sure don't reckon I can agree with you neither. I mean, well, just how come you say that colored folks don't have souls?"

"Because they don't, that's why."

"But why don't they?" I said.

"Tell him, Buck. Make old Nick here see the light," Ken said.

"Why, shorely," Buck said. "Y'see, it's this way, Nick. Niggers ain't got no souls because they ain't really people."

"They ain't?" I said.

"Why, o' course not. Most everybody knows that."

"But if they ain't people, what are they?"

"Niggers, just niggers, that's all. That's why folks refers to 'em as niggers instead of people."

Buck and Ken nodded at me, as if to say there wasn't anything more to be said on this subject. I took another pull at the bottle and passed it around.

"Well, looky here, now," I said. "How about this? My mama died almost as soon as I was born, so I was put to suck with a colored mammy. Wouldn't be alive today except for her sucklin' me. Now, if that don't prove—"

"No, it don't," Ken broke in. "That don't prove a thing. After all, you could have sucked titty from a cow, but you can't say that cows is people."

"Well, maybe not," I said. "But that ain't the only point of similarity. I've had certain relations with colored gals that I sure wouldn't have with a cow, and—"

"But you could," Ken said. "You could. We got a fella over in the jail right now for pleasurin' a pig."

"Well, I'll be dogged," I said, because I'd heard of things like that but I never had known of no actual cases. "What kind of charges you makin' against him?"

Buck said maybe they could charge him with rape. Ken gave him a kind of blank look and said no, they might not be able to make that kind of charge stick.

"After all, he might claim he had the pig's consent, and then where would we be?"

"Aw," said Buck. "Aw, now, Ken."

Ken said, "What you mean, aw, now. You tryin' to tell me that animals can't understand what you're sayin' to 'em? Why, god-dang it, I got me this little ol' beagle-terrier, and I can say, 'Boy, you want to go catch some rats?' and he'll leap all over me, barkin' and whinin' and licking my face. Meaning, natcherly, that he does want to go after rats. Or I can say, 'Boy, you want me to take a stick to you?' an' he'll slink off in a corner with his tail between his legs. Meanin' he don't want me to take a stick to him. An'—"

"Well, sure," Buck said. "But—"

"God-dang it!" Ken said. "Shut up when I'm talking! What the hell's wrong with you, anyways? Here I go an' tell Nick what a smart fella you are, and god-dang if you don't make a liar out of me right in front of him!"

Buck got kind of red in the face, and said he was sure sorry. He sure hadn't meant to contradict Ken. "I can see just how it happened, now that you explained it to me. This fella, he probably says to the pig, 'How about a little you-know-what, Piggie?' and the pig started squealing and twitchin' her tail, meanin' she was ready whenever he was."

"O' course, that's the way it happened!" Ken scowled. "So what'd you mean by disputin' me? Why for was you telling me he couldn't have had the pig's consent, and making a god-danged idjit out of yourself in front of a visitin' sheriff? I tell you somethin', Buck," Ken went on, "I was entertainin' some pret-ty high hopes for you. Almost had me convinced you was a white man with good sense instead of one of these big-mouth smart-alecks. But now I don't know; I purely don't know. 'Bout all I can say is you shore better watch your step from now on."

"I shore will. I'm shore sorry, Ken," Buck said.

"I mean it! I mean every god-danged word of it!" Ken frowned at him. "You ever go disputin' or contradictin' me again, an' you'll be out in the street scratching horse turds with the sparrows. Or maybe you think you won't be, huh? Maybe you're gonna start arguin' again, tellin' me you won't be out fighting them birds for turds? Answer me, you god-danged liver-lipped idjit!"

Buck sort of choked up for a moment, and then he said of course Ken was right. "You say the word, Ken, an' that's pre-zackly what I'd be doin'."

"Doin' what? Speak up, god-dang it!"

"S-Scratchin'"—Buck choked again—"scratchin' horse turds with the sparrers."

"The hot, steamy kind, right? *Right?*"

"Right," Buck mumbled. "You're a thousand per cent right, Ken. I—I reckon there ain't nothin' less appetizin' than a cold horse turd."

"Well, all right, then," Ken said, easing up on him and turning to me. "Nick, I reckon you didn't come all the way up here to hear me an' old stupid Buck jibber-jabberin' at each other. 'Pears to me like you got plenty of troubles of your own."

"Well, sir, you're sure right about that, Ken," I said. "You purely are, an' that's a fact."

"And you're wantin' my advice, right? You ain't like some smark-alecks that think they already know everything."

"Yes, sir," I said. "I sure do want your advice, Ken."

"Uh-hah?" he nodded. "Uh-hah. Go right ahead, Nick."

"Well, it's like this," I said. "I got this here problem that's been driving me plumb out of my mind. Couldn't hardly sleep nor eat it's been pesterin' me so much. So I fretted and studied an' I thought and I thought, and finally I came to a decision."

"Uh-huh?"

"I decided I didn't know what to do," I said.

"Uh-huh," Ken said. "Well, now, don't you go rushin' into it. Me an' old Buck here has got plenty on our minds, but we always got time to consult with a friend. Right, Buck?"

"Kee-reck! You're a thousand per cent right, Ken. Like always."

"So you just take your time an' tell us about it, Nick," Ken said. "I'm always willin' to lay aside the cares of my great office when a friend's in trouble."

I hesitated, wanting to tell him about Myra and her half-wit brother. But all of a sudden, it seemed too personal. I mean, how can you discuss your wife with another fella, even a good friend like Ken was. And what the heck could he do about *her*, even if I did tell him?

So I reckoned I'd better leave her out of it, and take up this other big problem I had. I figured it was one problem he could handle just fine. In fact, now that I'd kind of had a chance to get reacquainted with him, and I'd seen how he handled Buck, I knew he was just the man to take care of it.

FIVE

"Well, sir, Ken," I said. "You know that whorehouse there in Pottsville. Place over on the river bank, just a whoop an' a holler from town . . ."

Ken looked up at the ceiling and scratched his head. He allowed that he couldn't say that he did know about it, but he figured naturally that Pottsville had a whorehouse.

"Can't very well run a town without one, right, Buck?"

"Right! Why if they wasn't any whores, the decent ladies wouldn't be safe on the streets."

"Kee-reck!" Ken nodded. "Fellas would get all full of piss an' high spirits and take right off after 'em."

"Well, that's the way I look at it," I said. "But now I got this trouble. Y'see, there's these six whores, all nice friendly girls and just as accommodatin' as you could ask for. I really can't make no complaint about these girls. But along with them is these two pimps—one pimp for three girls, I guess—and those pimps are giving me trouble, Ken. They been sassin' me somethin' awful."

"Now, you don't mean that!" Ken said. "You don't mean t'tell me that these pimps has actually been sassin' the high sheriff of Potts County!"

"Yes, sir," I said, "that's exactly what they've been doin'. An' the bad part about it is, they sometimes done it in front of other people, and a thing like that, Ken, it just don't do a sheriff no good. The word gets around that you've been told off by pimps, and it don't do you no good a-tall!"

"Do tell!" Ken said. "You spoke the God's truth there, Nick! But I reckon you don't just let 'em get away with it? You taken some action against 'em?"

"Well," I said, "I've been sassin' em back. I can't say that it's stopped 'em, but I sure been sassin' 'em back, Ken."

"Sassin' 'em *back*! Why for did you do that?"

"Well, it seemed about right," I said. "A fella sasses you, why you just pay him off by sassin' back."

Ken sort of drew his mouth in, and shook his head. He asked Buck if he'd ever heard such a thing in his life, and Buck said he purely hadn't. Not in all his borned days.

"I'll tell you what you got to do, Nick," Ken said. "No, sir, I'll show you what to do. You just stand up and turn your back to me, an' I'll give you a ill-us-strated lesson."

I did what he told me to. He got up out of his chair, and hauled off and kicked me. He kicked me so hard that I went plumb out the door and half-ways across the hall.

"Now, you come back in here," he said, crocking a finger at me. "You just sit down there like you was, so's I can ask you some questions."

I said I guessed I'd better stand up for a minute, and he said all right, have my own way about it. "You know why I kicked you, Nick?"

"Well," I said, "I guess you probably had a good reason. You were trying to teach me something."

"Right! So here's what I want to ask you. Say a fella kicks you in the ass like I just did, why what do you do about it?"

"I don't rightly know," I said. "No one ever kicked me in the ass before, saving my daddy, God rest his soul, and there wasn't much I could do about it with him."

"But suppose someone did. Let's just say we got a hypocritical case where someone kicks you in the ass. What would you do about it?"

"Well," I said, "I guess I'd kick *him* in the ass. I guess that'd be about right."

"Turn around," Ken said. "You turn right back around again. You ain't learned your lesson yet."

"Well, looky," I said. "Maybe if you could just explain a little more—"

"You turnin' ongrateful?" Ken frowned. "You tryin' to give orders to a fella when he's trying to help you?"

"No, no, I ain't trying to do that," I said. "But—"

"Well, I should hope not! Now, you just turn around like I told you to."

I turned my back to him again; there just wasn't anything else I could do, it looked like. He and Buck both got up, and they both kicked me at the same time.

They kicked me so hard that I went practically straight up instead of forward. I came down kind of crooked on my left arm, and it hurt so bad that I almost forgot who I was for a moment.

I picked myself up, trying to rub my ass and my arm at the same time. Which just can't be done, in case you're thinking about doing it. I sat down, sore as I was, because I was just too dizzy to stand.

"Hurt your arm?" Ken said. "Whereabouts?"

"I'm not positive," I said. "It could be either the radius or the ulna."

Buck gave me a sudden sharp look out from under his hatbrim. Sort of like I'd just walked into the room and he was seeing me for the first time. But of course Ken didn't notice anything. Ken had so much on his mind, I reckon, helping poor stupid fellas like me, that he maybe didn't notice a lot of things.

"Now, I guess you learned your lesson, right, Nick?" he said. "You see the futility of not givin' back no more hurt than what you get?"

"Well, I sure learned some kind of lesson," I said. "So if that's the one you was teaching me, I guess that was it."

"Y'see, maybe the other fella can kick harder'n you can. Or maybe he's got a tougher ass an' it don't hurt him as much as it does you. Or say you got a situation like me an' Buck just demonstrated. Two fellas start kicking you in the ass, so's you get two kicks for every one you give. You get a situation like that, which is just about what you got figuratively speakin', why you could get the ass kicked clean off of you a-fore you had time to tip your hat."

"But these pimps ain't kicked me," I said. "They just been sassin' me, and shovin' me around a little."

"Same principle. Same principle, pre-zackly. Right, Buck?"

"Right! Y'see, Nick, when a fella starts doin' somethin' bad to you, the proper way to pay him back is t'do somethin' twice as bad to him. Otherwise, the best you got is maybe a stand-off, and you don't never get nothing settled."

"Kee-reck!" Ken said. "So I'll tell you what to do about them pimps. The next time they even look like they're goin' to sass you, you just kick 'em in the balls as hard as you can."

"Huh?" I said. "But—but don't it hurt awful bad?"

"Pshaw, 'course it don't hurt. Not if you're wearin' a good pair o' boots without no holes in 'em."

"That's right," Buck said. "You just be sure you ain't got any toes stickin' out and it won't hurt you a-tall."

"I mean, wouldn't it hurt the pimps?" I said. "Me, I don't think I could stand even an *easy* kick in the balls."

"Why, shorely, shorely it would hurt 'em," Ken nodded. "How else you goin' to make 'em behave if you don't hurt 'em bad?"

"You're actually lettin' 'em off pretty easy, Nick," Buck said. "I know I'd sure hate to be in the same room if any pimp sassed old Ken here. Ken wouldn't stop with just kickin' 'em. Why, a-fore they knew what was happening, he'd just yank out his pissoliver and shoot 'em right in their sassy mouths."

"Pre-zackly!" Ken said. "I'd send them sassy skunks to hell without no fooling around about it."

"So you're really being too easy on 'em, Nick. A god-danged sight easier than a proud, intelligent, upstandin' officer like ol' Ken. Ken would shoot 'em deader'n doornails, if he was in your place, and you heard him say so yourself."

"Right!" said Ken. "I sure wouldn't miss doing pre-zackly that."

Well . . .

It looked like I'd got what I came for, and it was getting kind of late by then. So I thanked Ken for his advice, and stood up. I was still just a little wobbly, though; kind of rocking on my heels. And Ken asked me if I was sure I could make it to the station all right.

"Well, I guess so," I said. "I sure hope so, anyways. It sure wouldn't seem right for me to ask you to walk me there after everything you've already done for me."

"Why, you don't need to ask!" Ken said. "You think I'd let you go all the way to the train alone, a fella that looks as peaked as you do?"

"Well, I wouldn't want to trouble you none," I said.

"Trouble?" Ken said. "Why, it's a positive pleasure! Buck, you just heist yourself up out of that chair, and walk Nick to the depot."

Buck nodded and heisted himself up. I said I sure hoped I wasn't putting him to any bother, and he said it wouldn't be no bother a-tall.

"Just so's you can bear with me," he said. "Know I can't be no ways as good a comp'ny for you as a fella like Ken."

"Well, now, I'm sure you'll be just fine," I said. "Bet you'll prove out a real interestin' fella."

"I'll try," Buck promised. "Yes, sir, I'll purely try, and that's a fack."

SIX

I had supper down near the depot, buying a whopping big meal for Buck along with my own. Then, my train came and Buck walked me down to the car I was riding in. Not that I couldn't have made it all right by myself—I was feeling pretty good about then. But we were getting along real fine, just like I thought we might, and we had a lot of things to say to each other.

I fell asleep almost as soon as I'd given my ticket to the conductor.

But I didn't sleep good. Dog-tired as I was, I drifted into a scary dream, the nightmare that was always a-haunting me. I dreamed that I was a kid again, only it didn't seem like a dream. I *was* a kid, living in the old rundown plantation house with my daddy. Trying to keep out of his way, and never being able to. Getting beat half to death every time he could grab me.

I dreamed I was ducking into a doorway, thinking I'd got away from him. And suddenly being grabbed from behind.

I dreamed I was putting his breakfast on the table. And trying to get my arms up when he flung it in my face.

I dreamed—I *lived*—showing him the reading prize I'd won in school. Because I was sure that would please him, and I just had to show it to someone. And I dreamed—*lived*—picking myself up off the floor with my nose bloodied from the little silver cup. And he was yelling at me, shouting that I was through with school because I'd just proved I was a cheat along with everything else.

The fact was, I guess, that he just couldn't stand for me to be any good. If I was any good, then I couldn't be the low-down monster that had killed my own mother in getting born. And I had to be that. He had to have someone to blame.

I don't fault him much for it any more, because I've seen a lot of people pretty much like he was. People looking for easy answers to big problems. People that blame the Jews or the colored folks for all the bad things that happen to 'em. People that can't realize that a heck of a lot of things are bound to go wrong in a world as big as this one. And if there is any answer to why it's that way—and there ain't always—why, it's probably not just one answer by itself, but thousands of answers.

But that's the way my daddy was—like those people. They buy some book by a fella that don't know a god-dang thing more than they do (or he wouldn't be having to write books). And that's supposed to set 'em straight about everything. Or they buy themselves a bottle of pills. Or they say the whole trouble is with other folks, and the only thing to do is get rid of 'em. Or they claim we got to war with another country. Or . . . or God knows what all.

Anyway, that's how my daddy was. That's the way I grew up. It's no wonder, I reckon, that me and the girls always got along so well. I reckon I really worked at getting along with 'em; sort of made a trade out of it without really knowing that I was doing it. Because a fella has to have someone that likes him. He just naturally has to. And girls are just naturally inclined to like a man.

I guess when you come right down to it, I was making the same mistake that those people I was talking about make. Because there ain't no bigger problem than love, nothing as truly hard to come by, and I was looking for an easy answer to it.

SEVEN

Well, sir, danged if I hadn't got back in Pottsville on just about the darkest night of the year. It was so dark that I could have had a firefly sitting on my nose and I wouldn't have been able to see it.

Of course, the dark didn't really bother me. The way I knew every nook and cranny of Pottsville, I could get to wherever I wanted to go if I was walking in my sleep. So the dark was really an advantage to me, rather than otherwise. If anyone was up and around, and of course there wouldn't be at that time of night, they wouldn't see where I was going and wonder why I was going there.

I walked right down the dark middle of Main Street. I turned south at the end of it, and headed toward the river. There was just a speck of light down that way, sort of a little blob bulging up out of the darkness. I figured it came from the whorehouse, or rather from the little pier behind it. Those two pimps would be sitting out there, I knew, taking the night air and drinking themselves stiff.

They'd be feeling their oats for sure by the time I got there. All sassy and nasty, and primed for meanness toward a fella that'd always been nice to them.

I struck a match, took a quick look at my watch, I began to walk faster. The steamer, *Ruby Clark*, was about due and I had to be on hand when it rounded the bend.

There'd been a pretty hard rain the week before; low river country, there's always a lot of rain. The wet was all dried up by now, because we get a lot of hot sunshine too. But the road had gotten rutted here and there, and hurrying like I was I brought my foot down where I shouldn't have.

I stumbled, almost taking a header before I could right myself. I paused, sort of getting my breath back, and then I whirled around. Straining my eyes and ears, scared stiff for a minute. Because I'd heard something. The same kind of clod-kicking sound I'd made, only not so loud.

I held my breath, telling myself that there couldn't be anyone following me. Knowing that even if there was someone back there, I was still protected by the darkness.

I stood stock still for two, three minutes. Then, I heard the sound again and I recognized it for what it was, and I almost laughed out loud with relief.

It was just some of those god-danged big night-beetles we have down here. They go swooping around, looking for each other, and then they come together in mid-air and go plunking down on the ground.

They can make a heck of a racket on a stilly night. If you're maybe just a little uneasy like I was, they can give you a bad start.

It was two or three minutes later when I got to the whorehouse. I tippy-toed along the walk which ran down the side of the place, and went around to the rear.

The two pimps were there, right where I thought they'd be. They were sitting down with their backs to the mooring posts, a dimmed lantern and a jug of whiskey between them. They looked at me owl-eyed as I came in out of the darkness, and then the one named Curly, a kind of dude-ish fella with kinky scalp-tight hair, shook a finger at me.

"Now, Nick, you know you're not supposed to come over here but once a week. Just once a week, and only long enough to pick up your graft and get."

"That's right," said the one named Moose. "Fact is, we're bein' mighty generous to let you come here at all. We got a reputation to protect here, and it sure doesn't help none to have a fella like you dropping around."

"Well, now," I said, "that's not a very nice thing to say."

"Oh, well, there's nothing personal in it," Curly said. "It's just one of those unpleasant facts of life. You're a crook, and it doesn't look good to have crooks around."

I asked him how come he thought I was a crook, and he said what else could I call myself. "You take graft, don't you? You're getting a dollar out of every five that comes in here?"

"But I have to," I said. "I mean, it's kind of a civic duty. If I didn't keep you people stripped down a little, you'd get too powerful. First thing I know, you'd be running the county instead of me."

Moose sneered and wobbled to his feet. "You two-bit clown," he said, "will you just get the hell out of here? Will you, or am I gonna have to make you?"

"Well, now," I said. "Well, now, I don't know about that. I figure that's a pretty mean way to talk to a fella that's always been nice to you."

"Are you gonna get or not?" He took a step toward me.

"You'd better, Nick," Curly nodded, pushing himself up. "You kind of make us sick to our stomachs, you know? It may not be your fault, but the air turns bad every time you show up."

Around the bend, I could see the lights of the *Ruby Clark*, and I could hear the whip of the paddles as it fought for the turn. It was that time, it would be that time any second now, and I unholstered my gun and took aim.

"Wha—!" Moose stopped dead in his tracks, his mouth gaping open.

Curly said, "Oh, now, Nick!" forcing a smile to his face. But it was the sickest smile I'll ever see.

That's one thing people always know, I guess. They know when they're going to die. And Moose and Curly knew that they were going to.

"Good night, ye merry gentlemen," I said. "Hail and farewell."

The *Ruby Clark* whistled.

By the time the echo died, Moose and Curly were in the river, each with a bullet spang between his eyes.

I waited on the little pier for a minute until the *Ruby* had gone by. I always say there's nothing prettier than a steamboat at night. Then I went back around on the catwalk, and headed for home.

The courthouse was dark, naturally, when I got there. I took off my boots and crept up the stairs. And I got in bed without waking anyone.

I fell asleep right away. A couple of hours later I waked up, with Myra shaking me.

"Nick! *Nick!* Will you please get up, for pity's sake!"

"Huh! What?" I said. "What's going on, Myra?"

But I heard it then, the pounding on the downstairs door. A fella would've had to be deaf not to hear it.

"Well, I'll be dogged," I said. "Now, who in tarnation can that be?"

"Well, go and see, darn it! Get down there before they wake poor Lennie up!"

I studied about it for a moment, staying right where I was while Myra went on nagging at me. Then I said I wasn't sure whether I should go downstairs or not, because why for would any honest person be pounding on doors at this time of night?

"It might be robbers, Myra," I pointed out. "Wouldn't be a bit surprised if that's who it was. I hear they do their robbin' late at night when decent folks is in bed."

"You fool! You stupid, spineless, cowardly slob! Are you the sheriff of this county or not?" Myra yelled.

"Well," I said, "I guess you could say that."

"And isn't it the sheriff's job to take care of criminals? Isn't it? Answer me, you—you—!"

"Well, I guess you could say that, too," I said. "I ain't thought much about it, but it sounds reasonable."

"You—you get down there!" Myra spluttered. "Doggone you, you get right down there this minute, or I'll—I'll—"

"But I ain't got no clothes on," I said. "Nothin' but my long-handled drawers. Wouldn't hardly seem right goin' to the door without no clothes on."

Myra's voice dropped so low that I could hardly hear it, but her eyes flashed fire. "Nick," she said, "this is the last time I'm going to tell you. You go to the door right this minute, or you'll wish you had! You'll really wish you had!"

The pounding was getting a lot louder by now, and someone was shouting my name, someone that sounded an awful lot like Ken Lacey. So, what with Myra carrying on like she was, I figured maybe I'd better go to the door.

I swung my legs over the side of the bed, and pulled on my boots. I studied 'em a minute, wetting my finger with spit and rubbing down a little scuffed place. I yawned and stretched, and scratched under my armpits.

Myra let out a groan. She snatched up my britches and flung 'em at me, so that the legs wrapped around my neck like a scarf.

"You ain't mad about somethin', are you, honey?" I said, getting the britches untangled and starting to draw 'em on. "I sure hope I ain't annoyed you no way."

She didn't say anything. Just started to swell up like she was about to explode.

"I got a trade-last for you," I said. "A fella was saying to me the other day, he said, 'Nick, you got the prettiest mother in town.' So I asked him who he meant, naturally, because my mama's been dead for years. And he said, 'Why, that lady you call Myra. You mean to tell me she ain't your mother?' That's just what he said, honey. So now you got to tell me something nice that someone said about me."

She still didn't say anything. She just leaped at me, sort of meowing like a cat, her hands clawed to scratch my eyes out.

She didn't do it, because I'd been kind of expecting something like that. All the time I was talking to her, I was easing back toward the door. So instead of landing on me, she came up against the wall, clawing the heck out of it a-fore she could come to her senses.

Meantime, I went on downstairs and opened the door.

Ken Lacey busted in. He was wild-eyed, heaving for breath. He grabbed me by the shoulders and started shaking me.

"Have you done it yet?" he said. "God-dang it, have you already gone an' done it?"

"Wh-what?" I tried to shake free of him. "Have I gone an' done what?"

"You know what, god-dang it! What I told you to do! Now, you answer me, you consarned idjit, or I'll beat it out of you!"

Well, sir, it looked to me like he was pretty excited about something. Might get himself in such a tizzy that he'd keel over with the frantics. So I just pushed him into my office and made him sit down at my desk, and I struck a lamp and made him take a big drink of whiskey. And then, when he seemed to be calmed down a little, I asked him just what it was all about.

"What am I supposed to have done, Ken? The way you're actin', you'd think I'd killed someone."

"Then you didn't," he said, his eyes hard on my face. "You didn't kill anyone."

"Kill anyone?" I said. "Why, what a riddicerlous question! Why for would I kill anyone?"

"And you didn't? You didn't kill them two pimps that was sassing you?"

"Ken," I said. "How many times have I got to tell you? Why for would I kill anyone?"

He heaved a big sigh, and relaxed for the first time. Then, after another long drink, he slammed down the jug and began to cuss his deputy, Buck.

"God-dang, just wait until I get hold of him! Just you wait! I'll kick his mangy ass s'hard he'll have to take off his boots to comb his hair!"

"Why, what'd he do?" I said. "What's old Buck gone an' done?"

"He frazzled me, that's what! Got me so god-danged excited an' worried that I was plumb out of my mind," Ken said, cussing Buck up one side and down the other. "Well, it's my own god-danged fault, I reckon. Had the proof right before me that he was a low-down maniac, but broad-minded like I am, I went and closed my eyes to it."

"How come?" I said. "What you mean you had the proof, Ken?"

"I mean I caught him reading a book, that's what! Yes, sir, I caught him red-handed. Oh, he claimed he was only lookin' at the pitchers, but I knew he was lyin'."

"Well, I'll be dogged!" I said. "I will be double-dogged! But what's Buck got to do with you being down here?"

So Ken told me how it had happened.

It seemed like after he left me, Buck went back to the office and began to fret out loud. Wonderin' whether I'd really be crazy enough to kill those pimps, which would leave Ken in a peck of trouble. The way Buck saw it—in his out-loud worryin'—Ken had told me I should kill 'em, and if I went ahead and did it he'd be just as guilty as I was.

He kept on fretting about it, Buck did, saying I just *might* kill the pimps because I'd always taken Ken's advice in the past, no matter how nutty it was. And then when he saw how upset Ken was getting, he said that the law probably wouldn't be too hard on him. Proba'ly wouldn't be hard on him, a-tall, like they would me, but maybe let him off with only thirty, forty years.

The upshot of it was that Ken finally tore out of his office, and caught the Red Ball freight to Pottsville. He hadn't had too nice a trip because the caboose, where he was sittin', had had an awful flat wheel. He said he was probably a lot sorer in the behind than I was from getting kicked, and all he wanted to do now was go to bed.

"I just had more'n one poor body can stand in a day," he yawned. "I reckon you can put me up all right, can't you?"

I said that I was right shamed, but, no, I couldn't. We just didn't have no place where an extra fella could be bedded down.

"God-dang it!" he scowled. "All right, I'll go to the hotel, then!"

I allowed that that might be kind of hard to do, seeing that Pottsville didn't have a hotel. "If it was daytime, you could bed at the Widder Shoup's place; that's what the travellin' salesmen do. But she sure wouldn't let you in at this time of night."

"Well, where the god-danged hell am I gonna sleep, then?" he said, "I sure as heck ain't sittin' up all night!"

"Well, let's see now," I said. "Danged if I can only think of but one place, Ken. A place that could bed you down. But I'm afraid you wouldn't get much sleep there."

"You just lead me to it! I'll do the sleepin'!"

"Not at the whorehouse you wouldn't," I said. "Y'see, the girls ain't had much business lately, and they'd all be mighty raunchy. Prob'ly be makin' demands on you all night long."

"Uh-hah!" Ken said. "Well, now! I reckon a fella can put up with anything if he has to. Nice young gals, are they?"

"No, they ain't," I said. "Most of 'em are fairly young, maybe seventeen, eighteen. But they got this one old gal that's every bit of twenty-one. And she just won't leave a fella alone! She purely won't, Ken, and it wouldn't be fair not to warn you."

A streak of spit was trickling down his chin. He brushed it away and stood up, a kind of glassy look in his eyes.

"I better be goin'," he said. "I better be goin' right this minute."

"I'll put you on the right road," I said. "But there's something you got to know first. About them two pimps . . ."

"Don't you worry none. I'll take care of 'em!"

"You won't have to," I said, "because they won't be there. They'll be off somewheres drunk by now, and they won't wake up until noon."

"What the hell, then?" Ken took a fidgety step toward the door. "If the girls think they ain't there—"

"But they *don't* think that. The pimps have got 'em kidded that they're watching the place day and night, which naturally makes it hard for the girls to relax and have fun like they want to. So—"

"Uh-huh? Yeah, yeah," Ken said. "Go on, god-dang it!"

"So here's what you do as soon as you go in. You tell the girls that you've taken care of the pimps real good, and that they won't be nosing around a-tall. You tell 'em that, and everything will be just fine an' dandy."

He said he'd tell 'em what I said to. (And as it turned out, he told them exactly that.) Then, he went out the door and across the yard, moving so fast that I could hardly keep up with him.

We crossed through the edge of town, and I lined him up on the river road. He went on by himself, then, without so much as a nod. And then I reckon he remembered his manners, because he turned around and came back.

"Nick," he said, "I'm obliged to you. Maybe I ain't been too nice to you in the past, but I ain't forgettin' what you've done here tonight!"

"Aw, pshaw," I said. "Comes to that, Ken, I ain't forgetting all the things you've done, neither."

"Well, anyways, I'm obliged to you," he said.

"Why, it was a positive pleasure doin' it," I said. "A positive pleasure, and that's a fact."

EIGHT

Ken showed up at breakfast time the next morning, looking mighty peaked and pale and wrung-out. But all shook-up as he was, he managed to toss a lot of flattery at Myra and to say a few kind words to Lennie, so she treated him pretty nice. Not real nice, because she knew he'd spent the night in the whorehouse—which was the only place he could have spent it—but as nice as a lady could treat a gentleman under the circumstances. She kept urging him to have something to eat, and Ken kept turning it down with thanks and saying that he hardly ever et anything in the morning but just a little coffee, which was all he wanted now.

"I got to watch my weight, ma'am," he said. "I ain't got a naturally handsome figure like you and your fine-looking brother."

Lennie giggled and spit at him; feelin' pleased, you know. Myra blushed and said he was just a great big flatterer.

"Me? Me, flatter a woman?" Ken said. "Why, I never heard the like!"

"Oh, you! You know I don't have a *really* good figure."

"Well, maybe not. But that's because you ain't fully developed yet," Ken said. "You're still a young girl."

"Tee-hee," Myra giggled. "You awful thing, you!"

"You just wait until you fill out a little," Ken said. "Wait until you're as old as your brother."

Well, sir, lies like that can take a lot out of a man even when he's feeling good. Which Ken sure wasn't. He was just carrying on out of habit, and from the looks of him he was just about to the end of his rope. Fortunately, it seemed to occur to Myra about then that she was being a little too friendly with Ken and that she was letting him get pretty gay with her. So she froze up all of a sudden, and started clearing away the dishes. And Ken said his thank-yous and good-byes, and I got him downstairs to my office.

I handed him a quart bottle of white whiskey. He took a long, long drink, gagged, gulped and leaned back in his chair. Sweat popped out on his forehead. He shuddered all over, and his face turned a few shades whiter. For a minute I thought he was going to be one sick man; all that lying and flattering to Myra had been just too much for him. Then, all at once, the color flooded back into his face, and he stopped sweating and shaking. And he drew a long, deep sigh.

"God-dang!" he said softly. "I shore needed that."

"Fella can't ride a horse with one stirrup," I said. "Have another one, Ken."

"Well, god-dang it," he said. "God-dang it, Nick, I don't care if I do."

He had a couple of more drinks, which brought the bottle down to about the halfway level. Then he said he guessed he'd better slow down a little bit. And I told him to just take his time, he couldn't get a train back home for a couple of hours yet.

We sat there for a minute or two, not saying much of anything.

He looked at me and looked away again, and a kind of shy-sly look came over his face.

"Mighty handsome young fella your brother-in-law," he said. "Yes, sir, mighty handsome."

"And he's an idjit," I said. "Anyways, he sure ain't quite right in the head."

Ken nodded and said, yeah, he'd noticed that. "But maybe that might not make too much difference to a certain kind of woman, you know, Nick? Say a woman that was a lot older than he was. A woman that was pretty ugly and pretty apt to stay that way."

"Well, I just don't know about that," I said. "I wouldn't say you were wrong but I sure wouldn't say you was right either."

"Well, maybe that's because you ain't real bright," Ken said. "Why, I'll bet you there's a woman right in this town that would really *pree-fer* Lennie to a fella like you. I ain't sayin' that you ain't a plenty good-lookin' fella yourself, but probably you ain't got as long a dingle-dangle as he has—they tell me them idjits are hung like a stud-hoss. And, anyways—"

"Well, now, I don't know about that," I said. "I ain't never had any complaints in that department yet."

"Shut up when I'm talkin'!" Ken said. "Shut up and maybe you'll learn somethin'! I was about to say that everything else being equal, which I doubt like hell in your case because all of them idjits have got dongs you could skip rope with, *but*—but irregardless of that a woman still might rather have a dummy pour it on her than a normal fella. Because she don't have to put on for him, know what I mean? She can boss him around. She can be just as haggy as all hell and twice as mean, and she can still get what she needs."

I scratched my head and said, well, maybe so. But I still thought he was wrong about Lennie. "I know for a fact that there ain't no woman in this town that's got any use for him. They pretend that they do, to keep on the good side of Myra, but I know they all hate his guts."

"*All* of 'em?"

"All of 'em. Except Myra, of course. His sister."

Ken snorted and ran his hand over his mouth. Then, he kind of got a grip of himself, and his talk slowed down a little. But he still couldn't get off the subject.

"Ain't much family resemblance between Lennie and your wife. Hardly know they was brother an' sister unless someone told you."

"That's right, I guess," I said. "Can't say that I ever thought much about it."

But I had thought about it. Yessir, I'd thought plenty about it.

"Was you acquainted with Lennie before you married? Know that you was goin' to have a idjit for a brother-in-law?"

"Well, no, I didn't," I said. "I didn't even know that Myra had a brother until afterwards. Came as quite a surprise to me."

"Uh-hah!" Ken snorted. "Well, don't be surprised if you get another surprise some time, Nick. No, sir, don't you be surprised at all."

"What?" I said. "How do you mean, Ken?"

He shook his head, not answering me, and broke out laughing. I laughed right along with him.

Because it was a pretty good joke, you see. *I* was a joke. And maybe I couldn't do anything about it right now, but I figured I would some day.

Ken took a couple more long drinks. I stood up and said maybe we'd better be going. "Got quite a little walk to the station, and I want you to meet a few fellas. Be a big treat for 'em to meet a big-city sheriff like you."

"Why, now, I bet it would be that," Ken said, staggering to his feet. "Prob'ly ain't every day they get to meet a real man in a pisspot of a town like this."

"Tell 'em how you took care of them two pimps," I said. "They'll be right impressed hearin' how you took on two pimps all by yourself, and gave 'em what-for."

He blinked at me owlishly. He said, what pimps, what the god-danged hell was I talking about, anyway? I said, the pimps I'd warned him about last night—the two that were bound to try to give him some trouble.

"Huh?" he said. "What? Did you tell me somethin' like that?"

"You mean you let 'em get away with it?" I said. "Ken Lacey took dirt from a couple of low-down pimps?"

"Hah? What?" He rubbed his hand over his eyes. "Who says I took dirt from pimps?"

"I knew you didn't!" I said, giving him a slap on the back. "Not Ken Lacey, the bravest, smartest peace officer in the state."

"Well," said Ken. "Uh, you shorely spoke a mouthful there, Nick. You shorely did, and that's a fact!"

"Any other man, I wouldn't have let him go over there last night. But I knew you could stand up to those pimps if they come at you with guns and knives. I knew you'd make 'em wish they'd never been born."

Ken put a stern look on his face, like that fella William S. Hart does in the movies. He squared his shoulders and straightened up, or as much as he could straighten with the whiskey wobbling his legs.

"What'd you do to 'em, Ken?" I said. "How did you settle their hash, anyways?"

"I, uh, I took care of 'em, that's what." He gave me a lopsided wink. "You know, I—*hic!*—took care of 'em."

"Good. You took care of 'em for good, Ken?"

"God-danged right, I did. Them's two pimps that won't never bother a white man no more!"

He started looking around for the whiskey bottle. I pointed out that he was holding onto it, so he had himself a couple more drinks, and then he held the bottle up to the light.

"Why, god-dang! Danged if I ain't drunk almost a whole quart of whiskey!"

"What the heck?" I said. "It don't hardly show on you none." And the funny part of it was that it suddenly didn't show much.

I'd seen him drink before, and I knew how whiskey acted on him. A fairly small amount of booze, say, a pint or so, and he'd get drunk as a skunk. He'd show it, I mean. But when he went over that certain amount—and up to a point, of course—he'd seem to sober up. He'd stop staggering, stop slurring his words, stop playing the fool in general. Inside, he'd still be dead drunk, but you'd never know it by looking at him.

He finished the rest of the whiskey, and we headed for the railroad station. I introduced him to everyone we met, which was a big part of the population, and he stuck out his chest and told everyone how he'd taken care of the two pimps. Or rather, he just said that he *had* taken care of 'em.

"Never mind how," he'd say. "Never you mind how." And then he'd wink and nod, and everybody would be pretty impressed.

We stopped to talk to so many people that it was only a couple of minutes before train time when we got to the station. I shook hands with him and then, before I realized I was doing it, I laughed out loud.

He gave me a suspicious look; asked me what I was laughing about.

"Nothing much," I said. "I was just thinkin' how funny it was you rushing down here last night. Thinkin' I might kill those pimps."

"Yeah," he grinned sourly, "that is funny. Imagine a fella like you killing anyone."

"You can't imagine me doing it, can you, Ken? You just can't, can you?"

He said he sure couldn't, and that was a fact. "If I'd stopped to think, instead of letting that god-danged Buck get me all riled up—"

"But it would be easy to imagine you doing that killing, wouldn't it, Ken? Killing wouldn't bother you a bit."

"What?" he said. "What do you mean, I—"

"In fact, folks wouldn't have to do any imagining, would they? You've as good as admitted it to dozens of people."

He blinked at me. Then the wild sweat broke out on his face again, and a streak of spit oozed from the corner of his mouth. And there was fear in his eyes.

It had soaked in on him at last, the spot he was in. Soaked clear through a quart of booze until it hit him where he lived and rubbed the place raw.

"Why—why, god-dang you!" he said. "I was just makin' talk! You know danged well I was! I never even seen those pimps last night!"

"No, sir, I bet you didn't." I grinned at him. "I'd bet a million dollars you didn't."

"Y-you—" He gulped. "You m-mean you did k-kill—"

"I mean, I know you're a truthful man," I said. "If you said you didn't see those pimps, I know you *didn't* see 'em. But other folks might think somethin' else, mightn't they, Ken? If those pimps' bodies was to crop up some place, everybody'd think that you killed them. Couldn't hardly think nothin' else under the circumstances."

He cussed and made a grab at me. I stayed where I was, grinning at him, and he slowly let his hands drop to his side.

"That's right, Ken," I nodded. "That's right. There ain't a thing you can do but hope. Just hope that if someone *did* kill those pimps that no one ever finds their bodies."

The train was coming in.

I waited until it came to a stop; and then, since Ken seemed too dazed to do it by himself, I helped him on.

"One other thing, Ken," I said, and he turned on the step to look at me. "I'd be real nice to Buck, if I was you. I got kind of a funny idea that he don't like you very much as it is, so I sure wouldn't do no more talkin' about making him peck horse turds with the sparrers."

He turned back around again, and went on up the steps.

I started back through town.

NINE

I'd been thinking it was about time to do some political campaignin', since I had a pretty tough opponent coming up for a change. But I figured there'd been enough going on for one morning, what with Ken's big talk; and, anyways, I just didn't have a campaign plan this time.

Always before, I'd let the word get around that I was against this and that, things like cockfighting and gambling and whiskey and so on. So my opposition would figure they'd better come out against 'em, too, only twice as strong as I did. And I went right ahead and let 'em. Me, almost anyone can make a better speech than I can, and anyone can come out stronger against or for something. Because, me, I've got no very strong convictions about anything. Not any more I haven't.

Well, anyway, by the time it got ready to vote, it looked like a fella wouldn't be able to have no fun at all any more, if my opponents were elected. About all a fella would be able to do, without getting arrested, was to drink sody-pop and maybe kiss his wife. And no one liked the idea very much, the wives included.

So, all and all, I began to look pretty good to folks. It was a case of nothing looking better than something, because all anyone had to do was listen to me and look at me a while to know that I wasn't against anything very much, except having my pay stopped, and that I wouldn't have enough gumption to do anything even if I did want to. I'd just let things go along like they always had, because there wasn't much point in trying to change 'em. And when the votes were counted, I was still sheriff.

I'm not saying that there weren't a lot of folks who really liked me. There *was* a lot of 'em, folks that I'd been kids with and who knew me as a nice friendly fella who was always ready to do a favor it if didn't put him out of pocket too much or offend someone else. But it seemed to me that I didn't have as many friends as I'd used to. Even the very folks I'd favored, them most of all, it seemed like, weren't as friendly as they had been. They seemed to kind of hold it against me because I *hadn't* cracked down on 'em. And I didn't know quite what to do about it, since I'd never really got the habit of doing anything, and I didn't know how I was going to get myself elected again. But I knew I was going to have to do *something*. I was going to have to do something or think of something entirely different from the stuff I'd come up with in the past. Or I'd be out of a job when fall came.

I rounded the corner from the depot, and turned into Main Street. Then I started to duck back off of it, because there was a heck of a racket a couple of blocks down the street, a lot of fellas jamming the sidewalk. It looked like a fight of some kind was going on, which meant that I'd better get out of sight before I had to arrest someone besides maybe getting hurt myself.

I started to dart back around the corner; then, somehow, I caught myself, and I went on down the street to where the ruckus was.

It wasn't really a fight, like I'd been afraid of. Just Tom Hauck beating a colored fella named Uncle John. It seemed like Tom had been coming out of the hardware store with a box of shotgun shells when Uncle John had bumped into him or vice versa. Anyway, he'd dropped the shells and some of 'em had spilled off into the street mud. Which was why he'd grabbed hold of the colored fella and started beating him.

I pushed myself between them, and told Tom to stop.

I felt kind of funny about it, because Tom was the husband of Rose Hauck, the gal who was so generous with me. I guess a fella always feels kind of funny in a situation like that; guilty, I mean, like he ought to give the fella any break that he can. Aside from that, Tom was a lot bigger than I was—mean fellas are always bigger than I am—and he was about half-loaded with booze.

About all Tom ever did was booze-up and go hunting. His wife, Rose, did most of the farm work when she wasn't laid up from Tom beating her. Tom would set her chores for her, before he went off on a hunting trip. They were usually more than a strong man and a boy could do, but if Rose didn't have 'em done by the time he got back, she was in for a beating.

Now, he pushed his big red face into mine, and asked me what the hell I meant by interferin' with him.

"You tellin' me a white man can't whip a nigger if he feels like it? You sayin' there's some law against it?"

"Well," I said. "I don't know about that. I ain't saying there is, and I ain't saying there ain't. But there's a law against disturbin' the peace, and that's what you're doin'."

"And what about him disturbin' my peace? How about that, huh? A god-danged stinkin' nigger almost knocking me off the sidewalk and making me spill my shotgun shells!"

"Well, now, there's some division of opinion about that," I said. "It looks like maybe you might have bumped into him instead of him bumpin' you."

Tom yelled that what was the god-danged difference, anyways? It was a nigger's place to look out for a white man and keep out of his way. "Just ask anyone," he said, looking around at the crowd. "Ain't that right, fellas?"

Someone said. "That's right, Tom," and there was a little murmur of agreement. A kind of half-hearted murmur, because no one liked Tom very much even if they did have to side with him against a colored fella.

It looked to me like they'd really rather be on my side. All I had to do was change the issue a little, make it between me and him instead of between a white man and a black.

"Where did you get that board you been beating him with?" I said. "It looks to me like it came out of the sidewalk."

"So what if it did?" Tom said. "You expect me to use my fists on a nigger?"

"Now, never you mind about that," I said. "The point is, you got no right to beat him with city property. Suppose you broke that board, then what? Why these good taxpayers here has got to pay for a new one. Suppose someone comes along and steps in that empty place in the sidewalk? These taxpayers has got to pay the damages."

Tom scowled and cussed, and glared around at the crowd. There wasn't hardly a friendly face among 'em, so he cussed some more and said all right, then, to hell with the board. He'd just get the harness straps from his horse and beat Uncle John with them.

"Uh-huh," I said. "I don't reckon you will. Not right now, anyways."

"Who's gonna stop me? What the hell you mean I won't do it right now?"

"I mean Uncle John ain't here right now," I said. "Kind of 'pears like he got tired of waitin' for you."

Tom's mouth gaped open, and he looked around wildly. Everybody began to laugh, because naturally Uncle John had skipped out, and the expression on Tom's face was a sight to see.

He cussed me; he cussed the crowd. Then, he jumped on his mare and rode away, heeling her so hard in the flanks that she screamed with pain.

I stomped the sidewalk board back into place. Robert Lee Jefferson, the owner of the hardware store, caught my eye and motioned me to come inside. I went in, and followed him back to his little office.

Robert Lee Jefferson was the county attorney as well as the store owner, there not being enough work in the job to interfere with his business. I sat down, and he told me I'd handled the situation with Tom Hauck real well, and that Tom would surely have a lot of respect for law and order from now on.

"In fact, I imagine the whole town will, don't you, Nick? All those noble taxpayers who observed the manner in which you maintained the peace."

"I guess you mean just the opposite of what you're sayin'," I said. "Just what do you think I should have done, Robert Lee?"

"Why, you should have arrested Hauck, of course! Thrown him in jail! I'd have been delighted to prosecute him."

"But what could I arrest him for? I sure couldn't do it for whippin' a colored fella."

"Why not?"

"Aw, now," I said. "Aw, now, Robert Lee. You don't really mean that, do you?"

He looked down at his desk, hesitating a moment. "Well, maybe not. But there are other charges you could have got him on. Being drunk in a public place, for example. Or hunting out of season. Or wife-beating. Or, uh—"

"But Robert Lee," I said. "Everyone does those things. A lot of people, anyways."

"Do they? I haven't noticed any of them being brought into court for prosecution."

"But I can't arrest everyone! Pretty near everyone."

"We're talking specifically about one man. One mean, no-good, drunken, shiftless, lawbreaking wife-beater. Why didn't you make an example out of him for other men of his type?"

I said I just didn't rightly know, since he put it that way. I just didn't know; but I'd do some studyin' about it, and if I came up with an answer I'd tell him.

"I already know the answer," he said curtly. "Everyone with a lick of sense knows it. You're a coward."

"Now, I don't know as I'd say that," I said. "I ain't sayin' that I ain't a coward, but—"

"If you're afraid to do your job by yourself, why don't you hire a deputy? The county provides funds for one."

"Why, I already got a deputy," I said, "my wife. I deputized Myra, so's she could do my office for me."

Robert Lee Jefferson started at me grimly.

"Nick," he said, "do you honestly think you can go on doing as you've been doing? Absolutely nothing, in other words. Do you really think you can go on taking graft and robbing the county, and doing nothing to earn your money?"

"Why, I don't see how I can do much else if I want to stay in office," I said. "I got all kinds of expenses that fellas like you and the county judge and so on ain't bothered with. Me, I'm out in the open all the time, brushin' up with hundreds of people whereas you folks only see one once in a while. Anyone that's put in trouble, why I'm the fella that puts 'em there; they don't see you until afterward. Anyone that needs to borry a dollar, they come to me. All the church ladies come to me for donations, and—"

"Nick . . ."

"I throw a big barbecue every night the last month before election. Come one, come all. I got to buy presents when folks has a new baby, and I got to—"

"Nick! Nick, listen to me!" Robert Lee held up his hand. "You don't have to do all those things. People have no right to expect them of you."

"Maybe they don't have a right," I said. "I'll go along with that. But what they got a right to expect and what they do expect ain't exactly the same thing."

"Just do your job, Nick. Do it well. Show people that you're honest and courageous and hard-working, and you won't have to do anything else."

I shook my head, and said I couldn't. "I just plain can't, Robert Lee, and that's a fact."

"No?" He leaned back in his chair. "And just why can't you, pray tell?"

"For a couple of reasons," I said. "For one thing, I *ain't* real brave and hard-workin' and honest. For another, the voters don't want me to be."

"And just how do you figure that?"

"They elected me, didn't they? They keep electing me."

"That's pretty specious thinking," Robert Lee said. "Perhaps they trusted and liked you. They've been giving you every chance to make good. And you'd better do it very quickly, Nick." He leaned forward and tapped me on the knee. "I'm telling you that as a friend. If you don't straighten up and do your job, you'll be out of it come fall."

"You really think Sam Gaddis is that strong, Robert Lee?"

"He's that strong, Nick. Every bit that strong. Sam is just about everything you're not, if you'll excuse my saying so, and the voters like him. You'd better get busy or he'll beat the pants off of you."

"Uh-*hah*!" I said. "Umm-*hmm*! Would you mind if I used your phone, Robert Lee?"

He said to go ahead and I called Myra. I told her I was going out to Rose Hauck's place to help her do her chores, so that Tom wouldn't beat her up when he got home. Myra said that that was just fine, her and Rose being such good friends—or so she thought—and she told me to stay as long as I liked.

I hung up the phone. Robert Lee Jefferson was staring at me

like I was plumb out of my mind. "Nick," he said, waving his hands, "haven't you heard a word I said? Is that your idea of doing your job—to go out and chore around the Hauck farm?"

"But Rose needs help," I said. "You surely ain't sayin' it's wrong to help her."

"Of course I'm not! It's nice of you to want to help her; that's one of your good qualities, the way you're always willing to help people. But—but—" He sighed and shook his head wearily. "Aaah, Nick, don't you understand? It isn't your job doing things like that. It isn't what you're paid for. And you've got to start doing what you're paid for, or Sam Gaddis will beat you!"

"Beat me?" I said. "Oh, you mean the election?"

"Of course, I mean the election! What the hell else have we been talking about?"

"Well, I've been thinking about that," I said. "I've been doing a lot of thinking about it, Robert Lee, and I think I've thought of an angle that will beat ol' Sam."

"An angle? You mean some kind of trick?"

"Well, you might call it that," I said.

"B-But—but—" He looked like he was about to explode again. "But why, Nick? Why not simply do your job?"

"Well, I thought a lot about that, too," I said. "Yes, sir, I really did a lot of thinking. Almost had myself convinced for a while that I actually should get out and start arrestin' people, and start actin' like a sheriff in general. But then I did some more thinkin', and I knew I hadn't ought to do nothing of the kind."

"But, Nick—"

"Because people don't want me to do that," I said. "Maybe they think they do, but they don't. All they want is for me to give 'em some excuse to vote for me again."

"You're wrong, Nick." Robert Lee wagged his head. "You're dead wrong. You've got away with tricks in the past, but they won't work this time. Not against a truly fine man like Sam Gaddis."

I said, well, we'd just have to wait and see, and he gave me a sharp look.

"Have you got some idea that Sam Gaddis isn't a good man? Is that it, Nick? I can tell you right now that if you have some idea of digging up some dirt on him—"

"I got no such idea," I said. "I couldn't dig up no dirt on Sam if I wanted to, because there just ain't none to dig."

"Good. I'm glad you realize that."

"No, sir," I said. "I know Sam's as good a man as they come. That's why I can't understand how all these stories about him got started."

"Well, that's fine. I—*what?*" He stared at me startled. "What stories?"

"You mean you ain't heard?" I said.

"Of course I haven't! Now just what are these stories?"

I made as if I was about to tell him, and then I stopped and shook my head. "I ain't gonna repeat 'em," I said. "If you ain't heard 'em, you sure ain't gonna hear 'em from me. No, siree!"

He took a quick look around and leaned forward, voice lowered. "Tell me, Nick. I swear I won't repeat a word you say."

"I can't. I just can't, Robert Lee. It wouldn't be fair, and there's just no reason to. What difference does it make if people are going around spreading a lot of dirty stories about Sam, as long as we know they're not true?"

"Now, Nick—"

"I tell you what I *am* gonna do," I said. "When Sam gets up to make his first campaign speech, come Sunday-week, I'm gonna be right up on the platform with him. He gets my moral support a thousand per cent, and I'm gonna say so. Because I know there ain't a word of truth in all them dirty, filthy stories that are going around about him!"

Robert Lee Jefferson followed me to the front door, trying to get me to say what the stories were. I kept refusing, naturally, the main reason being that I'd never heard no one say a bad word about Sam Gaddis in my life.

"No, sir," I said, as I went out the door. "I just ain't gonna repeat 'em. You want to hear any dirt about Sam you'll have to get it from someone else."

"Who?" he said eagerly. "Who should I ask, Nick?"

"Anyone. Just about anyone," I said. "There's always folks that are willin' to dirty a good man, even when they ain't got a thing to go on!"

TEN

I got my horse and buggy out of the livery stable, and drove out of town. But I was quite a little while in getting out to see Rose Hauck. I had a little business with Tom to take care of first, business that was kind of a pleasure, you know what I mean, and it was about an hour's drive to his favorite hunting place.

He was there, maybe a hundred feet back from the road, and he was doing his usual kind of hunting. Sitting with his back against one tree and his gun against another, and slugging down whiskey from a jug as fast as he could swallow.

He looked around as I came up on him, and asked me what the hell I was doing there. Then his eyes widened and he tried to get to his feet, and he asked me what the hell I thought I was doing with his gun.

"First things first," I said. "One thing I'm doin' out this way is to pay a visit to your wife. I'm gonna be gettin' in bed with her pretty soon now, and she's gonna be givin' me what you were too god-danged low-down mean to ever get from her. Reason I know she's gonna give it to me is because she's been doin' it for a long time. Just about every time you were out here hog-drunk, too stupid to appreciate what a good thing you had."

He was cussing before I had the last words out; pushing himself up against the tree-trunk, and at last wobbling to his feet. He took a staggering step toward me, and I brought the gun up against my shoulder.

"The second thing I'm gonna do," I said, "is somethin' I should have done long ago. I'm gonna give you both barrels of this shotgun right in your stupid, stinking guts."

And I did it.

It didn't quite kill him, although he was dying fast. I wanted him to stay alive for a few seconds, so that he could appreciate the three or four good swift kicks I gave him. You might think it wasn't real nice to kick a dying man, and maybe it wasn't. But I'd been wanting to kick him for a long time, and it just never had seemed safe until now.

I left him after a while, getting weaker and weaker. Squirming around in a pool of his own blood and guts. And then ceasing to squirm.

Then, I drove on out to the Hauck farm.

The house was pretty much like most farm houses you see in this part of the country, except it was a little bigger. A pitched-roofed shack, with one long room across the front and a three-room lean-to on the back. It was made of pine, naturally, and it wasn't painted. Because with the hot sun and the high humidity, you can't hardly keep paint on a house down here. At least, that's what folks say and even if it ain't so, it's a danged good excuse for being shiftless. The farm land, a whole quarter section of it, was as good as you'd find.

It was that rich, black silt you see in the river lowlands; so fine and sweet you could almost eat it, and so deep that you couldn't wear it out, like so much of the shallow soil in the south is worn out. You might say that land was a lot like Rose, naturally good, deep down good, but Tom had done his best to ruin it like he had her. He hadn't done it, because they'd had too much good stuff to begin with. But both the land and her were a long sight from being what they'd been before he got ahold of 'em.

She was hoeing sweet potatoes when I arrived, and she came running up from the field, panting for breath and pushing the sweat-soaked hair from her eyes. One heck of a pretty woman, she was; Tom hadn't been able to change that. And she had one heck of a figure. Tom hadn't been able to ruin her body either, although he'd sure tried hard. What he had changed was the way she thought—mean and tough—and the way she talked. When she didn't have to be on guard, she talked practically as bad as he did.

"Goddam, honey," she said, giving me a quick little hug and stepping away again. "Dammit, sweetheart, I won't be able to stop today. That son-of-a-bitch of a Tom gave me too much work to do."

I said, "Aw, come on. You can spare a few minutes. I'll help you afterward."

She said, goddammit, it wouldn't do any good if she had six men to help her. She still couldn't get through. "You know I want you, honey," she said. "I'm crazy for you, baby, and you know I am. If it wasn't for all this goddam work—"

"Well, I don't know," I said, deciding to tease her along a while.

"I guess I ain't real sure that you do want me. Seems like as if you did, you could give me a minute or two."

"But it wouldn't be a minute or two, darling! You know it wouldn't!"

"Why not?" I said. "It don't take no longer than that to kiss you a little, and give you a few squeezes and pats, an'—"

"D-Don't!" She moaned shakily. "Don't say those things! I—"

"Why, I'd probably even have time to hold you on my lap," I said. "With your dress sort of pulled up, so's I could feel how warm and soft you are where you sit down. And I could maybe sort of pull your dress down from the top, kind of slide it down from your shoulders, so that I could see those nice things underneath, and—"

"Stop it, Nick! I—you know how I get, a-and—I can't! *I just can't, honey!*"

"Why, I wouldn't even expect you to take your dress all the way off," I said. "I mean, it ain't really necessary, when you get right down to cases. With a tight-packed little gal like you, a fella don't have to do hardly nothing at all except—"

She cut me off, groaning like a spurred horse. She said, "Goddam! I don't give a damn if the son-of-a-bitch beats my tail off!"

Then, she grabbed me by the hand and began to run, dragging me toward the house.

We got inside, and she slammed the door and locked it. She stood leaning into me for a moment, twisting and writhing against me. Then, she flung herself down on the bed, rolled over on her back and hitched her dress up.

"What the hell you waiting for, honey?" she said. "Come on, darling, goddam it!"

"What you layin' down for?" I said. "I thought I was just goin' to hold you on my lap."

"P-Please, Nick!" She moaned again. "We've g-got no time to waste, so—*please*, honey!"

"Well, all right," I said. "But I got some news for you. Sort of a little secret. I think maybe I ought to tell it to you before—"

"Crap on the secret." She made a wild grab for me. "I don't want any goddam secrets! What I want is—"

"But it's about poor old Tom. Somethin' done went and happened to him . . ."

"Who gives a damn? It's just too goddam bad that the son-of-a-bitch isn't dead! Now—"

I told her that that was the secret: Tom *was* dead. "Looks like he got his guts blowed clear through his backbone," I said. "Looks like he stumbled over his gun when he was drunk, and blowed himself to glory."

She looked at me, her eyes widening, mouth working as she tried to speak. Finally, the words came out in a shaky whisper:

"You're sure, Nick? You really killed him?"

"Let's just say he had himself an accident," I said. "Let's just say that fate dealt him a crool blow."

"But he *is* dead? You're sure about that?"

I told her I was sure, all right. Plenty sure. "If he ain't, he's the first live man I've ever seen who could hold still while he was getting kicked in the balls."

Rose's eyes lit up like I'd given her a Christmas party. Then she threw herself back on the pillows, rocking with laughter.

"Holy Jesus, so the stinking son-of-a-bitch is really dead! I'm through with the dirty bastard at last!"

"Well, sir, it sure looks that way," I said.

"Goddam him! I just wish I'd have been there to kick him myself, the bastardly son-of-a-bitchin' whoremonger!" she said, adding on a few more choice names. "You know what I'd have liked to do to that dirty bastard, Nick? I'd have liked to take me a red hot poker and jabbed it right up the filthy son-of-a-bitch's—uh, what's the matter, honey?"

"Nothin'," I said. "I mean, maybe we ought to show a little more respect for ol' Tom, him bein' dead and all. It just don't seem quite fittin' to low-rate the dead with a lot of dirty names."

"You mean I shouldn't call the son-of-a-bitch a son-of-a-bitch?"

"Well, now, it don't sound real good, does it?" I said. "It don't sound nice a-tall."

Rose said it sounded just fine to her, but if it bothered me she'd try to watch her tongue. "That son-of-a-bitch caused enough trouble while he was alive without fouling us up afterward. Anyway, I'd do anything to please you, sweetheart. Anything you want, darling."

"Then, why ain't you doin' it?" I said. "How come you still got your dress on?"

"Goddam," she said, looking down at herself. "Rip the goddam thing off, will you, honey?"

I started ripping, and she started helping me with my clothes. And things were getting right to the most interesting point when the phone rang. Rose cussed and said to let the goddam thing go, but I said it might be Myra—which it was—so she stalked out in the kitchen and answered it.

She talked quite a while. Or, rather, she listened to Myra talking. About all Rose got to say was a lot of well-I-declare's and you-don't-say-so's and so on. Finally, she said, "Why, of course I'll tell him, Myra, dear. Just as soon as he comes in from the field. And you and Lennie take care of your sweet selves until I see you again."

Rose slammed up the phone, and came back to where I was. I asked her what Myra wanted, and she said it could wait, goddam it. There were more important things to do right now.

"Like what?" I said.

"Like this," she said. "*This!*"

So we didn't do no talking for quite a while.

Not until afterwards, when we lay side by side, holding hands and breathing in long deep breaths. Then, finally, she turned around facing me, her head propped up on her elbow, and told me about Myra's call.

"Looks like a day for good news, honey. First, that son-of-a-bitch, Tom, gets killed, and now it looks like you're a cinch to get re-elected."

"Yeah?" I said. "How's that, baby?"

"Sam Gaddis. The whole town's talking about him. Why, do you know what he did, Nick?"

"I ain't got the slightest idea," I said. "I always thought Sam was a mighty good man."

"He raped a little two-year-old nigger baby, that's what!"

"Mmmm? Male or female?" I said.

"Female, I guess. I—*ha, ha*—Nick, you awful thing, you." She laughed and gave me a squeeze. "But isn't it terrible, honey! To think of a grown man screwing a poor innocent little baby! And that's only one thing he did!"

"Do tell," I said. "Like which?"

Rose said that Sam had also cheated a poor widow woman out of her life's savings, and then he'd beat his own father to death with a stick of cordwood to keep him from talking about it.

"And that's only the beginning, Nick. Everyone's saying that Sam broke into his grandma's grave, and stole the gold teeth out of her mouth. Did you ever hear of such a thing? And he killed his wife and fed her corpse to the hogs. And—"

"Now, wait a minute," I said. "Sam Gaddis has never been married."

"You mean you just never saw his wife. He was married before he came here, and he fed her to the hogs before anyone could find out about her."

"Aw, come on, now," I said. "Just when is Sam supposed to have done all these things?"

Rose hesitated and said, well, she didn't know when exactly. But, by God, she knew he'd done 'em.

"People wouldn't just make up stories like that. They couldn't!"

"Couldn't they?"

"Why, of course not, honey! Anyway, most of the stories came right from Mrs. Robert Lee Jefferson, according to Myra. Her own husband told them to her, and you know Robert Lee Jefferson wouldn't lie."

"Yeah," I said. "It don't seem like he would now, does it?"

And I had to bite my lip to keep from laughing. Or maybe doing the opposite. Because it was really pretty god-danged sad, now, wasn't it? It was a god-danged sorry state of affairs.

Of course, it was all to the good for me. I'd thrown the bait to Robert Lee Jefferson, and he'd bit on it. He'd done just what I expected him to do—gone around, asking people what the stories about Sam were. Which had started them to asking other people. And before long, there were plenty of answers; the kind of stinking dirty dirt that people can always create for themselves when there ain't none for real.

And it made me kind of sad, you know? Really downright sad. I couldn't help wishing that Robert Lee hadn't taken the bait, and started asking questions. Which, in turn, had started piling up the dirt around a fine man like Sam Gaddis.

Yes, sir, I really sort of wished things hadn't worked out this way. Even if it did ruin Sam and get me re-elected, which it was just about certain to do.

Unless something went wrong. . . .

ELEVEN

It rained during the night, and I slept pretty good like I almost always do when it rains. Along about ten the next morning, when I was having a little second breakfast because I hadn't eaten much the first time but a few eggs and some pancakes and sausage, Rose Hauck called.

She'd been trying to reach me for quite a while, but hadn't been able to because of Myra's gossiping about Sam Gaddis. Myra talked to her for a couple of minutes, and then passed the phone to me.

"I'm afraid something's happened to Tom, Nick," Rose told me—just as if she didn't know what had happened to him. "His horse came home without him this morning."

"Is that a fact?" I said. "You think maybe I should go out and start looking for him?"

"Well, I just don't know, Nick," she hesitated. "If Tom is all right, he might be pretty mad if I sent the sheriff after him."

I said that was for sure, all right. Tom didn't like anyone butting in on his affairs. "Maybe he holed up somewhere on account of the rain," I said. "Maybe he's waitin' for it to dry up a little before he starts home."

"I'll bet that's it," she said, making her voice relieved. "He probably didn't have cover for the mare so he sent her home by herself."

"That's probably the way it was, all right," I said. "After all, he didn't tell you he was coming home last night, did he?"

"No, no, he didn't. He never tells me how long he's going to be gone."

"Well, don't worry none about it," I said. "Not yet, anyways. If Tom ain't home by tomorrow, why then I'll start lookin' for him."

Myra was making wild faces and motions, as if to say, what is it all about? I passed her the phone and there was some more jibber-jabbering, and she wound up by asking Rose to come have supper with us. "Now, you just must come, dear, because I've got all kinds of news to tell you. You can get a ride in with the mailman about four, and I'll have Nick drive you home afterward."

She hung up, shaking her head and murmuring, "Poor Rose. That poor, dear, sweet woman."

I said. "Why, Rose ain't poor, honey. That's a right good farm her and Tom has."

"Oh, shut up!" she said. "If you'd have been half a man, you'd have done something about Tom Hauck long ago! Put him in jail where he belongs instead of leaving him free to beat up that poor little helpless wife of his!"

"Why, I couldn't do that," I said. "I couldn't interfere between a man and his wife."

"No, you couldn't. You couldn't do anything! Because you're *not* half a man!"

"Well, now I don't know about that," I said. "I ain't saying you're wrong, but I sure ain't saying—"

"Oh, shut up!" she said again. "Lennie's more of a man than you are. Aren't you, Lennie, darling?"—she smiled at him. "You're Myra's brave strong man, aren't you? Not an old cowardy calf like Nick."

Lennie slobbered out a laugh, pointing a finger at me. "Cowardy calf, cowardy calf! Sheriff Nick's a cowardy calf!"

I looked at him, and he stopped laughing and pointing. He turned real quiet, and kind of pale.

I looked at Myra, and her smile stiffened and faded. And she was almost as pale and silent as Lennie.

"N-Nick—" She broke the long silence with a trembly laugh. "W-What's the matter?"

"Matter?" I said.

"The way you're looking. Like you were about to kill Lennie and me both. I—I never saw you look that way before."

I forced a laugh, making it sound easy and stupid. "Me? Me kill someone? Aw, now!"

"But—but you—"

"I guess maybe I was thinking about the election. Thinking maybe it wasn't a very good idea to be pokin' fun at me with the election comin' up."

She nodded her head quickly, and frowned at Lennie. "Of course, we'd never carry on like that in public. But—but probably it isn't a good idea. Even if we were just joking."

I thanked her for her understandin', and started for the door.

She followed me for a step, still kind of anxious; shook up from the scare I'd accidentally given her.

"I don't think you have to worry about getting elected, dear. Not with all the talk that's going on about Sam Gaddis."

"Well, I never believe in takin' chances," I said. "I always figure a fella ought to lean over backwards and put his shoulder to the wheel, and not count his chickens until they're hatched."

"Mrs. Robert Lee Jefferson said her husband said that you said you didn't believe the stories about Sam Gaddis."

"I don't. I don't believe a god-danged word of 'em," I said.

"But—she also said that he said that you said you were going to speak up for Mr. Gaddis. She said that he said that you said you were going to be on the speakers' platform with him, come Sunday-week."

I told her she'd spoken the truth, and that was a fact. "You talk to her again, you tell her that when she said that Robert Lee said that I said I was going to speak up for Sam Gaddis, she was a thousand per cent right."

"You fool—!" She caught herself. "But Gaddis is running against you, dear. Why should you do anything for him?"

"Now, that's quite a question, ain't it?" I said. "Yes, sir, that is *quite* a question. Reckon I'd tell you the answer if I didn't figure you'd have so much fun cipherin' it out."

"But—"

"Reckon I'd better be rushing back to my office," I said. "No tellin' what's been happening while I was away."

I went on down the stairs, pretending like I didn't hear her when she called to me. I went in my office and sat down with my boots up on the desk. And I slanted my hat over my eyes, and kind of dozed for a little while.

It was awfully peaceful. The mud was keeping most folks indoors, and the painters were taking the day off because of the wet, so there wasn't a lot of slamming and banging and calling back and forth from them. A fella could really rest for a change, and catch up on the sleep that he didn't get at night.

I rested and slept until noon, when I went upstairs for dinner.

Myra had got over her scare, and was about back to normal. She looked at me and said she could see I'd had a very busy morning, and she hoped I wasn't wearing myself out.

"Well, I'm trying not to," I said. "A fella like me, with the whole county depending on him for law and order, has got to watch out for his health. Which sort of reminds me. About me takin' Rose Hauck home tonight—"

"You're going to do it!" Myra snapped. "You're going to, so just don't try to get out of it!"

"But suppose Tom's there? Suppose he's mad about me bringin' his wife home, an'—an'—"

I squirmed, letting my eyes fall, but I could still see Myra glaring at me. At last she spoke, her voice shaky with hate and disgust.

"You—you thing, you! You miserable excuse for a man! I'll tell you this, Nick Corey! If Tom *is* there and you let him hurt Rose, I'll make you the sorriest man in the county!"

"Now, my goodness," I said. "My goodness gracious! You don't need to talk that way. I wouldn't stand by an' watch Rose get hurt."

"Well, you'd better not! That's all I've got to say! You'd just better not!"

I started eating, with Myra shooting me a suspicious look now and then. After a while, I looked up and said I'd just thought of something else about Rose. Suppose Tom came home after I left and wouldn't be around to protect her.

"He's bound to be pretty bad off," I said. "Stayin' away so long, he'll probably be twice as drunk and mean as he usually is. Makes me plumb shiver to think what he might do to Rose."

"Well . . ." Myra hesitated, studying over what I'd said and not finding anything to fault me for. "Well, I don't suppose it would look right for you to stay all night at the house. But—"

"Naw, I couldn't do that! I sure couldn't do that," I said. "Anyways, we don't know for sure when Tom's comin' home. Might be gone two, three days. All we know is he's gonna be plenty hard to get along with when he does get back."

Myra fumed and frowned, and said I should have done something about Tom long ago, and Rose wouldn't be in this position now. I said she was probably right, and it was just too bad we couldn't think of some way to give Rose some protection.

"Let's see," I said. "I wonder maybe if we could get her a watchdog, or—"

"You fool! Tom would kill it in a minute! He's killed every dog they ever had!"

"Mmm-hmm," I said. "God-dang if I didn't forget about that. Well, let's see, now. I'd know of just the thing if Rose was a different kind of person. More nervy, you know, instead of so meek and mild. But that's the way she is, so it just wouldn't do no good."

"What wouldn't do any good? What are you talking about now?"

"Why, a gun," I said. "You know, one of them things you shoot with. But it sure wouldn't do no good with Rose, her bein' scared of her own shadder, so—"

"That's it!" Myra cut in. "We'll get her a gun! She ought to have one anyway, a woman alone as much as she is."

"But what good will it do?" I said. "Rose wouldn't shoot no one to save her life."

"I'm not so sure about that—not if her life was at stake. At any rate, she could point it. Make that big brute of a husband keep away from her."

"Well, now, I just don't know about that," I said. "If you ask me—"

"I'm not asking you! I'm taking Rose out to get a gun this very day, so just finish your dinner and shut up!"

I finished eating, and went back down to my office. I rested and dozed some more, but not as good as I had in the morning. I was kind of puzzled with myself, you know, wondering why I'd wanted Rose Hauck to have a gun. Because, of course, I did want her to have one.

I tried to tell myself that it was just for her own protection, just in case someone tried to bother her. But I knew that wasn't my real reason. My real reason, I guessed, was something I hadn't quite figured out yet. It was part of something else, some plan-wishes I had for Myra and Lennie—and I hadn't quite figured out what they were either.

Maybe it don't seem to make sense for a fella to be doing things for a reason that he don't know about. But I reckon I've been doing it most of my life. The reason I went to see Ken Lacey, for example, wasn't the one I let on that it was. I'd done it because I had a plan for him—and you've seen what that plan was. But I didn't know it at the time I'd called on him.

I'd had a kind of a goal, and I'd figured that a fella like Ken could be a lot of help in bringing it about. But just how I was going to use him I wasn't even halfway sure.

And it was the same situation now, with Rose and the gun. All I knew was that they probably fitted into a plan for Myra and Lennie. But I didn't have no real idea of what the plan was; I purely didn't.

Except that it was probably pretty unpleasant . . .

Rose got to the courthouse around four o'clock that afternoon. I was on the lookout for her, and I got her in the office for a minute before she could go on upstairs.

She was looking prettier than I'd ever seen her, which was really saying something. She said she'd slept like a goddam baby all night long, and she'd woke up laughing, thinking about that son-of-a-bitch of a Tom being dead out in the mud somewheres.

"Did I do all right when I called up this morning, honey?" she whispered. "It sounded like I was really concerned about the dirty bastard?"

"You did just fine," I said. "And looky, baby . . ."

I told her about the gun, how it would look like she was worried about Tom beating her up when he came back—which, you see, would prove she didn't know he was dead. And she kind of hesitated for a second, giving me a quick frowny look, but she didn't argue about it.

"Whatever you say, Nick, honey. If you think it's a good idea."

"Well, it was actually Myra's," I said. "I just about had to go along with it, or it would have looked like I knew Tom wasn't coming back."

Rose nodded and said, "What the hell?" dismissing the subject. "Maybe I can take a shot at you some time, if you're not real nice to me."

"That time ain't never gonna come," I said. And I gave her a quick hug and a squeeze, and she went on up the stairs.

She and Myra went out a little later to get the gun, and stayed out until after five.

A few minutes before six, Myra called me, and I closed the office and went upstairs to supper.

Myra did most of the talking, like she always did; shutting me up whenever I said anything. About all Rose did was agree with her, putting in a word now and then about how wonderful and smart Myra was. And that was the same as usual, too. We finished eating. Myra and Rose started clearing up the dishes. Lennie looked at me to see if I was watching him—which I was, only he didn't know it—and then he made a sneak toward the door.

I cleared my throat to get Myra's attention, and jerked my head at Lennie. "How about that, honey?" I said. "You know what we agreed on."

"What?" she said. "What are you talking about now, for pity's sake?"

"About him goin' out at night," I said. "You know what he'll do, an' it just ain't a good idea with the election coming up."

Myra said, "Oh, pshaw. The boy's got to get a little air some time, doesn't he? You can't begrudge him that!"

"But we agreed that—"

"I did not! You just got me so mixed up I wasn't thinking what I was saying! Anyway Sam Gaddis is bound to be beat and you know it!"

"Well, I just don't see no use in taking chances," I said. "I—"

"Oh, shut up! Did you ever see such a man in your life, Rose? Is it any wonder that I'm half out of my mind from living with him?" Myra scowled at me, then turned to give Lennie a smile. "You go right ahead, honey. Have a good time, but don't stay out too late."

He went out, after a blubbery spiteful grin at me. Myra said I'd better go in my bedroom and stay if I couldn't make sense, which she was sure I couldn't, so that's what I did.

I stretched out on the bed, with the spread turned back so that my boots wouldn't soil it. The window was open, and I could hear the crickets singing, like they always do after a rain. Now and then a bullfrog would sound off with a loud *kerrumph*, like a bass drummer keeping time. Way off across town, someone was pumping water, *p-plump, whish, p-plump, whish*, and you could hear some mother calling her kid, "*Henry Clay, oooh, Hen-ry Clay Houston! You come home now!*" And the smell of fresh-washed soil was in the air, just about the nicest smell there is. And . . . and everything was fine.

It was so god-danged nice and peaceful that I dozed off again. Yes, sir, I went to sleep, even though I hadn't had a real hard work day and I'd managed to catch up on my rest a little.

I guess I must have been asleep about an hour when I waked up to the sound of Myra yelling and Lennie bawling, and someone talking to 'em—Amy Mason speaking her mind in a way that almost put your teeth on edge. Soft, but firm and cutting, like only Amy could speak when she had her dander up. You knew you'd better listen to what she was saying, when Amy spoke that way; you'd better listen and take it to heart or it would be too god-danged bad for you.

I knew it was having its effect on Myra, in spite of her yelling and trying to set defiant. She began to kind of whimper and whine, saying that Lennie didn't mean anything by peeking in Amy's window—he was just curious about people. Amy said she knew exactly what he meant, and he'd better not try any of his nasty tricks again if he knew what was good for him.

"I've already warned your husband," she said, "and now I'm warning you, Mrs. Corey. If I catch your brother at my window again, I'll take a horsewhip to him!"

"Y-You wouldn't dare!" Myra whined. "And you just stop hurting him! Let go of the poor boy's ear."

"Gladly," Amy said. "It makes my flesh crawl to touch him."

I cracked the door open an inch or so, and looked out.

Myra had her arm around Lennie, who looked red-faced and mad and scared as she patted him on the head. Rose was standing next to her, trying to appear concerned and protective. But I knew, knowing her so well, that she was laughing inside, tickled pink to see Myra catching it for a change. As for Amy . . .

I swallowed hard, looking at her, wondering what I'd ever seen in Rose after I'd had someone like Amy.

Not that she was any prettier than Rose, or built any better. You just couldn't fault Rose on prettiness or build no matter who you stood her up against. The difference, I guess, was something that came from the inside, something that kind of grabbed hold of you right around the heart, that left its mark on you like a brand, so that the feel of her and the memory of her was always with you no matter where you strayed.

I came bursting out of the bedroom and looked around, putting a real surprised look on my face. "What's going on here, anyways?" I said, not givin' anyone a chance to answer. "Why, good evening, Miss Mason. Is they some kind of trouble?"

Amy said no, they was not no kind of trouble; kind of mimicking me, you know. "Not now there isn't, Sheriff. The trouble's all settled. Your wife will tell you how to avoid any in the future."

"My wife?" I gave Myra and Lennie a studyin' look, and turned back to Amy. "Did my wife's brother do somethin', Miss Mason? You just tell me about it."

"Of course Lennie didn't do anything!" Myra snapped. "He was just—"

"Is your name Miss Mason?" I said. "Is it?"

"W-What? What?"

"I asked Miss Mason a question," I said. "In case you ain't heard, Miss Mason is one of the most prominent and respected young women in Potts County, and when I ask her somethin' it's because I know she'll tell the truth. So maybe you'd better not go contradictin' what she says."

Myra's mouth dropped open. She turned from red to white, and then back to red again. I knew she'd probably give me all-heck when she got me alone, but for the present she wasn't talkin' back. She knew she just hadn't better, what with an election coming up and Amy being so generally well-thought-of. She knew that someone like Amy could cause an awful lot of trouble, if they took a notion, and an election year was no time for trouble.

So Myra didn't give me any trouble, much as she felt like it, and Amy was kind of pleased by the way I'd acted, and said she was sorry if she'd said anything hurtful. "I'm afraid I lost my temper for a moment," she smiled, a little stiffly. "If you'll excuse me, I'll run along home."

"I'll walk you home myself," I said. "It's too late at night for a young lady to be out by herself."

"Now, that's not at all necessary, Sheriff. I—"

I said it certainly was necessary; me and my wife, we wouldn't have it no other way. "That's right, ain't it, Myra? You insist on me seein' Miss Mason home, don't you?"

Myra said yes, her teeth practically clenched together.

I nodded and winked to Rose and she winked back at me; and Amy and me left.

She lived right there in town, so I didn't get out the horse and buggy like I might have if her home had been a far piece off. Anyway, I wanted to talk to her and I didn't want her pulling away from me. And it's just about impossible for a woman to be standoffish when you're walking her home through the mud on a dark night.

She had to listen when I started telling her how Myra had hooked me. She said she just wasn't interested and it wasn't any of her business, and that sort of thing. But she listened anyway, because she couldn't get out of it. And after a couple of minutes she stopped interruptin' and began to cling closer to me, and I knew she believed what I was saying.

On the porch of the house, she flung her arms around me and I put mine around her, and we stood there in the darkness for a little while, just holding onto each other. Then, she sort of pushed me away, and I couldn't see her expression, but somehow I knew she was frowning.

"Nick," she said. "Nick, this is terrible!"

I said, "Yeah, I guess I have kind of messed things up, all right. I guess I've been nine kinds of fool, lettin' Myra scare me into marryin' her and—"

"That's not what I'm talking about. That could be solved with money, and I have money. But—but—"

"Then, what's botherin' you?" I said. "What's so terrible, honey?"

"I—I'm not sure." She shook her head. "I know *what*, but I don't know why. And I'm not positive it would make any difference if I did know. I—can't talk about it now! I don't even want to think about it! I—Oh, Nick! *Nick!*"

She buried her face against my chest. I held her tighter, stroking her head and whispering that everything was all right, that nothing could be so very terrible as long as we were together again.

"Now, it just couldn't, honey," I said. "You just tell me what it is, and I'll show you it don't really amount to nothin' at all."

She clung to me a little tighter, still not saying anything. I said, well, to heck with it; maybe we could save it for another time, when I didn't have to be in kind of a rush like I was tonight.

"You remember how I used to go night-fishin'?" I said. "Well, I was thinkin' maybe I might go tomorrow night, and it'd be kind of a natural mistake if I should wind up here instead of the river, because you ain't so awful far from it."

Amy sniffled, then laughed.

"Oh, Nick! There's just no one like you!"

"Well, I should hope not," I said. "The world'd be in a heck of a mess if there was."

I said I'd see her the next night, just as soon as it was good and dark. She shivered against me, and said that would be fine.

"But do you have to go now, darling?"

"Well, I guess I kind of should," I said. "Myra'll be wonderin' what happened, and I got to see Miz Hauck home yet tonight."

Amy said, "Oh, I see. I'd almost forgotten about Rose."

"Yeah, I got to take her home," I said, kind of grumbling about it. "Myra has done promised her I would."

"Poor Nick!" Amy patted my cheek. "Everyone's always imposing on him."

"Aw, I don't really mind," I said. "After all, someone's got to take care of poor Miz Hauck."

"How true! And isn't it fortunate that she has someone so willing to take care of her? You know, Nick, poor ol' Mrs. Hauck seems to be bearing up remarkably well under her troubles. She looked positively blooming, like a woman in love, one might say."

"Is that a fact?" I said. "I can't say that I rightly noticed."

"Come in for a while, Nick. I want to talk to you."

"I guess we better let it wait until tomorrow night," I said. "It's kind of late, an'—"

"Now! Tonight, Nick."

"But Rose—I mean, Miz Hauck—will be waiting. I—"

"Let her. I'm afraid it's not the only disappointment she's in for. Now, come in!"

She flung the door open and went in, and I went in after her. Her hand gripped mine in the darkness, and she led me back through the house to her bedroom. And it was a funny thing, her saying she wanted to talk to me, because she didn't do no talking at all.

Or hardly any.

Afterwards, she lay back and yawned and stretched; kind of fidgeting because I never could see good in the dark, and I was slow in getting my clothes on.

"Will you please hurry a little, darling? I feel all nice and relaxed and drowsy, and I want to get to bed."

"Well, you sure ain't got far to get," I said. "What was it you was wantin' to talk to me about, anyways?"

"About your grammar, possibly. You're no ignoramus, Nick. Why do you talk like one?"

"Just habit, I guess. Kind of a rut I've got into. English and grammar, I reckon, they're like a lot of things. A fella don't use 'em—he don't see no real demand for 'em—and pretty soon he loses the knack. Wrong is right for him, an' vicey versa you might say."

Amy's head shifted on the pillows, her eyes wide in her white face as she studied me.

"I think I know what you mean, Nick," she said. "In a way, I'm a victim of the same process."

"Yeah?" I said, pulling on my boots. "How you mean, Amy?"

"Or I'm beginning to be a victim," she said. "And, you know, darling, I rather like it."

I stood up, tucking in my shirt-tails. "Just what was you wantin' to say to me, Amy?"

"Nothing that can't wait until tomorrow night. In fact, I no longer think I'll have anything to say then."

"But you said—"

"And I said some other things, too, darling. Possibly you weren't listening. Now, you run along now, and I do hope pore ol' Miz Hauck ain't too disappointed."

"Yeah," I said. "I sure hope she ain't neither."

But I had an idea she was going to be.

TWELVE

The way I'd met Myra was at the state fair a few years ago. I was all dressed up like I always am when I go someplace, and even a god-danged fool could see I was doing plenty all right. Anyway, I reckon Myra seen it. And she didn't look so bad herself then; she'd gone to some pains to pretty herself up. And I didn't fight too hard when she latched herself onto me.

It was at this place where you throw balls at a colored fella's head, and if you hit him you won a prize. I was just doin' it because the fella that ran the place kept asking me to. It had seemed unobliging not to, but I sure didn't want to hit this colored man and I didn't. But I heard someone clapping their hands, and here was Myra, carrying on like I was the world's greatest pitcher.

"Oooh, I just don't see how you do it!" she said, simpering up at me. "Would you throw some balls for me, please, if I give you the money?"

"Well, I'd kind of rather not, ma'am," I said. "If you don't mind excusin' me. I was just quitting myself."

"Oh," she said, kind of letting her face sag, which didn't require much of an effort if you know what I mean. "I understand. Your wife is with you."

"Naw, that ain't it," I said. "I ain't married, ma'am; I just don't want to throw at that colored fella, because it don't seem right somehow. It ain't rightly decent, you might say."

"You're just saying that," she pouted and simpered. "It's your way of rebuking me for being forward."

I said, naw, that wasn't it at all; I really felt like I said I did. "I guess it's his job to get throwed at, but it ain't mine to do the throwin'," I said. "Anyways, a fella'd be better off without a job than one like this. If he's got to get hit to live, he ain't got nothing worth living for."

Myra put on a solemn face, and said she could see I was a really deep thinker. I said, well, I didn't know about that, but I was sure a thirsty one.

"Maybe I could offer you a lemonade, ma'am, seein' as how I can't favor you by throwing balls."

"Well . . ." She twisted and twitched and twittered. "You won't think I'm terribly forward if I say yes?"

"Why, you just said it, ma'am," I said, leading her toward the pink lemonade stand. "You just said yes, and I don't think nothing like that at all."

And sure enough I didn't.

What I was thinking was that she must have buggers in her bloomers or a chigger on her figger, or however you say it. It looked to me like something had better be done about it pretty quick, or her pants would start blazing and maybe they'd set the fairgrounds on fire and there'd be a panic with thousands of people getting stomped to death, not to mention the property damage. And I couldn't think of but one way to prevent it.

Well, though, I didn't want to rush into things. There just wasn't any need to rush, as far as I was concerned, because I was getting married to Amy the next week and she'd taken good care to provide for me until then. So I stalled around, trying to decide whether I really ought to do the only thing I could think of to do. You might say it really wasn't my problem if Myra did set the fairgrounds on fire, with thousands of innocent women and children getting killed. Because I was from out of town, and I'm a great believer in local rights—you know, like State rights—and Myra lived here in the city. Could be I might get into all kinds of trouble by interfering in a local problem, even if it was something that even a god-danged fool would be familiar with, and the local folks weren't doing nothing about it.

I took Myra to a few side shows, standing close to her while I tried to make up my mind. I took her on the merry-go-round and some other rides, helping her on and off and looking at her when her dress slid up, and so on and so forth. And god-dang if it wasn't long before I came to my decision.

Myra looked shocked when I whispered to her, almost as shocked as if I'd bought her a sack of popcorn.

"Why—why, I just wouldn't think of it!" She twisted and twitched. "The very idea, going to a hotel with a strange man!"

"But I ain't strange," I said, giving her a pinch. "I'm built just like the rest of 'em."

"Oh, you awful thing, you!" she giggled. "You're just terrible!"

"Why, I ain't neither terrible," I said. "Anyways, it ain't fair to say I am without more knowledge on the subject."

She giggled and blushed, and said she just couldn't go to a hotel. "I just couldn't! I really couldn't."

"Well, if you can't you can't," I said, getting a little tired of it all. "Far be it from me to urge you."

"But—but we could go to my rooming house. No one would think anything of it if you just came up to my room for a little visit."

We took a streetcar over to the place where she lived, a big white house a few blocks from the river. It was a very respectable place, from all appearances, and the people were too. And no one lifted an eyebrow when Myra said we were just going upstairs to clean up before we went out for supper.

Well, sir, I hardly touched that woman. Or, anyway, if I did touch her, I didn't do much more than that. I was ready to and rarin' to, and, well, maybe I did do a *little* something. But with all them clothes she had on, it was god-danged little.

All of a sudden, though, she pushed me off to the floor, starting to bawl and sob so loud you could hear her in the next block. I picked myself up and tried to shush her. I asked her what the heck was the matter, and I tried to pat her and calm her down. She shoved me away again, setting up an even bigger racket.

I didn't know what the heck to do. Anyways, I didn't have time to do anything before a bunch of the other roomers came busting in.

The women hovered around Myra, trying to soothe her and talk to her. Myra kept bawling and shaking her head, not answering when they asked her what the matter was. The men looked at me, and kept asking me what I'd done to Myra. And it was just one of those situations where the truth won't do and a lie's no help. Which fortunately there ain't many of in this vale of tears.

The men grabbed ahold of me and began to bat me around. One of the women said she was going to call the police, but the men said no, they'd take care of me themselves. They'd give me what I deserved, they said, and there were plenty of men in the neighborhood to help 'em.

Well, I couldn't really blame 'em for thinking what they did. I'd've probably thought the same thing in their place, what with Myra bawling and her clothes being messed up, and me not being in very good shape neither. They figured I'd raped her, and when a fella rapes a gal in this part of the country, he hardly ever gets to the jail. Or, if he does, he don't stay there very long.

I figure sometimes that maybe that's why we don't make as much progress as other parts of the nation. People lose so much time from their jobs in lynching other people, and they spend so much money on rope and kerosene and getting likkered-up in advance and other essentials, that there ain't an awful lot of money or man-hours left for practical purposes.

Howsoever, it sure looked like I was about to be the guest of honor at a necktie party, when Myra decided to speak up.

"I'm s-sure Mr. Corey didn't mean to do wrong," she said, looking around teary-eyed. "He's really a fine man, I'm sure, and he didn't mean to do wrong, did you, Mr. Corey?"

"No, ma'am, I sure didn't," I said, running my finger around my collar. "I positively didn't mean nothing like that, and that's a fact."

"Then why did you do it?" a man frowned at me. "This is hardly something that a person does accidentally."

"Well, I don't know about that," I said. "I wouldn't say you're wrong, but I ain't sure you're right either."

He started to take a swing at me. I ducked but another fella caught me by the shoulder and flung me toward the door. I went down on my knees and someone kicked me, and some others jerked me to my feet again, not being very gentle about it, and then everyone was hustling me out of the room and trying to sock me at the same time.

Myra said, "Wait! Please wait! It's all a mistake."

They slowed down a little, and someone said, "Now, don't upset yourself, Miss Myra. This skunk isn't worth it."

"But he wants to marry me! We were going to get married tonight!"

Everyone was pretty surprised, including me, and they were puzzled too, which I wasn't. It looked like I'd sold my pottage for a mess of afterbirth, as the saying is. I'd been chasing females all my life, not paying no mind to the fact that whatever's got tail at one end has teeth at the other, and now I was getting chomped on.

"That right, Corey?" A fella nudged me. "You and Miss Myra getting married?"

"Well," I said. "Well, it's like this, or at least that's the way I see it. I mean, uh—"

"Oh, he's so bashful!" Myra laughed. "And he gets excited so easily! That's what happened when—" She looked down at herself, blushing and brushing at her mussed-up clothes. "He got so excited when I said yes, I'd marry him, that—that—"

The women put their arms around her and kissed her.

The men slapped me on the back, and began shaking my hands. They said they were sorry they'd misunderstood the situation; and doggone it, couldn't a woman get a man in a heck of a lot of trouble without even halfway trying?

"Why, we might have had you strung up by the neck, Corey, if

Miss Myra hadn't set things straight! Now, wouldn't that have been a fine state of affairs?"

"Yeah," I said. "That would have been a good joke on me. But looky, fellas. About this marriage business—"

"A wonderful institution, Corey. And you're getting a wonderful woman."

"And I'm getting a wonderful man!" Myra jumped up and threw her arms around me. "We're getting married right tonight, because Mr. Corey just can't wait, and you're all invited to the wedding!"

It just happened that there was a preacher right up in the next block, so that's where we went—where everyone else went, I should say—and I got took. Myra dragged me along, with her arm hooked through mine; and these other folks brought up the rear, laughing and joking and slapping me on the back, and crowding on my heels so that I couldn't slow down.

I tried to sort of hang back, and they thought that was funny as all-heck. They thought the expression on my face was funny, and they practically went into hysterics when I said something like what was the god-danged hurry, and maybe we ought to think this over for a while.

It reminded me of one of those ceremonies you read about in ancient histories. You know. There's this big procession, with everyone laughing and carrying on and having themselves a heck of a time, and up at the head of it is this fella that's going to get sacrificed to the gods. He knows he'll get his ass carved up with a meat axe as soon as they stop throwing roses at him, so he sure ain't in no hurry to get to the altar. He can't get out of the deal, but neither can he put his heart into it. And the more he protests, the more people laugh at him.

So . . .

So that's what it reminded me of. A fella getting sacrificed for something that just ain't worth it.

But I guess a lot of marriages strike me the same way. Everything for show and nothing for real. Everything for public and nothing for private.

And that night, after me and Myra were in bed—I guess a lot of marriages turn out like that, too. Bawling and accusations and mean talk: the woman taking it out on the man because he was too stupid to get away from her.

Or maybe I'm just kind of sour . . .

THIRTEEN

I got my horse and buggy out of the livery stable, and drove back to the courthouse. Myra was jumping on me, wanting to know what had took me so long, almost as soon as I was inside the door. And I said I'd had quite a time getting things straightened out with Amy.

"I don't see why," Myra said. "She seemed calm enough when she left here."

"Well, there's quite a few things you don't see," I said. "Like why you should keep Lennie in at night so we wouldn't have messes like this."

"Now, don't you start in on Lennie!"

"I tell you what I'd like to start," I said. "I'd like to start home with Rose, so maybe we could all get to bed sometime tonight."

Rose said yes, she really should be going, and she thanked Myra for the dinner and hugged her and kissed her good night. I went on downstairs ahead of her, before I got into another argument, and she came running down after a minute or two and got into the buggy.

"Ugh!" she said, scrubbing at her mouth. "Every time I kiss that old bitch I want to wash out my mouth."

"You ought to watch that cussing, Rose," I said. "It's liable to slip out sometime when you don't mean it to."

"Yeah, I guess I should, goddam it," she said. "It's Tom's fault, the dirty son-of-a-bitch, but I'm sure as hell going to do my best to stop it."

"That's my girl," I said. "I can see you ain't going to have no trouble."

We were outside of town by now, and Rose moved over in the seat to snuggle up against me. She kissed me on the back of my neck and she put a hand inside my pocket and sort of wriggled it around; and then she kind of moved away a little, and gave me a funny look.

"What's the matter, Nick?"

"What?" I said. "How's that, Rose?"

"I said, what's wrong with you?"

"Why, nothing," I said. "Course I'm kind of tired and wore out from all the excitement tonight, but there ain't nothing really wrong."

She stared at me, not saying anything. She turned around in the seat, facing straight ahead, and we rode in silence for a while. At last she spoke, in a voice so low I could hardly hear it, asking me a question. I went cold all over, and then I said, "For gosh's sake! What a thing to say! You know Amy Mason ain't that kind of woman, Rose! Everyone knows she ain't."

"What the hell you mean she's not that kind?" Rose snapped. "You mean she's too goddam good to go to bed with you, but I'm not?"

"I mean, I just ain't hardly acquainted with the woman!" I said. "I barely know her to tip my hat to."

"You were gone long enough tonight to get acquainted!"

"Aw, naw, I wasn't honey," I said. "It just seemed like a long time to you, like it did to me. You know. Because we were just waitin' to get together tonight, and it seemed like a heck of a long wait. Why, honey, I was just itchin' and achin' for you from the minute you showed up today."

"Well . . ." She moved over a little in the seat.

"Why, for gosh's sake," I said. "What for would I want with Amy Mason when I got you? Why, it just don't make sense, now does it? There just ain't no comparison between the two of you!"

Rose came all the way over in the seat. She leaned her head against my shoulder, and said she was sorry, but I had acted kind of strange, and it did make her so goddam mad the way some men were.

"That goddam Tom, for example! The son-of-a-bitch just wouldn't leave me alone until I gave in to him, and then he goes out and screws everything that can't outrun him!"

"Tsk, tsk," I said. "I just can't understand fellas like that."

Rose squeezed me and kissed me on the ear. She gave me a little nibble on the ear, and whispered to me. Talking about what-all she was going to do to me when we got to her house.

"Myra wants you to stay a while, and make sure I'm all right.

Isn't that nice, mm? We can take our time, just you and me together for hours and hours. And, honey, we won't waste a minute of it!"

"Oh, boy," I said.

"It'll be like it never was before, darling!" She shivered against me. "Oh, honey, I'm going to be something special for you tonight!"

"Goll-ee," I said. "Goody, gosh-dang."

She went on whispering and shivering against me, saying that this was one night I'd never forget. I said I bet I wouldn't neither, and I meant every word of it. Because the way I was feeling, as hollow as a tree-bark whistle and like my back was broken in six places, there wasn't going to be no party when we got to Rose's house. Which meant that she'd know she'd been right about Amy. Which also meant that she'd probably take that gun she'd got today and shoot me right through the offendin' part. And with a memento like that, I sure wouldn't forget the night.

I tried to think of some way of stalling her. I looked up at the sky, which was clouding over again for a rain, and I saw a streak or two of lightning, and I thought, well, maybe a bolt would strike me, coldcocking me for the night, so that Rose would excuse me. Then I thought, well, maybe the horse would run away and throw me into a bob-wire fence, and Rose would have to let me off then, too. Or maybe a water moccasin would climb up in the buggy and fang me. Or—

But nothing like that happened. A fella never gets lucky that way when he really needs to.

We reached the farm. I drove on into the barn, wondering how much it would handicap a fella having a hole where I was going to have one. It seemed to me it would mess him up pretty bad in the things he needed to do most, and I climbed down from the buggy, feeling mighty glum.

I helped Rose down, giving her a smack on the bottom by way of habit. Then, I bent down behind the splashboard to unhitch the singletree, and the horse was fidgeting and switching his tail and I was saying, "Sooo, boy, soo, now." And then I thought of an idea.

I gave the horse a goose and made him jump. I drove my shoulder against the splashboard, making a heck of a racket like the horse had kicked it. Then I jumped out in the clear again, groaning and clutching myself.

Rose came running up, clinging to me by one arm as I staggered around doubled over. "Oh, honey! Darling! Did that goddam nag kick you?"

"Right in the you-know-what," I groaned. "I never had nothin' hurt so bad in my life."

"Goddam him to hell, anyway! I'll get a pitchfork and gut the brindle bastard!"

"Naw, don't do nothin' like that," I said. "The horse didn't go to do it. Just help me get him hitched up again, so's I can get home."

"Home? You're not going anywhere in your condition," she said. "I'm taking you in the house, and don't you argue about it."

I said, but, looky, now, it wasn't necessary to go to all that trouble. "I'll just go home and lay down with some cold towels on it, and—"

"You'll lie down here, and we'll see about the towels after I see what the damage is. It might be you need something else."

"But, looky, looky here, now, honey," I said. "It's kind of private, a thing like that. It ain't hardly something a woman should deal with."

"Since when?" Rose said. "Now, come on and stop arguing with me. Just lean on me and we'll go real slow."

I did what she said. There just wasn't anything else I could do.

We got to the house. She helped me back into the bedroom, made me lay down on the bed and started taking off my clothes. I told her she didn't need to take them all off, because the pain was just in the part that my pants covered. She said it wasn't any trouble at all, and I could relax better if I was all undressed instead of partways, and to stop butting into her business.

I said that it was my business that got hurt, and she said, well, my business was her business, and right now she was running the store.

She leaned down over the place where I was hurt, or supposed to be hurt, turning the lamp this way and that so that she could make a proper inspection.

"Hmmm," she said. "I don't see any bruises, honey. No breaks in the skin."

I said, well, it sure hurt, that's all I knew. "Of course a fella don't have to get hit very hard in that area to make him hurt to beat heck."

She said, "Let's see, now, you tell me where it hurts. Does it hurt *there*, or *here*, or *here*—"

She was awful gentle, so gentle that it wouldn't have hurt me in any of the places even if I *had* been hurt. I told her that maybe she'd better be a little more firm about it so I could make sure of where the pain was. So she pushed and pressed a little harder, asking if it hurt *there* or *here* and so on. And I let out an "Ooh" or an "Aah" now and then. But what I was feeling wasn't pain.

It didn't matter any more about Amy; me being with her that night, I mean. I was as ready and rarin' as I'd ever been, and, of course, Rose wasn't long in noticing the fact.

"Hey, now!" she said. "Just what's going on here, mister?"

"What does it look like?" I said.

"It looks to me like a big business recovery."

"Well, god-dang, gee-whillikins!" I said. "And right after a severe blow to the economy! You reckon we ought to celebrate the occasion?"

"What the hell you think? she said. "Just let me get these goddam clothes off!"

I snoozed a little while afterwards. No more than fifteen minutes, probably, because I'd rested quite a bit that day and wasn't really tired.

I came awake with Rose's hand biting into my arm, her voice a scary whisper. "*Nick!* Nick, wake up! Someone's outside!"

"What?" I mumbled, starting to roll over on my side again. "Well, leave 'em out there. Sure don't want 'em in here."

"Nick! They're on the porch, Nick! What—who do you suppose it—"

"I don't hear nothin'," I said. "Maybe it's just the wind."

"No, it—*listen*! There it is again!"

I heard it then; faint, careful footsteps, like someone moving on tiptoe. And along with them, a dull draggy sound, as if something heavy was being dragged up on the stoop.

"N-Nick. What do you think we'd better do, Nick?"

I swung my legs off the bed, and said I'd get my gun and have a look. She started to nod, and then she put out her hand and stopped me.

"No, honey. It won't look right your being here this time of night. Not with the lights all off and your horse put away."

"But I'll just take a little peek out," I said. "I won't show myself to no one."

"You might have to. You just stay here and keep quiet, and I'll go."

She slid quietly out of bed, and trotted into the other room, making no more noise than a shadow. I was pretty nervy, naturally, wondering who or what was up on the porch and what it might have to do with me and Rose. But the way she was taking things, sort of keeping out in front and leaving me in the background, was a big comfort. I thought about Myra's idea of Rose as someone meek and mild and ready to jump at her own shadow, and I almost laughed out loud. Rose could whip her weight in bobcats if she took a notion. She'd maybe let Tom get the best of her, but that just wasn't no way a fair match.

I heard the click of the key in the outside door.

I sat up, kind of poised on the edge of the bed, ready to move if she called to me.

I waited, holding my breath for quiet. There was another click, as Rose unlatched the screen, and then a rusty squeak as she pushed it open. Then . . .

It was a small house, like I've said. But from where I was to where she was was still quite a piece—maybe thirty feet or more. Yet that far away, I heard it. The gasp; the scared-crazy sound of her breath sucking in.

And then she screamed. Screamed and cussed in a way I don't ever want to hear again.

"N-Nick! Nick! The son-of-a-bitch is back! That goddam Tom's back!"

FOURTEEN

I grabbed for my pants, but the legs were twisted and the way Rose was carrying on, I didn't have no time to fool with 'em. Pants weren't what I needed anyway, with that god-danged Tom back. So I snatched up my gun, which I sure as heck did need, and ran for the door.

I tripped over a chair in the kitchen, almost taking a header against the wall. I righted myself, and dashed out to the porch. Then, I saw how things were—and they sure weren't good, all right, but they were a lot better than I'd expected 'em to be.

It was Tom's body that was there, not Tom. It had been left on the porch, face up, with the shotgun placed at the side. The beard had grown out some, because hair does go on growing for a while on dead people. He was all covered over with mud, and the middle of his body was just a big gutsy hole. His eyes were wide open and staring. The meanness was gone from them, but the fear that had taken its place was worse. Whatever death looked like, it sure didn't look good to him.

All in all, you might say he wasn't a very pretty sight. Nothing that would take first prize in a best-lookin'-fella contest. Old man Death had painted Tom Hauck in his true colors, and it wasn't an even halfway flattering portrait.

I couldn't really blame Rose for carrying on like she was. Almost any woman would have done the same, if her husband had come home in the middle of the night looking like Tom did. Rose had a right to raise a ruckus, but it wasn't helping things, particularly helping me to think. Which I was obviously in need of doing and fast. So I got an arm around her and tried to calm her down.

"Easy, now, honey, easy. This don't look so good, but—"

"Goddam you, why didn't you kill him?" She tore away from me. "You told me you killed the son-of-a-bitch!"

"I did, baby. He sure don't look like no live man, now does he? He couldn't be no more dead if—"

"Then who brought him back here? What goddam dirty bastard did it? If I get my hands on the son-of-a-bitch—"

She broke off and whirled around wide-eyed, seeming to listen for something. I started to say I wanted to get my hands on the fella, too, because just why the heck had he done this anyway? Rose told me to shut my goddam mouth.

"Now, honey," I said. "That ain't no way to talk. We got to be calm and—"

"There!" she yelled, pointing. "There he is! That's the son-of-a-bitch that did it!"

She leaped off the porch and started running. Racing up the lane that led from the house to the road. Her naked white body faded into the darkness. I hesitated, wondering if I shouldn't at least put my pants on, and then I thought what the heck, and I ran after her.

I couldn't see whatever Rose had seen. I couldn't hardly see nothing, it being so dark. But I did hear something—the squeak of wagon wheels and the soft plod-plod of horses' hooves on the muddy lane.

I kept running. Finally, the squeaking and the plodding stopped and I saw the white of Rose's body. Then, she was cussing and screaming again, ordering whoever it was to climb down off the wagon.

"Get down, you black bastard! Get down, goddam you! What the hell's the idea of bringing back that son-of-a-bitch of a husband of mine?"

"Miz Rose. Please, ma'am, Miz Rose. I—" It was the soft, frightened voice of a man.

"I'll show you, you son-of-a-bitch! I'll teach you! I'll peel your black ass right down to the bones!"

She was trying to tear loose a piece of harness strap when I ran up. I jerked her around, and she faced me wild-eyed, pointing shakily to the fella who stood at the side of the wagon.

It was Uncle John, the colored fella I mentioned earlier. He was standing with his hands half-raised, and in the darkness his frightened eyes seemed all whites. He kept them turned away, naturally, because a colored fella could get himself killed for looking at a naked white woman.

"H-He—he did it!" Rose began to bawl. "He brought the son-of-a-bitch back, Nick!"

"Well, now, I'm sure he didn't mean no harm by it," I said. "Howdy do, Uncle John. Nice evenin'."

"Thank you, Mistah Nick. I's feelin' tol'able thank you." His voice shook with fear. "Yes, suh, sho' is a fine evenin'."

"You son-of-a-bitch!" Rose yelled. "What'd you bring him back for? Why do you think we got rid of the dirty bastard, anyway?"

"Rose!" I said, "*Rose!*" and Uncle John's eyes rolled in his head and he said, "Please, ma'am, Miz Rose," and it sounded like a prayer.

He'd already seen a lot, a heck of a lot more than it was healthy to see. He sure didn't want to hear anything to go with it. Rose slipped away from me again, opening her mouth for another yell, and Uncle John tried to stopper his ears with his fingers. But he knew it was no good. He heard, and he knew that I knew it.

"It's not fair, Nick, goddam it! You go to all the trouble of killing the son-of-a-bitch, and this bastard brings him back!"

I slapped her across the mouth. She whirled and came at me, hands clawed. I grabbed her by the hair, lifted her off the ground, and gave her a criss-cross slap, backwards and forwards.

"You get the idea?" I said, letting her back down on her feet. "Now, you shut up and get back to the house or I'll give you the worst beating you ever had in your life."

Her hand went slowly to her face. She looked down at herself, seeming to realize for the first time that she was naked. Shivering, she tried to cover up with her hands, shooting a scared look at Uncle John.

"N-Nick. What—what'll we—"

"Go on, do what I told you to." I gave her a push toward the house. "Me an' Uncle John will handle this."

"B-But—but why did he do it?"

"I got an idea about that, too," I said. "You run along, now, and everything will be fine."

She hesitated, then scampered back up the lane. I waited until I was sure she was really gone, and then I turned around to Uncle John.

I smiled at him, and he tried to smile back. But his teeth were chattering so bad that he couldn't.

"Now, don't be scared, Uncle John," I told him. "You got nothin' to fear with me. Ain't I always treated you right, now, ain't I? Ain't I always done the very best I could by you?"

"Yes, yes, suh, Mistah Nick," he said eagerly, "an' I done right by you, suh, ain't I, Mistah Nick? Now, ain't that the truth, suh? Ain't I been a plumb good nigger for you?"

"Well, sir," I said, "I reckon I could call you that, all right."

"Yes, suh, Mistah Nick. Any of them bad niggers startin' trouble, I always comes an' tells you, suh. Any of 'em steal a chicken or shoot crap or get drunk or all 'em other things bad niggers do, I always comes right an' reports it to you, now don't I, suh?"

"Well, sir," I said, "I reckon you're right about that, too, and I ain't forgettin' it, Uncle John. But just what are you getting at anyways?"

He gulped and choked, swallowing a sob. "Mistah Nick, I won't say nothin' about—'bout what happen tonight. Hones', Mistah Nick, I won't say nothin' to no one. You just let me go an'—an'—"

"Why sure I will," I said. "Ain't keeping you from leaving now, am I?"

"Y-You really means it, Mistah Nick? You really ain't mad at me none? I c'n go home right now, an' just keep my big ol' mouth shut forevah an' evah?"

I told him that of course he could leave. But I'd feel a lot better if he first told me how he happened to be here with Tom Hauck's body.

"You don't do that, I might be kind of suspicious of you. I might figure you'd done something bad and was trying to hide it."

"No, suh, Mistah Nick! Doin' something bad was jus' what I didn't! I try to do good, an' then I get all mixed up, ol' foolish me an'—an'—oh, Mistah Nick!" He covered his face with his hands. "D-Don't be mad at me, suh. Uncle John, he don't know nothin' at all. He don't h-hear nothin' an' he don't see nothin', an'—an'—please don't kill me, Mistah Nick! Please don't kill ol' John."

I patted him on the back, letting him cry for a minute. Then I said I knew he hadn't done nothing wrong, so why would I want to do anything bad to him. But I'd sure be obliged if he told me just what *had* happened.

"Y-You—" He uncovered his face to look at me. "You really ain't gonna kill me, Mistah Nick? Honest?"

"God-dang it, you callin' me a liar?" I said. "Now, you just start talkin', and don't tell me nothing but the truth."

He told me what had happened, why he had brought Tom Hauck's body back to his farm house.

It stacked up just about the way I thought it would.

He had come across the body early that evening while he was out hunting 'possum, and he'd started to come into town to tell me about it. Then, with so many varmints around, he figured it might be best to bring the body in with him. So he'd loaded it on his old spring wagon, along with the shotgun, and headed for town again.

He was about halfway there when it struck him that it might be a pretty bad idea to show up in town with the remains; in fact, it was a god-danged bad idea to be caught even in the same neighborhood with them. Because a lot of people might figure he had a first-class motive for killing Tom. After all, Tom had given him a hard beating and intended to beat him again if he got within grabbing range. He just couldn't lead a very happy life as long as Tom was around, so it wouldn't be any surprise at all if he killed him. Anyways, Uncle John being a colored fella, he wouldn't get the benefit of any doubts.

Tom Hauck was completely no good, and the community was well shot of him. But they'd still lynch Uncle John. It would sort of be their civic duty, the way they'd see it; part of the process of keeping the colored folks in hand.

Well, so poor old Uncle John had got himself in a pickle. He couldn't take Tom's body into town, or even be seen with it. And Tom being a white man, he couldn't bring himself to just dump the body off in a ditch somewhere. There was only one thing he could do, as he saw it; only one thing that would be acceptable to Tom's white ghost and the All-Knowing God that he had been taught to believe in. He'd just take the dead man back to his own home and leave him there.

"Now, don't that seem fittin', Mistah Nick? You see how I figgered, suh? I reckon now, it sho' wasn't the right thing to do, seein' as how Miz Rose carry on so bad, an'—"

"Well, now, don't you worry none about that at all," I said. "Miss Rose was just upset seeing her husband dead, and pretty ugly-dead, at that. It's probably goin' to take her quite a while to get over it, so maybe we'd better move the body somewheres else until then."

"But—b-but you say I could leave, Mistah Nick. You say I jus' tell you the truth, an'—"

"Yes, sir, that's what we'd better do," I said. "So just you hurry up, and turn your wagon back around."

He stood there, head bowed; his mouth working like he was trying to say something. There was a long roll of thunder, and then a jagged flash of lightning, lighting his face for a moment. And somehow I had to look the other way.

"You hear me, Uncle John?" I said. "You hear what I tell you to do?"

He hesitated, then sighed and climbed up on the wagon. "Yes, suh, I hear you, Mistah Nick."

We drove back to the house. It began to rain while we were loading Tom's body, and I told Uncle John to stand on the porch until I was dressed so that he wouldn't get no wetter than he had to.

"You're probably kind of hungry," I said. "You want I should bring you a cup of hot chicory? Maybe a little pone or somethin'?"

"I reckon not, thank you, suh." He shook his head. "Miz Rose probably got no fire this time o' night."

"Well, we'll just build one up," I said. "No trouble at all."

"Thank you, suh. I guess not, Mistah Nick. I—I ain't real hongry."

I went on in the house and dried off with a towel Rose gave me, and it sure felt good getting back into my clothes. She was pestering me with questions while I dressed: what were we going to do and what was I going to do, and so on. I asked her what she thought; did she reckon she'd ever feel safe with someone knowing what Uncle John knew.

"Well—" She wet her lips, her eyes turned away from mine. "We can give him some money, can't we? Both of us will. That should, uh, well, he wouldn't want to say anything then, would he?"

"He takes a drink now and then," I said. "No tellin' what a fella will do when he gets enough booze in him."

"But he—"

"And he's a very religious fella. Wouldn't be at all surprised if he figured he ought to pray for us."

"You can send him away somewhere," Rose said. "Put him on a train and send him up north."

"He can't talk up there? He wouldn't feel more free to do it away from us than he would here?"

I laughed and chucked her under the chin, asking her what she was so squeamish about. "Here I thought you was a real tough woman. It didn't bother you at all about what happened to Tom."

"Because I hated the son-of-a-bitch! It's not the same with Uncle John, a poor nigger man who was just trying to do the best he could!"

"Maybe Tom was doing the best he could, too. I wonder if we did any better."

"But—but, Nick! You, why you know what the bastard was like."

I said, yeah, I knew, but I'd never heard of anyone killing Tom's wife, and Tom sleeping before and after with the party that did it.

Then, I laughed, cutting her off before she could butt in. "But this is different all right, honey," I said. "This you know about before it happens. It ain't something you learn about afterward, so you can say, well, what can I do about it, and it ain't really my doin'."

"Nick—" She touched my arm, sort of frightened. "I'm sorry I lost my head tonight, honey. I guess I can't blame you for trying to hurt me."

"It ain't really that," I said. "I reckon I'm just kind of tired of doing things that everybody knows I'm doing, things they really want and expect me to do, and having to take all the blame for it."

She understood; she said she did, anyway. She put her arms around me and held me for a little while, and we talked a couple of minutes about what would have to be done. Then I left because I had a pretty full night's work ahead of me.

I had Uncle John drive up in the back country, about three miles behind the farm. We unloaded Tom's body there, in the edge of some trees, and Uncle John and I took such shelter as we could a few feet away.

He sat down at the base of a tree, his legs being too wobbly to hold him up any longer. I hunkered down a few feet away from him, and broke open the barrel of the shotgun. It looked fairly clean, clean enough to be safe, anyways. I blew through it a couple of times to make sure, and then I loaded it with the shells I'd taken from Tom's pockets.

Uncle John watched me, all the begging and praying in the world in his eyes. I relatched the barrel, and sighted along it, and he began to cry again. I frowned at him, feeling pretty fretted.

"Now, what you want to carry on like that for?" I said. "You knew what I was goin' to have to do right along."

"No, s-suh, I believe you, Mistah Nick. You different f'm other white folks. I believe every word you say."

"Well, now, I think you're lyin', Uncle John," I said, "an' I'm sorry to hear you. Because it's right in the Bible that lyin's a sin."

"It's a sin to kill folks, too, Mistah Nick. Worse sin than lyin'. Y-You—you—"

"I'll tell you somethin', Uncle John," I said. "I'll tell you somethin', and I hope it'll be a comfort to you. Each man kills the thing he loves."

"Y-You don't love me, Mistah Nick . . ."

I told him he was god-danged right about that, a thousand per cent right. What I loved was myself, and I was willing to do anything I god-dang had to to go on lying and cheating and drinking whiskey and screwing women and going to church on Sunday with all the other respectable people.

"I'll tell you something else," I said, "and it makes a shitpot-ful more sense than most of the goddam scripture I've read. Better the blind man, Uncle John; better the blind man who pisses through a window than the prankster who leads him thereto. You know who the prankster is, Uncle John? Why, it's goddam near everybody, every son-of-a-bitch who turns his head when the crap flies, every bastard who sits on his dong with one thumb in his ass and the other in his mouth and hopes that nothing will happen to him, every whoremonger who thinks that piss will turn into lemonade, every mother-lover supposedly made in God's image, which makes me think I'd hate like hell to meet him on a dark night. Even you, particularly you, Uncle John; people who go around sniffing crap with their mouth open, and acting surprised as hell when someone kicks a turd in it. Yeah, you can't help bein' what you are, jus' a pore ol' black man. That's what you say, Uncle John, and do you know what I say? I say screw you. I say you can't help being what you are, and I can't help being what I am, and you goddam well know what I am and have to be. You goddam well know you've got no friends among the whites. You goddam well ought to know that you're not going to have any because you stink, Uncle John, and you go around begging to get screwed and how the hell can anyone have a friend like that?"

I gave him both barrels of the shotgun.

It danged near cut him in two.

FIFTEEN

What I wanted things to look like was that Uncle John had shot Tom with his own gun and then Tom had got the gun away from him and shot Uncle John. Or vice versa. Anyways, when I got to thinking about it afterward, it seemed to me that people weren't going to see it that way at all. Which meant that they were apt to start looking for the real killer. And for a spell there, I was pretty worried. But I didn't need to be. As plumb crazy as it was, with Uncle John getting killed almost two days after Tom and with both of 'em obviously dying almost the instant they was shot, it turned out no one thought anything of it. They didn't wonder at all about how one dead man could've killed another.

Of course, both bodies were wet and muddied up, so you couldn't say offhand just when they'd died; and we just ain't equipped to do a lot of scientific examination and investigation here in Potts County. If things look a certain way, folks usually figure that's the way they are. And if they'd had a mind to kick up a fuss about anyone, it wouldn't be Tom Hauck or Uncle John.

The plain fact was that no one much gave a good god-dang about either one of 'em. It was a plain case of good riddance to bad rubbish as far as Tom was concerned; and who cared about one colored fella more or less, unless it was some other colored folks, and who cared if they did care?

But I guess I'm getting ahead of myself a little . . .

I dropped the shotgun between Tom and Uncle John. Then, leaving John's horse and wagon where they were, I plodded back across country to the Hauck farm.

It was pretty late by that time, or pretty early I should say. An hour or so short of dawn. I hitched up, without going to the house, and headed for town.

The livery stable door was open, the hostler snoring like a buzz saw up in the hayloft. A lantern stood burning in a tub of sand, casting a flickering light along the row of stalls. I put up the horse and buggy without hardly a sound, and the hostler went on snoring. And I went out into the dark again, the dark and the rain.

There wasn't no one on the street, of course. Even without the rain, no one would have been out at that hour. I got to the courthouse, took off my boots and sneaked upstairs to bed.

The dry-warm felt awful good after them wet clothes, and I guess I was plumb wore out. Because I went to sleep right away, instead of tossing around fifteen, twenty minutes like I usually do.

Then, just about the time my head touched the pillow it seemed like, Myra started yelling and shaking me.

"Nick! Nick Corey, you get up from there! My goodness, do you want to sleep all night and all day, too?"

"Why not?" I mumbled, hanging on to the pillows. "Sounds like a danged good idea."

"I said to *get up*! It's almost noon, and Rose is on the phone!"

I let her get me up, and I talked to Rose for a minute or two. I said I was sorry to hear that Tom wasn't home yet, and I'd probably get out and take a look around for him, even if I wasn't sure that the sun would stay out and it wouldn't start raining again.

"I'll prob'ly do it, Rose," I said, "so don't you worry none. I reckon I'll prob'ly start lookin' for him today, even if it does start raining again and I spoil my clothes like I did last night, not to mention catchin' an awful cold. Or if I don't get out today, I'll sure do it tomorrow."

I hung up the phone and turned around.

Myra was frowning at me, tight-mouthed and disgusted-looking. She pointed to the table and told me to sit down, for pity's sake.

"Just eat your breakfast and get out of here! Start doing your job, for a change!"

"Me?" I said. "I do my job all the time."

"*You!* You stupid silly spineless fool! You don't do anything!"

"Well, that's my job," I said. "Not doing nothing, I mean. That's why for people elect me."

She whirled around so fast her skirts spun, and went out into the kitchen. I sat down at the table. I looked at the clock and saw that it was almost twelve o'clock, practically dinner time, so I didn't eat much except some eggs and ham and grits with gravy and seven or eight biscuits, and a bitty bowl of peaches and cream.

I was having a third cup of coffee when Myra came back in. She began to snatch up the dishes, muttering to herself, and I asked her if they was something the matter.

"If they is," I said, "you just tell me all about it, because two heads is better than one."

"You miserable—! Aren't you ever going to get out of here?" she yelled. "Why are you still sitting at the table?"

"Why, I'm drinking this here coffee," I said. "You look real close an' you can see that I am."

"Well—well, take it with you! Drink it somewhere else!"

"You mean you want me to leave the table?" I said.

"*Yes!* Now, go on and do it, for pity's sake!"

I said I plumb liked to be obliging, but if she studied it over she'd see it didn't make much sense for me to leave the table. "I mean, it's almost time for dinner," I said. "You'll be bringin' it in any minute now, so why for should I leave when I can set right here an' be all ready to start eatin'?"

"Y-You!" Her teeth gritted together. "*You get out of here!*"

Without no dinner?" I said. "You mean I got to work all afternoon on an empty stomach?"

"But you just got—" She choked up, and sagged down into a chair.

I said that was fine, she should sit down and rest herself up a little, and it didn't matter at all if dinner was maybe a minute or two late. And she said—

I don't know what she said. We just went on talking back and forth for a while, neither of us really listening to the other. Which didn't bother her any, since she never paid any attention to me anyhow, and to tell the truth I never actually paid a lot of attention to her, anyhow. Anyways, I couldn't have done it today even if I'd wanted to, because I was too worried about what would happen when Tom and Uncle John were found dead.

That's why I'd been pestering Myra, I guess. I didn't want to get out and face up to whatever was going to happen, so I'd start gigging at her. That was kind of habit with me, I reckon, taking it out on her when I felt bad or bothered. More of a habit than I maybe realized.

"Where at is Lennie?" I said, picking up the conversation again. "He don't hurry up he'll be late for dinner!"

"He's had his dinner! I mean, I fixed him a lunch before he left!"

"You mean he's outside when maybe the sun will stop shining pretty soon and it'll start raining to beat heck, and he'll probably spoil his clothes and get himself an awful cold?" I said. "Now, that ain't takin' very good care of your brother, honey."

Myra's face began to swell, kind of like she was blowing out her cheeks. She stared at me, her eyes popping, and god-dang if she didn't sort of tremble all over.

"Why for did Lennie go out in the daytime, anyways?" I said. "He can't peek in no windows when it's light."

"You!" Myra said, pushing herself up from the chair. "Y-You—" She pointed toward the door, her hand shaking like a leaf. "You get out of here, you hear me? GET OUT OF HERE!"

"You mean, you want me to leave?" I said. "Well, you should've said so sooner. Maybe given me a little hint."

I put on my hat, and told her to be sure and call me when dinner was ready. She made a wild grab for the sugar bowl, and I got on down the stairs pretty fast.

I sat down in my office. I tilted my hat over my eyes, and put my boots up on the desk. It looked to me like it was a good time to take a little nap, because people still weren't getting around much on account of the mud. But this was one day I just couldn't keep my eyes closed.

Finally, I stopped trying. There just wasn't much point to it with me so scared-worried. I figured the best thing I could do was to get things over with; get some fellas together and start the hunt for Tom. Then, whatever happened, I'd know what it was, at least, and I wouldn't have to fret myself anymore.

I got up and started for the door. The phone rang, and I went back to answer it. And just as I did, Lennie came busting in.

He was waving his arms, burbling and spitting all-the-heck over everything with excitement.

I waved him to simmer down, and spoke into the phone. "Just a minute, Robert Lee. Lennie just came in, and it looks like he wants to tell me somethin'."

"Never mind. I know what he wants to tell you," Robert Lee Jefferson said, and he told me what it was. "Now, you better get right down here and take charge."

I said I'd do that, and I did.

It was Henry Clay Fanning, a farmer who lived a couple miles south of the Hauck place, who'd found the bodies. He'd been out cutting cordwood at the time, and he'd just pitched 'em up on top of his load and brought 'em on into town.

"Didn't waste a minute," he said proudly, spitting snuff into the mud. "You reckon the county'll sort of take care o' me for my trouble?"

"Well, I'm not real sure they will, Henry Clay," I said, noticing how Uncle John's head was crushed between the wood and the wagon bed. "After all, you was comin' to town anyways."

"But what about that nigger?" he said. "A white man ought to get some kind of ree-ward for handlin' a nigger."

"Well, maybe you will," I said. "If not in this world, the next one."

He went on arguing about it. Some of the people in the crowd picked up the argument, debating it back and forth between themselves. They were about evenly divided on the subject, one group claiming that Henry Clay *was* entitled to a reward, and the other saying that a white that was fool enough to bother with a nigger didn't deserve nothing but an ass-kicking.

I grabbed hold of a couple of colored fellas, and told 'em to carry Uncle John's body back to his folks. And they kind of dragged their feet, but of course they did it. Then, me and Robert Lee and one of his clerks carried Tom into Taylor's Emporium, Furniture and Undertaking.

I told Robert Lee I'd kind of like his opinion on things, and he turned on me, looking sickish. "Can't you at least let me wash my hands?" he snapped. "Are you in such an all-fired hurry I can't even do that?"

"Not me," I said. "I ain't in no more hurry than ol' Tom is, and I sure don't see him bein' in one, do you, Robert Lee? Kind of hard to tell which is the biggest, ol' Tom or the hole in him!"

We all washed up in the rear of the Emporium, Robert Lee looking awful pale and sickish. Then his clerk went on back to the hardware store, me an' Robert Lee following him maybe ten minutes later. We couldn't make it any sooner than that, because Robert Lee had to make himself another quick trip and a long visit to the wash-sink.

He held himself straight and tight-lipped as we left, still as pale as a ghost. Then, just as we stepped out the door, Henry Clay Fanning latched hold of him.

That Henry Clay was a real case, what we call a cotton-patch lawyer down here. He knew all the privileges he was entitled to—and maybe three or four million others besides—but he didn't have much sense of his obligations. None of his fourteen kids had ever been to school, because making kids go to school was interferin' with a man's constitutional rights. Four of his seven girls, all of 'em that were old enough to be, were pregnant. And he wouldn't allow no one to ask 'em how they'd got that way, because that was *his* legal responsibility, it was a father's job to care for his children's morals, and he didn't have to tolerate any interference.

Of course, everyone had a pretty good idea who'd gotten those girls pregnant. But under the circumstances, there wasn't any way of proving it, and with Henry Clay being kind of mean-tempered no one talked much about it.

So here he was now, exercisin' his rights again. Grabbing Robert Lee Jefferson by the arm and whirling him around.

"Now, you see here, Robert Lee," he said. "Maybe that doggone Nick Corey don't know the law, but you do and you know god-dang well I'm entitled to a ree-ward. I—"

"What?" Robert Lee stared at him. "What did you say?"

"County pays a ree-ward for corpses pulled out of the river, don't they? So why don't I get a bounty for finding these? I not only found 'em, I haul 'em all the way into town an' get nigger blood all over my wagon, an'—"

"Answer me, you incestuous skunk! Did you address me as Robert Lee?"

Henry Clay said sure, he called him that, and what about it. "What you mean callin' me a—"

Robert Lee hit him in the mouth. Henry Clay sailed off the sidewalk and landed in the mud on his back. His eyes were open, but he didn't stir. Just lay there, breathing with a snuffling sound because of his bloody nose and mouth.

Robert Lee dusted his hands, nodded to me and entered his store. I followed him back to his office.

"Now, I feel better," he sighed, sinking down in a chair. "I've been wanting to punch that dirty cur for years, and he finally gave me an excuse."

I said I guessed Henry Clay didn't really know a lot about law, after all. "If he did, he'd know that calling you by your first name would be laying a predicate for justifiable assault."

"What?" He gave me a startled look. "I'm not sure I understood you."

"Nothin'," I said. "You sure gave him a punch, Robert Lee."

"Wasn't it a beaut? I only wish I'd broken his filthy neck."

"Maybe you'd better be kind of careful for a while," I said. "Henry Clay might try to get back at you."

Robert Lee snorted. "He doesn't have the nerve, but I wish he did. That's one man I'd enjoy killing. Imagine him calling me by my first name!"

"Yeah," I said, "just imagine that!"

"Now, about this other matter, Tom and Uncle John, I don't see much point in impaneling a coroner's jury in such a clear-cut case. The facts seem obvious enough, don't you agree?"

"Well, it sure is a clear-cut case," I said. "I don't know as I've ever seen such a clear-cut case of killing."

"Exactly. And everyone I've talked to has the same opinion. Of course, if Rose should insist on an inquest . . ."

"Or Uncle John's kinfolks . . ."

"Oh, now—" Robert Lee laughed. "Let's not be ridiculous, Nick."

"I say something funny?" I said.

"Well, uh," said Robert Lee, sort of clearing his throat. "Perhaps I chose the wrong word. I should have said impractical."

I looked blank, and asked just what did he mean, anyways? He snapped back that I knew very well what he meant. "No doctor is going to do a post mortem on a Negro. Why, you can't get a doctor to touch a live Negro, let alone a dead one."

"I reckon you're right," I said. "Just in case we had to, though, and I'm just asking for information, do you suppose you could get out a court order t'make a doctor do his duty?"

"We-el"—Robert Lee leaned back and pursed his lips—"I imagine that's something that one could do *de jure*, but not *de facto*. In other words you'd have a paradox—the legal right to do something that was factually impossible of accomplishment."

I said I'd be god-danged, he was sure one heck of a smart man. "I reckon my head's plumb bustin' from all these things you been tellin' me, Robbie Lee. Maybe I better run along before you give me some more information, an' it pops wide open."

"Now, you're flattering me," he beamed, standing up as I did, "which reminds me that I should compliment you on your conduct in today's affair. You handled it very well, Nick."

"Why, thank you kindly, Robert Lee," I said. "How does the election look to you by now, if you don't mind my asking?"

"I think you're a cinch to win, in view of the unfortunate talk about Sam Gaddis. Just keep on doing your job, like you did today."

"Oh, I will," I said. "I'll keep on exactly like that."

I left the hardware store, and sauntered back toward the courthouse, stopping now and then to talk to people, or rather to let them talk to me. Almost everyone had about the same idea about the killing as Robert Lee Jefferson. Almost everyone agreed that it was an open and shut case, with Uncle John killing Tom and then Tom, dead as he was, killing Uncle John. Or vice versa.

About the only people who didn't see it that way, or said they didn't, were some loafers. They wanted a coroner's jury impaneled, and they were ready and willin' to serve on it. But if they were that hard up for a couple of dollars, I figured they hadn't paid their poll tax, so what they thought didn't matter.

Rose had heard the news from probably two, three hundred people by the time I got back to the courthouse, and Myra said I had to get out to the Hauck place right away and bring Rose into town.

"Now, please hurry, for once in your life, Nick! The poor thing is terribly upset!"

"Why for is she upset!" I said. "You mean because Tom is dead?"

"Of course, I mean that! What else would I mean?"

"Well, I was just wonderin'," I said. "She was terribly upset last night when she thought he might be comin' home, and now she's terribly upset because she knows he ain't. Don't seem to make much sense somehow."

"Now, just you never mind!" Myra snapped. "Don't you dare start arguing with me, Nick Corey! You just do what I tell you to, or *you* won't make much sense! Not that you ever did, anyway."

I got the horse and buggy and drove out toward the Hauck farm, thinking to myself that a fella hardly got one problem settled before he had to take care of another one. Maybe I should have foreseen that Rose would be coming in and staying with Myra and me tonight, but I hadn't. I'd had too many other things on my mind. So now I was supposed to see Amy tonight—I'd just better see her if I *ever* wanted to see her again. And I was also supposed to stay at home—Rose would think it was god-danged peculiar if I didn't. And I just didn't know what the heck I was going to do.

They were a real problem, Rose and Amy. A lot bigger problem than I realized.

The farm house was all steamy and kind of smelly when Rose let me in. She apologized for it, nodding toward the black dress that was hung up over the stove.

"I had to give it a hurry-up dye job, honey. But the goddam thing ought to be dry pretty soon. You want to come into the bedroom and wait?"

I followed her into the bedroom and she started taking off her shoes and stockings, which was all she had on. I said, "Looky, honey. Maybe we shouldn't do this right now."

"Huh?" She frowned at me. "Why the hell not?"

"Well, you know," I said. "You're just now officially a widow. It just don't seem decent to hop in bed with a woman when she ain't hardly been a widow an hour."

"What the hell's the difference? You slept with me before I was a widow!"

"Well, sure," I said. "But everybody does things like that. You might say it was even kind of a compliment to a woman. But this way, when a woman ain't been a widow long enough to get her weeds wet, it just ain't respectful. I mean, after all, they's certain proprieties to observe, and a decent fella don't hop right on a brand-new widow any more than a decent brand-new widow lets him."

She hesitated, studying me, but finally she nodded.

"Well, maybe you're right, Nick. Christ knows I've always done my goddam best to be respectable, in spite of that son-of-a-bitch I was married to."

"Why sure you have," I said. "Don't I know that, Rose?"

"So we'll wait until tonight. After Myra goes to sleep, I mean."

"Well," I said. "Well, uh—"

"And now I am going to tell you a surprise." She gave me a hug, eyes dancing. "It won't be long now before we can forget about Myra. You can get a divorce from the old bag—Christ knows you've got plenty of grounds—or we can just say to hell with her and leave here. Because we're going to have plenty of money, Nick. Plenty!"

"Whoa, whoa now!" I said. "What the heck are you sayin', honey?" And she laughed, and told me how it was.

Back in the beginning, when Tom was still sugarin'-up to her, he'd taken out a ten-thousand-dollar insurance policy. Ten thousand, *double indemnity*. After a year or so, when being nice got tiresome, he'd said to hell with the policy and to hell with her. But she'd kept up the premiums herself, paying for them out of her butter and egg money. Now, since Tom had been killed instead of dying a natural death, she'd collect under the double-indemnity clause. A whole twenty thousand dollars.

"Isn't it wonderful, honey?" She hugged me again. "And that's only part of it. This is damned good farm land, even if that son-of-a-bitch was such a no-good bastard that he never put any improvements on it. Even at a forced sale, it ought to bring ten or twelve thousand dollars, and with that much money, why—"

"Now, wait a minute," I said. "Not so fast, honey. We can't—"

"But we can, Nick! What the hell's to stop us?"

"You just think about it," I said. "Think how it would look to other people. Your husband gets killed and right away you're a rich woman. He gets killed and you profit by it plenty, and you tie up with another man before his body's hardly cold. You don't think that folks would wonder about that a little? You don't think they might get some alarmin' ideas about her and this other man and her husband's death?"

"We-el . . ." Rose nodded. "I suppose you're right, Nick. How long do you think we'll have to wait before it will be safe?"

"I'd say a year or two, anyways," I said. "Prob'ly two years would be best."

Rose said she didn't think two years would be best. Not for her it wasn't. One year was going to be goddamned plenty to wait, and she wasn't sure she'd even wait that long.

"But we got to! My gosh, honey," I said. "We can't take no chances, right when we've got everything the way we want it. That wouldn't make no sense, now would it?"

"Everything isn't the way *I* want it! Not by a hell of a long shot!"

"But looky, looky, honey," I said. "You just agreed that we had to be god-danged careful, and now you—"

"Oh, all right," Rose laughed, kind of pouting. "I'll try to be sensible, Nick. But don't you forget I've got my brand on you. Don't you forget it for a minute!"

"Why, honey," I said. "What a thing to say! Why for would I want another woman when I've got you?"

"I mean it, Nick! I mean every word of it!"

I said sure, I knew she did, so what was she carryin' on about? She untensed a little, and patted me on the cheek.

"I'm sorry, honey. We'll see each other tonight, hmmm? You know, after Myra's gone to sleep."

"I don't see no reason why not," I said, wishing to gosh I could see a reason.

"Mmm! I can hardly wait!" She kissed me and jumped up. "I wonder if that goddam dress is dry yet."

It was dry. Probably a heck of a lot dryer than I was, what with all the sweating I was doing. I thought to myself, Nick Corey, how in the good gosh-dang do you get in these god-dang messes? You got to be with Rose tonight; you just don't dare not to be with her. And you got to be with Amy Mason tonight. Anyway, you're sure aching to be with Amy, even if you don't have to be. So—

But I did have to be.

I just didn't know it yet.

SIXTEEN

Myra was waiting for us at the head of the stairs when me and Rose arrived, and the two of 'em practically fell into each other's arms. Myra said, you poor, poor dear, and Rose said, oh, what would I ever do without you, Myra, and then they both busted out bawling.

Myra made the most noise, of course, even though it was more Rose's place to do it, and she'd been practicing all the way into town. There just wasn't no one that could beat Myra when it came to noise-making. She started to steer Rose into her bedroom, her eyes on Rose instead of where she was going, and she bumped spang into Lennie. She whirled and gave him a slap that almost made *me* hurt. Then she hit him again because he yelled.

"Now, you shut up!" she warned him. "Just shut up and behave yourself. Poor Rose has enough trouble without putting up with your racket!"

Lennie clenched his teeth to keep from bawling; I almost felt kind of sorry for him. Fact is, I felt real sorry for him, but right while I was doing it, I felt something else. Because that's the way I am,

I guess. I start feeling sorry for people, like Rose, for example, or even Myra or Uncle John or, well, lots of folks, and the way it eventually works out is it'd be a lot better if I hadn't felt sorry for them. Better for them, I mean. And I guess that's natural enough, you know? Because when you're sorry for someone, you want to help them, and when it sinks in on you that you can't, that there's too god-danged many of them, that everywhere you look there's someone, millions of someones, and you're only one man an' no one else cares an'—an'—

We were having an oven supper that night, which was a good thing since Myra was so long in the bedroom with Rose. Finally, they came out, and I patted Rose on the shoulder and told her she'd have to be brave. She rested her head against my chest for a moment, like she just couldn't help herself, and I gave her another pat.

"Now, that's right, Nick," Myra said. "You just take care of Rose, and I'll get supper on."

"I'll sure do that," I said, "me an' Lennie'll both take care of her, won't we, Lennie?"

Lennie scowled, blaming Rose naturally because Myra had hit him. Myra gave him a frown and told him he'd better watch his step. Then she went into the kitchen to take up supper.

It was god-danged good, being a company meal. Rose remembered to bust into tears now and then, and say that she just couldn't eat a bite. But she couldn't have put away much more without letting out her dress.

Myra filled up our coffee cups, and brought in dessert, two kinds of pie and a chocolate cake. Rose had some of each, shedding a few tears at intervals to show that she was just forcin' herself.

We finished eating. Rose got up to help, but of course, Myra wouldn't hear of it.

"No, sir, no, siree! You sit right down there on the settee, and rest your poor dear self!"

"But it's not fair to leave you with all the work, Myra darling," Rose said. "I could at least do—"

"Nothing, absolutely nothing!" Myra shooed her away. "You're going to sit down, that's what you're going to do. Nick, you entertain Rose while I'm busy."

"Why, sure," I said. "Nothin' I'd enjoy more than entertainin' Rose!"

Rose had to bite her lip to keep from laughin'. We went over to the settee and sat down, and Myra gathered up an armful of dishes and started for the kitchen.

Lennie was lolling on a chair with his eyes closed. But I knew they weren't closed tight. That was a trick of his, pretending to be asleep, and I guess he must have liked it real well because this was about the umpteenth time he'd tried to pull it on me.

I whispered to Rose, "How about a little kiss, honey?"

Rose shot a quick look at Lennie and the kitchen door, and said, "Let's have a big one." And we had a big one.

And Lennie's eyes and mouth flew open at the same time, and he let out a yell. "My-ra! Myra, come quick, Myra!"

There was a heck of a clatter as Myra dropped something in the kitchen. A stack of dishes, it sounded like. She ran in, scared out of her wits, looking like she expected the house to be on fire.

"What? What, what?" she said. "What's going on? What's the matter, Lennie?"

"They was huggin' and kissin', Myra!" Lennie pointed at Rose and me. "I seen 'em, huggin' and kissin'."

"Why, Lennie," I said. "How can you say such a awful thing?"

"You was too! I seen you!"

"Now, you know that ain't so!" I said. "You know god-danged good an' well what happened."

"Just what did happen?" Myra said, looking kind of uncertainly from Rose to me. "I'm—I'm sure there must be a, uh, mistake, but—"

Rose started crying again, burying her face in her hands. She got up, saying that she was going home because she just couldn't stay another minute in a place where people said such awful things about her.

Myra put out a hand to stop her, and said, "Nick, will you kindly tell me what this is all about?"

"They was huggin' and kissin', that's what!" Lennie yelled. "I seen 'em!"

"Hush, hush, Lennie! Nick?"

"T'heck with it," I said, sounding mad. "You can believe any god-danged thing you want to. I tell you this, though, this is the last god-danged time I try to comfort anyone when they're feelin' bad!"

"But . . . oh," said Myra. "You mean that . . .?"

"I mean that Rose got to feelin' real bad again," I said. "She started cryin' and I told her to just lean against me until she felt better, and I sort of patted her on the shoulder like any decent fella would. Why, god-dang it!" I said. "I did the same god-dang thing a while ago when you were right here in the room, and you said that was fine, I should take care of her! And god-dang, look how you're actin' now!"

"Please, Nick," Myra was all flustered and red. "I never for a moment thought that, uh—"

"It's all my fault," Rose said, drawing herself up real dignified. "I guess I can't blame you for thinking such terrible things about me, Myra, but you should have known that I'd never, never do anything to hurt my very best friend."

"But I do know it! I never had any such thoughts, Rose, darling!" Myra was practically bawling herself. "I'd never doubt you for a moment, dear."

"They're story-tellin', Myra!" Lennie yelled. "I seen 'em huggin' and kissin'."

Myra slapped him. She pointed to the door of his room, chasing him toward it with a couple more hard slaps. "Now, you get in there! Get right in there and don't let me see you again tonight!"

"But I seen—"

Myra gave him a crack that practically knocked him off his feet. He went stumbling into his bedroom, blubbering and spitting, and she slammed the door on him.

"I'm terribly, terribly sorry, Rose, darling," Myra turned back around again. "I—*Rose*! You take that hat right back off, because you're not moving a step out of here!"

"I th-think I'd better go home," Rose wept, but she didn't sound real determined. "I'd be too embarrassed to stay after this."

"But you mustn't be, dear! There's absolutely no need to be. Why—"

"But she does," I cut in, "an' I don't blame her a god-dang bit! I feel the same way myself. Why, god-dang it, the way I feel right now I get sort of self-conscious even bein' in the same room with Rose!"

"Well, why don't you get out of the same room then?" Myra snapped. "My goodness, get out and take a walk or something! No sense in you acting the fool, just because poor Lennie did."

"All right, I will get out," I said. "That god-dang Lennie starts all the trouble, and I get drove out of my own house. So don't you be surprised if I don't hurry back!"

"I'll be pleasantly surprised if you don't. I'm sure neither Rose nor I will miss you, will we, Rose?"

"Well—" Rose bit her lip. "I hate to feel responsible for—"

"Now, don't you trouble yourself another minute, darling. You just come out in the kitchen with me, and we'll have a nice cup of coffee."

Rose went with her, looking just a wee bit disappointed, naturally. At the kitchen door, she glanced back at me quickly, and I shrugged and spread my hands and looked sort of mournful. As if to say, you know, that it was too doggoned bad, but it was just one of those things, and what could you do about it? And she nodded, letting me know that she understood.

I got a pole and fishing line from under my bed. I came back out of the bedroom and called to Myra, asking her if she could pack me up a lunch because I was going fishing. And I guess you know what she told me. So I left.

There weren't many people on the street that late at night, almost nine o'clock, but practically everybody that was up asked me if I was going fishing. I said, why, no, I wasn't, and where did they ever get an idea like that?

"Well, how come you're carryin' a fish pole and line, then?" this one fella said. "How come you're doin' that if you ain't goin' fishin'."

"Oh, I got that to scratch my butt with," I said. "Just in case I'm up a tree somewheres, an' I can't reach myself from the ground."

"But, looky here now—" He hesitated, frowning. "That don't make no sense."

"How come it don't?" I said. "Why, practically everyone I know does the same thing. You mean to say you never took a fishing pole with you to scratch your butt with, in case you was up a tree an' couldn't reach yourself from the ground? Why, god-dang it, ain't you behind the times!"

He said, well, sure, he always did the same thing himself. Fact is, he was the first fella to think of the idea. "All I meant was that you shouldn't have no hook an' line on it. I mean, that part don't make sense."

"Why, shore it does," I said. "That's to pull up the back-flap of your drawers after you're through scratchin'. God-dang," I said, "it looks to me like you're really behind the times, fella. You don't watch out, the world will plumb pass you by before you know it!"

He scuffled his feet, looking ashamed of himself. I went on down the street toward the river.

I told one fella that, no, I wasn't going fishing, I was going to fasten on to a sky-hook and swing myself t' the other side of the river. I told another fella that, no, I wasn't going fishing, the county was putting a bounty on flying turds and I was going to try to hook onto some, in case they cleaned out the crappers when the train went by. I told another fella—

Well, never mind. It don't make no more difference than it made sense.

I got to the river. I waited a while, and then I began moving up the bank until I was about on a line with Amy Mason's house. Then, I started cutting back toward town again, dodging any house with lights in it and taking cover whenever I could. And finally I got to where I was going.

Amy let me in the back door. It was dark, and she took my hand and led me back to the bedroom. She flung off her nightgown there, grabbed me and held me for a minute, her lips moving over my face. She began to whisper, wild crazy things, sweet wild crazy things. And her hands fumbled with my clothes, and I thought to myself, god-danged, there just never was no one like Amy! There just ain't no one like her! And . . .

And I was right.

She made me know I was.

Then, we were lying side by side, holding hands. Breathing together, our hearts beating together. Somehow, there was perfume in the air, although I knew Amy never wore none; and somehow you could hear violins playin', so sweet and so soft, playing a song that never was. It was like there wasn't any yesterday, like there'd been no time before this, and I wondered why it should ever be any other way.

"Amy," I said, and she rolled her head to look at me. "Let's get away from this town, honey, let's us run away together."

She was silent for a moment, seeming to think the idea over. Then she said I couldn't think very much of her or I wouldn't make such a suggestion.

"You're a married man. I'm afraid you might have a great deal of trouble in getting unmarried. What does that make me, the woman who runs away with you?"

"Well, looky, honey," I said. "This sure ain't satisfactory, the way we're doin' now. We sure can't go on like this, can we?"

"Do we have a choice?" Her shoulders moved in a shrug. "Now if you had money—you don't, do you, dear? No, I thought not—you might be able to make a settlement with your wife, and we could leave town. But in the absence of money . . ."

"Well, uh, about that now . . ." I cleared my throat. "I reckon they's a lot of fellas that'd be too proud to accept money from a woman. But the way I look at it—"

"I don't have it, Nick, popular opinion to the contrary notwithstanding. I own a number of income properties, and the rentals enable me to live quite well by Pottsville standards. But they'd bring very little at a sale. Certainly not enough to support two people for the rest of their lives, let alone assuage the wounded feelings of a wife like yours."

I hardly knew what to say to that. Maybe, well, maybe my feelings was kind of hurt. Because I knew just about as much about the property she owned as she did, and I knew she was a lot better off than she pretended.

She just didn't want to get things squared up and go off with me. Or just run away with me like any woman should if she was really in love with a fella. But it was her money, so what the heck could I do about it?

Amy picked up my hand and put it on one of her breasts. She squeezed it, trying to press it into her flesh, but I didn't help her none, and finally she pushed it away.

"All right, Nick," she said. "I'll tell you the real reason I won't go away with you."

I said to never mind, I wouldn't want to trouble her none, and she snapped for me not to dare to be rude to her. "Don't you dare, Nicholas Corey! I love you—at least, it seems to be love to me—and because I do, I'm willing to accept something that I never thought I could accept. But don't you be rude to me, or I might change. I might cease to love a man who I know is a murderer!"

SEVENTEEN

I didn't say anything for quite a spell; just lay still where I was, wondering where that violin music had gone to and why I couldn't smell the perfume no more.

Finally, I said, "Just what are you talkin' about, Amy?" And I was just a little relieved when she told me, just a little, because it could have been a lot worse.

"I'm talking about those two men you killed. Those, well, pimps is the word, I believe."

"Pimps?" I said. "What pimps?"

"Stop it, Nick. My reference is to a certain night when you and I returned to Pottsville on the same train. Yes, I know you didn't see me, but I was on it. I was curious as to why you'd be going to the river at that time of night, dressed in your very best clothes, so I followed you . . ."

"Now listen," I said. "You couldn't've followed me wherever I went. It was doggoned dark that night that—"

"It was very dark for you, Nick. For a man who's never been able to see well at night. But I don't suffer from that handicap. I followed you quite easily, and I saw you quite clearly when you killed those two men."

Well . . .

At least it was better than her knowing I'd killed the other two. It didn't tie up with Rose in a way that I couldn't very well get out of. Which Amy would have known was the case if she knew I'd killed Tom Hauck. And which was still the case even if Amy didn't know about it.

For a minute or two, I almost wished I was running off with Rose and thirty thousand dollars plus, and t'heck with Amy. But my thinking that was just almost and I didn't even almost it very long. Rose just naturally took too much out of a fella, she was too demandin' and possessive, and she didn't have much of anything to give him back. She was one heck of a lot of woman, but when you'd said that you'd said it all. A lot of woman but a god-danged flighty one. A woman who was apt to lose her head just when she needed it most, like she had with Uncle John.

I rolled over and took Amy into my arms. She swam up against me for a moment, pressing every soft warm inch of herself against me, and then she kind of moaned and pulled away.

"Why did you do it, Nick? I told you I'd accepted it, and I have, but—why, darling? Make me understand why! I never thought you could kill anyone."

"I never thought I could neither," I said. "And I can't rightly say why I did it. They were just one more god-dang thing I didn't like, that I particularly didn't like. I'd been letting them go, like I let so many things go, and finally I thought, well, I didn't have to. There were a lot of things, most things, that I couldn't do nothing about. But I *could* do something about them, an' finally . . . finally I did something."

Amy stared at me, a little frown working up on her face. I gave her a pat on the bottom, and kissed her again.

"T'tell the truth, honey," I went on, "I really felt like I was doing the right thing for them fellas. They weren't no good to themselves nor nobody else and they must've known it, like anyone would know a thing like that. So I was doing 'em a pure kindness by fixing it so they wouldn't have to go on livin'."

"I see," Amy said. "I see. And do you also feel you'd be doing Ken Lacey a pure kindness if you kept him from going on living?"

"Him especially," I said. "A fella that mocks his friends, that hurts people just because he's able to hurt 'em—*Ken Lacey!*" I said. "What do you know about him?"

"Only one thing, Nick. All I know is that you somehow seem to have arranged things so that Sheriff Lacey will be blamed for the two murders that you committed."

I swallowed, and said I just didn't know how she figured that. "It sure ain't my fault if Ken comes down here an' gets drunk, and pops off all over town about what a tough fella he is. I figure that if a fella wants to get all the glory out of braggin', he has to take the blame along with it."

"I don't figure that way, Nick. I won't allow you to do it."

"But, looky," I said. "Why not, Amy? What's Ken to you, anyways?"

"He's a man who may be falsely convicted of murder."

"But—but I just don't understand," I said. "If you don't mind about me killin' them two pimps, why . . ."

"You haven't been listening, Nick. I mind about them very much.

But I had no way of knowing that you were going to kill them. In the case of Sheriff Lacey, I do know your plans, and if I allowed you to carry them out I'd be as guilty as you are."

"But"—I hesitated—"what if I just can't help myself, Amy? What if it's him or me?"

"Then, I'd be very sorry, Nick. It would have to be you. But that circumstance isn't likely to arise, is it? There's no way you can be incriminated?"

"Well, no," I said. "I can't think of none offhand. For that matter, there's a good chance them bodies will never be found."

"Well, then?"

"Well . . . god-dang it, Amy, it'd be a lot better to let things go like I planned!" I said. "A whole lot better. Why, if you knew that god-danged Ken Lacey like I do, some of the mean things he's done—"

"No, Nick. Absolutely, no."

"But, doggone it—!"

"No."

"Now, you looky here, Amy," I said. "It just don't look to me like you're in any position to be givin' orders. You got guilty knowledge, like they say in the courts. You know I killed those fellas an' you didn't say nothin' about it, so if you try to do it later you're incriminatin' yourself."

"I know that," Amy nodded evenly. "But I'd still do it, Nick. I'm sure you know I would."

"But—"

But I *did* know she'd do it, even if it got her hanged. So there just wasn't anything more to say on the subject.

I looked at her, with her hair spilled out on the pillows and the warmth of her body warming mine. And I thought, god-dang, if this ain't a heck of a way to be in bed with a pretty woman. The two of you arguing about murder, and threatening each other, when you're supposed to be in love and you could be doing something pretty nice. And then I thought, well, maybe it ain't so strange after all. Maybe it's like this with most people, everyone doing pretty much the same thing except in a different way. And all the time they're holding heaven in their hands.

"I'm sorry, honey," I said. "O' course, I'll do whatever you want. I wouldn't never want to do nothing else."

"And I'm sorry, too, darling." She brushed my mouth with a kiss. "And I'll do what you want. As soon as things here are a little more settled, I'll go away with you."

"Fine. That's just fine, honey," I said.

"I want to very much, dear, and I will. Just as soon as we can be sure that there are no loose ends here."

I said again that that was just fine, wondering what I was going to do about a great big loose end like Rose Hauck. Then I thought, well, I'd just have to face that problem when I came to it. And I put everything out of my mind but Amy, and I reckon she put everything out of her mind but me. And it was like it was before, only more so.

It was like nothing that ever was. Only more so.

Then, again we were layin' there side by side. Breathing together, hearts beating together. And suddenly Amy tore her hand out of mine, and sat up.

"Nick! What's that?"

"What? What's what?"

I looked to the window where she was pointing, at the drawn shade with its rim of flickering light.

Then, I jumped up and ran to the window, and tilted the shade back. And I guess I must have groaned out loud.

"God-dang," I said. "God-dang it to heck, anyway!"

"Nick, what is it, darling?"

"Colored town. It's on fire."

I guess I should have known it might happen. Because Tom Hauck *was* a white man, whatever else you said about him, and it looked like a colored fella had killed him. So some idjit would get the notion that "the niggers got to be taught a lesson," and he'd spread the word to other idjits. And pretty soon there'd be trouble.

I got dressed with Amy watchin' me worriedly. She asked me what I was going to do, and I said I didn't know, but I was sure going to have to do something. Because a thing like this, a sheriff bein' off fishing when trouble broke, was just the kind of thing that could lose an election.

"But, Nick . . . that doesn't matter now, does it? As long as we're going away together?"

"When?" I jerked on my boots. "You can't name no definite date, can you?"

"Well—" She bit her lip. "I see what you mean, dear."

"Might be a year or two," I said. "But even if it was only six months, I better be in office. Makes it a lot easier to wrap up any of them loose ends you mentioned than it would if I was just an ordinary citizen."

I finished dressing, and she let me out the back door.

I went back the way I'd come, down to the river, then up the river bank. And of course I didn't keep my fishing pole with me.

I came up on the far side of the Negro section, dirtyin' myself with some charcoal from the fire. Then, I mingled in with the crowd, beating at the flames with a wet toesack that someone had dropped.

Actually, there wasn't a whole lot of damage; maybe a total of six or seven burned shacks. What with the recent rain and no wind, the fire was slow in starting and it didn't have a chance to spread far before it was discovered.

I started telling some colored folks what to do, working right along with them. Then, I stood back for a minute, wiping the sweat from my eyes, and someone tapped me on the shoulder.

It was Robert Lee Jefferson, and he looked about as stern as I'd ever seen him.

"God-dang, ain't this something, Robert Lee?" I said. "No telling what might have happened if I hadn't been right here Johnny-on-the-spot when the fire broke out."

"Come along," he said.

"Why, thanks, Robert Lee," I said, "but I don't rightly think I can. This fire—"

"The fire is fully under control. It was under control long before you got here. Now, come along."

I climbed into his carriage with him. We drove to his store, and there were other carriages and buggies and horses tied up outside, and there were maybe half a dozen men waiting on the sidewalk. Important citizens like Mr. Dinwiddie, the bank president, and Zeke Carlton, who owned the cotton gin, and Stonewall Jackson Smith, the school superintendent, and Samuel Houston Taylor, who owned Taylor's Emporium, Furniture and Undertaking.

We all went inside. We sat down in Robert Lee's office, or I should say, everybody but me sat down. Because there just wasn't no place for me to sit.

Zeke Carlton started the meeting by slamming his fists down on the desk and asking just what the hell kind of county were we running. "Do you know what can come of a thing like this tonight, Nick? Do you know what happens when a bunch of poor helpless niggers gets burned out?"

"I got a pretty good idea," I said. "All the colored folks get scared, and maybe they ain't around when it comes cotton-pickin' time."

"You're tootin' well right, they're not! Scarin' them god-dam poor niggers could cost us all a pisspot full of money!"

"Your wife said you'd gone fishing tonight," Robert Lee Jefferson said. "At just what point on the river were you when the fire broke out?"

"I didn't go fishing," I said.

"Now, Corey," Stonewall Jackson Smith said firmly. "I saw you heading toward the river myself with a fishing pole and line. I'd say that was pretty conclusive evidence that you did go fishing."

"Well, now, I just don't think I can agree with you," I said. "I wouldn't say you was wrong, but I sure wouldn't say you was right, neither."

"Oh, cut it out, Nick!" snapped Samuel Houston Taylor. "We—"

"Take t'other night, now," I went on, "I seen a certain fella crawlin' into an empty freight car with a certain high school teacher. But I don't think that's conclusive evidence they was shipping themselves somewhere."

Stonewall Jackson turned fiery red. The others looked at him, kind of narrow-eyed, like they was sizing him up for the first time, and Mr. Dinwiddie, the bank president, turned to me. He was friendlier than the other fellas. He'd stayed pretty friendly toward me ever since the time I'd pulled him out of the privy.

"Just where were you and what were you doing there tonight, Sheriff?" he said. "I'm sure we'll all be glad to accept your explanation."

"Not me, by God!" said Zeke Carlton. "I—"

"Quiet, Zeke," Mr. Dinwiddie motioned to him. "Go on, Sheriff."

"Well, we'll start right at the beginning of tonight," I said. "I figured someone might try to start somethin' with the colored folks, so I got out a pole an' line and pretended to go fishing. The river runs right in back of colored town, you know, an'—"

"Yeah, hell, we know where it runs!" Samuel Houston Taylor

scowled. "What we want to know is why you weren't there to prevent the fire?"

"Because I had to make a little detour," I said. "I seen a fella sneakin' away from someone's house, and I thought maybe he'd pulled something crooked. It looked like something I ought to investigate, anyways, just to make sure. So I went up to this house, and I was about to knock when I decided it wasn't necessary and it might be kind of embarrassin'. Because I could see this housewife inside, and it was plain to see, as happy as she looked, that there hadn't been no kind of trouble. Aside from which she didn't have hardly no clothes on."

It was just a shot in the dark, of course. Sort of a double shot. I figured that with this many Pottsville citizens involved, someone was just about bound to be two-timin' his wife, or someone's wife was two-timin' him. Or else he was god-dang suspicious that she was.

Anyways, it sure looked like my shot hit home, because it was the dangest funniest thing you ever seen, the way they acted. All of 'em—or most of 'em, I should say—glaring at each other and trying to keep their heads ducked at the same time. All of 'em accused and accusing.

Mr. Dinwiddie started to ask just whose house I was referring to. But the others gave him a look that shut him up fast.

Robert Lee cleared his throat, and said for me to go on with my story.

"We can assume that you eventually reached the river, and you were there when the fire started. Then, what happened? What were you doing all the time that the rest of us were fighting the blaze?"

"I was trying to catch the fellas that started it," I said. "They came crashing down through the underbrush afterward, trying to get away, and I hollered for 'em to halt, they was under arrest, but it didn't do no good. They kept on running, and I chased 'em, yelling for them to stop or I'd shoot. But I reckon they knew I wouldn't, knew I wouldn't dare to, because they all got away."

Robert Lee wet his lips, hesitating. "Did you see who they were, Nick?"

"Well, let's put it this way," I said. "It don't make much difference whether I know who they were or not. As long as I didn't catch 'em, their names ain't important and it would just cause hard feelin's to say who they was."

"But, Sheriff," Mr. Dinwiddie said. "I don't see, uh—" He broke off, seeing the look that Zeke Carlton gave him. Seeing the looks of the others, his most important depositors.

Because I'd fired another shot in the dark, and it had hit even closer on target than the first one.

With a couple of exceptions, there wasn't a man there that didn't have a grown or a semi-grown son. And there wasn't a one of them young 'uns that was worth the powder it'd take to blow their nose. They loafed around town, puttin' up a half-way pretense of working for their daddies. Whoring and drinking and thinking up meanness. Any troubles that broke out, you could bet that either one of 'em or all of 'em was mixed up in it.

The meeting broke up, hardly anyone nodding to me as they left.

I followed Robert Lee out to the walk and we stood talking together for a minute.

"I'm afraid you haven't made yourself any friends tonight, Nick," he told me. "You'll really have to buckle down and work from now on, if you want to stay in office."

"Work?" I scratched my head. "What at?"

"At your job, naturally! What else?" he said, and then his eyes shifted as I stared at him. "All right, perhaps you did have to compromise tonight. Perhaps you'll have to again. But one or two exceptional cases don't justify your doing nothing at all to enforce the law."

"Well, I'll tell you about that, Robert Lee," I said. "Practically every fella that breaks the law has a danged good reason, to his own way of thinking, which makes every case exceptional, not just one or two. Take you, for example. A lot of fellas might think you was guilty of assault and battery when you punched Henry Clay Fanning in—"

"I'll ask you just one question," Robert Lee cut in. "Are you or aren't you going to start enforcing the law?"

"I sure am," I said. "I sure ain't going to do nothing else but."

"Good, I'm relieved to hear it."

"Yes, sir," I said. "I'm really going to start cracking down. Anyone that breaks a law from now on is goin' to have to deal with me. Providing, o' course, that he's either colored or some poor white trash that can't pay his poll tax."

"That's a pretty cynical statement, Nick!"

"Cynical?" I said. "Aw, now, Robert Lee. What for have I got to be cynical about?"

EIGHTEEN

The fire was on late Friday night, and it was almost dawn Saturday before I got home. I scrubbed myself up, and put on some clean clothes. Then I went out into the kitchen, and started to fix breakfast.

Myra came out fuming and fussing, asking me what in the world I was up to. I told her about the fire and how people were criticizin' me, and she shut up fast. Because she didn't want to be an ex-sheriff's wife any more than I wanted to be an ex-sheriff, and she knew I was going to have to do some humpin' or we might be.

She finished cooking breakfast for me. I ate and went downtown.

It being Saturday, all the stores were open extra early, and any farmers that weren't already in town were on their way in. They stood around on the sidewalks, their black cloth hats brushed and clean-looking, their Sunday shirts fairly clean, and their overalls ranging from middling-dirty to downright filthy.

Their wives wore starched-stiff sunbonnets and Mother Hubbards made out of calico or gingham. Their kids' clothes—except the kids that were old enough for hand-me-downs—were made out of meal sacks, with the faded labels still showing on some of 'em. Men and women, and practically every boy and girl over twelve, were chewing and spitting snuff. The men and boys poured the snuff down inside their lower lip. The women and girls used snuff-sticks, frayed twigs which they dipped in their snuff cans and then put in the corners of their mouths.

I moved around among the men, shakin' hands and slapping backs and telling 'em to just come and see me any time they had a problem. I told all the women that Myra had been askin' about 'em and that they just had to come and see her sometime. And I patted the kids on the head, if their heads weren't too high up, and gave them pennies and nickels, depending on how tall they were.

Naturally, I was busy with the townspeople too, doing my dangedest to make friends or to get back any I'd lost. But I couldn't be sure I did any better with them than I did with the farmers, and I couldn't be sure I did any good with the farmers.

Oh, almost everyone was pleasant, and no one was what you'd call downright unfriendly. But too many of 'em were cautious, kind of cagey when I hinted around at the subject of voting. And if there's one thing I know it's this: a fella that's going to vote for you don't lose much time in declaring himself.

I tried to run a tally in my mind, and it looked to me like the best I could hope for was a near-draw with Sam Gaddis. That was the best, despite all the dirty talk that was going on about him. And if he was that strong now, in spite of the talk, how could I be sure he wouldn't be even stronger in the run-off?

I ate some crackers and cheese for lunch, passing them around amongst the fellas I was talking to.

About two o'clock, I had to go out to the cemetery for Tom Hauck's buryin', but a passel of other folks went, too, by way of amusin' themselves, so you couldn't really say it was a waste of time.

I worked through the supper hour, eating some crackers and sardines and passing them around amongst the fellas I was talking to.

Finally, it got too late to work any longer. But by then, I was so keyed up from talking, so restless and high-strung that my nerves seemed to be standing on end. So instead of going home, I sneaked over to Amy Mason's house.

We went back into the bedroom. She held me off for a minute, kind of cold and peevish-actin', and then she seemed to change her mood suddenly. And we went to bed.

It happened pretty fast, considering how wore out I was. But afterwards my eyes drifted shut, and I seemed to sink down into a deep dark pit, and—

"Wake up!" Amy was shaking me. "Wake up, I said!"

I said, "Huh, whassa matter, honey?" And Amy said again that I was to wake up.

"Is that how little I mean to you? That you can fall asleep like a hog in a wallow with my arms around you? Or were you saving yourself for your precious Rose Hauck?"

"Huh? What?" I said. "For gosh sake, Amy—"

"Rose is staying at your place, is she not?"

"Well, sure," I said. "But just on account of her husband's death and buryin'. She—"

"And why didn't you tell me she was staying there? Why did I have to find it out for myself?"

"But, looky," I said. "Why the heck should I tell you? What's it got to do with us? Anyways, you already knew all about me an' Rose, an' it didn't seem to bother you none."

She stared at me, her eyes sparkling with anger, and suddenly turned her back to me. Then, just as I was about to put my arm around her, she turned and faced me again.

"Just what do I already know about you and Rose? Tell me!"

"Aw, now, honey," I said. "I—"

"Answer me! Just what do I know about you? I want to know!"

I said I'd just made a slip of the tongue, and there wasn't anything to tell her about Rose and me. Because of course, she didn't want to know about us. No woman that sleeps with a man wants to know that another woman is doin' it, too.

"I was just referrin' to the other night," I said. "You know, when you was teasin' me about Rose, and I told you there wasn't nothing between us. That's all I meant when I said you already knew all about us."

"Well—" She was anxious to believe me. "You're sure?"

"O' course, I'm sure," I said. "Why, my gosh, ain't we the same as engaged to get married? Ain't we goin' to go away together just as soon as we figure out what to do about my wife an' we're sure there ain't any kickbacks from them two pimps I killed? That's right, ain't it, so why would I be fooling around with another woman?"

She smiled, her lips kind of trembly. She kissed me, and snuggled up in my arms.

"Nick . . . don't see her anymore. After she's gone home, I mean."

"Well, I sure don't want to," I said. "I sure don't aim to, anyways. I sure won't see her, Amy, unless I just can't noways get out of it."

"Yes? And just what is that supposed to mean?"

"I mean, she's Myra's friend," I said. "Even before Tom got himself killed, Myra was always after me to give Rose some help, an' I felt sorry for her so I usually did. So it'll look awful funny if I stop all of a sudden, without even waitin' until she can hire a farm hand."

Amy was silent for a moment, thinking things over. Then her head moved in a little nod.

"All right, Nick. I suppose you will have to see her—one more time."

"Well, I'm not sure that'll be enough," I said. "I mean, it prob'ly will, but—"

"One more time, Nick. Just to tell her that she'd better employ some help because you won't be seeing her again. No"—she put her hand over my mouth as I started to speak—"that's it, Nick. Just once more, and never again. If you want me, that is. If you want to keep me from being very, very angry with you."

I said, all right, that's the way it would be. There just wasn't much else I could say. But what I was thinking was that Rose was going to have something to say about this, and I could get in just as much trouble by not heeding her as I could Amy.

Amy just wasn't giving me a chance, god-dang it! I was just as anxious to be shot of Rose as she was to have me. But it would take time and if I didn't have the time, if I could only see Rose once more . . .

"Nick, darling . . . I'm still here."

I said, "Yeah, danged if you ain't." And I hugged her close and kissed and petted her, putting a lot of enthusiasm into it. But I tell you frankly, I didn't feel much. And it wasn't just because I was so tired I could hardly lift a finger.

I'd been almost on the point of hitting on a plan, something that would not only take care of Rose without me seeing her more than once, but would take care of Myra and Lennie at the same time. And then Amy had spoke up, and the pieces of the plan had scattered every which way. And I knew I was going to have a heck of a time putting 'em together again, if I ever was able to.

"Nick!"—she was beginning to sound cross again—"you're not going to sleep again, are you?"

"Me?" I said. "Me go to sleep around a pretty thing like you? Now, what do you think?"

She let me out the door, so drowsy herself she could barely keep her eyes open. I sneaked back across town, and believe me, sneakin' is the word, because I was plumb wrung dry an' there wasn't enough juice left in me to wet a whistle.

I got to the courthouse, and slipped off my boots at the foot of the stairs. I sneaked up the stairs and got to my room, and got out of my clothes. Then, I slid into bed, careful as I could to keep the springs from squeaking. And I sighed and thought, Oh, Lord, how long, god-dang it? One cross is bad enough, but I hadn't ought to carry a whole god-dang lumberyard around with me!

Rose grabbed me. She swarmed all over me, and it was like her body was on fire.

"Goddam! What the hell took you so long, Nick?"

I tried to keep from groaning. I said, "Look, Rose we can't do this, honey. It's already Sunday morning."

"Crap on Sunday morning!" she said. "Who gives a damn what day it is?"

"But—but this ain't nice," I said. "It just ain't nice to fornicate on Sunday morning. Now, you just think about it, an' you'll see I'm right."

Rose said she didn't want to think about it, she just wanted to do it. "Come on, dammit!" she panted. "Come on! I'll show you whether it's nice or not!"

Well, I just couldn't, you know. At least, I thought I couldn't. And I guess the only way I managed to was because the good Lord gave me strength. He seen I was in a heck of a spot, like He naturally would, because if He'd noticed something like a sparrow fallin', He'd just about have to see the predicament I was in.

So He gave me strength, I reckon. Which—an' I don't mean to sound ungrateful—was about the *least* He could do.

NINETEEN

Rose went to church with Myra and me, Lennie staying at home because he didn't always behave too well in crowds. After the services, Rose and Myra went on home to get dinner ready, and I hung around to do a little handshakin' and baby-pattin' and back-slappin'.

Sam Gaddis was doing the same thing, a gray-haired middle-aged fella with a dignified look about him. The minister had given him a kind of indirect boost in his sermon, which was about casting stones and judge not lest ye be judged, and now he seemed to be getting a better reception than I was. People would turn their heads to look at him, while they were shaking hands with me. I'd slap 'em on the back and they'd sort of take it as a shove toward Sam. And there was one woman that yanked her baby away just as I was about to kiss it, so that I danged near kissed my own belt buckle.

It looked to me like a case of, if you can't lick 'em join 'em, so I eased my way through the crowd and grabbed Sam by the hand.

"I want you to know I'm a thousand per cent behind you, Sam," I said. "All these dirty stories going around about you, I know they ain't true, Sam, even if it sounds like they are, so you got my moral support a thousand per cent, and I'm goin' to be right up on the speaker's platform with you tonight to prove it!"

He said, "Well, uh," and cleared his throat awkwardly. He said, "Well, uh, that's certainly very nice of you, Sheriff. But, uh—uh—"

What he wanted to say was that he didn't want me within a thousand miles of him, let alone on the same speaker's platform. But the kind of fella he was, he didn't know how to say it.

"Well—uh, now—" he tried again. "I surely appreciate your offer, Sheriff, but wouldn't it be better if, uh—"

I slapped him on the back, cutting him off. I said, by golly, I was going to do it and he didn't need to worry about takin' favors from me, because I wasn't really doin' him one.

"I figure it's just the right thing to do," I said. "You might say it's something I got to do. So come tonight I'm goin' to be up there on the platform with—*oof!*"

Zeke Carlton shoved past me, digging his elbow into my ribs. He dropped an arm around Sam's shoulders, and jerked his head at me.

"I'll say it for you, Sam. You don't want Nick around you, because he's a sneaky, half-assed, triflin' no-good excuse for a sheriff, and you'd be hurt just by bein' seen with him, even if he didn't stick a knife in your ribs!"

Sam cleared his throat again, looking more uncomfortable than ever. Zeke glared at me, like he wanted to spit in my face.

I said, "Well, now Zeke, that ain't hardly no way to talk. Here it is Sunday, and we're still here on the church grounds, and god-dang if you ain't calling me names and using bad words like 'half-assed'."

"Balls!" he sneered. "Who the hell are you to be correctin' me? Why—"

"I'm the sheriff," I said, "an' it's my job to look out for wrong-doin', particularly seein' that the Lord ain't abused right in His own front yard. So you just better not do it no more, Zeke, or I'll by-golly march you right down to the lock-up!"

Zeke let out an angry snort; laughed on a shaky note. He looked around at the crowd, trying to swing them to his side. But we're a real God-fearin' community, like you probably gathered, and everyone was frowning at him or givin' him frosty looks.

That made him madder than ever. "Why, God da— gosh-darn it, don't you see what he's trying to do? He's trying to get at Sam through me! He knows I'm backing Sam so he wants to make trouble for me!"

"Now, that just ain't so," I said. "You know it ain't so, Zeke."

"The hell—the heck it ain't!"

I said, no, sir, it sure wasn't and he knew it as well as I did. "I leave it to anyone here," I said. "If they ever knew me to do a man dirty or even say so much as an unkind word about another fella as long as they've lived. Just ask anyone. I'll leave it up to them."

Zeke scowled and muttered something under his breath. Cuss words, it sounded like. I asked Sam if he thought I was out to harm him, and he scuffled his feet and looked embarrassed.

"Well, uh, I'm sure you wouldn't, uh, do so—uh—"

"Right," I said. "I wouldn't. In the first place, it just ain't my nature to hurt another fella, an' in the second place I know it wouldn't do no good. Because I figure you can't be hurt, Sam. The way I see it, you're as good as elected right now."

Sam's head snapped up. He kind of waved his hands, helplesslike, like he didn't know whether to pee or go blind. And if *he* was surprised, he sure had plenty of company. Everyone else was staring at me, their eyes popped open. Even Zeke Carlton was struck dumb for a moment.

"Now, see here, Nick—" he spoke up at last. "Now, let's get this straight. Are you saying that you're concedin' the election to Sam?"

"I'm saying that I'm going to," I said, raising my voice. "I'm concedin' to Sam just as soon as he answers one question."

Zeke asked what kind of question. I said a very simple question, stalling a minute to get as big a crowd as I could.

"A very simple question," I repeated. "One that's already on everyone's lips, you might say, and that Sam would have to answer sooner or later."

"Well, come on!" Zeke scowled impatiently. "Ask it! Sam don't mind answering questions, do you, Sam? Sam's life is an open book!"

"How about that, Sam?" I said. "I'd like to hear you speak for yourself."

Sam said, "Well, uh, yes. I mean I'll be glad to answer your question. Uh, anything I can, that is."

"Well, this is about them dirty stories people are tellin' on you," I said. "Now, wait a minute! Wait a minute, Zeke, Sam"—I held up my hand—"I know them stories ain't true. I know Sam wouldn't rape a little colored baby or steal the gold teeth out of his grandma's mouth or beat his pappy to death with a stick of cordwood or rob a widder woman of her life's savings or feed his wife to the hawgs. I *know* a fine fella like Sam wouldn't do nothing like that. So all I'm asking is this; this is my question . . ."

I paused again, gettin' everyone on their toes. I waited until you could have heard a weevil crapping on a cotton boll, and then I asked my question.

"All right," I said, "here it is. If them stories ain't true, how come them to get started? How come almost everybody claims they *are* true?"

Sam blinked. He opened his mouth, and then he closed it again. And he and Zeke looked at each other.

"Well, uh," Sam began. "I, uh, I—"

"Now, hold up there!" Zeke butted in, turning to me. "What do you mean everybody's saying they're true? Who the hell's everybody?"

"I stand corrected," I said. "I reckon everybody ain't sayin' it, when you get right down to cases. Prob'ly ain't no more than two, three hundred people that are sayin' it. But that still leaves the same question. How come even two, three hundred people are sayin' it *is* true that Sam raped a little colored baby an' beat his pappy to death an' fed his wife to the hawgs an'—"

"Never mind, dammit!" Zeke grabbed Sam by the arm. "Come on, Sam. You don't have to answer no damn-fool question like that."

"Well, of course, he don't have to," I said. "But I should think he'd want to. Don't rightly see how he can get elected sheriff if he don't answer."

Zeke hesitated, scowling. He shot a glance at Sam, then gave him a nudge.

"All right, Sam. Maybe you'd better answer."

"Uh, well, of course," Sam nodded. "Uh, what was the question again, Sheriff?"

I started to tell him, but someone behind me interrupted.

"You know the question, Sam! How'd them stories about you get started? How come folks say they're true if they ain't?"

There was a loud murmur of agreement, with people nodding and nudging each other. Sam cleared his throat to speak, and there was another interruption. A catcall from the outskirts of the crowd.

"How about that nigger baby, Sam?"

The crowd looked at each other, embarrassed, snickering, or outright guffawing. All at once there were catcalls from half a dozen different directions.

"Where's them gold teeth, Sam?" and "Did you just screw that widder for her money, Sam?" and "What'd you do with them hawgs you fed your wife to?" and so on. Until everything was in an uproar of shouts and laughter and bootstampings.

I let it go on for two, three minutes, letting these here good Christians work themselves up to the proper pitch. Then I held up my arms and called for quiet, and finally I got it. But it was restless, you know. The kind of quiet you get just before a storm.

"Now, Sam," I said, facing around to him again. "You reckon you fully understand the question, or do you want me to repeat it?"

"Uh, well—"

"I'll repeat it," I said, "an' you listen closely, now, Sam. If you didn't rape any little defenseless colored babies or beat your poor ol' pappy to death or feed your sweet, trusting wife that you'd sworn to protect and cherish to the hawgs or—if you didn't do none of them dirty low-down things that make me sick to my stomach to think about, how come so many folks say you did? Or puttin' it briefly, Sam, how come folks say that you done things that would out-stink a skunk and that you're lower down than a puke-eating dawg, if it ain't true? Or puttin' it still another way, are you sayin' that you're telling the truth an' that everyone else is a dirty no-good liar?"

Zeke Carlton hollered, "Now, wait a minute! That's not—" But he was hollered down before he could say anything more. Everyone was yelling for Sam to answer, to let him do his own talking. I held up my hands again.

"Well, Sam, what's the answer?" I said. "We're all waitin' to hear it."

"Well—" Sam wet his lips. "Well, uh—"

"Yeah," I said. "Just speak right up, Sam. Why are people sayin' those stories are true, if they ain't?"

"Well . . ."

Sam didn't have an answer. You could almost smell him sweatin' blood to think of one, but he just couldn't. Which wasn't no surprise to me, of course, because how could anyone answer a question like that?

Sam kept trying, though. He was on maybe about his sixteenth try when someone flung a prayer book, hitting him spang in the mouth. And that was kind of like a signal, like the first crack of lightning in a storm. Because the air was suddenly full of prayer books and hymnals, and everyone was shouting and cussing and trying to get their hands on Sam. And all at once he disappeared like he'd been dropped through a trap door . . .

I sauntered on home.

I thought, well, it was just as well that I wouldn't be on the speaker's platform tonight at Sam's meeting because Sam wouldn't be there neither because there wouldn't be no meeting because Sam wouldn't be a candidate no more.

I thought, well, that was at least one nail out of my cross, and maybe, if I kept on being upright and God-fearin' and never hurting no one unless it was for their good or mine, which was pretty much the same thing, why then maybe all my other problems would get straightened out as easy as this one had.

We ate Sunday dinner, Rose and Myra and Lennie and me. Rose was supposed to go home that afternoon, and I said I'd sure be proud to take her as soon as I'd rested myself a little. But naturally I didn't take her.

I couldn't, you know, since I could only see her one more time. Just once to do something about her. And that plan had come back to me again—the plan for doing something about her and Lennie and Myra at the same time. But it wasn't something that I could pull off on Sunday afternoon, or any afternoon; it had to be at night. And, anyways, I had to study some more about it.

Myra called to me after about an hour. Then she came into my bedroom and called some more, shaking me until the whole bed almost fell apart. And, of course, it didn't do no good at all.

Finally, she gave up, and went back out into the other room, and I heard her apologizing to Rose.

"I simply can't wake him up, dear. He's just dead to the world. Not that it's any wonder, I suppose, considering how much sleep he's lost."

Rose said, yes, it wasn't any wonder, was it?, her voice kind of flat. "Well, I really hadn't planned on staying over tonight, but—"

"And you don't have to," Myra declared. "I'll just take Lennie and drive you home myself."

"Now, that's not necessary," Rose said quickly. "I don't mind—"

"And I don't mind taking you. I really don't, darling. So you just get yourself ready—*Lennie, go wash your face*—and we'll be on our way."

"Well," said Rose. "Well, all right, Myra, dear."

They left a few minutes later.

I yawned and stretched and turned over on my side, all set to go to sleep for real. I started to doze, just started to, and I heard someone coming up the stairs.

It was a man, judging by the footsteps. I started to turn back on my side again, thinking, well, t'heck with him, it's Sunday afternoon an' I'm entitled to a little rest. But you just can't ignore no one when you're sheriff, Sunday or whatever day it is. So I flung my feet over the side of the bed, and got up.

I went out into the living room and flung open the hall door, just as he was about to knock on it.

He was a city-dressed fella, tall and thin with a nose like a fish-hook and a mouth about as big as a bee's-ass.

"Sheriff Corey?" He flashed an identification card at me. "I'm Barnes, the Talkington Detective Agency."

He smiled, his bee's-ass mouth stretching enough to show one tooth, and it was like getting a glimpse of an egg coming out of a pullet pigeon. I said I was plumb proud to meet him.

"So you're with the Talkington Agency," I said. "Why, god-dang if I ain't heard a lot about you people! Let's see now, you broke up that big railroad strike, didn't you?"

"That's right." He showed me the tooth again. "The railroad strike was one of our jobs."

"Now, by golly, that really took nerve," I said. "Them railroad workers throwin' chunks of coal at you an' splashin' you with water, and you fellas without nothin' to defend yourself with except shotguns an' automatic rifles! Yes, sir, god-dang it, I really got to hand it to you!"

"Now, just a moment, Sheriff!" His mouth came together like a buttonhole. "We have never—"

"And them low-down garment workers," I said. "God-dang, you really took care of them, didn't you? People that threw away them big three-dollar-a-week wages on wild livin' and then fussed because they had to eat garbage to stay alive! I mean, what the heck, they was all foreigners, wasn't they, and if they didn't like good ol' American garbage, why didn't they go back where they came from?"

"Sheriff! Sheriff Corey!"

"Yeah?" I said. "You got something on your mind, Mr. Barnes?"

"Certainly I have something on my mind! Why else would I have come here? Now—"

"You mean you just didn't drop in for a little chat?" I said. "Just to maybe show me your medals for shootin' people in the back an'—"

"I'm here to inquire about a former resident of Pottsville! A man named Cameron Tramell."

"Never heard of him," I said. "Good-bye."

I started to close the door, Barnes held it open.

"You've heard of him," he said. "He was known locally as Curly, and he was a pimp."

I said, oh, I said, oh, yeah, sure, I'd heard of Curly. "Ain't seen him for a spell, come to think of it. How's he getting along, anyways?"

"Now, Sheriff"—he grinned at me with his eyes—"let's not spar with each other."

"Spar? What do you mean?" I said.

"I mean, Cameron Tramell, alias Curly, is dead, as you well know. And you also know who killed him."

TWENTY

I had him come in, and we sat in the living room while he explained about Curly. It seemed that both bodies had been washed up, Moose's as well as Curly's. But no one was interested in Moose, whereas they were plenty interested in Curly. And the people that was interested in him was his own family, one of the best families in the South. They knew he was no good, naturally; in fact, they'd paid him to stay away from 'em. But still he was "family"—still part of 'em—and they meant to see to it that his murderer was hanged.

"So here I am, Sheriff . . ." Barnes forced a smile. "Perhaps we don't see eye to eye on everything, but, well, I'm not a man to hold a grudge, and I'm sure neither of us wants to see a murderer running loose."

"I know I sure don't," I said. "If I see any murderers runnin' around loose, I'll arrest 'em and throw 'em in jail."

"Exactly. So if you'll tell me the name of the man who killed Curly . . ."

"Me?" I said. "I don't know who killed him. If I did, I'd arrest him an' put—"

"Sheriff! You *do* know who killed him. You've admitted it."

"Not me," I said. "*You* said that I knew, not me."

His mouth pinched together again, and his eyes along with it. With that fish-hook nose, his face looked like three clods on a sandbank with a plough cutting through them.

"Approximately one week ago, on the morning after Curly was killed—"

"Now, how do you know it was the morning after?" I said. "Ain't no one can say that unless it was the fella that killed him."

"I know this, Sheriff. I know that your friend, Sheriff Ken Lacey, openly boasted on the streets of this town that he had taken care of Moose and Curly, meaning he had killed them. And you were with him at the time of this boasting, this claim that he had murdered these two men, and you gave your hearty approval to it."

"Oh, yeah," I laughed, "now I remember. That was a little joke of Ken's an' mine. Had ourselves a peck of fun with it."

"Now, Sheriff—"

"You think it wasn't?" I said. "You think that a fella who'd killed two men would walk around the streets braggin' about it, and that I, an officer of the law, would just pat him on the back for it?"

"Never mind what I think, Sheriff! The events I have described *did* take place, and on the night previous to them—the only night Sheriff Lacey spent in Pottsville—he stayed at the river whorehouse, and he there boasted to the inmates of the house that he had fixed Moose and Curly good and that he had taken care of them good, and so on. In other words, there is incontrovertible evidence that approximately one week before Moose and Curly were found dead, on the *only* night Sheriff Lacey spent in Pottsville, he did declare himself to be the murderer of the aforesaid Moose and Curly."

"Uh-hah," I said, making myself sound real interested. "Now, this in-con-tro-watchmacallit evidence you speak about. Would that be the unsupported word of these whorehouse gals?"

"It's not unsupported, dammit! There's Sheriff Lacey's bragging the following morning, and—"

"But he was just jokin', Mr. Barnes. I put him up to it."

Barnes' head snapped back, them little old eyes of his glaring at me. Then he darted it forward again, like he was going to hook me with his nose.

"Now, you listen to me, Corey! Listen to me good! I don't intend to—to—" He broke off suddenly, shook himself like a horse shaking off flies. Then his face twisted, and screwed up and unscrewed, and god-dang if he didn't smile. "Please excuse me, Sheriff Corey; I've had a rather trying day. I'm afraid I lost track of the fact, for a moment, that we're both equally sincere and intent in our desire for justice even though we may not act and think alike."

I nodded and said that I guessed he was right all right. He beamed and went on.

"Now, you've known Sheriff Lacey for years. He's a good friend of yours. You naturally feel that you have to protect him."

"Uh-uh," I said. "He ain't a friend of mine, and if there was any way I could pin them two murders on him I'd be plain proud to do it."

"But, Sheriff—"

"He *was* a friend of mine," I said. "He stopped bein' one even before that night he came down here an' rousted me out of bed and got me to point out the way to the whorehouse to him."

"Then he did go there!" Barnes rubbed his hands together. "You can testify of your own knowledge that he did go to the whorehouse on the night in question?"

"Why, sure I can," I said. "It's the plain truth, so why couldn't I testify to it?"

"But that's wonderful! Wonderful, Sheriff! And did Lacey tell you why he wanted to go to the—no, wait a minute. Did he say anything that would indicate that he was going to the whorehouse for the purpose of killing Moose and Curly?"

"You mean then, that night?" I shook my head. "No, he didn't say anything then."

"But he did at some other time! When?"

"That day," I said, "when I was over to his county on a visit. He said that pimps was one thing he just didn't have no use for, and that he believed in killin' 'em on general principles."

Barnes jumped up, and began pacing around the room. He said that what I'd told him was wonderful, wonderful, and it was just what he needed. Then, he stopped in front of me an' shook his finger sort of playful.

"You're quite a tease, Sheriff. Almost made me lose my temper, and I'm a man who prides himself on self-control. You had this vital information all along, and yet you appeared to be defending Lacey."

I said that, well, that was the way I was, a real card. He glanced at his watch, and asked me what time he could get a train into the city.

"Oh, you got lots of time," I said. "Better'n a couple of hours. Best thing you can do is stay an' have supper with us."

"Why—why, that's very kind of you, Sheriff. Very kind."

I got some whiskey out of the office, and we had ourselves a few drinks. He started talking about himself, him and the detective agency, me throwing in a word now and then by way of leading him on, and his voice began to get kind of bitter. It seemed like he hated what he was doing. He knew exactly what Talkington was, and he couldn't make no excuses for it. It was a downright hateful outfit, and he was part of its hateful doings, and he hated himself because he was.

"You probably know what I mean, Sheriff. Even a man in your job has to close his eyes to some very bad things."

"You're right about that," I said. "I have to close 'em if I want to stay on bein' sheriff."

"And do you want to? You've never thought of taking up another line of work?"

"Not for very long," I said. "What else would a fella like me do anyways?"

"Exactly!" His eyes lit up and they began to look a lot bigger. "What else can you do? What else can I do? But, Nick—excuse me for being familiar—my name's George, Sheriff."

"Glad to know you, George," I nodded, "an' you go right on calling me Nick."

"Thank you, Nick"—he took another drink of whiskey. "Now, here's what I was going to ask, Nick, and it's something I've worried about a great deal. Does the fact that we can't do anything else—does that excuse us?"

"Well," I said, "do you excuse a post for fittin' a hole? Maybe there's a nest of rabbits down in that hole, and the post will crush 'em. But is that the post's fault, for fillin' a gap it was made to fit?"

"But that's not a fair analogy, Nick. You're talking about inanimate objects."

"Yeah?" I said. "So ain't we all relatively inanimate, George? Just how much free will does any of us exercise? We got controls all along the line, our physical make-up, our mental make-up, our backgrounds; they'll all shapin' us a certain way, fixin' us up for a certain role in life, and George, we better play that role or fill that hole or any god-dang way you want to put it or all hell is going to tumble out of the heavens and fall right down on top of us. We better do what we were made to do, or we'll find it being done to us."

"You mean it's a case of kill or be killed?" Barnes shook his head. "I hate to think that, Nick."

"Maybe that's not what I mean," I said. "Maybe I'm not sure what I mean. I guess mostly what I mean is that there can't be no personal hell because there ain't no personal sins. They're all public, George, we all share in the other fellas' and the other fellas all share in ours. Or maybe I mean this, George, that I'm the Savior himself, Christ on the Cross come right here to Potts County, because God knows I was needed here, an' I'm goin' around doing kindly deeds—so that people will know they got nothing to fear, and if they're worried about hell they don't have to dig for it. And, by God, that makes sense, don't it, George? I mean obligation ain't all on the side of the fella that accepts it, nor responsibility neither. I mean, well, which is worse, George, the fella that craps on a doorknob or the one that rings the doorbell?"

George threw back his head and roared with laughter. "That's priceless, Nick! Priceless!"

"Well, it ain't exactly original," I said. "Like the poem says, you can't fault a jug for bein' twisted because the hand of the potter slipped. So you tell me which is worse, the one that messes up the doorknob or the one that rings the bell, and I'll tell you which got twisted and who done the twisting."

"But—but suppose the same person does both?"

"It ain't likely," I said. "As a fella that's had to deal with plenty of high jinks, and god-dang if I don't feel I'm living in a joker's paradise sometimes. I can say that these little chores is usually divided up. But if that wasn't the case, George, then we've opened up another field of obligation and responsibility. Because this fella had to eat before he could crap, didn't he, and where did the food come from?"

"We went on talking and drinking until Myra came home.

She fixed supper for George and me, she an' Lennie having already eaten at Rose's place. George was real courtly to Myra. God-dang if she didn't look almost pretty the way he shined up to her, and god-dang if he didn't look almost handsome because he done it.

Then we finished eating and I walked George toward the railroad station, and things weren't so nice any more. We were friendly, but it was just one of those have-to-be things. There wasn't no real warmth or liking in it.

I reckon that's the bad part of whiskey, you know?—the bad part about a lot of good things. Not the indulging in 'em, but the not being able to indulge. The afterwards, when the ol' familiar taste of piss is back in your mouth, and you want to spit it out at everyone. And you think, god-dang, why for did I want to be nice to that fella? And I bet he thought I was a god-danged fool.

George was looking kind of glum and let-down; kind of frowny and thoughtful. Then, Amy Mason crossed to our side of the street, and I introduced her, and George perked himself up again.

"You have a fine sheriff here," he said, clapping me on the back. "A very fine officer, Miss Mason. He's helped me solve a very important case."

"Indeed?" said Amy. "What kind of case, Mr. Barnes?"

And George told her, adding on that he just wouldn't have had a case against Ken if it hadn't been for me.

"I'm sure it wasn't an easy thing for him to do, either," he said. "It's never easy for one officer to incriminate another, even if they are not friends."

"How true!" Amy said. "And I'm sure it will become even less easy as time goes on. By the way, Sheriff, will you stop by my house this evening? I think I've seen a prowler around."

I said I'd be tickled to death to stop by, and she mustn't feel like she had to set out no coffee or cake or nothing because I wouldn't want her troubled.

She said she wouldn't be troubled at all, sort of tossing her head at me. Then, she went on, and George Barnes and I went on toward the station.

Way up river, the train was whistling for the crossing. George shook my hand and gave me a bee's-ass smile, and thanked me again for my help.

"By the way, Nick. It's just a matter of form, of course, but you'll be receiving a subpoena within the next day or so."

"A subpoena?" I said. "Why for will I be receiving one of those?"

"As a prosecution witness against Ken Lacey, naturally! The chief prosecution witness, I should say. We'd certainly never get a conviction without you."

"But what am I going to testify against him about?" I said. "What's old Ken supposed to have went and done?"

"*What's he supposed to have done?*" George stared at me. "Why—what are you trying to pull, anyway? You know what he's done!"

"Well, now I reckon I forgot," I said. "Maybe you wouldn't mind tellin' me again."

"Now you see here!" He grabbed me by the shoulders, teeth gritted. "Don't you go dumb on me, Corey. If you want money, all right, but—"

"I'm really plumb puzzled, George." I eased out of his grip. "Why for would I want money?"

"For stating under oath what you've already told me privately.

That Ken Lacey murdered Cameron Tramell, alias Curly!"

"Huh?" I said. "Now, wait a minute, George. I didn't tell you nothin' like that."

"Oh, yes, you did! You certainly did tell me that, in so many words. You told me—"

"Well, maybe you got that impression," I said. "But never mind about that, never mind what I told you. The important thing, I reckon, is what I didn't tell you."

"And what was that?"

"This," I said. "The morning after Ken Lacey left, I saw Moose an' Curly alive."

TWENTY-ONE

It was Sunday morning. Early-early Sunday morning. Way off somewhere in the country, I could hear a rooster crowing, but I figured he was probably just dumb—or doing it for exercise, because it was at least an hour before dawn.

Yes, sir, it was plumb quiet, and not a creature was stirrin', you might say. Except for me, shifting my buttocks a little on the bed now and then so's I would stay comfortable. And except for Rose.

She was out in the kitchen, it sounded like, fixing herself a cup of coffee. Then there was a clattery-clash, and I reckoned she must have thrown the cup against the wall, and then I heard a mumbled string of words that had to be curses.

I yawned and stretched. I sure was needing some sleep, but I guess I'm always in need of sleep like I'm always in need of food. Because my labors were mighty ones—ol' Hercules didn't know what hard work was—and what is there to do but eat and sleep? And when you're eatin' and sleepin' you don't have to fret about things that you can't do nothing about. And what else is there to do but laugh an' joke . . . how else can you bear up under the unbearable?

It was a cinch that cryin' didn't do no good. I'd tried that before in my agony—I'd cried out as loud as a fella could cry—an' it hadn't done no good at all.

I yawned and stretched again.

Sunday in Pottsville, I thought. Sunday in Pottsville, an' my sweetheart is going to leave me, and I hope it don't grieve me. My eyes plumb deceive me, an' no one'll believe me.

And I thought, god-dang it, Nick, if you didn't already have your work cut out for you, you could be a poet. The poet laureate of Potts County, by dang, and you could make up poems about piss tinkling in pots and jaybirds with the bots and assholes tying knots and . . .

Rose came in, and stood beside my bed.

She looked down at me, biting her lip, her face twisted like a handful of clay that a baby has played with.

"I just want to tell you one thing, Nick Corey," she said. "And don't think you're not getting off lucky, because I'd be doing a lot more than talk to you if I could. I'd see you swinging by your neck, you dirty bastard. I'd tell about you killing Tom, and goddam you, I'd laugh my head off when they strung you up, an'—an'—"

"I thought you were just going to tell me one thing," I said. "Seems to me like that's about a dozen."

"Screw you! I'm not going to tell you what I was going to say because I'm a decent woman. But if I wasn't, you know what I'd say? You know what I'd do to you, you rotten son-of-a-bitch? I'd heist a leg and pee in your ear until it washed out that stinking pile of crap you call brains!"

"Now, you just watch out now, Rose," I said. "You just better watch out or you'll be saying something dirty."

She started bawling, and stumbled back out of the room.

I heard her as she dropped down on the lounge, bawling and sniffling. And after a while she began to mumble to herself. Wondering out loud how *anyone*—meaning me—could do such a terrible thing.

And what could I have said except that it wasn't easy; it sure wasn't easy. And how could I explain what I didn't really understand myself?

Well?

But this is what had happened.

TWENTY-TWO

After I'd taken George Barnes to the station last Sunday, I stopped by Amy Mason's house. I knew I'd better explain that I'd just been kidding in front of Barnes—that I didn't have no intention of letting Ken Lacey get blamed for killing those pimps. But the way she hopped on me the minute I showed up, I hardly had a chance to say anything.

"I warned you, Nick!" she blazed at me. "I warned you not to do it! Now, you'll have to bear the consequences!"

"Now, wait a minute, honey," I said. "What—"

"I'm going to send a telegram to the governor, that's what! Right tonight! I'm going to tell him who actually did kill those two, uh, men!"

"But Amy, I didn't—"

"I'm sorry, Nick. You'll never know how sorry I am. But I'm going to do it. I can't allow you to commit a murder—and framing Sheriff Lacey would be murder—that I know about in advance."

I finally managed to make her listen to me, to tell her that I wasn't even halfway planning to frame Ken. "It was just a joke, see? I was just leadin' Barnes on for a good hard letdown."

"Yes?" She looked at me sharply. "You're sure about that?"

"Sure I'm sure. You should have seen his face when I told him I'd seen them pimps alive the day after Ken was down there."

"Well . . ."

She was still sort of suspicious, still not quite convinced that I didn't have some scheme for framing Ken without getting myself in trouble. Finally, I got kind of impatient, and I said I wasn't really flattered to have her doubtin' my word when she didn't have no reason to.

"I'm sorry." She smiled and pecked me on the cheek. "I believe you, dear, and I'll tell you something else. If I hated Sheriff Lacey like you do, I'd probably want to kill him, too!"

"Hate?" I said. "What makes you think I hate him?"

"Now, darling, it sticks out all over you. What did he ever do to you to make you feel that way about him?"

"But I don't," I said. "I mean, I don't hate him. I mean, it ain't what I feel about him that matters. It's what he is, you know; the things he's done to others. I—well, it's kind of hard to explain but—but—"

"Never mind, dear." She laughed and kissed me again. "You're not going to do anything to him, and that's all that matters."

But it wasn't all, you know? Not by a long shot. I'd've sworn that I never held no malice toward no one, never a speck of hatred. Or if I ever had felt sort of a teensy twinge of dislike, it hadn't been the motivatin' factor in whatever I'd done.

That's the way I felt about myself, anyways, until Amy'd said what she'd said. And now I was kind of worried. I could put Ken Lacey out of my mind, since I wasn't going to take any action against him. But the others, well, they were all part of the same pattern, weren't they? And if I'd been showing spite toward Ken, then maybe I'd been doing the same thing with them.

And maybe, in the case of what I was about to do, the people I was about to take care of . . .

But it had to be done, I reckoned. It had to be, and I didn't have no choice in the matter.

I was willing to let things ride; I'm long sufferin', you might say. But they wouldn't have it that way.

Rose was callin' Myra every day, hinting that she needed me to do this or that for her. And Myra kept naggin' at me to go out and do what Rose wanted done (which wasn't what Myra thought it was). And Amy was insistin' that I couldn't see Rose but one more time—no more, or else. And Lennie had taken one of his spells of tagging after me, and spying on me. And—

And finally it was Saturday night, last night, and I couldn't hold out no longer. They were all asking for it! And like the Good Book says, Ask and ye shall receive.

It was about eight in the evening, about an hour after sunset.

I came running down the cotton rows, half-stooped, which didn't conceal me much because it was a low stand of cotton. In the dusk, just about anyone nearby could see me, and they didn't even have to be too nearby. And that was the way I wanted it.

Lennie didn't like to walk. Ordinarily, he'd never go outside the town limits. It had really been a job to act sneaky and creepy enough to tote him way out here to Rose's place.

I came out of the cotton, and made a dash toward the house. Out of the corner of my eye, I could see Lennie rising up in the field. Gawking openly, as I reached the house and pounded on the door. He really thought he had me now, Lennie did; he had me and Rose. He'd caught me sneaking into her house at night, so pretty soon now he was going to do some peeking. And then he'd go back to town with a fine story to tell Myra. A real juicy story about her own husband and her best friend.

That was just the way I wanted it.

That was the way I'd planned it.

Lennie was going to get a story for Myra, all right, but it would be a lot nastier than he figured on.

"Nick—" Rose opened the door. "What—where have you been, anyway? Why didn't you come out last—"

"Later." I squeezed inside and closed the door. I kissed her, keeping her mouth closed until I knew she was ready to listen. "I couldn't come any sooner, honey, because I been workin' on a plan. It's a way to get rid of Myra and Lennie, and I've already taken the first step an' now I'm goin' to need your help. So here I am, askin' for it. You don't want to give it, you just say so and we'll just forget all about gettin' rid of 'em and go on like we been doin'."

"But, by—what—" She was willing but confused, puzzled. I'd talked fast, acting excited and running my words together, and I had her nodding even while she was frowning and wondering what the heck it was all about.

"Well, forget it," I said, turning toward the door. "Just forget I asked, Rose, an' I'm sorry I troubled you."

"No, wait! Wait, honey!" She grabbed onto me. "I just wondered what—why—but I'll do it, honey! You just tell me what it is!"

"I want you to wait a couple of minutes," I said. "Then, I want you to go outside and grab Lennie an'—"

"Lennie!" She let out a frightened gasp. "D-Did he—"

"He followed me out here. I egged him into doin' it, because that's part of the plan. So you grab him and haul him inside, and then you tell him what I tell you to."

I told her what to say, the gist of it, that is. She turned pale, lookin' at me like I'd gone out of my mind.

"N-Nick! That's—that's crazy! I couldn't—"

"Sure, it's crazy," I said. "It's got to be crazy, don't you see?"

"But . . . oh," she said, and her eyes narrowed a little. "Yeah, I can see how it might—but, Nick, honey, what about the rest? How does—"

"There ain't time to tell you, now," I said. "You just go on an' take care of Lennie, an' I'll explain everything afterward."

I turned and went into the bedroom, seeming to take it for granted, you know, that she'd do what I told her to.

She stayed where she was for a moment, fidgeting uncertainly. Frowning and maybe a little frightened. She took a step toward the bedroom, on the point, it looked like, of calling out to me. Then she suddenly faced back around, crossed to the door, and went outside.

Dimly, I heard running sounds. The fast scuffle of footsteps on the hard-packed clay of the yard. I heard a holler as she grabbed hold of Lennie, and I heard him burbling and giggling as she dragged him into the house. Tickled pink with himself, but just a mite scared along with it.

They came into the kitchen. I stood back out of sight, watching and listening.

"All right," Rose said, her eyes pure poison as she looked at him. "What were you doing sneaking around here?"

Lennie giggled and smirked, putting his hands over his mouth, lattice-like. Then, he said me an' Rose was really going to catch it.

"You just wait, I'm gonna tell Myra on you! I seen him! I seen ol' smarty Nick! He come sneaking out here so's you 'n' him could do somethin' nasty!"

"You mean screwing?" Rose said. "What's nasty about screwing?"

"Ooh!" Lennie pointed a shaky finger at her, his eyes popped as big as saucers. "Now, you done it! You're really gonna catch it now! I'll tell Myra you—"

"What's the matter?" Rose said. "You screw Myra all the time, and don't tell me you don't, you stupid-looking jackass! That's what makes you goofy, banging her so much. You've tossed it to her so often you've thrown your ass out of line with your eyeballs!"

I almost busted out laughing.

That Rose! There just wasn't no one like her, god-dang it! In less than a minute, now, she'd got Lennie so mixed up that he couldn't have found his butt if it'd had a bell on it.

He pointed his finger at her again, shaking all over. Rubbing his eyes with his other hand as he started to blubber.

"I *deed* not! I do not! I never done nothin' like that, an'—"

"The hell you didn't! You're not her brother, you're her boy friend! That's what she keeps you around for, to diddle her fiddle. Because you're low-hung and she's high-strung!"

"It a-ain't n-neither! I *de-ed* not! You—y-you're just a m-mean ol' storyteller, an'—"

"Don't lie to me, you liver-lipped bastard!" Rose shook her fist in his face. "I've seen you pouring it on her! I climbed up one of those ladders the painters are using and peeked in the window, and goddam, you were pounding it like a drum. The way you were banging the bunghole, you damned near fell in!"

Well, god-dang. It was better than a circus. And it just went to show what a fella could do when he really put his mind to it.

Here you take a common everyday thing like fornication, which, like the fella says, can be a pretty fleeting pleasure. But if you can just take the idea of it, you know, and start tossing it around amongst the right people, or the wrong ones, dependin' on your viewpoint, why then you can get something pretty god-dang unusual. Something like what was going on here.

A heck of a lot of laughs—plus the means of getting some people to get rid of themselves, when there ain't no way for you to get rid of them.

"I'm g-gonna tell M-Myra!" Lennie blubbered. "I'll tell jus' what you said about her, every dirty m-mean word an'—"

"Cow's ass?" said Rose, like she was sayin' "How's that?" and, "Suck which?" Like she was sayin' "Says which?" "You and Myra better stop playing tickle the pickle, boy, before you bat your brains out with your balls."

"I'm gonna tell Myra!" Lennie bawled, stumbling toward the door. "You're gonna get it!"

"Tell her she may be a hole, but you're no post," Rose said. "Tell her you'll tickle her ass if she'll whistle 'Old Black Joe.' "

She gave Lennie a shove. It knocked him clean out the door and off the porch, and he landed sprawling in the yard.

He picked himself up, blubbering and rubbing his eyes. Rose gave him a final cussing, accusing him and Myra of a whole blast of dirty things. It kind of made me wince to listen to her, it was that dirty. What she'd said before sounded downright complimentary by comparison.

She came back in, slamming the door. I gave her a hug, and told her she'd done just fine.

"Now, are you beginnin' to get the picture?" I said. "Lennie never leaves town. He's not only too danged lazy to do any real walkin', but he's scared to get very far off by himself. Myra knows this. She knows he'd be just about as likely to flap his arms and fly as he would to come way out here to your place. So what happens when he goes home and tells Myra he *has* been out here?"

Rose said, "Mmm," nodding her head slowly. "She probably won't believe him, right? But what—"

"She won't believe him," I said. "Leastways, she'll have some awful strong doubts he's telling the truth. Then, he tells her all the dirty things you said about her, about her and Lennie sleepin' together and so on. And how can she believe that? How can she believe that her very best friend, a perfect lady, would all of a sudden start talking dirty about her?"

"Mmm-hmm," Rose nodded again. "She can't believe that he came out here, in the first place, and she can't believe what he says happened here. The way she sees it, he'll just have made it all up, and he'll probably get his ears boxed for lying. But—"

"Not just lying," I said, "but god-danged dangerous lyin'. The kind that breaks up homes, and gets people killed. And Myra won't want to chance the risk of it happening again. She'll figure he's taken a real bad turn for the worse, and she'll have to put him away somewhere like she's sometimes threatened to."

"Huh!" Rose gave me a startled look. "When did Myra ever do anything like that? Why she can hardly bear to let Lennie out of her sight!"

I said Myra had threatened to put him away a couple times, when she got extra mad at him, and, yeah, she couldn't hardly bear to let Lennie out of sight. "That's why she's never done anything about him, because she'd want to be with him wherever he was and she didn't want to leave Pottsville. Now, though, she's got no choice. He goes and she goes, too."

Rose said she just wasn't sure about it. It sounded good but you couldn't depend on it working out that way. I said that, well, of course we'd have to help things along a little.

"Myra's bound to tell us about it, and naturally, we get pretty blamed worried. And the worrieder we get the worrieder she gets. We're real concerned about what Lennie might do next, you know, like maybe taking a meat axe to people instead of just lying about 'em. Or setting houses on fire. Or chasin' little girls. Or—well, don't you fret about it, honey." I gave her a squeeze, and a pat on the bottom. "Everything's goin' to work out fine, just absolutely fine. I ain't got a doubt in the world about it."

Rose shrugged and said, well, maybe so; I knew Myra better than she did. Then, she snuggled up to me and bit my ear. And I kissed her, and pulled myself away.

"Lennie ain't a real fast walker," I explained. "I aim to cut cross-country and beat him back to town. Just in case, you know."

"Just in case?" Rose frowned. "In case of what?"

"In case we need a clincher. Something that'll sweep the last doubt out of Myra's mind, if she should have a doubt. It ain't even remotely likely that she will have. But when Lennie gets to the courthouse, just pantin' to tell Myra about me bein' out here, ain't it a pretty good idea for me to be sittin' in my office?"

Rose had to admit that it was, much as she hated to have me leave.

I promised we'd get together in a day or so. Then, I beat it out the door before I had to talk any more.

Naturally, I didn't go back to town. I already knew what was going to happen there. What I wanted to see was what was going to happen here, although I already had a pretty good idea, and maybe to help it along a little if it needed helpin'.

I circled around through the fields until I reached the lane that came up from the road. Then, I hunkered down beside it in a clump of scrub mulberries, and waited.

About an hour and a half passed. I started to worry a little, wonderin' if I could have been wrong, and then I heard the squeak of buggy wheels coming on fast.

I parted the bushes and peeked out. Lennie and Myra swept by, Myra clutching the horse's reins, Lennie's head lolling back and forth on his neck. He was carrying something on his lap, a black, box-like thing, and one of his hands clutched something that looked like a stick. I scratched my head, wonderin' what the heck the stuff was—the box and the stick—and then the buggy had rolled past me, up and out of the lane and into the farmyard.

Myra whoa-ed the horse to a stop. She and Lennie climbed down from the buggy, and she trailed the reins over the horse's head to keep it from wandering away. Then, she and Lennie crossed the yard and went up on the porch.

She banged on the door. It opened after a minute, and the lamplight outlined her face, white and purposeful-looking. She started to go in, then she took Lennie by the shoulder and shoved him in ahead of her. And at last I saw what he was carryin'.

It was a camera—a camera and one of them sticks that you explode flash-powder in for taking pictures indoors.

TWENTY-THREE

I jumped up and started for the house. About the first step I took, my foot caught in a root and I fell sprawling with the wind knocked out of me. For a minute or two, I didn't even have enough breath to groan, and when I finally did manage to pick myself up, I couldn't move very fast. So it was maybe all of five minutes before I got to the house, and found a window where I could hear and see.

Well, sir, it was a funny thing, a funny-terrible thing, a strange-crazy thing. Because what caught my attention wasn't what you'd have thought it would be at all. Not Rose, scared and dazed and wonderin' what the heck had gone wrong. Not Lennie and Myra, smilin' and spiteful and enjoyin' theirselves. Not something that was in the room itself. Not somethin' but nothing. The emptiness. The absence of things.

I'd maybe been in that house a hundred times, that one and a hundred others like it. But this was the first time I'd seen what they really were. Not homes, not places for people to live in, not nothin'. Just pine-board walls locking in the emptiness. No pictures, no books—nothing to look at or think about. Just the emptiness that was soakin' in on me here.

And then suddenly it wasn't here, it was everywhere, every place like this one. And suddenly the emptiness was filled with sound and sight, with all the sad terrible things that the emptiness had brought the people to.

There were the helpless little girls, cryin' when their own daddies crawled into bed with 'em. There were the men beating their wives, the women screamin' for mercy. There were the kids wettin' in the beds from fear and nervousness, and their mothers dosin' 'em with red pepper for punishment. There were the haggard faces, drained white from hookworm and blotched with scurvy. There was the near-starvation, the never-bein'-full, the debts that always outrun the credits. There was the how-we-gonna-eat, how-we-gonna-sleep, how-we-gonna-cover-our-poor-bare-asses thinkin'. The kind of thinkin' that when you ain't doing nothing else but that, why you're better off dead. Because that's the emptiness thinkin' and you're already dead inside, and all you'll do is spread the stink and the terror, the weepin' and wailin', the torture, the starvation, the shame of your deadness. Your emptiness.

I shuddered, thinking how wonderful was our Creator to create such downright hideous things in the world, so that something like murder didn't seem at all bad by comparison. Yea, verily, it was indeed merciful and wonderful of Him. And it was up to me to stop brooding, and to pay attention to what was going on right here and now.

So I made an extra hard try, rubbing my eyes and shaking myself, and finally I managed to.

"—a goddam liar!" Rose was yelling. "I didn't say any such of a goddam thing!"

"Tsk, tsk." There was a possum grin on Myra's face. "Such language. I'm beginning to think you're not a very nice girl, after all."

"To hell with what you think! Who wouldn't cuss, having you and that idiot show up at this time of night!"

"You mean you didn't expect us?" Myra said. "Did you think I'd let you talk that way about me, and not do anything about it?"

"But I didn't talk about you! Lennie's lyin'! Lennie wasn't even out here tonight!"

"Wasn't he? Then what was his handkerchief doing out there on the porch? One of the extra-big, double-thick kind I make for him because the poor dear's always slobbering."

Myra went on grinning, watching the fear spread over Rose's face. Rose stammered that she was lying, that she hadn't found Lennie's handkerchief on the porch. But she had, all right. I'd put it there myself.

"Well?" Myra said. "Well, Rose?"

Rose was caught, and she must have known it. The rough talk she'd been using was a dead giveaway in itself. But like a scared person will, she kept on trying.

"W-Well . . ." She bobbed her head jerkily. "All right, Lennie *was* here. I caught him sneaking around the house and it scared me, and I guess I talked pretty rough to him. But—but I certainly didn't say those dirty things that he says I did!"

"Didn't you?"

"No, I didn't! How many times do I have to tell you?"

Myra laughed, a mean scary laugh that even made me shiver. She said that Rose didn't have to tell her any times, because a lie didn't gain anything by repetition.

"Lennie's telling the truth, dear. He doesn't have the imagination to make up a story like that."

"B-But—but—"

"And you don't have the imagination either. You couldn't have invented the story, any more than he could. Which means—well, I don't know how you found out, but you obviously did. And that's the important thing, isn't it? That and making sure that you don't do any talking to anyone else."

Rose stared at her, slowly shaking her head, her voice a harsh sickish whisper. "I—I d-don't believe you. Y-You and Lennie. I *just don't believe you!*"

The fact was, I was pretty shocked myself. Because I'd guessed the truth; I'd been pretty sure of it. But that wasn't nowhere near the same as knowin' it.

"I don't believe you," Rose repeated shakily. "Why—why would you—"

"Oh, stop pretending," Myra said. "You found out about us, and you were foolish enough to tell Lennie. As for the why of things, you're going to find that out, too, and very shortly. That is, of course, if you're similarly attracted to him."

She motioned to Lennie. He fastened the camera around her neck with a strap, and she fiddled with the settings for a minute, getting it like she wanted. Then he poured powder into the flash-stick from a can in his pocket, and carefully handed it to her.

Rose stood staring at them.

Myra let out another one of her mean-scary laughs. "Don't worry about your picture, dear. I'm really quite professional with a camera. In fact, I made quite a bit of money that way before I was married, quite a bit. You'd be surprised at the sums people paid me for certain pictures that I took of them."

Rose shook her head, seeming to shake off her fear for the moment. She said that Myra was going to get a surprise if she didn't drag her ass out of there.

"Now, beat it, you baggy old bitch! Take your buggy boy friend and clear out of here before I forget I'm a lady!"

"In a moment, dear. Just as soon as I take your picture—with Lennie."

"Take my picture! Why, goddam you—"

"Mmm-hmm, take your picture. With Lennie. It'll be much safer than killing you, and every bit as effective at keeping you quiet, and—*tear her clothes off, Lennie*!"

Lennie's hand darted out before Rose could move. It caught in the front of her dress and ripped downward, taking the underclothes along with the dress. Before you could blink an eye, she was standing in a puddle of rags, naked as a baby jay.

Lennie burbled and choked on his own spit, and about a pint more spilled over his chin. Myra gave him a lovin' look.

"She looks very good, doesn't she, darling? Why don't you see if she really is?"

"Guh, guh—" Lennie hesitated doubtfully. "M-Maybe she hurt me?"

"Now, of course she won't hurt you," Myra laughed. "You're big and she's little, and anyway I'm here to protect you."

"Guh, guh—" Lennie still hesitated. He'd ripped Rose's clothes off, but just doing that, just the one quick grab, didn't take much guts. He wasn't quite ready to go the rest of the way, even with Myra to nerve him up and tell him it was okay. "W-What—how I do it, Myra?"

"Just grab her and throw her down," Myra said, and then, sharply, forcing him to obey before he could think, "*Grab her, Lennie!*"

Rose had been standin' sort of stunned since her clothes were ripped off. Glazed-eyed, too stupefied even to try to cover herself.

But then Lennie grabbed, hugging her to him, slobbering over her, and everything was changed. She came to life like a turpentined bobcat, screaming, clawing, kicking and pounding. Lennie got hit and clawed in about a dozen places at the same time, not to mention a kneein' in his crotch and a kicking on his shins.

He fell away from her, blubbering and clutching himself. Rose darted into the bedroom and slammed the door, and Myra hauled off and kicked Lennie in the tail.

"You big boob, go after her! Break the door down!"

"I'm a-scairt," Lennie whined. "She hurt me!"

"I'll hurt you a lot worse!" Myra twisted his ear by way of demonstration. "I'll beat you black and blue if you don't do what I tell you. *Now, break that door down!*"

Lennie began to shoulder the door. Myra stood right behind him, urging him on, telling him what would happen if he didn't mind her.

The lock gave. The door banged open, Lennie following it with his rush and Myra following him. And . . .

And so I reckon I never will know what was in Myra's mind. Or what wasn't in it. Whether she'd forgot about that pistol she'd helped Rose buy, or whether she thought that Rose wouldn't dare use it. Or whether she was so danged mad and determined to put Rose in a fix that she just wasn't thinking.

No, sir, I'll never know what she thought or didn't think. Because just about a second after the bedroom door busted open, she and Lennie were dead.

They came stumbling backward into the living room when Rose started shooting, falling over each other, going down to the floor together in a tangled heap. They were already dead then, I reckon, but Rose kept on firing—like she was shooting fish in a barrel—until the gun was empty.

I climbed in the buggy and started for town, ponderin' over the strange workings of Providence. What I'd really sort of figured on was that Myra would kill Rose, and then Myra and Lennie would have to skip town, because I would be absolutely impartial even if they were sort of kinfolks and I'd do my dangedest to see that they were punished even if I had to shoot 'em while they were trying to escape. Which would probably be the best way of winding things up.

But this would be all right, I reckoned. It would work out just as well with Rose killin' Myra and Lennie.

I put the horse and buggy in the livery stable, listening to the hostler snore away in the hayloft. I went back across town to the courthouse, and everyone was long-gone in bed of course and it was like there wasn't no one on the earth but me.

I went upstairs to the living quarters, and drew the shades down tight. Then, I lit a lamp and got myself a cup of cold coffee from the stove, and eased down on the lounge to drink it.

I finished it, and carried the cup back into the kitchen. I toed my boots off and stretched out on the lounge to rest. And the downstairs door slammed open and Rose came pounding up the steps and busted in on me.

She'd run all the way into town on foot, I reckon, and she was wild-eyed and crazy-lookin'. She sagged against the door, heaving for breath, pointing a shaking accusin' finger at me. It was all she could do for a moment, just point.

I said howdy-do to her, and then I said it was all right, me and her bein' friends, but it really wasn't perlite to point at people.

"I thought you ought to know that," I said. "It not only ain't polite, but you might poke someone in the eye."

"Y-You!" she said, fighting for breath. "You—you—!"

"Or if they was real tall folks," I said, "you might poke 'em in some other bodily orifice, which could be plumb embarrassin' for you, not to mention the danger of getting your finger caught."

She took a long, shuddery heave. Then she came over to the lounge and stood over me. "You you you son-of-a-bitch!" she said. "You you you rotten stinking bastard. You—you goddamned whore-mongerin', double-crossing, low-down, worthless, no-good, mean, hateful, two-timing ornery—"

"Now, god-dang it, Rose," I said. "Danged if it don't almost sound as if you was mad at me."

"*Mad!*" she yelled. "I'll show you how mad I am! I'll—"

"Better not holler so loud!" I said. "Folks might be roused into coming up here to find out what's going on."

Rose said to let 'em come, but she lowered her voice. "I'll damned well tell them what's going on, you dirty bastard! I'll tell them just what happened!"

"And what would that be?" I said.

"Don't you play dumb on me, damn you! You *know* what happened! You were outside all the time, because I heard you when you drove away! You let it happen! You stood by watching while I had to kill two people!"

"Uh-huh?" I said. "Yeah?"

"What the hell do you mean, 'Uh-huh yeah'? Are you saying that you didn't do it, that it didn't happen that way? That you didn't lan the whole thing, an'—an'—"

"I ain't sayin' nothin' like that at all," I said. "All I'm saying or rather askin' is what you're goin' to tell folks. What kind of a believable explanation are you going to put together for them two dead bodies you got in your house and the blood all over the floor, and the fact that even an idjit could prove they was shot with your gun? Because no one's goin' to believe the truth, Rose; they just ain't goin' to believe no such wild story. You just think about a minute, and you'll see that they won't."

She opened her mouth to speak, to call me some more dirty names I guess. Then she seemed to have some second thoughts on the matter, and she sat down quietly at the side of the lounge.

"You've got to help me, Nick. You've got to help me cover this up some way."

"Well, now, I don't rightly see how I could do that," I said. "After all, you're guilty of murder an' fornicatin' and hypocrisy, an'—"

"Huh! *Wha-at!*" She glared at me. "Why, you fork-tongued son-of-a-bitch! You call me names after what you've done! And I don't suppose you're at all responsible, are you?"

"Not a speck," I said. "Just because I put temptation in front of people, it don't mean they got to pick it up."

"I asked you a question, damn you! Who planned those murders? Who tells a lie every time he draws a breath? Who the hell is it that's been fornicating with me, and God knows how many others?"

"Oh, well," I said. "It don't count when I do those things."

"It don't count! What the hell do you mean?"

I said I meant I was just doing my job, followin' the holy precepts laid down in the Bible. "It's what I'm supposed to do, you know, to punish the heck out of people for bein' people. To coax 'em into revealin' theirselves, an' then kick the crap out of 'em. And it's a god-danged hard job, Rose, honey, and I figure that if I can get a little pleasure in the process of trappin' folks I'm mighty well entitled to it."

Rose stared at me, frowning.

"What is this?" she said. "What kind of nutty talk is that?"

"Well, now, I guess it does sound kind of nutty," I said, "but that ain't hardly no ways my fault. By rights, I should be rompin' on the high an' the mighty, the folks that really run this country. But I ain't allowed to touch them, so I've got to make up for it by being twice as hard on the white trash an' Negroes, and people like you that let their brains sink down to their butts because they couldn't find no place else to use them. Yes, sir, I'm laborin' in the Lord's vineyard, and if I can't reach up high, I got to work all the harder on the low-hangin' vines. For the Lord loveth a willin' worker, Rose; He liketh to see a man bustin' his ass during workin' hours. And I got them hours cut way, way down with eatin' and sleepin', but I can't eat and sleep all the time."

I'd let my eyes drift shut while I was talking. When I opened them Rose was gone, but I heard her moving around in Myra's room.

I went to the door and looked in.

She'd stripped out of her clothes, and was trying on some of Myra's. I asked her if she was figurin' on going somewhere, and she gave me a look that would have fried an egg.

"Am I going somewhere," she said bitterly. "As if you didn't know what I was going to do, what I *have* to do!"

I said I reckoned she'd be taking the dawn train out of town, because no one would see her leave that way and she'd have a full day's start before I got excited and worried about Myra and Lennie and got around to discovering that they was murdered.

"Of course, that dawn train don't carry passengers, they just got a water-stop here. But I reckon them trainmen will be proud to let you ride when they see how friendly you are. I bet they won't charge you a cent, which makes things pretty nice since you don't have no money you can put your hands on."

Rose bit her lips; shook her head wonderingly.

"You're actually enjoying this, aren't you? You're getting a kick out of it!"

"Not really," I said. "It's just part of my job, you know, to gloat over folks in trouble."

"Nick," she said. "What's happened to you? When did you get like this?"

I said, well, sir, if she meant when had the truth been revealed to me, it had been happenin' for a long time. Bit by bit, I'd been given a glimpse of it, and now and then I'd think I knew what it was, and now an' then I was just mystified and scared. I didn't know from what for, and I'd get the idea that I must be goin' crazy or something. And then, tonight, at her house, as I stood outside of myself plannin' things, and then as I'd watched what I'd planned take place, it was sort of like someone had pulled a trigger in my mind and there was one great big flash of light, and at last I saw the whole truth; at last I saw why things were as they were, and why I was as I was.

"I saw it all, honey," I said. "I saw the truth and the glory; and it ain't going to be nearways so bad for you as you might think. Why, a gal like you can make herself a mint in them river towns, just doin' what you like to do, and I never knew no gal that done it any better. And speakin' of that, and as long as we won't be seein' each other no more, I've got no objection to cleaving unto you for five to ten minutes even if you are sort of a fugitive from the law."

Rose snatched up the alarm clock from the dresser and flung it at me. It smashed against the wall, and what I mean is it *really* smashed.

"Now, god-dang it, Rose," I said. "How the god-dang heck am I goin' to wake up in time for church?"

"Church! *Church!*" she moaned. "You going to church after—after—! Oh, you son-of-a-bitch! Oh, you sneaky, tricky, lying, mealy-mouthed bastard!"

"Now, there you go again," I said. "There ain't no sure use of pretendin' no longer, 'cause now I *know* you're mad at me."

She cut loose with another blast of cuss words. Then, she whirled back around to the mirror, and began fussin' with the dress she was trying on.

"It's that Amy Mason, isn't it?" she said. "You're getting rid of everyone so you can marry her."

"Well," I said. "I got to admit I've been studyin' about it."

"I'll bet you have! I just bet you have, you double-crossing skunk!"

"Yes, sir," I said. "I've been studyin' about it, but the fact is I can't make up my mind. It ain't that she's a sinner, because she's one of the quality an' they got their own laws and rules and I don't have to bother with 'em. But I'm afraid marryin' her might interfere with my work. Y'see, I got my job to do, Rose; I got to go on bein' High Sheriff, the highest legal authority in Potts County, this place that's the world to most people here, because they never see nothin' else. I just got to be High Sheriff, because I've been peccul-yarly an' singularly fitted for it, and I ain't allowed to give it up. Every now an' then, I think I'm goin' to get out of it, but always the thoughts are put in my head and the words in my mouth to hold me in my place. I got to be it, Rose. I got to be High Sheriff of Potts County forever an' ever. I got to go on an' on, doin' the Lord's work; and all He does is the pointin', Rose, all He does is pick out the people an' I got to exercise His wrath on 'em. And I'll tell you a secret, Rose, they's plenty of times when I don't agree with Him at all. But I got nothing to say about it. I'm the High Sheriff of Potts County, an' I ain't supposed to do nothing that really needs doing, nothin' that might jeopardize my job. All I can do is follow the pointin' of the Lord's finger, striking down the pore sinners that no one gives a good god-dang about. Like I say, I've tried to get out of it; I've figured on runnin' away and stayin' away. But I can't, and I know I'll never be able to. I got to keep on like I'm doin' now, and I'm afraid Amy would never understand that or put up with it. So I misdoubt I'll be marryin' her."

Rose gazed at me in the mirror. She studied me for a long time, puzzled, angry, frightened, and then she shrugged and rolled her eyes.

"Oh, brother!" she said. "What a bull artist!"

"Now, god-dang it, Rose," I said. "You just think about it a little and it'll make plenty of sense for you. Ain't it logical that I should appear here in Potts County, which is just about as close to the asshole of creation as you can get without havin' a finger snapped off? And don't I have to be just another fella—just a man, like I was the first time—and don't I have to act like one, just the same as anyone else? When in Potts County, do what the Potts County folks do, like the fella says. An' if you want to promote anyone to glory, why do it privately, because people want logical explanations for everything, particularly for the miracle of promotin' people to glory."

Rose made a farting noise with her lips. "Brother!" she said again. "Are you ever full of crap!"

"Now, don't you say that, Rose," I said. "Please, please don't. I've been a long time figuring things out, and now I finally done it; I finally explained things to myself, and I had to explain 'em, Rose, or go crazy. An' even now, sometimes, I find a doubt or so creepin' in, and I can't stand it. I honest to God can't stand it. So, please, honey, please don't . . . don't . . ."

I turned and stumbled off to my bedroom.

I prayed mightily and pretty soon I got a grip on myself, and my doubts went away. I prayed mightily and the strength flowed back into me, and I didn't hardly mind at all the times that Rose was fussin' and cussin' at me. And I could even have kissed her goodbye when she left, and maybe've given her a pinch or two, if she hadn't threatened to brain me if I so much as touched her.

TWENTY-FOUR

I went to church like always, and I was asked to sing in the choir like I'd been doin' up until the time it had looked like Sam Gaddis was going to beat me out for sheriff. So I sang out loud an' clear, shouting the praises of the Lord, and god-dang if I didn't practically raise the roof with Amens when the minister started preachin'. I reckon I must've prayed and shouted an' sang louder than anyone in the church, and after everything was over the minister wrung me by the hand and called me Brother, and said he saw the spirit was truly in me.

"And where is good Sister Myra today? Not ill, I hope."

"Well, no, I reckon not," I said. "She and Lennie drove out to see Sister Rose Hauck last night, and I didn't discover until this morning that the horse had run off and come back to town by hisself. I guess that's what happened, anyway, because the horse is in the stable an' she and Lennie ain't come home yet."

"Yes?" He frowned a little. "But haven't you phoned the Hauck house?"

"Oh, I didn't see no point in that," I said. "I couldn't have picked her up, anyway, before church and I sure didn't want to miss church. I figured I'll probably drive out in time to bring her in for the evenin' services."

"Yes," he said, still kind of frowning. "Well . . ."

"Hallelujah!" I said. "Praise the Lord, Brother!"

I went on home, and fixed myself a bite to eat. Then I washed up the dishes, and put 'em away, and after I'd done that I went into my room and dropped down on the bed. Just laid there, doin' nothing in particular and not workin' very hard at it.

I found a long hair sticking out of my nose, and I jerked it out and looked at it, and it didn't look particularly interesting. I dropped it to the floor, wonderin' if falling hair from fellas' noses was noted along with fallin' sparrows. I raised up on one cheek of my butt, and eased out one of those long rattly farts, like you never can get rid of when other folks are around. I scratched my balls, tryin' to decide at what point a fella stopped scratchin' and started playin'. Which is an age-old question, I guess, and one that ain't likely to be solved in the near future.

I listened, tryin' to hear Myra out in the kitchen. I started puzzlin' over where Lennie might be, and thinking maybe I ought to go out and look for him before he got into trouble. I wondered if maybe I shouldn't take a run out to see Rose, and pleasure her up a little if Tom wasn't at home.

It seemed like a good idea, the more I thought about it. And I was clean out into the living room before I suddenly remembered; and I dropped down hard into a chair, and buried my face in my hands. Trying to sort things out. Trying to fit them back together in the only way they made sense.

Buck came in—Ken Lacey's deputy, you know. I was kind of befuddled for a minute, so absorbed with fittin' things together that I couldn't quite place him. But there was the gun hangin' from his hip and his deputy sheriff's badge and his long leathery face, so of course I remembered pretty fast.

We shook hands and I told him to set down. "I bet you prob'ly run into my wife downtown," I said. "I bet she told you just to come right on up here and walk in without knockin', because I wouldn't mind a bit, didn't she?"

"Nope," said Buck.

"You mean it didn't happen that way?"

"Yep," said Buck.

"Yeah?"

"Yeah," said Buck. "What happened was I was huntin' me a skunk, and when I'm a-huntin' skunk I don't stand none on ceremony. I just bust right in wherever I smell him."

"Well," I said. "Well, now. How you standin' all this weather?"

"Tol'able. Just tol'able."

"You reckon it's goin' to get any hotter?"

"Yep," said Buck. "Yes, sir, it's goin' to get a lot hotter. Wouldn't surprise me none if it got so hot for a certain fella that didn't keep his bounden bargain with me that he just naturally won't be able to stand it."

I got a bottle out of the sideboard and filled a couple of glasses. He took the one I handed him, and threw it against the wall.

"Like to keep my hands free," he explained. "Kind of a habit with me when I'm around a fella that don't keep his bounden agreements."

"Buck," I said. "I just couldn't do it! I was willin' to but it was just plumb impossible!"

"No, it wasn't," Buck said. "Moresomeover, it ain't."

"But you don't understand, god-dang it! I possolutely couldn't do it because—"

"Ain't interested in no becauses or whys or whichfores," Buck said. "You 'n' me had a bargain, and I done my part in gettin' Ken down here. Now you do your part an' drop that rope over his neck, or I'm goin' to put it around yours."

I told him that would be a pretty trick to see, but maybe he'd better not attempt it. "Might be you'd get it around your own neck."

"Maybe," Buck said. "But then I reckon not. I reckon I could go right on a-playin' a part, like I got so much practice doin' around Ken Lacey."

"Such as?" I said.

"Such as bein' in such a state of fear and tremblin' that I didn't dast do anything when you told me you was goin' to kill them two pimps. Also, along with being feared and trembly, I was just plain stupid, and I didn't reckon there was no way we could ever convict you until this fella, George Barnes, came along and he don't like you none at all nohow an' I figure he could somehow prove the truth with me tellin' him what it was, an' also swearin' to it."

"Buck," I said. "Listen to me, Buck . . ."

"Uh-huh." Buck shook his head. "I et a peck of dirt a day, every day I worked for Ken Lacey. Et so much dirt that I could feel it seepin' out of me, and I couldn't hardly bear to hug my kids no more nor t'sleep with my wife for fear it would rub off on them, and they couldn't never get clean like I figured I couldn't never get clean. Well, now, I got a chance to stop eatin' it and put Ken Lacey under six feet of it. And don't you try to stop me, Nick. You try to stop me, and t'me you're just Ken Lacey; you're his twin brother, spoonin' the dirt into me every time I open my mouth, and I just can't eat no more. I just can't, by God, I CAN'T EAT NO MORE DIRT! I C-CAN'T—"

His jaw snapped shut. He brushed his nose with his sleeve, his eyes burnin' into mine. "That's it, Nick. I'd rather it was Ken, but it's goin' to be you or him."

I took a drink from my glass, giving him time to get calmed down a little.

Then I told him why he couldn't do it, revealin' who I was for the first time. He didn't seem a speck surprised, beyond raising his eyebrows for a second. The fact was, I guess, that he probably thought I was jokin' or crazy—he didn't care much which. An' I suppose I should have expected that—because what would you have thought?—but I was still a mite disappointed.

I told him again, just to make sure he'd heard me right. He shook his head, sayin' he reckoned I was wrong.

"Prob'ly got yourself mixed up with that other fella," he said. "The one with the same front initial."

"That's right, Buck!" I said. "That's right! I'm both, don't you see? The fella that gets betrayed and the one that does the betrayin' all in one man!"

He didn't seem even nowheres near convinced. I jumped up and went over to the window, thinkin' that maybe I would see a sign.

But all I could see was a couple of dogs, frolickin' around and sniffing each other.

I stood watching them, and I guess I laughed out loud without knowin' it.

"That grave-dirt ticklin' you?" Buck drawled. "You already got one foot in it, you know."

"I was just watching a couple of dogs out here," I said, "and it reminded me of a story I heard one time. You ever hear it, Buck?—I mean why dogs always go around sniffing each other's asses?"

Buck said he hadn't heard it. "Can't say that I'm real interested in hearin' it, neither, just in case you was figurin' on telling it."

I said, that, well, sir, accordin' to this story, all the dogs in the world held a convention back in the beginning of time, their purpose being to set up a code of conduct, like maybe it shouldn't be fair to bite each other in the balls and so on. And there was this one dog that had a copy of Robert's Rules of Order that he'd got somewhere, prob'ly at the same place Cain got his wife. So he automatically became chairman, and the first thing he done was to declare the entire convention a committee of the hole. "Fellas," he says, "canines of the convention. I don't want to tread on no honorable dogs' paws, so I'll just put it this way. When we go back in them smoke-filled rooms to caucus, I'm sure we don't want to smell nothing but smoke, and the best thing to do it seems to me is to pile our assholes outside, and if someone will make a motion to that effect, I'll certainly be glad to put a second to it." Well, sir, it seemed like such a danged good idea that every dog in the convention jumped up to make the motion, so the chairman declared it passed by acclamation, and there was a brief recess while all the dogs went outside to stack up their assholes. Then, they went back inside t'carry out their business. And god-dang if a heck of a storm didn't blow up out of nowhere, and it scattered them assholes every which way, mixin' 'em up so bad that not a one of them dogs was ever able to find his own. So that's why they still go around sniffing butts, and they'll probably keep on until the end of time. Because a dog that's lost his ass just can't be happy, even if one of 'em is pretty much like another, and the one he has is in good working order.

"What I'm saying is this, Buck," I said. "Hang on to your own ass, and don't try to get Ken's. For all you know, he may be eatin' a lot worse than dirt and I may be too, and you'll be a lot happier like you are."

"Is that all you got to say?" Buck said, and I could hear him getting up from his chair. "You're sure that's all you got to say?"

I hesitated, thinkin' I should be able to come up with somethin'. Because it was all so clear to me. Christ knew it was clear: love one another and don't screw no one unless they're bending over, and forgive us our trespasses because we may be a minority of one. For God's sake, *for God's sake*—why else had I been put here in Potts County, and why else did I stay here? Why else, who else, what else but Christ Almighty would put up with it?

But I couldn't make him see that. He was as blind as the rest of 'em.

"Well, Nick? I ain't waiting much longer."

"And you don't have to, Buck," I said. "You don't have to because I finally come to a decision. I've been a long time comin' to it; it's been the product of thinkin' and thinkin' and thinkin', and then some more thinkin'. And dependin' on how you look at it, it's the god-dangest whingdingest decision ever made, or it's the skitty-assed worst. Because it explains everything that goes on in the world—it answers everything and it answers nothing.

"So here it is, Buck, here's my decision. I thought and I thought and then I thought some more, and finally I came to a decision. I decided I don't no more know what to do than if I was just another lousy human bein'!"

JAMES CRUMLEY
THE COLLECTION £9.99

The Wrong Case
The Last Good Kiss
Dancing Bear

Collected here for the first time with a new introduction by the author, James Crumley's three dazzling crime novels present raw slices of American life, cut from the beating heart of a nation, and demonstrate why he is regarded as the finest crime writer of his generation.

'Undoubtedly the rightful heir of Chandler or Ross Macdonald. Compared to these novels, most other contemporary writers seen anaemic or artificial by comparison' – *Weekend Telegraph*

'As Chandler said of Hammett, he can write scenes that seem never to have been written before. With the death of Ross Macdonald and on the strength of just three novels, Crumley has become the foremost living writer of private-eye fiction' – *Crime ad Mystery Writers*

'Carefully plotted suspense . . . like Dashiell Hammett's books, they take realism beyond the limits of their chosen genre, showing us a darker, more provoking vision' – *Times Literary Supplement*

'One of the finest books of American fiction of any sort ever to grace a bookshelf' – *Time Out*

JAMES M. CAIN

THE FIVE GREAT NOVELS

£8.99

The Postman Always Rings Twice
The Butterfly
Serenade
Mildred Pierce
Double Indemnity

James M. Cain is the third member of the trio which had such enormous influence not only on the writing of detective fiction but on the novel, on film and on the way America was viewed. Like Chandler and Hammett, Cain wrote about crime, but unlike them he wrote from the point of view of the criminal and with a sense of bitter, even savage, realism which is entirely his own.

'These novels represent a kind of native American expressionism, in which vivid elements familiar from pulp fiction are recast by a transcendent starkness, and in which literary embellishment is eschewed, with the result that they seem all the more metaphoric. It is no accident that movies based on three of them helped to define the genre known as film noir; or that Camus used *Postman* as his model for *L'Étranger*' – *New York Review of Books*

'Nobody else has ever quite pulled it off the way Cain does, not Hemingway, and not even Raymond Chandler. Cain is a master of the change of pace' – *Tom Wolfe*

'Cain has established a formidable reputation of furious pace, harsh and masterful realism, tough, raw speech right out of the mouths of the people' – *Saturday Review*

'A poet of the tabloid murder' – *Edmund Wilson*

THE WALTER MOSLEY OMNIBUS

WALTER MOSLEY £9.99

Devil in a Blue Dress
A Red Dress
White Butterfly

The first ever Walter Mosley collection contains three complete cases for Easy Rawlins – African-American war veteran turned private investigator – who was born on the bad side of 1950s LA. With his jive-talking, unlicensed and very unofficial detective, Walter Mosley has turned the private-eye novel on its head and confirmed his place as one of the most exciting and original voices to come out of America this decade.

'Easy Rawlins is real and his world is as believably alive as anything in fiction' – *Sunday Times*

'An excellent craftsman, Mosley's finely tuned sentences and masterful handling of the traditional techniques of the novel distinguish him as perhaps the most important black literary figure to appear on the scene since James Baldwin's death' – *Guardian*

'We sense that here is the real world we are hearing about for the first time. The most exciting arrival in the genre for years' – *Financial Times*

'Astonishing virtuosity, upending Chandler's LA to show a dark side of a different kind' – *Sunday Times*

'The find of the 1990s' – *Daily Telegraph*